"What are you wearing under this dress?" he asked, his mouth brushing hers, the words whisper-soft.

Not what she expected him to say. "E-excuse me?"

His teeth sank into her lower lip, making her yelp. "Focus."

On what? The demon club? The humans dying downstairs? The fact that you're a fucking vampire? Where should I begin?

He sighed, his forehead falling to hers. "Astasiya, we have very little time to sort this before the Conclave. I need you to work with me. Both our lives depend on it. What are you wearing?"

She cleared her throat, her hold on his neck tightening as if needing his support to respond. And maybe she did. This was all a lot to take in. "A, uh, thong," she managed to say. "And a strapless bra."

One of his hands drifted from her hair to her waist, then down to her ass. His palm flattened and forced her to arch up into him. A breath hitched in her throat at the feel of his growing arousal.

He's turned on… here… now?

She trembled, the heat of his body seeping into her cool skin, warming her blood. They were standing rather close. And he smelled amazing, as always.

Anywhere else, in the dark, she'd have kissed him. But here…

"The dress will have to stay, then," he said, the disappointment evident in his voice.

She frowned. "What's wrong with my dress?" It hit her midthigh and clung to her curves. She looked good in it.

He ignored her, his mouth brushing hers in a chaste kiss as his hips pressed firmly into hers.

Definitely aroused.

"You're going to see things tonight that will make you want to scream, but you must remain calm and quiet. Mortals who overreact die, and they die badly."

"Wh—"

Issac lifted her off the ground one-handed, her legs wrapping around him automatically for balance. And, oh God, that placed his thick erection right against the scrap of lace between her thighs.

Any other place and time, her body's instinct to move against him would have won out, but not now. The shiver that traversed her spine was from his words, not his touch.

Mortals who overreact die. Her arms tensed around his neck.

Issac had already admitted that her involvement as his pawn would likely lead to her death. And now…

I'm going to die here.

IMMORTAL CURSE SERIES

BLOOD LAWS

FORBIDDEN BONDS

BLOOD HEART

Immortal Curse Series

Books 1 - 3

USA Today Bestselling Author
Lexi C. Foss

Immortal Curse Series Books 1-3

Editing by: Outthink Editing, LLC

Cover Design By: Manuela Serra

Model: Thom Panto

Photography: Wander Aguiar Photography

Published by: Ninja Newt Publishing, LLC

Print Edition 2.0

ISBN: 978-1-68530-116-3

Blood Laws

USA Today Bestselling Author
Lexi C. Foss

PRETERNATURAL BEINGS

Fledgling (noun): The child of a male Ichorian and a human female, who has not yet been reborn as a Hydraian; they do not typically possess supernatural or psychic gifts until their immortal rebirth.

Hydraian (noun): An immortal offspring of a male Ichorian and a human female, who possesses two supernatural or psychic gifts and does not require human blood to survive.

Ichorian (noun): An immortal being of unknown descent who possesses one supernatural or psychic gift and requires human blood to survive.

Immortal (noun): A general noun designating a being who does not age and is immune to natural human death.

Seraphim (noun): A being who belongs to the highest order of angelic hierarchy.

KEY TERMS

Arcadia: Notorious Ichorian club in New York City that also serves as the primary meeting location for the Ichorian government.

Blood Laws: A series of ordinances created by the Ichorian governing board in response to the Treaty of 1747.

Catastrophic Relief Foundation (CRF): A global humanitarian aid organization headquartered in New York City with a secret paramilitary unit designed to destroy rogue supernaturals.

Conclave: The Ichorian governing board.

Edict: A law or rule issued by the High Council of Seraph.

Elders: The original Hydraians who also serve as the Hydraian governing board.

Fated Line: Seraphim who can foresee the future.

High Council of Seraph: Seraphim governing board.

Nizari: Ancient Ichorian assassins who hunt and kill fledglings.

Nizari Poison: A green substance notorious for killing fledglings and preventing their rebirth.

Sentinel: A soldier in the CRF unit designed to slaughter rogue immortal beings.

Treaty of 1747: An armistice between Hydraians and Ichorians to cease fire and live in their designated areas. Those who opt to cross these boundaries do so at their own risk.

"An unknown power is surfacing. She will possess the strength and will to destroy us all unless certain measures are put in place to curb her inclinations."

–Prophetess Skye

By order of the Ichorian Conclave, the below behaviors are forbidden:

The intentional creation of fledgling immortals through procreation with human females

Knowingly allowing fledgling immortals or Hydraians to exist on Ichorian soil

Consorting with Hydraians in any capacity, unless otherwise negotiated by birthright and rank

PROLOGUE

"Ready?" Astasiya's angel friend asked, gesturing to the house before them.

She shook her head, not ready at all. He had told her these new people would be her parents. But she didn't want new parents. She wanted her old ones back. Right now.

"They'll protect you, just like your parents did."

She bit her lip, her focus on the door so unlike the one at home. "But Momma keeps talking to me," she whispered. "She needs help."

So much heartbreak.

Sadness.

Momma's all alone.

Astasiya's lips trembled. The dreams scared her the most. All that water with nowhere to go. She drowned over and over and over.

And it hurt. So, so much. Astasiya woke screaming every time, that madman's eyes fresh in her mind.

They were just supposed to play hide-and-seek. But Daddy never came for her. She tried to find him instead, and she did, but her angel friend appeared and took her to a safe place with lots of trees. He promised to keep her safe, like he always did when he visited.

But Momma isn't safe.

"I'll search for your mom," he said to her now, his voice soft yet stern. "While you live here, okay? And then one day, we'll go find her together."

"Promise?" she asked. 'Cause if he did, then he'd have to see it through. Because that's what Daddy always told her—*a promise can't be broken.*

"I vow it," her angel friend replied, squeezing her hand. "We'll find her."

She nodded. "Together."

"Together," he agreed.

"Gabriel," a soft voice whispered through the cool air, causing the hairs along Astasiya's arms to dance. She couldn't see anyone other than the angel holding her hand, but she could *feel* the new presence.

Another angel. This one was misting like her momma sometimes did when they played hide-and-seek. Technically, it was cheating because Astasiya couldn't see her momma when she did that. Just like the unfamiliar angel who had joined them without revealing herself.

Astasiya's heart gave a big jump in her chest, her lips wobbling again. *Can Momma mist under water? Does she have her wings?*

"Astasiya," her angel friend murmured. "You won't remember me when we meet again, but I will make sure you know the truth when the time is right."

Her eyebrows crinkled. That didn't make sense. "But I know you."

"Yes, but to keep you safe, I need you to forget me. For now." He looked toward the space where the chiming voice originated—at the invisible angel.

Astasiya wished she could see, but she wasn't old enough yet. Had to be a grown-up, her parents always said. But she so badly wanted to see the feathers, especially the blue ones her daddy once described.

"Your mother has the most beautiful wings, little angel. A light blue with traces of white and sapphire. You'll see them one day."

"Everything from this week, including Osiris if she saw him," her angel friend said to the empty space.

"What about the death?" the chiming voice asked.

What color are your wings? Astasiya wanted to ask, but she knew it was rude to interrupt. She'd ask when they finished talking.

"She needs that to grow," he replied. "And Ezekiel needs to be the villain."

"I can do that. Anything else?"

"Yes. Give her doubts about Caro's true nature."

"That's going to be difficult."

"Indeed, that's why I called the best memory manipulator in existence for assistance." His light eyes met Astasiya's again with a sadness in them that reminded her of her dreams. "Consider me your personal Seraphim, Astasiya. I'll always be watching over you." He kissed her on the forehead and straightened. "Now, Vera."

The air tingled with energy. *That feels weird.*

"Already started," the chiming voice whispered.

I don't understand, Astasiya tried to say, but her lips didn't move. Something felt… weird. Like floating. Another dream? But she didn't want to sleep. Not yet.

These people, who were they? Her new parents.

No. She had parents.

They… they died.

No, they didn't!

Momma… water…

Their house went up flames. Her mother and father inside.

That's not… It didn't… What are you doing?

Black eyes, flickering with gold embers.

Drowning…

She shivered. That face belonged to the devil. He lit a match and watched them burn. Astasiya had been trapped, hiding, watching it all happen. Every scream. Her name from her mother's mouth.

In my dreams, she calls for me. Not de—

There was nothing she could do. Just watched them die. A horrible, painful death. That's what happened when Astasiya persuaded—those around her were hurt.

No! Daddy said it wasn't my fault!

Except, maybe, no. She shouldn't have compelled that man for the ice cream. Her parents were found because of it. She would be found, too, if she ever did it again.

They'd kill her.

Just like her parents.

She had to be good. She had to behave. She had to hide.

With her new family. The Davenports.

Astasiya blinked. Her head felt funny. Like she'd fallen down and hit it.

Momma?

She sniffled. No. Her momma was gone. She'd never see her again. And not because of the misting game. Or were those part of her dreams? Astasiya scrunched her nose, confused. It all felt so… *wrong.*

"Goodbye, little sister," a voice whispered in the wind, causing her brow to pucker.

What was that?

The doorbell rang, startling her from a daze. Had she just done that? Her fingers curled at her sides. She must have because no one else stood out here. Someone had just dropped her off.

So fuzzy.

And cloudy.

"Astasiya?" a warm voice greeted, the female before her unfamiliar, but her eyes were kind. She smiled, holding out a hand. "Welcome home, sweetheart."

Home.

She frowned. *This isn't my home.*

But she belonged here now. Because her parents died.

That's not…

"Oh, Henry! Astasiya is here!" The woman sounded so happy. So welcoming. She even smiled a nice smile.

Trustworthy.

Astasiya felt her lips curl. This could be okay. Maybe she'd stay.

But Momma needs me… She just couldn't remember why. Something about water. No, a fire. It engulfed them, killing them, leaving her here.

With the Davenports.

Her new parents.

My new home.

CHAPTER ONE

Fate Comes Knocking

Seventeen Years Later

"Good morning," Jeffrey greeted, smile firmly in place.

Stas Davenport didn't know how the elderly man always appeared so cheery. And in New York City, of all places. No one smiled here, especially not at this ungodly morning hour.

"Hi," she replied, forcing her lips upward. "Just here for Owen." *Who couldn't be bothered to meet me at the café for coffee.*

"Of course, miss." He never called her Stas even though he knew her name. "Go on up. I'm sure he's expecting you."

"Thank you." Stas managed another grin before stepping into the waiting elevator.

You better be awake, Stas typed as the doors closed. *And holding a coffee cup with my name on it.*

No reply.

He'd texted her this morning reminding her to come over. If he fell back asleep afterward, she'd kick his ass.

After her coffee, of course.

She selected his floor and narrowed her gaze at the numbers overhead.

"Let's meet Saturday at seven," she mimicked, doing a poor impersonation of her friend's voice. "No interruptions that way." Fuck. Not even her internship at the Catastrophic Relief Foundation (CRF) made her move around this early. Maybe she'd nap on Owen's couch while he practiced his dissertation. The slides for his presentation were all correct. He just needed to follow along.

She glanced at her screen again as she stepped out onto his floor.

Still no reply.

He totally went back to sleep.

Well, he wouldn't be sleeping for long.

She slid the phone back into her pocket, preparing her fists for a beating against his door. Except a man dressed in a tailored suit stood in her way, his focus on his hand.

Stas frowned. *Odd.* Owen usually preferred bulky, blond men, not athletically lean males. This one was much taller than her close friend's usual conquests, and prettier, too, in an aristocratically perfect kind of way.

She could see the appeal, especially in the way his suit pants cut across his strong thighs.

"So, you're why Owen's running late this morning," she said in greeting. "I suppose I can forgive him, as long as there's coffee waiting."

Striking blue eyes met hers, making her heart skip a beat.

Pretty had been too feminine a word.

Gorgeous was the more accurate adjective.

His high cheekbones and chiseled jaw were a deadly combination with those midnight irises. Lizzie would be elbowing her repeatedly right about now, her not-so-subtle way of calling attention to a handsome man. Good thing Stas left her back at the condo.

The elegantly dressed male glanced over her, his gaze exuding indifference before returning his attention to the phone in his hand.

Not even a hello.

Doorman Jeffrey would be so disappointed.

"Right, well, nice to meet you, too." She couldn't help the sarcastic note at the end. Not smiling, she understood. Outright ignoring someone, especially after fucking her friend, qualified as rude.

His alluring gaze shot upward, holding her in place when she would have moved around him for the door. "You're talking to me?"

Stas glanced up and down the empty hallway, her brow furrowing. "Who else would I be talking to?"

He cocked his head to the side, renewed interest flaring in his pupils. "You can see me." Not a question, but a statement.

A tingle crept down her spine, centering at the base and flaring outward across her skin. She almost shivered, her breathing uneven.

Something's not right.

She couldn't tell what. Just an inkling. An instinct. It curdled against her insides, kicking up her pulse.

I should—

The man pushed off the wall, his over-six-foot frame dwarfing her five-foot-eight one.

"You really can see me," he repeated. "How intriguing." His deep voice held a touch of a foreign lilt that she couldn't put her finger on. *English, maybe?* But not exactly. The accent seemed aged somehow.

"Uh, yeah. I can see you." She doubted he escaped much female notice, but his personality left a bit to be desired.

Her lips flattened as the stranger began to circle her, his midnight gaze roaming over her slowly and purposefully, touching on every curve and detail along the way. She swallowed, his blatant appraisal causing the hairs along her arms to dance in warning.

That is not how a gay man looks at a woman.

"Are you one of Jonathan's new toys?" he asked. "Come to review the details before the authorities arrive?"

"Jonathan?" *What the hell is this guy talking about?*

"Hmm, perhaps not, then." His irises finally returned to her own. "I doubt he'd send such a young candidate to survey the scene. Too brutal an introduction, but what is life without death?"

Her blood chilled. *Okay. Owen brought home a crazy person.* A good-looking one, sure, but the man was clearly mad.

"Right." She took a step away from the lunatic and another toward the door. "I'm just going to go in and talk to Owen now. You have a good day, okay?"

She took a third step, her fist raised to knock—

The air whooshed out of her as she was yanked backward into something hard. Her lips parted on a scream, only to be covered by a warm palm. A band of steel came around her middle, holding her arms in place when she tried to squirm.

Stas blinked.

What the fuck just happened?

Owen's door remained closed beside her as she faced the hallway.

The man stood behind her, his chest to her back, his solid arm around her waist, and his hand over her mouth.

How?

"Shh." Warm lips brushed her ear. "I'm not done with you yet."

His tense form held hers with ease, his back brushing the wall behind him.

Oh, hell no. Gorgeous man or not, she was not okay with being held against her will.

She threw her elbow backward just as the door beside them opened.

Thank. Fuck. Her muscles relaxed, relief settling over her shoulders. *Owen would—*

Her nose twitched. *What is that smell?*

So acrid.

So potent.

So *familiar.*

Burning flesh. A distinct scent, one she would never forget, and it was coming from inside her friend's apartment. Vivid memories overwhelmed her, locking her in place.

Her parents screaming in the flames, telling her to hide.

An evil man with eerie gold-flecked eyes.

Laughter.

Death.

"He says to leave it," a deep voice announced, stirring her from her memories, her palms clammy. "Someone will discover it soon."

"Works for me," a second male replied, grunting.

Both stepped through the threshold from Owen's apartment in matching black outfits, their hulking sizes far more intimidating than the male behind her. Not that she trusted him any more than she trusted them.

The one with lighter hair wiped his hands against his dark pants. He looked like the kind of man who went by Hank, while his olive-skinned friend was more of a Brutus.

And neither of them appeared the helpful sort.

They exuded an air of danger and malice, not because of the guns proudly displayed on their belts, but because of the grim satisfaction radiating from their expressions.

Stas froze. *What have you done to Owen?*

Because she knew that scent. It reminded her of death.

No. That's ridiculous. Maybe he burned breakfast, or popcorn, or *something.*

But then who the hell are these guys and why are they here?

A chill skittered down her spine, her heart in her throat.

Don't panic. It could—

She held her breath as Hank turned to close the door. Why he scared her more than the man behind her did, she didn't know. It was all driven by instinct.

And he would see them in three, two…

He looked right at them.

Nothing.

"All right, let's go." It was directed over her head.

Oh, right. Because they're working together.

Of course they're working together.

Why else would the deranged man be here, holding me against my will? He'd clearly been waiting for these goons in the hallway.

I just need my mouth free, then I can get to Owen.

"Nah, something seems off out here." Brutus searched around them. "You feel it?"

Hank glanced up and down the corridor, his gaze passing over them in the process. "Yeah, I feel it. It's probably a residual from that." He gestured at Owen's door.

Stas shivered, not liking the insinuation or the stench still wafting around them. *What happened? Where's Owen?* she wanted to demand. She started to squirm, only to be held tighter by the man behind her, his palm practically smothering her mouth.

Does he know what I can do?

Are they here for me?

Impossible.

Brutus shuddered. "Yeah, that was bad."

Hank didn't seem as bothered and continued walking. "Let's just go."

Yeah, no thank you.

Stas had played this game of quiet mouse long enough. All she needed was to free her mouth. One demand would solve the problem.

Wiggling hadn't worked.

So she stomped her heel against the man's expensive shoe instead, eliciting a wince from him. She lifted her foot in an attempt to loft a kick backward into his shin and only met air.

Her shoulder blades protested as her captor slammed her into the wall. Hard.

Fuck.

She struggled to move but couldn't. Both of her wrists were in one of his hands above her head. The rest of her was pinned between the wall and his body. Her chest heaved against his at the wasted effort. She would have screamed, but his other hand had never left her mouth.

Blue fire swirled in the depths of his gaze, the intensity of it scattering goose bumps down her arms. Fury poured off of him in waves, intoxicating her, thrilling her, terrifying her.

Who are you? she wanted to ask. *What are you doing to me?*

"What the fuck was that?" Brutus stared right at her, his murky eyes emanating confusion.

Stas waited for her captor to reply, but he didn't. He seemed to be concentrating very hard on holding her against the wall despite her lack of a struggle.

"Probably one of the neighbors waking up. We gotta go, dude." Hank stood at the top of the stairwell. "Now."

"Nah, that was something else…"

"Man, I'm leaving with or without you. Your choice." He went through the door, leaving Brutus in the hallway. His dull eyes passed over them again without focusing. Almost as if they weren't actually there.

Her heart skipped a beat.

He can't see us.

The male's irritated expression said, *Finally.*

Oh…

His earlier statement, "*You can see me,*" suddenly took on a whole new meaning.

Her eyes went wide. *No… That's not possible.*

And yet, entirely plausible.

Stas knew better than anyone that the supernatural existed. Not the kind kids enjoyed reading about or the stuff of fairy tales, but the real kind. The scary kind. The kind that killed.

But she'd been so careful. No one knew about her psychic talents—no one alive, anyway.

The door to the stairwell slammed, the finality of it shuddering down her spine.

Blue eyes burned into hers, the intensity stealing her breath away. *He's one of them—a supernatural.* And now he knew she existed.

Her father's smile had been so sad…

"You have to play today, little angel. For me and your mom. Just in case the bad men come, okay?"

"'Cause of the ice cream?" she whispered, her heart breaking. Daddy always said not to use compulsion on strangers. Bad things happened. Now the bad men were coming. Because of her.

"No, darling, not the ice cream. The bad men who might come will be here for me and your mom, not you. So you have to stay hidden and wait for me to find you, just like all the other times we played."

Except it hadn't been anything like the other times. Because a bad man did come—a supernatural one—and he burned her parents alive.

She couldn't blink. Couldn't move. Couldn't think.

It had finally happened.

The supernaturals had found her.

She needed to fight, to flee, but her limbs refused her. There wasn't any point.

Because she stood no chance, just like her parents that day.

This is my ending, not my beginning.

Today is the day I die.

~*~

Issac Wakefield did not like complications.

And the woman he held up against the wall? She definitely qualified as one.

Why he felt the need to hide her from the two Conclave lapdogs was beyond him. He almost let her fall into their sight when she tried to kick him, but instinct forced him in another direction.

She's immune.

Issac could manipulate everyone's vision, including that of Hydraians and Ichorians. Yet, this woman had *seen* him. That implied his gift didn't work on her.

Fascinating.

And from what he could tell, she had no idea.

Her pulse practically sang to him, her fear alluring to his predatory drive. He thought maybe Jonathan had caught wind of the recent assassination and sent a pet out to investigate. It could have explained her immunity, but her poor fighting skills and paling expression suggested a lack of training. And Jonathan would never allow one of his experiments to wander about without defensive skills.

So what are you? he wondered, holding her gaze.

He slowly removed his hand from her mouth, knowing the other Ichorians were no longer in hearing range. "What's your name?" It seemed a solid starting point and an easy enough query to answer.

She gaped at him, her lips moving without sound.

Shock.

Fantastic.

He released her and she nearly fell. Of course, she could be faking it, but his centuries of experience said otherwise. This woman had no idea what world she'd just stumbled into.

Issac almost felt sorry for her. Now that he knew of her existence, everything in her life would change. It already had.

"What are you doing here?" he tried again. The woman had seen right through his glamour, which meant she'd seen his face. He couldn't just leave her in the hallway. Not without understanding who and what she was, and why she'd chosen today to appear. It felt very orchestrated, which again had him thinking about Jonathan. This was exactly the kind of trap he would set.

"I… I…" She shuddered, her arms wrapping around herself.

Well, he supposed this was better than screaming.

He could knock her out and deal with it after he completed his task. It wouldn't take him long to review the scene, unlike the two Conclave minions who had spent over an hour in Owen Angelton's apartment.

Someone had clearly tipped off Osiris. If Issac hadn't shown up in the middle of their investigation, he'd have thought the two idiots killed Owen. But no. The Hydraian died before they arrived. And Lucian, the Hydraian King, wanted to know how it happened. He hadn't even been aware that his immortal was residing in the city until a distress call arrived early this morning.

Jacque had gone in first, the teleporter was good friends with Owen. Alas, he'd arrived too late, the message having been delayed by an unknown cause. Mateo was looking into it now.

And Issac was here to finish the investigation, the location too dangerous for any of Lucian's men to thoroughly review it for themselves. Case in point, the departing Ichorians downstairs.

"Wh-what are you?" she stammered.

His eyebrows rose. "The better question is, what are *you*, darling?" A fledgling, perhaps? It seemed appropriate considering she could *see* him.

Her face paled even more, her lips gaping like a fish again.

Right. They were just wasting time. He'd complete his mission and then deal with the traumatized woman. "Let's go inside," he suggested, opening the door.

She gagged as the acrid air wafted into the hallway.

He grabbed her wrist and tugged her inside, closing the door behind them. This way he could at least hear her if she tried to escape. Because the last thing he wanted to do was have to track her down after this. It would be much easier if she just stayed put until he was ready to deal with her.

"Oh God…" Her eyes clouded with dark embers, taking on a distant gleam, her knees collapsing beneath her and sending her to the ground. A glance into the kitchen confirmed why. Blood and glass littered the tile, indicating the struggle started there. And it seemed to have triggered a memory of some kind from the girl trembling on the floor.

Definitely not moving anytime soon.

Issac took advantage of her collapsing mental state by using the time to visualize the scene in the kitchen.

He pictured the dark-skinned male standing in the kitchen, pouring himself a glass of wine, just as the door burst open. The blood evinced a fight. Natural. Understandable, even. But what prompted the distress call to Lucian? It seemed a bit out of sequence. If Owen knew he was in danger, he wouldn't pour himself a glass of wine while he waited for the inevitable.

No.

Something wasn't quite right here.

Issac followed the light from the windows, down the hall, and into the small living area, his stomach twisting at the scene before him.

Owen's head—or what was left of it—appeared carelessly tossed on top of the coffee table with his charred remains on the recliner beside it.

Blood, innards, and other unmentionables were scattered about, making it bloody difficult to determine a safe walking path. While he adored Lucian and considered him a brother, he was not about to soil his shoes in the name of friendship.

"Wait," the woman called out, the whispering of her jeans suggesting she was trying to stand. "Hold on." She stumbled into the room, her green eyes glowing with the fight he'd witnessed in her earlier. Her mouth fell open at the sight on the table and chair, her palm going to her abdomen. "Oh my God…"

"Not God, darling," he murmured.

But she didn't hear him, her stomach heaving as she ran to the bathroom. She clearly knew her way around because she chose the right door on her first try, the sound of her emptying her insides following soon after.

The ghastly scene had been too much for her. Issac remembered a time when he may have reacted the same, but death had long since lost its impact on him. People died every day. Sometimes naturally, sometimes not.

And Owen definitely fell into the latter category.

Someone had clearly tortured the Hydraian. For information? Not likely. He was too young an immortal to know much. Which meant someone wanted to make a statement. But what?

Issac eyed the remains, searching for evidence or a clue.

The misshapen head on the table didn't resemble the man he once knew—his brown hair and dark skin replaced by a ball of gore with a gaping hole in the center.

The methods were reminiscent of a Conclave assassination, but Osiris didn't order this hit. If he did, he wouldn't have sent his henchmen to investigate this morning. This was either the work of a rogue Ichorian teaching a Hydraian a lesson or something else entirely.

Regardless, the murderer was definitely nonhuman.

"Owen," the woman moaned as she returned, tears trailing down her face. "What the fuck did you do to Owen?"

He gaped at her. "You think I did this?" He nearly snorted. "I had no cause to harm him. I'm merely here as an emissary to find out what happened."

"What?" Her face crumpled, reason not fully registering over her blatant emotions. "Why would someone do this?"

"Why does anyone do anything?" he countered, focusing on a series of photos decorating the fireplace mantle. *Ah, I see.* "You were friends," he surmised. *Definitely not a minion of Jonathan's.* But it also suggested Owen had been in New York for quite a while. *What were you doing in the city?*

"Who are you?" she breathed, her palm against her chest.

His lips twitched. She didn't recognize him? "Well, I may just let you live after all." Lucky day and all that.

A buzzing caught his attention before she could reply. He navigated through the bloody mess toward the origin, careful not to touch anything crude.

Crouching down, he found the source beneath the couch.

A cell phone. Using a trick Mateo had taught him, he unlocked the main screen and started scanning through the text messages.

"You must be *Sassy Stas*," he guessed, reviewing the most recent text message regarding coffee. She'd mentioned something about it in the hallway as well.

A glance over his shoulder confirmed his suspicions. Her focus had fallen to the item in his hands, her lips trembling at having her name disclosed. Part of him wanted to console her, to tell her he meant her no harm. While the other part of him refused to lie. Because he would most certainly harm her if he needed to.

She gagged at the head on the table, averting her eyes to the ceiling—the only surface of the room not coated in blood splatter. She swallowed visibly, her cheeks taking on a greenish tint again. If he didn't say something to snap her out of it, she was liable to be sick again, perhaps even in the living area. And wouldn't *that* be incriminating.

He stood and read one of the texts from Owen's screen. " '*You better be awake. And holding a coffee cup with my name on it.*' Hmm, no coffee, just a corpse with a cell phone displaying your name. If you don't contact the authorities, I'm guessing you'll be their first house call. Woman deprived of caffeine kills friend—has a nice ring to it for a story, yes?"

Some of that emerald fire he'd witnessed earlier returned to her gaze, a faint blush overcoming the sick pallor of her skin. "Who *are* you?" She winced at the dead body and took a step back. "*God.* I can't." She stumbled into the hallway wall. From the way her nose wrinkled, he gathered the stench and sight were both affecting her.

He left her to console herself and scrolled through the other messages as well as Owen's contacts. Nothing out of the ordinary, but he pocketed the phone anyway. Mateo might see something he couldn't. He could also dust it for prints to find out who messaged Stas this morning since it was clearly sent after the Hydraian's death.

Someone wanted her to find the body.

But that someone couldn't have known Issac would be here, too. Only Lucian knew about this visit, and anyone he would have told would be a trusted confidant.

Issac ventured into the bedroom, finding more photos and other items that confirmed Owen's tenure in the city. The textbooks on his desk were for a journalism or political science degree program, based on the titles. Not a lot of useful information, just a notebook filled with scribbles and a laptop.

"How long have you known Owen?" he asked as he reentered the living area. The blonde had collapsed near the front door, her arms wrapped around her knees.

She eyed him warily. "Why?"

He cocked a brow, not used to repeating himself. "How long?"

"Since freshman year," she mumbled. "Almost six years."

That long? Lucian would not be pleased.

"What was he doing here?" Issac wondered out loud.

"Studying," she whispered. "We were supposed to graduate next weekend."

"Graduate," he repeated, recalling the textbooks from Owen's room. "From?"

She swallowed and shook her head, whether in rejection or because she couldn't speak. From the defiance he'd witnessed early, he guessed the former. While clearly traumatized, a fire still lurked in her gaze, one that screamed challenge.

"Stas," he murmured, cocking his head to the side. "Is that short for something?"

She glowered up at him, confirming his suspicions. Now that the initial shock of her friend's death had faded, her senses were returning, and with them came anger. "Why?"

No sense in lying to her. "So I can find you later."

She snorted and hugged her knees to her chest. "Good luck."

He shrugged. "I'll just find out from the police report, then."

She started, her gaze widening. "What?"

"Well, clearly someone wanted you to find the body. You have, which—"

"Wait?" she interjected. "Someone wanted me to find him?"

Had she not figured that part out yet? "Who do you think sent you a text this morning? Because it wasn't Owen. He's been dead for nearly four hours, give or take." Issac based the math on his senses. The blood was dead for far too long to be viable. Hence the reason he and his brethren could wander the Hydraian's flat. Had the blood been fresh, it could still be toxic. Alas, the lethal properties had died with their owner.

"*What?*" The color drained from her pale cheeks. "You're saying someone texted me from his phone *after* they killed him? *Why?*"

"Best guess? To ensure he was found. It would only take a few glances at his message history to see who he talked to most. You." Which begged the question, why had Owen befriended her? Did he, too, notice her penchant for being immune to Ichorian gifts? Was she resistant to Hydraian abilities as well?

"Which means," he continued, "phoning the authorities is the next step. Feel free to do that now, as I'll be leaving momentarily." And he'd track her down afterward. If he'd learned anything in his long life, it was to involve the cops early, let them draw up their ridiculous conclusions, and work behind the scenes to solve the real crime.

They'd never suspect Stas anyway. The strength required to rip a man's head from his neck and burn a body was nonhuman, and her athletic form didn't possess the necessary strength or mental stamina for such things.

Besides, they were clearly friends. Her presence here wouldn't be abnormal, though they'd likely want to know all about Owen's history.

"The police," she groaned, as if just realizing their importance. Most humans would call right away, but her instincts had led her astray. Why?

"Yes, the police," he said, brow furrowing. "I'm surprised you haven't tried to call them already." He half expected her to when she'd stumbled back into the foyer.

"I was a little busy." She waved a hand toward the apartment, her face paling again. "Damn it."

Right. She'd been sick from the shock.

Still, most would have thought to call. Fascinating that she didn't, or perhaps she thought he would. In that case… "I wouldn't suggest discussing my presence here." Even if she realized who he was, no one would believe her. A renowned billionaire over what appeared to be a college student? She didn't stand a chance in hell.

She didn't acknowledge his request, just stared at him. "How did you know Owen?"

"I didn't." Not well, anyway.

"Then why are you here?"

As if he would tell her that. "We'll catch up after you handle the authorities because, by my calculations, you were seen downstairs entering long enough ago that they will question what took you so long to call." Osiris's minions—Michael and Cain—had graciously left the doorman alive after altering the camera footage. It worked to Issac's benefit as well, leaving absolutely no trace of him in this building. While he could manipulate visual sensors in humans, he could not alter technological proof, such as a video evidence, of his presence.

"God, it's happening all over again," she whispered, her fingers threading through her long blonde hair and tugging harshly. "I can't do this. Not again. Not after…"

She trailed off, leaving him wondering what incident she was referring to. The last Hydraian death in the city had taken place long before she was born. Most of them were smart enough not to venture here, not with it being the heart of Ichorian territory. One could only push the treaty so far.

"Again?" he prompted, curious.

She shook her head as tears gathered behind those beautiful eyes again. Real pain etched into her features, stirring a strange urge to console her. Issac understood that agony far too well, having experienced substantial loss himself. It's what kept him motivated and inflamed his need for revenge.

It was why he resided in this city when he could live anywhere in the world.

And while a part of him wished to impart some wisdom to her, he had none. Only a drive to keep moving, to continue plotting, and to seek justice.

"Call the police," he told her. "I'd not recommend mentioning me," he repeated. "Or the two men from earlier," he added, thinking about how Cain and Michael had covered their tracks. "Your story won't be corroborated by any evidence and will only leave you looking insane."

That seemed to strike a chord in her, because her nostril's flared. "And if I mention you anyway?" she asked, her gaze hardening. "You'll come after me?" she guessed.

He smiled. "I'll be seeing you again regardless of what you say to them, darling." It didn't matter whether she gave him a name or not. Mateo would hack the system to find everything he needed to know. Besides, he had her phone number in Owen's phone. He had all the breadcrumbs he needed to learn more about this mystery woman and her unique ability to see through his glamour.

Stas sighed, her head falling back against the wall, her expression resigned. No fight or argument, just acceptance. She pulled her phone out of her pocket, her eyes locking on his. "If you're going to leave, do it now."

At least she'd managed to pull herself back together, a feat considering their surroundings. But this one was familiar with death. He'd bet his life on it.

"I'll see you soon, darling," he murmured, opening the door. His fingerprints were untraceable, making his exit easy.

"Yeah," she muttered after him, her phone already dialing.

He considered staying to listen in on her conversation with the authorities but didn't want to risk her seeing him again this soon. The police report would give him the information he needed.

Then Mateo would work his magic on her background.

Stas.

Hmm, Issac really hoped that was short for something because the name just did not fit the unique woman.

Time would tell.

Until then, he had a call to the Hydraian King to make.

CHAPTER TWO

Caught in the Act

The woman didn't mention Issac or Osiris's lapdogs, stating she found the door slightly ajar when she arrived. Her omissions intrigued him, but not nearly as much as the rest of her portfolio.

Astasiya Davenport.

Adopted seventeen years ago by Susan and Henry Davenport in Havre, Montana. Whereabouts prior to adoption unknown.

Now twenty-four years old. NYU master's degree candidate set to graduate at the end of this semester—in less than two weeks.

CRF intern in the marketing department.

Roommate to Elizabeth Watkins, daughter of renowned George Watkins—an asshole to the highest degree.

Issac grew more curious with every detail he learned about Astasiya from her dossier. He'd memorized all of it, including her transcripts and familial history. All in preparation for seeing her again.

She had a lot of explaining to do.

And soon.

Issac brushed his thumb across his bottom lip as he eyed Astasiya and Elizabeth from the shadows of the Kimmel Center auditorium.

He'd cloaked his presence from everyone around him but remained conscious of Astasiya's ability to see through his glamour. Hence his position behind her, leaning against the wall. If she turned, she'd see him. Fortunately, the dean of the College of Political Science held her attention as he spoke about Owen Angelton from the podium at the front. There were photos of the Hydraian everywhere, all smiles, most of them including Astasiya.

The phone records confirmed the age of their friendship—nearly six years, just as she'd said.

Lucian had been astonished to learn his immortal had been lurking in renowned Ichorian territory. Issac purposely withheld the details about Astasiya, wishing to learn more about her himself first.

She could prove useful.

Or maybe she'd played him all along.

Her proven ties to Jonathan suggested the latter. The redhead beside her damned her even more. But something about Astasiya felt genuine, innocent in a way that Issac couldn't help but wonder about her true purpose here.

Elizabeth wrapped her slender arms around Astasiya's neck after the dean finished, her hug expressing a firm friendship between them. "Just say the word and we're out of here." The words were faint but clear.

"I'm okay," Astasiya replied, the tension in her body betraying the lie as she pulled back. "It's just all these memories, you know?"

"Like the photo they used from freshman year?" Elizabeth snorted. "I can't believe they chose that one."

"It was a good day. A good week, really."

"Duh. It's when you met me." The redhead smiled, her peculiar genetics fully on display. Issac wondered if she knew about her birthright. Did Astasiya know? Their history extended as far back as the one Astasiya had with Owen. That couldn't be a coincidence. "Seriously, we can go if you need to," Elizabeth added, her expression sobering.

"I'm okay, Liz. Being out is what I need right now. Owen wouldn't want me, or any of us, to sit at home."

Elizabeth nodded. "True, he—"

"Lizzie!" A gaggle of girls had approached, their dyed hair and made-up faces a stark contrast to Astasiya's natural look. They all reached for Elizabeth, pulling her away into their circle and leaving Astasiya staring after them with a sardonic twist of her mouth.

Disapproval, not envy. And a slight touch of humor.

Issac agreed with her entirely, especially as the women begin sobbing over Owen's untimely demise. He suspected the females barely knew the immortal.

Astasiya, however, clearly knew him.

He lifted the program up to hide his features, stepping back into the wall just as she turned. Her sweet scent taunted his nostrils, the lure of her blood exciting his instincts.

Definitely a fledgling.

So who created you? he wondered as he followed her.

The minds of the room were easy to manipulate, his presence here lost in the recesses of their thoughts. He likened it to a room littered with televisions all set to the same channel as he wove through the crowds after Astasiya.

She remained lost in thought, not sensing the predator in her wake—a fatal error. He could snap her pretty little neck with a flick of his wrist. Thankfully, she was of more use to him alive.

A curvy woman with bouncy curls stepped into his quarry's path, her round face smothered in tears. She sobbed some story about Owen that had Astasiya cringing and taking a step back. The words continued flowing, none of them intelligible.

"Stop crying," Astasiya demanded. Her shoulders seemed to tighten even more with the words, her upper body stiff. "I mean, just, it's going to be okay… It's…"

But the girl had ceased her blubbering, her gaze eerily unfocused. "Sorry," she mumbled, taking her leave.

Issac frowned after her. *How odd.*

"Fuck," Astasiya muttered to herself, her steps faster now.

Until yet another female waylaid her from the side. A reporter with overdone lips and hair bigger than the room.

He nearly snorted.

Tabloids belonged to the devil.

"I heard through the grapevine you and Mr. Angelton were close. What can you tell me about his social activities?"

"Yeah, I'm not interested. Thanks, though." She tried to maneuver around the pushy woman, but a set of manicured nails snagged her arm.

"Is it true he was gay?"

Astasiya winced, causing Issac to take a step forward. It seemed it was time for him to intervene. She'd not be pleased to see him, but it had to be better—

"Let me go," she said, her voice low and steady. A cascade of energy seemed to follow, alerting his senses.

The reporter released her immediately, her expression filled with shock.

Astasiya didn't miss a beat, her legs quickly carrying her out of the room.

Issac stood motionless, shocked at the display of power.

All fledglings were gifted with two supernatural abilities, but they couldn't access them until their resurrection—until their Hydraian rebirth.

Just like Ichorians couldn't access their inherent talent until their own death and reawakening.

But this woman could compel.

How was that even possible?

She wasn't a Hydraian yet. And definitely not an Ichorian. He'd sense it in her blood.

What are you, Miss Davenport?

Or better yet, who *are you really?*

He trailed after her engaging scent, requiring answers. She maintained ties to Jonathan, lived with a renowned experiment, and had befriended the late

Owen Angelton. Too many coincidences when wrapped up with her ability to persuade others.

Not a typical human. Far from it.

Issac caught a glimpse of her disappearing into a nearby classroom, her hands fisted at her sides. He entered silently, closing the door behind him without a sound as she stared blankly at the vacant room.

His lips parted, but her rounding shoulders silenced his words.

She reminded him of a broken raven in that black dress, her body curling in on itself as she fought not to cry.

That hint of innocence slammed into him again, confusing his instincts.

She mourned Owen's loss.

A true friend.

Not an act, because she thought she was alone here.

He leaned against the wall, crossing one ankle over the other as he surveyed her long, slender legs—exposed by the dress—and her supple curves. A gorgeous woman, especially with that thick mane of hair.

Time to play this from a different angle.

He waited until her breathing evened, and murmured, "Well, that was enlightening."

Astasiya's hand flew to her chest as she whirled around. "Jesus," she managed on a harsh exhale. "You scared the shit out of me."

Issac slid his hands into his pockets and cocked his head to the side. "I'm curious. How old were you when you realized you could bend others to your will?"

She paled. "What?"

"Oh, come now, Astasiya. Feigning ignorance doesn't suit you. Order me to do something instead. I dare you."

She froze instead, her full lips parting, her slender arms locking at her sides. All signs that confirmed his suspicions. Not only that, but she was very aware of her gift as well.

"I thought the hysterical woman might just be emotionally mad," he said, pushing off the wall to saunter closer to her. "Persuasion is a rare gift, after all." An understatement. Issac knew of only one other with the ability—Osiris.

And wouldn't he be pleased to learn of Astasiya's existence.

A fledgling who could compel without having been turned.

The things Issac's kind would do to her… Correction, the things *he* should do to her…

Alas, no.

Not just yet.

He tucked a stray blonde strand behind her ear, reveling in the way it made her pulse skip a beat. "The scene with the reporter—telling her to let you go—was clear compulsion, Miss Davenport." He'd witnessed it countless times during Conclave meetings. She certainly possessed the power of persuasion, a dangerous ability in the wrong hands, indeed.

She swallowed. "How long have you been watching me?" The steady quality of her voice impressed him, especially with the way her heart thundered in his ears—a calling card to his kind.

"Long enough." He allowed his gaze to roam, admiring the elegant lines of her dress and the way it hugged her curves. Gorgeous. Athletic. The type of woman he'd entertain in his bed before leaving in the morning. Except this one possessed something more, something that piqued his interest in a way few others had throughout the centuries.

Her pupils flared as he met her gaze again, her heightened breaths an indication that his open perusal of her assets had not gone unnoticed. And the subtle hint of interest in her green irises told him the attraction was mutual.

But he doubted she'd be as easy as his usual conquests.

And he liked that about her.

"It's customary for one in my position to kill you on sight," he informed Astasiya, deciding not to lie to her. "Fortunately for you, darling, I'm not an admirer of our archaic laws."

Fear tinged the air, her tongue darting out to lick her lips. Yet her expression hardened, as if she was struggling not to lay a retort at his feet.

Fascinating.

All it would take was a command and he'd back off, yet she remained quiet. Nearly stoic. Unfazed.

"You really have no idea what you are, do you?" The prospect of a fledgling walking about with persuasive abilities intrigued him immensely, so much so that he smiled. "Amazing. You were adopted at age seven, yes? Surely you learned something from your birth parents before that point?"

Her fingers curled at her sides, her shoulders tensing. "I learned not to trust the supernatural world."

"Yes, I'm guessing the house fire was a cover story." He'd read about it in the report. "Very nice of the Davenports to take you in, though." He considered her carefully, searching her features for tells to decipher truth from lies. "Does anyone else know what you can do?"

She folded her arms, her bare skin brushing his suit jacket in the process. If she wanted him to step back, she'd have to try harder.

Astasiya cleared her throat, her pupils narrowing. "It's not something I go around advertising, no."

"Then you clearly want to live."

"Most people do," she replied, her voice flat and emotionless. Too bad for her that he could *hear* the escalated rhythm in her chest.

And it was bloody intoxicating.

"Are you going to get to the point of this visit anytime soon, or do you plan to tell me more things I already know about myself?" she demanded, causing his lips to curl.

Feisty.

He approved.

"Tell me, darling, would you like to know more about your unique talents?" It was a test phrased as a query. What he really meant was, *Do you know what you are?*

The slipping of her bravado answered him immediately.

No. She had no idea.

And now he'd baited her, because curiosity flashed across her features, and a longing that nearly fractured his plans. It wasn't nice to play with fragile toys, and while she exuded a tough exterior, a delicate essence lurked beneath her skin.

One that gleamed with hope as she asked, "You can tell me?"

"I can," he admitted. "For a price."

The hint of hope died, replaced by a flash of annoyance. She glanced over him, her lips flattening into a line of disapproval. Not the usual look women gave him, especially when dressed in an expensive suit.

"You don't look like someone who needs the money."

Ah, right, she's still clueless. He chuckled and considered fondling the strand of hair brushing the side of her breast. It would be soft, addictively so.

"I do love that you have no idea who I am," he confessed. It felt like an eternity had passed since he last hid from humanity. Hopefully, his reasons for being in the city and in the spotlight would diminish soon—something this woman just might be able to assist him in accomplishing. Especially with her connections and otherworldly ability.

"You know, a name would help with that," she snapped.

He smirked. "No, I find I like the anonymity." He leaned into her space, his eyes holding hers. "But do let me know when you figure it out."

"By, what, calling you?" she asked sweetly.

Humor touched his chest. "You could try." But even if she found his name, no one would put her through to his phone without permission. Maybe he'd add her name to the approved list, just for fun. Maybe he wouldn't.

She pursed her lips. "Can you tell me who killed Owen and why?"

Probably not, but… "I can tell you all sorts of things." And he could always work with her to determine the culprit behind Owen's demise. Lucian would benefit from the information as well.

"For a price," she repeated, amusing him more.

"Indeed."

She considered, her brow furrowing. He wondered if she would try to demand some answers out of him. That would spoil his plans, but he knew how to answer evasively, had been doing it for years with Osiris. And once she realized that, she'd hopefully take him up on his offer. Because he *wanted* her to agree, to enable him to have the opportunity to learn more about her unique background and talent.

And to determine if she was yet another product of Jonathan's lab.

Like her roommate.

"What do you want from me?" she asked, her voice holding a touch of uncertainty.

He admired her neckline again and the way her dress stopped at her thighs. Magnificent, long legs ending in a pair of heels that accentuated her calves. "Money is not the only form of payment, darling," he murmured, meaning every word.

Why not mix a little business with pleasure? Assuming she agreed, of course.

And the flush creeping up her neck said she did.

She swallowed, her tongue darting out to lick her lips again as if readying them for his mouth.

Fear, he found, lent well to foreplay. He gave in to his desire to fondle the loose strand of her hair beside her breast, his fingertips purposely brushing her dress along the way. Her nipples beaded beautifully beneath the fabric in response, another tell of her mutual interest.

Something to play with later.

"I'll be in touch when I decide what I desire." He gave her hair a subtle tug, releasing it. "Until then, I strongly suggest you keep that psychic gift of yours under control. You never know who might be watching, darling."

CHAPTER THREE

Demons and Nightmares

So much pain. It pierced Stas's chest, *suffocating her so severely she couldn't help but reach for the source of the agony.*

"I'm okay, little angel," her mom assured. "I'm okay."

"Mom hurts," Stas whispered. "Bad hurt."

"I know, baby. But I'm okay." Her mom pulled her into her arms, holding her tight. "I love you."

"I love you too, Momma."

A game of hide-and-seek.

Go play.

Go hide.

Don't come out.

That's what Daddy had said.

And she listened because he always liked to play. She went to her favorite spot in the trees, waiting, but he never came.

She waited and waited and waited.

But nothing.

"Daddy?" she whispered, peeking through the branches, her forehead marred with a frown. He should have found her by now.

Stas crept out of her spot, quietly. He'd told her not to come out until he found her. She'd promised. Maybe she should stay.

But what if he couldn't find her? She'd chosen a real good spot this time. Her lips twitched to the side. He probably just needed a little help.

She took a few more steps, her nose twitching at the smoke wafting through the trees. A fire.

Oh no!

Her little legs carried her fast toward the flames, her heart beating in her chest. But a hand stopped her, holding her back, caging her as her parents screamed.

Cruel black eyes flecked with gold.

A sinister smile.

Her parents burning, the agony of their deaths ripping Stas in two.

Momma! Daddy! But her voice refused her, a prisoner to her own body, forced to watch their suffering. She could do nothing, not even as Owen joined them, his face contorted on a scream.

The smell…

The heat…

It consumed her, ringing a bell in her head, forcing her to—

Stas threw her phone across the room, her body convulsing violently.

Fuck.

It'd felt so real. Her limbs shook from the exertion of her fight, her shoulder burning as if the hand actually held her now, not just in her nightmare. She shuddered, her knees tucked into her chest.

Not again.

Not now.

But ever since finding Owen in his apartment, she'd been unable to sleep without the night terrors.

So fresh.

So new.

So cruel.

She hadn't saved them. She hadn't saved Owen.

Not that she could have. Not that she'd known. But the torment of it all stole her breath, left her limbs quivering in the bed, her body fighting for air as she, too, burned with her parents and friend.

"I hate this," she whispered. "I fucking hate this."

She pulled a pillow over her head. It felt like a truck was attempting to parallel park on her skull. Forward, backward, crushing every bone. She cursed a blue streak when her alarm continued to sound from the ground.

I'm going crazy.

It had to be the guilt. She should have told the police the truth about the two men in Owen's apartment, about the stranger who held her against the wall. What if they found something? The man said there wouldn't be any evidence, but what if he lied?

She pressed the pillow harder into her head.

If they found out she'd lied, she could be accused of working with the murderer. But her instincts had held her back, an old part of her believing that the cops really would think her insane if she mentioned the men.

Just like they did when her parents died.

They called it a house fire—an accident. Even when she screamed and cried and told them a man had burned her parents alive, no one *listened* to her. The deranged stories of a child, using her imagination to tell an outlandish tale. It left an inherent distrust in her heart, one that she hadn't considered in years but felt rise to the surface when the police arrived at Owen's apartment.

Don't say anything. They'll just think you're crazy.

She couldn't live through it again, so she'd given them a version of the truth—that she'd come over to study with Owen, found his door ajar, and discovered his dead body inside. The shock had rendered her useless, making her sick, before she could finally place the call.

And they believed her.

She showed them the text message.

They confirmed it was sent after his death and asked if she'd seen his phone.

She lied and said she hadn't.

Then *he* found her at the memorial service, the demon with all the answers.

Yes, a fucking demon. That's what she'd decided to call her mystery suit man since he wouldn't give her his fucking name.

She growled into her pillow, her mind fracturing from the lunacy of her life. This did not happen to normal people.

Normal people can't compel.

Not helping!

"Stas?" Lizzie knocked on the door softly, likely having heard whatever screams Stas had let loose during her nightmare. "You all right in there?"

"Yeah." Ugh, her throat felt like sandpaper. "I'm fine."

"Uh, okay. I'm making coffee."

Such magical words. Her roommate knew her way too well. "Thank you, Liz."

Stas removed the pillow and blinked up at the ceiling.

It's Sunday morning.

Graduation day.

She glanced at the clock.

Henry and Susan Davenport were expecting her in less than an hour. And they had an afternoon of activities planned, all meant to take her mind off of Owen and to celebrate her accomplishments.

It sounded like hell.

But her adopted parents had flown in from Montana to celebrate.

Lifting a hand to her aching skull, Stas padded into the bathroom.

Well, didn't she look fantastic. Tangled hair, bloodshot eyes, sunken cheeks with sleep marks etched into her fair skin.

Nothing a good old-fashioned shower can't fix.

* * *

Wishful thinking because the shower didn't fix anything. Not even Stas's makeup could hide the dark marks beneath her eyes, but at least she rocked the dark blue dress and matching heels.

She didn't bother drying her hair, opting for coffee instead. Caffeine worked wonders.

Walking into the kitchen, she found Lizzie dressed in a lavender dress and white heels, holding Stas's favorite mug. "One teaspoon of brown sugar already added."

"I love you." A sentiment meant for her best friend and the liquid gold inside her cup. Stas took a fortifying sip and smiled. *See? Everything's better now.*

Her roommate scanned her with discerning brown eyes, her pink-painted lips scrunching to the side. "Still not sleeping well?"

Stas sat down at the breakfast table, sighing. The coffee seemed to be helping her head heal, but not her soul. "Nightmares," she admitted softly. "I hate them."

"About your birth parents again? Or Owen?" Lizzie knew a little about Stas's history with sleepless nights because they lived together. There were only so many times a woman could wake up screaming before the other demanded an explanation. But they grew less and less common over time.

Now they were back in full force.

"Yeah." Stas shuddered as an image of Owen's head rolled through her mind. Literally. Still on fire and rolling.

"I'm sorry," Lizzie whispered.

Stas's hand tightened around her coffee mug. "I'm sorry, too." For her birth parents. For Owen. For lying to the authorities. For allowing a demon to leave her tongue-tied in a classroom. For—

"Do you want anything besides coffee? There's some quiche in the fridge from yesterday." Most days, Lizzie acted more like a mom than a roommate. Sometimes it drove Stas nuts. This morning, she appreciated it.

"That sounds great." She started to stand, but her best friend beat her to it.

"You keep working on that caffeine binge. Can't have a grumpy Stas today."

She snorted. *Can't argue with that logic.*

Taking another fortifying sip of the liquid heaven left Stas feeling warm and relaxed. She should marry coffee. It'd probably satisfy her more than a man ever could, except maybe a certain blue-eyed demon. Similar to the one smoldering up at her from her roommate's society magazine.

Stas choked on her last sip, snatching the paper from the other side of the table.

Sapphire gaze. Chiseled jaw. Broad shoulders. Tapered waist. Sexy as sin.

A literal male advertisement for men's fashion.

No. An article.

About her demon.

"*Holy shit.*"

Lizzie turned around, her focus falling to the magazine in Stas's hand. "Oh,

I know, right? I mean, I guess he's handsome and wealthy, but calling him one of New York's hottest bachelors is a bit of a stretch, isn't it? Just because his dad, like, created the CRF doesn't mean he's going to inherit the company." She huffed as she set a plate in front of Stas and collapsed into the seat across from her. "False advertising, if you ask me."

She gaped at her best friend. "What are you talking about?"

"Tom." She gestured at the tabloid. "And I can't believe they used that picture of him." She shook her head. "That man rocks a suit way better than army garb."

Stas blinked back to the article. Tom Fitzgerald's wide grin flashed up at her from the opposite page. "Huh." He and her demon were in the same featured article. She read the title on the front.

New York's Ten Hottest Bachelors.

Issac Wakefield was listed at number two. The thirty-four-year-old billionaire was the CEO of Wakefield Pharmaceuticals. Apparently, he inherited the company from his father at the young age of twenty-five. No wonder he expected her to recognize him. Almost everyone would, except Stas rarely followed this gibberish. She preferred business articles, of which she'd read several about his company, but she'd never thought to look for a photo of the CEO.

"This is insane," she marveled. Her demon was a billionaire playboy who masqueraded as a murder scene detective. *Because* that *happened in real life.*

"I know!" Lizzie slammed her coffee cup down. "Did you read the part about how he's ready to settle down?" She forced a laugh. "Yeah, right. That man is married to his job."

Stas focused on the other article so she could see what her best friend was going on about. "It's not a bad picture." He actually looked pretty good in those fatigues, with his muscles on display, his sandy hair windswept, his dimples flashing.

My demon has dimples too.

Not that she cared to think about that.

She refocused on the words, ignoring the temptation to glance at Issac's photo again.

"They captured his personality pretty well, Liz. The article calls him a hero for his time overseas, saying it's admirable that he took a job in the CRF paramilitary unit rather than on a business team." A Sentinel, as the CRF called him. Most of the men recruited for that section had military backgrounds, making Tom a perfect candidate considering he spent several years in the Special Forces. He could have gone into a government agency, but his father owned the CRF. It also paid better since it was privately owned and funded.

Lizzie's snort did not match her housewife appearance. "Yeah, a true humanitarian."

"Come on, Tom's not that bad." Stas pushed the article back across the table before she gave in to the urge to study Issac again. *Not happening.*

"I know. That's exactly the problem." A deep sadness overcame Lizzie as she gazed at Tom's picture. Every other male in this city noticed her feminine charms except the one man she actually wanted. Hell, Lizzie could prance around in a skimpy swimsuit and the former sniper still wouldn't see the supermodel in front of him.

Lizzie closed the magazine, her expression holding a touch of resolve as she met Stas's gaze.

"I don't like that look," Stas started, her quiche uneaten before her.

"Yeah, so, speaking of Tom… he's coming to dinner tonight."

Stas groaned at the mention of the dreaded after-graduation dinner. She would rather gouge her eyes out with a spoon than spend an evening with the Watkins family. It was bad enough she saw them once a month for brunch with the Fitzgeralds—a tradition, which started over twenty years ago, that she was roped into during her first year at Columbia.

"Oh, no, you're not backing out of dinner," Lizzie said before Stas could even suggest it. "Our parents are going to finally meet. They missed each other at our Columbia graduation, something I *know* you orchestrated, but they are meeting this time."

"To be fair, they were busy giving you this condo." A multimillion-dollar property on the Upper West Side. Somehow, they felt giving it to her would make up for all the years they mistreated her growing up. Stas wondered what gift they had in store for their only child tonight as she graduated with her master's degree in education.

"Yeah, a convenient excuse." Her gaze narrowed. "They're meeting tonight, Stas. You're not bailing on me."

Stas put her head down on the table. Owen was supposed to have been her date tonight, to help keep her sane. And also to celebrate his own graduation.

Which was clearly not happening now.

"This week sucks," she grumbled. An immature statement, but true.

"Want to order pizza afterward and binge on chick flicks all night?" Lizzie asked, a note of childlike hope in her voice. She'd not be eating much during dinner, not with Lillian Watkins present. The willowy woman strictly controlled Lizzie's diet, claiming it to be her motherly right. *Bitch* didn't even begin to describe her or the way she'd tormented her daughter's self-esteem throughout the last two decades.

Which, of course, meant Stas had no choice but to attend dinner. Someone had to protect Lizzie. Still, that didn't mean she couldn't negotiate a little something here. Peeking up at her best friend, Stas arched a brow. "Can we order one with pineapples and ham?"

"Sure, one of the pizzas can be Hawaiian. I'll pick the other two." Lizzie possessed a love for Italian food that never managed to go to her hips. Amazing, really. She could eat five pints of ice cream a day for a month and still resemble a supermodel.

"Pizza for a week?" Stas mused. "All right, deal."

CHAPTER FOUR

Dinner Crashers

"Are you all right, sweetheart?" Susan Davenport asked for the fifth time today.

Stas loved her adoptive parents to death, truly, but this line of questioning had to stop. She was close enough to breaking down without the constant check-in on her feelings.

"I'm okay, Mom," she lied. Graduating without Owen this morning had created a bruise on her heart, which left her aching all afternoon.

He's really gone.

She knew that. But the reality of it… She swallowed, refusing to do this here. If she cried, her mother would demand she return to Montana—a threat that had been looming since she told her adoptive parents about Owen's death.

"It's all right to mourn, hon," her father murmured, his hand on her shoulder. "I know it's a big day and all, but you can feel sad, too."

And I do. Trust me, I do.

But tears solved nothing.

She wanted to know who killed him and why. Something the billionaire demon might be able to tell her.

No. Not a good idea.

Except she hadn't been able to stop thinking about him all day. Now that she knew his name, he was suddenly accessible.

One phone call.

One agreement.

He might be able to tell her.

"Stas?" her father asked, his brow furrowing.

"I'm okay," she repeated. "Really."

Their expressions said they didn't believe her.

Good thing she had a distraction plan in place. "The Watkinses and the Fitzgeralds are already here." She gestured to the table in the corner of the dining room where they always sat.

"Are we late?" her mother asked, glancing at her watch.

"No, they're always early." Much to Stas's chagrin. They constantly made her *feel* late. "Come on, I'll introduce you."

Everyone stood to greet them. Doctor Fitzgerald first, his suit immaculate as always and his fatherly grin in place. Tom second, his charming features clearly marking him as his father's son. Then the Watkinses and Lizzie.

Everyone shook hands, Susan blushing fiercely when Doctor Fitzgerald complimented her by saying she didn't appear old enough to have a daughter Stas's age.

It was true.

The Davenports had been in their early twenties when they adopted Stas. But not many knew the truth, so no one clarified the relationship. It wasn't so much a secret as it was a sensitive subject. Stas always referred to them as *Mom* and *Dad* out loud.

"Congratulations on your graduation, ladies," Doctor Fitzgerald said as everyone settled into their respective seats.

"Thank you," Lizzie said softly from beside Stas. Lillian sat on the other side, her expression as constipated as ever. The woman seriously needed to stop investing in face-lifts; it was only making her appearance worse. And her husband, well, he could stand to lay off the sweets. Not that he seemed bothered as he snagged a roll from the center basket.

"How'd your interview go the other week, Stas?" Doctor Fitzgerald asked, his dark eyes crinkling at the sides. The man didn't look a day over forty, despite having a twenty-seven-year-old son.

"It went well," she said, relieved to discuss something normal and non-Owen related. "Human Resources said the job is mine once I finish the security process." Which included passing a polygraph this week. Hopefully, they didn't ask about anything crime-related because she was pretty sure lying to the cops during a murder investigation qualified.

"That's right. You're the one who got our Stas a job at the CRF," her father chimed in.

"Oh, your daughter did that all on her own." Dr. Fitzgerald smoothed a hand over his suit jacket. "I just helped open a few doors, is all." Because he was the CEO and creator of the CRF, she was willing to bet he did a hell of a lot more than that, but she accepted the compliment with a smile.

"The marketing director adores her," Mister Watkins put in with a self-satisfied nod toward Dr. Fitzgerald. "Very pleased with the recommendation."

"But she has to take a polygraph?" her father asked as a tingle itched at the base of her spine. Subtle, but pressing, and prickling the hairs along her arms.

She glanced at the entrance as Issac Wakefield sauntered into the restaurant dressed in yet another suit. Black jacket, pants, and shoes, and a maroon shirt open at the collar.

With a gorgeous female ornament on his arm.

Her matching dark red dress boasted a V-neck created for a woman with her body type, her breasts proudly on display and barely contained. The back was equally as sinful, dipping to her ass, which swayed as she walked.

Well. So much for Stas's theories about what Issac wanted from her. He clearly already had what he needed in the sexual department.

She barely noticed the shorter male who walked in behind him with his arm wrapped around a similarly dressed model.

"Stas?" her father's voice brought her back to the table.

"Yes?"

"I was asking for your thoughts on the polygraph." He arched a brow.

"I've already given you my thoughts on it," she replied, unsure of why he was bringing this up again. "It's part of the job requirements." The CRF was a privately owned humanitarian organization with ties to various government agencies. It seemed standard practice to require a polygraph, as many of the positions dealt with classified information.

"Yes, but isn't it a bit intrusive for a civil employee?" her father pressed.

Says the high school principal who advocated for athletic drug testing, she thought, recalling the citywide argument regarding invasion of privacy.

"I mean, I can understand employees who handle government documents undergoing the security clearance process, but not everyone else," he added.

"Trust me, if we could avoid it, we would in a heartbeat. Do you have any idea how expensive it is to run a top-secret security clearance on every potential employee?" Dr. Fitzgerald rubbed the back of his neck. "It's not cheap."

That seemed to appease her dad a little, but he still pursed his lips.

"We really appreciate everything you've done for our Stas," her mom interjected, changing the subject before her father could say anything more on the topic. He'd made his feelings on the security process known from the beginning, but Stas didn't understand why he was making such a big deal of it. She didn't have anything to hide.

Well, except for her persuasive problem.

And lying to the cops at Owen's crime scene.

Okay, so she harbored a few secrets, but surely she could pass a polygraph. Right? Maybe?

She glanced at the demon who knew her darkest confidences yet remained a complete stranger to her. He raised a brow in greeting, then tilted his head toward his gorgeous date. Her lips were at his ear. Whatever she said seemed to amuse him, because his lips twitched. The familiar intimacy between them left a sour taste in Stas's mouth, causing her stomach to churn.

This was the Issac she read about in the article—the desired bachelor. He clearly had a different woman on his arm every night.

So what does he want from me?

She forced herself to refocus on the conversation at the table. Something about Tom's recent mission overseas where he helped deliver food and water to a group of orphaned children. She could feel her mother melting into a puddle of goo beside her, while Lizzie focused on her salad plate. The menu was always set before they arrived, a nine-course meal organized daily by the chef.

"Well, it's good to know Stas is working for such an amazing organization," her mother said, her cheeks flushed. "It's hard having her so far away, I mean, but some of my worrying is eased by knowing she has a family here."

"It's been our pleasure, I assure you." Dr. Fitzgerald winked at Stas.

"Of course, the whole thing with Owen has me a bit on edge."

Stas groaned. "Oh, Mom, please don't."

"What? I'm concerned for your safety, Stas. Your friend was *murdered*."

As if she didn't know that. "It's not…"

Sapphire eyes met her own over her father's shoulder.

Oh, shit.

"Well, isn't this a small world?" Issac said by way of greeting, his lips quirked up into a devious smile as he moved around the table to stand directly behind her, his hands settling on the back of her chair.

Lizzie started hitting Stas's thigh. She assumed the repetitive tapping was Lizzie-code for *Oh. My. God.* But Stas couldn't move. She couldn't even breathe.

"Wakefield." Tom's shoulders were rigid. "Can we help you with something?"

"Oh, I've been helping myself just fine lately, but thank you, Thomas." His palm slid to her shoulder, branding her bare skin and sending a jolt of electricity through her heart. "I apologize for interrupting. I only wanted to congratulate Astasiya on her graduation this morning."

Dr. Fitzgerald raised a dark blond brow. "You two are acquainted?"

Stas wondered the same thing, but about Tom and Issac. Maybe they both attended a "Hottest Bachelors of New York" club. Her lips twitched at the thought.

"We met through a mutual acquaintance," Issac replied. "Owen Angelton. You've no doubt heard of him, yes?" He brushed her pulse with his thumb in a proprietary move that heated her neck.

What are you doing? she wanted to ask.

Dr. Fitzgerald steepled his long fingers on the table, his posture relaxed. "Yes, we were just discussing that. He was supposed to be your date tonight, right, Stas?"

Thanks for the reminder. She cleared her throat. "Uh, yeah, he wanted to meet everyone." She shook the cobwebs from her brain and tilted her head back to meet Issac's gaze. "Thank you for the congratulations, Issac." She used his first name on purpose and found she rather enjoyed saying it out loud.

His responding grin stole the breath from her lungs. Holy crap, a man should not possess such a smile. It could be dangerous for women with certain heart conditions.

"Of course, darling." He squeezed her shoulder before refocusing on her parents. "I don't believe we've had the pleasure of meeting. I'm Issac Wakefield."

"Uh, right. These are my parents. Susan and Henry." Her mother looked ready to faint under the directness of Issac's gaze. Her father, however, seemed to be missing the guns he kept at home. *Great.* They were making assumptions about their relationship.

"A pleasure," Issac murmured. "Do you mind if I steal your gorgeous daughter for a moment?"

Her eyes narrowed up at him. *What game are you playing?*

"Not at all," her mom replied, her excitement palpable.

Stas fought the urge to groan.

Her mother wasn't vain, just excited by the prospect of her daughter seeing someone. Stas's dating history could be counted on one hand. Not for a lack of trying by the male population, but because she just didn't date. School always took precedence.

"Astasiya?" The hand on her shoulder lifted, palm up, a gesture for her to stand.

Well, it wasn't as if she had a choice in the matter. "Excuse me," she said, standing without taking his hand.

"Gentlemen"—Issac's attention shifted to the Fitzgeralds and Lizzie's dad—"always a pleasure."

He pressed his palm into the small of her back, burning a hole through her satin dress as he guided her through the restaurant. Stas would have a lot of explaining to do when she returned. Her leg had taken a steady beating from her best friend's fist the entire time Issac stood behind her. The *"Oh. My. God"* code had changed to *"What the hell is going on?"* after he announced their acquaintance.

The demon escorted her into a dark corner near the elevators of the reception area. She turned right before the wall and put her hands on his sturdy chest when he would have advanced another step closer. "Thanks for that, Issac. They're going to think we're dating now." Which they definitely were not ever going to do.

Warm fingers wrapped around her wrists. "I decided what I want as payment."

Her eyebrows met her hairline. "And you had to tell me now?"

His heated gaze slid slowly over her, taking in every inch of her dress along the way. She fought a resulting shudder, not wanting to react to his nearness or the intimacy of his touch.

Why did he have to be so damn good-looking? Like a supermodel standing inches from her with his perfectly sculpted, aristocratic features.

And those damn eyes…

"You look beautiful in this dress, darling." The accented endearment had her hackles rising.

"Yeah? Your date looks beautiful in her dress too, Issac."

She took a step back into the wall as he advanced on her. The hands on her wrists kept her from pushing him back as he crowded her personal space. Sandalwood mingled with bourbon, a tantalizing combination.

"This is not—"

"Clara is not my date," he interjected, his broad shoulders and substantial height cutting off her view of the restaurant's lobby and forcing her to focus solely on him. "When did you figure out my identity?"

"This morning."

"How?"

"Apparently, you're one of New York's hottest bachelors." Her face warmed at the admission of how she discovered his name. "Lizzie likes society magazines."

His chuckle caressed her in a way it shouldn't, causing her to squeeze her legs together in protest. *This man is fucking potent.*

"Not at all how I expected, but I'll accept it." He stroked his thumb against her wrist. "Were you surprised?"

"Yes."

"Good, I adore that about you. Which brings me to what I want, assuming you still wish to strike a deal with me." More circles against her skin. Each one hot and branding and distracting.

Why did he have to be so close to her?

Every inhale drew his scent closer and every exhale felt too hot.

He came here with another woman.

Who he claims isn't his date.

That's irrelevant.

But he knows what you are…

She swallowed. Not only that, but he had offered to tell her. For a price.

Just this morning she chastised herself for even considering a deal, but now, well, now she wanted answers. Again.

"Will you help me find out who killed Owen?" she asked. Because she knew in her heart the authorities wouldn't be able to solve this case, not after the way they reacted at the crime scene. They just kept muttering the word *impossible* and scribbling nonsense in their books.

Issac tilted his head. "You care more about Owen than your own heritage?"

"I care about both," she clarified. "And I want answers to both."

He released her wrists and rested his arm against the wall over her head while gazing down at her. "Demanding more from me before knowing what I require?"

She didn't back down. "I'm giving you my terms."

"What about mine?"

Her heart hammered in her chest at his nearness, his lips only a few inches from hers. "Name them."

He smiled, indicating those were the words he desired to hear. "I want you, Astasiya."

The image of him stripping off her clothes and taking her up against the wall flashed behind her eyes, making her knees go weak. *That can't be what he means.* The man obviously didn't need to trade answers for sex. "I'm not following."

"Hmm, how to phrase it." The hand lying at his side moved to her hip, his opposite arm still over her head, while her limbs remained limp at her sides. All her focus was on inhaling enough oxygen to keep her brain working. "I need certain individuals to believe we're dating, and for that to work, I require your voluntary participation."

Okay, not at all what she expected him to say. "Why the hell would you want to do that?"

"Maybe I like you."

She narrowed her gaze. "Or maybe you have an ulterior motive."

"Maybe it's both." He shifted closer, the heat from his body seeping into her skin and influencing her in dangerous ways—like encouraging her to tilt her head back as he lowered his mouth to hover over hers.

"Dating for information," he whispered. "A simple quid pro quo situation. You help me and I'll help you."

"How is our pretending to date going to help you?"

The devil grinned in his gaze. "Does the why really matter when I have the answers you seek?"

Did it? She wasn't sure. "If I agree, will you tell me what I am?"

"Hmm." His attention drifted to her mouth, his pupils flaring. "I will after our first date."

"Not now."

He shook his head. "Payment first, then answers." His palm slid up her side to wrap around the back of her neck. "Now, do we have a deal?"

For years, she'd sought an explanation for her unnatural talent. And this man—demon—was the closest she'd come to understanding her condition. He might be able to tell her how her parents died. And Owen.

All she had to do was play along.

A few dates.

Gather some intelligence about the supernatural world.

Find out what happened to her friend and her family.

All by pretending to be Issac Wakefield's girlfriend. Not exactly a hardship. She just had to keep her emotions in check, which wouldn't be a problem. Stas didn't do love or relationships.

"Okay," she agreed softly. "Dating for information. I accept."

"Brilliant." His fingers knotted in her hair, his thighs aligning with hers. "Just one more thing."

She swallowed, her breathing shortening. "Which is?"

He smiled. "This."

"Th—"

His mouth silenced hers, his tongue sliding between her parted lips with the expert ease of a man used to possessing a woman.

And fuck, he tasted divine. Like the finest bourbon, smooth and hot, and edged in age.

Her thighs clenched, her stomach tightening, his kiss dominating her in a way she'd never experienced. One swipe of his tongue and he owned her. Which shouldn't be possible. Not when she knew the truth about him.

Not human. Not real. All a charade.

But the heat pressing into her lower belly certainly felt *real.* As did the way his palm tightened against her neck, holding her for his sensual assault.

He took her slow at first, thoroughly introducing her to his preferences and skill before emboldening the kiss. Each stroke embodied a mixture of warning and promise, telling her just what to expect from him between the sheets. Issac would take what he wanted, when he wanted it, however he wanted it. She had no choice but to accept him, her body succumbing to his every will.

How is it possible to feel so entirely owned from just a kiss?

He branded her.

Controlled her.

Caressed her.

And released her just as her arms encircled his neck.

His hand was still in her hair, his mouth only a breath away from hers. "Thomas." The growled name vibrated her chest.

She blinked. *Thomas?*

"I'm only going to say this once." Issac's broad shoulders blocked her view of what sounded like a furious Tom. "Release her."

Arousal swam in the depths of Issac's gaze. He brushed his lips against her temple and her ear. "Consider our deal sealed." A breath of words meant for her alone. "Is there a problem, Thomas?" he asked, louder now, as he moved to her side, his arm sliding around her lower back.

Tom, Stas thought, frowning. No one ever called him Thomas. Then again, no one called her Astasiya, either. It seemed her demon harbored a dislike of nicknames.

"Go back to the table, Stas." The command in Tom's tone startled her. In the six years she'd known him, he'd never spoken to her like that.

"Excuse me?" she asked, daring him to say that to her again.

"Now, Stas."

Her eyebrows shot up. He'd gone full military officer on her, using a tone he usually reserved for work. Why the sudden protectiveness? Yes, he treated her like a sister, just like Lizzie, but whom she dated wasn't his business.

Not really dating.

Also not the point.

As if hearing her thoughts, Issac nibbled her neck. The look Tom gave him in response screamed murderous intent. What the fuck was wrong with him?

"It's all right, darling," Issac murmured against her throat. "We'll catch up properly later."

"Like hell you will," Tom replied.

Stas gaped at her friend, mortified and at a complete loss for what to say.

"You can stand down now, Sentinel," Issac said, the heat of his body leaving her side. "I'll see you soon, Astasiya." The insinuation in his tone had her stomach clenching. His lips had seared her being, leaving her with a promise of so much more.

It's a charade, she reminded herself. *He's just playing with you.*

But that kiss had certainly felt real…

Tom glowered after her demon, his body tense, his expression darkly serious.

Stas hit his arm to grab his attention and to refocus her own. "What the hell is wrong with you?" Her fingers tingled from the punch, his biceps far too solid. She knew he worked out, but damn. He resembled a rock beneath the suit.

Tom's dark brown gaze reminded her of molten lava as he stared down at her from his over-six-foot height. "He's not who you think he is, Stas."

Yeah, she already knew that. "I can take care of myself, Tom."

"He's bad news," he continued. "You can't date him."

Stas had never been the type to take orders well. "I'm not having this conversation with you." His intentions might be in the right place, but he had no right to dictate her personal life.

"Yes, you are. Tell me you won't date him."

"I'm not going to do that."

"Yes, you will."

"Do you even hear yourself right now?" she asked. He sounded insane.

"I'm just looking out for you."

She sighed, understanding. Issac showed up with a woman on his arm, only to end up kissing Stas outside of the restaurant. Not exactly Boyfriend of the Year material, especially in her friend's eyes. Still, it wasn't any of Tom's business what she did in her personal life.

"How do you know him?" she asked, changing the subject.

His expression darkened. "Through work."

"Wakefield Pharmaceuticals donates drugs to the CRF?"

He snorted. "Hell no. Look, he's not a good person, Stas. Which is why you need to stay away from him."

And back to the original topic. "I make my own decisions, Tom."

He folded his arms, his expression dubious. "Well, you're making a bad one."

She shook her head, done. "I love you, but I'm not talking to you about this anymore." She brushed past him before he could reply, refusing to say another word. The deal was done. She'd play Issac's game in exchange for answers. Nothing more, nothing less.

The demon in question raised a glass to her as she walked by, as if to say, *Cheers, darling.*

Yeah. Cheers, she thought back at him. *I need a drink.*

~*~

"You're toying with an innocent girl's life," Aidan remarked as he sipped his brandy with an elegance only acquired by time.

"Perhaps," Issac replied as Astasiya reclaimed her seat at the table in the corner of the dining room. That blue dress of hers clung to every curve and revealed a pair of legs that were designed to be wrapped around a man's waist. Preferably, his. "He does appear surprised by our acquaintance, yes?" he asked, switching topics.

"It's genuine," Clara murmured, her perceptive blue eyes on their former ally. Her knack for sensing emotions was why he'd invited her to dinner tonight. "The whole table is shocked." Which meant Jonathan hadn't sent Astasiya to meet him that fateful morning at Owen's apartment. He suspected that to be the case, but he still desired confirmation. Now that he had it, his plan could move forward.

"She's your type," Anya noted, her perfect lips taunting him with a smile. The woman adored flirting, hence the revealing dress she wore displaying all her ample assets. The dark beauty held nothing back. Aidan was a lucky man. "We all know how you feel about natural blondes," she added.

"Except this one seems conflicted." Clara frowned. "I don't think I've ever seen a woman react to you like this, Issac. It's quite phenomenal, really."

He started. "I thought you couldn't sense her?" From what he'd surmised, Astasiya was impervious to supernatural gifts.

"Well, no, I can't, but this one doesn't stare at you in adoration like all the others do."

He followed her gaze to the blonde in question and grinned when he found Astasiya glowering at him. Yes, this woman had spirit. One of her many positive traits. The elder Fitzgerald caught him looking and lifted his brow, his curiosity clear. Brilliant. That marked Issac's secondary goal for the evening as accomplished.

Aidan cocked his head to the side. "She might be useful, Issac."

"Yes." In more ways than one. He could enjoy her company while also using her to exact revenge, and if she lived, he'd give her to Lucian. The Hydraians would be thrilled with the addition of her persuasive power.

"Perhaps you should try not to get her killed?" Aidan suggested over his glass of brandy.

Issac studied the man he considered to be his father, the one who always seemed to know his thoughts and plans before they were fully contrived. "Casualties are a consequence of war, Aidan. You know that better than anyone."

"Ah, but is it her war to fight?"

Issac didn't hesitate. "It is now."

CHAPTER FIVE

Security Clearances Are Bullshit

"Lizzie?" Stas called as she dropped her purse by the door. "Why does it look like Valentine's Day threw up in your condo?"

There were flowers everywhere.

All shades, sizes, and scents.

"Liz?"

No reply.

Stas ventured into the formal dining area, then the kitchen, and down the corridor to the master suite. Lizzie sat inside with her bare feet kicked up on the desk, her computer keyboard in her lap. She didn't glance up from the screen as she asked, "Did your parents make it to the airport okay?"

"Yeah." It took some reassuring, but they eventually got on the plane. She understood their concerns. However, Stas had never been the type to hide from her fears.

Which was exactly why she'd agreed to date a demon.

He came from a world that fueled her nightmares, but he also possessed all the answers. If he wanted to harm her, he would, with or without her permission. She might as well use him in the same manner he intended to use her.

"So, uh, why does the condo look like a flower shop?" Stas asked, her nose crinkling from the floral aroma.

Lizzie shrugged. "I don't know. Maybe ask your *boyfriend*."

"What?" *The flowers are for me? From Issac?* "Why?" Was he trying to give her Valentine's Day–themed nightmares?

Her roommate moved the keyboard to her desk. "There's a card by the vase of exotic lilies in the kitchen. Why don't you go read it?"

Right, still mad about the Issac thing.

"By the way, he's not my boyfriend," Stas grumbled as she left for the kitchen with Lizzie right behind her.

"Uh-huh."

"I didn't lie to you, Liz."

"No, you omitted it. I've been trying to get you to go on a date for six years. What happened to *I'm not interested in my MRS degree*?" Lizzie's tone went high as she parroted Stas's favorite excuse for not dating. She went out sometimes and didn't mind sex.

Well, occasionally.

Okay, hardly ever.

To be fair, her experiences weren't something to brag about. With the exception, maybe of last night, and that'd only been a kiss.

Stas found the card on the counter and read it.

I'll pick you up at six o'clock tomorrow. -Issac

Cocky much? Tomorrow was her security interview. What if it ran over?

"For the record, *this*"—she handed the card to Lizzie—"will be our first date." Assuming she agreed to the high-handed proposal. *Of course you will, idiot.* "And I didn't tell you I met him because I didn't realize who he was until yesterday." Something she already explained after dinner last night.

Lizzie chewed her lip, considering. "What are you going to wear?"

"I don't know. Jeans and a tank top?"

Manicured nails clicked on the counter. "Try again."

"A skirt?"

"And?"

"A tank top."

Lizzie sighed dramatically. "What am I going to do with you?"

"Help me get ready for my date?" she offered, knowing her best friend lived to play beauty consultant. Stas enjoyed fashion as much as the next woman, but no one knew clothes better than her roommate. The woman lived and breathed high society, and if anyone could prepare Stas for a night with Issac Wakefield, it was Lizzie Watkins.

"You need me," her best friend said.

"I do," Stas admitted.

Lizzie tapped her jaw, pensive. "All right, you're forgiven pending an afternoon of chick flicks, wine, and leftover pizza."

That sounded like a horrible way to spend her Monday off. *Not.* "Deal."

Lizzie held up a finger. "*And* you wear the outfit of my choosing on your date tomorrow. I'll put it on your bed before I go to work." She managed an after-school program for underprivileged kids, meaning she wouldn't be home when Stas left tomorrow. And the wicked gleam in her best friend's eyes said whatever outfit she had in mind would double as a punishment.

"You drive a hard bargain, Liz."

Her roommate held out her hand and wiggled her fingers. "Deal?"

I'm so going to regret this, but what choice do I have? She shook Lizzie's hand. "Okay, deal."

* * *

"Have you ever committed a serious crime?"

Stas swallowed. *Don't think, just answer.* "No." *Breathe in, one, two. Breathe out, one, two.* Her reflection in the one-way mirror gave nothing away. She remained poised, confident, and aloof.

The polygrapher—Agent Stark—wrote something down beside her while the machine ticked loudly in her ears.

Don't think, she repeated to herself. If she allowed herself to consider—

No. Stop thinking.

"Have you ever met an Ichorian?"

Oh, this again. The first time he'd given her this question, she'd asked him to define *Ichorian.* He'd stopped the test and reminded her that some of the questions were meant to throw her off, hence the made-up phrases and words.

Now she knew how to answer. "No."

Again with the ticking.

And the scribbling.

They'd been doing this for hours, round and round, question after question.

Does he know about Ow—

Stop thinking!

She focused on her reflection again, studying her blouse. So much more conservative than the outfit Lizzie had picked out for her date later.

Oh, much safer.

Stas pictured the dress as she answered all the same queries.

Have you ever traveled to Greece?

No.

Have you ever manufactured, purchased, or sold drugs?

No.

Have you ever met a Hydraian?

No.

"This now concludes round six of the security interview for Astasiya Davenport. Recording to end in three, two, one..."

A click resounded through the room, causing her shoulders to sag. The contraption around her abdomen dug into her bra, but she didn't care. This whole ordeal was far more exhausting than she anticipated.

"We're done," Stark said, his tone emotionless. He pushed away from his desk and helped extract her from the polygraph instruments without a word. "Follow me" was all he said.

Man of many words.

His muscular stature reminded her more of a military man than a business professional. He possessed a commanding air, one that sent a chill down her spine. This was not a person to defy or piss off.

If he suspects I lied… She swallowed. No. She couldn't think about it. Or Owen. Or the fact that lying to the authorities was most definitely a serious crime. *It's over. It's fine. Everything's going to be okay.*

And what would he do anyway? Drill her about a crime she may or may not have committed?

Except, lying could cost her this job.

Better than ending up in prison for omitting information.

Stark stopped abruptly to knock on an all-white door that matched the pristine corridor. It felt so clinical in the lower levels of the CRF, reminding her of a vacant hospital. No one wandered down here. No paintings or door signs. Just vapid walls revealing a maze of rooms with the occasional security camera dotted above.

The marketing department upstairs was an entirely different world, filled with windows overlooking Manhattan, colorful cubicles, and smiling faces. Perhaps Stark should pay the floor a visit. His stern features could use a little brightening.

A petite woman with darker features and caramel skin opened the door, her gaze lifting to Stark without faltering. "Sentinel."

"Doctor," he returned flatly. "Astasiya Davenport is here for her medical examination."

She gingerly lifted the sleeve of her lab coat and blinked down at her watch. "You're early."

"Her polygraph finished sooner than expected."

Does that mean I passed? Or failed? Stas wondered.

The doctor studied him for a long moment, his expression as stoic as ever. "I see," she said slowly, joining them in the hallway and closing the door behind her. "Then I'll proceed with the exam, if you wouldn't mind…?"

He nodded.

Something passed between them. Something unpleasant.

Clearly a history here. Maybe they used to date?

Stas suppressed a shiver at the wrongness, chalking it up to their clinical surroundings. It just felt so cold down here.

"Astasiya, I'm Doctor Patel." The doctor held out her hand. Despite the smaller size, she delivered one hell of a shake. "If you'll follow me, please."

Stark didn't say anything, but Stas could feel his light eyes on them as they walked down the hall. A glance back at him confirmed her suspicions, the knowing glint in his gaze causing her stomach to churn.

It's just nerves.

Or I failed spectacularly.

But he couldn't know about Owen. No one did except for her demon.

"This way," Doctor Patel said, opening a door to the left.

Stas followed her inside, swallowing the bile rising in her throat. Everything about this felt wrong. *It's the guilt.* There was no other explanation. Yet, what was she supposed to do? Admit everything during the polygraph? She'd come off as a lunatic and would definitely not obtain her clearance for the job afterward.

"All right, have a seat." Doctor Patel gestured to the exam table. Such a simple request, yet Stas's feet resembled lead as she moved across the room. Goose bumps pebbled her skin, her insides twisting at some subtle threat she couldn't diagnose.

What the hell is wrong with me? It's just a physical exam.

"Let's start with your medical history," Doctor Patel said from her computer in the corner. She asked a few standard questions, none of which were all that intrusive, yet Stas still felt that prickle of unease at the back of her neck. Something that told her she was being watched. Carefully.

Paranoia.

It had to be.

This was the CRF, the company she'd interned with for almost a year. The renowned humanitarian agency owned by Doctor Fitzgerald, who had been nothing but a mentor to her for the last six years.

She clearly needed more sleep.

"Vitals," Doctor Patel continued, taking Stas's blood pressure, checking her lungs and heart, and drawing blood for a panel.

All standard.

All completely acceptable.

Until she revealed a tray of syringes.

"What are those for?" she wondered out loud.

"A few common vaccines." Dr. Patel explained as she retrieved a clipboard from the desk. "It's mandatory for CRF employees. You never know when you might have to travel for a work assignment."

"I wasn't aware my position required travel."

"It's standard procedure here." Dr. Patel handed Stas the clipboard with a few documents attached. "These are the consent forms. They explain the three different types of shots that will be administered today and their potential side effects. Review and sign, please."

Stas's brow furrowed. It seemed more prudent for an employer to inoculate employees after they were cleared for hire. Or maybe even wait until the first business trip. Vaccinations weren't exactly cheap.

"You can always deny them," Dr. Patel added, her near-black eyes eerily observant. "But I'll have to note that in your medical exam records."

Meaning Stas might not be given a security clearance if she didn't agree. Add that to a potentially failed polygraph, and, well, she could kiss her job offer goodbye. Not even Doctor Fitzgerald could fix that problem for her—all of this was mandated by the government, not his company. And those contracts were what kept the CRF alive.

Might as well at least see what vaccinations they were requiring.

Hepatitis. Pretty standard.

Typhoid fever. Not as familiar, but she'd heard of it.

She frowned at the last one. "Nizari fever?"

"It's a recent development." Excitement lit up Doctor Patel's features. "We're seeing a lot of cases in Asia right now, actually. Hence the requirement."

"Oh." It all seemed a bit extreme, but this was the CRF. Globally renowned and respected, and also the company Doctor Fitzgerald had founded. He wouldn't inject his future employees with anything life-threatening. Besides, Stas had never been sick in her life. Not even a common cold. A few shots wouldn't kill her.

She signed the documents and removed her blouse, leaving her clad in a thin tank top that did nothing to protect her from the cool, sterile air.

"Perfect." Doctor Patel readied Stas's arm for the first injection. "Hepatitis is given in three doses, so you'll need to come back for the next two. The details will be with your new-hire paperwork." She administered the shot while speaking and finished with a Band-Aid.

"Okay," Stas replied, noting the requirement to follow up later.

"This might sting a bit," the doctor warned as she inserted a needle with a peculiar-looking green liquid. "This is for typhoid."

Why is it gre—

Ow!

Sting was an understatement. It felt like the woman had just inserted ice directly into Stas's vein. She bit her lip to keep from crying out. Nerves frayed as the medicine worked its way through her body. It took significant effort not to shiver when the coolness settled around her chest.

"What did you say that was for?" she asked, her voice higher than intended.

"Typhoid. And this last one is for the Nizari."

Another syringe filled with green.

Odd.

She opened her mouth to ask for more time, when Dr. Patel injected her with a shot of liquid fire.

Fuck!

Stas shook from the impact. Cold met heat, causing her mind to fracture beneath the conflicting directives from her nerves.

What in the ever-loving…?

Wow, she was dizzy.

The room swam around her, the lights blinking in and out of sequence. She blinked, her lips parting on a question that her numb tongue refused to help her deliver.

This can't be a normal reaction.

"All done." Dr. Patel's voice sounded far away.

Stas squinted at the tiny woman. *What?* Had she just given her a fourth inoculation? *No, only three on the table. Right?*

"How are you feeling?"

Horrible. Somehow, Stas forced the word "fine" through her dry lips.

"Good. I just need to chart a few things and then Agent Stark can escort you back upstairs."

Stas mouthed, "Okay," welcoming the distraction. Because walking right now was a no-go.

A numbing sensation slithered over her, centering in her chest and expanding outward. She stole a deep breath, hoping to dispel the feeling.

It only worsened.

This can't be a good sign.

But the doctor remained blissfully unaware as her fingers flew across the keyboard in the corner.

Stas closed her eyes and focused, willing her body to accept whatever had been injected into her veins. She could lie down when she returned home. Not here.

It was probably just her nerves catching up to her.

Yes, that had to be it. The guilt brought up by the polygraph coupled with her general unease in the underground of the CRF. She'd feel better as soon as she stepped outside the building. Hell, even off the elevator onto the first floor.

Stas rolled her shoulders, her limbs tingling. But she could feel her arms again—a good sign. Clearly, all just in her head.

She slid from the table to test her ability to stand, and her hands locked onto the exam table to keep her from swaying. Dots danced before her eyes, but she remained upright. A few blinks later and her wits returned, just in time for the doctor to face her.

"You're a little pale. Are you feeling okay?" Frown lines marred Doctor Patel's forehead, but her gaze held a touch of eagerness that sent a chill down Stas's spine.

There is something not right with this woman. How Stas knew that, she couldn't say, but she'd never denied her instincts. Ever.

"Just a little light-headed," she said, forcing a small smile. "It's been a long day." *Can she hear the slight slur in my voice? Or is that just my imagination?*

Dr. Patel studied her for a little longer than was comfortable. "Let me go get Agent Stark, okay?"

Stas nodded once, making the world spin.

Standard vaccinations, my ass.

She'd be researching that Nizari whatever later. After some sleep.

At least the numbness had worn off, leaving her more nauseated than weak. But still dizzy. She focused on re-dressing and forced another friendly exchange when Doctor Patel returned with Agent Stark.

They said some things.

Hopefully nothing important, because she barely heard them. Hardly even paid attention to Stark escorting her back upstairs. Fortunately, he didn't speak much, just instructed her on when and where to scan her badge. He led her to the familiar four-story glass lobby of the CRF and handed over her purse.

Where did you find this?

"Welcome to the CRF, Stas," he said, his light green eyes capturing hers. A hint of familiarity hit her, causing her heart to flutter.

I know you…

Because he just did her polygraph.

Right. Yeah. "Thanks," she said. Or she thought she did, anyway.

With another forced smile, or maybe a grimace, she turned toward the flags decorating her exit. The creepy one in the middle grabbed her attention first, as it always did.

Memento Mori, it said in a fancy scrawl. *Remember that you must die.*

Why, thank you, creepy flag, she thought as she pushed through the doors.

She moved on autopilot, relying on her ten months of experience traveling between the CRF headquarters and Lizzie's condo. Two trains. Walking. Central Park. Oh, Seventy-Ninth Street. Home.

I can sleep now, she thought numbly, half walking, half slouching. *Or maybe I should go to a hospital.*

"Astasiya?"

Her gaze came up from the sidewalk to find Issac leaning against a sleek black car parked outside of Lizzie's building. Another suit. Of course. At least she had on a blouse and skirt this time. Or did she leave her blouse behind?

She lifted her arm.

Nope.

It was on.

When did I do that?

"Are you all right?" the cultured voice asked, causing her to squint in his direction.

Is he real? She tilted her head. *Looks pretty real. Sexy, too. No, we don't like demons. But this one is nice. Oh, he asked something…*

She blanked on what he wanted to know, not that her mouth felt all that capable of replying. Her tongue felt too big, and wow, the world was really moving, wasn't it? She couldn't distinguish up from down from sideways. Everything started to tilt upside—

Hands gripped her shoulders, causing her to stumble back a few steps. *Issac.* Damn, he moved fast. She could have sworn he stood over ten feet away from her just a few seconds ago.

"Your security interview was today. Did that include a medical exam?" His voice pierced the fog, his handsome face far too close to hers.

"Uh." She had to focus. *What did he ask? About my medical exam?* "Yup. Lotsa shotsss."

"Were any of them green?"

"Creepy green." She shivered. "Cold green. Then sooo hot." *Like you.* Ah, she had to stop that. Maybe not looking at him would help. *Oh, yes, closing the eyes…* A slap against her cheek had her flinching and glaring upward at the too-handsome offender. "Ow."

"I need you to stay awake."

Whoa, they were flying.

No, she was flying.

As in, no longer standing but still moving. In his arms, surrounding her with sandalwood and peppermint and lulling her into comfort. She rested her head against a muscular shoulder, only to be jolted awake and set on something leathery. *I'm in his car.*

"Talk to me," he said from beside her. *Is he already driving?*

"I don't feel right."

"I can see that, darling. Tell me about the vaccinations."

She yawned. "Cold. Fire."

He replied with something, but the pounding in her ears overshadowed his sexy accent. Black painted her vision as her head hit something soft. A pillow? She didn't know. Didn't care. Exhaustion consumed her entirely.

No more pain.

No more dreams.

Just… sleep.

~*~

Issac studied the injection sites on Astasiya's arms, noting the discoloration of her veins. She felt cold—too cold—and her breathing was far too shallow.

She's dying.

"Fuck." This couldn't be happening. But here she was, lying in his bed… dying.

Because of me.

Those three words reverberated in his mind, leaving him helpless at her side. He never meant for this to happen, never expected Jonathan to go to such lengths. Yes, sometimes innocents were a casualty of war. He'd said that just the other night, and still believed it.

But this was a casualty he intended to fix.

No matter the cost.

Hence the incoming presence beside him.

"This better be important, Wakefield," Lucian said as he appeared with his teleporter, Jacque.

Issac didn't bother with pleasantries, jumping right to the point. "Look." He lifted Astasiya's hand to show them the inky green lines crawling up her arm. "Is that what I think it is?"

Lucian eyed Astasiya's skin with interest and knelt beside her for a closer examination. His big hand enveloped her wrist, twisting it one way and then the other. "Nizari poison."

Jacque's dark eyebrows shot up into his moppy hairline. "A fledgling? In New York City?"

Issac ignored the teleporter and focused on the issue at hand. They could discuss her heritage later. "I think it's a variant of the venom." The Nizari assassins didn't know she existed because Issac never reported her existence to the Conclave. And as fledglings were rare these days—a result of the lethal Ichorians killing most of them before their immortal rebirth—most of the assassins were retired.

"It's not the Conclave," Lucian said, his lips flattening. "The mark is too obvious."

Yes, the Nizari were known for making fledgling deaths look like accidents. "I think it's Jonathan." No one else would have any reason to test her ancestry. Of course, this implied that he *knew* about her ability to compel. "The CRF gave Astasiya immunizations as part of her medical exam today. She said they were green," he added while listening for her vitals. *So slow. Too slow.*

"Who is this woman, Issac?" The command in Lucian's tone, coupled with his muscular stature and hard stare, would bring most men to their knees in submission. Women, too.

But Issac didn't heel to anyone, least of all Lucian. They were family, after all, despite living on opposite sides of the immortal coin.

"She's a long story that we don't have time for right now." His phone buzzed, security calling from the lobby. *Finally.* Issac answered and told them to let his physicians up. "I have two of my best infectious disease clinicians coming in to evaluate her. I need you to give them everything you know." Both doctors were on his payroll at Wakefield Pharmaceuticals, and they specialized in orphan drugs. Between their skill sets and Lucian's familiarity with the Nizari venom, they might be able to save Astasiya's life.

"Why didn't you report her presence?" Lucian pressed. "She's a fledgling, and therefore mine. You know the rules, Wakefield."

Sometimes Issac really hated the man he called a brother. "I'm not debating this right now, Lucian. I need you to help my physicians save her life. Then we'll discuss her history and how I know her." He dialed Mateo before Lucian could reply.

His progeny picked up on the first ring. "Sire?"

"I need you to break into the CRF's database and retrieve whatever information you can on Astasiya's medical exam."

A second of hesitation passed before Mateo replied, "When I do this, they may detect my virtual presence." A subtle warning.

Mateo was the only being in existence with the technical wherewithal to hack *anything.* And Issac had kept the extent of his abilities a secret for years, hoping to use him as a trump card at the right moment.

It seemed today was now that moment. Because while the young Ichorian possessed the talent to attack a corporation from inside the system, the woman dying in Issac's penthouse flat could hurt his opponent from a much more vulnerable place.

The perfect revenge.

"I'm aware of the risk," Issac replied, his mind already made up. *She must live.*

"Of course, Sire. I'll send the records to your personal file."

"Thank you, Mateo."

He hung up just as his health care professionals arrived. Jacque went to retrieve them, leaving Issac alone with his old friend. Those hard emerald eyes told Issac exactly how Lucian felt about the situation. As the Hydraian King, he wasn't used to being kept in the dark, let alone ordered around.

"You and I are going to have a very long conversation once this is over." Lucian's tone brooked no argument.

"Save her first."

"Fine."

A violent shiver wracked Astasiya, drawing attention to her rising fever. The damp washcloth Issac had placed on her forehead before everyone else arrived wasn't doing a damn thing. His doctors rushed over to assess her, forgoing the usual greetings. *Thank fuck.*

"I'm going to need a few things." Lucian listed them for Jacque. "And bring Alik. Every moment I spend in this city is a risk to my life." He leveled another sharp glance at Issac, his sacrifice clear. New York City wasn't safe for Hydraians, let alone their King. "I need B and Jay, too," he added.

"On it." The teleporter disappeared, something the researchers failed to notice, as they were too engrossed in tending to Astasiya.

In his bedroom.

Not a guest room.

The decision had been made without thought. An oversight for him to evaluate later.

"You owe me," Lucian said, scribbling something down on a notebook one of the researchers had handed him.

On the contrary, Lucian, Issac thought. *Once you realize how powerful she is,* you *will owe* me. *Assuming she survives.*

CHAPTER SIX

Helpful Hydraians

"Start talking, Wakefield." Lucian stood beside Astasiya's comatose form, his thick arms folded over his chest, legs spread. Balthazar sat in the corner chair, while Jayson and Alik stood by the windows, their stances guarded. Every moment they stayed here put all their lives in jeopardy, but it had taken nearly two hours to stabilize Astasiya's vitals.

Now her life was in the hands of the researchers who had left only moments ago to prepare a makeshift remedy at the lab.

Either it would work or it wouldn't.

What if it doesn't?

She appeared so helpless and alone in Issac's bed, her hair fanned out around her in a halo of gold. A foreign part of him longed to lie with her, to provide her with any semblance of comfort he could, if even for a moment. Odd considering he never wanted to hold anyone, not even sexual partners. He preferred his space, hence his requirements to keep women out of his quarters.

Yet, he hadn't hesitated to place her in his bed.

He still didn't know why, didn't truly wish to consider the cause. It had just felt right to carry her here rather than to one of the guest suites. As if he felt compelled to watch over her, to protect her.

"Fascinating," Balthazar murmured from the corner chair, his lips curled at the edges. The mind reader could hear every thought in the room—no, within the entire building and well beyond it—and was clearly listening to Issac now.

Fuck you, Issac thought at him, edging the words with sarcasm.

Anytime, he mouthed back at him. Somber moments be damned, the man oozed sex in everything he said and did, and he certainly didn't discriminate when it came to bed partners.

Never going to happen. A phrase Issac had thought at the male many, many times. Not that it would deter Balthazar in the slightest. One flash of his sinful gaze sent most women to their knees—men, too. Pair that with his athletic physique and the thousands of years of experience under his belt, and, well, most didn't stand a chance against his charm. Yet, he never tempted Issac. Females, specifically natural blonde ones, were Issac's preference. Like the woman in his bed.

Lucian cocked an eyebrow. "I've done everything I can to ensure her survival, Wakefield. I want an explanation. Now."

Right. Procrastinating the discussion served little purpose. Might as well start from the beginning. "Her name is Astasiya Davenport. We met the morning of Angelton's murder."

Issac relayed the story of their fateful introduction, including details about her immunity to his gift for visual manipulation, and the evidence suggesting her long friendship with Owen.

"Mateo pulled the police records," he continued. "Then additional files on her history. She was adopted at age seven by a couple who lives in Havre, Montana, and it seems someone went to great lengths to cover up her life before that moment. She moved to New York to attend the university, which is where she befriended Owen, as I already mentioned. That's also where she met the young Elizabeth Watkins, who later introduced her to the Fitzgeralds."

Jayson and Alik turned from their perches by the floor-to-ceiling windows at the mention of the infamous names. As Elders, they were considered to be the most powerful of their race, which was why they were here. Allowing their King to visit the most dangerous city in the world for Hydraians went against the grain, but their lifelong friendship with Issac circumvented the rules. These men were family, and no treaty or war would ever put them on opposite sides of the playing field.

"She knows Jonathan," Lucian said, scratching the blond stubble dotting his chin. "Which can only mean one thing. You're using the girl to get vengeance for Amelia."

"I am." The words tasted bitter in his mouth, mainly because he felt responsible for her current situation. He only meant to pique Jonathan's interest. Which he clearly succeeded in doing since the lunatic tried to poison the poor woman.

"But she's a fledgling," Lucian added.

"Yes," he confirmed, aware of what the Hydraian King really wanted to know. Fledglings were rare, and one as powerful as Astasiya was even rarer. "In addition to being resistant to psychic gifts, she has a persuasive talent."

Jayson frowned. "Meaning what? She can coax people into doing things?"

"Not coax. Command. Like Osiris." Stunned silence met his words. Osiris was the most powerful Ichorian in existence. Suggesting her gift rivaled the notorious immortal's spoke volumes about her potential. She would be unstoppable after her rebirth.

"You're telling me, that as a fledgling, she has the power to *command*?" Doubt colored Lucian's tone.

"I observed her use of persuasion twice in casual conversation. It was natural and effective." *And sexy as hell.*

Issac's focus shifted to her prone form. Her heartbeat comforted him only a little. The machines were doing their jobs of keeping her alive, but he had no way of knowing how long it would last.

The urge to lie beside her overcame him again, but he swallowed it. Now wasn't the time to show weakness. Not when he needed to negotiate.

"You're soft on her," Balthazar noted in an unhelpful manner. "I mean, I can see why. Even half-dead she's gorgeous, but it's not like you to delve deeper than the surface, Wakefield. She must be phenomenal in bed." Issac tried not to think about it, but the smile that slipped over those too-perfect lips told him his thoughts came over loud and clear. The bastard let out a low whistle. "Wow. He hasn't fucked her yet. No wonder he wants her to live so badly." At Lucian's cocked eyebrow, the mind reader waved a hand. "Yeah, sorry, carry on."

"Tell me more about her relationship with the Fitzgeralds and why you think she can be used against Jonathan," Lucian said, the rock band logo on his shirt peeking through his folded forearms. Even dressed casually, the man exuded authority. Not that Issac would ever bend to him, but on this, he'd compromise.

He relayed what he knew, which wasn't much, yet enough to explain how the girl could be useful. "We all want revenge, and I think Astasiya could be the key," he concluded.

Jayson twirled a knife between his long fingers. His shoulders and muscular stature rivaled the others, but beneath it all was a calm lethality underlined in charm. A dangerous combination, one that aided him well when on a mission to assassinate someone. "Can't we just kill the son of a bitch and get it over with?" he asked, his tone far too pleasant for the words.

"Don't look at me," Alik replied. He was the shortest of the group, at just six feet tall, and also the deadliest. "I voted to slaughter him six years ago when he left Eli's head on that godforsaken table beside his headless body holding Amelia's ashes. Talk to the *King*. He's the one who said it was better to wait."

Lucian rolled his eyes at the jibe. The Elders and Issac were among the few who could harass the man about his *regal title*. No one else would dare.

"From what you've told me, she's not going to be easily swayed to our cause," Lucian said, his expression thoughtful, assessing. "Which also means she's not going to be quick to join us in Hydria, either."

An intelligent deduction, and accurate.

"Astasiya requires a slow introduction to our world. It's the only way to build trust, especially after this." Issac considered the woman in his bed, wondering if she dreamt in her deep sleep. Her immunity to his gift made it impossible for him to know, something that intrigued him more than it should. "I'm up for the challenge of teaching her."

"I'm sure you are." Another unhelpful comment from the mind reader in the corner.

Lucian flashed him a speculative glance. "You realize trusting an Ichorian to mentor and groom what could be the most powerful Hydraian in existence goes against the grain, yes?"

Issac snorted. "Don't be an ass." He might not be a Hydraian by blood, but he was a respected member of their society. They trusted him, and for good reason. "Do you remember that time you asked me to trust Eli not to accidentally kill my only sister?" Technically, Amelia was Issac's half sister since they had different fathers. Semantics.

Lucian's blond brows rose. "You mean the one who also happened to be my sister?" Because they shared a birth father—Aidan. The same man who raised Issac as a youth and eventually turned him into an Ichorian.

"Not the point," Issac replied.

"Entirely the point."

"Whatever. Don't be a dick. You know I'm more than capable of mentoring her, Lucian."

"Because you did such a fantastic job mentoring Tristan."

He had to go there. "Tristan has no place in this conversation." Issac's progeny needed some work, but he wasn't *that* bad. "My gift for controlling vision might not work on her, but it works on everyone else. I'll keep her hidden, introduce her to our world at the right pace, and convince her to help our cause."

"That's a hefty task for the CEO of a billion-dollar enterprise." This from the corner again. Balthazar clearly had a death wish tonight. "I would be better suited for the job. My slate is clean, and you know she won't be able to resist this face."

Not after I disassemble it. "No." Flat. To the point. And nonnegotiable. The mind reader could not—*would not*—go anywhere near Astasiya. Ever. He'd try to fuck her, not teach her. "No," Issac repeated. "End of."

"Worried about your competition, Wakefield?" Balthazar's taunt made Issac's hands curl into fists.

"I'm worried you'll be too busy seducing her to teach her anything." *There, that was a fair argument.*

"On the contrary, I could teach her all sorts of things." The deep tenor of his voice implied *what* he intended to show Astasiya. If anyone would be giving her a tutorial around the bedroom, it would be Issac. Not Balthazar. "This territorial thing you've got going on is cute," the mind reader added, smirking.

Careful, Issac warned. One psychic punch would black out the bastard's sight and leave him curled in the fetal position on the floor—a visual tactic Issac had used on the mind reader many times in their long history.

Balthazar blew him a kiss and waggled his dark eyebrows before looking at the man in charge. "I vote we leave her with Wakefield, Luc. There's more going on in that head of his than he's admitting out loud, or even to himself."

"I'll bear that in mind, B." Lucian's biceps bulged as he combed his fingers through his blond hair and then down his face. "Before I agree to anything, I want some clarification."

"Regarding?" Issac prompted.

"You met Astasiya at Owen's apartment, which means two things. First, you kept her existence from me on purpose until now. And second, she knew Owen. Who else knows about her?"

Ah, this is going to start an argument. "Aidan, Clara, and Anya know, but only because I needed backup for…" He trailed off as Astasiya's heartbeat changed.

It was a reassuring rhythm in the back of his mind, until it wasn't.

Issac knelt by the bed and wrapped his fingers around her wrist. *Weak. Too weak.* Alarms sounded from the machines, making his stomach lurch. *Don't do this to me, Astasiya.*

Balthazar joined him, hand on his shoulder. "I need you to move," he said, his teasing nature subsiding to the powerful man beneath the jovial veneer. He'd attended medical school several times, providing him with the knowledge and abilities to treat Astasiya's condition.

It had been Lucian's primary argument for Balthazar being here.

And despite the man's irritating habits, Issac trusted the mind reader when it came to matters of life and death.

Keep her alive, Issac thought at him, moving out of his way. It grated to defer to someone else, to place his faith in another to do what was needed.

But I can't help her. The words bounced around his skull, making him wince. The Nizari poison killed fledglings. No rebirth. No future as a Hydraian. Nothing. Her death would be permanent.

The ache in his chest reminded him of the day he found Amelia's ashes. An inane reaction to a woman he met less than two weeks ago.

Humans died every day.

His relationship with Astasiya was young at best. He knew little about her aside from the research. Her resilience intrigued him, and their brief kiss foreshadowed a passion well worth the seductive effort, but beyond that, what did he know about her?

She's intelligent.

Brave.

Gorgeous.

Dying…

"That's not good enough." Lucian was on the phone. "No. She's not going to make it. Bring what you have and we'll improvise." He hung up and joined Balthazar's efforts to resuscitate Astasiya.

She'd stopped breathing.

Issac collapsed in the corner chair in the sitting area of his room, his head in his palms as he listened to her waning pulse.

This is your *fault*, his subconscious reminded him.

He made decisions every day that impacted the lives of others, but this one grated on him. Left him feeling… *guilty*.

Innocents died in war every day.

Why did this one bother him?

The loss of whom she could have become?

A hard thud brought his head up. Electricity flowed through the room as everyone waited to see how her heart responded to the paddles against her chest.

It was too silent.

His Ichorian senses picked up on the tiniest thump, followed by another. *Her heartbeat.* The rhythm sounded off, wrong, unhealthy.

"It's only temporary," Balthazar said in his doctor voice, the one void of teasing and seduction. Medicine was one of the few things he took seriously. "I'm honestly surprised she's still alive. Most fledglings die within an hour or two, and she was injected almost eight hours ago."

"She's resilient," Lucian said, frowning. "Do you think Owen knew about her?"

"Yes," Issac replied softly, his body frozen as he focused all his energy on her pulse. *Such a sweet sound.* "Their phone records suggest they've been friends for almost seven years. No way he was around her that long and didn't notice what she could do." Not when Issac figured it out during their second meeting.

"So he knew her for as long as he lived in the city?" Jayson whistled low and shook his head. "That's incriminating."

"It is indeed." Lucian checked something on the machine and gave Issac a nod. "You already know my answer, Wakefield. I'm trusting you to protect what's mine, assuming she lives."

Issac didn't care for the verbal claim. She wasn't an object to be owned or a weapon to be used.

Except isn't that what you're planning to do with her?

Fuck off.

"You know I will," he said, addressing Lucian's comment.

"I do. And you'll call me the second anything changes."

"Of course."

Lucian started to fiddle with one of the cords, then dropped it and pinned Issac with a stare.

And here comes the comment about me talking to Aidan before him, in three, two . . .

"Oh, and the next time you discover a powerful fledgling roaming the streets of New York City? You better tell me before you talk to Dad."

"Duly noted, but let's focus on helping this one survive first." That was all he could think about right now. He needed her alive. He would consider the why of it later.

Lucian nodded. "Fair enough."

CHAPTER SEVEN

A Slow Introduction

Stas's nose twitched and her stomach growled.

Bacon.

Oh, yes, please.

Lizzie loved to make brunch on the weekends, and Stas adored her for it. Especially when bacon was involved.

Stas stretched her arms and legs, feeling a dull ache inside that left her frowning. She felt exhausted despite the nightmare-free sleep. Odd.

She reached over to grab her phone from the nightstand and hit a fluffy pillow instead. Groaning, she rolled closer and tried again. More pillows.

What the hell? Her bed wasn't this big. She blindly patted around. It wasn't this soft, either.

And what the fuck am I wearing? Yoga pants and a tank top. Stas never wore those clothes to bed.

Yawning, she forced her eyes open for a look around.

Floor-to-ceiling windows with a magnificent view of the Hudson River greeted her.

She flew upward, causing her head to spin. "Ow," she managed through her dry throat. Shit, she felt awful. Like a hangover, but worse. Lying down again helped marginally, her vision no longer blurring.

A high ceiling—not common in Manhattan apartments—met her gaze.

Mahogany tones decorated the oversized bedroom suite, and glass doors led to a terrace outside.

Okay, so she was in a building with views of the Hudson River to one side and Manhattan to the other.

Definitely *not* Lizzie's condo.

Stas inched upright and rested against the dark wood headboard, admiring the mahogany tones of the room. Very masculine. A familiar suitcase rested on the floor in the corner beside her purse.

How did I get here?

And when?

She took several deep breaths, calming the spinning in her head. Despite the strange surroundings, she felt safe. An odd sensation, considering, but her instincts rarely failed her.

The familiar scent of sandalwood reminded her of a certain demon, too.

Stas frowned, trying to recall her last memory. Something about the polygraph, being concerned with the serious-crimes question. Everything after that was fuzzy.

Had she drunk too much afterward on her date with Issac?

That would explain her memory loss and presence here, except she rarely overindulged in alcohol. Although, Issac could likely easily drive her to that point. And that would explain the hangover-like throbbing in her skull.

I hope we didn't... yeah.

No, definitely not.

Stas would be naked if they did, not dressed for yoga. And his side of the bed—or what she assumed to be his side—was perfectly made.

Assuming I'm in Issac's room.

She swallowed, her throat reminiscent of sandpaper.

God, she needed water before she figured all this out.

Bathroom.

There, near the glass doors.

Of course, it was across the room.

With a sigh, she slowly slid from the silky bedding. Black spots flashed in her eyes at the undesired movement. Definitely dehydrated and hungover. Great. What had Issac done to push her to drink this much?

Unless he drugged her.

No. No, he wouldn't do that.

Not that she knew him well enough to know for sure.

Her brow crumpled as she gingerly stepped toward the all-marble bathroom. A stack of towels sat on the expensive countertop, the oversized shower behind her a standing invitation. But the giant tub beside it appealed to her more.

Water first.

She grabbed a glass tumbler—there were three—from beside the left sink and filled it to the brim before downing all the contents. The *W* etched into the crystal of her glass further confirmed her whereabouts.

W for Wakefield.

Three cups later, she felt slightly better, but not great.

Although, the brown stone tiles of the shower looked even more inviting now, as did the multitude of showerheads. A glance in the mirror confirmed her need for a wash even more—tangled hair, sunken eyes, pale skin.

"I look like shit," she said to herself, her voice raspy despite the water.

With a shake of her head, she locked the bathroom door, undressed, and took advantage of the gorgeous bathroom.

It was as she ran a bar of soap over her arms that she noticed an array of colors smattered along her skin. They resembled week-old bruises.

"What the fuck?" she breathed, eyeing her inner elbow and bicep in horror. "*What the fuck?*"

A face flickered in her mind, a short woman with dark hair. Something about injections. And an all-white room.

Stas's legs began to shake, her heart hammering in her chest.

She swallowed and grasped the stone wall for support, the hot water doing little to dispel the chill overwhelming her skin.

Her stomach roiled with a memory she couldn't quite grasp, her mind refusing to release the details.

But something bad had happened.

That's how she ended up here.

What did Issac do to me? She frowned, the thought not quite right. Somehow she knew he didn't harm her. Someone else had.

Stas quickly finished her shower, needing answers. She combed her hair with a brush from one of the drawers, then wrapped a towel around herself before venturing back into the room for the suitcase she'd spotted in the corner. Inside was everything she needed—jeans, tank top, toiletries.

Who packed this?

They'd even included her matching lace undergarments—a penchant she considered to be a secret.

Did Lizzie do this?

Stas quickly dressed before searching her purse for her phone.

Several text messages appeared featuring a conversation between her and Lizzie that she didn't remember ever having.

I guess that date went well, then. You can thank me for the dress advice later.

Stas frowned. She didn't remember wearing the dress.

Thank you, Lizzie, was the reply. In Stas's name. From her phone. But she couldn't for the life of her remember this conversation.

So where is he taking you for the week? Lizzie had asked next.

It's a surprise, she'd apparently replied.

Stas snorted. Definitely a surprise, as she had no flipping idea how she arrived or when or where she even was right now. Aside from in Manhattan.

Well, check in every now and then so I know he hasn't kidnapped you permanently, Lizzie had messaged.

You know that wouldn't entirely be a bad thing, Liz...

Who are you and what have you done with my Stas?!

It's Issac... He's just... The words that followed had Stas's jaw dropping. There was no way in hell she would ever say *that* about a man. "Oh, hell no." She started toward the door, when she noticed the date on her screen.

And froze.

Friday.

Wasn't yesterday Tuesday?

"What the fuck?"

Her legs were moving again with purpose, out the door, down the hallway lined with windows, and into a great room the size of Lizzie's condo.

This place is huge.

And it faced the Hudson River, with towering ceilings above, indicating her location at the top of the building.

An oversized couch with two matching recliners faced a mounted television that would make the entire male population drool. A wall of bookcases graced the opposite wall with an oversized U-shaped couch.

The refined elegance and masculine textures were very Issac.

So where is he?

She hung a left between the two seating areas, toward what appeared to be the foyer, and found another hallway just before it that led to the kitchen—a kitchen Lizzie would obsess over. Marble counters and tiles, hardwood cabinets, an island large enough to host a dinner party, and a half-naked Issac beside the stove.

Flipping a pancake.

In a towel.

Her lips parted, her brain fracturing.

Defined shoulders and a wide, muscular back tapered into a lean waist that disappeared into a blue cloth wrapped loosely around his hips. Fresh water droplets hung from his messy dark strands and dripped over skin that was tanner than she expected. The note of chlorine in the air suggested he'd just come from a swimming pool.

How? Why? Where?

Her tongue felt thick in her mouth as he moved from the stove to the island to pick up a plate.

The front was even better than the back—all rippled, lean muscle. And a dusting of hair leading her eyes on a happy trail to the impressive bulge beneath the towel.

"You look refreshed." Amusement underlined his tone and darkened his eyes to an alluring sapphire she could easily lose herself in. "I'm almost done making breakfast. Would you care for a cup of coffee?"

Gorgeous. Half-naked. And offering her coffee.

I must be dreaming.

"Yes," she whispered, unable to think or focus beyond the offering before her. And she wasn't even sure *what* she was accepting, either. Him? The towel? Coffee?

He handed her a cup with a knowing smirk.

She managed a quiet "Thanks" before diving into the life-reviving fuel. The dark blend with fruity notes warmed her raw throat and chest, eliciting a deep sigh of contentment.

This is exactly what I needed.

What about answers?

Her eyebrows lifted. Shit. The demon had completely distracted her practical senses.

She joined him at the island, her back to the counter as he chopped up what appeared to be a fruit salad. A fucking fruit salad. Like they were in some sort of alternate dimension where they played house together.

"What the fuck is going on?" She meant to ask that the second she saw him, but his lack of clothing derailed her focus. *Maybe this is all just one very fucked-up dream?*

"You have no idea how thankful I am to hear that tone, Astasiya." He sounded so casual and at home, like they did this together every day and his walking around in nothing but a towel was completely normal. He flipped a pancake and turned off the burner before crowding her against the island. With one hand on either side of her hips, he stared down at her. "I'm not sure how to word this without sending you into a fainting fit."

"I don't know what that means, so start talking." *God, my throat hurts.* She took another sip of her coffee, abundantly aware of his nearness and the heat flaring off his bare chest.

His forearms flexed beside her, drawing attention to the muscular masterpiece on display before her. She needed to find him a shirt or something before she lost her mind, because *wow.* And did he have to stand so close?

"The short of it is, you nearly died, but my team of clinicians saved your life."

Okay, forget the damn towel.

"I *what?*" *Did he just say I almost died?* This had to be a dream. Or a different reality. *Something.* Because her almost dying seemed way too far-fetched.

Except I did lose several days of memory.

And the healing bruises…

"The important thing is, you survived. As for the how of it, well, it appears the CRF has manufactured their own version of Nizari poison." The coffee cup fell from her hand and landed in one of his. She didn't have time to contemplate his insane reflexes. Her mind was too busy dissecting his words. "How about you sit down, I'll serve breakfast, and we'll discuss this over food. The physicians said you need to eat, and I'm starved after my swim."

It sounded rational enough, but she needed more information. *Now.* "Why would the CRF try to poison me?"

He used a hand on her lower back to guide her toward the dining area and pulled out a chair at the oversized table. "That is one question I can't answer."

"Why not?"

"Because it would be speculation on my part." He returned to the kitchen to continue preparing food while she chugged one of the glasses of water sitting on the table. Using the pitcher in the middle of the two place settings, she refilled her cup and hastily gulped down the refreshing liquid before pouring herself a third glass.

Meanwhile, Issac set a few items on the table.

Her brow furrowed. "Baked beans?" That's *what you want to ask about?* Clearly, her mind had up and died.

And apparently so had she.

Fuck.

"It's an English thing," he replied, already heading back to the stove.

"Right." She picked up the coffee mug that had miraculously followed her to the table—compliments of Issac—and noted the slight hint of sugar. *He knows how I take my coffee.* Only her roommate knew that detail. "Who sent all those texts to Lizzie?"

"Hmm, I believe Balthazar did," he replied, his focus on food preparations.

"And who the hell is Balthazar?" she demanded.

"He was one of the physicians looking after you this week."

"You let a stranger talk to my best friend?" *And you thought that would be okay?*

"He's not a stranger." He brought over a frying pan. "He's an old friend whom I occasionally want to punch in the face. Pancake?"

"Sure." *Why not?* She chewed her lip as he added one to her plate and put two on his own. "Okay, I can accept the texts because they kept Lizzie from worrying. But what's a Nizi-whatever?"

"Nizari," he corrected as he brought over a skillet of eggs and bacon, adding two spoonfuls to the space beside her pancake. Then he placed several scoops on his own breakfast array.

Domestic Issac.

I'm totally dreaming.

But why the hell would I dream this?

Issac brought over the fruit bowl and took the seat across from her at the very long, oversized table for twelve.

Okay, seriously, the man really needed to put on some clothes. Those abs were lethally distracting and only half-hidden by the table, and she needed to focus.

"A Nizi-ari-thing almost killed me," she said slowly. "I don't even know what that means."

"Nizari," he corrected again with a chuckle. "Eat something first, and I'll tell you what you want to know."

"I'd rather you tell me now." The scent of bacon taunted her senses while her stomach churned from all the water she'd imbibed. Or maybe it was just the realization that she'd almost *died. What the ever-living hell?*

"Eat," he told her, demonstrating with a few bites of his own.

"Explain," she countered.

His lips twitched. "Nice try, darling. Your health matters more to me at the moment. I spent a great deal of money in resources to ensure your survival, and we will follow the doctors' instructions. Now *eat.*"

Her gaze narrowed at the command in his tone. "I deserve an explanation."

"And I intend to provide one once you're sufficiently fed."

Fucking games. "You told me I almost *died,* and you're going to make me wait for an explanation? Fuck you."

He sighed, setting down his fork. "Astasiya, this is not a two-second discussion." His midnight gaze traveled over her. "The physicians said you're healing remarkably well, which I suspect is a result of your genetics. Those bruises on your arm were fresh a few hours ago, but look days old now. And it would appear the Nizari poison is out of your system. But to maintain your healing, I need you to eat."

She glowered at him. Fine. She'd eat. Using her fork, she cut off a piece of the pancake on her plate—blueberry—and took a bite.

Stas had every intention of swallowing it immediately in a show of defiance and demand, but the flavors on her tongue forced her to savor it. Because wow, whatever he did to that pancake surely fit the definition of *decadence.*

Even the eggs were delicious.

Okay, so she was hungry.

Very hungry.

But she also wanted answers.

"What's a Nizari, Issac?" she asked after washing down some of the food with a glass of water. He had resumed eating while she gave in to the temptations on her plate. It hadn't been her intent, but the flavors, paired with her growling stomach, forced her hand. Literally.

Issac regarded her while chewing, his chiseled jaw flexing with the movements. He picked up his coffee, taking a long sip, eyeing her the whole time. "How about we make a deal?"

Her eyebrows lifted. "What kind of deal?"

"I'll tell you what you need to know, but not everything. Not yet, anyway."

That sounded like a horrible idea. "Why the hell would I agree to that?"

"For several reasons, the foremost being you're not ready to know everything yet, and the second being you still owe me a few dates. Dating for information, remember?"

"I think my almost dying voids our deal."

"It voids nothing, but I'll give you the details you need, and I'll continue to give you information as we date."

Her fists clenched. She wanted to throttle him. "Tell me what the hell a Nizari is, Issac." Stas wove a hint of compulsion into her tone, causing his nostrils to flare.

"It's a poison that was developed by an elite group of Conclave assassins who used it centuries ago to slaughter fledgling immortals after realizing their threat to the Ichorian race. The assassins were referred to as the Nizari. Hence, the elixir they created was named after them. However, the one used on you was a variant, not the pure substance." His gaze narrowed. "Now, compel me again, darling. I dare you." The threat lingering in his tone was lost to her chaotic thoughts.

Conclave.

Assassins.

Ichorian. Hadn't her polygrapher mentioned that term?

"Fledgling immortals?" she managed to ask out loud, her brow crumpled.

"Yes. It's what we call your kind. Fledgling for short." He waited for her to comment, but she had nothing, her mind running all the words in a loop, searching for some aspect of familiarity.

Nothing.

Issac ate another bite, leaving her to her thoughtful silence.

Maybe he'd been right about the need for slow information because none of what he'd said made a lick of sense. All she'd gathered so far was that someone had tried to poison her. And apparently her *kind* was referred to as *fledgling immortals.*

Is he implying I'm immortal?

But he also said she'd almost died.

"How are you feeling, Astasiya?" he asked softly after nearly finishing his plate. "I know this is a lot to take in, but I mean physically."

That seemed like a safer topic, one she could actually understand and focus on.

How was she feeling?

"Dehydrated," she decided. "My throat is sore, my head hurts like I'm hungover, and I think this might be the first time I've ever been sick." She frowned at that last part. *It's also the first time I've ever almost died, apparently.*

How is this my life?

"You've never been sick?" he asked. "Not even a cold?"

"No." Something she chalked up to always keeping herself in decent health, but was likely related to her… *immortality. I'm a fledgling? And assassins want me dead?* "Can we go back to why the CRF would want to hurt me?" Because she couldn't wrap her head around that. All she remembered was her polygraph. Had something happened after that?

"I suspect the CRF used the Nizari poison on you to test your bloodline. But as I said earlier, that's speculation on my part."

"When?" she asked, completely lost.

"When they administered your vaccines during the physical exam." He frowned at her. "Do you not recall telling me about the green shots?"

That woman's face flickered through Stas's thoughts again. A tray. Needles. A pristine room. Something about papers and weak explanations. "It's fuzzy," she admitted, worrying her lower lip and shaking her head. "I don't remember much after the polygraph."

"Well, it seems the CRF gave you a series of inoculations, one or several of which were a manufactured compound of the Nizari poison."

"But why?"

He sighed. "To test your fledgling bloodline, or that's my theory, anyway."

Right. Speculation. And he'd already said that.

But it didn't make sense. Why would a renowned humanitarian agency dabble with poison that killed fledglings? They didn't even know about immortals, right?

"Have you ever met an Ichorian?"

Wasn't that the term Issac had used just moments ago?

"What's an Ichorian?" she asked.

"What I am," he replied smoothly.

"And…" She paused, thinking back over his explanation. "They kill fledglings?" *Like me?*

"Yes." No hesitation. No hint of remorse. Just a straight response paired with an unreadable expression.

Well, shit. She licked her lips, considering. She could ask him why he didn't just let her die, but she suspected he would answer evasively. He wasn't ready to admit her purpose here, or he would have told her already. He didn't strike her as the kind of man who waited when he wanted something.

"During my polygraph, the agent asked me if I knew any Ichorians," she said slowly, pairing what Issac had accused the CRF of doing to her with her experience during the security process. There had to be a logical association, one that didn't equate to them trying to kill her. This was Doctor Fitzgerald's organization. The man she considered her mentor. The father of one of her friends. He would never hurt her.

"I'm not surprised. Did the polygrapher ask about Hydraians as well?"

She blinked. "Yes." That had been the other term Agent Stark mentioned. "What's a Hydraian?"

"Your future," he answered vaguely.

"Meaning?"

He smiled. "Astasiya, I'm thankful you're alive, more than you know, but that doesn't mean I'm going to answer every question."

"That makes you an ass."

He folded his arms over his bare chest, drawing her attention to all those defined ridges of muscle decorating his abdomen. "Sure. An ass who saved your life and made you breakfast."

"That's not fair."

Issac leaned toward her, his blue eyes narrowing. "Who said anything about fair?"

He stood to casually stretch his arms over his dark head. Every sinewy inch of him not covered by the towel was on display, something she suspected he'd done for her benefit.

Amusement flirted with his lips, confirming her suspicions, as he lowered his hands.

Devious man.

Demon.

"Hmm, I'm feeling generous," he murmured. "So I'll answer something you haven't actually asked yet. Not with your mouth, anyway."

"Yeah? And what's that?" She couldn't help the sardonic note in her tone, irritated with his evasiveness. He'd barely told her a damn thing. The damn—

His towel dropped.

"A swimsuit, darling," he said with a wink before turning to leave.

Stas tried to scowl. She really did. But the swim trunks showcased strong legs and an exquisite ass. The man was walking perfection.

"Oh, and don't go anywhere," he called back to her over his shoulder—a muscularly lean shoulder that melted into a sexy-as-fuck backside. "We're not done yet."

He disappeared, taking the gorgeous sight with him.

Stas groaned, her forehead hitting the table as she attempted to beat some sense into her brain. She *never* swooned, but Issac, well, he'd certainly awakened some feminine-nonsense gene inside of her.

Lizzie would be so proud. After years of only having passing interests in men, Stas finally found one undeniably attractive. And it was one she most certainly should not be fawning over.

Damn demon Ichorian.

Whatever the fuck that all meant.

Ugh, she was in trouble. She needed to follow him and demand more answers, but pissing him off, especially after he saved her life—assuming that was true—didn't seem like the smart play. While her command earlier had worked, he'd clearly been irritated. And his explanation hadn't made an ounce of sense, really.

Still, she had one answer.

I'm a fledgling immortal.

This man, being, Ichorian, whatever, clearly had the answers she'd been searching for the last seventeen years. Too bad he wouldn't just give her all the details now. There had to be a reason, something she wasn't understanding.

The CRF?

What would have happened during her polygraph if she had admitted to knowing an Ichorian?

She drummed her fingers against the tabletop. Issac's accusations regarding the CRF didn't marry up to the organization she knew and adored. How would a humanitarian organization know anything about the elixir that almost killed her? They were involved in international affairs, not supernatural nonsense. Issac had admitted it was speculation, meaning it may have been someone else who poisoned her, but who?

He saved me. That part radiated true within her heart, igniting another question. *Should I trust him?* Her instincts whispered, *Yes*, but common sense held her back.

She needed more information—information Issac didn't want to give her yet.

Fine.

They'd play this little game.

And if that didn't work, she'd tie him to a chair and compel him to give her answers.

CHAPTER EIGHT

Gifts from Hydria

Issac paused on the threshold of his living area to admire the view of Astasiya lounging on his favorite couch. All that glorious blonde hair was pulled over one shoulder, leaving her neck exposed.

The innocent gesture taunted the predator within him, exciting his hunting instincts.

He hadn't fed in nearly two weeks, a long time for an Ichorian. But he'd been slightly preoccupied by the female on the couch. Maybe he should snack on her, provide her with the true definition of his kind.

Vampire—a word he loathed.

Monster.

Fallen angel.

She shifted, pulling her jean-clad legs beneath her, not yet sensing his presence. Something had consumed her attention. It appeared to be a book of sorts.

What did you choose, darling?

Issac finished fastening his cuff links while approaching the beauty on the couch. He moved silently behind her to peer over her shoulder, Astasiya too engrossed in her book to sense him.

What he saw in her lap made his blood run cold.

It wasn't a book at all, but a photo album. One that held cherished memories he preferred not to revisit.

"Where did you find that?" he demanded. Because it didn't belong here.

Stas's fingers trembled as she touched the page. "You knew Owen." Her softly spoken words alleviated the pressure in his chest, but only slightly.

"We were acquainted, yes. Did you find that on the bookshelf?" He would bet good money Jacque put it there. *Damn teleporter.* He loved leaving little reminders of Hydria all over Issac's condo. A not-so-subtle hint to visit.

"You told me you didn't know him." Accusation underscored her tone.

Issac couldn't recall his precise phrasing. Had he implied he didn't know Owen? "We weren't so much friends as we were acquaintances."

Laying his jacket over the back of his couch, he sat beside her.

She traced the photo, her lower lip trembling. Ah, the date, yes. Not to mention the attire. She'd clearly identified a key element in Owen's existence—his immortality.

"I don't miss the fashion of that decade," Issac murmured, noting the bell-bottom jeans and flowery shirts in the photo.

"He was an Ichorian, too?" she guessed.

"Not quite, no."

Her full lips curled downward. "This photo looks like it's from the seventies. It's decades old." A clear deduction that didn't require his confirmation. She looked at him. "If he wasn't an Ichorian, then what was he? Because he obviously wasn't human if he still looked twenty-something today."

"He was a Hydraian."

She continued to stare at him. "Okay, so what's the difference between a Hydraian and an Ichorian?"

"Telling you that would require defining Ichorian." Which he couldn't do yet.

A slow introduction would foster trust and understanding, something they required between them for this partnership to work. If he told her everything now, she'd run screaming.

Or worse, she'd go straight into Jonathan's waiting arms.

And Issac couldn't risk that, not when he was so close to achieving his goals.

Yet, he'd seen the look in her eyes when he mentioned the very likely scenario of the CRF trying to poison her—doubt. Until he broke that barrier, they couldn't move forward. Her faith was too intertwined with the Fitzgeralds and Watkinses to listen to him. He planted the seed of doubt by speculating about the CRF's intentions. It would be up to her to put the puzzle pieces together now.

"Okay." Annoyance flashed in her green eyes, making him want to kiss her. "So are there more types I should know about?"

"It depends on who you ask. Ichorians and Hydraians are the most prominent, but there are those who believe Seraphim still walk the earth. They're rare and supposedly the creators of my race, but I've never met one."

"Seraphim." Her lips twisted. "Like angels?"

"Why are you giving me that look?" It held traces of laughter and surprise, offending him slightly. "Are you surprised I may be a descendant of the divinity?"

"It...well..." She bit her lip, her eyes crinkling with mirth. "I sort of nicknamed you *demon* when you wouldn't give me your name."

Oh. He grinned. "You gave me a pet name."

"No, I gave you a *name* when I didn't have anything else to call you."

"It's cute." The indignant look she gave him was adorable as well. *So feisty.* "Ichorians are descended from a fallen Seraphim, or so the rumor says, so it's still appropriate." He brushed his knuckles down the curve of her neck. Her soft skin blushed a pretty shade of pink in response. "Mmm, I like my pet name."

"It's *not* a pet name." She flipped to the next photo and his smile died.

He didn't know Owen well, but Amelia did. She knew all the Hydraians.

"He looks so happy here," his blonde murmured, not realizing the turmoil building in his chest.

Issac would be sending this particular reminder back to Jacque.

"Do you know why he was killed?" Astasiya asked while turning the page to display another memory. The blue eyes staring up from the page haunted Issac's soul. He didn't need the fresh reminder. Not today. He took the album from her and closed it.

"I have my suspicions, but nothing concrete." He stood and returned the album to the shelf, his touch lingering on the familiar binding. Amelia's creativity was etched into every groove. There were hundreds of these books in Hydria. Jacque knew what he was doing when he dropped this particular one off. It seemed a call to the young teleporter would be required this afternoon.

"Who is she?" Astasiya asked, her arms folded tightly around her stomach from her position on the couch. "The woman in all those pictures, I mean."

Issac longed to change the subject, but the memories troubling her gaze reminded him too much of his own. This woman understood loss. Not just Owen, but her birth parents as well. The information Mateo provided said they died in a house fire. Clear human fabrication. Whatever happened to her parents weighed heavily upon her. It was evident in the way she studied him now.

"My sister, Amelia." He held out a hand to help Astasiya stand. It served as an excuse to touch her, one she accepted with minimal hesitation despite the shocked expression on her face. Questions brewed in her eyes, ones he had no interest in addressing. Ever.

Besides, they had business to discuss.

"I have to attend a gala tonight, and I would like to take you with me," he told her. "As my date." He dropped her hand and feigned fixing his already immaculate tie. The blood-red color suited his current mood. Having a delectable yet unavailable woman in his bed for three nights was enough to drive a sane man mad. He would definitely need to feed soon. Too bad what he wanted wasn't on the menu.

Issac retrieved his jacket from the back of the couch and put it on while she considered his request.

"Okay," she said slowly. "But only if you give me five more answers to whatever I ask and tell me what an Ichorian is."

His lips curled, intrigued. *Playing with fire, are we, darling?* He welcomed the challenge, especially after that unfortunate walk down memory lane. This—negotiating—he could do. "Are you trying to make a deal with me, Miss Davenport?"

Fierce green eyes met his, provoking all manner of inappropriate thoughts. Like what they would look like in the throes of passion. "No, I'm giving you my terms."

He nearly laughed. No woman ever gave him terms for a date. Not that this necessarily qualified since he considered it more of a business arrangement. They needed to be seen in public together for his plan to work, and to put to rest any suspicions the CRF had about her reacting to the Nizari poison. Winning her over in the process would be an added bonus, one that would make her more helpful.

"I will give you two answers." He tucked a soft strand of her hair behind her ear and let his fingers drift down her neck. "And I will consider defining Ichorian more clearly for you." *By showing, not telling.*

She licked her lips and shook her head. "Three answers and you define Ichorian now."

He moved into her personal space, gripping her hip with one hand to hold her in place when she tried to move away. Their foolish conversation had already gone on longer than he intended. "We leave at seven." He bent so their mouths were a hairsbreadth apart. "And I will only answer your three questions after the gala, not before or during."

Her breath fanned his lips, encouraging him to close the gap between them. But he waited, wanting her consent first.

She gave a tiny nod, her lips grazing his. "Okay." A single word that he took to mean so much more than it really did.

His free hand tangled in her hair as he took her mouth with his. There was nothing tentative about his movements, all power and demand, and she melted into him the way she had the other night at the restaurant. Only this time he didn't hold back. Wrapping his arm around her waist, he pulled her closer and devoured her.

Three days of having her near, but so far away, fucked with his senses. He wanted this woman on a near-lethal level despite hardly knowing her. But when did he ever truly know his conquests?

I want to know her, he thought, deepening their kiss. *Very, very badly.*

She moaned, her tongue engaging his in a sensuous dance that fueled the need growing inside him. Every touch, every stroke, every nip made his intentions clear.

I want you.

And I will have you.

Her body responded in kind, already yielding to his experience and desire.

His hand tightened in her hair, holding her closer. He left nothing to the imagination, showing her exactly who he was and what he would demand, and she didn't back down, meeting him move for move, showing him exactly what kind of lover she would be.

An equal.

Fierce.

Confident.

Her sweet arousal teased his senses, demanding more. Mmm, he longed to take her up on that unspoken offer. Alas, this was only meant as a proper introduction to his needs and intentions. He hardened the kiss, proving his dominance in a single swipe of his tongue against hers. She groaned in response, succumbing to his touch and command.

Oh, yes, they would pair well in the bedroom.

He eased back slowly, showing her with his eyes how she affected him. Promising her more. Vowing to finish this. *Soon.*

"Hmm, I would continue this discussion, but you need to be seen in public." He nipped her lower lip, not hard, just a soft tease for them both.

"Public?" she repeated, her expression dazed.

"Yes." He nuzzled her nose, his palm sliding to the back of her neck. "It will help dispel any uncertainties surrounding your reaction to the Nizari poison."

She blinked, some of the fog lifting from her heated gaze. "You think someone noticed my reaction?"

"It's possible, but seeing you alive and healthy will negate any suspicions. Which is why my driver is waiting downstairs to take you out for an afternoon of pampering." He brushed his lips against hers, enjoying the shiver it evoked from her. "Try to be ready by seven."

"I'll just take the subway home. I have a few cocktail dresses in my closet. I don't need any *pampering*." She made little air quotes with her fingers before gripping the lapels of his jacket. The possessive action warmed him inside, as did her words. A woman denying his gifts provided such a rare experience. He rather liked it, not that he planned to allow it.

"It's nonnegotiable, darling. I've already arranged everything and requested a friend to pull a few dresses for you to choose from."

"Should my closet be insulted?"

He grinned. "No, I rather enjoyed going through your clothes, especially your lingerie. Someone has a lace fetish." He nipped her bottom lip again as she struggled for a response. She'd failed to ask about her suitcase, something he attributed to her general alarm and confusion over the week's events.

"You were in my room?" she finally asked, her voice breathy.

"It was that or dress you in my clothes." An appealing thought, actually. The woman would look fantastic in a pair of boxer briefs and a white T-shirt. No bra or panties, just his clothes against her flesh. Mmm, he would tease her nipples through the thin fabric with his mouth until her taut peaks were visible beneath the shirt.

A beautiful image, one that left his pants a little tight.

He stepped away before he made the image a reality. Astasiya needed time to recover. He also didn't have enough time to indulge in her the way he desired. Perhaps later, after the gala. Something to anticipate.

"Do I want to know how you got into the condo?" she wondered.

"Probably, but I'll have to count it as a question and you owe me a date first." He patted her on the ass because he could, and started toward the foyer. "Enjoy your spa day, darling."

"I don't remember agreeing."

"I don't remember offering a choice." He called over his shoulder. "See you at seven."

Chapter Nine

Smile for the Cameras

She's in the condo.

Issac read the text message from his driver, Benjamin, as he exited Wakefield Pharmaceuticals' headquarters.

He typed a reply saying they would be ready for pickup in twenty minutes. It was only a five-minute walk to his condo building, and he'd changed into his tuxedo at the office. One of the perks of owning the company and the Wakefield Pharmaceuticals' building meant he had another penthouse with a full bedroom and en suite bathroom. Not that he used it often. He much preferred his place off Chambers Street.

He ran a hand over the silk lapel of his buttonless jacket, approving of his Italian designer's creation. The wool kept him a bit warm for this June evening, but the overall fit worked. He'd paired it with a black vest, silk button-down, and trousers. Black on black—his trademark gala attire.

"Evening, sir," Paul greeted as he opened the door to the condo building. It was always "sir" or "Mister Wakefield" no matter how many times Issac suggested otherwise.

"Hello, Paul." He gave the man a nod as he headed toward the elevators.

There were only two condos on his floor, both of which he owned. The larger one he used for himself, while his guests stayed in the smaller residence.

Astasiya, however, waited inside his suite, an intimacy he reserved for only his closest friends and family. She'd stayed in his condo for several days already, nearly died there, so why not give her full rein? It would make her more comfortable.

And yes, perhaps a small part of him enjoyed having her in his space.

Not that he cared to investigate that feeling. There was no future for them. She didn't know that, but he did.

He entered the condo and followed the sweet aroma of lavender and soap to the great room. Astasiya stood by the windows, admiring the view. The evening hours always provided a glorious sight, but he couldn't be bothered to appreciate it now. Not with the gorgeous blonde standing before him.

Sapphire silk hugged her curves, flowing over her long legs to the floor. Two thin straps were all that kept the fabric from falling, leaving her entire back exposed to his touch. The hairstylist had piled Astasiya's blonde hair up high on her head, exposing her neck and making him regret that he'd not had time to feed today.

She'd be taunting him all night.

Perhaps he would return the favor in a slightly different way.

"Hello, darling," he murmured, trailing his fingers down her spine. Her resulting shiver caused his lips to curl. "You're stunning."

"And you look more expensive than you usually do" was her greeting.

Cheeky minx.

His hand fell to her hip as she turned. The slit up her left leg exposed her upper thigh and provided a glimpse at the silver heels she wore. They added several inches to her height and lengthened her already long legs. *Glorious.*

"How was your afternoon?" he wondered, caressing her hip with his thumb. The designer dress certainly met his approval for the evening, though he'd have preferred a dipping neckline to the sweetheart cut.

"The pampering was all right, I suppose." Delight played over her full lips.

Cheeky indeed. "Just all right?"

"It was an experience."

He grinned. "Are you ready for another?" Issac could think of several entertaining activities for the evening, none of them just *all right.* One such activity? Finding out what color lingerie she'd selected. No bra, clearly, but he could feel the faint hint of lace against her hip. He traced the seductive texture with his thumb to the small of her back.

Her pupils dilated, the unveiled suggestion stirring her interest. "Maybe."

Not exactly consent, but he could work with it.

He placed his palm against her bare back, her skin warm beneath his touch. "Shall we?"

Not waiting for a reply, he applied just enough pressure to encourage her to move with him. She did and grabbed a black clutch from the table as they passed it.

"So where is this gala?" she asked as they entered the elevator.

"The Pierre." The flare in her gaze told him she knew of it. Most New

Yorkers did. It was a popular place for events. "Benjamin is driving us."

"The tall, chatty guy who took me all over the city today?"

"That would be him." The old man started working for Issac over a decade ago. A kind soul he paid handsomely to keep quiet about his personal affairs. Talkative he might be, but he understood the value of secrets.

"He doesn't get the night off?" she asked.

"Not tonight." Issac didn't feel too bad about it; the man had been given most of the week off. A result of Issac staying cooped up in his condo waiting for a certain blonde to wake up.

The gray-haired man greeted them as they exited the building, and opened the limo's back door.

"What happened to the car?" Astasiya asked, referring to the four-door vehicle Issac's driver typically used for daily errands.

"I upgraded it," Benjamin replied, grinning.

"Some upgrade," she said as Issac helped her into the limo.

Two flutes of champagne waited for them inside. He handed her one after settling beside her and took the other for himself. "To experiences, darling."

"I have no idea why we're doing this, but sure." She tapped her glass against his and took a healthy sip. "I hope there's food at this event."

"You could say that." These galas were more about the alcohol than the sustenance.

She groaned. "It's going to be one of those hoity-toity affairs, isn't it? With artistic food meant for looking at and not eating?"

"You sound familiar with them. Have you attended one?" He'd never seen her at a charity event, but then again, he usually attended these affairs with a date, so he may not have seen her.

No. Not true. Issac definitely would have noticed her.

"Yeah, no. Not my scene, but Lizzie's been to several. She always complains about the food afterward."

Always piquing his curiosity and surprising him. "Why isn't it your scene?" he wondered out loud. Most women adored lavish affairs.

"I'm more of a movie-date or coffee-date kind of a girl."

"Go on." He made a show of getting more comfortable and widened his legs enough to press his thigh against hers. It was the left one, exposed by the slit in the dress. His hand itched to settle there, slide his fingers beneath the silk, and explore. He busied himself with finishing his champagne and pouring a new glass instead.

"You know, typical stuff. Like spending Friday night at home with a book or watching a movie. I don't like the whole socialite thing. That's Lizzie's scene."

"Yet you appear to be fully ingrained in their world."

"Only by association."

"That's all it takes."

"But it's not *my* scene. I only tag along to keep Lizzie company."

He considered. "Your friendship with Elizabeth is interesting." The Watkinses were social climbers, their daughter a notorious CRF science experiment—not that anyone knew, of course. The stunning redhead wasn't related to her parents at all, something she seemed oblivious to. He wondered when George and Lillian would break the news to her. Allowing her to attend university and work full-time could not be their ultimate plans for the poor girl.

Though, she had met Astasiya in the process.

Was that an accident or something done on purpose?

"How did you meet Elizabeth?" he asked.

"We met during our freshman year at Columbia. She was my assigned roommate. It was awkward at first. She likes pink, I mean *really* likes pink, and hugs, and she can be a bit boy crazy. We had a few ground rules to work out, but she's become my best friend over the years." She smiled. "She's Lizzie."

Ah, so potentially an arrangement then if Elizabeth was her roommate. Interesting. "And that's how you met the Fitzgeralds?"

"Yeah. Sunday brunch. It's a monthly tradition. I think it started before Lizzie was born."

"I'm certain it did." George helped create the CRF and was one of the few who knew what the organization was designed to do. "How are you feeling, by the way?" He'd meant to ask earlier but had been too caught up in her dress. She appeared perfectly healthy, all her bruises healed. A happy circumstance of her immortal heritage, no doubt.

Astasiya swallowed the last bit of her champagne and set it on a table off to the side. "Physically? I feel fine."

"And emotionally?"

"Well, I'm a mix of pissed off, confused, and overwhelmed."

"All reasonable reactions." He leaned over her to set his glass beside hers. Her pulse leapt, enticing the Ichorian within him. Hmm, she needed to add *aroused* to her emotional list.

Issac extended his arm across the top of the seat behind her head while gently tracing the slit of her dress with his opposite hand, crowding her, testing her boundaries.

"I do like this dress," he murmured, studying her reactions.

"That's good, because you paid for it." The confident words almost hid the breathy quality of her voice. Almost.

"Does that bother you?" he asked softly, referring to him paying for her outfit. He typically sponsored his dates' attire for events because he required a certain level of fashion and expense to maintain his public image. However, the spa treatments and allowing the woman to pick her own dress were not typically included in the routine. That had been for her benefit and her benefit alone.

"Not really, but only because I don't know how much you spent on it all. They wouldn't let me pay for anything." She said that last part with an adorable glare. She didn't like him taking care of her. Too bad because he had no intention of stopping anytime soon.

"You would be the first woman to ever complain about that in my presence," he admitted.

"We've already gone over the part about me not being a socialite. Besides, we're not really dating."

"No?" It certainly felt like they were. At least tonight. His thumb slipped beneath the silk, lightly brushing her inner thigh.

"No, it's a business deal. Although, I really don't know what you're getting out of it."

He leaned in closer, his palm sliding up her leg. Her shuddering breath fanned his lips. "Are you sure about that, Astasiya?"

~*~

Stas forgot how to speak, her tongue useless inside her mouth.

That look, the one in his sapphire eyes, set her blood on fire. She fought the urge to clench her thighs, knowing he'd feel her reaction. But fuck, she needed something, *anything*, to alleviate the ache stirring inside her.

This is so wrong.

Yet, nothing had ever felt more right.

If she tilted her head just an inch, their mouths would touch. The temptation had her licking her lips, yearning for a taste. His all-black ensemble was lethally seductive, the vest hugging his muscular torso and highlighting the physique she knew lurked beneath.

His palm branded her thigh, his thumb drawing delicious circles against her bare flesh.

They should just skip the gala and stay here all night.

Except she'd wanted something from him earlier, a thought or question that had weighed on her mind all day.

Fuck if she remembered it now, not with his alluring scent mingling with her every breath.

The champagne was not helping.

Neither was the hot male cage surrounding her.

His arm dropped to her shoulders. "By my calculation, we have about five minutes before we hit Sixty-First Street," he whispered against her parted lips. "Not nearly enough time."

"We could just not go," she suggested, her voice holding a husky quality she'd never heard before.

This man was unraveling all her layers, exposing a part of her she'd never truly explored.

A very sexual part that failed to heed reason.

Her hands went to his chest, the pads of her fingers reveling in the feel of silk against stone. As much as she adored the tuxedo, she wanted to remove it, to explore his bare skin and the ridges of his abdomen.

"A tempting offer," he breathed. "Consider this a prelude."

She opened her mouth for him, accepting his tongue as he thrust inside, taking command in a way that was all Issac.

Her heart raced.

Everything tingled.

And fire licked across her skin, radiating from his palm on her leg.

Devastating, dominating, determined.

Stas lost herself to his embrace, completely intoxicated by Issac's kiss. He lifted her onto his lap, forcing her to straddle him. He palmed the back of her neck, holding her in a way that allowed him the deepest access to her mouth.

She forgot how to breathe.

Forgot how to think.

Her nails embedded in his silky shirt, holding on for dear life, as he devoured her to completion.

Oh God…

She needed more, her lower body shivering with a craving only Issac could satisfy. He kept his grip on her neck while his other hand returned to her thigh, sliding upward beneath the fabric to the lace beneath.

"Issac," she sighed, willing his fingers to move a few inches south to where she desired him most.

"Fuck," he whispered, reclaiming her mouth.

Yes, she thought, writhing over him, searching for purpose.

A flash brightened the air, followed by another.

What? She tore her mouth from his to peer out the tinted windows, her jaw dropping at the line of photographers standing outside the limo in front of them.

"They can't see inside," Issac said softly.

She shivered both from the feel of the hot, aroused male beneath her and the realization that she was about to be surrounded by vultures with cameras. "Shit." Her shoulders stiffened, the reality of their impending situation cooling her heated blood. "Can't we just go to the movies like a normal couple?"

Issac's chuckle vibrated through her as he removed his hand from her thigh. "We're a couple now, are we? I thought this was a business deal, Astasiya."

She swatted his chest and climbed off of him. "You know what I mean."

He leaned over to fix her dress with the ease of a man who tousled women in limos often. Not something she wanted to think about.

His focus went to her hair as he said, "I have to make an appearance tonight; otherwise, I would take you home and do *normal couple* things to you." His blue eyes met hers to mock those two words before he continued messing with her hair. "How do you feel about art?"

"Uh." *Art?* "It's not something I know much about."

"Then we'll skip the auction. I'm not much of an art connoisseur anyway."

"There's an art auction?"

"It's a gala, darling. The auction is a fundraiser for tonight's charity." His fingers trailed down her neck to her arms. "There you are, gorgeous as ever."

His English lilt intensified the compliment, making her warm all over. If anyone was *gorgeous*, it was him in that tux.

He smiled. "Three, two…" The door opened beside him.

A middle-aged man wearing a penguin suit greeted Issac by name, his smile bright.

"Evening, Claude. How are the wife and kids?" Issac asked as he stepped outside.

Stas frowned while the man answered, his tone jovial. *Issac must visit the hotel frequently to be so familiar with The Pierre's staff. How many dates has he entertained here?*

Does it matter?

Not really, no.

"Brilliant. Happy to hear they're doing all right," Issac said, his hand appearing in the doorway.

An invitation to escort her into the frenzy that waited outside.

Cameras.

Vultures.

Most of them were waiting, but a few were already taking photos of the famous Issac Wakefield.

And now he wanted her to join him.

Just one night.

She'd be known as the random blonde on his arm, not nearly as notable as all the models and famous actresses who typically accompanied him to these types of affairs. Which, of course, meant they'd all be comparing her to them. *No pressure.*

He peered down at her with a humored look. "Scared, darling?"

Yes. "No."

His lips curled. "Liar."

She took his hand to prove him wrong and allowed him to assist her out of the limo. Lightning flashed around her before she could level a retort, causing her to shelter her eyes. Issac wrapped his hand around hers, guiding it downward between them and exposing her face to the onslaught of hungry photographers.

"Just breathe." His lips brushed her ear as the hand not holding hers slid around her waist to hold her close. "And maybe smile."

"Why, because you always smile?" she retorted.

"Meaning?"

"You never smile in photos." She must have gone through thousands of event photos while researching him Monday night. Never once did he grin, or even crack a smile. "So why should I smile?"

A hint of amusement flickered through his dark blue eyes. "What else did you learn about me, Astasiya?"

"Nothing useful."

"My net worth didn't intrigue you?"

She snorted. "Assuming it's even true, no. Your biography read like a page out of the playboy handbook."

His resulting laugh sent a shiver down her spine. Such a lovely sound, one that caused her lips to curl in response to his open charisma.

Tightening his arm around her, he kissed her on the temple before returning his mouth to her ear. "Your honesty is refreshing."

"Does that mean you'll repay the favor?"

"Perhaps later." He nibbled her neck before returning his attention to the photographers. They were eating up his display of affection, making her wonder if this was the real him or an act.

With the ease of a professional used to navigating paparazzi, he angled them closer to the entrance, pausing every few seconds for another photo. He made a show of grinning for the cameras. There were going to be a lot of broken hearts tomorrow when the pictures surfaced, because Issac's smile, paired with that tux, was devastatingly beautiful. Stas paled in comparison at his side but did her best to pose along with him while the media shouted questions at Issac.

"Tell us about your date."

"Give us a name!"

"How did you meet?"

She lifted up on her toes to whisper in his ear. "Doesn't this exhaust you?"

He trailed his fingers up her exposed spine to fondle a strand of her hair as another photographer snapped their picture. "I doubt I will ever tire of having my hands on you, darling."

"I think we're past pickup lines, Issac."

"I don't use *lines*, something I believe I demonstrated in the limo. Or do you require another, more public demonstration?" The hand playing with her hair moved to her neck. He dipped her back, his opposite hand grabbing her hip to hold her steady as he lowered his mouth to hers. "I'm happy to oblige." He spoke each word against her lips, eliciting a shiver from deep within.

Lights flashed around them as he held her just out of view of their audience. The questions continued, sailing over their heads, all unanswered.

"What's her name, Issac?"

"Who is she?"

"How long have you been seeing each other?"

Oh God. If Issac had done all this with the goal of distracting her from almost dying this week, he'd succeeded. She couldn't decide if she wanted to hide forever or kiss him.

"I think I might have to hurt you," she said, meaning it.

"You could try." He pulled her upright, aligning her body with his. "I would very much enjoy punishing you for it."

Desire pooled in her belly. It went against all her ingrained ideals to be turned on by the thought of being *punished*, but her hormones weren't on the same wavelength as her brain. She would be having a serious discussion with her common sense later.

"Smile, darling. Your natural blush is quite lovely." He returned her to the view of their spectators and gave them all another adorable grin. Warmth crept up her neck as she forced her lips to curve upward.

These were not pictures she wanted to see tomorrow.

"Well done," Issac whispered as he escorted her into the palatial lobby of the hotel. Several employees stood by, but Issac bypassed them all, leading Stas to an opulent room with over fifty dining tables set up before a center stage. Chandeliers hung from vaulted ceilings, and candles decorated the walls between lavish red curtains. The ornate tiled floor gave the room a classical appeal, dating the hotel's wealth and grandeur.

Issac escorted her to a table near the middle of the room with a clear view of the podium, where she left her purse. Several recognizable celebrities mingled around them, suggesting the wealth and influence of the charity. A number of them greeted Issac by name as they sauntered by, acknowledging him as part of the beautiful-people club.

I so do not belong here, she thought as he handed her a flute of champagne from a passing waiter. His lips quirked at whatever expression she wore.

"Cheers, darling," he murmured, tapping his glass against hers.

She took a fortifying sip in response, enjoying the bubbly sensation against her throat. "This is quite the life you lead, Issac."

"The night's only begun." He kept his arm around her, holding her close while he socialized with the guests. She gathered this forced conversation was a pre-dinner requirement since no one had bothered taking a seat in the full room. A few waiters wandered around offering appetizers, but a subtle shake of Issac's head told her not to try one.

"Plastic tastes better," her demon whispered before continuing a conversation with some politician. She knew *demon* was no longer the appropriate term, but it suited him too well to stop using it. *Okay, so maybe it is a pet name.* Not that she would admit it out loud.

He introduced her to each newcomer, but most of them ignored her in favor of the handsome CEO of Wakefield Pharmaceuticals. She didn't mind, preferring to watch him work. This was his world, where he thrived in seducing the crowd while inspiring appreciative grins from all over the room.

"Stas?" The familiar voice gave her pause.

She'd called Lizzie this afternoon to ask for pointers about the gala tonight. It served as a way for her to explain where she'd been all week and to stay on her best friend's good side. But it never occurred to her that Lizzie wasn't her only friend who attended high-society events.

Until now.

"Hey, Tom," she greeted, smiling at his handsome appearance. The man wore a tux very, very well. Lizzie's jaw would be on the floor. Alas, Stas preferred his usual attire of jeans and a leather jacket—his comfort zone.

Silence fell around them, making her realize they'd interrupted Issac's conversation with a couple of politicians. Or were they actors? She couldn't tell anymore.

But Tom knew them all, shaking their hands, addressing them formally, and sharing several smiles.

There really is a hottest-bachelor club, and both of them are clearly members. The appreciative looks from around the room agreed with Stas's thoughts.

When Tom's focus reached her demon, his easy grin fell. They didn't shake hands. "Wakefield."

"Thomas."

Testosterone radiated between them, causing the hairs to dance along Stas's exposed neck. Issac's arm flexed against her lower back, holding her closer while Tom narrowed his gaze.

Yeah, this isn't awkward at all, boys. And everyone around them seemed to feel the same way, their intrigued gazes on the two men. Did Issac and Tom have a history of disliking one another? Because the lethal air emanating from Tom made her skin crawl in warning.

He's livid. Why?

"How kind of your father to give you the weekend off," Issac said, breaking the tense silence.

"Oh, don't let the suit fool you. I'm always working," Tom returned.

The words sent a chill down Stas's spine.

Seeing her friend had felt so natural, so incredibly normal, that she hadn't thought at all about the relation to him and *work*.

The CRF.

The organization that may or may not have tried to kill her.

Shit.

What if it's true? That they really did try to kill me?

Had it only been this morning that she woke up after nearly dying?

The harsh reminder made her shiver. All the pampering and grandeur of today had distracted her from real life.

A life she almost lost.

What am I doing here?

What if they know?

Is it even true?

Did they really try to poison me?

Nothing felt real, almost as if this was all a dream. She didn't know what or whom to believe, and the fact that she seemed fine now didn't help matters.

What really happened?

Issac nipped her neck and brushed his lips against her ear. "Breathe. You're safe."

Yeah? I don't feel very safe. Not with Tom glowering at her demon like that.

Doctor Fitzgerald approached from the left, his expression holding a touch of adoration—a stark contrast to the irritation vibrating from his son.

"Hello, Stas," Doctor Fitzgerald greeted, kissing her cheek. "You look lovely, dear. Issac." He nodded.

"Doctor," Issac returned, smiling. "Good to see you."

They shook hands while Doctor Fitzgerald replied, "Likewise."

Some of the tension dissipated as the crowd refocused on the renowned humanitarian. Everyone wanted a piece of him, just like Issac, leaving Stas again on the sidelines to observe.

She expelled a long breath, her heart beating a chaotic rhythm against her rib cage.

Pull it together, she whispered to herself. *It's all just speculation. Doctor Fitzgerald is a friend, mentor, father figure.*

And he proved it by charming the crowd around them, his smile genuine and reaching his dark eyes. Tom remained at his side, ever the dutiful son, mimicking his father in kind. They really could have passed as brothers, Doctor Fitzgerald not looking older than forty. It only added to his appeal, as several of the women around them seemed to notice. His wife had died over a decade ago, leaving him very, very single.

This world is—

"The good doctor is receiving an award tonight," Issac murmured against her ear. "They're also sitting at our table."

She glanced at him sideways. "Thanks for the warning." Sarcasm underlined each word. He could have given her a heads-up in the limo.

Amusement brightened his gaze. "You're welcome, darling."

"This is the second time I've seen you two together this week," Dr. Fitzgerald mused, breaking from the crowd. Genuine curiosity lit his handsome features, his lips twitching at the sides. Unlike the man beside him, who appeared to be contemplating the best way to disfigure her demon.

"Worried I might steal her?" Issac asked, his lips brushing her cheek, earning him a harder glare from Tom.

What is his problem? she wondered. Issac might not be Boyfriend of the Year material, but he wasn't *that* bad.

Jealousy popped into her head as a potential cause, but she quickly tossed it out. Tom treated her like a younger sister, just as he did Lizzie.

No. Something else was at play here. But what?

Dr. Fitzgerald arched a dark blond brow. "Should I be worried?"

"Absolutely," Issac replied against her neck, his possessive touch causing her to shiver. *Careful, Stas. Just a business deal.* "Are you ready to eat, darling?" he asked softly, ignoring all the eyes on them and focusing on her.

More than a few of their spectators wore surprised expressions, including Dr. Fitzgerald. Stas's stomach fluttered and heat crawled up her neck. She much preferred being the ignored arm candy to being the center of attention.

"Sure," she managed to reply, her throat dry. A light buzz hummed in her head from the two glasses of champagne she'd consumed on her empty stomach. So yes, she should probably eat something, too.

"Brilliant." Issac engaged the others in a few parting words, his smile enigmatic. When the Fitzgeralds joined the conversation, she had to fight the urge to fan herself. The three of them were magnetism on steroids. Further proof that this was not her world. Not by a long shot.

"Shall we?" her demon asked when the crowd dispersed.

Dr. Fitzgerald led the way. Tom lingered for a moment longer before he finally turned to follow his father. Stas took a step, only to be pulled back into Issac's side.

"Don't mention your reaction to the immunizations." The words were a breath against her ear, so low she almost missed them. "If they ask, the inoculations made you queasy, but you were otherwise fine."

Her stomach clenched, the stark reminder drizzling ice through her veins.

Human Resources had left her a voicemail during her hair appointment today. She passed her security exam, and they wanted to schedule her orientation.

That was what she meant to tell Issac. She wanted to know why he suspected the CRF's involvement in her near-death experience because he never actually told her.

This whole day had been a fairy-tale escape from reality.

And now that reality sat several feet away at a table they were all meant to share for dinner.

"Are you implying they know about the poison?" she asked, studying Issac's face for something, anything, that would give her reason to believe him. To suspect the man she considered a role model of having any involvement in her experience this week.

Because if his company truly was poising potential employees, he would know about it.

He'd never authorize such methods. Would he?

"I'm warning you that anyone could be listening," Issac replied softly. "Do you understand?"

She did, but that wasn't what she'd asked. "Does he know or not, Issac?"

"That's not for me to say. Observe and learn." He brushed his lips over hers, holding her gaze with an intent that made her heart race. "Trust me."

CHAPTER TEN

Dangerous Romance

Observe and learn.

Stas could do that.

Issac sat on her left, his palm resting on her upper thigh. His warm fingers caressed her bare skin through the slit of her dress while he engaged Doctor Fitzgerald in a conversation about the stock market. She gathered they shared similar investment strategies. Their easy candor also suggested they were friends, something Issac had failed to mention.

Yet, he'd accused Doctor Fitzgerald's company of trying to kill her.

One would think a friendship with the organization's CEO might be a useful detail, or a point of discussion.

Nope.

It left Stas irritated and confused, and that casual touch against her leg really needed to stop because it only bewildered her more.

So remove his hand.

Such a simple idea, one her mind understood where her body didn't.

I'm going insane.

"So, how is Aidan?" Doctor Fitzgerald asked as he set his napkin down on the table. He'd finished his food, while hers remained mostly untouched. Not because she disliked the taste, but because her appetite appeared to be nonexistent—a complication of her nerves rioting inside. The last thing she wanted to do was eat and be sick all over the table.

"He's well, which, of course, you already know," Issac replied, his thumb still against her skin.

Doctor Fitzgerald grinned. "Yes, true. I was surprised to see him at dinner the other night."

"That's one word for it," Tom remarked. He sat between his father and a young blonde woman. Her name began with a *T*. Tina? Taylor? Tiffany?

Whoever she was, she belonged to the family who filled out the rest of their table. All blondes, though Stas suspected the mother might dye her hair to match. She possessed a fake quality that several others in the room rivaled.

"Yes, he considered stopping by to say hello but didn't want to make the table uncomfortable," Issac said with a pointed look at Tom.

Doctor Fitzgerald chuckled. "Something you had no problem doing, hmm?" He winked at Stas, the indication clear.

They're talking about graduation dinner. Aidan must have been the male at Issac's table.

"Ah, well, I had a reason to stop by." Issac squeezed her thigh as he tilted his head toward her. "My beautiful woman."

She snorted. *Cheesy line.*

He must have sensed her thoughts because his fingers trailed higher, his thumb nearly caressing the edge of her lace thong. The actions were hidden by the table, his expression politely bored.

Stas fought the urge to squirm, not wanting to draw attention to herself, but holy hell, her skin was on fire.

"I'll extend your regards to Aidan," Issac said smoothly. "He's in town for another week or so."

Goose bumps scattered down her legs as he began to sketch a foreign pattern against her flesh. Every upward swipe caused her muscles to tighten, the taunting motion so incredibly inappropriate. Yet, her hands refused to react, her fingers curling into her palms instead as she fought the sensations he stirred inside.

This is wrong.

I shouldn't be enjoying this.

There's clearly something wrong with me.

She glanced at him, catching the wicked twinkle in his gaze. And it hit her—the purpose. Not necessarily to seduce, but to distract. She'd been unnaturally quiet through dinner, hardly touching her food, something that wasn't like her at all. Something others who knew her might notice.

He wanted her to relax.

Or maybe he wanted to take her mind off her situation.

Devious man.

She almost grabbed his wrist, but his thumb finally found the fabric between her legs. A subtle brush, one that caused her nipples to stiffen and her breath to catch.

So decadent and wanton, and not her at all.

What is this man doing to me?

She squeezed her legs together, realizing too late that the move trapped his hand.

Shit. This—

The clearing of a throat had her glancing at Doctor Fitzgerald. He gazed at her expectantly. She must have missed a question.

"Uh, I'm sorry, can you repeat that?" The breathless note in her voice seemed to amuse her demon. His lips twitched as his gaze dropped to her breasts—slowly, purposefully.

If she could move her legs, she would kick him. But she'd trapped his fingers between her thighs. Who knew what he'd do if she released him.

"I asked if you heard from Human Resources yet on your start date," Doctor Fitzgerald said.

Her heart dropped to her stomach, her limbs loosening. Issac slid his palm down to her knee and gave it a gentle squeeze, playtime over. His touch, however, meant everything to her. *I'm here*, he was saying. And she believed him. An indication of trust that surprised her enough to clear the cobwebs from her throat and allow her to reply.

"Yeah, they called today to schedule my orientation, but I received the voicemail too late to phone them back." Mostly true. She hadn't wanted to call them back, unsure of what to say.

"Fantastic. The clearance process can take so long that I was worried it might be a few weeks before you heard anything. Are you excited?"

She tried for a smile and hoped it translated. "Of course."

A round of applause saved her from commenting further as a short, white-haired woman took the podium to introduce the evening's keynote speaker. Stas recognized the name, but not the man who approached. He had a nice voice, one that carried and captivated as he highlighted various humanitarian efforts throughout the world and commended the committee who organized this event. Stas gathered by the end that the gala's purpose revolved around raising money for various relief organizations.

The elderly woman took the podium again to thank a few key sponsors, including Wakefield Pharmaceuticals and the CRF, who were both noted as top-level supporters. There were a few other items mentioned to draw out the program before she finally moved on to announce this year's recipient of the Humanitarian of the Year Award.

Everyone clapped as Doctor Fitzgerald made his way to the stage, his popularity amongst the gala attendees evident. He grinned before holding up a hand to quiet the warm welcome. Charismatic and commanding, he calmed the audience with that gesture alone.

"Good evening. I can't even begin to say how honored I am to be here tonight, receiving the Humanitarian of the Year Award. I honestly don't feel I deserve it, as I'm only doing what my heart tells me to, and really all the hard work is done by a team of ten-thousand-plus employees. I just show up every day and try to direct them." He gave a self-deprecating laugh that earned him several grins throughout the ballroom.

He continued speaking, the adoration and respect palpable throughout the room.

With each word, he reminded Stas why she idolized him. Why she wanted to work for him. Why she *trusted* him. He was magnanimous and humble, and not the kind of man who would authorize poisoning his employees.

There had to be another explanation.

Maybe someone else poisoned her on her way home Tuesday. The whole afternoon was fuzzy, making it entirely plausible that someone slipped her something without her knowing. That made more sense than her employer trying to kill her. The CRF wasn't even related to the supernatural world. They had no reason to give her the Nizari serum because they didn't know fledglings existed.

Except…

"I suspect the CRF used the Nizari poison on you to test your bloodline." Was it only this morning Issac spoke those words? They implied the CRF might know about the supernatural, but he never explained his suspicion.

He's wrong. He has to be wrong.

Six years of knowing the enigmatic man onstage trumped a fake two-week *relationship* with a demon. Stas didn't even know how to define *Ichorian*, for crying out loud.

Maybe Issac saved her life… or maybe he was toying with her.

This whole arrangement made no sense. *Dating for information.* She saw the way other women looked at him. Issac Wakefield didn't need to bribe a woman for a date. There was more to this that she didn't know.

Because he won't tell me anything.

Annoyance bubbled inside her, every passing moment making her want to turn and demand answers right now. He'd distracted her earlier with his seductive touch and smile and general sex appeal. Ridiculous. She'd never allowed a male to corrupt her in this way, and she'd be—

The crowd erupted into a standing ovation, pulling her back to the stage, where Doctor Fitzgerald stood with a slight flush painting his cheeks. He never could take praise very well, always deferring to others he felt deserved it more.

Not a killer.

Or a psychopath.

Unlike the demon beside her, whom she found outside a murder scene.

Owen...

Why was Issac there that day? He never explained, just kept her in suspense while forcing her into this charade for answers. Answers he didn't seem all that keen on giving.

But he did save my life.

Maybe.

"Aidan and Osiris would approve," Issac murmured as Doctor Fitzgerald rejoined them.

"Yeah? Maybe you'll try for it next year," her mentor replied, smirking.

"Not bloody likely."

History radiated between them, underlined in a palpable fondness that left her even more flabbergasted. How could Issac possibly suspect the CRF of trying to kill her? Unless he knew something about the organization that she didn't.

Ugh, she was thinking in circles and giving herself a headache.

The older woman stood at the podium again, making parting comments about the art auction and recommending everyone keep drinking champagne and wine. While Stas agreed wholeheartedly in the alcohol plan, she needed to take a breath. Alone.

"I'll be right back," she said quietly, excusing herself for the restroom.

She found it just outside the doors and quickly grabbed an embroidered cloth towel from the stack. *Definitely a fancy hotel.* Running it beneath cool water first, she used it to dab at her face, frustrated by the two splotches of pink decorating her cheeks.

Alcohol mingled with confusion created a decidedly unattractive look.

Just breathe, she told herself. *This is almost done. Then you can demand some answers.*

Or maybe just march back to the table, grab Issac by the arm, and growl a few demands in his ear.

No. That'd just create a scene, and she preferred to stay hidden.

She tossed the cloth into the basket by the door and walked out to find Tom waiting for her. He leaned against the wall, one foot crossed over the other and his hands tucked into his pockets. Lizzie would have swooned at the sight, his blond hair messy as if he'd just run his fingers through it several times.

But there was nothing attractive about the fury radiating in his gaze as she approached him.

"The Arcadia, ten o'clock tomorrow night. Go there, then tell me if Wakefield's still worth it." Tom pushed away from the wall and started down the hall. She caught his arm.

"Tom, what—"

"No, Stas." He shook her off and leveled her with one of the harshest looks she'd ever received from him. She took a step back. This was the man who led rescue missions all over the world, the domineering leader, not the big brother she knew and adored.

"Don't give me that wounded look. I've tried to warn you, but you won't listen. So go tomorrow and see for yourself. I suggest you wear something black. Call me when you're ready to talk about it."

His long strides ate up the hallway too fast for her to keep up.

"Tom, hold—" She cut off the command, knowing it would have forced him to halt in place. A dark part of her yearned to take over and demand he listen, and she almost did. But she knew better. People died when she used her abilities.

Like my parents.

Tom didn't pause or glance backward, just followed the stairs down to the lobby instead, bypassing the ballroom.

Her heart stuttered, her heels rooted to the floor. *What am I supposed to do with that?*

Doctor Fitzgerald walked out of the ballroom, frowning after the direction his son had headed. "Did Tom just leave?" he asked when he realized she stood only a few feet away from him.

"I think so," she said, swallowing.

He sighed and gave her an apologetic shake of his head. "I hope he wasn't too hard on you. Issac isn't his favorite person."

"I've gathered that."

"Don't worry. He'll come around." He put a hand on her shoulder and rubbed it in a fatherly way. "I meant to check in on you this week to ask how you're feeling."

Her brow furrowed. "Feeling?" she repeated, warning bells sounding in her head.

He nodded. "Yeah, I saw you leaving the building Tuesday and you didn't look like yourself. Was everything all right?"

Every muscle in her body threatened to lock in place, but the hand on her shoulder forced her to remain calm. If she reacted outwardly in any way, he'd sense it. "Yeah, it was the shots. They upset my stomach."

Shock lit his features. "Shots?"

"From the medical exam."

"You were given injections during your exam?" Did he look uneasy, or was that her imagination?

"Uh, yeah. Doctor Patel said my job might require travel."

His blond eyebrows met his hairline. "Really?"

Not a comforting reaction. "So, uh, that's not normal, then?"

"No, it most certainly is not. Inoculations are meant for our paramilitary unit only." He let go of her shoulder to pull out his phone. He typed while he spoke. "I'll be meeting with the medical director first thing Monday. This is news to me."

Her muscles went weak as all the tension left her body. If the CRF really did try to poison her, Doctor Fitzgerald hadn't known about it.

"Anita should have asked you basic questions, taken vitals, and let you go," he continued. "The vaccinations didn't negatively impact you at all, did they?"

Her lower back tingled, right around her birthmark. She fought the urge to scratch it while considering how to reply. Part of her yearned to tell him the truth, but instinct pulled her back from that leap of faith. There were too many missing pieces in this puzzle to trust anyone. He'd never believe her anyway, and she really didn't want to have to prove it by using her persuasive gift.

She cleared her throat. "Honestly, I felt a little woozy after the exam, but I slept it off."

"You felt sick afterward?"

More tingling. So annoying.

"Yeah," she admitted. "I felt pretty nauseated when I got home, but I think it was the stress of it all." Her stomach twisted with the lie, the wrongness of omitting the truth physically paining her. She really needed to change the subject, or maybe just alter it slightly. "So, uh, you think she followed the wrong protocol on purpose?" *Does that mean Doctor Patel knows I'm a fledgling?*

Ice drizzled down her spine at the thought.

What if Issac hadn't been the only one who saw her compel that reporter after Owen's memorial? He'd told her to be careful, that there might be others watching. What if he'd issued the warning too late?

"I'm not sure, but I promise to personally look into it," Doctor Fitzgerald said.

"Thank you."

"No need to thank me, Stas. I'm truly sorry this happened."

"It's not your fault."

"Well, not directly, anyway, but I still take ownership for it." He studied her closely, his brown eyes edged in concern. "I really hope we won't lose you over this. You're going to be very successful at the CRF."

"No. No, of course not." She shook her head as if to dispel the foolish notion. Although, a part of her thought perhaps she should walk away and never look back. But she'd never been one to run away, even when she should. "I'm very thankful for the opportunity," she added, forcing a smile.

At least she knew the CRF hadn't tried to kill her.

Just, maybe, Doctor Patel.

Which meant *someone* suspected Stas of being a fledgling.

"You earned it," Doctor Fitzgerald said, his smile crinkling his warm eyes. He gestured toward the ballroom. "I'll let you get back to your date, even if I think you can do better." What a dad-like thing to say.

"Thanks, and congratulations on your award. It's well deserved."

His cheeks flushed. "Thank you, Stas."

He went off in the direction of his son, while she ventured into the ballroom.

Their table was empty.

Where did you go, demon man?

She searched the room, spotting him near the dance floor in the company of three supermodels.

The tightness in her stomach grew, knotting uncomfortably as she started toward them.

This was the man she'd read about—the perpetual playboy, already picking out his next date despite still being on this one with her. Of course, this wasn't real, just a business arrangement.

One where he fondled and kissed her a lot.

Maybe he did that with all his business partners.

"Ah, darling, there you are," he said, holding his hand out for her as she approached. "Ladies, if you'll excuse me, I promised to give Astasiya a tour of the hotel."

Stas fought the urge to roll her eyes as all three women pouted. What did they think he was going to do, invite them along?

He linked his fingers through Stas's and led her away from the trio of simpering debutantes.

"Are you sure you don't want to finish your interview?" Stas asked, batting her eyelashes. "I don't mind waiting." She could peruse some art. Not that she would understand any of it or could afford it, but it would serve as a distraction while he flirted.

"My interview?"

"You know, for your next conquest, or date, or whatever you call them."

He paused to study her, his luscious mouth curling upward. "Hmm, yes, green is not your color, though it does match your beautiful eyes."

"What?" That line didn't even make sense.

"Jealousy, darling. It's not very becoming."

Her eyebrows shot upward. "Did you just accuse me of being jealous?"

He pulled her along beside him, his amusement evident. "No accusation necessary."

"I'm *not* jealous."

"Whatever you say."

"I'm not." What was there to be jealous of? This was his life. She knew that.

"Don't fret, darling. I'm here with you, not them."

"Right, as part of a business arrangement," she reminded him, ignoring the *fretting* part. "And where are we going?" They were heading toward the lobby exit.

"To complete our *business arrangement* in the limo."

"We're leaving? I thought we were going on a tour." Not that she particularly cared, but the hotel was gorgeous and a historical site.

He stopped again, this time raising a perfectly sculpted brow. "I only said that to maintain my image, but if you want to grab a hotel room, I would be happy to oblige."

She gaped at him. "Are you propositioning me?"

"You were the one expressing regrets over our missed tour. Who propositioned whom in that scenario?"

"You're impossible. You know that, right?"

His grin was too damn alluring. "We can conclude our agreement in bed or in the limo. Which do you prefer, Astasiya?"

With a growl and a muttered curse, she pulled him toward the doors. *Tempting demon.* Her common sense wouldn't stand a chance in bed with him, and she needed to focus. There were too many unanswered questions between them.

Benjamin stood waiting by the limo outside with the door open. She murmured a hello and climbed inside. Issac sat right beside her—despite the spacious backseat—and draped his arm over her shoulders. At least he'd left her thigh alone this time. His burning touch made it difficult to think.

"So, it's okay to leave this early?" she asked as the limo inched forward. It seemed early.

"The sizable donation I left excused us from the art auction, which means we can search for something more edible to eat. I'm craving Italian, but I'm open to other suggestions." That explained his eagerness to leave. He was hungry. *Typical male.*

"Does that mean I have to wait until after dinner for answers?"

He considered while toying with one of her blonde strands. "I suppose you've upheld your side of our bargain for the night. What would you like to know, Miss Davenport?"

"Everything."

"I believe our arrangement was for three questions."

"Fine."

~*~

Astasiya was adorable when frustrated.

That little growl she gave Issac in The Pierre lobby almost had him hoisting her over his shoulder and carrying her upstairs to a room. It wouldn't be the first time he booked a suite after a gala, but tonight he craved something different.

He wanted her in *his* bed—a foreign concept, one he'd never indulged in before.

But Astasiya was special, different, a new challenge he would thoroughly enjoy conquering.

He *liked* her. Perhaps more than he should. However, wasn't that half the fun?

She remained thoughtful beside him, her fight subsiding as she contemplated what questions to throw his way. He waited patiently, using the time to pull the pins from her hair. Although he enjoyed her updo, he wanted to see those natural blonde waves of hers on full display.

When he plucked the last pin free, he combed through the thick strands and luxuriated in the soft, alluring texture. All men had a trait they adored; for Issac, it was natural blondes. A night of passion would cure this intoxicating desire for her, but for now, he chose to revel in it, allowing the attraction to consume him.

He should wait, should ensure her trust first, but he wanted her. And he would have her.

Then they could return to business.

His phone vibrated, causing him to sigh. He used his free hand to remove it from his jacket and read the incoming message.

A summons. Of course. Issac nearly rolled his eyes at the timing of it all.

He could ignore Osiris, but it would be prudent to accept and play along. For now. He slipped the mobile back into his jacket pocket and pressed a button to talk to Benjamin.

"Change in plans, mate. We need to take Miss Davenport home. I believe you have the address."

His driver confirmed and Issac closed the connection.

"Sorry, darling, where were we?" He moved his hand to her neck to massage the tense muscles there. "Right, you were about to ask me a question, yes?"

"What do you want from me, Issac?" she asked, the words spilling from her mouth. "What are you really using me for?"

Her questions struck a deep chord, tugging at his chest. That wasn't what he expected her to ask at all, especially not while he'd been in the process of seducing her. "You think I'm using you?"

"I know you are, but I don't know why. Is it because I'm a fledgling?"

It would be so easy to refuse her, but this she deserved an answer to. Even if it wasn't an answer he wanted to give. He continued rubbing her neck, moving upward into her scalp, in an attempt to ease some of her tension where his words could not.

"This isn't about you," he started softly. "Not necessarily, anyway. I'm righting a wrong, and fate placed you in the center of my plans. You see, you're quite literally the perfect pawn."

The pink flush in her cheeks died as her body stiffened beside him, her muscles tense again. His words might not be what she wanted to hear, but they were at least true. He could have lied, but for what purpose?

"Are you going to elaborate on your plans?" she asked.

"I will when you're ready."

"Any idea when that will be?"

Considering how well the evening went… "I suspect it will be very soon."

She studied him for a long moment, a war of emotions dancing behind her gorgeous gaze. Whatever she wanted to ask, she wasn't sure she desired the answer. But he caught when her curiosity won in the end. "Are you going to get me killed, Issac?" Such a quiet query, spoken in a way that said she already knew his response.

This had definitely not gone according to plan.

He expected her to demand a definition for *Ichorian*—something he'd intended to give her. Not questions about his plans or how they may impact her life.

Are you going to get me killed?

He swallowed. "It's a distinct possibility, yes." Of course, she would wake up immortal. A loss for him, but a gain for her. She had the potential to become a powerful Hydraian, if Lucian allowed it.

"Then why bother saving me?"

His lips flattened. What a ridiculous waste of a question. "Because I need you alive."

"But only until you're finished with your plans."

"Well, yes." Then she would be free to accept fate whenever she liked.

Her hands balled into tiny fists, her frustration evident. That, he could have accepted. What he didn't like were the tears that flickered in her eyes—eyes that were too beautiful and fierce to showcase such pain.

Hurting her had never been his intention but seemed to be an inevitability. Just because his plan might kill her didn't mean he wished death upon her. He found her company rather enjoyable, a rarity these days. She made him laugh. The last person to do that was Amelia.

He waited for the pain that usually arose with thoughts of his sister.

Nothing.

Odd.

Perhaps the movement of his plans had granted him a reprieve. Tonight had been a spectacular success, something to be celebrated.

But the tear rolling down Astasiya's cheek dampened his celebratory mood. She flicked it away and turned to look out the window.

"I didn't mean to hurt you," he said softly.

"I'm fine."

Issac gripped her chin and forced her to look at him. Her vivid gaze startled him.

Astasiya wasn't hurt.

She was furious.

The tension in her shoulders and the mutinous line of her jaw both indicated she wanted to throttle him.

"You're angry," he said, sounding like a complete fool for uttering the obvious.

"And you're perceptive," she retorted.

The limo came to a stop just outside her building. Seeing it, she opened the door beside her and jumped out without waiting for Benjamin or saying another word.

Issac climbed out on his side and cut her off on the sidewalk.

"I'm sorry; did you want a thank-you?" Hostility poured off her in waves.

He frowned. "This bout of childishness is not attractive."

Her expression told him that was the wrong thing to say, despite it being the truth. "Childish? You think I'm being *childish*? You know what? Fuck you." She moved around him and marched off in a manner he considered to be the definition of immature.

Eyes rolling heavenward for patience, he started after her. She made it through the lobby before he caught her by the elbow. He maneuvered her into the elevator and hit the button for her floor. "Right, I can see you're furious with me and no amount of groveling is going to fix that quickly." So he did the only thing he could do.

He kissed her.

Hard.

When her lips parted in protest, he took full advantage and showed her with his tongue what he couldn't say with words.

He wanted her.

The thought of her dying burned him despite it being her fate. They had little time to share together, and wasting it being angry over words wasn't acceptable. Most women preferred honesty, and he'd given her just that.

Because he cared.

Because he needed her to know the truth.

Because he longed to enjoy these short moments with her.

Issac cradled her face between his hands, kissing her soundly, begging her to reply in kind. *Needing* her to respond.

Don't block me out. Not over this. Not yet.

Astasiya sighed, a low moan of approval escaping her throat as her nails dug into his suit jacket. Not to push him away, but to pull him closer. An emotional battle raged inside her. He could feel it in the way she poured her frustration and anger into the kiss, the sharpness of her grip on his tux.

She was angry.

But she still wanted him.

If only they could take this back to her bedroom, he could make this right. The summons was in thirty minutes. Not nearly enough time.

The elevator doors opened.

He backed her out and up against the wall, not giving a damn who might see them. He ground his hips into hers, letting her feel the evidence of his desire, needing her to know that while he considered her the key to his success, that wasn't all she meant to him. It might just be lust, but that had to be better than nothing. It had to be enough.

Astasiya's tension lessened with each stroke of his tongue against hers until she melted into his embrace, succumbing completely to his will.

He knew how to work with this, his hand sliding to her breast to tweak her hard nipple through the dress. She arched into him on a groan, all inhibition thrown to the wind. He did it again because he could, reveling in her response and taking full advantage of the thin silk. Her breast fit perfectly in his hand.

The thin straps of her gown taunted him.

One tug and the fabric would pool around her waist.

Alas, that was a temptation to be fulfilled another night.

He broke the kiss despite wanting to do the opposite and palmed her cheeks.

"You seem to mistake truth for what I want to happen," he whispered. "Fate has a path for you that doesn't involve me. I'm only borrowing you while I can. Please don't waste it by staying angry over a few honest answers."

Arousal illuminated her gaze while fiery embers ignited in her pupils. She was turned on and angry. A heady combination that had him reconsidering his evening plans.

"You only saved me to use me," she accused.

"I saved you because I need you."

"To fulfill your plans that might get me killed."

"All mortals die eventually, Astasiya."

Some of her ardor died. "*That's* how you justify it?"

He closed his eyes and tried to find his old friend, forbearance. This was why he only *fucked* women. Emotions were complications he avoided. Yet he felt compelled to placate her. When did he start caring so bloody much about hurt feelings?

"You're a fledgling, Astasiya. When you die, you'll be reborn a Hydraian. *That* is how I justify it." He pushed away from her and led the way to her door. She trailed a step behind him, then leaned against the wall beside her residence.

"You're saying when I die, I'll become immortal?" she asked as he pulled her clutch from his jacket pocket. She'd left it on the table earlier in the evening, and he worried she might forget it. Her eyes widened as he handed it to her, confirming his thoughts on the matter.

"Yes, a Hydraian," he replied.

"Then why bother saving me this week if I would just wake up?"

"Because the Nizari poison was specifically designed to make sure you wouldn't." He tucked a strand of her hair behind her ear. "I believe you are over your quota for the evening, darling. I'll be out of touch for the remainder of the weekend." He didn't allow her a chance to reply, just pulled her in for a kiss before starting down the hallway. "Sleep well, Astasiya."

Her muttered curse followed him all the way to his meeting. He was going to have some serious groveling to do when he saw her again.

Chapter Eleven

The Soultaker

Tom suggested Stas wear something black. What he'd failed to mention was the lingerie part.

She stood off to the side of the dance floor in a clingy black dress she thought would work for a nightclub. Almost all the other women here were in bras and skirts, or less. Translucent black seemed to be the better wardrobe requirement.

Stas sipped her drink while the deep bass of the Arcadia vibrated through her limbs, her nerves frayed.

What did Tom want her to see here?

Something about Issac, clearly. But he'd claimed to be busy the rest of the weekend. Had he meant he would be busy *here*? Because it was pretty obvious what this club catered to—sex. She'd caught several couples on the leather couches lining the walls already engaged in passionate affairs, hence her presence at the edge of the dance floor, where it was safe.

Except most of the people before her seemed to be taking pointers from the seductive beats playing overhead.

She searched the entire lower level for her demon, all the suit-clad males blending together with the pass of her gaze. A roped-off staircase near the middle led up to a VIP area, somewhere she couldn't access.

Are you up there, Issac?

Is this where you come when you need a break from toying with me?

She suspected Tom wanted her to catch Issac here, hooking up with another woman. Stas didn't exactly want to see that, but she could use the reminder of their business arrangement. Last night's date had felt a little too real, at least until he'd ruined it with the truth.

"You're quite literally the perfect pawn." His words reverberated through her heart, making her even more furious. Not necessarily at him, but at herself. Because at some point in the last week, she'd developed *feelings*. And those *feelings* were not acceptable.

She knew better.

This wasn't a real relationship. He needed something from her, plain and simple. They just happened to also be attracted to one another, a complication that could be solved by one night in his bed.

Or maybe a weekend.

Unless her emotions latched on, which they seemed to be doing.

She scanned the lower level once more, focusing on the dimly lit bar, and then the couches again. If she found Issac with another woman—

Awareness prickled her spine, her senses picking up something.

No, not something, *someone*.

There.

At the top of the stairs, dressed in an all-black suit like every other male in this club. Yet he owned it in a way the others never could.

And damn if he didn't look good.

She stepped to the side, admiring him as he descended with two other men. No women. Her shoulders relaxed, her stomach loosening at the sight of him without a date.

Not the right reaction.

Fuck off.

The three men garnered attention around them as they hit the bottom floor, several women already turning their way, but the trio moved through all of them with ease, their disinterest clear.

Stas stepped to the side, trying to keep them in her sights, when a finger boldly traced her spine, setting off her pulse.

Danger, her instincts whispered, her skin tingling with alarm. An unspoken threat had lingered in that brazen touch, stirring unease inside her.

"Hello, lovely." A low murmur against her ear, barely audible over the music. "Care to dance?"

She didn't even need to turn around to know the answer to that. *No.* But another caress of her back said this one wouldn't be swayed easily.

"I'm actually looking for someone," she replied while stepping out of his reach and to the side, where she nearly tripped over her own heels.

Oh, fuck.

It was the guy from Owen's apartment.

The one she'd nicknamed *Hank*.

"I'm looking for someone too," he replied, his muddy gaze sliding over her neckline and lower to her exposed legs.

She swallowed. Twice. Working on a reply that wouldn't come out in a screech. Because holy shit, he'd somehow been involved in Owen's death. Or at least the world that killed him.

"Sorry," she said, clearing her throat. "I meant I'm meeting someone." Those words usually worked, but Hank remained unfazed, his lips twitching at the side. The words seemed to go right through him as he moved into her personal space. She took a step back into a wall of male and spun to the side. The glass fell from her hand, shattering on the floor.

Brutus. His lecherous gaze stroked over her while Hank crowded her from the other side, both men trapping her with an ease that made her stomach churn.

Do they recognize me? She'd been in several of Owen's photos and had been friends with him for years. *What do they want?*

"What did you find, Mike?" Brutus asked, lifting his stubby finger to fondle a strand of her hair.

"Something delicious," Hank—or rather *Mike*—replied from behind her.

Her pulse raced, the need to duck out of their masculine cage clawing at her insides. But as she stepped to the side, they followed, edging her closer to the couches, and farther from the exit.

"It's cute. She thought my asking her to dance was a request." Mike sounded genuinely amused.

"I guess she's not into the gentlemanly thing, so should we get right to the point?" Brutus's lips were far too close to her neck, his words damp against her skin.

"That's certainly how I'm interpreting it," Mike replied, grabbing her hip, pulling her ass up against his groin.

"You really don't want to do this," she said, meaning it.

Command them to release you, the devil on her shoulder whispered.

Consider the consequences, her common sense replied.

One demand and they would have to leave her alone, but it wouldn't be subtle enough for them not to notice. And the last thing she needed was these two becoming aware of her persuasive abilities. They were probably about as human as Issac.

"Upstairs?" Mike asked.

"Yeah, she seems like a screamer. Do your thing, buddy."

How about we not…

"Gladly." Mike whirled her to face him, his grin menacing.

She pressed against his chest, not at all impressed by the stench of smoke surrounding him. "Really, I don't want—"

"Gentlemen," a new voice greeted, the owner standing just behind Mike. "I do hope you're planning to share."

Forest-green irises met hers, his face immediately familiar. *One of the men walking down the stairs with Issac.* Momentary relief flooded her, followed swiftly by dread. Cruelty lurked in this man's features, providing him with a lethal edge that matched his sharp, athletic form.

"She is a tempting morsel, indeed," he added with a smirk that sent a chill down her spine.

What kind of needs does this club cater to? Because she was starting to think this place might be a dungeon of sorts, for unwilling participants.

"Back off, Tristan," Mike growled, his grip tightening. "We found her first." Challenge lurked in his voice, his muscles flexing. Brutus joined him, his stance and presence menacing.

Tristan smirked, arrogance dripping off him as he ran his gaze lazily over the other men. He stood a few inches shorter, but violence radiated off him. The other two were more bodyguard types, all intensity and bulk. Tristan's lack of concern told her just what kind of man lurked beneath the suit.

"Did you, though?" he asked, cocking his dark head to the side. "I fear you might be wrong about that." The two brawny males visibly stiffened as a familiar warmth caressed her back. Tristan lifted his gaze to the one behind her. "You need a better leash for your pet, Issac."

A palm grabbed her hip, yanking her backward and away from Mike.

"Indeed," Issac murmured, his opposite hand circling her neck to hold her captive against him. "Thank you, Tristan."

"Sire." Tristan bowed his head and took his leave.

Mike and his friend stuck around, their eyes locked on the demon behind her with a mixture of uncertainty and resigned reverence.

"Gentlemen, my apologies for the misunderstanding." Issac's lips skimmed her thundering pulse, the heat from his body burning her back. "This one belongs to me."

What? I belong to no one.

But yeah, she wasn't going to argue right now. Not with him saving her from the two goons in front of her. Whatever they'd planned for her upstairs was definitely worse than being manhandled by her demon.

"S-sorry, Wakefield," Mike stuttered. "We didn't know she was yours." He put his hands in front of him, his expression contrite.

"Yeah, we didn't mean anything by it," his buddy added. "We're really sorry."

The two groveling idiots took a step backward, their gazes downcast.

They were terrified.

Stas frowned. What had them scrambling to get away from her demon? Sure, he maintained a daunting presence, but this was more than mere intimidation. They were *submitting* to him.

"An oversight on my part, I assure you. You're forgiven." Tension radiated at her back. Issac was livid. At her?

Mike and Brutus excused themselves in a similar fashion to Tristan, inclining their heads in a gesture of respect, before prowling about for another victim.

The fingers curled around her throat tightened. "What are you doing here, Astasiya?"

She tried to turn to face him, but he held her in place. A jolt of simmering electricity flashed through her veins, leaving her breathless and mute in his arms. The display of dominance should have pissed her off, yet it left her feeling… conflicted.

"Answer me," he demanded.

Right. Her presence at the Arcadia. She couldn't exactly tell him she'd come here searching for him at Tom's advisement. "Don't most people go to clubs to dance?" she asked, feigning innocence. A ridiculous excuse, one he had to see right through.

"I don't see you dancing," he growled, the sound rumbling through her ears, heightening that sizzling energy flowing through her.

"That's because I'm being manhandled," she replied, ignoring the sensations his nearness provoked and focusing on her sarcastic tendencies.

"This is not a game." The low pitch of his voice caused her to squirm, visions of his bedroom materializing behind her eyes. That was the kind of tone a man used in bed. An experienced one. A male who knew how to properly fuck a woman until dawn.

God, I need this to end. I can't focus around him, this attraction—

Issac bit her ear, interrupting her thoughts and sparking new ideas.

What would that mouth feel like on other parts of her body? He seemed to enjoy nibbling. Her nipples tightened at the prospect of him focusing his attentions there.

Think of last night. How he called you a pawn.

Her blood cooled.

Yes, that's what she needed to remember. His intentions with her.

"Who told you to come here, Astasiya?"

"Why do you care?" she countered, her voice higher than she intended. He evoked a response from her unlike any other. Not that her limited experience was much of a comparison.

"Because whoever sent you here is trying to get you killed."

She frowned. Tom wouldn't put her life in danger. He might be angry with her, but he still cared about her.

"Look around you," Issac said, angling her toward the back of the room.

She much preferred the view of the dance floor and the door. "I'm not really into voyeurism, Issac." She tried to look away, but the hand on her neck held her in place.

"Watch."

Not having much choice, she studied the threesome occurring on the couch nearest them. The mostly naked woman seemed to be enjoying herself with one man at her exposed breast and another beneath her skirt. Her dark head was tossed back in bliss while both men worked her over with frantic mouths.

"Is this what you're into, Issac? Kinky shit?" she asked, wondering if this was what Tom meant for her to see.

"Oh, darling, you have no idea what I'm into." The gentle kiss Issac laid on her neck belied his furious tone. "Look closer. What are they really doing?"

Swallowing, she eyed the ménage à trois again.

More ecstasy.

Mouth opened on a cry of… pain?

Her brow furrowed. *Is that blood?*

She sucked in a breath, her eyebrows lifting. The man at the woman's chest was lapping up a trail of dark liquid pooling from an open wound over her nipple.

And the one between her legs wasn't angled right.

They're not pleasuring her.

They're drinking from her.

Oh, what the fuck?

Two couches over, a foursome of three women and one man in a similar position. His mouth parted, eyes closed, one female on her knees bobbing her head while the other two suckled his neck and bare chest.

Vampires.

"Yes, you see it now, don't you?" Issac's harsh whisper heated her cooling skin, his lips at her throat. "Now tell me why you're here. Who sent you to die, Astasiya?"

"No." She tried to shake her head, but his grip forbade the movement. "He wouldn't. He just wanted…" Wanted her to what? Realize Issac wasn't human?

Her pulse leapt.

That would imply Tom *knew*.

How could he know something like that? Her knees shook, her limbs threatening to give out. Because if Tom knew, Doctor Fitzgerald knew, which would imply the CRF…

She couldn't finish that thought, her vision darkening before her eyes.

Issac's speculations…

No. No way.

She couldn't believe any of it. There was no way Tom knew what she would find here.

Then why send me?

Fuck.

"Thomas," Issac snarled against her ear. "That's what he told you in the hallway last night. To come here."

She barely heard him, her focus on the nightclub. The feeding. The vampires. Everywhere. On the couches, against the back walls, on the dance floor, even at the bar.

She'd missed all of it in favor of finding Issac.

Tom had led her to a blood den.

A club meant for demons.

"An Ichorian club," she realized out loud, her voice barely audible. That was the only explanation for this, for Issac's presence, why Tom told her to come here.

Her stomach twisted.

Why not just tell her the truth? Why put her at risk like this?

"Indeed, it is," Issac confirmed softly. "Come, I—"

"Is there a problem, Issac?" The cultured voice came from her right, interrupting Issac.

Stas hardly registered the newcomer, her gaze still on the couches. She spotted a third group—two men fucking a woman between them while openly feeding from her neck. Her face had taken on an unhealthy ashen tint rather than a euphoric one. *She's dying…*

"No problem, Osiris. Just having a conversation about what happens to women who are disobedient." Issac's harsh words drew her attention to the bald man standing before them. Dark brows, olive skin tone, harsh jawline, all wrapped up in a dangerous aura that sent a shiver down her spine.

The slight tightening of Issac's grip told her to stay quiet, a warning she didn't need.

This man was a predator.

A threat.

And ancient.

She shivered, her instincts telling her to run. This male could hurt her. Badly. And the cruelty lurking in his green eyes said he'd enjoy it.

He studied her intently, his gaze seeming to memorize every line and detail as if searching for her very soul. The slight pinch in his mouth suggested he found her lacking as he finally returned his attention to Issac.

"Eager to join us, is she?" he asked, his accent distinctly other. *Old. Very, very old.*

"Something like that," Issac replied.

"Bring her tonight. We could all use a diversion, and your punishments are always so creative."

The way he said it, so cold and calculating, scattered goose bumps down her arms. *This* was the man in charge. No question. And he would kill her without remorse. She could see it in the way he regarded her.

As an object beneath him.

A toy.

Just a passing amusement.

How could Tom send her here knowing the danger this place possessed?

Issac stroked his finger down the column of her throat as he considered the proposal. Her pulse raced as she waited, wondering what he would do, if he even had a choice. "As much as I would enjoy providing some evening entertainment, I fear her punishment will be for my eyes only tonight," he mused softly. "She's made me quite hungry, and I don't feel up to sharing."

"Disappointing." From the look he gave Issac, she could tell this man didn't appreciate being *disappointed.* "Bring her anyway."

She recognized the power in those three words, the familiar note of persuasion one she often heard in her own voice. *He can compel.* Even she felt pressured to obey, despite not knowing where he wanted Issac to take her.

Holy shit.

"Of course, Sire," Issac replied smoothly.

Tristan had used that term earlier. *Sire* must be a term of reverence or superiority, similar to how one would address a king.

"We'll see just how eager she is to join us afterward," Osiris mused.

Ancient eyes met hers, freezing her inside. She couldn't even breathe, let alone speak.

"I suggest you behave, little one. Issac is not known for his mercy—a trait I admire deeply." With that solemn warning, the man sauntered over to the staircase and ascended it. The guards bowed their heads as he passed, adding to his air of authority. *Yes, definitely the one in charge.*

Her chest ached from the lack of air, her throat burning beneath Issac's touch.

"Not a word," he whispered against her ear. "You need to do exactly what I say. Now walk with me."

Cool air met her neck as he dropped his hold, her lungs still not working the way they should.

I need to get out of here.

Except Issac guided her in the opposite direction, one of his hands meeting the small of her back to propel her forward—toward the same staircase Osiris had ascended.

Oh God…

Her legs locked, her heels cementing to the ground, but a subtle push against her spine forced her to move alongside Issac. Up the stairs. Past the nodding guards—no bowing. When one of them eyed her with unveiled interest, she stepped closer to Issac's side, seeking his protection and warmth.

He kept walking, guiding her upward into the VIP lounge filled with more couches and chairs. One of the patrons waved, her striking features familiar.

Clara.

The woman's face broke into a wide grin at Issac's approach, only to fall when she noticed his arm around Stas.

Issac shook his head once, earning him a pouty face from the woman.

This must have been whom he'd been entertaining before venturing downstairs with his two friends. It didn't take a genius to figure out what they'd all been up to, not with Clara wearing a black negligee and nothing else.

I see. This was what Tom wanted her to discover—Issac with Clara at the Arcadia. That made more sense than him sending her into a demon club.

Or maybe that was just her hoping for the best.

Issac led Stas into a rear hallway lined with doors, causing her to frown back at the reception area. A booth, in the open, surrounded by people, seemed like a much better plan.

He stopped at a random door, twisted the knob, and practically pushed her inside. She opened her mouth, but no words slipped past her lips.

Because she didn't know what to say or where to start.

The door slammed with a finality, shrouding them in darkness and silence.

"I-Issac," she whispered, her heart in her throat.

She squeaked as he grabbed her and pushed her up against the wall, his hands in her hair, his mouth a hairsbreadth away from hers.

It happened so fast.

Too fast.

Stealing her breath and her fight all at once.

"There are cameras everywhere," he warned, a dark edge highlighting each word. "And they all have night vision, so put your hands on me and make it look like you're enjoying this."

She swallowed and lifted her arms to wrap around his neck. *This is Issac. He won't hurt me. He needs me.* If she told herself that enough, she'd believe it. Maybe.

"What are you wearing under this dress?" he asked, his mouth brushing hers, the words whisper-soft.

Not what she expected him to say. "E-excuse me?"

His teeth sank into her lower lip, making her yelp. "Focus."

On what? The demon club? The humans dying downstairs? The fact that you're a fucking vampire? Where should I begin?

He sighed, his forehead falling to hers. "Astasiya, we have very little time to sort this before the Conclave. I need you to work with me. Both our lives depend on it. What are you wearing?"

She cleared her throat, her hold on his neck tightening as if needing his support to respond. And maybe she did. This was all a lot to take in. "A, uh, thong," she managed to say. "And a strapless bra." Both black and lacy, but she didn't add that part.

One of his hands drifted from her hair to her waist, then down to her ass. His palm flattened and forced her to arch up into him. A breath hitched in her throat at the feel of his growing arousal.

He's turned on… here… now?

She trembled, the heat of his body seeping into her cool skin, warming her blood. They were standing rather close. And he smelled amazing, as always.

Anywhere else, in the dark, she'd have kissed him.

But here…

"The dress will have to stay, then," he said, the disappointment evident in his voice.

She frowned. "What's wrong with my dress?" It hit her midthigh and clung to her curves. She looked good in it.

He ignored her, his mouth brushing hers in a chaste kiss as his hips pressed firmly into hers.

Definitely aroused.

"You're going to see things tonight that will make you want to scream, but you must remain calm and quiet. Mortals who overreact die, and they die badly."

"Wh—"

Issac lifted her off the ground one-handed, her legs wrapping around him automatically for balance. And, oh God, that placed his thick erection right against the scrap of lace between her thighs.

Any other place and time, her body's instinct to move against him would have won out, but not now. The shiver that traversed her spine was from his words, not his touch.

Mortals who overreact die. Her arms tensed around his neck.

Issac had already admitted that her involvement as his pawn would likely lead to her death. And now…

I'm going to die here.

"It's imperative they believe you're human," he whispered, his groin moving in a sinful circle against her. Such a subtle move, but one that sent tingling sensations through her entire body despite his words.

I should not… This cannot… Oh, he just did it again…

"I need to know you understand me." His peppermint scent seeped through her parted lips as he spoke the words against her mouth, stoking a forbidden fire inside her.

Pull yourself together, Stas.

This isn't the right place.

Just ignore—

His hard length caressed her hot center again, causing her to arch against him in a blissful mix of confusion and need. The heady combination left her light-headed, lost, unable to focus.

Who knew fear could be such a turn-on?

"Astasiya." He punctuated her name by nipping her lower lip, causing her to cry out. Whether in protest or because she liked the other things he was doing to her, she didn't know.

Reality started to blend with desire, making it difficult to discern right from wrong. It was as if her mind had shut down in favor of her body's needs. So much easier to rely on than to think about what she'd learned, what she'd observed, or the fact that she may very well die here.

"They cannot find out what you are," he growled against her mouth. "Both of our lives depend on it."

His words registered through the haze of passion clouding her mind. "No persuasion," she repeated. That seemed like common sense considering their surroundings. As did not giving in to her baser needs. *Logic.*

"One last thing." Issac licked her bottom lip, eliciting a stinging sensation. His bite had broken the skin, and the way he laved the wound now sent tingles down her spine.

Why does that feel so good?

"You can't enter the Conclave unmarked."

"Conclave?" she repeated.

"A meeting of sorts for Ichorians." His tongue traced a pattern against her mouth before dipping in to dance with hers.

What are we doing? she wanted to ask. *Why are we doing this?*

Instead, she kissed him back, welcoming the reprieve from her mind, needing a break from the danger lurking around them.

Not smart.

I don't care.

Think.

No.

She gave in to the urges, her mouth moving against his without restraint. It felt so natural, so calming, so *real.* Every embrace between them seemed experienced somehow, as if they'd been kissing each other for years. She already knew him, his wants, his needs, his desires, and she unleashed that knowledge with her mouth.

He groaned, his hips grinding against hers, their passion no longer an act, but true. One palm remained against her waist, his other wrapping around her nape. He slid his lips across her cheek to her throat, his exhale warming her skin.

"It's either this or we both die," he whispered. "And I'm particularly fond of living."

"Issac?" she breathed, uncertain of what he meant.

"Forgive me, darling."

Chapter Twelve

Broken Blood Laws

What the hell was Thomas Fitzgerald thinking sending Astasiya here? The bloody idiot threw her right into the middle of an Ichorian haven.

Fuck.

Issac wanted to torture and maim the imbecile, but first, he had to focus on protecting Astasiya.

By marking her.

His lips skimmed her pulse, the delectable scent taunting his senses. He meant to feed yesterday, or earlier this evening, but hadn't, his tastes for this woman all that drove his desires. And now he had her pinned against a wall, his mouth against the very artery he craved.

Consent mattered to him.

The rolling of her hips against his, despite the confusion underlying her voice, provided him with the acquiescence he required. Not all consensual cues were spoken; some were given through body language, and Astasiya's lithe form sang of approval, of a yearning just as fierce as his own.

"I need to bite you," he whispered. "To mark you as mine to protect you."

She swallowed, her hesitation palpable. After a beat, she breathed, "Okay."

His incisors ached from that one word alone, her blood so close, so potent, so *perfect.* He sank his teeth into her skin, breaking the surface swiftly and efficiently and eliciting a sharp squeak of protest from her throat. It was quickly replaced by a heady moan as he unleashed the endorphins into her bloodstream—a mechanism used by Ichorian kind to help subdue their prey.

Astasiya's arms tightened around him, her lower body arching and seeking purpose against his cock.

Mmm, what he wouldn't give to be inside her right now, to feel her slick walls tightening around him as he fucked her into oblivion. That was how he preferred to feed, but tonight required a more delicate introduction, one that would leave her well sated while only providing him with the sustenance he needed for survival.

She tasted amazing—sweet with a hint of fiery power that called to his very soul.

Such a unique flavor, unlike any he'd ever sampled.

Addicting.

Powerful.

A few pulls of her blood rejuvenated his spirit, energizing him in a way it shouldn't. Not yet. It usually took a few pints. But her essence, *fuck*, it was amazing. He swallowed more, savoring every drop, loving the way her heartbeat accelerated as if wanting him to devour her.

Astasiya groaned, her lower body pressing into his as the euphoria from his bite lit her on fire from within.

Fucking glorious.

A younger Ichorian would be lost to her responding passion, especially one who had gone so long without feeding, but he held himself in check, ensuring her pleasure while indulging in her blood.

Her head fell back against the wall, eyes glazing over in confused bliss. Balancing her between his torso and the wall, he slid his palm from her luscious ass to her exposed thigh, delighting in the energy traversing between them.

So perfect.

Delicious.

More…

He explored upward, eliciting a gasp from her as he found the lace undergarment adorning her hip. Her penchant for lingerie was fast becoming his favorite trait about her. If only he had time for a preview.

Alas, he'd kept the lights off for a reason.

If she saw the torture instruments surrounding them, she'd fall into a fainting fit.

"Issac." His name on her lips undid something inside of him, his control hanging on by a thread.

He wanted her more than anyone he could remember ever wanting before.

Maybe it was the moment.

This place.

Her.

He didn't know. Didn't care. He just wanted to rip the thong from her body and take her. Hard. Fast. To possess every inch of her and stake his claim. The possessive need overwhelmed him, calling to the predator inside and sending a tremble through his limbs.

This is dangerous.

Issac never felt this way for anyone, never even bedded a woman twice, but Astasiya had him wrapped up in a web of sensation carefully woven with feelings he couldn't even begin to define. As if his very purpose on this planet was to be with her.

I hardly know her.

But she's already mine.

The thought shook him to his core, forcing his teeth from her skin on a shudder so violent it was a wonder he kept her against the wall.

Her whimper confirmed he wasn't alone in the passionate struggle.

A weekend in bed. That's what they required, all he would allow, to kill this unhealthy obsession between them. But first, they had to survive the Conclave.

Issac traced the tempting line of lace beneath her dress, allowing himself one last indulgence. *So alluring. So gorgeous. So ready.*

"If we live through the night, I want to see what these look like without the dress," he whispered, his tongue tracing the marking on her throat. He left her purposely unhealed, needing everyone to know whom she belonged to, even if just for tonight. "If I had it my way, we'd be on our way to my bed right now, Astasiya. I want to devour every inch of you."

"Yes," she hissed, her agreement a welcome sound in his ear.

He took her mouth with his own, binding the agreement between them with his tongue.

She would be his—soon.

He would possess her.

Worship her.

Mark her in a way no other ever could.

And he promised her that with his lips, carving his name into her very being.

She was his, for now. No one else would touch her, taste her, or fuck her. Only him. Astasiya responded in kind, solidifying the vow, the heat pouring off her sinking into his skin, to his blood and soul.

This was never his intention, an infringement on his plans, but he cared fuck all about everything now. Only their survival mattered tonight.

An image of a clock flashed in his mind, courtesy of Tristan. He followed it up with a vision of the door, a silent way of saying that he and Mateo both stood in the hallway waiting. Issac manipulated the picture to show five minutes on his wristwatch. He wasn't done here yet.

With a final thrust of his tongue, he broke the kiss and pressed his forehead to hers, loving the way her exhales feathered over his lips.

Since when do I enjoy embraces such as this?

He shook off the bizarre, undesired feelings and focused on the task at hand—remaining alive.

"Ground rules," he started softly. "Do not speak to anyone even if they speak to you. Do not comment on anything. Do not react. Do not scream. And most importantly, do *not* use your talent for persuasion. If you break any of these rules, we both die. Do you understand?"

Her pulse kicked up a notch, flaring the mark he left on her neck.

He frowned. His predatory response to mortal fear didn't appear, only a foreign urge to console her. *This woman has clearly broken me.*

Yes, part of the blame fell on him for her presence here. Had he properly warned her of his kind, she'd not have felt the need to explore. And now she might die as a result. Or worse.

However, Thomas deserved substantial credit for her being here.

Yet it was up to Issac to protect her.

And I will. No alternatives. She would not die here tonight.

He grabbed her hips and helped untangle her limbs from his body, encouraging her to stand on her own. Her nails dug into his suit jacket, her heart rate shooting higher. Terror poured off her, the reality of their situation settling between them.

Issac cupped her cheek and brushed his lips over hers softly, tenderly, providing the only semblance of support he could offer. "You're in the heart of my world right now, Astasiya, and it's not kind to mortals. Especially those with psychic abilities."

Another kiss, this one lingering as her pulse slowly calmed, her grip on his clothing loosening, her body melting once again.

"You have to do what I say and trust me," he whispered against her mouth. "Can you do that?"

She remained quiet, her expression invisible in the dark. Predator he might be, but night vision was not one of his strengths. Unfortunate, considering the situation, as he enjoyed the way her eyes telegraphed her thoughts. Particularly as he couldn't access her mind in the way he could everyone else's.

"I'll protect you, Astasiya. You have my vow, but I need your cooperation for this to work."

"You need me alive," she finally said, her voice careful.

"I do," he agreed, his fingers sliding to the back of her neck, tightening. "But more importantly, I *want* you to live." An admission that cost him more than she'd ever know. Because he'd just confessed something to her he'd not wanted to disclose to himself.

I don't want to lose her.

A dangerous, lethal realization, one he would pay for dearly later.

Alas, that was a concern for another time. Tonight, he already had his hands full.

"Oh." A puff of air against his lips followed by more silence.

His palms began to perspire, his heart in his throat. They could not leave this room until she agreed. But if they were late…

He winced at the line of thought.

Being late was not an option. "Astasiya—"

"Yes," she interrupted. "I'll trust you. Tonight."

His shoulders fell, his forehead finding hers again. "Thank you." He meant it, something that seemed to surprise her, as she stilled against him.

He busied himself with fixing her dress, pulling the fabric over her ass—something she'd yet to do after he set her down—and running his hands over her sides to ensure it was in the right place. Then he adjusted his own clothes, specifically his pants, and ran his fingers through his hair.

The rumpled look would serve them well.

As would the fresh bite on her neck.

No one would question his intention with her, though they would be curious. Issac never brought pets to the Conclave. Ever. That alone would garner quite a few stares.

Issac pulled Astasiya's blonde waves over one shoulder, leaving his mark exposed. *This is the best I can do.* "For what it's worth, I'm sorry."

He opened the door before she could reply and linked his fingers through hers to pull her into the hallway before she could glance around the room they'd just occupied. It would only worsen matters, and he finally had a grasp of control between them, one he desired to keep.

Mateo and Tristan stood just where he expected them, the picture of elegance and superiority against the hallway wall.

"Miss Davenport," Mateo greeted, his charming grin in place as he openly tested Astasiya. "Lovely to finally meet you."

She glanced at Issac, deferring to him. That couldn't have been easy, but it confirmed she'd heard his rules. A good sign if they wanted to survive the night. Oddly, however, he missed her voice already. *Strange.*

"Oh, look at that. You trained your pet," Tristan said.

Issac gave the jackass a hard look. Sometimes he wished one could disown progeny, but turning Tristan into an Ichorian made him responsible for the bastard, even when he chose to be an ass. As he clearly intended to be now.

"Well done, Issac," Tristan added, smirking.

Issac lifted Astasiya's hand and placed a kiss against her wrist, a formal declaration of ownership in his world. "Astasiya, I believe you've already met Tristan. Might I introduce my other progeny, Mateo?"

She gave Mateo a small smile but didn't say anything.

Brilliant.

Unfortunately, this was just the easy part.

"Shall we, Sire?" Mateo asked, gesturing down the hall.

"Yes," Issac replied, squeezing Astasiya's hand once more for reassurance.

Tristan led the way, stopping when they reached the elevator and stepping inside when the opulent gold doors opened. These led to the underground. The only other way downstairs was through Osiris's private quarters. He owned this building. Hell, the Ichorian owned half the city. He was the most powerful being of their existence, and ancient, too.

Tension radiated through Astasiya's arm as they exited, her fledgling instincts no doubt picking up on the danger emanating from their destination.

Many humans died here.

Particularly those with unique abilities or those who had seen too much. Astasiya fell into both categories.

Issac despised the Conclave and its purpose—a standard show of status and authority, meant to establish the Ichorian hierarchy. He attended to protect his progeny from potential challenges. Centuries of lessons had taught his lesser brethren not to test his bloodline, but there were a select few who craved power beyond reason.

They entered through the traditional arch, the auditorium already bustling with darkly dressed Ichorians mingling near their designated seats. Aidan sat waiting in the front row with Anya draped across his lap. Clara and Nadia were behind him, engaged in conversation.

The three-story room fit over two hundred Ichorians comfortably, the marble columns and beige walls lending an opulent feel that belied the gruesome intention of the theater. And overseeing it all was a mural of angels painted into the ceiling in shades of blue.

Such blasphemy.

Aidan lifted his gaze from the gorgeous woman in his lap to greet Issac as he approached. His shrewd gaze landed on Astasiya, the lack of surprise a result of having seen them waltz through the VIP lounge only thirty minutes prior.

"Osiris was disappointed that you refused his offer to entertain, Issac," Aidan said in lieu of a greeting, the words holding a hidden meaning. "But I reminded him of your proclivity for private affairs."

Hmm, yes, refusing Osiris's wishes earlier was a risky decision. Fortunately, the hunger radiating from Issac's pores explained his ungiving mood. Even the master Ichorian would have sensed and understood that.

Although, apparently, he'd expressed his frustration to Aidan. And if Issac followed Aidan's comments correctly, he'd handled the issue on Issac's behalf.

"Cheers," he said, thanking him for fixing the problem. The last thing Issac wanted was a required punishment ceremony.

"Seeing your new toy up close, I can understand why you want to keep her to yourself," Aidan added, his green eyes—identical to Lucian's eyes—danced appreciatively over the woman frozen at Issac's side.

"Might I introduce Astasiya?" he offered, glancing down at his gorgeous blonde. "Aidan is my Sire. He made me who I am today." He added the last part for her benefit because she wouldn't know what *Sire* meant.

"A pleasure, dear." Aidan gave her a gentle smile before focusing on the two men climbing the stairs. "Tristan, Mateo, how do you feel about the potential new addition?"

Interesting.

Issac never mentioned wanting to turn Astasiya—an impossibility due to her bloodline. Which meant Osiris must have inferred that little lie from Aidan's words during their conversation. It would have helped to explain why Issac didn't want to punish her before the masses. He wouldn't want a future progeny to appear weak in any way.

Clever ruse, Issac thought, his lips twitching.

"Thrilled," Tristan deadpanned. "Issac could use another blonde in his life. Clearly." He stroked Clara's hair while giving Astasiya a pointed look.

All right. Issac narrowed his gaze. A conversation with his progeny would definitely be needed because that comment was unfounded and unnecessary.

Tristan didn't appear contrite in the slightest as he sat beside Clara. She immediately draped her legs over his and laid her head on his shoulder. Her empathetic ability left her craving physical contact, something Issac's best friend had no problem providing despite the platonic nature of their relationship.

"Well, I think she suits Issac's tastes," Mateo said. He gave Aidan a polite bow and took the chair beside Tristan.

Astasiya remained silent at Issac's side, eyes trained on him, awaiting instruction. He pulled her closer to brush his lips against her temple. His silent way of reassuring her. He followed it up with a squeeze, hoping she understood that he had a part to play next.

"Come," he said, his voice stern as he tugged her with him to the chair beside Aidan. He sat and yanked her down onto his lap, the show of force required for those around them.

Placement in the room indicated power. The rows at the back contained the weakest of their kind. Strength increased with each step toward the bottom, where the oldest and most powerful bloodlines resided. Aidan's ancient blood paired with his progeny's psychic talents put them in the front two rows.

"She's delicious, Issac," Anya murmured, her dark irises raking over Astasiya with abandon. Her full lips curved. "I'm Anya, by the way. I look forward to getting to know you very well."

"Let's not terrify the poor girl, love," Aidan murmured, nipping Anya's ear.

She swung her leather-clad legs around to straddle him, her arms wrapping around his shoulders. "Then entertain me a different way."

"Happily," Aidan replied against her mouth.

Issac chuckled and focused on situating Astasiya in a more comfortable position on his lap. Several interested gazes followed his movements, many accompanied with raised eyebrows. Most lovers shared chairs, making his choice typical. The fact that it was *him* sharing a chair was what garnered so much attention. In his over three hundred years of existence, he never brought a human with him to the Conclave.

Not that he minded.

Actually, he rather liked the way she felt against him, her head against his shoulder and her legs draped over his.

Mine.

At least for tonight.

Issac kissed the mark on her neck for everyone to see and secured her in his arms. He'd done what he could to ensure her survival.

The rest was up to her.

CHAPTER THIRTEEN

Master of Ceremonies

The auditorium gave Stas the creeps.

It sat deep underground, like some archaic ceremonial ring surrounding a center stage with one lonely chair. Oh, the adornments of gold and the white tile floor gave it an expensive feel, but she sensed the history lurking here.

The hint of death.

The terror.

And she had a front-row seat from Issac's lap.

This situation far outweighed the worst-case scenario she pictured for the evening—catching Issac in the act with another woman.

An underground colosseum filled with demons gathering around a black-and-white marble stage never once crossed her mind.

The throne in the center had seen better days. Blood stains. Charred material. A stone back. *People die there*, her instincts whispered. *They burn.*

She shivered as a vivid image of Owen flashed behind her eyes.

Unrecognizable head on a table.

Skin burnt to a crisp.

The horror he must have experienced…

What if—

A light tug on her hair drew her attention to the hard body beneath her and the arm wrapped around her waist. She met Issac's blue gaze and noted the admonishment there.

Control your reactions, he seemed to be saying. Likely because he could feel her pulse racing, or perhaps even heard it.

She reached up to touch the mark on her neck, only to have her wrist caught between his fingers and brought to his mouth for a nibble.

Don't, his eyes said.

Okay.

He released her hand and palmed her nape to pull her down for a kiss. Not the soul-destroying kind, but the comforting kind. A soft brush of his lips. An attempt to help her relax. Or perhaps he meant it as a show for their audience, because she could feel all their eyes on them. Observing. Studying. She shivered against him.

This whole room freaked her out.

All the attention on them didn't help.

I'm surrounded by demons.

The same demons who may have killed Owen.

The same demons who did *kill my parents.*

Oh God…

Was the culprit here? The man with the gold-flecked black eyes?

Her heart stopped.

What if he recognized her?

What if someone here knew about her friendship with Owen?

She'd end up in that chair, the throne in the center of the room.

"Mortals who overreact die, and they die badly."

Issac's palm squeezed, his lips trailing over her cheek to her ear. "Relax," he whispered. "Your fear is seducing the room."

Because *that* helped.

"You're mine, Astasiya. No one will touch you without my permission." He nipped her earlobe hard enough to bleed, something she assumed was more for show than a reprimand.

Or maybe he did mean to punish her.

She didn't know because she barely knew *him.*

"Trust me," he added on a breath, as if sensing her thoughts. "*Please.*"

That last word gave her pause. It came off as a near-silent plea, a word she doubted Issac said often. She moved back to catch his gaze and caught a flicker of emotion before a mask of casual elegance took over his features.

The air chilled behind her.

Issac nodded his chin at the center, telling her to refocus and pay attention.

The show was about to start.

Osiris's ancient green eyes captured hers as she turned, freezing her in place. His lips curled into a cruel smile that had her digging her nails into the skirt of her dress. Issac remained completely relaxed beneath her, one arm wrapped around her to support her lower back, his other falling over her lap to conceal her hands. Her legs dangled off his left knee, leaving her cradled against him like a child. But as that seemed to be the norm of the room—she'd noticed several others in this position upon entering—she didn't question it.

Silence fell over the room, the auditorium lighting dimming, confirming her theory about Osiris being the one in charge. Because he stood in the center of the marble floor, hands clasped before him, the stage lights flickering to life around him.

Several people—Ichorians, she guessed—scrambled to their seats.

Displeasure radiated from Osiris as he watched the latecomers take their seats, his lips flattened, his chiseled jaw clenched.

"Lucinda," he called into the stillness.

A curvy female seated a few chairs down from Aidan smiled, her painted lips a cruel red color that matched her hair. "My love?"

Osiris flicked a hand in the general direction of the last man to arrive.

Issac's arm tightened, providing her with a subtle warning as a lanky man went up in flames several rows back. His shriek tore through the room, sending her heart into a chaotic rhythm.

Fire.

Momma screaming.

Daddy writhing in agony.

That cruel man's laugh echoing across the yard.

A pinch to Stas's side brought her back to the auditorium, her gaze finding Issac's and holding for a beat. He gave nothing away, but that small touch told her he'd caught her drifting.

Deep red nails twirled in her peripheral vision, the fingers belonging to Lucinda. She circled them once, twice, then paused at Osiris's nod.

The flames died, sending the burnt man—still alive—to his chair on a grunt.

No one spoke or moved. Not even the women on either side of the victim, each of whom had specs of ash dusting their clothing.

They're used to this, Stas realized, swallowing. *This happens often.*

"Blake, is it?" Osiris's tone resembled frost in the already chilly room. "Next time, arrive punctually, or I'll let Lucinda play with you until the next Conclave."

The curvy female's lips curled with feline grace, her eyes screaming *sadistic bitch.* She wore a black teddy—similar to many others in the room—and a pair of metal cuffs linked to a set of chains. Stas followed the metal to the two collared males behind her.

Note to self: stay far away from that one.

"Now, where were we before I was so rudely interrupted?" Osiris continued, his commanding presence overpowering the room. "Right. Some of you may be aware that we recently underwent a breach in our beloved city. A Hydraian masquerading as a graduate student, of all things."

Stas stopped breathing.

Owen…

A Hydraian—something Issac had confirmed—graduate student.

What did Osiris mean by "breach"? Were Hydraians not allowed in the city?

Like Fledglings?

"Now, you may be wondering, as I did, how he went undetected." Osiris paused as if waiting for someone to guess. No one replied. "It's quite troubling, really. You see, I've recently learned that one of our own helped him hide. And as you all know, that's a direct violation of our sacred Blood Laws."

Whispers flooded the room, ranging from outraged to shocked. Osiris appeared politely interested, but the slight twist of his mouth suggested he approved. No, not just approved, *expected* this reaction.

A theatrical man, thriving on chaos.

Issac twirled a strand of her hair around his finger, studying it with a bored expression. Not at all concerned or entertained by the proceedings. *An expert at controlling his facial tells.*

"Yes, shocking, I know," Osiris said over the crowd. "And what's more shocking, the culprit's currently sitting in this room."

The murmurs escalated, exciting the master of ceremonies. He grinned—the gesture charismatic yet underlined in evil intent, a contradiction that sent a chill down her spine. This man knew how to seduce a crowd, and he enjoyed it.

"So who would defy one of the oldest orders of our kind and assist a Hydraian?" He scanned the room while slowly rolling up the sleeves of his dark shirt, revealing tanned forearms corded in muscle. "Of course, I could demand the damned step forward, but where would be the satisfaction in that? I'm curious to see if anyone can work it out alone first. Whom here would you accuse?"

The shouts started immediately.

Some in foreign languages.

Some in English.

All including names.

Issac's chuckle vibrated Stas's side, his fingers still combing through her hair. "Well, this ought to be entertaining," he said.

"Indeed," Aidan agreed, his gaze roaming the room in interest. Anya seemed equally piqued.

They think this was fun?

The energy in the room shifted from calm stillness to chaos as pandemonium ensued. Threats littered the air, causing the hairs along Stas's arms to dance.

Magic.

She could taste it, the magnetism calling to her inner gift, itching her to play. Stas swallowed, her throat reminding her of cotton balls.

I need to get out of here.

It wasn't safe.

Issac's lips brushed her pulse, nipping at the bite on her neck. Surely, he could feel her heart racing. He probably wanted her to calm down. But how? Violence tinted the auras of every single person—demon—in this room. They wanted to argue, to brawl, to *harm.*

Osiris raised his hand, silencing the room instantly.

Sweat dotted Stas's spine despite the cold temperature of the auditorium, the lethal atmosphere humming over her skin. *Someone is going to die tonight.*

"It's fun to learn how we really feel about each other, isn't it? I imagine some of you may be leveling challenges later this evening, hmm?" He chuckled, that charismatic grin in place. "Alas, I failed to hear the guilty party's name among the accused. Not surprising, really. I never would have guessed it myself." His eyes danced tauntingly over the audience. "Well, before we get to that, another matter of business first. Mike?"

Stas's heart dropped to her stomach. *Mike.* She didn't want to see him again.

But the burly man sauntered into the room holding a metal leash. He gave it a harsh tug, eliciting a yelp from the other end.

Oh my God. Issac caught Stas's hand before she could lift it to her mouth, his arms tight around her, reminding her to remain calm.

But on the other end of that leash was a frail woman.

Her dark head bowed.

Dressed in chains.

Crawling across the floor like a fucking dog.

Stas's stomach heaved, the alcohol she'd imbibed earlier threatening to expunge itself onto the floor.

Issac squeezed her hand, not in a gentle or reassuring way, but in warning. Things were about to get worse. *Fucking fantastic.* She wasn't sure how much more she could take.

"What's your name, sweetheart?" Osiris asked, his voice deceptively gentle as he stroked the woman's sunken cheek. Her dark features and caramel skin hinted at the foundations of a beautiful woman. But whatever these assholes had done to her had turned her into a shell of skin and bones with no substance.

"*Fuck you.*" Despite the woman's frail condition, her voice carried through the dark room.

"Intriguing name," Osiris replied, inspiring several laughs from the audience. "A result of conditioning, I'm sure." His smile died as he looked to the man holding the metal leash. "Now, who was it that brought her to your attention?"

"Jarod."

"Ah yes, Jarod." All part of the show, he searched the crowd and flashed a jovial grin at a tall male lurking near the back of the room. "Good man, please come join us."

Jarod meandered down to the stage with long, sure strides. He bowed low, kissing the olive skin of Osiris's hand before standing upright.

"You found this one in a brothel, yes?" Osiris asked.

"Yes, S-sire," Jarod stuttered, his meek voice not at all matching his impressive build.

"Only adds to her name." Osiris smirked at the laughs his crude statement garnered. "In any case, you noticed she had a peculiar ability, did you not?"

Stas's lungs stopped working.

A gifted mortal surrounded by Ichorians.

"It's customary for one in my position to kill you on sight," Issac had said what felt like years ago.

Was Stas about to learn what he meant by that? To witness exactly what his kind did to fledglings such as herself?

"I-I did, Sire. Her t-touch was hypnotic," Jarod stammered.

Stas frowned. A prostitute with a hypnotic touch? How was that considered evidence?

"Ah, how very intriguing. Have you or the others been able to re-create it, Mike?" Osiris asked.

Mike flashed a lascivious glance at the woman. "I don't know about hypnotic, but her touch sure is inspiring."

Ugh, gross.

"Not exactly proof, then." Osiris tapped his chin. "If only we had someone here who could sense immortal bloodlines." He smiled, his focus shifting over the crowd with a knowing gleam. "Oh, but we do, don't we? Sierra, love, why don't you join us?"

Chapter Fourteen

A Gift for Words

Ice held Stas captive, refusing her the ability to move or breathe.

An Ichorian with the ability to sense immortal bloodlines.

Fledglings.

Me.

Issac had listed all the ground rules, never once mentioning that someone might be able to sense her. An oversight? Or because he didn't consider the approaching woman a threat?

He didn't seem at all bothered, his body just as relaxed as before. He was even drawing patterns against her thigh with his thumb.

She forced herself to inhale. If he wasn't concerned, then she would be fine. Right? She exhaled through her nose. Okay, yes, this would be fine. Everything would be fine.

If she told herself that enough, she might just believe it.

"What do you think, dear?" Osiris asked as a woman with black slacks and a tank top joined him on the stage. She had to be the most conservatively dressed woman in the room.

Something about her struck Stas as familiar. Short blonde spikes, metal bar through her nose, short, plump, hmm… *Where do I know you from?*

Sierra's hand wavered a little, belying her confident stance, as she touched the brunette. Anticipation stirred in the air, everyone awaiting her verdict.

"I sense nothing, Sire," Sierra finally said, releasing the woman.

"Really?" Osiris's expression indicated surprise to the crowd, but it appeared too contrived. The slight flattening of the mouth, imperceptible to the back of the room but noticeable to those in the front, suggested he held something back.

Or maybe Stas was just starting to understand his tells. Something about him struck her as familiar, too. Like she *knew* him from a different life. *I'm clearly losing my mind.*

"She's not a fledgling, Sire." Sierra bowed her head and turned to leave, a flush creeping into her cheeks.

Oh, shit.

In two seconds, she would spot Stas.

Would she recognize—

"*Stop.*" Power buzzed through the room, singeing Stas's senses. It felt so familiar, calling to her own ability to compel. "Don't move until I tell you to."

Stas's lips parted, understanding finally dawning. She'd felt the urge to obey once before tonight. To feel it again contradicted coincidence.

Osiris can definitely *compel.*

Just like me.

Only his gift appeared to be far more powerful.

"Carl, join us." Another demand, tightening her stomach into knots.

No restraints. The man just wielded his gift like a whip, controlling the room with mere words.

This was one of Stas's darkest concerns—that she could someday give in to the sinful instincts brewing inside her. Compelling others could easily become addictive, and a very wicked part of her enjoyed it.

A lanky male dressed in the trademark black strode down the stairs across the room, his expression blank. He didn't acknowledge Sierra as he stepped onto the stage, merely arched a thick, bushy brow at Osiris after bowing his head in respect.

"Are you aware of your progeny's evening activities?" Osiris asked.

"Sierra bartends at Louie's."

Stas's lips parted at Carl's mention of Owen's favorite bar. She went there regularly with him. *Is that how I know Sierra?*

"Yes, indeed she does," Osiris agreed. "And do you know who was a frequent visitor of the establishment?"

Oh God… Stas had been right before. *This is all about Owen.*

Issac's thumb drew a circle against her lower abdomen, his touch burning through her dress. *Remain calm*, it said. *Don't react.*

She swallowed, trying to heed his advice, recalling all his warnings.

Breathe, she told herself. *Breathe.*

"Owen Angelton," Osiris said, confirming what she already knew. "You see, I've been trying to piece it all together, and I recently discovered that he frequented your progeny's club on a weekly basis. Yet, she never mentioned a word to me. Interesting considering her ability, is it not?"

Carl's stony mask didn't falter, his beady black eyes refusing to acknowledge the trembling woman frozen a few steps away from him. Fear radiated from Sierra, suggesting she would run if she could.

But Osiris's persuasion kept her feet glued to the floor, forcing her to face the open ridicule growing in the crowd. They were all piecing together the accusation, realizing that Sierra had been the Ichorian who aided Owen. And they were not happy.

"Jarod, you're a telekinetic, right?" Osiris asked.

The lanky man's nod was unsteady. "B-but only with objects of a certain weight and within d-direct line of s-sight."

"Right. Useless. Go back to your seat." A cold assessment that had Jarod cringing, his shoulders hunching over in defeat.

Stas almost pitied him. Almost.

At least until she remembered the woman on the floor covered in chains.

The bastard deserved a lot worse than being called out for his lacking ability.

"Oh, and, Jarod?" Osiris called as the cowering male started up the stairs. "Good prostitutes are all hypnotic. That's how they make their money. Try not to waste our time at the next Conclave."

Stas half expected him to use the fiery redhead to underline his statement, but he flicked his wrist in dismissal instead, his focus returning to the "hypnotic prostitute" on the floor.

"Now, what do I do with you?" he mused, tapping his chin. "It's possible you're gifted, but how will I know for sure? Can't trust anyone these days. Decisions, decisions." Movement from Stas's right startled her. Aidan's hand waved just once, low over the armrest, but enough to draw notice. "You have a suggestion, Aidan?"

All eyes turned in their direction, causing her skin to crawl. The lack of response in Issac's posture indicated he wasn't surprised by Aidan's boldness. Osiris seemed to share the sentiment, his expression showing mild interest.

"An auction," Aidan said.

He couldn't mean to auction off a human? Like an object?

Except the gleam in Osiris's gaze told her that was exactly what Aidan had just suggested. He seemed quite pleased—too pleased—by the idea. "When?" he asked.

"After the trial. To lighten the mood and perhaps inspire the famished?" Aidan spoke the words so calmly, as if they were debating the weather, not a mortal life. Anya demonstrated her approval by nipping Aidan's lip when he finished speaking, and he flashed her an indulgent smile before redirecting his focus to the stage.

Demons.

No, vampires.

They were talking about auctioning off an innocent woman as if she were property, not a living, breathing human being. *Who does that?*

"Excellent." Osiris snapped his fingers in Mike's direction. "Give the girl to Aidan. He'll watch her until the auction."

"Happily," his minion said, tugging harshly on the leash.

The woman gagged, her knees scraping over the ground as she crawled along behind him. "Assss," she hissed under her breath, causing Stas's eyebrows to lift.

This female was a fighter. Being beaten, starved, and dragged around by a metal leash hadn't dampened her fire in the slightest, as was evidenced as she continued to curse and mutter obscenities at Mike.

"Charming," Issac remarked, his tone cold and chilling her to the bone.

No remorse.

No concern.

Just a flat comment followed by a snort of disgust as the prisoner growled crudely at Anya—who had taken control of the leash.

"Indeed," Aidan replied, sounding just as frigid as Issac.

"Hmm, I don't know," Anya murmured, running her gloved fingers through the woman's dark mass of tangled hair. "I rather like the feisty ones."

Stas's stomach churned at the display, her blood freezing in her veins.

"Do try to contain your gifts, yes?" Osiris said, his affectionate gaze on Anya.

She waved her leather-clad hand at him, mischievousness dancing across her striking features. "I'm wearing protection."

Several chuckles vibrated around the room, including one from Issac. His hold around her abdomen loosened just enough for him to draw his fingers up and down her side.

The touch warmed her through the fabric, confusing her instincts. Part of her longed to cuddle closer, to seek his comfort and lean her head against his shoulder. Yet logic held her in place.

I should hate him, not trust him.

Except he'd warned her tonight would not be easy. And it wasn't his fault she sat here.

No, the blame lay at Tom's feet and her own. She never should have come here. If only—

Osiris's hand clamped around Sierra's throat, freezing Stas midbreath. He dragged the woman backward and tossed her unceremoniously into the chair while Carl observed emotionlessly.

Oh God…

The worst had yet to come, the truth of that lurking in Osiris's smile as he addressed the crowd. "Let the trial begin."

~*~

Sierra's screams echoed through the room as Osiris slid the razor across her mutilated skin.

This was one of the ancient immortal's favorite methods of torture, something he reserved for those he planned to kill. It didn't matter what the woman said, she would die tonight.

Astasiya remained rigid on Issac's lap, her nails biting into her palms. She'd clearly ascertained that Osiris could compel, something the Ichorian had made obvious when he commanded Sierra to sit in the throne without restraints while he skinned her alive.

A violent shudder had rocked Astasiya as a result, her understanding and horror palpable.

Issac had done everything he could to distract her from the stage before them. Fondling a lover during a ceremony such as this was expected and allowed, as many of his kind preferred the darker pleasures in life. Not Issac, but his brethren didn't need to know that.

He nipped Astasiya's shoulder, shifting her focus from the gruesome scene back to him. Her dilated pupils showcased her terror while her heartbeat remained normal. He hoped that was because of the diversions he continued to offer her—little kisses, bites, and touches.

"Why was Owen in New York City?" Osiris demanded for the fifteenth or sixteenth time. The bastard could just compel the information from Sierra, but he adored entertaining. And Issac's brethren thirsted for blood, furious at one of their own for breaking the precious Blood Laws.

Fucking archaic laws.

They were established after the Treaty of 1747 as a defensive measure. The Hydraians had grown too powerful, hence the reason the Ichorians lost. So the new plan was to prevent the Hydraians from amassing more power by cutting them off at the source.

Forbidding the creation of fledglings meant no new Hydraians could exist.

The rules against consorting with Hydraians was just an additional measure to ensure Ichorians and Hydraians didn't develop any *new* partnerships. Those of certain birthrights were grandfathered in, their relationships allowed to remain so long as they didn't break the treaty. Ergo Issac and Aidan were permitted to contact Lucian and the others.

Of course, that didn't mean Issac could invite the Hydraian Elders to New York City.

And that definitely didn't grant him the right to a relationship with Astasiya—a known fledgling.

Complicated laws.

Bullshit rules.

With very serious consequences.

"I don't know!" Sierra screamed, referring to Owen's purpose in the city.

"Truth," three women said in unison. They stood just behind Osiris, having been called down for their aptitudes for mind reading. Whenever one of them expressed even the slightest hint of doubt in Sierra's answer, Osiris repeated the question while removing another layer of skin.

Poor Sierra would have very little skin left to remove soon. Osiris had already divested her of her clothing and scalped her. The areas he focused on now were ones that would drive a sane person mad. And the hysteria in Sierra's gaze said she was well on that road to insanity.

"A pity he didn't tell you why he was in New York," the ancient murmured as he wiped the razor against a towel Carl held beside him.

Sierra had divulged very little information, only noting that Owen had paid her handsomely to keep his presence a secret and to provide him with notice of any upcoming Conclaves. Everything else she mentioned was inconsequential.

Osiris clearly knew she was out of details, the last several rounds meant to be a statement more than anything else. A lesson to those considering disobedience.

Like me.

Alas, Issac chose his path centuries ago, choosing to ally with the Hydraians while remaining in New York as an informant. Because while a treaty may exist between the races, everyone knew it was temporary.

One day, the agreement would fall. And Issac wanted to be able to provide his family and friends ample notice of that day.

So he played this game, attended the Conclaves, and worked his own angles.

A leathery bit of skin fell to the floor—the remainder of Sierra's thigh.

Astasiya swallowed, her attention having drifted back to the throne. Another question hung in the air, this one about whether or not Sierra knew of anyone else in the city aiding Hydraians. She responded in the negative between shrieks while the hive of mind readers confirmed her truthfulness.

Issac and Aidan were very good at keeping their personal affairs private.

No one suspected a thing about them, and they would keep it that way.

Osiris sighed theatrically and stood, trading his weapon for a clean towel from Carl. Having Sierra's maker involved in the ceremony only added to the punishment because, technically, the man could speak up on her behalf, attempt to negotiate a lesser sentence. That he said nothing spoke volumes about the kind of immortal he'd become and what little care he had for those he'd turned.

Issac would never allow his progeny to suffer in this manner.

Aidan wouldn't either.

"Tristan, would you mind?" Osiris asked while cleaning his hands with the bottle of water Carl had brought him.

"Of course, Sire," Tristan replied, instantly silencing the room.

This was why no one challenged Aidan's bloodline. Between Issac's aptitude for manipulating vision and Tristan's ability to control sound, they were a formidable team. Couple that with Anya's gift for killing by touch and Aidan's gift for intelligence and strategy, and they were unstoppable.

Astasiya shifted, her wide eyes lifting to Tristan in wonder and awe, clearly grasping what he'd just done.

Tristan sat lounging in his chair, petting Clara's arm. He gave Astasiya an indulgent look. "Impressed, pet?" he taunted, mouthing the words at her.

Her responding expression said, *Yes.*

Issac drew his finger down her spine and pressed his lips to her throat again, claiming his mark. It should have stirred unease inside him, yet all he felt was immense satisfaction. He was enjoying this charade far too much, but fuck if he cared enough to stop. After the evening they'd endured together, he'd earned a little pleasure in their situation.

"I'm assuming no one else has any final questions or last words for the accused?" Osiris's voice carried an ominous chill.

Sierra's seconds are numbered.

Issac wrapped his palm around Astasiya's neck, forcing her to study him, not the stage. She didn't need to see this next part.

Sierra's mouth parted on a silent scream, her eyes wild. She couldn't move, Osiris's command having paralyzed her from the neck down. He'd only allowed her head to move, requiring her voice, which Tristan now silenced.

A horrible, excruciating way to die.

Issac couldn't even imagine how much it had to hurt to remain seated from a command while in such pain. Osiris certainly knew how to put on a show.

"Well, hearing none, I think it's time to deliver punishment," Osiris said.

Because skinning the woman alive had clearly not been enough for him or the audience. Howls of approval followed, eliciting a grin from the mastermind on the stage.

Meanwhile, Astasiya began to tremble, something Issac attempted to dispel by tightening his grip on her neck. She remained cradled against him, her ass on his groin, her legs over the armrest. There was only so much he could do to hide her reactions, such as the goose bumps pebbling up her bare legs.

He nuzzled her throat again, attempting to mask her reaction as one of arousal, not fear—the two were closely related, after all.

"Sierra, Ichorian daughter of Carl, I find you guilty of breaking one of our most sacred laws," Osiris announced, his authoritative voice adding to the theatrics. "Consorting with Hydraians is a crime punishable by death. Carl, as is custom, I leave you with the honors. You know what to do."

Ah, a way to punish them both. Forcing an Ichorian to kill his progeny was a punishment in itself, one Issac could never accept.

But Carl left the room without a word, returning several minutes later with a ceremonial sword and a bottle of alcohol.

There were only two ways to kill an Ichorian—destroy the blood flowing through their veins or poison one by forcing them to ingest Hydraian blood.

Sierra had already started to heal enough for her mind to grasp Carl's intentions, her eyes pleading with her soundless mouth. He ignored her and instead showed the overproof hard liquor label on the bottle to the audience. Upon a few murmurs of approval, he upended the contents over her head.

Issac's palm slickened against Astasiya's skin, but his grasp remained firm. She would not handle this next part well.

Hell, she'd not handle *this* part well.

Sierra's agony was palpable, the alcohol sliding over her exposed flesh.

Despite anticipating the scene, Issac's stomach still churned. He'd witnessed this dozens of times over his life span, but it never grew easier. Osiris, however, seemed quite pleased. Eager, even.

Carl picked up Sierra's discarded shirt and pulled a lighter from his pocket, flicking it to life and lighting the fabric on fire.

This was the part Issac sought to protect Astasiya from, having noticed her reactions to Lucinda's little trick earlier.

Astasiya is afraid of fire.

Given the history of her parents, he couldn't blame her.

Carl tossed the flaming shirt onto Sierra's lap, the alcohol spreading the blaze rapidly over her form, destroying her. And still, she didn't move because of Osiris's command.

Astasiya stopped breathing, sensing the massacre behind her. Issac pressed his lips to hers, again attempting to hide her reactions from the room. He refused to let her end up on that stage, no matter the cost. Everyone would assume him infatuated, an oddity in his life, but one he accepted.

Consider me mad with lust. It's not exactly a lie.

He held Astasiya to him when she tried to pull back, her fear heightening.

Not yet, darling, he wanted to tell her. *Give it another minute.*

The sword glinted in the light, Carl slicing it through the air, putting Sierra out of her misery while her body still burned.

Astasiya's nails bit into the jacket covering Issac's forearm, which lay across her lap. He released her mouth and neck, having kept his lips there to keep her from screaming. She immediately turned, her spine rigid as she found Sierra's mutilated corpse.

Fortunately, the majority of the fire had died off, leaving her burnt and headless in the chair. Similar to Owen.

Which meant someone with Conclave knowledge had killed him. The mystery nagged at Issac, not feeling right. This whole evening had been about the Hydraian lurking in New York City, Osiris's displeasure over not knowing clear.

So who killed the Hydraian if not an Ichorian?

Osiris kicked Sierra's head across the floor, giving it an offending glance for having soiled his shoes. "Let this be a lesson to you, Carl. I allowed you to clean up your mess this time. I won't be so lenient on your next offense."

"Thank you, Sire." Carl bowed, then left the room, sword and bottle in hand. The body continued to smolder in his wake.

Astasiya's breathing evened, but she continued to clutch Issac's suit jacket. He flattened his palm against her thigh, giving it a gentle squeeze to remind her of his presence. If it helped, she didn't show it, her focus on the stage.

If only he could tap into her mind, he could alter the scene before her, help to lessen the impact. Although, he suspected she wouldn't appreciate that. His blonde was a fighter, the type of woman who chose to face her fears rather than run from them. That much he ascertained last night at the gala. She could have demanded he take her home and answer her questions, but she stayed beside him instead.

Osiris clapped his hands twice, his smile wide. "Now, let's have some real fun."

Astasiya tilted her head, her attention returning to Issac. The purpose of tonight's lesson lurked in her gaze, as did a hint of dismay. He'd told her during their second meeting that it was customary for one in his position to kill her kind. She now understood just what he risked in breaking that rule.

Why? she seemed to be asking.

Of course, she already knew the answer—he needed her alive. But it did indeed go deeper than that. Deeper than he cared to admit, even to himself.

"You all know how this works," Osiris continued, gesturing to the prostitute and giving Anya a knowing smile. "Bring her forward."

"Happily." Anya stood, her stilettos clacking over the marble as she dragged the human along behind her. Mike gingerly accepted the handle, careful not to touch Anya despite her wearing gloves. Rather than return to her seat, she remained on the stage.

Osiris arched a brow at Aidan, who shrugged. "She decided she wants a new toy. You know I can't say no to her."

"It's going to make this a very short auction," Osiris replied, glancing around the auditorium. "Is there anyone here who wishes to duel Anya for property rights?"

Astasiya had gone stiff again, but it wasn't so much fear Issac sensed from her as it was rage. While he preferred that emotion to terror, he needed her to calm down and conveyed that with a nip against her ear. She startled and glanced back at him again.

Calm down, he told her with his eyes.

"Anyone?" Osiris called again, sounding disappointed.

Anya had slipped off a single glove to study her ruby nails. "Cowards, the lot of them."

Osiris chuckled. "I think everyone is tired of dying by your hand, dear."

She pouted. "But it's been so long since my last challenge. I'm starting to get bored."

"Perhaps you can find entertainment in your new pet," Osiris offered, his tone and manner indulgent. She could literally poison the blood through a single touch, a rare gift that he adored and used on occasion.

"Does that mean I win?" Such a brilliant actress, she even sounded hopeful.

"Yes, dear. I don't think anyone is willing to take the risk." He sounded disappointed, but he grinned as Anya skipped over to the woman on the floor. She crouched down to trace her bare finger over the woman's mouth.

"Ow!" She yanked her hand back and waved it in the air. "She bites!" Her dark head swiveled in their direction. "Oh, Aidan, she's perfect."

The fond smile he gave her belied his shaking head. "I don't know what I'm going to do with you, sweetheart."

Issac smirked, feigning amusement for the charade at play. "I think we all have a pretty good idea of exactly what you'll do with her."

Astasiya flinched, clearly not appreciating the humor in his tone. It was all for show, but she'd have no way of knowing that since he never explained any of this to her.

"Anya's touch is lethal," he murmured against her ear as the woman in question dragged the human across the stage again. "That's why no one will challenge her."

"Sit," Anya commanded before sliding back into Aidan's lap.

The human on the floor didn't exactly obey so much as collapse into a heap, her fight depleting.

Just hang on, Issac thought at her. *You'll be all right.*

"Well, this wasn't nearly the diversion I hoped for," Osiris mused. "Does anyone have any grievances they wish to air? Punishment to deliver, perhaps?" He blinked long lashes in their direction on the latter inquiry, his question pointed.

No way in hell was Issac dragging Astasiya up on that stage.

Knowing how Osiris preferred to play, Issac maintained a bored expression, neither shaking his head nor nodding. If he showed no outward reaction, the older Ichorian would grow bored.

Several shouts graced the air, a disagreement being voiced from across the room. Osiris shifted focus with interest, his curiosity piqued.

Ah, a power struggle.

Issac nearly rolled his eyes at the blatant stupidity of his brethren.

Energy flickered across the auditorium, Ichorians using psychic powers to dismantle their challengers. A few ended up on the stage, fighting to prove their worth and status.

No one attempted to test their luck with Aidan's line.

Astasiya calmed with each passing minute, seemingly more comfortable with Ichorians harming one another. She almost appeared bored by the end, or perhaps just so emotionally exhausted that she could no longer feel.

It'd been hours since she last spoke. Issac found he missed her voice. He missed *her*.

Brushing his lips against her temple, he guided her closer to his chest, encouraging her to lay her head against his shoulder. She didn't fight him, didn't even flinch, her body melting into his as if it always belonged there.

Definitely fatigued.

It took significant energy to suppress natural instincts, something he knew all too well from centuries of experience.

Fights continued throughout the room, spoiling the pristine marble floors.

Blood.

Smoke.

Unmentionables.

Astasiya seemed oblivious to it all, having lost herself to her own thoughts. It concerned him to see her so broken, the mental abuse of the evening taking its toll.

Don't leave me, darling. We're not through yet.

The challenges withered, the bloodshed done.

Osiris seemed pleased with the outcome, enough that he excused the room, ending what had turned into a very long Conclave.

Finally.

Issac roused Astasiya on his lap, her eyes having fallen closed some time ago. She blinked, her green irises holding a dark note that disturbed him. He would fix that soon.

"She did well," Osiris said, approaching them.

"Mmm, yes, she did." Issac nuzzled her neck, expecting her pulse to spike, but it remained steady. *Too steady.* As if she no longer cared, the night having deadened all her instinctive reactions.

Not good…

Osiris assessed her slowly, thoroughly. Aside from a shallow swallow, she didn't outwardly react, both pleasing and concerning Issac.

Had she figured out how to mask her reactions already? Or had tonight left her so fractured she could no longer feel?

"Any idea what her talent will be?" Osiris asked.

Issac nodded, having already thought of a clever truth should this question arise. "She has an affinity for language, so likely something vocal."

"Fascinating. Do let me know when it's done." Osiris's statement implied he approved of Astasiya joining the Ichorian ranks.

Too bad that was an impossibility. "Of course," Issac said out loud, knowing those were the words his leader desired.

Osiris refocused on Astasiya and gave her a doting smile. "It was nice to make your acquaintance, young one. I look forward to knowing you better in the centuries to come." He didn't wait for a response, meandering toward the other side of the room to begin chatting with another group.

CHAPTER FIFTEEN

The World Has Gone Silent

"We're dismissed." The words were a breath against Stas's ear. They should have elicited relief, but she felt nothing.

For years, she knew this world existed and what it could do, had witnessed the darkest heart of it when her parents were burned alive. But tonight's live horror show took her expectations to a whole new level of hell.

Pure evil existed here.

Demons.

Blood.

Torture.

Strong hands went to her hips, helping her to stand on numb legs. An arm wrapped around her waist, holding her close to a hard, masculine body.

Lips brushed her neck, words whispered in her ear.

She heard nothing.

Understood nothing.

They started walking, Issac's palm against her lower back, his body between her and the macabre scene. Not that it helped. Sierra's remains were forever burned into Stas's mind.

So similar to Owen.

To her parents.

She shivered, thinking about how much this world had taken from her. And she didn't understand why. Not entirely, anyway. Something about laws and an ancient history she knew nothing about.

Issac possessed all the answers.

Do I still want those details?

Not right now. Maybe not ever.

The night air ruffled her hair. *We're outside.* Another fact that should have calmed her, yet nothing happened. Her heartbeat remained a dull thud in her ears, her hands cool, her body moving without her direction.

Issac opened a door, guiding her inside and onto a leather seat. *His car.* He could take her anywhere he wanted. That should have provoked some semblance of fear, a question, *anything*, but she didn't have the energy to try. What did it matter? This world was destined to kill her anyway.

On a throne.

Surrounded by hungry demons.

Having her skin stripped from her bones.

Burnt to a crisp.

She gagged, the acrid scent still very much alive in her nose. God, would she ever rid it from her clothes? Her hair? Her *skin*?

Issac's palm squeezed her thigh, his other hand on the steering wheel, already driving. How did she keep losing time? Or was he moving faster than her mind could comprehend?

She closed her eyes, too exhausted to debate the semantics.

"Astasiya, what did I tell you about using your persuasive talent?" Daddy's brow lifted in that way that meant she was in big trouble.

She bunched her mouth to the side, thinking. "Not to use it on strangers," she admitted slowly. "But I wanted that ice cream and he wouldn't give it to me."

"That's not a reason to demand it."

She folded her arms. It seemed like a good reason to her. The ice cream man had chocolate and she loooved chocolate. "But you demand Mom do things alllll the time that she doesn't want to do because you want something."

Momma didn't say anything, but her eyes sparkled as she waited for Daddy to reply.

"What I do with your mom is very different and private. Do I persuade strangers?"

Astasiya pinched her lips again and slowly shook her head. No. "We don't show strangers."

"And why don't we persuade strangers?" he asked, his voice soft and soothing.

"'Cause they don't understand and can make bad things happen."

And bad things did happen.

They died.

A warm palm cupped her cheek, stirring her from her memories. A blink outside showed they were parked near Lizzie's building.

Stillness surrounded them, the late hour leaving Seventy-Ninth Street quiet.

"Do you want to talk about it?" Issac asked softly, his thumb tracing her skin.

She frowned. *Do I?* "I..." She cleared her dry throat, the sandpaper texture a result of hours of disuse. "No." She didn't want to talk at all.

Issac studied her for a long moment before opening the door. He appeared beside her too quickly, pulling her from her seat and guiding her to the building's entrance without a word.

"Key?" he asked.

He didn't remark on the placement as she pulled the item from her bra. She hadn't wanted to carry a bag tonight. Good thing, too, because she probably would have left it behind and then that psychopath would have her address. If he didn't already.

She trembled at the thought, Issac's palm against her skin doing nothing to dispel the chill overwhelming her body.

Osiris knows my name.

What if he came for her? Did he sense her fledgling status?

"Do let me know when it's done?"

What did that even mean?

"Is Elizabeth home?" Issac asked. They were already outside her door.

She frowned. When did they even go into the elevator?

"Astasiya," he murmured, his hand on her face again. "Is Elizabeth home?"

Lizzie? Stas shook her head. Her roommate volunteered one Saturday night a month at a children's shelter in Harlem. She wouldn't be back until late tomorrow morning.

Which meant Stas would alone tonight.

Her stomach churned at the realization, the nightmares already playing behind her eyes. *Oh God…*

The door opened.

She disabled the alarm on instinct, moving on autopilot to the kitchen. *Water.* She needed a big glass of it. Followed by some alcohol.

Issac followed her, his jacket having disappeared with his tie.

Did he leave them in the car? Her closet? She couldn't even remember if he wore them inside.

Whatever. She chugged her cup, not caring at all what he thought of her inelegance, and poured herself another. It cooled her throat, easing the burn with each gulp. She closed her eyes, her shoulders falling, her back resting against the refrigerator.

Her stomach rumbled, the tightening in her gut reminding her how many hours had passed since her last meal. As if she could eat something now, or ever again. The mere thought of it made her nauseous.

No. No food.

"Talk to me, Astasiya," Issac murmured, the heat of his body seeping into her pores as he stood beside her.

She didn't look at him.

Didn't reply.

Because she had no idea what to say. Or perhaps she had too much to say.

"Please, love." He tucked her hair behind her ear, his touch lingering against her neck.

His bite.

God, she had a fucking vampire in her kitchen.

No, a demon.

An Ichorian.

Whatever the fuck any of that even meant. They burned people alive after skinning them. Certainly *not* angels despite what Issac had told her about descending from one. *Seraphim.*

She nearly laughed, the hysterical summarization taunting her sanity.

"Talk to me," he urged, his thumb tracing the column of her throat. "I miss your voice."

He misses my voice? He was the one who told her she couldn't speak all night.

Fucking rules.

Laws.

Trials.

A tear slipped from her eye that he caught with his thumb, brushing it to the side. His lips pressed against her forehead, his arms wrapping around her as he pulled her into a hug.

She couldn't return the embrace, her arms too stiff, the glass still in her hand.

"I never meant for you to witness any of that," he whispered, his hand rubbing her back. "It's a harsh world, but there are moments of light. If you allow me, I'll introduce you to some of them."

Stas snorted. *Light? Yeah, right.*

He sighed, pulling back to cup her cheeks between his hands, his dark eyes capturing hers as they opened. "Please tell me what you're thinking."

Her eyebrows rose. "You want to know what I'm thinking?" The words sounded normal now, unlike in the car, her throat properly working again. But they were also edged in an incredulity she couldn't hide.

Relief flourished in his features. "Yes, I very much would."

"Okay." She could do that. "I'm thinking about this." She pointed to the bite mark on her neck. "And about how Ichorians are apparently vampires, not angels. I have no idea what the fuck a Hydraian is, but obviously, they're not welcome here. And helping one, or a fledgling like me, earns the culprit a death sentence. But not just any standard sentence. No, you're burned alive. Like my parents. And Owen."

Images of charred flesh flashed behind her eyes. Fuck, she felt queasy. Like, really, really queasy.

She spun to set the glass in the sink and gripped the counter beside it, lowering her forehead to the cool marble. Issac gathered her hair away from her neck, the air cooling her skin.

Stas swallowed once. Twice. Calming her insides and willing the contents of her stomach to stay there.

"Your parents were murdered in the same style as Owen and Sierra?" he asked softly.

Of course he chose that topic. "Yes."

"You witnessed it?"

"I was hiding in the fucking trees while that monster tortured and maimed my mother, then set my father on fire for her to watch." Her knees wobbled, her mother's screams haunting her thoughts. Stas had wanted to go to her, to help her, but a hand had held her back. *Whose?* she wondered for the millionth time. Her mind refused her, only providing her with a partial memory that felt altered on some level she couldn't understand. Psychologically she understood it was a defense mechanism, her seven-year-old self's way of protecting her, but one day, she'd break down that wall and remember everything.

She rolled her forehead against the marble, aware that she must look deranged, and not caring. The cool texture felt good against her clammy skin.

"It's believed that Ichorians descend from a cursed line of fallen angels, and the curse requires my kind to drink human blood to survive. Not daily, or even weekly, but enough to remain breathing. Some indulge in it more than others." Issac's thumb brushed her pulse. "This mark declares you as mine."

Startled by his admission, she stopped moving her head. "Why?"

"To protect you."

She straightened slowly, his words slowly registering.

He gripped the counter on either side of her hips as she turned to face him. "Do you want to know how a fledgling is created?" he asked.

She nearly rolled her eyes but refrained due to the headache brewing behind them. "You know I do."

"By a male Ichorian parent, which means your father was an Ichorian. The fact that you *knew* him as a child tells me he broke several Blood Laws. He not only created a fledgling, meaning you, but he also allowed you to live. I'm guessing that is what brought about his death sentence. Your mother was just a casualty of being with the wrong man."

She stiffened, her hands tightening into fists at her sides. "Are you saying it's their fault for being brutally murdered? That they brought about their own fate by creating me?"

"Of course not. Their fate was the fault of antiquated Ichorian laws."

Not what she expected him to say. She relaxed marginally, her limbs beginning to tingle from fatigue. She really should have removed her shoes at the door. Because *ow*.

"So, you don't agree with the rules," she said, noting his tone.

"You being alive makes that obvious."

True. Except… "You're only keeping me alive because I'm the *perfect pawn*." The words tasted bitter in her mouth, as did the memory of him saying them. Was that only last night? Because it felt like a year had passed since the gala.

"Hmm, I see that bothered you." He tilted his head, gaze thoughtful. "You are indeed the perfect pawn, Astasiya. But that's not why I risked my life for you tonight." He brushed a strand of her hair away from her face, his thumb tracing her cheek. "I meant to introduce you slowly to my world, to not overwhelm you. Alas, that's no longer possible."

She swallowed. "Yes, I think tonight was the equivalent of being thrown into the deep end of the pool." And Issac had been her life raft.

"I'd liken it more to the darkest depths of the ocean, but yes." He pulled her to him, wrapping his arms around her. "There is still so much you don't yet understand."

An understatement. Her head fell to his chest as she returned his embrace. It felt so natural, so right, to melt into him, to borrow his strength, to bathe in the heat of his body.

This is so wrong.

He's a demon.

His friends took home a human slave, for fuck's sake.

She stiffened at that last thought. "What will happen with the girl?" she asked, his button-down shirt muffling her words.

"The prostitute?"

She nodded, not sure she wanted the answer, but needing it all the same.

"She'll be saved," he murmured, his fingers combing her hair. "Another aspect you don't yet understand that I intend to rectify. But trust me, she's safe."

Trust me. Two words that requested so much of her. This man had evaded her questions at every turn while also providing her with more information on the supernatural than anyone else in her existence ever had.

A conundrum that left her dizzy.

And in her current state, she couldn't ponder it much more. Stas needed a few hours of sleep, to recharge and face another day.

Her legs shook, her limbs threatening to give out on her. Holding back her emotions all evening had taken a toll not just on her mind but also on her body.

She was fucking exhausted.

Her eyes closed, her breathing steadying. The bedroom was so, so far away. She didn't have the energy, didn't want to even try, just wanted to lie here for a few moments and rest.

"I can't," she whispered, her fingers curling into his shirt. "Issac, I… I can't."

He must have understood her because he lifted her into his arms, carrying her with ease to her room. That he knew which one was hers confirmed he'd been here before, which she already knew—he'd packed her a suitcase earlier this week.

Only a few days ago?

Time was moving abnormally slow for how fast everything seemed to be happening.

Her mattress reminded her of heaven as he set her down. Pajama pants and a tank top seemed to appear beside her seconds later, his concerned expression flickering in and out of focus.

"Can you dress yourself?" he asked softly. "Or would you like assistance?"

So formal.

As if he hadn't just asked if he could remove her clothes. Of course, he hadn't meant it that way. Maybe he should. No. No, that wasn't a good idea at all. Except it sounded like an amazing plan to forget everything.

Okay, yeah, that's not happening.

Stas forced herself to sit up and twirled her finger, signaling him to turn around. He smirked but did as she requested.

Wait, he should probably just leave…

She'd handle that in a minute.

Shoes first—on the floor. Good.

Dress next. She reached around to fiddle with the zipper, tugging on it unsuccessfully. Damn. This was one of those dresses where she had to zip it up in the front, then twist it because the damn hook sat right between her shoulder blades.

She huffed a breath.

All right. Either she slept in the dress or she asked him to help. And as he'd already offered, she might as well take advantage.

"Can you help me unzip my dress?" It came out rougher than she intended. She blamed the exertion of trying to grasp the zipper for her shortness of breath.

He rotated and eyed the fabric glued to her body. "I'll need you to stand."

Right. Yeah. This really wasn't an ideal position at all.

He held out a hand to assist her, which she only accepted because she didn't trust herself not to face-plant on the carpet. Who knew emotional burnout carried similar side effects to drinking too much alcohol? Because she felt drunk as fuck.

Issac gathered all her hair over one shoulder and traced the material along her upper back to the zipper, then drew it down far too slowly. Almost hypnotically so. Or maybe time was messing with her head again. She really couldn't tell the difference anymore, her reality fracturing into a sea of absolute madness.

The dress loosened around her top, causing her hands to lift automatically to keep it against her chest as he exposed more of her spine.

Almost there.

Any second now.

His lips caressed the back of her neck, eliciting a shiver from deep within. She nearly dropped the dress, her instincts to melt into him overriding logic, but his touch disappeared in the next breath.

She glanced over her shoulder to find him facing the wall again, hands in his pockets.

Stas swallowed, a hint of disappointment pricking her chest. A reaction that made absolutely no sense whatsoever. This was neither the time nor the place. Not to mention, she'd hardly enjoy it in this state. And neither would he.

Dropping her dress, she pulled on the pajama pants and tank top, and collapsed on the bed from the exertion. She couldn't remember a time when she'd been this tired.

"I'm decent," she managed to say with a yawn.

"Not the adjective I'd use to describe you," he replied as he sat near the headboard of the bed. "Come here, love."

Love. She puzzled over the word, not sure she heard it right. Though it was a very English thing to say, and his accent clearly thickened with the term.

He raised an eyebrow when she didn't move, and patted the pillow.

Demands in the bedroom never bothered her. Actually, she preferred them.

And this one was not an exception to the rule.

She crawled up to the pillows ungracefully and curled into a ball beside him as he pulled the blankets over her. *Mmm, so nice. Comfortable. Warm.*

His fingers ran through her hair, his lips against her forehead. "I'm sorry about your parents, Astasiya. I'm sorry about tonight, too. And Owen. If I could change fate's cruelty, I would."

She lifted her eyes to his, lost in the cloudiness of the moment. "Is it always that way? Your Conclaves?"

He sighed, lying down beside her on top of the blankets, one arm hooking beneath his head as he stared at the ceiling. "The Conclave is our governing board, so to speak. A show of power to keep everyone in line and they only occur when someone breaks a Blood Law."

"How many Blood Laws are there?"

"Three primary rules, all involving fledglings and Hydraians." He glanced sideways at her. "As you may have guessed, my kind is not fond of the other immortals."

"And you?" she asked softly. "How do you feel about Hydraians?"

"I think that should be obvious to you by now given what I've already stated about the archaic laws." His dark lashes fell, fanning his defined cheekbones. "Good night, Astasiya."

She blinked at him. "You're staying?" *Wait, why is he even here?*

"Apparently."

"Why?"

"It feels right." He looked at ease, like he stayed in her room all the time.

"And you typically sleep in a dress shirt and pants?" It wouldn't surprise her. She rarely saw him in anything else.

One eye peeled open to look at her. "Are you giving me permission to undress?"

"Depends. What do you have on under that?"

He grinned, lowering his lashes again. "Go to sleep."

With you in my room? "Easier said than done." Except, his presence here did feel right. Like a comfort she'd never known. As if destiny had placed him here with a purpose—a good one.

She frowned, uncertain if her instincts were fried from the insanity of the day or if a moment of clarity had surfaced.

Regardless, she needed to sleep.

If Issac had wanted to hurt her, he could have done so several times over. Instead, he seemed to keep saving her.

Because he needs me alive.

Or maybe… maybe he wants me alive, too.

Banishing the inane thoughts, she reached over and turned off the lamp, shadowing the room in darkness.

After a few hours of rest, she'd be able to think more clearly and figure out why she thought Issac staying over was a sound idea.

Yes. Good plan.

Too drained to think anymore, she closed her eyes.

And fell into the dark abyss.

Chapter Sixteen

Water Nightmares

Stas couldn't breathe.

Thick black bands held her legs hostage as she tried to kick to the surface. Water clogged her airways, trapping her screams inside.

Yet, she lived.

Her body begged for oxygen.

Her skin decaying from years—decades—of living beneath the surface.

Her blonde strands resembling ash.

Everything hurt. Her heart, most of all. She missed *him*, her other half, her—

Oh, not again. Please, not again!

Slipping. Dripping into the world of nothing. Dying. Again.

Except she didn't; she remained waiting, her consciousness nagging at the obvious.

This isn't really happening.

The water swirled around her, a whirlpool of sensation whirling her into an inky hell and throwing her into a spotlight glistening off marble tiles.

Osiris.

He sat on the throne, his cruel lips twisted in delight. A bloody razor sat beside him and a scalp of blonde hair. Stas touched her head, feeling the blood and gore, her lips parting on a silent scream no one could hear.

Oh, fuck, he found her! He knew!

And now she sat bound to the chair, leather ropes holding her down as he chuckled maliciously before her. She sobbed, begging him to stop, not wanting to die like this, here and now. She didn't mean to fall into this world, didn't know why she existed.

Please don't! Please, not again!

Astasiya! Find—

Stas flew upward on a gasp, her lungs screaming for air. Her throat felt sore, used, horribly raw. She couldn't swallow, couldn't breathe fast enough, her heartbeat in her ears.

"Astasiya." The voice penetrated the drumming only barely. Masculine. Deep. Familiar.

Heat enveloped her, hands on her face, lips in her hair.

She struggled, alarmed by the presence of another, only to inhale the soothing scent of sandalwood. *Issac.* She collapsed against him, her face meeting his bare skin, his arms forming a protective shield around her back.

He's here.

I'm safe.

Stas shuddered, bits and pieces of the too-real nightmare flashing behind her eyes. A deep ache stirred in her chest, her mother's broken features so clear and vivid in her mind. It'd been her mother tied to that chair, begging for help before drowning all over again.

"He wouldn't let her move," she whispered on a sob, the vision flickering between her mother and Sierra. "The razor…" She buried her face against his shoulder, needing his familiarity and warmth.

"I know," he murmured, stroking her hair down to her back. "But you're safe here. I won't let that happen to you, Astasiya."

The vow in his voice circled her heart, soothing some of the pain radiating through her body. Still, Osiris's eyes haunted her, his malicious smile as he wielded that blade forever ingrained in her memory.

Just like the man who burned her parents alive.

She didn't see him tonight, had searched for him, wondering if he'd appear. Some part of her knew he wasn't there, the part that swore she'd recognize him without even seeing him. He had a lethal presence about him—a memorable one.

Issac's lips brushed her temple, his hands sliding over her, providing the comfort she craved. It went against reason to trust him, to give in to the lure of his protection, yet she did it with ease, as if they'd been doing this all their lives.

I trust him, she realized. Perhaps not logically, but she did nonetheless. Her breathing slowly returned to normal, her gaze clearing as Issac continued to caress her, his touch working magic against her back and neck.

She swallowed, her palms and legs informing her of his current state. He'd undressed while she slept, leaving him clad in only a pair of boxers. One of her thighs had lodged between his, the top of which absorbed the heat of his groin. And her hands had ended up on his bare shoulders, clutching his strength.

I'm cuddling a nearly naked Issac. In my bed.

"I can't remember the last time I had to wake someone the old-fashioned way," he said softly, completely unaware of the shift in her mind and the fresh wave of warmth flooding her veins. "Your immunity to my gift is quite tiresome."

She cleared her throat, her brow furrowing, not following his comment. "Your invisibility?"

"My invisibility?" he repeated.

"Yeah, your gift, right?" How would that help wake her up?

He chuckled, the sound warm and affectionate and not at all helping to dispel the heat flooding her body. "That's cute. Invisibility isn't my gift." He started massaging a tense spot on her neck, sending tingles down her spine.

Oh, so not helping with the attraction problem, but definitely not going to ask him to stop. Because wow, that feels… mmm.

"I control vision," he continued, his fingers working her muscles with expert precision. "The day we met, I was hiding my presence from everyone in the building by controlling their sight. Except it didn't work on you. I tried to access your visual receptors tonight, and I mean, I *really* tried, but your nightmare eluded me. Your mind is dark to me."

"You control vision in real time, like what I see right now, and in dreams?"

"My gift extends to the dream realm, yes. Vision is about what your eyes allow you to see, and those sensors are connected to the brain. I manipulate the part of the mind that tells a person *what* he's seeing or how to interpret an image. That extends to the imagination as well, such as how someone might picture something. I can make a person think he's sleeping when he's not, based on the dream playing out inside his head. Which is why I tried to access your nightmare—to stop it—but as I said, I can't touch your mind."

She blinked. Okay, visual manipulation was far more impressive than invisibility.

And he had hidden his presence in Owen's building by manipulating everyone's sight? Several hundred people lived in that apartment building. How many of them did he control that morning?

This is why others fear him, why they respected him at the Conclave.

What a terrifyingly powerful ability.

"I'm immune?" she asked, part alarmed, part relieved.

"Yes, to all power, it seems."

She lifted her head to look at him, but the darkness of the room hid his features. "Is that normal for a fledgling?"

"No, not at all. You're the first I've ever met. However, Aidan told me about someone he knew long ago with a similar ability."

"He knows about me?"

"Of course."

His quick, nonchalant answer made her shiver. Aidan reminded her too much of Osiris. They both possessed an air of age about them that lent to a disregard for humanity. His callous suggestion to auction off a mortal woman marked him as one of the last people she ever wanted to see again, but apparently, he knew about her. That didn't bode well for her future.

She rolled onto her back, away from Issac's magical hands, needing a moment. The way she accepted his comfort unnerved her. Trusting him defied rational thought. Their acquaintance nearly killed her, something he admitted might happen again, and he was using her.

He also saved my life at least twice now.

She almost growled, frustrated and exhausted by the confusion rioting inside her.

A glance at the clock showed she slept two hours at most. Not nearly enough, not after everything she'd been through.

Issac shifted beside her, his palm cupping her cheek as he hovered over her, removing the space between them. "Hmm, you and I are going to have a very long talk tomorrow, love."

Love. What happened to *darling*?

"However," he continued softly, his mouth lowering to hers. "We require more rest first, and fortunately, I know exactly how to help us achieve that."

She parted her lips with a reply that he interrupted with his tongue. Her heart stopped beating, her breath frozen.

He started slow, his tongue gliding against hers in a way that coaxed her into returning the kiss. Each slide and dip caressed her senses, causing her pulse to kick-start into a rhythm that bowed to his control. It decelerated when he went soft and accelerated when he deepened their embrace, his palms sliding down her neck and arms.

God, this man knew exactly how to destroy her, to plow through every wall, to bring her to her knees with a simple stroke of his mouth over hers. Each nibble and lick fractured another brain cell, leaving her mindless beneath him, and captivated.

He was fast becoming her darkest addiction, his touch something she craved more than air itself. Right and wrong fled her system, leaving a puddle of desire in their wake that only he could satisfy. She no longer cared about anything or anyone—except him.

And to release all those emotions, all that pain, was a gift in itself, one she couldn't refuse.

"More," she moaned. "More, Issac." Because if he stopped at just kissing her, she'd kill him. They'd danced around this attraction for too long. Fuck everything else, all that had happened, she wanted relief. "Please."

"Don't worry, love. I'm going to give you what you need," he whispered, his lips hot against hers. "What we both need."

His thigh slid between hers, pressing into the most sensitive part of her.

Yes…

She moved closer, her hips undulating beneath his, seeking the friction she so badly craved.

Dangerous. Wrong. Wanton.

But she gave in to the allure anyway, seeking the comfort he offered.

"Yes, love." His palms slid up her sides, beneath her top. "That's it." He peeled off her strapless bra, tossing it to the floor and revealing her breasts to the night air. "You're gorgeous," he whispered, his lips on her neck. "Utter perfection."

She threaded her fingers through his thick hair, her other palm against his shoulder.

So strong.

So soft.

So… *mine.*

The thought came unbidden, nearly derailing her from the moment, but the pinch against her nipple captured her attention, eliciting a groan from deep in her chest. *Fuck.* His hands really were enchanted. He knew exactly how to touch her and where, both rough and gentle, his strong thigh flexing between hers.

"Issac…" His name a prayer and a promise, wrapped up in a sultry voice she hardly recognized. Already she felt a sensuous storm brewing inside her, culminating in her lower abdomen. No one had ever done this to her, brought her this close, without *really* touching her.

But then again, none of her previous lovers rivaled Issac in any way.

His lips traced a wet path down her chest, his tongue teasing her stiff peaks. It made her want to explore him in kind, causing her palm to drift down his muscled back to his firm ass. The silky texture of his boxer shorts teased her fingertips, sliding across her skin as she ventured around to the front to palm his impressive erection.

He hissed her name, his teeth scraping her skin.

She stroked him through the fabric, only to find her wrist captured and pulled over her head. Her lips parted on a complaint that he swallowed with his mouth. His lower body settled between hers, the head of his cock right against her clit. And when he pressed into her, she saw stars.

Oh, fuck…

So close…

The minimal clothing between them didn't matter, not with him moving like *that.*

Her nails bit into his biceps, her back arching as she thrust upward, chasing the sensation tingling throughout her body.

Just.

One.

More.

"Now, Astasiya," he growled, his teeth sinking into her lower lip.

God, that voice, coupled with the things he was doing to her, pushed her over the precipice into oblivion. Sensual energy unlike anything she'd ever experienced flooded through her, his tongue absorbing each of her moans as he drove her to madness.

She quivered.

Quaked.

Exploded.

Her vision going dark and then light, every part of her melting beneath his assault. And then she was floating, lost in a cloud of bliss she never wanted to come down from.

"Glorious," he murmured, his lips tracing her jaw to her throat. "You're amazing."

His praise warmed her in a way she didn't expect. She should be the one commending him, not the other way around.

Because wow.

He sent her to heaven and back without really touching her. It was a testament to his skill and her lack of recent experience. Or maybe the culmination of all the foreplay between them.

His tongue laved her bottom lip before his mouth took hers in a kiss underlined in unspoken words. *Feelings.* They were walking a dangerous rope, this connection between them bordering on something decidedly deeper than mere lust.

It wrecked her.

Floored her.

Excited her.

"Sleep well," he whispered, pulling her against him, his hot arousal against her thigh.

"But—"

"Shh." He nuzzled her hair, tightening his hold. "Another time, Aya. We will have many more nights together. Trust me."

Aya? She wanted to ask him what he meant, but her yawn dispelled her ability to speak. Mmm, in the morning. She'd ask him then.

If she remembered.

Chapter Seventeen

Afternoon Ride

Astasiya's heartbeat changed, signaling her awareness. Her abrupt intake of air had Issac's lips twitching, but he remained otherwise still, his arm draped loosely across her waist.

He never held women like this, nor did he ever sleep beside one, but he rather enjoyed waking up with Astasiya snuggled up against him. His cock enjoyed it, too, especially as she stretched.

She froze as her ass brushed his groin.

Yes, darling, that would be for you.

Except they couldn't do anything about it right now. Elizabeth had returned home an hour ago, hence the reason Issac was wide awake now.

Astasiya shifted slowly, as if to not disturb him. He allowed it, deciding to give her the moment to herself she seemed to need. She crept quietly away from the bed and closed the door to the bathroom behind her.

He chuckled, sitting up with a shake of his head. Most women fawned over him, desiring to please him with their mouths and bodies just for a few minutes more of attention. Astasiya, however, couldn't get away from him fast enough.

The challenge she provided thrilled him. As did many other aspects of her body and mind.

Rolling out of bed, he pulled on his trousers and picked up his phone from the nightstand. Lucian had replied to the text he sent last night, agreeing to a meet.

Brilliant.

This whole slow-introduction idea with Astasiya had clearly not worked out as planned, so they needed a new course.

Checking the current hour, Issac sent back a message with a reasonable arrival time and pocketed the device.

The water flipped on in the bathroom, giving Issac pause as he began buttoning his shirt. Joining Astasiya in the shower would be most pleasing. He pictured the water trickling over her naked skin and his tongue following a droplet to the delicious juncture between her thighs. Mmm, an activity for later today if all went as planned. Because if they started now, they'd never make the meeting he'd just arranged.

Needing a distraction, he made her bed and left the room in search of Elizabeth Watkins. His curiosity over the woman had piqued when she appeared seemingly from nowhere at the age of eighteen.

From all that he'd observed, she appeared to know nothing about the supernatural. An impossibility, it seemed, with her birthright and those who surrounded her. She even had a Sentinel detail assigned to her security, something she definitely knew, as Issac had seen her speaking to them more than once.

He found her in the kitchen, humming over the counter as she whipped something in a bowl. Her summer dress seemed better suited for a day out with friends, not an afternoon at home, but Elizabeth seemed to fancy high fashion. She even wore stockings.

"Hello," he said with a slight knock, hoping not to startle her too much.

She squeaked, jumping backward and flinging what appeared to be egg all over the cherry wood cabinet.

So much for not surprising her.

"Sorry, Elizabeth, I didn't mean to cause alarm. Here, let me help." He reached for the paper towels by the sink, but she grabbed the roll before he could reach it.

"I-I have it," she stuttered, her brown eyes round, her cheeks pink. "You just caught me off guard." She was already wiping up the mess and bending to retrieve what appeared to be specialized wood cleaner.

Issac frowned. He knew she was an experiment of sorts, but she acted so incredibly human. Well, a clone of a housewife, anyway. *What did Jonathan do to you?*

"I, uh, was making an egg casserole," she explained, gesturing to the mixture and then the flaky pie crust beside it. "Stas loves bacon and eggs. Hopefully, you do, too, because I doubled the recipe."

He leaned against the counter, arms folded. "You knew I was here."

She tossed out the paper towels and began fiddling with her mixture again. "The expensive jacket and tie in the hall closet gave you away." She smiled at him over her shoulder. "Stas isn't dating anyone else who can afford that brand."

Oh, now that was an interesting statement. "Who all is she dating?" he wondered aloud, his eyebrow arching.

Elizabeth giggled, the sound one he heard far too often from simpering beauty queens, but hers came off as more genuine. "No one. Stas doesn't date."

"She doesn't?"

"Well, it seems she does *now*." She poured the mixture into her dish, adding a layer of cheese to the top. "But no, she didn't date much throughout college, too consumed with her studies."

Excellent segue. Thank you, darling. "Because she was focused on her future with the CRF."

Elizabeth snorted. "I guess, yeah." She put the casserole in the oven and started the timer. "Definitely not my first choice."

The muttered words surprised him. "What, working at the CRF, you mean?"

A faint red crept up her neck. "Sorry, I didn't mean for you to hear that."

And now he was very intrigued. "Your distaste for the CRF?" Which he heard clearly in her voice. "Or the comment about it not being your first choice?"

Her cheeks matched her auburn hair, her eyes widening. "I really need to learn to just not speak, like, at all."

"That would be a shame, as you have a lovely voice." He meant it as a compliment, not in a flirtatious manner but in a friendly one. "Why do you dislike the CRF?" he pressed, changing the subject back to what he really wanted to know. *Is this all a charade? Do you know what I am? Is your friendship with Astasiya by coincidence or on purpose?*

Elizabeth chewed her lip. "I don't not like it."

"But you're clearly not their biggest fan either," he pointed out, reading her body language and tone. If this was an act, then the woman deserved an award for her performance because the female radiated innocence. Especially in the way she continued to blush and lower her gaze.

"They just… I know how consuming they can be. I grew up with a father who was never home, and I don't want that for Stas. I hope she can find a balance. That's all."

Her words floored him, particularly the way she spoke about her father—George. Almost as if she truly believed she grew up with him working all the time.

Oh, there were birth records and other official documents that indicated she grew up with the Watkinses. But that family had been under surveillance for over two decades, and Elizabeth didn't appear in those videos or notes until six years ago.

Except it seemed she was completely unaware.

She appeared quite human.

Were his instincts wrong? Could she be the result of something else? Why go through the hassle of creating a history for someone who has no otherworldly powers or purpose?

One thing he knew for certain—she was not related to her parents.

But the experiment piece he now had to question. They all just assumed the CRF created her because where else would she have come from? Yet her mannerisms and emotions didn't suit that theory at all.

Are you a failed project at the CRF? A sleeper agent of some kind? Or something else entirely?

"So, uh, yeah. I'm happy for her, and it's nice to see her dating, too." Elizabeth's eyes sparkled over that last part, her lips pulling upward into an eager smile. "I saw the photos from the gala. How did you talk her into wearing that dress?"

"My stylist picked it out for her."

Elizabeth gave him a look. "Yeah, I figured that much. But how did you get Stas to wear it?"

He wasn't following. "Why wouldn't she wear it?"

"Uh, because it would have cost a fortune."

What kind of man did Elizabeth think him to be? "She didn't pay for it." He'd never force a date to buy their own gown.

Elizabeth made a noise in the back of her throat. "No, that's not— Okay. Let me start over. How did you convince Stas to let you buy her a dress? And not just any dress, but *that* dress? I can hardly get her to borrow my shoes, and they have nothing on that designer label. So how? How did you do it?"

Such a trivial topic and so very human. *She really has no idea who or what I am, does she?* Because anyone else in this situation would never think to question such a frivolous detail. "I didn't give her a choice."

She considered that, her lips scrunched to the side. "I see." She tapped her chin with a manicured nail. "You didn't tell her how much it cost."

"The topic didn't arise, no."

"And she didn't recognize the label, because it's Stas, and she wouldn't." She laughed and shook her head. "I'm very impressed. I hope she keeps you around."

"Thank you, I think."

"It's a compliment." She busied herself with the coffee maker, grabbing three mugs from the cupboard. "Can I offer a suggestion?"

"Yes." That didn't mean he'd take it, but this woman did appear to be Astasiya's true best friend. Not because of outlying circumstances, but because of pure fate. *Fascinating.*

"Never give her a price tag. Ever. Especially if you plan to dress her up again."

"You're recommending I not mention the cost?" he asked, sensing Astasiya's nearing presence. Her delectable blood sang to his senses, reminding him of how she tasted. He desired more. He desired *her.*

"I'm just saying she might not be as appreciative as your other more, uh, *money-savvy* dates. She's not ignorant or anything, just not…"

"Shallow?" he offered, aware that Astasiya lurked in the hallway now, listening.

"Right. That's a good word, or *materialistic*. She's not a fashion person, if that makes sense."

"Duly noted." He paused, waiting for his blonde to enter. Hmm, it seemed she wanted to hear more. All right. Then he'd continue pressing Elizabeth about her life and purpose in this world. "Astasiya hasn't told me what you're doing post-graduation?" He phrased it as a question, hoping she would elaborate from there.

Are you going to work for your father?

For Jonathan?

Or is your purpose darker? What are they planning to do with you?

And more importantly, what exactly are you? Because she wasn't an Ichorian or a Hydraian, from what he could tell. For all intents and purposes, she came off as completely human. Which couldn't be the case at all with her family history and ties to the CRF.

"Oh. I'm working with a kids' shelter in Lower Manhattan, and I volunteer with one in Harlem, too. That's where I was last night, but I work for the other full-time."

"Teaching the underprivileged?" That wasn't at all what he expected.

"Yeah, I lead their reading and writing programs."

"Very commendable." He meant it. "How do George and Lillian feel about it?"

Astasiya's pulse escalated, his question clearly striking a nerve. She appeared in the doorway, her expression concerned.

"Yeah, they don't like it much," Elizabeth replied, nose scrunching. "Oh, hey, Stas."

Issac smiled. *Eavesdropper*, he accused with his eyes.

The look she gave him screamed defiance. *What are you going to do about it?*

He shrugged, not at all bothered. Given the direction of their relationship, he had nothing left to hide.

"Casserole is in the oven," Elizabeth added.

"Yes, you live with quite the master chef, Astasiya," he murmured. "I'm impressed."

Astasiya grinned, approval radiating in her expression. He'd clearly said the right thing, and that pleased him far more than it should.

"Yeah, I sort of love her," she admitted, giving her roommate a side hug.

"Sort of?" Elizabeth gave her a reproachful look. "You adore me."

"It's true," she agreed.

"My sister would have liked you a great deal," Issac said, surprising himself with the words, yet meaning them. "She loved cooking and baking." Amelia spent most days in the kitchen, always entertaining and feeding everyone. His lips actually curled with the thought, astounding him. Usually, thoughts of his sister resulted in pain.

"You have a sister?" Elizabeth asked, brow furrowing.

"I had a sister, yes. It's not well known." Because he didn't contrive his new public image until after her death, and at that point, it wasn't worth the trouble of painting her backstory.

Elizabeth openly cringed. "Oh. I'm sorry."

"No need to apologize. She passed some time ago." And he certainly didn't want to elaborate on that right now. He smiled at Astasiya, needing a new topic. "I want to take you somewhere today. Interested?" He wouldn't exactly accept a negative response, but he'd negotiate as needed.

She cocked her hip against the kitchen table, expression curious. "That depends on where we're going."

He could withhold the truth or dance around it, but after last night, he felt compelled to be honest with her. Always. "The Hamptons."

Her eyebrows rose as Elizabeth nearly dropped the cream she'd just pulled from the refrigerator.

"The Hamptons," Astasiya repeated. "Why?"

"I'm expecting some friends, and I would like for you to join us." At her incredulous look, he added, "Might be an informative experience."

Understanding darkened her gaze. "Friends like the ones I met last night?"

"Similar, but much more hospitable."

"I assume that means you'll miss dinner tonight?" Elizabeth directed the question to her roommate.

"Fitzgerald and Watkins dinner," she translated on a groan. "Don't we get a reprieve? We just ate with them last weekend."

"That's what I said, but my mom said it's mandatory. For me, anyway, not you."

Astasiya looked positively pained, her expression falling. "I… I don't know if I'm ready for another dinner with them. But if you need me to go, Liz, I can."

"Oh, no." Elizabeth straightened, her gaze filling with purpose. "You totally go to the Hamptons when Issac Wakefield asks you to go to the Hamptons." She winced, seeming to remember the man she addressed by full name stood in the room. "Uh, I mean, you should go."

So much more nonchalant and natural, causing him to smile.

"I agree with Elizabeth," he said. "When I ask you to go somewhere, you say yes. Beautifully accurate advice."

Astasiya gave him a look. "Not biased at all."

"Naturally not, no," he murmured.

Elizabeth cleared her throat. "So, uh, do I just tell them you're together?"

"I've not agreed to go yet," Astasiya pointed out.

"She means yes," Issac translated.

"Like in a relationship or just a date?" Elizabeth asked, her focus completely on him.

"Both," he replied, wishing he could be there to see the look on all their faces at dinner. Maybe he'd ask Mateo to hack into the dining room security feeds, just for a laugh.

"You don't do *relationships*," Astasiya said, her cheeks bright with color.

"I also don't see a woman more than once, yet here we are," he pointed out.

"You can't be serious."

His lips curled into a taunting grin. "I'm very serious, love." *Especially when it comes to you.*

Elizabeth smiled. "So, I can refer to you as her boyfriend, right?"

Astasiya looked positively affronted by the notion. "Seriously—"

"Absolutely," Issac replied, cutting her off.

She sputtered. "I don't get a say in this?"

"No."

Elizabeth squealed and clapped her hands. Her yellow sundress flickered beneath the kitchen lights as she skipped around, her happiness making him smile. *Definitely a genuine friendship.* And it seemed she approved of him, too.

"Chick flicks and whatever pizza I want for a year," she announced, pointing a finger at Astasiya and waggling it. "And *you* have to pay for it all." Another squeal followed by an impressive ballet move that had Issac really wondering about her history and upbringing.

Where did she learn to dance like that?

"Oh God." Astasiya's head fell to the wall behind her as she shook it back and forth. "I can't believe you remember that."

"Of course I do. I've waited six very long years for this moment. Freakin' finally!"

"What am I missing?" Issac asked, completely enamored by the display between them.

"Oh, please don't," Astasiya groaned.

"Stas swore up and down that she would *never* have a boyfriend. It wasn't *her thing*, and she has no interest in her *MRS degree*." She used her fingers to quote Stas. "We made a bet that whenever she got a boyfriend, she would let me choose movies and pizza for a year, at her expense. That was how sure she was that she would never date."

"Hey, I dated."

"Oh, that Jake guy so did not count. You went home with him after that wedding. That's not a date. That's called a hookup."

Bright splotches of pink painted Astasiya's features. "Lizzie!"

"Okay, fine, Pete kind of counted. You went out with him twice, but he wasn't a *boyfriend*, and you didn't even sleep with him. And then there was that one guy, uh, Brian? Brandon? Whatever. He lasted for, like, two seconds before you got bored, and then—"

"Oh my God, just stop!"

"Oh, like he cares. He's a walking tabloid." Her cheeks reddened. "No offense."

"No offense taken, darling," Issac said, his mouth hurting from smiling so much. "However, please, do continue. This is all very enlightening."

"No," Astasiya snapped.

"The only other one was that Paul guy who wouldn't leave you alone, and none of it counted, but you're finally dating. Like, *really* dating." Elizabeth started dancing again.

"I daresay dear Elizabeth is more excited than you are," he noted.

Astasiya glowered at him. "Oh, I'm just thrilled." She moved to grab some plates as the timer on the oven sounded, and paused at something resting on the counter.

Issac glanced over her shoulder to read the headline.

Mystery Woman Coaxes Smile from Billionaire Playboy.

He was already laughing before she grumbled, "You've got to be fucking kidding me."

"Oops," Elizabeth said, grimacing.

Issac plucked the magazine from her hands and tossed it in the bin, where it belonged. "Ignore it, love."

She gave him a look. "The headline is wrong. You only smiled for show."

"If that's what you want to believe, then so be it." He knew the truth and that was all that mattered. Cupping her face, he pulled her closer, needing an answer. "Now, will you go with me today? Please?"

"To the Hamptons."

"Yes."

"To meet more friends."

He nodded. "You'll like them. They remind me of you and Owen."

Her eyebrows lifted at the subtle context underlying his words, and he nodded again at the silent question in her eyes. *Yes, they are Hydraians.*

"Please, Astasiya?" he asked softly. "Come with me today. You won't regret it."

She swallowed, a hint of emotion flickering in her gaze. "Okay," she whispered.

"Brilliant." He smiled, pleased. "We'll go after we finish eating."

"Okay," she repeated.

"Go pack a few things," he added, aware of their audience. "We might stay a few days."

"What?"

"Trust me." He couldn't elaborate in front of Elizabeth. She clearly knew nothing about his world, despite her surroundings, and he wouldn't change that for her.

Astasiya held his gaze for a beat, more of that emotion spilling through her expression. She finally nodded, agreeing. "I'll grab a bag."

Elizabeth stood behind them, the casserole already on a cooling rack. She grinned widely as Astasiya turned.

"Stop gloating, Liz," she muttered.

"*Pretty Woman* and a pizza with extra pepperoni. That's my first order," she replied.

"I hate you."

"You love me."

"Uh-huh." Astasiya grabbed her and hugged her tight, her words low as she added, "Call me if you need me tonight. You know I'll be there."

Something akin to relief graced Elizabeth's features, her expression turning somber. "I know. Thanks, Stas. But go have fun. You deserve it."

"Thank you," Astasiya replied, leaving the room. "I'll be back in a few minutes." She glanced at him. "With a suitcase."

He smiled. "Brilliant."

CHAPTER EIGHTEEN

Will You Dance with Me?

Issac hadn't visited Wakefield Manor in several years, his memories of the grounds tainted by that day in the ballroom.

The day he found Eli's headless body holding an urn of Amelia's ashes.

With each approaching mile, the ache in his gut grew stronger. He didn't want to do this, but the woman beside him required it.

Astasiya remained quiet and unaware in the passenger seat, taking in the summer scenery. The Hamptons were truly gorgeous, with all the manor-style homes and white picket fences. His estate rested on the water, a few streets over. Amelia had loved the beach, spending hours lounging in the sun with Eli at her side.

He swallowed, taking the turns and driving on autopilot.

The familiar gates loomed ahead, a *W* etched in the middle. He pulled a device from the glove box and clicked the button. The iron moved slowly, opening up the driveway. Usually, he went left at the split to park in one of the garages, but as he had a guest today, he bypassed it for the loop around the fountain in front of the mansion.

Fifteen bedrooms.

Just as many bathrooms.

Several living areas.

A pool house equipped with two pools.

And a guest home.

The abundance of space had been required to accommodate the parties Amelia enjoyed throwing here during the summers, many of the Hydraians choosing to stay overnight. They were just far enough outside of New York City to feel safe, especially with the security system at Issac's estate—built by Mateo.

He parked in the cobblestone drive outside the front and smiled as Robert opened the French doors. Issac could have phoned ahead with a warning, but he opted to surprise his estate manager instead. The ruddy color on the rotund man's cheeks said Issac had achieved that goal in spades.

"Welcome to Wakefield Manor," he murmured, setting his sunglasses on the dash and unbuckling his seat belt.

"It's gorgeous," she breathed, her eyes on the oversized windows and brick siding.

While he agreed, he didn't comment and instead unbuckled his seat belt as his door opened.

"I couldn't believe it when I heard the gate open," Robert said, bouncing on his heels just outside the car. "My Cherie is going to be thrilled."

Issac chuckled and stepped out to shake hands with the much shorter man. "How are the children, Robert?"

"Oh, Rebecca is married and just had a baby, making me a proud granddaddy to an adorable new granddaughter. She inherited all the fairer genes from Cherie's side of the family, too."

Issac had listened while walking around the car to open the door for Astasiya. "That's fantastic, Robert." He held out a hand for her, which she accepted as she joined him and stood by his side. "Why didn't you tell me?"

"Well." The man clasped his hands over his rotund belly. "Whenever we talk, it's usually about business. Didn't want to waste your time with family news and all that."

"You becoming a grandfather is hardly a waste of my time, Robert," Issac replied, disappointed that he would feel that way.

"Maybe, maybe." He rocked back and forth with the words. "So, who do we have here?" he asked, his hazel eyes crinkling as he studied the blonde at Issac's side.

"This is Astasiya Davenport. Astasiya, this is Robert Allmond. He lives here."

Robert blew a raspberry. "He means I live over there." He pointed in the direction of the guesthouse near the garages. "Cherie and I just keep up the grounds for Master Wakefield. Speaking of which, I better go tell her you're here. You know she's going to expect you to stay for dinner."

"Yes, I'm expecting company as well. Lucian and likely a few others."

"Oh!" Robert hopped with excitement. "I'll ask Shelly to help me ready some of the guest rooms. She's back from college for the summer."

Ah yes, the youngest of the Allmond family. "Is she enjoying Duke?" Issac asked, curious.

"Loving it, of course. I'll make sure she stops by to thank you."

Issac waved him off. Paying her tuition had been a natural favor. The Allmond family took amazing care of his estate, and he returned the favor in kind. "There's no need for that, but I would enjoy an update. I haven't seen her since she was thirteen or so?"

That seemed to calm the man a bit, his hand coming up to scratch his jaw. "Yeah, about that long, huh? I was starting to think the next time I'd see you would be at my funeral."

"Foolish thoughts."

"Not for an old man, they're not." There was a hint of chastisement in that statement that twisted Issac's heart. *Fair point.* "Okay, so four or five rooms will do? Yours as well?"

"I'll handle mine, but if you wouldn't mind the others?"

Robert puffed out his chest. "Master Wakefield, I've had six years of nothing to do other than keep the dust from settling around here. I do not mind one bit, and you can bet Cherie will feel the same."

Has it only been that long? It felt like a century had passed since Issac last set foot on these grounds.

"Thank you, Robert," he murmured.

"My pleasure, sir." He bowed and scampered off down the driveway.

Issac chuckled after him, shaking his head. He'd missed the jovial man, perhaps more than he realized.

"You have a manservant," Astasiya said, eyebrows raised. "And apparently a house in the Hamptons you don't use often. At least I know the tabloids were right about your net worth."

He snorted. "Hardly, on all accounts." He tugged her toward the still-open doors of the house. The Hydraians wouldn't arrive for another hour or so, which gave him plenty of time to change and give her a proper tour.

A twinge of excitement dispelled his unease, the idea of showing off a bit appealing to him far more than it should.

"Uh-huh. So why are we here, again?" she asked, her eyes dancing over the three-story foyer as they entered.

"To meet friends, but first, I need a shower." If Lucian or Balthazar found him like this, there would be comments galore. Issac never wore the same suit two days in a row, and the stubble across his jaw would certainly indicate his lack of a proper shave. That, he might keep, but the rumpled appearance required replacement.

"Not liking the whole walk-of-shame look?" she teased, a devious twinkle in her gaze. So much better than the dead eyes from last night.

He pulled her close, his lips brushing her ear. "Or liking it too much."

Her breath hitched, a slight pink creeping into her fair skin. She cleared her throat. "I mean, I guess I can keep myself entertained. Anything off-limits I should know about so I can start there?" Her voice held a sultry edge to it that lit his blood on fire.

He would have her beneath him.

Tonight.

Issac let her see that in his expression as he slowly perused her legs—exposed by her jean shorts—and her clingy tank top. She swallowed as he met her gaze, recalling her question about anything being off-limits.

"Only the master bedroom," he lied, knotting his fingers in her hair to guide her into a kiss. Fuck, he wanted her now. The last few days had been torture, his need for her escalating by the second. But he had to change first. He traced her lower lip with his tongue, allowing himself one final taste of her before stepping back. "I'll find you."

~*~

Issac disappeared down the hall rather than up the stairs.

Stas gazed left and right, surrounded by opulence and wealth. Above her hung a chandelier that glistened from the sunlight streaming in through the windows.

"Wow," she breathed. This place was unreal. Everything held a note of extravagance, even the furniture. She was almost afraid to touch anything.

Closing the front doors, she followed Issac's path, curious, and found herself in a vast dining area with doors that overlooked a huge porch. And beyond it, a pool. Not just a dipping pool, but a full-length water arena equipped with waterfalls and various plant life that she felt sure were not native to New York.

She should have brought her swimsuit.

The row of trees lining the back of the property hid the beach and ocean from her view, but she knew Issac's estate was situated on the water. She could smell it outside.

A kitchen Lizzie would have fainted at the sight of joined the dining area, expanding outward to showcase several ovens and stoves, two refrigerators, and an island that doubled as a dining table.

She snapped a picture with her phone, sending it to her roommate. Because wow.

Continuing her journey, she found another seating area near the back of the house with more doors that led outside to the patio, and ended her journey at a set of oversized doors. Finding them unlocked, she twisted the knob and froze.

Two stories of windows stared back at her from three angles. Thick velvet curtains were tied into the corners, granting her a magnificent view of the property and the ocean beyond.

"Holy fuck," she breathed, twirling in the oversized ballroom. No furniture or decorations in here, just a polished hardwood floor with a grand piano in one corner.

She left her sandals and purse by the door and padded barefoot into the room. Another one of those chandeliers hung above her from the vaulted ceiling. Definitely a room designed for entertaining and dancing.

Stas twirled in the center, picturing masquerade balls and parties in this room. It wasn't her usual scene, but she'd enjoy watching one. Especially if Issac were a star performer.

Having no training and not caring whatsoever, she danced around the room, letting go of the last twenty-four hours and just *being*. She felt light and carefree, as if she hadn't almost died last week. The Conclave disappeared, along with her troubles, and when she opened her eyes to find Issac leaning against the doorjamb, all she could do was smile. He brought her here. He did this. And it'd been so worth it for even the few moments of freedom she'd found in this room.

He'd traded his suit for a pair of jeans and a fitted gray shirt. No shoes. Hair damp. It was the most casual she'd ever seen him, aside from this morning when she woke up to his mostly naked body.

"This was Amelia's favorite room," he said, his voice soft. "She used to dance in the center where you're standing now while Eli played the piano."

"Eli?"

"I guess you could say he was my brother-in-law. He and Amelia never married, but they were romantically involved for centuries." Meaning his sister had been an immortal as well. Stas supposed she could have guessed that from the photo books in his condo. All those photos were decades old, yet Owen remained the same in all of them. Because he was a Hydraian. Did that mean Amelia had been one as well?

Fledglings were created from an Ichorian father and a mortal mother. Then fledglings became Hydraians—the enemies of Ichorians.

Stas frowned. She understood the creation bit but couldn't fathom a reason for why Ichorians would loathe their children. That part made no sense.

And what's more, Issac didn't seem to have an issue with fledglings or Hydraians. So why did he break all the rules? There were clear consequences, as she observed last night. Yet, here she stood in a ballroom while he fussed with an electrical board on the wall beside the door.

She was about to ask him when music began playing overhead, drawing her attention to the speakers. The lights flickered overhead next, setting a romantic mood in the room.

"Amelia taught me how to dance when we were young," he said over the music, sliding a wooden panel to cover the electrical switches he'd just altered. "She claimed it was the best way to win a woman's heart. I always said I had no interest in a woman's heart."

He sauntered onto the floor, extending his hand as he approached.

"Care for a demonstration, my lady?" he offered.

"You're asking me to dance?"

"Amelia would scold me if I didn't."

"Would she scold me for refusing?" she asked, even as she accepted his hand.

He chuckled. "She definitely would, yes." He caught her hip with his free hand and pulled her closer. "And I should warn you, my sister was known to make many grown men cry. I don't recommend upsetting her. Now put your other hand on my shoulder."

She did as instructed. "Okay, but I'm warning you, I'm not a great dancer."

He walked her two steps backward, then one to the side, as if testing that theory. "Not an issue. It's all about the leading, love."

"Uh-huh." He wouldn't be saying that when she kept stepping on his feet.

Issac seemed to take her words as a challenge, as he proved his point by moving her across the floor with a few subtle nudges of his hand against her hip. His hand in hers helped as well, as did the slow beat of the song. He'd clearly chosen this one on purpose.

"Good," he praised as they returned to their starting place. "Now, let's make it interesting."

His palm slid from her hip to the small of her back, the gentle pressure encouraging her to shift with him as he introduced her to a slightly faster rhythm. She mimicked his motions, keeping pace with him and smiling when she realized this wasn't nearly as hard as she expected.

"I don't know how you're doing this, but I'm dancing." And she wasn't terrible, either.

His lips twitched as he lifted the hand holding hers and led her into a twirl. She gasped as he caught her around the waist with his opposite arm, her pulse racing at the fluidity of his movements.

Okay. Issac could dance. Like, really, legitimately dance.

"Mmm, yes, I daresay, Astasiya, you move quite well." He spun her around him again, this time dipping her close to the floor before righting her against him. "Amelia would approve."

Her breathing escalated as he picked up the pace to match the new song. Each touch and brush of his hand caused her hips to sway with his, her body syncing in time with his and following his lead entirely.

Issac twirled her, bringing her back to his front, his hands on her hips holding her to him.

"I bought this estate for Amelia," he murmured against Stas's ear. He slowed their swaying as the music melted into a sensual tune. "She wanted to be closer to me but couldn't stay in the city. So this was the best alternative. I thought it would keep her safe." He rotated Stas back around to face him and gazed down at her. "I was wrong."

Despite the emotion thickening his voice, he continued their movements, whirling her about the floor with an ease that spoke of years of training. Stas's pulse quickened with every twirl, her body trusting him to catch her. He never missed a beat, his tempo in line with the rhythm regardless of the song. She wondered if this was his outlet, his way of moving through the pain.

"What happened?" she finally asked, her voice breathy from all the activity.

"Jonathan happened." Lifting her hand, Issac propelled her into a twirl that was faster and harder than the others. She spun twice before he caught her against him, her heart fluttering at the intense contact. "He made it look like the Conclave did it."

She swallowed, her feet missing a step as ice drizzled down her spine. "Like Owen?"

Issac masked her stumble with another spin, helping her to rebalance and continue. "Yes, the same methods."

They danced in silence for a long moment, her mind processing his admission. "So you think Jonathan killed Owen?"

"I've considered it," he murmured, slowing their momentum to a sway that seemed to fuse their bodies together. "But everything with Jonathan requires a motive, and I cannot think of a reason for him to have killed Owen."

Well, Stas couldn't think of a reason for *anyone* to kill Owen. But it seemed this mysterious Jonathan had a penchant for arranging murder scenes into a Conclave-like setting.

So, who is Jonathan? Another Ichorian? Whoever he was, she doubted she knew him. Although, she must have some tie to him if Issac felt she could help him in seeking revenge. "What was his motive for Amelia and Eli?" she wondered out loud.

"I believe he wished to incite a war. The Hydraians are very protective of their Elders, of which Eli was one."

"An Elder?" she repeated.

"Yes, the oldest of the Hydraian race. There were five. Now there are four."

"So by killing him…?" It turned into a question because she couldn't puzzle it all out.

"Hydraians and Ichorians have long been at odds with one another, something you may have gathered last night during the Conclave. However, there's a truce of sorts in place. Assassinating an Elder, someone the Hydraians held very dear to their hearts, was a surefire way to invoke an emotional need for retaliation. Add Amelia, and, well, it's a wonder Lucian could control his Hydraians."

"I'm not sure I completely follow," she admitted. "But I understand the gist of what you're saying: Jonathan had a motive."

"Yes."

"And how did you figure out it was him?"

"Ah, that is a much longer story." He twirled her with the words before pulling her flush against him again. "The short version is, a bottle of red wine tipped me off. I found it in the fridge, not fully chilled, and it came from a vineyard only one person I know fancies."

"Jonathan." A reasonable guess considering what he said before about Jonathan having killed his sister.

"Indeed," he replied. "There were other factors at play, but I'm positive he had a hand in my sister's murder."

"What happened when you accused him?" she wondered, curious as to why or how the man still lived. Given what she'd observed of Issac's world, his kind wasn't afraid to kill. And Issac certainly had the motive to seek revenge.

"Nothing, as I've not informed him." He dipped her backward, his lips at her neck. "I've let him think that I believe the Ichorians killed my sister."

Her eyes flew to his as he righted her again, her breasts against his chest. "Why?" she asked, breathless.

"Because the best revenge takes time and careful planning. It requires the perfect pawn." Another pivot ending in a dip that brought her dangerously close to the floor. Her chest heaved against his as he held her there, his body bent over hers as her hair brushed the polished wood.

"Me."

"Yes." He slowly guided her upward, her body flush with his. "But last night changed everything. You meeting Osiris was a consequence I never could have predicted."

"Meaning what? I'm no longer the perfect pawn?"

"Oh, you're still perfect for my plans." The hand on her back drifted lower, sliding over her curves. His lips were a hairsbreadth from hers. "But I'm rather fond of you being alive." She shivered at the heat in his voice. They were no longer moving, just locked in an intimate embrace that left her craving more.

Clapping shattered the moment, a low whistle added for effect. "Not bad, Wakefield," a deep voice praised. "Not bad at all."

Chapter Nineteen

Blood Ties

Balthazar, Issac mentally growled, not at all amused.

"I give it a seven point eight out of ten on the seduction scale," the mind reader informed Issac as he lowered the music to a soft background murmur. "Points deducted for a lack of disrobing and missed opportunities for light petting."

"You're an ass," Issac said, stepping in front of Astasiya.

"I'm only trying to be helpful. Shall I demonstrate the disrobing part while you take notes?" The suggestion underlying his voice had Issac narrowing his gaze.

Fuck. Off.

Balthazar grinned wickedly instead, intent and sin dancing across his features. "Oh, I wouldn't go that far, sweetheart. I'm always up for a good challenge."

Issac frowned. "What?" That didn't even remotely make sense. And since when did Balthazar refer to Issac as *sweetheart*?

Amusement played through Balthazar's dark eyes. "I'm replying to your little blonde vixen's lascivious thoughts. You've unleashed quite the fancy in that one."

Astasiya's gasp had Issac glancing over his shoulder. She peered around him at Balthazar, her expression boasting shock and dismay.

Hmm, most women reacted like this when first meeting the sensual Elder. The man practically oozed sexual intent, and his outward confidence confirmed his ability to follow through. Issac shook his head, giving the mind reader a knowing look. "Nice try, Balthazar. She's immune to immortal gifts."

"Sounds like a performance issue, Wakefield. Might want to get that checked out because I hear her loud and clear. She's a fan of your ass, in case you were wondering."

Issac studied Astasiya, who now wore several shades of red.

"You're practically screaming it, sweetheart," Balthazar added, causing her lips to part.

Somewhat telling, but not. "You're going to have to do better than that." Sensing a woman's interest in another man didn't require mind-reading abilities, especially for someone as old and as experienced as Balthazar.

Balthazar's chuckle echoed across the room. "Now she thinks you're arrogant. Which, by the way, sweetheart, I've seen his ass, and I can firmly say he's well within his rights to be arrogant about it."

Astasiya blanched, her face giving everything away. Even Issac could tell what she was thinking.

All right, Balthazar. You want to prove you can really read her thoughts? Let's go for something harder.

The mind reader gave him a look that said, *Challenge accepted.*

"What are the names of your birth parents, Astasiya? Their real names?"

"Why?" The word came out on a breath, as if shocked he would ask. "What do they have to do with anything?"

"Caroline and Seth," Balthazar said, disapproval radiating from the downward angle of his lips. "That wasn't very nice, Wakefield."

Astasiya took a step to the side, her focus on the mind reader leaning against the wall. He'd chosen a casual outfit, as always, of jeans and a maroon shirt. This was why Issac had chosen to dress down—he knew the Hydraians would arrive in similar attire.

"How did you know that?" she asked, her hands shaking at her sides.

Okay, that had been the wrong question to ask, clearly. Because she appeared ready to fall apart.

Balthazar tapped his head. "Mind reader, sweetheart."

"Impossible," she breathed, accusation lurking in her gaze as she faced Issac. "You said I was immune to Ichorians and their psychic gifts."

"You are." Of that he was certain.

"Then explain him?" She pointed at the smirking male across the room.

"He's not an Ichorian, but a Hydraian like Owen." A thought occurred to him, shifting his attention back to Balthazar. "Who else is here?" Maybe someone else could test a gift on Astasiya to see if this was just a fluke or if her supernatural resistance only applied to Ichorians.

"Ash and Jay. Jacque went back to get Luc a few minutes ago. And yeah, I think you should run that theory by your leggy blonde before you test it."

Issac's jaw clenched. "Get the fuck out of my head." *Or I'll play in yours.*

"It's just been my experience—of which I have a few millennia more than your three centuries—that most women don't like men thinking for them." He winked at Astasiya, which only pissed Issac off more.

Stop flirting with her.

Balthazar seemed amused, his eyes saying, *I've only just started.*

"What theory, Issac?" Astasiya demanded.

I fucking hate you, Balthazar, he thought while pinching the bridge of his nose. The damn mind reader adored throwing Issac off his game, like a perpetual competition with no true winner. Because truthfully, they rivaled each other in many, many ways.

"You're immune to Ichorian gifts, but Balthazar's ability to read your thoughts suggests you might not be immune to Hydraian gifts. The only way to test that theory would be to have other Hydraians use their respective talents on you." There. That sounded scientific and sound.

Except the raising of her brows said she didn't agree with that logical idea at all. "You want to make me a guinea pig?"

"You could really use some work on your bedside manner, Wakefield."

"Oh, do shut up." Issac envisioned punching Balthazar in the face and forced the image into the mind reader's visual preceptors. The bastard staggered sideways on a gasp, only to shift the opposite way as Issac cast another visual spell—this one showcasing a hit to the stomach.

"As for you," he added, turning to Astasiya. "I thought you might want to test your immunity against psychic abilities in a safe environment. But what do I know?" He stalked out of the room in search of Lucian.

Astasiya needed someone reasonable to introduce her to Hydraian life. Not the seductive Elder with only one goal in mind.

Touch her and I'll kill you, Issac thought at him, knowing Balthazar could hear him. He didn't really mean it.

Or maybe he did.

Fuck, this woman had him tied up in knots over absolutely nothing and everything. He just felt so out of sorts around her, as if he were trying to fix something elusive.

No, that wasn't it.

He felt threatened.

Not by her, but by Balthazar.

Issac paused in the hall, startled. He *never* felt this competitive with anyone, least of all the Elder. So why now? Why her?

Because she'll never truly be mine…

His lips flattened. Since when did he care about the long term? Was it the element of the forbidden that taunted him into these thoughts and feelings? The fact that their relationship was a true impossibility, therefore making it safe to yearn for more? But why bother? Issac preferred one-night stands, easy relationships with no strings or expectations. Why would Astasiya be any different?

He shook his head. *This isn't me.* He needed to rein in these wayward inclinations and refocus on the task—to introduce Astasiya to the future.

And for that, he needed Lucian. Her destiny.

~*~

Okay, someone's angry, Stas thought, gaping after Issac. He'd just stormed out of the room, his shoulders tense, hands fisted at his sides.

And whatever he'd just done to Balthazar... wow. The man was still recovering, hands on his knees, his breathing harsh.

"Why is he so pissed?" she asked, confused as hell. She didn't want to be the object of an experiment. Was that really so infuriating?

"No, it's my fault," Balthazar said, coughing. "I underestimated his fondness for you and pushed too far." He shook his head and finger-combed his dark hair, righting himself. "Not that I regret a minute of it."

His licentious gaze made her snort. Sure, he was attractive—almost lethally so—but she only had room for one too-gorgeous man in her life right now.

"I'm more than mere looks, sweetheart," he murmured, his tone one that alluded to silky sheets and long nights spent naked between them. "Why else would your Issac feel so threatened?"

She swallowed. *First, not* my *anything. Second, I'm not even going to consider the first comment.* Because if she did, she might believe him, and the last thing she wanted to do was fantasize about a *mind reader.*

"Ah, but fantasy makes it all so much more interesting." Sensuality seemed to ooze from his pores, his handsome face and deep voice a combination that no doubt brought most women to their knees. "Men, too," he added for her.

Her gaze narrowed. "You must get the biggest headache reading minds all the time."

"He loves it," a deep voice drawled from the doorway. "B?"

"She's not a threat, but I would be happy to search her more thoroughly." The wicked twinkle in his gaze only added to the smile he flashed her.

A charmer—not in a creepy way but in an experienced way.

This man knew how to seduce women, and if she weren't so wrapped up in Issac, she might be more intrigued.

"That won't be necessary," the newcomer replied, stepping into view.

Her lips parted. *Are all of Issac's friends gorgeous?* Because fuck, she couldn't handle more of these guys. She had enough between Balthazar and Issac. Now she had a third.

Lizzie would be losing her shit.

Stas just, well, stared.

"Can you give us the room?" the new male asked, his authority clear in both tone and stature. Tall, broad shoulders, sturdy jaw dusted in blond stubble, and emerald eyes that seemed to pierce her to her very soul.

Why does he look so familiar? She tried to place the features, but the connection refused her. It wasn't *him* she recognized, but something about him.

"Be careful with this one, Luc," Balthazar warned as he walked by him. "Issac has her all riled up." He glanced back at her, devious energy smoldering in the depths of his chocolate irises. "I look forward to getting acquainted, Stas. Let me know when you're ready for a real immortal."

The new male demigod—because what else could she call these guys? (They certainly weren't human)—shook his head with a chuckle while shutting the door.

"B will never learn," he said, more to himself than to her.

B is a nickname for Balthazar. Got it.

And what was this guy's name? She'd been too consumed by his size and striking features to hear it. Those features only grew more powerful and gorgeous as he approached her.

"I'm Lucian, but call me Luc." He held out a palm that was twice the size of hers.

Yep, definitely some sort of god. "Stas," she managed on a squeak as she shook his hand.

He released her from his hold, his shake firm and quick. "Yes, I know." He flashed her a devastating smile that had her taking a sharp breath.

Okay, so not only did Issac belong to the hot-bachelor club, but he also seemed to be part of some sort of secret society for lethally attractive men. This… was distracting.

"You can't read minds, right?" she asked, realizing that her thoughts were going south fast.

"No, my gift is more strategic. Some call me omniscient, but it's not the correct term. I also possess a sensual talent, but it's not relevant to our discussion."

"Oh." A sensual talent? Like a supernatural-style gift or just an overconfident statement about his bedroom skills? Given Balthazar's introduction, it seemed appropriate to assume the latter.

What is with these men? No, not men. Gods.

"I hear you're gifted with persuasion," he said, his words dumping a figurative bucket of ice water over her head. "That's a very unique talent, even more so since you can apparently already access it."

She swallowed, unsure of how to reply to that. *Where's Issac?* He mentioned telling Aidan about… Her eyes widened. *That* was how she knew this man. "You look so much like Aidan." The words left her mouth without thought.

"Yes, he's my father." His eyes crinkled with his smile. "You met him last night, right? During the Conclave?"

Her palms were clammy. "I… yes." Wait, did those rules still apply here? She took a step back. *Is this man an Ichorian? One who knows about my gifts? Oh, fuck, is he here for me?* She searched the room, expecting more of them to appear, but hoping Issac would be among them. *Where did he go?*

"Relax," Luc murmured, holding up his hands in a placating gesture. "I'm not your enemy, Stas. I'm actually very much your ally."

Yeah, she doubted that. Not after the introduction she received last night, courtesy of Osiris.

"Issac has explained that you're a fledgling who will one day become a Hydraian, right?"

She didn't trust him enough to answer that, so she said nothing instead.

"I'm a Hydraian, Stas," he said softly. "The oldest, actually. Aidan is my Ichorian father, who created me with a mortal mother several millennia ago."

Her lips parted. "Several…" She couldn't finish that phrase. *How old is this guy?*

"Balthazar, whom you just met, is nearly as old. I met him during a time you can't even begin to fathom, and we've existed together for thousands of years. It may seem impossible right now, but you can trust us, and you will. Because we're your future."

Issac chose that moment to open the door, his expression far less irritated than before. "When I mentioned bringing some of the others, I didn't realize you intended to invite an army to my house."

Luc grinned. "You're just sour that B tagged along."

"One of these days, I'm going to shoot him."

Luc shrugged. "He'll wake up."

"I know. That's precisely why I've not bothered." Issac stopped beside the blond male, their contrasting appearances giving her whiplash. Women everywhere would weep at the sight.

This sort of thing should be illegal.

"I was just introducing myself to your Stas, as she's apparently unfamiliar with my name." A hint of accusation lurked in those words.

"Yes, we've not yet touched on Hydraian hierarchy." His sapphire gaze captured hers. "Lucian is the eldest of his kind. Thus many refer to him as their King."

Luc rolled his eyes. "Great introduction."

"It's true."

"It's ridiculous and you know it," Luc replied, not at all amused. "They consider me a leader because of my vast experience."

"He remembers everything," Issac added helpfully. "He's omniscient."

"See, this is what I referred to earlier, Stas. Everyone makes this assumption about my gift, but it's really just that I store every detail from every experience, of which I've had many due to my age."

"Otherwise known as omniscience."

Luc shook his head. "Not by definition, which sta—"

"Okay," Stas interrupted, grimacing when both men focused on her. "Sorry, I need some clarifications."

"Then you're definitely in the appropriate company," Luc replied, smiling. "What can I clarify?"

Uh, everything. But she chose to start with the basics. "What are the rules for today?" It was something Issac should have covered with her prior to this introduction.

"There are none," Issac replied. "This meeting defies them all."

Because Hydraians and Ichorians weren't supposed to consort with one another. Right. "Isn't that dangerous?"

"Absolutely." This from Luc. "But you're well protected here."

"Hence the Guardians taking over my kitchen," Issac muttered.

Luc chuckled. "I'm fairly certain the majority of them came to see you, not to protect me. You're missed on the island."

They shared a moment, some hidden conversation flowing between them that left Issac nodding. "I should visit more."

"Yes. You should." The command in Luc's tone startled Stas. This man truly was a leader, and it showed in the way he gripped and squeezed Issac's shoulder. But something else lurked between them, something brotherly.

Aidan is Luc's biological father.

Aidan also turned Issac.

Did that make them family?

"Where does Amelia fit in all this?" she wondered out loud, earning her an arched brow from Issac.

"My sister is dead."

"Right, I know. I'm just…" She winced, uncertain of how to word it. "This is all, well, confusing."

"Aidan is my father," Luc said, repeating what she already knew. "He was also Amelia's birth father. Making her a Hydraian, just like me."

That was the connection she needed. "So you're all friends because Aidan created you."

"Yes, but not quite." Issac scratched his stubbled jaw, his expression thoughtful. "My father died when I was two. Then my mother—a widow—met Aidan a year after, and he became her consort of sorts because my mother didn't wish to give up her title and fortune. Amelia was born shortly after."

Meaning Amelia and Issac shared a mother. "And then Aidan turned you into an Ichorian later."

He nodded. "Precisely. I grew up with him as my father figure, even referred to him as such for many years. Which is why I consider Lucian a brother."

Luc grinned. "In a world of black and white, there is also gray."

"Yes. So perhaps now you see why I'm not a fan of our archaic laws, hmm?" His lips quirked at the sides.

"Why have the laws to begin with?" she asked, still uncertain of that part. "I mean, why would fathers want to hurt their children?" Because clearly they did. Case in point—Owen.

"Ah, families have fought over much less throughout existence. But in this case, it's the oldest reason known to man: fear." Luc's gaze took on a faraway gleam, seeming to lose himself in the past. It was then that she saw it—his age.

Like Osiris.

Luc resembled a normal man. Well, a ridiculously handsome man captured in the body of a god. But not exactly *old.*

Yet those eyes held thousands of lifetimes of knowledge.

"What are they afraid of?" she asked softly, both curious and confused.

"Power," Luc murmured, still seemingly lost in his own mind. "And blood."

She frowned. "I don't understand."

He blinked, refocusing on her. "Hydraians are dually gifted, while Ichorians are singularly powerful. That's how the jealousy began, long, long ago. Our kind inherits the talents from their fathers and their mothers, both of which manifest during rebirth. Many thought to use us, even isolated us on an island. But then they realized the darkest secret of all, something we kept hidden for nearly two thousand years."

Issac's face was artfully blank, his gaze almost bored. Very unlike Stas, who felt as if Luc had left her on the edge of her seat. "What was the secret?" she asked, hoping he would tell her.

"Our blood is toxic to Ichorians," Luc replied. "Which means, Stas, that once you're reborn as a Hydraian, you will be hunted by every Ichorian in existence. Because not only can a single drop of your blood kill one, but you'll also be able to persuade them to drink it."

Chapter Twenty

A Crumpled Charade

Issac caught Astasiya's hip as she swayed, his gaze locking on Lucian. He could have eased her into that truth rather than flaying her alive with it.

"But… But…" She touched her neck, gingerly stroking the healed mark against her skin. It had disappeared overnight, something that disappointed him more than it should.

"You're a fledgling," he reminded softly, his lips at her ear. "Your blood isn't venomous to me yet."

She clutched his shirt, burying her face against his chest as he wrapped his arms around her. Lucian raised his brows, the display of affection evidently surprising him.

"Let's prepare for dinner," Issac suggested, knowing Cherie and Robert would be over soon with a feast. "We can discuss more later." Because they were nowhere near done yet. They hadn't even skimmed the surface.

"Can I have a moment?" Astasiya whispered. "Please?"

"Of course, love." He kissed her temple and signaled for Lucian to leave with a nod of his head. *I'll handle it.*

The much older man nodded. "I look forward to getting to know you better, Stas."

She didn't return the sentiment, her body shaking against Issac.

Lucian didn't press, merely left the two of them alone, the door closing quietly behind him.

"We're alone," he murmured, stroking his fingers through her hair. "I know this is a lot to take in and understand. It's why I wanted to introduce you to it slowly." Because he knew it would overwhelm her, specifically when she realized her future—not just that she would become a Hydraian, but also a powerful one. Perhaps the most powerful in existence.

She would have many enemies.

Fortunately, she would be equipped to handle herself. There was a reason the Elders survived as long as they did, and they would teach her as they had many others throughout their millennia of existence.

Rendering me useless to her.

He pushed that thought away, focusing on the trembling woman in his arms. "Ask me anything," he whispered. "I'll answer it."

She shook her head, her arms twisting around his waist. "I don't even know where to start."

"You could ask me when or how immortality will occur." That's what he wanted to know when Aidan first told him about this world. "And I would tell you it's your decision. You won't become a Hydraian until you die, even if it's a decade from now. As long as your bloodline remains, you'll be reborn."

"My bloodline?"

"Hmm, yes, it's speculated the immortality lives in our blood. Destroying it, such as by fire or severing the flow to the mind, are two ways to kill an immortal, including a fledgling."

She shuddered. "The Conclave."

"Yes, the ceremony is driven by the final death—the only way to guarantee an immortal will not awake."

"Owen…"

He nodded. "Exactly, yes. Whoever killed him knew how to ensure he would be unidentifiable to the authorities, and never rise again. I suspect the same was applied to your parents."

"Yes." She fell silent, her body no longer quivering. He continued combing her hair and lightly rubbing her back, offering what minimal support he could.

"Lucian and the others are nothing like the immortals you witnessed last night," Issac promised. "Have dinner with them and give them a chance to prove it to you. I'm certain you won't regret it."

She cleared her throat and finally looked at him, her eyes clear. "I have so many questions, Issac."

"I know, and the others and I can answer them. We won't lie to you. *I* have never lied to you." He added the last part to prove a point, to remind her that he'd done everything in his power to earn her trust, even when trying the slow approach.

Astasiya studied him for a long moment, her wariness evident in the way her nostrils flared. But eventually she nodded, the motion tentative. "All right."

He wrapped his palm around the back of her neck and pulled her into a kiss, needing to taste her. Tonight would change everything. She'd learn more about her destiny, which didn't involve him.

She's not for me.

His gut ached with the thought, his grip tightening as if to hold on to her for just another moment. He'd never felt this way about anyone, had never desired to be this close to another. But Astasiya had changed him on an irrevocable level.

He wasn't fond of it.

Preferred to avoid it.

A night in bed could cure them both, or worsen it.

Maybe I should end it now, before this feeling deepens.

Her tongue slipped into his mouth, distracting him from his thoughts, her talented mouth returning his kiss.

Oh, fuck the idea of pushing her away.

No, he wanted her closer.

He wrapped an arm around her waist, holding her in the position he preferred, and devoured her. Her nails bit into the back of his neck as she clung to him, hanging on as he kissed her beyond reason. This was how he would take her body—hard and thorough. All night. Until they both couldn't walk, and then he'd do it again. Because he needed her out of his system, and their time together was limited.

"Aya," he breathed, the nickname falling from his tongue unbidden. It came to him last night, and hell if he cared to analyze it now. If there wasn't a room full of Hydraians waiting for them, he'd take her now. "Fuck, I want you."

Her shuddering exhale tasted of mint, necessitating another kiss, this one longer and harsher.

He unloaded his conflicting emotions into it.

Frustration.

Confusion.

Apologizing for last night and the Conclave.

Expressing gratitude for her survival.

Sealing it all with a hint of anger for causing him to feel this way, for making him second-guess his plans and reprioritize his needs… for *her.*

And ending it with a whisper of a pledge for more. Later. As soon as they finished dinner.

Her pulse beat in time with his as he pressed his forehead to hers. Their breaths mingled, both coming in pants.

"That…" She swallowed. "I… Yes."

He chuckled. "What are you agreeing to, love?"

"You. This. Whatever this is."

He cupped her cheek, brushing his lips over hers. *It can't last*, he wanted to say but couldn't, his lips refusing to utter the words he normally had no problem saying. *One night. No strings.* He said that to every woman he ever fucked. But the phrases clung to his tongue, refusing to be released.

Issac cleared his throat. "We need to go to dinner first." A coward's excuse, but he required the distance. This *connection* between them was confusing his senses. Being around his family and friends would help. She needed to meet them all as well.

"Okay." Disappointment lurked in her tone, but she nodded. "Dinner."

~*~

Stas sat beside Issac, her heartbeat thrumming in her ears. She'd expected a horror show, or fighting, or some sort of power challenge. Not laughter. Or love. Or light teasing.

These immortals acted… normal.

Like friends.

No, closer than friends.

Like family.

A very good-looking family. Even the females were flawless. Stas was starting to understand Issac's theory regarding descending from angels. Because yeah, they possessed a heavenly appearance, as if marked by the gods themselves.

Their names were all beginning to run together, but Luc had taken the chair beside her while Balthazar sat at the head of the table. Everyone else filled in the spaces between, and few lounged outside, enjoying the evening breeze on the illuminated patio.

"Syrup shots," one of them was saying, her big eyes on Issac. Her name began with a G. Gretchen? Greta? Georgia?

"You're joking," he replied, glancing over her head at Luc. "Tell me she's joking."

"There is nothing wrong with maple shots."

"There is everything wrong with maple shots," Issac fired back. "Syrup belongs on pancakes, not in a bloody glass."

"It belongs on waffles, actually, and you shouldn't knock my invention until you try it."

Issac shook his head, his disgust clear. "I'll pass, thank you."

"But it works!" the woman said, her excitement clear. "He demonstrated them last month in…" She trailed off, frowning at Balthazar. "Where did we go?"

"Aruba," he murmured. "You'd have enjoyed the body-shot display, Wakefield."

"Not with maple shots, no," Issac replied, his arm around Stas's chair, his thumb brushing her shoulder. They'd already eaten, the immortals proving to have hearty appetites. And now it seemed they were playing a game of catch-up, going through stories she knew nothing about.

Such as this one about maple syrup that she gathered Luc had turned into some sort of liquor.

The banter continued, providing such a different atmosphere than what she expected. An almost average night, minus the abnormal beauty and hints of immortality floating around the room.

Issac sipped his wine, chuckling and shaking his head at his friends. He was much more relaxed than last night. This felt real, as if he'd given her a glimpse into the true Issac Wakefield. Surrounded by Hydraians.

And breaking all the rules.

Now that she understood why Ichorians disliked Hydraians, the Blood Laws Osiris had mentioned made sense. Learning about Issac's familial ties helped her comprehend why he risked so much as well, why he'd kept her alive.

But he never told her about his plans for revenge or how he planned to use her.

"So, Stas, tell me about your job at the CRF," Luc said before taking a swig of his beer. The table fell silent at the request. She hadn't said much since introductions, and even then only a polite hello. They probably wondered if she could speak.

"Uh, I work with the marketing team. I started as an intern last year, but they just offered me a full-time position a few weeks ago." Not all that interesting yet everyone gaped at her. "I, uh, just passed my security exam. So I start next week." Assuming she remembered to call Human Resources back tomorrow.

"Hmm." Luc nursed his beer, his gaze pensive. "Issac mentioned you're close with the CEO and his son. How did you meet?"

"Through my roommate, Lizzie. Her father works at the CRF too."

"Ah yes. Elizabeth Watkins. I've not yet had the pleasure, but I know of her. What did you say she's doing?" The question went over her head to Issac.

"She's teaching," he replied.

"Teaching?" Luc repeated. "That's… unprecedented."

"Indeed."

Stas frowned between them. "What's unprecedented about teaching?" Lizzie adored kids. It seemed a natural path for her to pursue education.

"It's just not what I would have expected," Luc said. "With her upbringing and all, I mean."

"If you mean because she grew up with Lillian, then I understand." But something told her that's not what he meant at all. "How do you know of Lizzie?"

"Not the right question. How about a new route?" he suggested. "What is Doctor Fitzgerald's first name?"

What? "John. Why?"

He nodded. "Commonly short for Jonathan, yes?" The innocence underlying Luc's tone didn't match the intelligence radiating from those sharp green eyes.

She nearly snorted at the inane commentary when she realized *what* his words implied. Her gaze shot to Issac, who sat beside her, swirling his red wine, awaiting her reaction.

"*No.*"

"Afraid so" was all he said. So casual. So nonchalant. So uncaring.

She pushed back from the table, knocking his arm from her chair. "No."

"He tried to ignite a war between our worlds. I assume you've informed her?" Luc's voice still held that note of innocence to it.

"I have." Issac. Still nonchalant.

Stas's hands fisted at her sides, her breath coming in erratic puffs. "No. I don't believe you."

"He tried to make it look like the Conclave, thinking it would incite my kind to finally seek revenge against our makers, the Ichorians. With Eli being an Elder and Amelia being my half sister, it almost worked. Issac was the one who realized what really happened. He saved a lot of lives in the process." Luc's rendition of the story matched Issac's from earlier, but she refused to accept them.

"You're wrong." Doctor Fitzgerald would never do that. He was her mentor. Her friend. Tom's father. "It's not true."

"Unfortunately, it is," Issac said, standing.

She took several steps back until she came up against a wall, her head swaying back and forth, rejecting his claim. Not Doctor Fitzgerald. He was world renowned for his humanitarian efforts. How could they accuse him of being a murderer? "You're wrong," she whispered. "He wouldn't—"

"I'm not wrong, Astasiya. The Sentinel program that Thomas belongs to, the very one *Jonathan* manages, is a military unit whose primary task is to hunt and kill rogue supernaturals. And—"

"They perform humanitarian missions," she interjected, her blood running hot. "I've done the press releases for them, Issac. I've seen the photos."

"You've seen what Jonathan allows you to see, Astasiya. And while, yes, they may perform some missions for media purposes, they're designed to take out immortals. Why do you think they gave you a full medical checkup?"

"Doctor Fitzgerald said that was an error."

"And you believe him?" he pressed. "Did he ask you if you had any adverse reactions?"

"Well, yes, because he *cares* about me."

He shook his head sadly. "No, Astasiya. He doesn't. He cares about my perceived interest in you, and he tested that theory with the Nizari poison."

"He's telling the truth, Stas," Luc added softly. "Think about it for a minute. Why would Jonathan try to provoke a war?"

"He wouldn't," she whispered, tears prickling her eyes. "*He wouldn't.*"

"He would." Issac sounded so emotionless, so certain of his accusation. "If a conflict between Ichorians and Hydraians was to ever spill over into the mortal realm, who would be there waiting with a solution?"

"The CRF's Sentinel program," Luc replied.

"Which has been researching immortal-killing weaponry for the last three decades," Issac added. "It's ingenious, really. War is good for business, and Jonathan knows that better than anyone."

"You're lying." The words came out on a choked sound, her voice failing her. "You're friends." She saw him with Dr. Fitzgerald. They shared jokes and stories like old colleagues. How could he accuse his *friend* of doing this?

Because he's right, her subconscious whispered.

She shoved the voice to the back of her mind, refusing to hear it. Doctor Fitzgerald would never do this. He didn't know anything about the supernatural.

Yet, Tom sent me to an Ichorian club.

Because he knew what she'd see.

Not Issac with another woman, but drinking blood.

Which implied—

"Remember what I told you just hours ago?" Issac asked, breaking into her thoughts. "The best revenge takes careful planning. Jonathan thinks I blame the Conclave and therefore trusts that our relationship is intact. He's comfortable. Exactly where I want him to be."

She shook her head, trying to clear it, but he kept talking.

"Think, Astasiya. What humanitarian organization subjects its civilian staff to full-blown security clearances? How about the Nizari poison that almost killed you? Do you think that's standard for all employees, because I'm guessing it's not. I'm betting that Jonathan requested his medical staff administer it after he saw us last weekend. Our little kiss did not go unnoticed, and neither did my unabashed pursuit of you. Jonathan and I have known each other for centuries. I don't date women. I fuck them. My interest in you only piqued his curiosity."

An arrow through the heart would have hurt less.

This explained all the attention, the black-tie event, the kiss in the hallway at the restaurant. He meant it all for show, something she knew already, but his abrupt confirmation still burned a hole through her chest. His blatant lack of remorse turned her inside out. He just stared at her with an expectant look, waiting for her to understand the validity of his words.

The security clearance she understood. Several government agencies required it.

But the questions about Hydraians and Ichorians during her polygraph provided damning evidence. One could be a coincidence, but two demonstrated a knowledge of this world most mortals didn't possess.

She trusted Doctor Fitzgerald, knew he would never hurt her, yet he had been interested in her reaction to the vaccinations. Because he cared, or had something else driven his interest? What would he have done if she'd admitted to becoming sick? Kill her?

She shivered. For six years, she looked up to him. He wasn't a cruel man. He couldn't be building an army. How would he even be getting away with it? Wouldn't Osiris know and do something to stop him? The master Ichorian didn't seem to handle rebellion well, and this would be the epitome of defiance.

Her head spun, a battle waging in her mind.

Loyalty fighting logic.

Desire brawling with truth.

The facts are damning.

Everything she'd learned over the last week painted Doctor Fitzgerald in a guilty light. Did he really authorize the Nizari poison? Did he suspect her of being a fledgling? Or was that standard protocol? Only he could tell her. Would he admit it?

Wait, did Issac say he's known Jonathan for centuries?

Is Doctor Fitzgerald immortal?

He didn't look a day over forty, yet Tom, his son, was twenty-seven. And Tom clearly knew about the supernatural world. Because his father told him? Because Tom himself was also immortal?

Fuck. She squinted her eyes closed, her vision spinning.

If all this was true, then Tom had sent her to the Arcadia not to find Issac cheating on her but to show her demons existed.

He sent me to a fucking slaughter.

Stas stumbled to the side, her equilibrium tilting.

She couldn't do this anymore. She needed a break. A fucking drink. To run. To… To… *Something.*

Issac lifted a hand, causing her to flinch.

"Don't fucking touch me," she growled. He lost that privilege when he admitted to her purpose in his life. A *perceived interest* to *pique Jonathan's curiosity.* Well, he'd fucking succeeded.

Issac scowled, her command clearly registering. Because yes, she'd threaded those words with power. And now he couldn't touch her. Too bad she had no idea how long it would last.

The narrowing of his eyes scattered goose bumps down her arms. That look told her to run. Fast.

And she did, taking off down the hall toward the ballroom. She skidded to a stop by the closed doors, her purse and shoes nowhere to be found.

Issac sauntered down the hall toward her as she turned, his expression one of unveiled annoyance.

"Where's my purse?" she demanded.

"Why? Are you going somewhere?" he asked, his voice the epitome of calm. And that just pissed her off more.

"Not yet." She walked around him, aware that he still couldn't touch her.

"And where will you go? To Jonathan? To tell him you're a fledgling and hope he uses you for research instead of killing you outright?"

She stopped at the back staircase, refused to turn around. "That would just suck for you, wouldn't it? All that work you put into your pawn, just to lose it to the man who supposedly murdered your sister?" Water welled in her eyes, blurring her vision. "Well, I'm sorry you wasted your precious fucking time. Now, where's my purse?"

"In the pool house with your suitcase," he said, somehow driving the knife further into her gut. He couldn't even offer her a room in his home? She nearly laughed. No, those were for family and real friends. She was just the pawn in his game, a woman he wanted to fuck, but nothing more.

Why does that hurt? I never wanted a relationship. Neither did he.

But the truth slapped her across the face, leaving her weak in the harshest of ways.

Swallowing her pride, she went through the patio doors near the rear of the house and ignored all the Hydraians seated on the patio. Walked down the long path by the pool to the house beyond it. A kitchen with a breakfast nook was situated just inside the doors, a bowl of fruit on the table.

How fucking welcoming, she thought, hating it immediately.

A set of double doors were open beyond it, displaying a huge room with a four-poster bed.

Ah yes, the bed Issac had likely planned to fuck her on before heading back to his room in the house. Well, she despised that too.

She pulled her phone from her purse as Issac came to stand beside her, arms folded over his chest.

Why was he even here? Hadn't he said enough? She knew her purpose now. Not exactly how he'd intended to execute his plan, but it wasn't like she planned to stick around to hear about it.

There was only so much damage her heart could take in one day. Stupid mercurial organ, falling for a man she had no business falling for.

He's a demon, for crying out loud.

The waterworks threatened again.

Ugh, I'm losing my fucking mind.

Refocusing on her phone, she noticed several missed calls from Tom and a text from Lizzie telling her dinner went okay. She hadn't realized how late it was until she read the time. It would be well after midnight by the time she returned to the city. Then what would she do? Confront Doctor Fitzgerald? Talk to Tom?

A hysterical laugh threatened to bubble out of her.

The phone trembled in her hand. She didn't know who to call.

She couldn't bring Lizzie into this mess.

Owen was dead.

She no longer trusted Tom.

Her parents were too far away, not that she would allow them anywhere near this world.

A cab would do, but she wasn't sure where to go. What little money she had wouldn't last long.

Fuck.

She texted her roommate back with a quick, *I definitely won't be home tonight. Don't worry about me.* She didn't give a location because she didn't know where to go.

Her throat tightened. Dropping her phone into her purse, she let the bag fall to the floor.

I have no one.

Even if Issac was wrong about the CRF, she couldn't risk going back to the city. Not after everything she now knew. It'd been a miracle she'd survived this long as a fledgling in the middle of Ichorian territory.

"Talk to me," Issac said, standing a few inches behind her.

She swallowed, refusing to turn, not wanting him to see the tears glistening in her eyes. "Why?"

"Because I need to know you're okay."

Are you fucking kidding me? Of course I'm not okay. She took a deep, fortifying breath instead and muttered, "I'm fine."

"Your little show of persuasion out there says otherwise." His warmth cocooned her back, his step forward silent on the plush carpet.

Don't touch me, she begged. Because if he did, she'd break. Stas couldn't handle her body caving to him, not after everything he revealed. He toyed with her emotions just to pique the interest of Doctor Fitzgerald.

"*I don't date women. I fuck them.*"

The words prickled her heart, straightening her backbone. She took a step away from him but faced him. *Let him see the emotion in my eyes. It's not like it matters.*

"I know you don't really care." The defeated note in her voice couldn't be helped. All she wanted was to be left alone, and he wouldn't even grant her that. "So why even bother? Just go back to your dinner party. It's not like I'm going anywhere. You can even take my phone if it makes you feel better. I'll be fine."

The latter was a lie. She would never be fine, at least not inside. Outside she could pretend. She mastered the art of concealing emotions at a young age. That would come in handy now.

"I know you're not going to run, Astasiya. That's not why I'm standing here."

Wrapping her arms around herself, she sighed. "Then what do you want from me?" What would it take to get him to leave her alone?

He started to lift his hand but dropped it. Those beautiful eyes almost looked troubled. An act, no doubt. She didn't understand it, couldn't determine the purpose.

"You never handle anything the way I expect you to," he murmured. "It's amazing."

Wow. Okay. "Happy to amuse you. Can you kindly fuck off now?" It came out as a question rather than a demand.

His eyes widened. "You're furious with me."

How good of him to notice, she thought, arching a brow.

"Because I told you the truth about Jonathan?"

She just stared at him. He couldn't be serious. "Why are you still pretending to care? Do you get some sort of sick pleasure from it? Trying to see how long you can toy with your little pawn before it finally breaks?"

"Astasiya—"

"No. This charade thing is done. You made yourself very clear. Your feigned interest piqued Doctor Fitzgerald's curiosity. Given that he nearly killed me with that Nizari crap, I'd say you did a fine job. What I don't understand is why you're still standing in front of me, acting like you give a shit when we both know you don't."

Silence.

A fire lit his blue irises, making her stomach flip. She wasn't sure if he wanted to kiss her or kill her. The intensity pushed her back a step, the back of her knees hitting the nightstand.

"While true that my interest in you also intrigued Jonathan, there is nothing *feigned* about it. If I could touch you right now, I would demonstrate thoroughly." He uttered each word slowly and precisely, his gaze smoldering.

I... I don't know how to reply to that.

"Do you understand why Lucian is here?" he continued, not giving her a chance to speak. "The danger you were in last night, well, let's just say I haven't felt that way in a very long time. That's why I called Lucian. He's here to help you become a Hydraian and to help keep you alive."

She bit the inside of her cheek. That's what he meant about her packing a few things, but he phrased it as a choice. Like she *might* decide to leave. "But what about your revenge?" That was the whole point of their association.

He palmed the back of his neck. "It seems my desire for you to live trumps my need to avenge my sister's murder."

He opened the drawer of the dresser beside them and pulled out a pair of swim trunks. She frowned at it. Storing swimwear in the pool house made sense, but there were other clothes beside it.

Issac took several steps toward the door before pausing, not meeting her gaze. "I'm going for a swim. Let me know if I need to find somewhere else to sleep tonight. I'll understand if you need space."

He closed the door behind him, disappearing from view.

His parting words had her studying the room around her. Dark, masculine tones, an oversized bathroom with a Jacuzzi tub, and beyond it a walk-in closet filled with suits.

Her lips parted, the obvious clues having been missed due to her emotional state.

This is Issac's room.

Chapter Twenty-One

Making Waves

Okay, I may have overreacted.

Stas stared at the vaulted ceiling from Issac's bed, her lips twisted to the side. The shock had slowly melted into mortification at how she'd behaved. Because yeah, she'd definitely taken out her frustration on Issac. Which he sort of deserved, but not really.

It may have started as a charade, but the attraction between them wasn't a lie. He'd proven that several times. And he'd again confirmed he cared about her by following her to his room, where she found her suitcase and purse.

Still, he should have told her about Jonathan from the beginning. That would have saved them a lot of confusion and heartache.

Would you have believed him?

Ugh, she hated that voice. Such doubt. Such irritation.

And so right.

Because she wouldn't have believed him at all. She wasn't even sure she did now. All the evidence backed up his claims, but her heart longed to reject the truth. Once she gave in, she'd have to admit that Doctor Fitzgerald was a monster, and she wasn't ready for that.

She dug her palms into her eyes, the temptation to scream hitting her hard. Why did this have to be so difficult? Why her? Why was all this happening?

Because I'm a fledgling.

My blood will be toxic to Ichorians, like Issac.

The same man who had seemingly chosen her over his need to avenge his sister, a woman he clearly loved.

"I'm an idiot," she muttered to herself. She'd accused him of not caring when he clearly did. And now he'd left her in his room.

She needed to find him. To talk to him. To apologize.

Right.

No time like the present.

She rolled off the oversized mattress, the tile cool beneath her feet. The window above the kitchen sink showcased the beach, and the moon shining brightly over the water, causing her to pause and admire the view. She wondered if the curtains along the back of his room revealed the same view or if those covered windows overlooked the trees.

Hmm. Stas would investigate later.

Her musings shifted as she found Issac in the pool, swimming laps. He seemed to cut through the water, his strokes measured and sure, surprising her. She knew he enjoyed the sport after the towel incident from the other day but had no idea he excelled at it.

But of course he did.

The man exemplified perfection in every way.

She tested the water with her toes and found the temperature to be pleasant enough. Sitting on the edge, she allowed her legs to dangle over the side, her focus on the sexy swimmer gliding across the pool.

He completed another lap before stopping in front of her. The water hit him mid-torso as he stood, making the depth around five feet or so. He pulled off his goggles and tossed them onto the deck beside her, his expression wary.

"I may have overreacted," she admitted. "I'm sorry."

His shoulders visibly relaxed. "You don't need to apologize, love. It's a lot to take in."

"Which is why you preferred the slow approach," she said, understanding that now. "I just wish you'd have told me your suspicions about Jonathan sooner."

"Would you have believed me?"

A question she'd asked herself more than once in the last hour. "Probably not," she admitted, drawing a circle in the water with her finger. "A part of me still doesn't, even now."

"Do you require more proof?"

She shook her head. "No, I think what I need is more time." She twisted her lips to the side, unsure if that would really help or not. "There's something I don't get." Well, there were a lot of things she didn't comprehend yet. But on this topic, something really stuck out to her. "Osiris is all about rules, right? Why would he let Doctor Fitzgerald create an elite immortal-killing unit in the heart of Ichorian territory?"

"Ah, a question we've been contemplating for nearly three decades. He's clearly worked out some sort of arrangement with Jonathan, though we're not sure what." He pushed onto his back, his hands sculling beneath the water to keep himself afloat as his legs came up.

She tried not to admire the rippled abdomen on display.

And she failed miserably.

The man's body was a moving distraction.

"Aidan believes Osiris has hired Jonathan's team to target specific immortals, and in return, he allows the Sentinel unit to exist."

"So Jonathan is an immortal," she said, having already guessed as much.

"An Ichorian, yes."

"And Tom?" He looked too much like his father to be adopted.

"A fledgling, just like you," Issac confirmed. "Which is why we're certain Jonathan has an arrangement with Osiris—because he's allowed Thomas to exist."

"So…" She paused, swallowing. "Tom knew what he was doing when he…?"

"Sent you to the Arcadia?" Issac finished for her. "Yes. Although, I don't think he knew about the Conclave. But he definitely knew the activities and behavior common in the club."

She expected as much given everything she now knew. "So he wanted me to find you with another woman." Not necessarily in the throes of passion, but to catch him *feeding*.

Issac lifted a shoulder, still treading water. "That, or more likely, he wanted you to see the world I belong to. I rarely feed at the Arcadia, if ever. And I certainly didn't last night. Not until you arrived."

Her heart skipped a beat at the memory of his bite. She hadn't understood it at first. Then, by the time she realized what he was doing, she could hardly think.

It'd been so intense.

Addictive.

Crippling her mind and thoughts, stealing her from reality, and sending her to a place she'd never been.

A place she would happily visit again.

"Does…?" Heat crept up her neck. "Does it always, uh, feel like that?"

"It can, yes." Sin danced across his features, curling his lips. "Care for another bite, love?"

Such a loaded proposition, one that warmed her in a way it probably shouldn't. "Maybe," she managed, her throat dry.

He stood again, a dark emotion flaring in his midnight irises, one that sent off a flurry of butterflies in her lower abdomen. That was the kind of look a man gave a woman before he devoured her.

She started to scramble backward, but he caught her by the ankle and yanked her into the water.

Shit!

Completely submerged.

Hair and all.

She pushed up from the bottom of the pool. *Fucking demon.*

Spitting out a mouthful of water, she glowered at the laughing male beside her. "What the hell was that for?"

"Payback for earlier."

She snorted and splashed him, the move automatic and far more playful than she intended.

He slowly wiped the droplets from beneath his eyes, then narrowed his gaze in her direction. "All right, Aya."

He lunged for her.

With a shriek, she kicked onto her back to escape him, unsure of what he intended to do. But he was much faster, grabbing her hip with one hand and fisting her wet hair with the other. He tugged her to him, his body hot and hard in all the right places.

"Issac…" She put her hands on his shoulders, winded from her poor attempt at outswimming him. "Let's talk about this."

"Talk?" He arched a brow. "All right, then. For the record, I do not appreciate edicts of any kind, especially ones that forbid me from touching you."

Okay, not what she expected him to say. "I, uh, I'm—"

His mouth took hers in a punishing kiss that seemed to vibrate through her, stroking her very soul. *Holy wow.*

He'd kissed her several times over the last few days, but this one threatened to blow her mind. So much frustration and heat and pent-up *need.* His grip tightened, holding her exactly where he wanted her, ravaging her mouth, destroying her, claiming her.

She trembled against him, lost to his will, silently begging him for more.

But he pulled away, his forehead touching hers, their exhales mingling. "Not being allowed to touch you was physically painful. Please don't do that to me again, Astasiya."

If this was the expected result? "No promises," she breathed. She'd take a dunk in the water any day if it meant ending up in his arms.

"Mmm, then I better take advantage of touching you while I can." He led her backward beneath the waterfall, effectively hiding them from view of anyone outside. Her back met the wall, his body caging hers. "You're decidedly overdressed, Astasiya. How about we fix that?"

His hands fell to her tank top, giving it a tug.

"Yes," she managed, her voice husky.

Devious intent darkened his features as he guided the fabric over her head, casually tossing it aside without a glance. His thumb stroked the button of her jean shorts next, flicking it open and pulling down the zipper without faltering.

Her heart was in her throat, a thundering cacophony of beats in her ears.

He tugged the material from her hips, sliding it downward with the ease of a man used to undressing a woman, the water providing minimal resistance as he went.

Flames erupted inside her, igniting her veins and sending a tremor down her spine. By the time he finished his task, she could hardly stand, her knees threatening to buckle.

"I truly adore your penchant for lace, Astasiya," he murmured, his focus on her blue bra, his palm on her ass. He lifted her one-handed, forcing her to wrap her legs around his waist. "You questioned my desire earlier. Are you questioning it now?" He punctuated the words by grinding his hips into hers, his erection hot and hard against her.

Fuck.

She arched into him, wanting to feel more, to put this intense passion between them to the ultimate test. Her lips parted, but all that escaped her was a moan that sounded a lot like his name. Issac captured her mouth once more, his lips bruising against hers, his tongue fucking her mouth the way she wanted him to take her body.

Oh, he'd held back before.

Now? He gave her everything.

She felt branded.

Owned.

Possessed.

Every touch stoked the need inside her, enflaming her with a passion no one had ever come close to sparking.

"Issac," she breathed, needing more.

They still wore too many layers.

Her nipples chafed against the bra, causing her to whimper. Not enough friction. Not enough *Issac.*

Desire controlled her every move. One hand went to his hair, the other to his back, enjoying the feel of him. All hard, hot male pressed up against her, just begging her palms to explore every muscular inch.

His hands returned the favor in kind, sliding up to palm her breasts. She arched into him on a groan, meeting the delicious hardness settled at the apex of her thighs. He rotated his hips, hitting her most sensitive spot and shooting sparks through her system.

"Do you feel how badly I want you?" he asked, his lips whispering over hers.

"Yes," she hissed. If he'd just remove the rest of their clothes, he'd feel how much she wanted him, too. Damn, she needed to free him, to *feel* him. Her fingers traced the ridges of his abdomen to the happy trail leading to the edge of his swimsuit.

"No." He grabbed both wrists and held them over her head in one hand, the devil smoldering in his gaze.

Her complaint came out as a gasp as he pressed into her, his arousal nudging the place she desired him most. *Too many fucking clothes.*

"How does it feel to not be able to touch something you want, Aya? Does it burn you the way it burned me?"

She shivered at the possessive hold and nipped his bottom lip in protest. "I could command you to let me go," she said, her voice drowsy with lust.

"But that requires you to have a voice." His mouth covered hers, taking her slowly, making his point clear. His free hand returned to her breast before drifting down toward the sweet spot between her thighs. He found her clit through the fabric, pressing it with his thumb.

She cried out against his lips, evoking a grin from him.

"Try commanding me now, little fledgling." His teasing tone made her want to do just that, but he distracted her by rolling the pad of his thumb in a sensuous circle, her hips bucking in response.

A growl caught in her throat as he pressed harder, energy humming up and down her spine, her abdomen overheating. "*Fuck.*"

"Another demand, love?" He removed his thumb, eliciting a curse from her very soul. "Is this what you want?" he asked, sliding his fingers beneath her panties to part her slick folds.

"Oh…" Her hands fisted, her head falling back against the wall on a groan.

He was killing her in the most delicious way, his fingers teasing her into oblivion while only barely brushing where she desired him most.

She bit her tongue to keep from screaming, her need overwhelming all of her senses.

So close.

Just right.

Not enough.

"Issac." It came out as a plea as she writhed against him, her body on fire. "Please."

He bent to nibble one of her aching nipples through the lace, intensifying the sensations and worsening them. It almost hurt, but it felt so, so good.

His thumb found her clit again, pressing down hard and bringing her to the precipice, only to disappear just before she could fall over the cliff into oblivion. His teeth sank into her nipple, evoking a scream from her throat.

"Issac!" she cried out, trembling with need, tears glistening in her eyes. "Fuck! What do you want?" she asked, begging now. "An apology? For me to promise never to compel you again?" It fucking hurt to be brought to the point of no return only to be denied.

"No, darling." He kissed her hard and ripped the lace from her body, leaving her naked and gasping against him. "Keep your hands there." He pressed her wrists into the wall beside her hips.

God, this man was going to wreck her. Inside and out. Heart, body, and mind. It terrified her, floored her, excited her.

He slowly removed his swimsuit, inch by inch, revealing his gorgeous form to her gaze.

And damn, every part of him was perfect. Long. Lean. Strong.

She shuddered, desperate to explore him but fearing he would stop if she did. Stas couldn't bear if this ended now. She'd surely explode. Ruined. Destroyed. Expired.

Her limbs shook from the onslaught, electricity humming like a live wire through her very being. One stroke and she'd combust.

She wanted him inside her. Now. If only—

"I admire your persuasive talent, love," he whispered, his lips against her jaw. "Even when used on me." He knotted his fingers in her hair, his mouth brushing hers. "Never apologize for what you can do." His fierce words only added to the sensations building inside of her.

"Okay," she managed, her throat dry, her legs quivering around his waist.

"Touch me," he mouthed, his cock hot and heavy against her lower abdomen.

Finally.

She grabbed his shoulders, sliding her hands down his back to his ass and back up again. Silk. Muscle. Man. Her own personal heaven.

His palms went to her thighs, his arousal prodding her entrance.

She arched into him in invitation. "Yes…"

Her nails bit into his back as he pushed forward, his gaze holding hers.

The intimacy of it nearly undid her, his intensity almost unbearable. There were so many unspoken emotions lurking in his blue eyes, emotions she knew were rivaled in her own.

But she couldn't look away.

Not even as he slid deeper, all the way to the hilt, filling her almost to the point of pain.

He took her mouth in a thorough kiss, his body still against hers, giving her a moment to adjust. Her minimal experience hadn't prepared her for him—for this.

"Aya," he whispered, the nickname tasting sweet on her tongue. "What are you doing to me?" he asked, wonder in his voice.

She parted her lips, only to find them occupied again, his mouth memorizing and training hers for his use alone. Every kiss, every caress translated to a claim, her body slowly submitting to him.

I'll never want another.

Only Issac.

She'd never experienced such passion with another, never knew it existed. But as his hips began to shift, she learned a whole new dance of life. One underlined in adoration and overwhelming sensation.

God, he can move.

She threaded her fingers through his hair, holding on as he took her without remorse, fucking her the way only Issac could. There would be bruises tomorrow. She didn't care. Not when it felt so incredibly raw and true and amazing.

"Fuck," he groaned, his lips falling to her neck, his teeth scraping her pulse without breaking the surface.

Her thighs clenched around him, the heat inside climbing to insurmountable heights.

So hot.

Burning.

Need.

His hand drifted between them, his thumb finding her clit and pressing down. "I want to feel you fall apart." His voice was rough and growly and so fucking arousing. "Come for me, love." He intensified his thrusts while circling her bundle of nerves, the heady combination too much for her senses.

I'm falling.

Too much.

Oh, fuck.

"Issac." Her nails bit into his back, needing to hold on as a tumultuous wave of energy shook her very being. It heightened, grew, all centered in her lower abdomen and spreading. It hurt, tightening all her muscles.

"Now, Aya." The command in his tone shattered her, spiraling her into a tornado of heated oblivion that blinded her vision.

She couldn't move.

Couldn't breathe.

Couldn't think.

Only feel. Her heart hammering in her chest. Her lungs burning. Her lips parted on a soundless scream.

She squeezed her legs, capturing him, her mouth against his shoulder, her arms around his back. He drove himself into her, his penetrating movements only prolonging her ecstasy as he slammed her hips against the wall. Each stroke set off a new quake, her limbs shaking and burning around him.

He groaned her name, his muscles stiffening beneath her touch, his orgasm exploding inside her. The heat of it sent another shock wave crashing through her, shaking her to her very core.

Stas panted, her exertion overwhelming and exhausting, and yet so very exhilarating.

Issac kissed her, his mouth worshiping and adoring, her name murmured between nips and licks. He remained hard inside her, the water still rippling around them from his exertion.

We just fucked in the pool, she realized dizzily. And water resistance hadn't impacted him in the slightest. *What can he do on a bed?*

"I need more," he whispered, as if reading her mind. "Much, much more."

She undulated her hips, silently urging him to proceed. She'd be sore tomorrow. But who the hell cared? She'd enjoy every minute of the sensual ache, thinking of Issac the entire time.

He grinned against her mouth. "In the bedroom, love. I want to taste every inch of you."

Chapter Twenty-Two

A Lesson in Exclusivity

Issac couldn't stop touching Astasiya.

She slept soundly beside him, exhausted from their night in bed. The woman was fucking flawless, meeting him move for move and kiss for kiss.

He'd entertained numerous women over the centuries, but none of them aroused him like the woman sleeping in his arms. Even now, his cock desired more, pressing against her ass, urging him to wake her with an orgasm.

But they had company, something he suspected she wouldn't be pleased about when she woke up.

Issac kissed her neck, her bare shoulder, and along her arm as he slid his palm down her stomach to the apex between her thighs. She squirmed, her heartbeat escalating in his ears.

"We missed breakfast," he murmured, guiding her onto her back, his lips against her hip. "A shame, really, as I'm starved. Someone kept me up all night."

Perhaps he could coax her into a good mood so his news of who had dropped by for a visit wouldn't be so upsetting. He nipped her skin, tracing a path along her lower abdomen with his tongue.

Bedroom eyes gazed down at him, her pupils dilated from sleep and flickering with wonder. "Oh God…"

"Mmm, no. Issac," he corrected, smiling against her skin.

"Fuck." She clutched the silk bedsheets on either side of her waist, her gorgeous breasts on display from the sunlight streaming in through the translucent curtains.

He licked the sensitive space between her legs, teasing her, adoring her, memorizing her. "Good morning," he murmured, his lips grazing her mound. "Or should I say 'afternoon'?"

"I'm... You're..." She shuddered, her thighs tensing as he settled between them.

"I'm what?" he asked against her damp flesh, her arousal taunting him in the most sensual of ways. "Hungry? Yes."

"That's—" She bowed off the bed, whatever she'd been about to say wrapped up in a moan as he tasted her. He'd wanted to do this last night, had meant to lick every inch of her, but the sight of her in his bed had derailed his focus. Being inside her had become his obsession, his primary goal of the evening.

Now, he wanted to worship her the way she deserved.

His guests could wait.

One night hadn't been enough. Hell, a month wouldn't suffice at this point. This woman was under his skin, his new addiction in life.

He devoured her, loving the way she writhed and moaned. Her hands moved to his hair, holding him to her, encouraging him to explore more, to take her over the edge. Rather than oblige, he shifted out of her reach, eliciting a guttural growl in response.

"Tease," she accused, her breath harsh.

He grinned against her inner thigh before moving upward to her breasts. They were flushed and aroused, just the way he liked them. He took a tender bud deep into his mouth and rolled it with his tongue.

"I want you to shatter so hard that you think of me all day, Aya." He bit the sensitive peak, evoking a whimper of need from her. Oh, he loved that sound. He inspired another by nibbling her breast, her pleasure addictive.

"Tell me what you need," he whispered sliding down again, his tongue dipping into her belly button. "My hands? My cock? My tongue?" The last word was spoken right against her swollen clit.

"Yes," she hissed. "Yes."

He slipped a finger through her wetness, teasing her. "Yes?" he repeated. "Yes what?"

"Just touch me, Issac," she begged, her words healing a wound deep inside him. Being told he couldn't have what he desired had physically hurt. Her plea now counteracted the command from last night, lifting a bruise from his heart he hadn't realized was there. He *needed* to caress her, to adore her, to please her.

His lips closed over her sensitive bud, and she cried out his name.

Yes.

He swirled his tongue over it before sucking her hard into his mouth, causing her to buck against him.

So beautiful.

So gorgeous.

So *mine.*

He'd never felt this possessive over anyone, but Aya awoke the predator inside him, the one who desired her more than any other. And she was his. Writhing. Wet. Willing. In his bed. Where she belonged.

Issac's palms skimmed her legs, her abdomen, and breasts, urging her to come, needing to feel her pleasure beneath his touch and tongue. He sensed her teetering, her muscles clenching around him, her body frozen on the precipice.

And falling.

His name a scream in the air.

Her fingers gripping his hair, her body trembling, coming undone in the most gorgeous sight he'd ever witnessed. Fucking beautiful. Glorious. And he wanted to see it again. He wrung every drop from her, waiting until her quakes shifted to quivers, and climbed up to cage her between his arms.

"I absolutely adore hearing you say my name like that." He kissed her thoroughly, allowing her to taste herself on his tongue. "And I'm going to enjoy hearing you say it again just like that later." He would do so now, but she wasn't ready for him again yet. Just pressing his cock against her center had her wincing. "Mmm, we need to get ready. Shower with me?"

Her brow furrowed. "But… don't you… I mean, shouldn't we, uh, finish?" She cleared her throat, her cheeks flushed with color.

"You're quite charming when flustered." He brushed his lips over hers before rolling off of her and standing, hand palm up, waiting for her. "That was for you, love. The shower is for me."

"Oh…" She pushed up onto her elbows, her eyes roaming over him with interest.

He chuckled and scooped her up off the bed, tired of waiting, and headed toward the bathroom. "We have people waiting for us."

"What? Who?"

"I mean, I realize I fucked the sense right out of you, but did you miss Lucian and all the others at dinner last night?" He set her on the counter, his hands gripping the marble on either side of her thighs.

She narrowed her gaze. "That's a bit cocky, isn't it?"

"Confident," he corrected, smirking. "And also, true." He went to the walk-in shower to turn on the water and found the items they needed under the sink. "Can you stand yet, darling?"

"So arrogant," she muttered, sliding to her feet. "We'll see if I return the favor now."

"Who said that's what I have in mind?" He pulled two oversized towels from the cabinet to set aside on the heat rack before stepping onto the stone floor of the shower. "Join me, Aya. If you dare." She brought out a playful side to him that he barely recognized after centuries of disuse.

Astasiya made him feel young.

Alive.

Buoyant.

Her arms slipped around his waist as she entered the shower, her breasts against his back. "I'm not afraid of you."

His lips curled. "That sounds like a challenge."

"Take it however you want."

He angled the showerheads over both of them and turned in her arms. She tilted her head back beneath the spray, her eyes closed, her expression angelic. He slid his mouth over hers, needing to kiss her, his dick throbbing against her lower belly. Fuck, he wanted her again. And again. Alas, he meant what he said. This wasn't about reciprocation but about a different type of seduction.

Threading his fingers through her hair, he combed through the long, damp strands while gently teasing her lips with his tongue. She sighed against him, her hands exploring his back.

"Mmm, I could kiss you forever, it seems," he whispered, picking up the shampoo. "But we need to talk about today." He lathered a healthy amount into his hands and ran his palms over her head, taking care of her in a way he rather enjoyed.

"What about today?" she asked, gazing up at him through thick lashes.

"Well, first, a few others have arrived." He rinsed the suds from her hair and repeated the actions for himself before picking up the soap.

"Who?" she asked as he guided the bar over her arm, painting suds over her skin.

"Aidan and his harem, as well as Tristan and Mateo."

"Harem?" she repeated.

"Anya, Nadia, and Clara." Technically, the latter wasn't involved with Aidan sexually, but Issac didn't want to go into that topic now.

"He has a harem?"

"He created them all, yes." Issac slipped the soap between her breasts, taking tender care of her core and loving the way her nipples beaded in response to his teasing touch.

"So they're like your siblings?"

He nearly laughed. "Hardly. He may have turned them, but our relations are somewhat estranged. I grew up with Amelia and knew Lucian at a young age, while Aidan's newest additions came from different occurrences throughout the last few decades. We're all friends, of course, but I don't consider them family." Especially Clara. That would be wrong on a variety of levels.

Issac soaped the tops of her thighs and knelt to reach the rest of her legs before telling her to spin so he could approach her from behind.

"How is an Ichorian created?" she asked, curiosity evident in her tone.

"It's a blood exchange process that ends in death and subsequent resurrection," he said, his focus catching the mark at the base of her spine as he massaged her ass with both hands.

"So not through procreation," she continued, causing his gaze to snap up.

"What?"

"Well, you said an Ichorian mating with a human creates a fledgling. Fledglings become Hydraians after their rebirth—which I interpret to mean they wake up immortal after dying?"

"Yes," he confirmed, his attention shifting back to the mark on her skin. He traced it with his finger. Small, heart-shaped, almost like a tattoo, but not quite.

"What happens when an Ichorian has sex with another Ichorian?"

"Aside from sharing pleasure?" *Assuming both parties are into that kind of thing.* "Nothing. Ichorian females are infertile, and my kind are immune to disease."

"What about a Hydraian and a mortal?"

"Hydraians are also infertile." He stood and finished soaping off her back, the blemish imprinted in his mind. "And before you ask, so are fledglings." He rotated her to face him. "Which is why we didn't use protection." With humans, he always wore a condom. Astasiya didn't require it, something he very much enjoyed and would be taking advantage of again soon.

She bit her lip, nodding. "Probably should have discussed that pre-sex."

He smiled and helped her rinse the suds from her skin. "There wasn't anything to discuss, love. I can't impregnate you, nor would diseases impact us."

Another nod. "Well, that's good, then."

He handed her the soap. "Your turn."

Delight radiated from her expression. "Yes, please."

She started with his abs, causing him to smile. He hadn't given her much opportunity to touch him last night, his hands too busy controlling hers as he took her in various ways. All of which she enjoyed, as did he. So much so that he'd completely missed the symbol on her lower back.

Astasiya lathered his chest, his arms, and continued lower, her fingers wrapping around his base to give him a firm stroke.

"Careful, darling, or I'll accept that as an invitation."

"Just being thorough," she replied, all innocence, aside from the sinful intent dancing in her gaze. She fisted him again, squeezing harder this time, her palm slick and confident against his shaft.

"You're playing a dangerous game, love."

"Me?" She batted her eyes at him. "Never."

Another stroke that had his balls tightening, his abdominal muscles clenching. Part of him wanted her to continue. The sadist in him preferred to wait, to delay his gratification until they had more time to prolong the experience.

He caught her wrist, stilling her movements. "Keep pushing and you'll end up on your knees with my cock down your throat." Not an idle threat, which she must have seen in his features because she shivered.

"I… I might enjoy that." Soft words.

He smiled. "If we didn't have everyone waiting on us, I'd test that statement." And enjoy every fucking minute of it.

Her grip loosened. "Why are they waiting on us?"

Hmm, time to kill the fire brewing between them. He'd reignite it later. "Because they want to talk about your future, and I believe Aidan has news on Owen."

She froze. "Owen?"

Issac took over soaping his body. "Indeed. He sent me a series of visions when he arrived, Owen being one of them."

Her brow furrowed. "Visions?"

"My gift, Aya." At her continued frown, he added, "I'm constantly tapped into everyone's vision, within a certain mile radius, of course. As my Sire, I'm very attuned to Aidan."

"Miles?" she asked, her lips parted in awe.

"Roughly one or two, depending." He swapped the soap for some conditioner, applying it to her hair first.

"That must be overwhelming," she said after a minute.

He chuckled, recalling his early days. It'd been an absolute nightmare learning control, but residing in London for a few months had done the trick. "I liken it to having the tele on in the background without sound. Switching them all to the same channel is an easy skill. It's making them see different things that can be more cumbersome."

"And what you did to Balthazar?" she asked as he rinsed her hair.

He smirked, recalling the way he'd handed Balthazar his ass yesterday. An overreaction, sure, but the bastard deserved it. "Child's play."

Issac rinsed his hair and brushed his lips against hers once more before shutting off the water. Her eyes glimmered with questions, causing him to arch a brow. "Is there something you want to know, love?"

She nodded slowly, her cheeks reddening.

"And?" he prompted, intrigued.

"You didn't… We didn't…" She pinched her lips to the side. "You didn't bite me again. Last night, I mean."

He wrapped a freshly warmed towel around her shoulders, grinning. "I typically only feed every two weeks or so. But if you're craving a bite, I'll be happy to oblige." He nipped her chin playfully.

"And you usually feed during sex?" she asked as he grabbed his own towel.

"Yes." He met her gaze. "Is this where you ask about my experience?" Because he really didn't want to have that conversation.

She shook her head. "No, I'm well aware of your playboy reputation. As you said, you don't date women, you fuck them, right?"

"Hmm." He caught her around the waist and yanked her to him. "I'm not sure I like that tone, Aya."

"Just stating facts." The bitter quality in her voice had him narrowing his eyes further. "And what does *Aya* mean?"

"It's my nickname for you," he murmured, his palm wrapping around the back of her neck. "Just yesterday you protested Elizabeth referring to me as your boyfriend. And now, your mood has soured over a few experience-related questions. Why?"

"Those are two very unrelated topics."

"Oh?" He tightened his hold around her when she made to step backward. "Allow me to relate them, then. You don't want me to be your boyfriend, yet you ridicule my relationship behavior. So which is it?"

"I don't…" She shook her head. "What are you asking me?"

This was why he avoided dating. Too much confusion and emotions. But with Astasiya, he found he wanted that.

While he hadn't realized it yesterday, her outright rejection had hurt a bit. Never in his life had he ever considered a romantic relationship with anyone. Then the first one he desired to truly court—Astasiya—had seemed quite affronted by the proposition of a label.

"Would you like me to be yours exclusively, or not?" he asked, tired of dancing around this topic. Either she admitted her feelings ran as deep as his own or she laughed him off.

Her eyebrows rose. "Like seriously date? Not just a charade?"

"If this were a charade, love, we wouldn't have just spent a night fucking in my bed." She was the first woman he'd ever entertained here. Typically, he reserved his Hamptons estate for family and friends only, since Amelia and Eli were the primary inhabitants. Until recently, anyway.

"Oh." Her cheeks pinkened. "You want this to continue."

"That is the general idea, yes." And he'd really appreciate a more telling response on the prospect sooner rather than later. He couldn't be the only one who felt this intensity between them.

"Exclusively," she added.

"Now you're just repeating my phrases." He released her to run a comb through his hair before handing it to her. "That mark on your lower back—how long have you had it?"

She looked taken aback by the abrupt subject change, but as she didn't seem ready to discuss their future, he switched to a more practical topic.

"I… The what?"

He pressed his palm to her lower back over the towel, rubbing the spot to the left of her spine with his fingertips. "There's a heart-shaped blemish here, and I'm wondering how long you've had it."

Her brow crumpled. "Uh, my birthmark? Forever. Why?"

"I don't think it's a birthmark." He kept replaying the image in his head, the details too exquisite and contrived to be of natural occurrence. "I think it might be a rune."

"A *what*?"

He didn't bother repeating the term. She'd heard him. "With your permission, I'd like to show Aidan and Lucian. They'll be able to confirm for sure."

She blinked. "You want me to let them examine my lower back?"

"No." He tapped his head. "I can provide the detail they need."

"Ah, right." She started combing her hair, her lips curled down. "I mean, if you think it's useful, then okay. But only my lower back, Issac."

He chuckled and kissed her temple on his way to his closet. "As if I would ever share the rest of you with anyone." He meant that in a multitude of ways. The idea of another seeing her naked, or worse, *touching* her, had his fists curling around the jeans he'd just picked up.

No. Definitely not sharing her. Ever.

Except, one day he'd have to. Because a Hydraian and Ichorian relationship was too risky to consider.

So we'll date until we tire of each other.

That would work.

Astasiya didn't have to join the Hydraians tomorrow. She could wait a year, or five.

He selected a gray shirt, his movements stiffer than intended. Clearing his throat, he reentered the bathroom to find Astasiya pulling up a lacy blue thong from her suitcase. She added a matching bra that had him regretting having to join the others in the main house.

"You're killing me," he said, his voice hoarse.

Her gaze ran over his bare torso to the towel wrapped around his hips. "Likewise." She sauntered toward him, a smile in her eyes. "Yes, Issac."

"Yes what?" He hadn't asked her a question.

"I want you exclusively." She went onto her toes to kiss him softly. "Feel free to bite me anytime." She nibbled his lip and took a step back, her hooded gaze nearly undoing him.

He dropped his clothes and pulled her into him again, his mouth on hers. She couldn't just say that and wander off. No. He needed to feel her promise against his lips, to taste it with his tongue, to memorize the words with his heart.

She grabbed his shoulders, her nails claiming him as she dug them into his skin.

He had no idea what they were doing.

But fuck if he cared.

For the first time in his life, he allowed emotion, rather than logic, to drive him, and he followed the sensations to his very soul.

A handful of images flashed in his head from the others, as well as a timer that Tristan seemed to be imagining.

Countdown, Issac translated, slightly irritated by the clear intention to interrupt.

With a sigh, he slowly released Astasiya, his forehead falling to hers. "The others are getting impatient."

"You can hear them? Like, telepathically?"

"God, no. That'd be awful." He shuddered at the thought. "I just *see* them. Tristan, specifically. He's planning his interruption."

"The Ichorian who can control sound."

"That'd be the one," he murmured, stepping away to retrieve his clothes as a buzzing sounded through the room.

"What the hell is that?" Astasiya asked, her gaze darting back and forth.

"Tristan being an impatient ass," he growled, pulling on his jeans. He sent his progeny an image of his middle finger, and the noise stopped.

"That's… Is he outside?"

"No, he's in the main house."

"Is he able to manipulate sound for miles the way you can influence vision?" she asked while rummaging through her suitcase.

"Yes. Our powers rival one another." He ran his fingers through his hair, not caring at all to style it. "I suspected what he would be able to do based on his affinity for music. He was actually quite famous in the late eighteenth century, renowned for his skill with a harp. I met him in New York, during one of his visits. He fancied the States, you see, and, well, the rest is history between us."

"Eighteenth century," she repeated, a few articles of clothing in her hands. "Do I even want to know how old you are?"

He chuckled, amused. "Nearly four hundred, which is quite young compared to Aidan and all the Elders. They've experienced several millennia, Aidan being the oldest of us all."

"I… This… Yep. Completely surreal." She shook her head and focused on choosing an outfit.

She donned a blue sundress that hit her midthigh, and left her hair damp over one shoulder. No makeup. No styling. Just all-natural woman, which he appreciated considering his usual female company.

Pulling his shirt over his head, he walked over to nibble her pulse.

"You're gorgeous, love," Issac whispered.

"Even with my supposed rune?" she asked, her tone teasing. "Which, by the way, they're going to tell you is a birthmark."

"Are they?" He gazed down at her. "Care to wager on that?"

She laughed. "Yeah, I have about ten dollars in my purse, but why not?"

"You know I'm not interested in money," he reminded her, pressing his hips into hers. "But I'll wager other, more pleasurable activities."

She licked her lips, intrigue flashing in her features. "Such as?"

"Hmm." He pressed his lips to her ear. "If I'm right—which I am—then I get to fuck you however and wherever I want."

"And when I'm right?" It came out breathy.

"You can tie me up tonight and do whatever you want." Which he wouldn't enjoy nearly as much as being in charge, but he could concede to her for an evening. Not that he would need to. The mark was most definitely a rune.

"Yeah, I'll take that bet," she agreed.

"Brilliant." He nipped her lower lip. "Ready to face the others?"

She scrunched her nose, clearly not ready at all. "There are no rules, right?"

"Oh, I can come up with some, if you like." He wrapped his hand around her throat, giving it a gentle squeeze. "Maybe later in the bedroom."

She swallowed, her pupils dilating. The interest flaring in her gaze intrigued him. They would definitely be exploring that later. "I meant with the Ichorians," she said, her voice husky.

I know. His palm slid upward to cup her cheek. "You're free to do whatever you want, love. We're surrounded by friends here."

"Your friends."

"They'll become yours as well, over time." He kissed her gently, lingering. "Can you do something for me?"

"Depends on what it is," she whispered, her lips moving against his.

"Hear them out," he replied, just as soft. "Let them show you who they are before you judge them. And remember, your decisions will always be your own. No one can make them for you. All right?"

She was quiet for a long moment, a million emotions flashing through her features. But eventually she nodded. "I can try, yes."

Chapter Twenty-Three

Once upon a Time

Stas's resolve to try for patience and understanding went out the window when she entered the house. Her grasp on Issac's hand tightened, her legs threatening to give out beneath her.

The female auctioned during the Conclave sat at the dining table with her arms wrapped around her middle. Incredulity radiated from her dark irises. At least she appeared to be in better health—minus her frail state. But someone had clearly offered her a shower and clothing.

"Ah, Stas," Luc said from the head of the table. "I was just telling Eliza about Hydria."

Eliza? That must be the woman's name.

"Hydria?" Stas repeated.

"It's where they all live," Eliza replied, her voice far stronger than Stas expected. "An island near Athens."

Luc nodded. "Yes. It's technically owned by Greece. However, we're self-sufficient and report the bare minimum to the Greek authorities to maintain citizenship status. Everyone on the island has a job, whether it be in Athens proper, part of the security system, or other, more lucrative means."

"Investments," Issac added as he took the chair catty-corner to Luc. He held out the one beside him for Stas, his indication clear. *Join me.*

The only reason she didn't protest the request was because of the food on the table—cheese, fruit, and a relish tray. Her stomach growled at the sight, her fingers snagging a raw pepper as she sat down.

He smiled as she ate, the gleam in his gaze suggesting he knew what had inspired her appetite. Their midnight snack and early-morning post-sexathon meal hadn't been enough.

Issac poured her a glass of water from the pitcher on the table while saying, "When you live forever, you invest and watch the money grow. That's the lucrative side Lucian is referring to, which is a skill set I've cultivated over the last few centuries."

"Yes, Issac is one of our advisors on the subject, having amassed billions over the centuries." Luc shrugged. "No one wants for anything, but we do support each other."

"So you can live forever and you all choose to work," Eliza said, sounding very unimpressed. "How boring."

The Hydraian King's lips thinned. "Survival requires even the most menial of tasks. It's a strategy that works."

She snorted. "Okay, so my work history involves sex. What will my job be on your island?" Sarcasm colored her tone and radiated from her eyes. A clear defense mechanism, one Stas understood all too well.

"My suggestion? College, to acquire a more marketable skill that will benefit everyone." Luc leaned back in his chair, his muscles flexing with the movements.

"You don't find sex to be an adequate skill?" Feisty energy poured off Eliza. This woman had spirit, even after the Ichorians tried to break her.

Speaking of which… "Where are Anya and Aidan?" Stas asked softly, her focus shifting to Issac while Luc and Eliza continued their conversation beside them.

"In the living area with the others." He wrapped his arm around the back of her chair, leaning in close, his voice equally hushed. "It's been a while since we were all together."

She started to nod, then frowned. "So this isn't a unique occurrence?"

"No, we used to gather more frequently before Amelia and Eli passed."

"In the Hamptons?"

"Sometimes. The location shifts. Aidan and his harem currently live in Vancouver, while I've resided along the East Coast for the last century or so. The Hydraians are just off the coast of Athens, as Lucian said. Jacque's ability to teleport facilitates matters, at least now. He's actually quite young for an immortal, only a hundred or so."

Teleporter.

Right.

She shook her head to clear it. "Okay, help me understand this. You all gather like this, frequently, despite the Blood Laws urging you not to? Does Osiris know?"

"If he did, we wouldn't be here having this conversation right now."

Fair enough. "But you just risk it anyway?"

"We're family, Aya. You have to realize that up until the eighteenth century, Hydraians and Ichorians lived in peace. The war between our kinds started when Ichorians realized the threat lurking in Hydraian blood."

"War?" she repeated, her eyebrows lifting.

"It didn't last long," Luc cut in. "Also, I'll add, the only reason we lived in peace, as Issac calls it, is because the Ichorians put us all on an island—Hydria—and withheld resources. They wanted us weak, to cripple our dual gifts, but what they created was a brotherhood founded by the desire to live. We knew for over three thousand years that our blood could kill an Ichorian. However, we kept it quiet and safeguarded the secret, knowing they would round us up and kill us. And instead, we worked as a cohesive unit to become stronger so when the inevitable happened, we could protect ourselves."

"The Ichorians tried to eradicate the Hydraians," Issac murmured, his thumb brushing her bare shoulder. "They failed miserably. Not only were they outmatched in power, but several Ichorians refused to fight. Including myself and many others with personal ties to Hydraians."

"In the end, Aidan, Osiris, and I drew up the Treaty of 1747—a tentative agreement evoking peace." Luc leaned forward, hands clasped on the table. "The Blood Laws were created as a result, to deter fraternization between the immortals."

"Yes, Osiris is a clever leader," Issac added. "He's biding his time, breaking down the relationships built over the centuries through fearmongering, and, we believe, will one day lead another attempt against the Hydraians. Hence the reason Aidan and I and the others play nice and attend the Conclave meetings."

"You're playing the role of double agent," she translated, completely awed by the history and purpose he just detailed. "I don't know whether to call you brave or suicidal."

He chuckled and tugged on a strand of her hair. "I'll accept 'brave.' As I told you the other night, I have no intention of dying."

A collection of giggles coming from the hallway interrupted them as Balthazar entered with his arms around Anya and Clara. All three of them were dressed for the pool, or maybe a magazine spread. For a sexy magazine. Because the girls were in thongs and tops that barely covered their breasts, and the man between them… *wow.*

"Oh, you're here!" Clara bounced over to Issac's chair and wrapped her arms around him from behind, her lips against his cheek.

He grabbed her wrist to press a kiss to her hand. "Yes, just rehashing history with Lucian."

Clara didn't move, her breasts firmly pressed into Issac from behind, her lips still near his face. The ease with which she touched him indicated a history, one that soured Stas's stomach.

Yes, they'd just discussed exclusivity.

But this, well, she didn't like it. Not one bit. Especially the part where Issac kept holding Clara's hand.

"You should invite Aidan," Clara said, a smile in her too-blue eyes. "You know how he adores a jaunt through the past."

"I do," Issac agreed, releasing her. Finally. "Are you off to have a swim?"

"Balthazar challenged us to a round of water volleyball." She flipped her long blonde hair over her shoulder as she stood, cocking a model-worthy hip at the man in question.

"I merely suggested a friendly game," he murmured, his arm still around Anya. "The girls took it as a challenge. Luc, you in?"

"I'll have to pass for this round," Luc replied, disappointment evident in his tone. "Are Jay and Alik playing?"

A snort from the doorway had him looking over his shoulder at a man in a leather jacket and jeans—the attire far from appropriate for the hot summer day. "Why the fuck would I play volleyball?"

"Because it's fun?" Clara suggested.

The athletically lean male folded his arms and gave her the kind of smolder that could silence the room. "Fun would be driving to the city and slaughtering some Ichorians."

Clara shivered. "Always so dark."

Yes, that was an apt description. Lethal energy radiated from the man, one Stas didn't recognize as having joined them for dinner last night. Another Ichorian? Or a Hydraian?

"Alik," Balthazar said. "Meet Stas. Stas, this is Alik. He likes to brood more than socialize."

"And you all wonder why?" the male—Alik—replied, pushing off the doorway. "I'll be out patrolling with Jeremy. At least he understands the value of silence."

Nice to meet you, too, Stas thought at his back.

"Don't take it personally, sweetheart." Balthazar gave her a soft smile. "Alik isn't a fan of being this close to Ichorian territory, and he's feeling protective."

"He's an Elder," Issac added. "One of the four I mentioned as the oldest of Hydraians. Balthazar, Lucian, Alik, and Jayson."

"Present," a new voice said as another godlike male joined the room clad in a swimsuit. "I thought we were playing a game in the pool?"

"We are, but we stopped to chat while waiting on you." Balthazar gave him a grin. "Ready to strip some women?"

"Always."

"I thought you said this was a friendly game." Anya batted her eyes demurely.

"Of strip water volleyball, yes." Balthazar smiled, his dimples making his face even more breathtaking.

Yep. Totally giving in to the angel myth because how else is this much beauty in a room possible?

"Then why the hell are we still standing here? I can't wait to make you parade around the deck naked." Anya gave him a little push that earned her a laugh.

"If all you want is a show, just ask," he said, heading toward the door.

The newcomer smirked. "Like B needs a reason to lose his clothes."

"Right back at you, Jay. Now, let's teach the girls a lesson." Balthazar opened the back door, leading Anya and the one called Jay—which Stas assumed was short for Jayson—outside.

"It's like Hydria just exploded in my dining room," Issac remarked.

"You miss it," Clara accused, winking at him. "Admit it."

"Never."

"Liar." She blew him a kiss and flounced over to the exit. "Oh, and this new emotion? You wear it well. I like it." Her gaze rose to Stas. "Thank you for brightening his aura. I hope to know you better soon."

She disappeared before Stas could fathom a reply. Which probably would have been… *Huh?*

"Clara's an empath," Issac explained.

"And bubbly," Eliza muttered. "Like, overly bubbly." She visibly shuddered.

Stas grinned. Now, this woman? Yeah, this woman Stas could see herself befriending in a heartbeat.

"Right, shall we move this discussion to the living area?" Issac suggested. "I believe Aidan has a few matters to discuss, and there's something I want to show you both." He squeezed her shoulder with the words, his intention clear.

My birthmark.

Which he thought was a rune.

Why the hell would I have a rune on my back?

Luc's eyebrows rose. "I'm intrigued."

"I thought you might be," Issac murmured, his lips tilting.

Had he just shown Luc a glimpse of it with his mind? The way the Elder's green eyes focused on her, she suspected he did.

Both men stood, Issac holding his hand out for Stas. "Aya?"

"Can I have a minute with Eliza first?" she asked, hoping he would allow it.

He didn't hesitate. "Of course, love. We'll be in the other room." He gave her shoulder another squeeze before leaving with Luc at his side. "It's a rune, isn't it?"

"Show me a more detailed view," the Hydraian King replied.

"When we're all together, I will." Issac's words drifted down the hall. "I want Aya to hear the results."

She smiled, pleased that he wanted her involved.

Then she remembered their bet.

Right. He wanted to win, and to gloat if he did. *Devious demon.*

"Stas or Aya?" Eliza asked, tilting her head to the side.

"Stas," she confirmed. "Eliza, right?"

The woman nodded. "You were there, weren't you?"

"At the Conclave?"

Another nod.

"Unfortunately." Stas almost felt ashamed, not that she could have changed fate. "I'm sorry about what was done to you."

Her nostrils flared, anger flashing through her features. "Don't fucking pity me."

"No, I know. I mean, I'm not…" She trailed off because, yeah, she had felt bad for her. And yes, that was tied to pity. *I need to start this over.* "Okay, you're right. It's just…" *No, not a good route.* "Have they been, uh, nice to you? The Ichorians, I mean."

A note of understanding cooled her expression, but the irritation still lurked in her dark gaze. "You want to know if you can trust them."

"Sort of. I don't know. It's all been a bit overwhelming." An understatement. She looked at the ceiling and then back at Eliza. "Did they tell you I'm a fledgling?"

"Yeah, they mentioned it. Apparently, we're pretty rare."

Stas blinked. "We?"

The other woman stared at her. "Uh, yes. *We*. I'm a fledgling, too. Didn't you know that?"

"I thought Sierra said you weren't one? That the idiot who accused you was just an inexperienced asshat?"

Eliza's lips curled. "'Inexperienced asshat,' not a bad description." Then her smile faltered, a memory haunting her eyes as she dropped them to the table.

Stas saw it then, the broken woman hiding behind a charade of bravery—a coping mechanism for whatever had happened to her. Which was why pity infuriated her, because she had to be perceived as strong.

Stas understood that, had experienced something similar when her parents died.

This world had been cruel to them both.

"So you're a fledgling," Stas mused, trying to bring Eliza back to their conversation. "Are you able to do anything special now?"

"What do you mean?"

"Like, do you have any gifts?"

Eliza lifted her focus from the table, her mouth curling down at the edges. "No. Luc said they won't present themselves until I become a Hydraian."

Oh. Stas had hoped she might know what it's like to hide a gift in the mortal world for years. Alas, it seemed Stas was still alone on that front. "So how do they know you're a fledgling?" she wondered out loud.

"Aidan had someone—one of Luc's Hydraians—test my bloodline somehow. I guess she has a similar gift to the woman from the, uh, Conclave. The one who could sense immortal genetics or whatever." Eliza twisted her lips to the side. "You don't think they'd lie about it, do you?" Her eyebrows rose. "Oh, sorry, I didn't mean—"

"I don't think they'd lie," Stas interjected. "But I understand why you might not believe them." Because she felt the same way.

A moment passed between them, a mutual respect.

They were one and the same.

Yet completely different.

"They've treated me very kindly," Eliza said after a long moment. "As soon as we left that night, Aidan gave me his jacket. They allowed me to shower. Gave me clothes." Her gaze fell again. "They held me while…"

While I cried, Stas inferred, her heart breaking for the woman.

She swallowed the reaction, hiding it, not wanting Eliza to sense her pity again.

"You're very strong," Stas whispered, emphasizing the other emotion flourishing inside her. Admiration. "Stronger than most women I know." She reached across the table to squeeze her hands, but Eliza quickly pulled back, her aversion to touch evident.

Of course. Stas should have expected that.

"Maybe we should go see what they're discussing," Eliza said, standing, her limbs quivering. "Make sure they're not talking about us."

"Sure," Stas agreed, recognizing a wall when she saw one.

Eliza wanted space.

Stas comprehended that need better than most.

She pushed away from the table and joined her in the hallway, careful to keep physical distance between them.

"Stas?" Eliza whispered, pausing on the threshold. Her midnight irises lifted, a glimmer of respect shining in their depths. "Thank you."

Chapter Twenty-Four

A Financial Trail

Issac held his arm out for his Aya as she entered. He sat on the love seat across from Aidan, Lucian, and Mateo.

"Such a good pet," Tristan mused from the recliner in the corner as Astasiya joined Issac. "Coming when the master calls her."

Astasiya stiffened, her sharp gaze going to Issac's asshole of a best friend. "Excuse me?"

"Ah, but she speaks." Tristan tsked. "Such a pity, Issac. I prefer them silent."

"Then it's a good thing she's not yours," Issac returned, a hint of censure in his voice. One his progeny ignored.

"Not my type, I'm afraid." He eyed Eliza, who had chosen a chair against the wall, her legs tucked beneath her.

Hmm, yes, Tristan preferred submissive females, the kind who fancied pain over pleasure. He wasn't gentle by any measure of the imagination, and while Issac might enjoy dominance in the bedroom, hurting a lover didn't appeal to him.

"The feeling is mutual," Astasiya replied, distaste clear in her tone.

"Such disrespect." Tristan pressed a palm to his chest, feigning an affronted look. "This one is certainly a downgrade, Issac. Especially considering your usual fare."

"Careful," Issac warned, his arm tightening around Astasiya.

"When have you ever known me to mince words?" Tristan tossed back. "Just stating a clear observation."

"You're just sour over losing your wingman," Nadia said from the stairs. Ash and Jacque were behind her, all three of them dressed in swimwear. Balthazar must have requested more players for his shenanigans outside.

"No, I'm trying to understand how he could find this option more attractive than Clara, who was literally made for him." So callous. So nonchalant. But the devious twinkle in Tristan's gaze demonstrated his intention to hurt, and the gasp at his side said the verbal barb was translated and received.

"That's enough," Issac stated, done with this ridiculous banter. "Either fuck off or shut your goddamn mouth." He would deal with his disgruntled progeny later, the fuckwit. "Aidan, Mateo, what did you find on Owen?"

The energy in the room shifted, Tristan's shock at having been dismissed evident in the way he didn't retort or move. Nadia, Ash, and Jacque quietly slipped down the hallway toward the pool.

"As you know, Eliza is in fact a fledgling," Aidan started, reiterating the topic they'd been discussing before Astasiya and Eliza joined them. "Which I found curious since Sierra claimed her not to be one during the Conclave."

"Making it a good thing Osiris never asked for clarification during the trial," Issac added. Because the mind readers would have caught on to the lie.

"Indeed," Aidan agreed. "But it was strange, right? Why would she lie? So I tasked Mateo with finding out more about Sierra and her ties to Owen. What he found was, well, fascinating."

Mateo slid a tablet across the coffee table, the screen displaying some sort of legal document—a deed. Issac lifted the item, reading through the details as Mateo said, "The bar Sierra worked at was owned by Owen. He purchased it over twenty years ago."

"What?" Astasiya asked, joining Issac in reviewing the documents. "Why?"

"While a fascinating question in and of itself, there's something even more pressing. *How*?" Aidan asked. "Owen was too young to have amassed the wealth required to purchase a property in Manhattan, so how did he acquire it?"

Issac flipped the tab, seeing the answer as Mateo voiced it. "A shell corporation," his progeny said. "Called Gabriel."

As someone well versed in setting up such organizations, Issac had never heard of this one. "Who owns it?"

"I don't know." Those three words were rare, particularly in regard to Mateo's ability to find every detail known to man in cyberspace.

"As in you've never heard of him, or you can't find him?" Issac asked.

"The latter. Whoever set it up is one of the best I've ever seen. The work reminds me of a previous mystery."

"Jonathan," Issac translated. "We've always wondered how he acquired the funds to create the CRF," he added for Astasiya's benefit. "Whoever granted him the funds is a ghost. Mateo can't find any trace of the benefactor."

"Yes, only mentions of him in certain CRF project files," Mateo muttered, his frustration over this particular puzzle evident. "And this new corporation, Gabriel, has the same feel. No bank accounts, no names, not even a place. Almost as if it exists in space."

"How is that possible?" Astasiya asked.

"Great fucking question," Mateo replied, running his fingers through his short blond hair. "There's always a trail. *Always*."

"Mateo harbors a gift for technology that goes beyond the standard hacker and into the supernatural," Issac explained softly as he passed the tablet back to Mateo. "He manages most of my accounts as a result. He's well versed in moving properties and money around, creating identities, and so forth. But for him to not be able to trace a lead speaks of divine intervention."

"Another immortal," she replied.

"Yes, exactly." He shifted his attention to Aidan. "This suggests a link between Owen and Jonathan."

"It does," he agreed. "Which provides a potential motive if a working arrangement between them went sour."

"What I have trouble grasping is a purpose for their partnership," Lucian said, his expression artfully blank. Hearing that one of his Hydraians may have been working with the infamous CRF CEO had to hurt.

"I can't find anything in the CRF files that addresses that point," Mateo said, his eyebrows drawing downward. "But there's a part of his servers I can't seem to reach."

That was news to Issac. "Since when?"

"I imagine it's always been the case," he replied. "I discovered the wall when searching for information on the Nizari poison last week. The medical research side was easy, most of the researchers leaving a multitude of back doors for me to pass through. But there's a vault deep inside that I can't access with my psychic abilities."

"Similar to the ghost trail," Issac replied, drumming his fingers against his knee. "Is there any way around it?"

"Not without going inside the CRF, which we can't do for obvious reasons."

Issac nodded. "The runes."

Jonathan had somehow crafted a layer of magic to secure the perimeter. Ichorians and Hydraians would be defenseless inside, stripped of their powers, and essentially mortal. Issac had seen the markings outside, etched into the stone pillars adorning the iron gates. They circled the property. And bore similar notations to the design against Astasiya's lower back.

"That reminds me," he murmured, pressing his lips to her ear. "May I show them now, love?"

She blinked at him, her eyes holding a myriad of questions. "My birthmark?"

He nodded.

"I… If you think it's relevant." A touch of incredulity lined her words. "I mean, I doubt it's related."

"I beg to differ." It all seemed very much connected. Owen befriending

Astasiya. Her roommate-pairing with Elizabeth during their freshman year. Obtaining employment at the CRF. "There are a lot of links, Aya."

She studied him for a long moment, her uncertainty melting to concern. "You think Owen befriended me on purpose."

"It's starting to sound that way, yes."

"Okay, but that implies the CRF knows about me, that Jonathan knows I'm a fledgling."

"Yes, it does."

"Then why wait until the security exam to test the theory?" she asked. "Why go through all the hassle of a six-year friendship?" She shook her head. "No, it doesn't feel right. Owen... He was one of my best friends. I *knew* him."

"Except you didn't know he was a Hydraian," Issac pointed out softly, rubbing her upper arm as he secured his hold around her. "It's possibly a coincidence—Owen having a similar financial supporter capable of hiding his tracks, like the CRF does—but it all feels too close, too purposeful. Even Elizabeth being your roommate is a bit contrived considering her ties to the CRF."

"Lizzie?" Astasiya pulled back, angling her body toward him. "Now you think Lizzie befriended me on purpose, too?" The squeak at the end of her voice pierced his heart. He hadn't meant to upset her. Again.

"Your friendship with Elizabeth is too heartfelt to be fake," he said quickly. "I'm suggesting that someone may have coordinated your living arrangements, that your pairing as roommates may not have been fate so much as designed."

"When did you meet Owen?" Lucian asked before she could reply. "Was it after you met Lizzie Watkins?"

"Yes, but there's no way she's in on it. And Owen..." She shook her head. "No. We're... we *were* close friends. He cared about me. I'm sure of it. He'd never hurt me."

"Perhaps Jonathan became aware of you through the random housing assignment and tasked Owen to get to know you better," Aidan suggested. "I wonder if Jonathan requested Owen to do something in regard to you that he refused."

"Such as administer the Nizari poison?" Lucian said, scratching his jaw. "Actually, that provides ample motive. If Owen suspected Stas of being a fledgling, which I imagine he would have had to after six years of knowing her, then he'd know the cost of administering the poison."

Aidan nodded. "And because he cared about her, he declined the task."

"Thereby earning his death," Lucian finished. "It's exactly the kind of retaliation Jonathan prefers, especially when a minion doesn't do his bidding."

"Indeed." Aidan focused on Issac. "Show me the rune."

Astasiya shook beside him, her fingers trembling as she twisted the cloth of her dress against her thighs. "He...he died because of me?" she whispered, her big green eyes looking to Issac as if she needed him to deny it. "You think D-Doctor Fitzgerald...?"

"We don't know for certain, but it does seem plausible, yes."

"H-how? W-why?" She swallowed. "H-how do we…? I mean, there isn't proof. We c-can't know for—"

An alarm sounded on Mateo's tablet, silencing the room.

Issac's progeny lost himself to the technology, his fingers dancing over the screen with a dexterity few possessed. He managed the security of Issac's estate, his strategically placed devices monitoring the grounds and nearby surroundings for any potential threats. The system activated whenever Issac or Amelia entertained Hydraians on the property, a fail-safe to ensure everyone remained alive and protected.

"Tom Fitzgerald is a mile away," Mateo said, his focus on the screen. "He seems to be alone."

"What?" Astasiya gaped at him. "How could you possibly know that?"

"Facial recognition," Mateo murmured without looking up. "I have all potential threats cataloged and categorized to notify me when in proximity."

"Like…" She cleared her throat. "Does it include all Ichorians?"

He nodded. "Of course."

"Their faces?" she pressed, causing Issac to frown, curious as to what she truly wanted to know.

"Yes, well, no." Mateo typed something and bent over the screen. "He's definitely headed our way." He finally straightened, meeting Astasiya's gaze. "The program has no pigment, just bone structure and dental records. Think skeletons, but alive. Would you like to see it?"

She grimaced. "No, not really."

"What did you want to know, love?" Issac asked, holding her close.

"I, uh, I was just thinking." She paused, her fingers clenching the fabric of her dress. "I thought, maybe, if he has all the Ichorians, I might be able to find the man who killed my parents."

Ah yes. He imagined she would want to know his identity.

"You saw the man who murdered your parents?" Aidan asked, head tilted. "What did he look like? Perhaps Lucian or I have met him."

With their penchants for remembering every detail of their lives, it would seem quite probable they could help Astasiya identify the killer. If only Issac could see the vision in her mind.

"That'll need to wait," Mateo said, standing. "Tom just turned onto the street outside the gate. He's definitely on his way here, and he's not trying to hide it."

"Who's Tom?" Eliza asked, having been quiet and studious by the wall throughout the conversation.

"A friend of Astasiya's," Issac replied. "Who also happens to be a Sentinel with the CRF."

"Like the humanitarian organization?" She frowned. "Is that the company you keep talking about?"

"Yes, they have a paramilitary unit that specializes in assassinating immortals," Lucian summarized as he stood. "I'll brief you more on it later." He held out a hand for her. "We need to join the others, just in case Tom has brought a surprise with him."

Balthazar and Jayson entered at that moment, towels wrapped around their damp waists. The mind reader must have heard the thoughts inside and set everyone in action.

"Is Eli's armory unlocked, Wakefield?" Jayson asked.

Issac nodded, sending them upstairs with Ash and Anya right behind them.

It seemed the pool party had moved inside.

Amelia would be positively appalled by the wet footprints across her marble foyer.

Sorry, he said, glancing upward on instinct.

"Can you at least tell me why we're going upstairs?" Eliza asked, her arms wrapped around her middle, shaking. "Please?"

"For protection," he replied, his voice coaxing and tender and very unlike the authoritative one he typically favored. "The Hydraian who used to live here maintained a fully stocked weaponry, which my people are going to use if Tom has brought anyone with him."

She didn't look very convinced. "And what are we going to be doing?"

"Talking." He held out his hand again. "There's still so much for you to learn, but you can trust me."

"They're not going to hurt Tom, right?" Astasiya asked, her voice tight and distracting Issac from the couple across the room. "They can't hurt him, Issac. They… He's…" She swallowed. "He's still my friend."

"He sent you to the Arcadia."

"I know, b-but… Please, Issac. Don't let them hurt him. Maybe he just wants to talk." The plea in her gaze had him sighing.

"All right. No one will touch him unless he enters aggressively," he vowed. He made his voice loud enough for everyone to hear him on the ground level.

Balthazar, don't hurt the nitwit. Aya wants to talk to him first. Despite their differences, Issac trusted the mind reader to spread the word to his cohort. On this, they would share a side.

"I'm too racked to be bothered, really. What with the edict not to kill and all." Tristan's Irish lilt always became more pronounced when agitated. "How very unlike you," he added, the words pointed.

"Maybe you should have stayed in the city," Issac replied flatly, done with his childish behavior.

His best friend narrowed his gaze, then chose to say nothing as he joined the others upstairs.

Smart man.

"Tom's at the gate," Mateo informed just as the buzz sounded from the security panel against the wall. "And he's alone."

"Well, it seems Thomas is braver than I anticipated," Issac murmured, standing. "Let him through."

Chapter Twenty-Five

Queen on the Board

Fuck, why is he here?

Stas stood beside Issac in the foyer, Aidan and Mateo just behind them with guns in hand. A few other Hydraians lurked about, all with names she couldn't remember.

Tension radiated through the room, not at all helping the ache in her stomach.

Owen working with Doctor Fitzgerald.

Lizzie potentially being set up as her roommate.

How long has the CRF known about me?

Was any of it even true? She felt in her gut that they were missing something vital, some key piece of information that would exonerate both her best friends.

And Tom.

Yes, he sent her to the Arcadia.

However, she knew he cared about her. She couldn't be that blind to emotions and instincts; otherwise, she'd been living in a lie for the last six years. Stas refused to accept that, refused to believe it.

"Let me talk to him first," Issac said softly.

She eyed him warily. "Why?"

"To determine his intentions." He pulled her close, his lips at her ear. "And to give you an opportunity to prepare for whatever you need to say to him."

She studied his expression, soft and knowing and filled with understanding. How was it possible for someone to comprehend her on this level? To know what she needed before she realized it herself?

She started to shake her head to clear it, then realized it came off as a denial. "Okay," she said and swallowed. "But I want to listen."

"Of course." He gestured to a stop behind the door, and she moved just as Tom knocked, his fist loud against the wood panel. "Ready?" Issac asked.

Not really. She nodded anyway because what choice did she have? Besides, she wanted the truth. She needed to know.

Did the CRF really try to kill me?

"Thomas," Issac greeted, opening the door.

"Where is she?" Tom demanded, the voice that of the commander, not her friend.

"By 'she,' I assume you mean Astasiya?" Issac used a taunting tone, one she suspected had Tom glowering at her demon.

"If you turned her, I swear to whatever god you believe in that I will kill you."

She stole a breath, the words a blunt confirmation of what she already knew, but to hear it so clear in his voice was an entirely different beast. It meant he really did send her to the Arcadia to witness Ichorians feeding. And what about the Conclave?

"With what?" Issac asked, sounding bored. "That CRF-modified pistol on your hip? That would imply you are able to see well enough to shoot. Or do you plan to use that fancy silver knife tucked into your boot? Again, requires sight, something I have no problem taking away if you threaten me again."

Silence met his words.

Stas's stomach churned, her palms clammy as she fisted them at her sides.

He knew.

He knew *and he still sent me there.*

How could he do that to me?

"Tell me she's okay," Tom finally said. "Please. Tell me she's okay."

Her heart stuttered at the worry in his tone, the first indication that he actually did care, that maybe he hadn't meant to do this to her. God, why did this have to be so confusing?

"She's fine," Issac replied, folding his arms. "What the bloody hell were you thinking, sending her to the Arcadia?"

Tom expelled a long breath, his relief palpable even through the door. "Fuck, I wasn't thinking. I let my emotions, my anger, take over. I just wanted her to catch you, you know, doing your thing."

"My thing?" Issac repeated, sounding bored. "What thing is that, Thomas? What exactly did you hope for her to see?"

"Feeding, asshole. I wanted her to see what you are."

"To what purpose, exactly? Other than endangering her life, of course."

"Goddammit, Wakefield. Just let me talk to her. I know she's here."

"Do you?" Issac arched a brow. "And how do you know that?"

"Her phone," Tom growled. "Come on, just… I need… I need to apologize. And I need to see for myself that she's okay."

"I'm fine," she said, moving to Issac's side, tired of hiding. "He hasn't turned me. You can go now." Because the headache brewing between her eyes didn't need more fodder, nor did she know what to say to him.

He sent her to the Arcadia to catch Issac feeding.

Well, hell. A conversation would have been a much safer alternative.

She frowned. *Wait, if Tom sent me to the Arcadia to find out about Issac, then that means he assumed she didn't know about Ichorians.*

Didn't that contradict the theory about the CRF being aware of her fledgling status? Unless they assumed her to be ignorant of the supernatural world?

"Stas." Tom started forward, but Issac blocked him by placing himself between them.

"Easy there, Sentinel. I didn't invite you into my home."

"I want to talk to her."

"About what?" she asked over his shoulder.

"Privately."

Issac folded his arms again. "Not going to happen."

"I'm not going to do anything to her," Tom said. "Come on, Stas, you've known me for almost seven years. I didn't know it was a Conclave. They don't happen often. I went to the club the minute I realized what was going on, but I was too late."

"For what it's worth, he's telling the truth about that last bit. He was waiting outside the Arcadia when we left. He even followed us back to your place, which is why I stayed the night." He stepped to the side, his shoulder braced against the doorjamb. "It's also worth noting that it is not only stupid but also extremely risky for a Sentinel to stand outside the Arcadia. Especially one who happens to be the son of the CRF's creator. The bounty on Thomas's head is quite high. Essentially, he did risk his life to check on you as he is also doing now."

Her brows rose. "And you didn't mention this earlier because…?"

"Because his showing up didn't change the fact that he nearly got you killed."

"You still should have told me." Not that there'd been a lot of opportunity with all the other conversations.

"I'm telling you now."

She didn't have the energy or will to argue over something so trivial. He told her now, when it counted, even though he could have omitted the truth. "Okay," she said, stepping into his side to lay her head against his shoulder.

Tom observed the exchange without commenting, his expression artfully blank.

"Why didn't you just tell me what he was?" she asked.

"Would you have believed me, Stas?"

Another indication that he expected her to be ignorant of the supernatural world. *Something's not right.* If the CRF knew about her fledgling status, then so would Tom, as the CEO's son. Yet, he'd just suggested doubt over what she would believe.

Why would he suspect that if he thought she was part of that world already?

"You're probably right," she said slowly, the lie burning on her tongue.

"He's told you about the CRF, right?" Tom asked. "What we do?"

Issac seemed to still beside her, his hesitation something she understood. He didn't want her to mention his accusations against Jonathan. That, she could do.

Stas shrugged to keep it nonchalant. "No, not exactly. But some things were implied."

"Did he mention that we hunt down rogue supernaturals who are causing issues in the mortal world?"

That wasn't exactly how Issac described it, no. "He mentioned that the military unit is equipped to handle immortals," Stas offered instead.

"Is that why you're hiding here? You're afraid we'll hurt you for finding out?"

"Will you?" *Your organization already tried to kill me once.*

"Of course not. You know me better than that."

Do I? she wondered. "Maybe," she said after a beat, still deciding his intentions. "But you've known about this for how long without telling me?"

"You weren't cleared to know, Stas."

Meaning the CRF doesn't know what I am, or they would have killed me automatically. "So you sent me to a nightclub to clear me?"

He palmed the back of his neck. "It was a discreet way of telling you."

"A discreet way?" Issac repeated. "Thomas, she met Osiris as a result. Was that discreet enough for you?"

Tom's eyes widened. "She met Osiris?"

"Oh, yes. And what's worse, she bloody intrigued him. Why do you think she's here?"

"Shit." He began to pace, his hands in his hair. "Fuck, you have to let me take her, Wakefield. She'll be safer at headquarters and you know it."

Issac snorted. "I don't need to let you do anything." He gazed down at her. "It's not my choice."

She stared back at him. "It's an option?" *To go to the CRF?*

"Yes, but it takes you back to the city." *Where it would be unsafe,* he seemed to add with his eyes.

"How would the CRF keep me safe from Osiris?" she wondered out loud, her question more for Issac than Tom.

But Tom was the one who answered. "We have wards and other security protocols that will keep him out."

"So I would have to live there?" She didn't like the sound of that at all.

"Not necessarily." A vague answer. "How about you come back with me and I'll explain how we can protect you? It's the least I can do for getting you into this mess. Then, if you aren't interested, I'll drive you back here myself."

"You expect me to trust that?" she asked, incredulous.

"I expect you to trust *me*. How well do you know him, anyway? You really think he'll help you before he helps himself? A man who comes from a long line of fallen angels?"

"I prefer *demon*," Issac murmured, his lips twitching at the reference to the so-called pet name she'd given him. "But whatever works."

"Has he explained why he drinks blood yet? A curse from the gods, right, Wakefield?"

"Is that why you stopped by, Thomas? For a history lesson?"

"Stop." Stas needed a minute to process, to gather more information on this decision. It was one she shouldn't be considering at all, but something still felt wrong. She needed more details, proof, *something*, to validate all the allegations. "If I go with you, you tell me everything. If I don't like it, I get to leave," she reiterated. "Yes?"

Tom nodded.

"And does your dad know you're here?" she asked, trying to figure out where Doctor Fitzgerald fit with this inane idea.

"No, but he knows about the club. And, uh, he's kind of pissed at me. Like, livid." He looked decidedly uncomfortable. "He loves you, you know. Like a daughter. It's a little weird, but I get it. You're family, Stas. You know you can trust us. Just think about it. Give me a chance to make this right. Please."

Movement caught her attention, Mateo waving his hand. *Five minutes*, he mouthed. Until what, she had no idea.

But Issac must have understood the cryptic hand maneuver because he said, "Astasiya needs a few minutes to decide."

"I thought you didn't make choices for her?" Tom countered.

"He doesn't," Stas said quickly. "But he's right. I need a few minutes to think about everything. You owe me at least that much, Tom." *And it seems Mateo wants to say something.*

Tom expelled a long breath, his shoulders falling. "Fine. Yes. You're right. I'll just… I'll be in my car. But will you tell me either way?"

She nodded, her chest aching a little at the sadness in his expression. "I will."

"Okay." He swallowed and took a step back, turning toward his car, then stopped. "Stas?"

"Yeah?"

"For what it's worth, I'm sorry. And I'm glad you're okay." Sincere words that pierced her resolve.

That was the look and tone of the friend she'd known for years.

Contrite.

Desperate.

And heartbroken.

"I'll be in my car," he added softly.

Issac shut the door before she could reply, his jaw clenched. "What is it you're trying to show me, Mateo?" he demanded, the irritation in his tone surprising her.

The blond male took a step backward, his palms up in the air. "Okay, hear me out before you reject the idea."

~*~

Hear him out?

"Start talking. Quickly, mate." Because from what Issac had inferred from the images rolling through his mind, Mateo wanted to send Astasiya on some sort of reconnaissance mission through the CRF headquarters.

"What's going on?" she asked, glancing between them. "What did I miss?"

"Tell her," Issac encouraged, folding his arms.

Mateo cleared his throat, his already pale face losing color. "This presents us with an opportunity. Tom wants to take her back to CRF's headquarters, right? Where the servers are? If Stas can get close enough to them, I could hack into the system the old-fashioned way."

"What would that require?" Aidan asked, his stance casual beside Mateo.

"All she needs is a device—which I can procure relatively quickly—and to find either the server room or a proper host connection."

"Host connection?" Stas repeated, her brow furrowed. "What does that mean?"

"Like a master computer with access to all the files," Mateo explained. "I imagine Jonathan has one."

"With his controlling nature? It's an absolute certainty that he does." Aidan scratched his jaw. "So you're suggesting Stas go with Tom and help you access the files that are blocked via unknown means. How certain are you that this method will work?"

Mateo didn't hesitate. "About eighty percent, give or take."

"You want to risk Astasiya's life over a plan with less than a one hundred percent presumed success rate?" Issac snorted. "No."

"Hold on," she said, focusing on Mateo. "Tell me exactly what you would need so I understand what you're asking of me."

"Okay." Mateo pulled his wallet from his jeans pocket and found a nickel, handing it to her. "You'll need to hide something of this size in your purse or in your pocket and place it near Jonathan's computer. It should provide me with the access I need, assuming he has host files on his system. If not, then you'd need to find the server room, which I imagine is in the basement somewhere, in a temperature-controlled room—"

"And shrouded in security, no doubt," Issac added in a growl. "There's no bloody way she'll find the server room without being caught, Mateo."

"Your faith in me is inspiring," she muttered.

"It's not meant to be personal, love. Just stating the obvious. Jonathan is renowned for his security. Case in point, Mateo can't access certain files and he's a bloody Ichorian with supernatural technical skills."

She considered him and nodded. "Issac's right. I've been down there once, and it's a maze of white halls littered with security cameras. Finding the server room would be next to impossible."

"But if Jonathan invites you to his office for a chat…?" Mateo prompted.

"I could place this near his laptop," she agreed, holding up the coin. "Assuming I can get it through security. They scan all personal items through the machine, and there are metal detectors, too."

"I can work with that, but I would need the evening to prepare. I might even be able to make it into a card of sorts. Hmm." His gaze turned inward, his voice taking on a dreamy quality. "Oh, I could add a camera to your wardrobe, take video of the underground." He smiled, taking back the nickel and putting his wallet away. "Yes, architectural design. Stas could provide us with brand-new details about the layout."

Issac just stared at him. "Have you lost your bloody mind?" He was asking an untrained operative—Astasiya—to go on a suicide mission. "If Jonathan even senses her intentions…" He couldn't finish the thought, the ideas too horrific for his mind. "Absolutely not."

"Do you think there's information on Owen in those files?" Astasiya asked, ignoring Issac. "Maybe even Amelia?"

"I think there's a reason Jonathan is using a magical encryption to hide certain documents, and I would bet they're related in some fashion, yes." Mateo glanced at Aidan. "Do you agree?"

The eldest among them stared off into space for a long moment, strategy and intelligence radiating from his ancient gaze. He slowly nodded. "Yes, it is the most logical of explanations. Whatever he is hiding via supernatural means is something he wants no one to see." He blinked, refocusing on Issac. "Mateo's idea is worth considering. This is a unique opportunity to gather intelligence from the inside, which is what you desired all along."

"He's right," Astasiya murmured. "You wanted to use me for revenge, and this proves I really am your perfect pawn."

His gut clenched at the words, his heart skipping a beat. "Aya…"

"No, it's okay," she continued, gazing at him with eyes that showed her very soul. "I know you've changed your mind, but Mateo's right. If Doctor Fitzgerald was working with Owen, I deserve to know. I *need* to know, Issac. And those files might just have the answers."

"And if they don't?" he countered. "Then what?"

"Then we're right back where we started," she replied, grabbing his hand. "But at least we'll know what's in those files."

He shook his head. "I'm not willing to risk you over a *what-if*, Aya. There has to be another way."

"It's not your decision, Issac," she said softly, stepping into him and catching his other palm with hers. "Tell me, do you trust Mateo?"

An unfair question, particularly when voiced in front of his progeny. Issac sighed, his shoulders falling. "Mateo has never failed me." True words, ones that brought pride to Mateo's features. "So yes, I trust him."

"Then I trust him, too," Astasiya replied, squeezing his hands. "I need to do this, Issac. Not just for me, but for Owen."

"You'll risk your life in search of answers?" He tilted his head to the side. "Think about what you're saying, Aya. Think about what Jonathan could do to you. The Nizari poison was just a preliminary measure. He's been experimenting on immortals for over a decade."

"It's true," Aidan said, the voice of reason. "We don't know exactly how he's doing it, but the technology he's given the Sentinels is too advanced for human invention. Not to mention the runes."

"And those details, are they hidden?" she asked, her attention going to Mateo. "Can you access them?"

He shook his head. "Only superficial details with vague names regarding assets."

"Meaning these research projects are likely part of the classified files you can't reach," Astasiya inferred.

"Yes," Mateo agreed. "That's my theory."

"Theory," Issac repeated, disgusted with the word. "Not proven. Not scientific. Not fact. You'd be risking your life on a *theory*, Aya."

She swallowed, her gaze returning to his. "I'd be risking my life on a lot more than a theory, Issac. You want me to believe all these accusations about Doctor Fitzgerald, but I can't without more proof. I need to see him again, to really know that it's true." She cupped his cheek. "You're asking me to criminalize my mentor, the man who helped me with my career path, the one who has treated me with the utmost respect since I met him nearly seven years ago. Yes, the information you've provided is damning, but I need to know with certainty that he's evil. It's the only way I can help you achieve your revenge."

"But I don't want to use you in that way, Aya. I don't want to lose you." Didn't she understand? This was no longer a game of chess. Real emotions were on the board, with Aya front and center, and he couldn't risk the pawn who had become his queen. "Astasiya, you're worth more to me than vengeance."

Fuck, he could hardly believe the words falling from his lips, but they were true. Revenge—a quest of the past. He couldn't lose Astasiya, not over this, not over something he recruited her into. Issac would never forgive himself.

"I know," she whispered, lifting to brush her mouth over his. "Which is why I have to do this. It's no longer about you, but about me. If everything in my life has been a lie these last few years, I *have* to know. Trust me to do this. Please."

"It's not about trust," he replied, his arms folding around her back. "It's..." *It's about fear.* He didn't want to lose her. *But she's not even mine.* Not really. Exclusivity was one thing, a future entirely another.

Still, in regard to Mateo's plan to infiltrate the CRF...

Fuck.

Logically, Issac understood the idea. It was the best chance they had at gaining insight into their enemy's inner fortress. But risking Astasiya had him shaking his head, doubt creeping in. "I can't lose you," he said again.

"I can do this," she urged. "But I need you to believe in me."

"Oh, Aya. It's not about faith. It's the matter of not being able to protect you in the CRF." The last time she went in there without him, she came out poisoned. That had bothered him. Now he feared it would destroy him.

What the hell is wrong with me? Issac didn't do this with anyone. He always lived by his own code, allowing others to do the same. But the idea of Astasiya entering that building alone, without him, unsettled him immensely. Only a few weeks of her acquaintance and he already felt as if she'd bonded to his soul.

How is that even possible?

A tender emotion brushed her features. "Have you forgotten that I know how to protect myself? All it takes are a few demands."

"That's assuming your gift works in the underground," he replied, his mouth thick with foreign sensations. "Ichorians and Hydraians are essentially made human inside those walls. What will they do to you?"

"She's already mortal," Aidan said. "The runes shouldn't apply, as they're designed for immortal bloodlines."

"Shouldn't or won't?" Issac asked, his grip on Astasiya's hands tightening.

"I'll be okay, Issac," she whispered. "Let me trust my instincts. Please? Can you trust me?"

His heart leapt into his throat.

There was only a handful of people he ever trusted, and two of them were dead. But a fragile part of him, one he hadn't known existed until he met Astasiya, already trusted her, too. It was the same part of him that cared for her.

"What about Osiris?" he asked, going for a different tactic. The ancient Ichorian harbored a variety of homes, but he frequented the city often.

"He scares the shit out of me," she admitted. "But, Issac, I can't let fear drive my decisions. This is the right move." Spoken like the strong woman he knew her to be. One of the many traits he admired about her. "I'm not naive. I know going with Luc is my safest option, but I'm not ready yet. Not until I know the truth. Not until I find out what really happened to Owen."

Resolve shone bright in her features.

Astasiya would go with or without his support.

Either he respected her decision or he fought it.

Issac sighed. He'd never allow her to put herself in a life-threatening situation while thinking he didn't have her back.

"Oh, Aya." He gripped the back of her neck and pulled her in for a kiss, etching every foreign emotion and unspoken thought into her mouth with his tongue. She gripped his arms, holding him closer, returning the favor and devastating him with her own feelings.

It was as if they'd bonded on a level not of this earth, his soul aligning magically with hers, dancing somewhere in space.

He couldn't define it.

Didn't understand it.

Refused to ponder it.

Just embraced it.

My Aya… He deepened the kiss, not caring at all that they had an audience, ignoring everyone and everything around them. They were creating a pact, one that required him to give where his instincts desired to take.

She would always be in charge of her own decisions.

He'd never take that away from her.

Even when he craved control and longed to keep her safe.

But she had to follow her heart, to learn for herself, and he understood that more than he wanted to admit. Telling her wasn't enough. She needed to *see.*

"Come back to me, my Aya," he breathed against her lips. "Promise me you'll come back to me."

Her lashes fluttered open. "You're trusting me?"

"Yes," he whispered, nuzzling her. "Do what you need to do." It killed him to say it, but grounding her would be wrong. His Astasiya was born to fly.

Chapter Twenty-Six

Technical Mayhem

Issac stood outside the door, giving Astasiya space as she spoke to Thomas in the driveway. From the Sentinel's expression, he wasn't crazy about her proposal. Too fucking bad for him because Issac wasn't budging on this stipulation.

Tristan joined him, hands in the pockets of his trousers, his shrewd gaze on Astasiya. "If I caused offense earlier, I apologize."

Issac snorted. "Lies do not become you." He faced the man he considered his best friend. "But while you're here, mind telling me what has your knickers in a twist? You never care about who I fuck. Why the sudden change?"

"Because she's more than a fuck," Tristan replied. "You took her to a Conclave, Issac."

"Not by bloody choice, I didn't." Osiris had compelled him to bring Astasiya. There was no alternative.

"You risked your fucking life for her—all of our lives."

"Something you did not take issue with at the Arcadia," Issac pointed out. "If I recall, you assisted me rather willingly."

"As is my duty, even when my best lad is away with the fairies."

Issac narrowed his gaze, not at all appreciating the accusation regarding his mental state. "And what would you have had me do instead, hmm?" There'd been no other option. He couldn't just hand her over to the likes of Osiris.

Tristan knew that.

"It's not so much the decision as it's your reactions," he said flatly. "The lass is in your head. Soon your heart. And she's nowhere near good enough for you."

"Not good enough?" Issac repeated, his brows lifting. "Under whose authority was that decision made?"

His progeny faced him, his expression emotionless. "What kind of future do you have with her? She's a fledgling."

"I'm very aware of what she is, Tristan." And also how it impacted their relationship. "Is that your basis for disliking her, then? That she's a future Hydraian?" Those types of issues never bothered Tristan in the past. Issac didn't understand why they should now.

"I don't give a flying fuck about that. What concerns me are your feelings for the lass. You're letting her change you, making decisions based on emotions, not sense, and all for a temporary fuck. This will not end well, Sire."

Ah, there it was, the underlying reason for Tristan's concern—that Astasiya would change Issac on an irrevocable level. Possibly, yes, she'd already begun the process. But it was for him to fret over, not Tristan. "It's my business to sort, not yours."

"Then sort it," Tristan replied. "Because from my vantage point, you appear to be falling for the lass, and hard. And your relationship is an impossibility."

"What makes you think I'm unaware of that?" he countered, slightly irritated by the censure in Tristan's tone. "Do you truly think I'm ignorant of our predicament?"

"Being aware of the truth and accepting it are two very different sentiments, Sire." Tristan took a step back, his gaze flicking to an approaching Astasiya. "Enjoy her while you can, but guard yourself."

He left before Issac could reply.

Fortunately, Astasiya hadn't overheard a word of it.

He held open his arms for her, and she stepped into them on a sigh, her forehead falling to his chest as Thomas drove off.

"I take it he agreed, then?" Issac inferred, his lips in her hair.

"Yeah. He's going to set up a meeting for noon tomorrow."

"That should provide Mateo with enough time," he murmured, his grip tightening around her. He still couldn't believe he'd agreed to this. The logic and motive behind it were sound. The execution was what concerned him.

Fortunately, they had two of the best strategists in the world on the case. If anyone could develop a foolproof plan, it was Aidan and Lucian. With Mateo's technical expertise, there shouldn't be any issues.

Unless Jonathan threw a play none of them expected, which was entirely likely.

"I saw you talking to Tristan," Astasiya murmured, pulling back to meet his gaze. "He's not my biggest fan, hmm?"

Right. She would be wondering about this. "He's protective."

"And seems to think you're destined for another woman?" she prompted, eyebrow arched.

Issac sighed, his fingers teasing the ends of Astasiya's hair. "Clara is just a friend. But yes, Aidan created her as a gift—for me." He palmed the back of her neck before she could step away. "Don't, Aya. There's nothing between us, only a long friendship with no desire for an intimate future."

Her gaze narrowed. "What about an intimate past?" Of course she would go there.

"If you're asking if I've fucked her, the answer is yes. Only once. And neither of us was particularly fond of the outcome." He tightened his hold as she tried to move away. "I won't apologize for my history, love. All I can do is pledge fidelity going forward, which I've already done."

"You could have warned me."

"Perhaps, but that would imply I consider it an important topic. Which I do not." Unlike his progeny who decided to mention the issue—one Clara and Issac hadn't discussed in decades because neither of them perceived the other in a sexual manner. "She's a friend and nothing more. A fact Tristan knows but decided to disregard to provoke unwarranted strife." He tilted his head. "Don't let him win, Aya. Please."

She studied him for a long moment and shook her head. "Your best friend is an ass."

He snorted. "I'm well aware."

"Yet you're still friends."

"He has his moments." Issac loosened his hold and brushed his mouth over hers. "There's no one else, Aya. Only you. I swear it."

She relaxed against him, her lips lingering against his. "I think you should take me to bed and prove it." The taunt was a whispered invitation that heated his blood. "We have all night, right?"

"Mmm, yes, we do. And I know of just the right distraction to keep us both occupied." He smiled against her mouth. "Something to take our minds off all the heavy discussion."

He really just wanted to see her naked again. Perhaps in another shower, or just in his bed, or on the table in the kitchen. Hmm, all three appealed to him. It would give them a night of pleasure before having to head back into the city tomorrow morning.

Issac could do with a bout of passionate fun, maybe even a bite.

Otherwise, he would waste the evening worrying about something he couldn't control.

Yes, he'd much rather spend it living and cherishing every moment.

"Now you're just teasing me," she accused, her hands falling to his hips as she tilted her head back. "But let me guess, does it involve my birthmark? Because I'd still like to win that bet."

His lips curled. "Actually, I'd just thought to take you back to the pool house for a few hours of sensual treatment and food, but now that you've reminded me, I would like to declare a winner." Which would be him, naturally.

"Sensual treatment?" she repeated. "I think I prefer that now."

"Too late, love. You've already inspired the idea." He caught her hand and pulled her alongside him. "Let's put this bet to rest, then I can put you to bed."

She snorted. "What a line."

He paused, arching a brow at her. "Is that your way of requesting a demonstration, love?" He backed her into the door, his hands on her hips, his thigh sliding between hers. "Just because we're in the company of friends and family doesn't mean I won't ravish you right here and now." The words were against her parted lips, his grip tightening. "Say the words, Aya. I dare you."

She shivered, her fingers digging into his shirt. "I—"

The turning handle had Issac pulling her to him just as the doors parted, a grinning Balthazar on the other side.

"Professional tip, Wakefield. Feed her a proper meal first. Then ravage her again. Provides better energy and increases enthusiasm." He glanced down at her, a wicked glint in his gaze. "And from what I overheard last night, you are quite passionate, sweetheart. When you're ready for a real immortal, you know where to find me."

A glorious pink overcame her cheeks as Issac arched a brow. "Did you miss my performance last night? Because I believe I left her more than satisfied. Over and over again."

Astasiya gasped, her eyes widening.

"Oh, I heard it," he replied, his lips curling. "I rated it a nine until you failed to feed her prior to the shower."

"I was busy eating—"

"Okay, yeah, we're not having this conversation," Astasiya said, sliding between the two of them to enter the house. She paused just inside the door, her face turning an even deeper shade of red. "*Fuck*."

"That is the topic at hand, yes," Balthazar murmured, walking past her to join their audience in the living area. Most were gazing at Astasiya with interest, which had been the cause of her stumbling to a halt.

Issac closed the door before circling his arms around her from behind, his lips at her ear. "Ignore, Balthazar, darling. The rest of us do."

When she didn't speak or move, he kissed her cheek.

Time for a subject change.

"Aidan, Lucian, do you have a moment?" he asked. They were deep in conversation with Mateo, his blond head bent over his tablet, as usual.

The father and son duo glanced up at the same time, their faces so similar, yet one slightly more aged than the other. Neither of them favored facial hair, which only aided in their resemblance.

"Yes?" Aidan prompted.

"The rune," Lucian said, fully in tune with Issac, as always. Not due to mind reading, just a habit of knowing him well. "He wants us to look now."

"Ah yes." Aidan blinked. "Show us, Issac."

He telegraphed the image with ease while resting his chin on Astasiya's shoulder. Heat radiated from her cheeks, suggesting she'd not yet forgiven him for bantering with Balthazar. Issac could have thought the words instead, but saying them out loud felt so much more refreshing. Particularly after the bastard's blatant proposition.

As if Issac would share.

"Not something you ever considered an issue in the past, Wakefield," the mind reader said, smirking. He'd taken the seat beside Eliza, his arm stretched out over the back of the couch, carefully not touching the woman.

Although, she seemed to be comfortable with the proximity because her body was angled toward him. Not in a sexual manner so much as a comforting one.

Balthazar's secondary ability to control emotion would come in handy in her situation. He also tended to be rather tenderhearted in these circumstances, marking him as the perfect confidant. Amelia always did adore him in a familial way.

Issac did not share that opinion. *Astasiya is mine. Fuck off.*

Balthazar chuckled, his too-handsome face causing several of the females in the room to take notice. Astasiya, thankfully, was too focused on Aidan and Lucian to notice.

The two omniscient beings were chattering in an old language, a dead one from the sounds of it. They tended to regress when lost in debate and theories.

Issac waited them out, knowing one of them would eventually return to the future with his findings. "I believe I'm winning, Aya," he whispered against her ear. "I hope you're ready to take another shower. That's where we'll start."

She quivered, her soft intake of air confirming she'd visualized his words. He longed to see in her mind, to manipulate her vision with just what he intended.

Her. Wet.

Soft.

Willing

Palms against the wall.

His cock sliding into her from behind, his lips against her neck.

Mmm, yes, that was exactly how they would start. He allowed her to feel the stirrings of his arousal around her ass, grazed his teeth against her pulse.

The clearing of a throat brought his head up, his attention falling upon an expectant Aidan. "We have follow-up questions," he said.

Of course they did. "Which are?" Issac prompted.

"Does the mark ever bother you, Stas?" Lucian asked, his green eyes holding a faraway gleam that matched his father's.

Both were lost to their gifts, sorting through thousands and thousands of years of knowledge and experience, all while maintaining a conversation in the present. That sort of power was what qualified Lucian to lead and what kept Ichorians from challenging Aidan. Playing against an omniscient strategist was a fool's errand, indeed.

"Uh, no, not really," she replied.

Aidan didn't appear to like that answer. "Issac, can you try to manipulate her vision for me?"

Seemed a waste of time, but he nodded anyway and gave it a go. Astasiya squirmed a little, likely uncomfortable with the idea of being a test subject. Then she stilled, her lips parting.

"Oh, shit…" She spun in his arms, her gaze widening. "Do it again."

He frowned. "All right." He came up against another black wall of nothing, her mind completely shut off to him.

Her eyebrows were in her hairline. "My back… it… it tingles."

Lucian and Aidan were nodding, their conversation flowing again in a foreign language no one in this room understood. After several minutes of suspense, Lucian tilted his head to the side, his focus on Astasiya. "Have you ever seen a Seraphim, Stas?"

"A Seraphim?" she repeated, moving to Issac's side. "Issac said they were rare."

"Extremely rare," Aidan agreed. "I haven't seen one in several thousand years. I started to suspect they were extinct, but that mark suggests otherwise. When did you first notice it?"

"Uh, as a kid? It's a birthmark." Frown lines marred her brow. "Are you suggesting a Seraphim put a rune on my back?"

"Yes," they both replied at once.

"Why?"

"First guess, to protect you from Ichorians." Aidan shifted focus. "Have we tested Hydraian gifts on her thoroughly?"

"Only mine," Balthazar replied.

Aidan scratched his chin, his gaze searching. "Where's Jacque?"

"'Sup?" the teleporter appeared, a piece of pizza in his hand. "Heard my name from the kitchen."

"Stas, would you mind letting Jacque teleport you across the room?" Aidan asked. "To test your mark?"

She gaped at him. "You want me to let some guy I don't know teleport me?"

Issac pressed his lips to her temple. "Jacque's harmless, darling. Trust me."

"I'm not sure whether to be offended or pleased by that," the teleporter said around a mouthful of food.

"His manners, however, leave much to be desired," Issac added.

Jacque shrugged. "You try teleporting people back and forth all day across the world and tell me if you're not feckin' starved, yeah?"

"Across the world?" Astasiya repeated. "Yeah, no. Nope. Find someone else."

"I can always try it." The deep voice came from the hallway as Alik entered with a bottle of beer in his hands.

Issac tensed. "That's not—"

"Did you just speak in my head?" Astasiya asked, her eyes wide.

"Not immune," Alik summarized, collapsing into a chair beside Balthazar. "I can try my other gift if you're not satisfied."

"No," Issac said flatly.

"What's his other gift?" Astasiya wondered out loud, then shook her head. "Never mind, I don't want anyone else in my head."

Considering Alik could cripple an army with a thought, that was a wise decision.

"Did your mark tingle at all when Alik telepathically spoke to you?" Aidan asked.

She stiffened and shook her head. "No, not then or now. Stop doing that."

Alik shrugged, sipping his bottle, completely unperturbed.

"And no, don't do that either," she added, shuddering. "No wonder you're so… *dark*."

"Keeps me alive," Alik replied. "As well as everyone else."

Well, he must have answered her question about his ability to mentally torture hundreds of minds at a time. Brilliant. That would certainly warm Astasiya to the Hydraians.

"The protection rune is specific to Ichorians, then," Lucian was saying, in English this time, to Aidan. "Why?"

"I'm more interested in the how of it," Aidan replied. "What do we know about her ancestry?" The question seemed to be directed toward Issac.

"Just the names of her birth parents. Are you thinking they knew a Seraphim?" Issac rubbed Astasiya's arms while he spoke, her skin pebbled with goose bumps.

"Yes. It's possible her father knew one and requested a protective marking to help keep her alive." Aidan crossed one ankle over his knee. "I'd love to know what he negotiated in trade for such a precious gift. The higher angels hate Ichorians."

"Why?" she asked.

"Because we're considered an abomination to the angelic race." Aidan said it so casually, as if everyone knew that. "Do you remember meeting anyone unique in your childhood? Someone with an otherworldly air or poor communication skills? Seraphim don't socialize much with mortals, or anyone really. *Stoic* and *abrupt* would be good descriptors."

"Uh." She swallowed. "Not ringing any bells."

"What about your parents? Do you remember anything about them, Stas? Anything unique?" Lucian asked.

She pinched her lips to the side. "My father could compel. My mother…" She trailed off, slowly shaking her head. "It's… My memories have always been unreliable, fuzzy in nature."

Lucian and Aidan shared a look. "Memory tampering?" the eldest suggested.

"Possible," Lucian agreed. "We'll need to dive into that more."

"Indeed." Aidan switched to their archaic words again, the two of them lost to their minds. Mateo sat blissfully beside them, working on his plans for tomorrow.

The others all seemed to be melting into their own conversations as well.

"Do you have any other questions?" Issac asked, his arm sliding around Astasiya's shoulders.

"Not yet," Aidan and Lucian said together before returning to their discussion.

The question had been for Astasiya. "And you?" Issac whispered, his lips against her ear.

"What language are they speaking?"

He chuckled. "Honestly, I have no idea. They revert back to dead languages when they get excited about something." He kissed her shoulder. "It's rare for them to be presented with a learning opportunity."

"Because they know everything."

"Not so much know everything as they remember everything they've ever learned."

She glanced up at him. "That's terrifying."

"And amazing," he added, drawing his finger across her jaw. "In any case, they'll let us know if they figure anything out, but I'm guessing that rune of yours will remain a mystery."

"And why's that?"

"Because only the Seraphim who gave it to you can tell us why." The only thing they knew for certain was the marking protected her from Ichorian gifts.

Her expression fell, her lips curling down at the sides. "Oh."

He lifted her chin upward with his thumb, his lips brushing hers. "You look like you could use a distraction right about now."

"I just found out my birthmark isn't a birthmark at all," she whispered. "A distraction would be great."

"There's food in the pool house."

"I'm more interested in the bed." Soft words, confidently spoken.

She'd just revealed the seductress she kept hidden away deep inside. The one who favored lace and craved his bite.

And oh, how his demon side approved.

"Yes, and I do believe I won." He allowed his gaze to roam over her slowly. "Anywhere and however I want, yes?"

She visibly shuddered, her eyes taking on a bedroom quality he adored. "I think I'm going to enjoy this distraction."

"That's the idea." He pressed his lips to her ear, his words for her alone. "I'm going to start by fucking that delicious mouth of yours, then we'll make it more interesting. Now, follow me."

Chapter Twenty-Seven

Testing Boundaries

This is a bad idea.

The thought reverberated in Stas's mind as they neared the CRF headquarters. She fought the urge to fiddle with the top button of her blouse—the one that Mateo had sewn on this morning.

A camera.

That would link back to his tablet.

She swallowed. He promised the metal detectors wouldn't catch anything, and the button looked real enough.

Just like the item in her pocket.

A business card with Issac's contact information as CEO of Wakefield Pharmaceuticals on the front and his masculine handwriting scrawled across the back.

But between the paper edges was something that would allow Mateo to hack into Doctor Fitzgerald's system, so long as she placed the item close enough to his computer.

Issac squeezed her leg, his palm resting against her upper thigh as he navigated the Manhattan streets. "You don't have to do this, Aya."

Oh, but she did. They were missing something, some key detail. Every fiber of her being vowed that Owen never meant her any harm, even when they first met.

Of course, she felt the same way about Doctor Fitzgerald despite the evidence to the contrary.

"It's the only option," she said softly, more to herself than to Issac. "I'm just nervous, is all."

That the card in her pocket might set off some alarms.

That someone might notice the button.

That she might get caught.

That I might not like the truth.

She shivered, goose bumps pebbling her arms despite the warm summer day.

The electricity dancing across her skin intensified as the looming glass towers of the CRF appeared before them, a variety of flags decorating the courtyard out front.

"Last chance, love," Issac murmured, his hand moving to the shifter between them.

"I have to do this." The conviction in her voice didn't match her churning insides.

He nodded, slowing as they approached the gated entrance. "When we pass the guard stand, my gift will no longer be viable."

"Issac, this—"

"I want you to test your gift on me when I park inside, Aya. We need to know that it works."

"This isn't the plan," she gritted out.

"Plans change." He uttered the words while steering into place in front of the gate. "Let me do the talking."

Her stomach twisted, the small breakfast she'd eaten this morning threatening to make a reappearance. She bit her lip to keep from demanding him not to do this, knowing it was too late when a guard tapped on the passenger window. Another approached the driver's side. Pistols strapped to their hips.

Issac rolled down the glass and removed his sunglasses to peer up at the security officer beside her side of the car. "Good morning," he greeted, his tone deceptively pleasant. "I'm dropping off a guest for Jonathan Fitzgerald. I think you'll find he's expecting us."

The robust man didn't even look up from his clipboard as he asked, "Name?"

He didn't hesitate. "Issac Wakefield."

Two almond-shaped eyes popped up, his dark eyebrows rising. "I— I need to phone this in."

"Of course," Issac replied. "We'll wait." He relaxed into his seat as if he hadn't just alerted CRF security that an Ichorian wanted entry.

She had so many questions.

So many concerns.

But the open windows kept her quiet.

While one soldier went into the booth to make the call, the other stroked his weapon, his focus on Issac.

Were his gifts already moot?

She glanced at the stone columns on either side of the entrance, roughly five feet before them. *Are there runes etched into the rock?* she wondered, searching for patterns that her eyes refused to identify.

"He's clear," the male called from the booth. "Fitzgerald will meet them in the parking lot."

By the casual use of the surname, Stas assumed he meant Tom.

"Cheers," Issac said as the gates opened. The windows closed around them as he shifted forward through the stone pillars, his shudder visible as they passed.

"Have you lost your fucking mind?" she demanded, furious.

"You're allowed to put your life at risk, while I'm not?" he countered, his sideways glance one of admonishment and disbelief. "That is not how this will work between us, Aya."

"Damn it." Her fists clenched, her heart beating a mile a minute.

If something happens to him…

If they catch him…

God, she'd never forgive herself.

"Issac," she whispered. "You can't do this. Not for me."

"It's already done." He navigated into the parking lot off to the side of the building—an area reserved for diplomats and VIPs. Apparently, Issac qualified.

Unless this was a trap.

Would the Sentinels run out to grab him?

In broad daylight?

She glanced around the vacant lot, noting the normal afternoon air and the lack of movement.

Just a typical work day with a handful of empty cars.

"You asked me to trust you, Aya. Now it's your turn to do the same." His arm came around the back of her seat, his body angled toward her, the car humming beneath them. "Command me to do something, love."

She continued to survey their surroundings, while Issac appeared completely relaxed beside her.

No worries.

Not even a frown line in his forehead.

"How are you so calm right now?" she asked, her nerves straining her voice.

"Who says I am?" He tugged on a strand of her hair, forcing her to look at him. "Command me to do something," he repeated. "I need to know your gift is unimpacted by the wards. Please." A hint of emotion deepened his irises to an alluring sapphire, his expression otherwise blank.

He's concerned not for himself but for me.

She didn't know how to feel about that. No, that wasn't right. Of course she did. Because she felt the same way. They were surrounded by potentially dangerous elements, and all she cared about was his safety, not her own.

"I want you to do everything you can to leave the CRF grounds the second I shut the passenger door." Persuasion laced through her words, the demand as natural as speaking. She sensed it seep into his pores, his very being, saw the flash of recognition in his gaze, the acceptance in the flare of his pupils.

"Well played." He wrapped his palm around the back of her neck, pulling her closer. "Sexy as fuck, too." He kissed her hard, his tongue conveying some sort of hidden message, a secret she couldn't grasp. Not with her mind whirring, her body chilled from the very real possibility that Issac could be caught, or worse.

"You need to go," she whispered urgently. "It's not safe here."

"I could say the same to you, love."

"My gift is fine. I'll be okay. I promise."

He pressed his forehead to hers. "And now that I know that, I feel marginally better about leaving you here. There is one item I would like to request, if you'll entertain it?"

"Don't ask me to retract my demand." Because she wouldn't. Which proved she believed his accusations about the CRF. Otherwise, she wouldn't be so panicked.

And I'm about to waltz into the viper's den.

"No, it's something more personal." His thumb brushed her pulse. "You've healed from the Conclave. I want to re-mark you. It's a sign of devotion, one Jonathan will both understand and respect. It will also provide proof of our ongoing affair."

"You want him to know I'm yours," she translated.

"I do," he admitted softly. "Because it means if he hurts you, he'll have to contend with me. And considering the tenuous nature of our relationship, I don't see him wanting to draw more attention unto himself."

She understood what Issac truly desired—to protect her. This was a way to help him feel more confident about the situation, to know he'd done everything in his power to keep her safe aside from entering the building with her.

How had their charade melted into such intensity? Or had it been that way from the beginning? A part of her, some foreign sliver inside, had bonded to him on a level that superseded existence. That piece of her urged her to deepen the connection, to allow him this simple favor.

Because whatever he craved, she craved, too.

She nodded, understanding him in a manner that surpassed logic. "Can you make it quick?" she asked softly, aware of their location, but also knowing why he needed this.

"Not a statement most women say around me, but yes, I can." He nuzzled her jaw, his hand already pulling her hair to the side. "Just know I'll want more later."

"You could have fed last night," she reminded him, her voice huskier than she intended. They'd spent most of the evening hours lost between the sheets, even enjoyed dinner in bed—a dinner Issac had prepared.

But he never bit her. Even when she offered.

"Mmm, but I did." The words were spoken against her throat. "I licked every inch of you, Aya. And I intend to do it again tonight." His incisors pierced her skin, the sharp prick giving way to a sensation of euphoria that stole her breath.

She clutched the lapels of his jacket, her heart hammering in her chest.

Oh... This was inappropriate. Wrong. Not the right place. Yet the indecency of it only heightened the moment.

His name fell from her tongue, both a warning and a plea wrapped up in one. Stas couldn't decide if she wanted him to stop or keep going. But he made the decision for her, pulling away with a satisfied gleam in his eyes.

He cupped her cheek. "Jonathan would be a fool to touch you now."

A sharp rap on the window caused her to jump away from Issac, her gaze flying upward to Tom just outside her door.

Shit.

Issac rolled down the glass. "Thomas."

"Wakefield," he returned. "Brave of you to enter the grounds."

Her demon arched a brow. "I could say the same about you venturing into my estate."

"Touché." Tom stuffed his hands into the pockets of his jeans. "I appreciate you dropping her off. You've been noted as a nonthreat and will be permitted to leave without issue."

"Much appreciated." Issac reached over for her hand, giving it a gentle squeeze. "I just need one more minute with Astasiya."

Tom nodded, taking a step back. "I'll be on the sidewalk." He pointed to the path running alongside the building. Not waiting for confirmation, he left as the window slid upward.

"Your edict still stands," Issac murmured. "I'll leave as soon as you step outside."

She blinked. "You can feel it?" Odd that she couldn't. Except, she never really did. Would her control over it improve when she became a Hydraian?

"Mmm, it would seem your desire for me to escape unharmed is strong." He removed his hand, a smile on his lips. "I'm actually quite flattered, as it shows you care."

She unbuckled her seat belt. "Like you needed that to know."

"You're not the only one new to these emotions, Aya," he said softly. "Be safe. Please."

She paused with her hand on the handle, looking back at him.

What if I never see him again?

Don't think like that.

"Issac—"

"Don't, Aya. Don't say anything else. You're coming over this evening. No arguments."

She swallowed, nodding. "Yeah. After the meeting. I'll be there."

"You'd better." He lifted his hand, his fingers light against her chin. "Be safe, my Aya."

"I'll see you soon," she promised.

"I know." He ran his thumb over her bottom lip, then pulled her in for a searing kiss that imprinted him on her soul. "Don't hide the mark." He gathered her hair over one shoulder while he spoke. "And remember what you can do."

"I will," she whispered, opening the door. "Now safely leave the grounds." That twinge of compulsion stirred inside her, punctuating her words on instinct alone.

"Call if you need a pickup, Aya."

"Okay." She grabbed her purse and shut the door, refusing to say goodbye. It felt like a bad omen.

Something tugged against her soul as he put the car in drive, her heart in her throat as she watched him exit the lot.

She needed him to be safe.

To leave without issue.

Walking quickly to the corner, she watched as he navigated the grounds, not a single person or object in his path.

Then he was at the exit.

The gates lifted.

Electricity hummed over her skin as he passed through the cement columns unscathed, her breath leaving her on a sigh.

"I'm a man of my word, Stas," Tom said, having joined her. "You know that about me."

She glanced up at the much taller man, taking in the sincerity and hurt lurking in his eyes. "It's hard to know who to trust right now," she admitted. "All the lies. The secrets. This secret world of immortals." She shook her head, tears pricking behind her eyes as the emotions of the last few weeks caught up to her at once. "I don't know right from wrong or up from down anymore."

"Ah, Stas." He wrapped his arms around her in a hug filled with adoration, brotherly love, and affection. Such familiarity. Such warmth. "I'm so sorry." Soft words saturated with such heartbreaking honesty that she couldn't help but return the embrace.

"You're going to make me cry," she accused, knowing full well it wouldn't be him at all, but the stress of their situation. God, she couldn't decide if she wanted to weep or scream or run like hell.

But Tom was right. She *knew* him. He may have kept a huge, devastating secret from her, but hadn't she done the same? She hid her ability to compel from everyone, even her closest friends.

"Will you ever forgive me?" he asked, his heart in his voice. "For the other night?"

That all depended on what happened today, what she learned inside the walls of the CRF. "I can try," she said instead, unable to voice the truth.

Another secret between them, joining the vault with countless others.

How could she be angry with him for hiding a world from her when she was guilty of the very same crime? Even now, she intended to help Mateo break into the CRF records.

It's the right thing to do.

Is it, though?

Maybe. Yes.

She sighed, stepping back, meeting his troubled gaze. "I'm ready to see your dad." To determine the truth once and for all.

He nodded. "He's waiting for you, too. Let's go." He gestured for her to follow, his much longer legs carrying him across the concrete in wide strides. She kept pace, gripping her purse as her breakfast churned in her stomach.

This is it.

Deep breaths.

The creepy black flag hanging over their heads seemed to taunt her entry. *Memento Mori.* White cross. A curse of death.

And not the omen she needed right now.

"You'll need to check your purse and your phone," Tom said conversationally, standing beside the metal detector just inside the entrance.

She nodded, placing her bag on the conveyor belt.

The card seemed to burn in her pocket, as did the tiny camera on her blouse—one she'd forgotten about until just now.

Mateo promised it would pass the scanners.

She hoped he was right.

Tom walked through, the system blaring loudly in response, mocking her.

Perspiration dotted her spine, her hands, her brow. *Oh God…*

The officers said nothing to Tom, completely aware of who he was and not caring at all that he'd set off the alarms. He wore a pistol on his hip, something no one seemed to mind.

Had he brought that outside because of Issac? Or did he always carry a firearm?

"Stas?" he prompted, his expression concerned.

"Sorry," she mumbled. "I, uh, just expected them to make you go back through."

He chuckled and scratched the days-old stubble dotting his jaw. "They're used to me setting it off, aren't you, boys?"

Two of them snorted. The third just looked bored.

Right.

So, he always kept a weapon on his person.

Good to know.

"You can go through," one of the security guards said, his shoulders twice the width of hers. Not because he was overweight. No. That was all muscle.

Noting all their younger ages and stature, she finally put something together.

They weren't security guards at all, but Sentinels. Like Tom. Hence, the easy camaraderie between them and militaristic features—short hair, clean-shaven, athletic forms.

How had she never noticed that before?

Because you didn't know the organization might be evil.

"Stas?" Tom gave her a look, one filled with curiosity and concern. Because she was acting like a crazy person, frozen beside the metal detector.

That doesn't make me look guilty at all.

She forced a laugh. "It's been a really long weekend."

His features softened a bit, understanding bright in his chocolate eyes.

A couple of employees entered behind her, likely returning from an early lunch break.

Now or never, she told herself. *I really hope you did your job, Mateo.*

She crossed the threshold.

Chapter Twenty-Eight

Truth and Deception

The rhythmic drumming in Stas's ears drowned out all sound around her, including Tom's voice as he handed her a temporary badge from the security desk.

She slid the lanyard over her head.

Nothing happened.

No one tackled her.

They didn't request a pat-down.

Just a bunch of nodding Sentinels, two of which smiled at her warmly.

Mateo's devices hadn't set off the alarm.

I'm losing my mind over nothing, she realized, mentally shaking herself. What if all this was a complete misunderstanding? Yes, the CRF dabbled in the immortal world. But maybe Issac and the others had the wrong opinion on it.

"Ready?" Tom asked after securing her bag with the Sentinels.

She nodded. "Yes."

"Cool. Follow me." He led her to a bank of elevators on the other side of the three-story lobby and swiped his badge. "You went down here for your polygraph, yeah?"

Unfortunately. "And my medical exam."

His brow furrowed. "Medical exam?"

"Yeah, with Doctor Patel."

His expression darkened, almost to the point where she wanted to step backward. "Doctor Patel gave you a medical exam?"

The elevator dinged before she could reply, her throat suddenly dry.

Tension tightened his shoulders, his square jaw clenched as he scanned his badge to select the lower level. "What did she do during your exam?" he asked as the doors closed before them.

Stas swallowed. "Standard things, at least until the vaccines."

He muttered a curse, shaking his head. "*Fuck*."

"Your dad said it's not common procedure."

"It's not," he growled. "Not at all."

Her pulse quickened as they stepped into the underground cavern of endless white hallways. A sensation of wrongness crept over her, similar to how she felt during the Conclave. Except Issac wasn't here to protect her this time.

She caressed the mark on her neck, the two pinpoints against her skin providing a false sense of comfort.

"This way," Tom muttered, his steps clipped.

They took a different path from her last visit down here, one that led them through a room of armed military men.

Oh, I hope you all are seeing this, she thought, remembering the camera against her blouse. *Because this can't be normal.*

There were so many guns and cameras and mirrors. Every wall. Covered in thick two-way glass.

Energy crawled over her skin. Not the good kind, but the bad kind.

"You're breaking protocol, Fitzgerald," a deep voice said from their left. Two brawny arms corded in muscle crossed a burly chest that left her gulping.

Not the kind of man you want to piss off.

"Bite me, Hawthorne." Tom swiped his badge against another door to lead her away from the hostile guards.

"They seemed friendly," she said as he took a left down a dimly lit hallway. No cameras this way. Interesting.

"They're assholes." He kept moving, his boots shuffling against the white tile until a familiar blond male turned the corner with a raised eyebrow. "Where is he?" Tom asked by way of greeting.

"Where do you think?" Light green eyes flickered her way. "Miss Davenport."

She swallowed, unnerved by that knowing gaze. *He* knew about her exam because he'd taken her to Doctor Patel. "Agent Stark."

Tom glanced between them. "You two know each other?"

She wiped her clammy palms against her black pants. "Yeah, he was my polygrapher."

Skepticism deepened the creases in Tom's brow. "I didn't know you moonlighted as a polygrapher, Stark."

"Only when requested," he replied, walking away.

Stas frowned after him. "If he's not a polygrapher, then what does he do?"

Could he have been involved in her poisoning somehow?

"You don't want to know," Tom replied. He took an abrupt turn down another corridor void of surveillance and stopped at a door a few feet down, knocking twice. It cracked open, just enough for Doctor Fitzgerald to see them.

Tom cocked his head toward her. "I told you she was fine." Flat words accompanied by a somewhat hostile stance.

Well, that's new. Every time the two men interacted, she caught only respect and admiration. However, the Tom standing beside her now radiated fury.

What gives?

"Thank God," Doctor Fitzgerald said, his relief palpable. "I just need to finish up this conversation, Stas. But I'm looking forward to catching up with you."

"Me, too," she lied, forcing a smile.

"Take her to my office" was all he said to Tom before shutting the door.

Wow. Okay. Definitely some tension here.

"It'll be my pleasure," Tom gritted out, his gaze narrowed at the letters etched into the wood.

A-7.

Stas wondered what they meant and whom Doctor Fitzgerald might be talking to in the room. Whoever it was, Tom didn't seem to approve.

He stalked off down the hall—still white with no cameras—and opened a door at the end of it. "He means his office down here," Tom explained.

Does that mean the computer Mateo needs is in here? she wondered, entering the reasonably sized space. An oversized oak desk took up a quarter of the space with a collection of chairs around it—two in front, one behind—and a table for four sat in the corner.

Two computer monitors.

One laptop between them.

That had to be what Mateo needed.

Tom palmed the back of his neck, noticing her inspection. "Yeah, it's not as swanky as the one upstairs, but no one really sees this one except the Sentinels."

"You mean the humanitarian military personnel who are not actually conducting humanitarian missions?" She couldn't help the sarcasm, particularly after seeing the army waiting underground for intruders.

What are they guarding in this area that requires that much firepower?

"There are still humanitarian missions, Stas. We've saved people from some pretty fucked-up situations. If you thought the Arcadia was bad, you should see some of the other Ichorian dens." He looked pointedly at her neck. "As you obviously know, they require blood to stay alive. Most of them call it a curse, but there are some who luxuriate in it more than others." Disdain tainted his tone.

"You don't seem to like them very much."

"I detest them."

After what she saw during the Conclave, she could understand why.

Tom sat in one of the chairs across from Dr. Fitzgerald's desk and waved at her to take the other, putting her closer to the laptop. Mateo said he needed the card within a foot of it. She estimated the current distance at just over two.

"What all did Issac tell you about the immortal world?" Tom asked, tucking his hands behind his head in a way that accentuated the strength in his arms.

"He explained the difference between Hydraians and Ichorians. And he mentioned the Blood Laws." As well as a lot of other shit she couldn't repeat.

"I assume he didn't paint the CRF in the kindest light."

"Not exactly, no."

He smirked. "Yeah. They don't care much for our technology."

"Why's that?" The immortals had mentioned something about it being beyond human invention, meaning the CRF had employed supernatural means of some sort.

"Because we develop instruments that can kill them." He brought up his ankle to rest on his opposite knee. "They're immortals with psychic gifts. All we have—as humans—is our strength and agility and, now, weapons."

Except you're a fledgling, she thought. *And not exactly human.*

Doctor Fitzgerald chose that moment to enter, a towel in his hands as if he'd just been drying them off. "Do you mind giving us a few minutes, Tom? I'd like to speak with Stas privately."

A chill settled across the room, Tom frozen for too long a moment as he glowered at his father. Doctor Fitzgerald returned the look with a steely gaze of his own, his dominance filling the office with an almost ominous air.

Stas wasn't so sure she wanted Tom to leave. Not with this version of her mentor in the room.

"Yes, *sir,*" Tom said, standing. He left with a not-so-subtle slam of the door.

Um... This was not the father-son duo she knew.

"I can't tell you how relieved I am to see you here, Stas." Instead of taking the chair behind the desk, Doctor Fitzgerald leaned against it with his legs crossed at the ankles a few inches from her. His nearness didn't normally bother her, but it did today. She felt caged between him and the wall, like he feared she might run.

Do I have a reason to?

Dressed in black slacks and a pale blue dress shirt, he resembled the Doctor Fitzgerald she respected and adored. He even had the same genuine smile.

Why did he suddenly feel like a stranger to her?

"Tom tells me you had an eventful weekend," he continued, his soft brown eyes falling to the mark on her neck.

"That's one way to describe it." She preferred *intimidating* or *paralyzing* to *eventful.* "Honestly, I would rather get to the point and talk about the Sentinel program."

I want to talk about you.

And I also need to figure out how to place this card close enough to your laptop.

He chuckled and shook his head. "I've always enjoyed your directness, Stas." He pushed off the desk, walked around it, and settled into his chair. Lacing his long fingers together on the desk, he leaned forward.

"The CRF still does everything you've been told; it just also does a little more. There's a humanitarian wing that caters to those in need, helps with search and rescue missions, and delivers aid. That's all true. What the general public isn't aware of is we also have an elite group of Sentinels who dabble in supernatural affairs. Tom, as you now know, belongs to the latter. From your expression, I gather Issac already told you all of this?"

"He did."

"I see." He narrowed his gaze. "Did he also mention his involvement in your medical exam?"

Uh… "What?" *How much does he know? About my reaction to the Nizari venom? Does that mean he did try to poison me?* Ice drizzled through her veins. *Oh, I never should have come here. I never—*

"Hmm, I can see he didn't." Doctor Fitzgerald typed something into his keyboard and switched on one of his monitors. What appeared to be an interrogation video displayed across the screen. "After what you told me Friday night, Agent Stark and I had a long chat with Anita Patel. Needless to say, we learned who gave her the directive to administer the vaccinations." His gaze snagged hers for a moment, his lips tightening. "I'm sorry, Stas, but you're not going to like this."

She sat forward to better see the video. He hit Play.

Doctor Patel appeared in her lab coat, sitting across the table from two suit-clad men. Agent Stark appeared to be bored, while Doctor Fitzgerald wore a hostile expression—similar to the one he just gave his son.

"You recently administered a medical exam to Astasiya Caroline Davenport," Doctor Fitzgerald said, giving the dates and details of her security interview. They went over a few documents before he reached the heart of the matter. "You gave Miss Davenport inoculations meant only for paramilitary personnel when her file clearly indicated *civilian.* Further, it appears you dispensed vaccines that are not part of our paramilitary exam protocols. Nizari poison, if the surveillance feeds outside of the exam room are correct. Do you deny any of this?"

Apathy painted the woman's features in harsh shades, her lack of concern evident. "No."

Stark's expression remained unchanged, his gaze steady. "Who gave you the Nizari poison, Anita?"

"The man who hired me to give it to her."

"And who hired you?" he asked in the same monotone from Stas's polygraph. The man took stoic to a whole new level.

"Issac Wakefield." The answer was clear and concise and sent a shock down Stas's spine.

What?

No.

That wasn't possible.

He *saved* her.

Unless…

Unless saving her was the point. To poison her and then rescue her. To give her a reason to be wary of the organization he intended to get revenge against while simultaneously instilling a deep-rooted trust in him as her savior. An ingenious plan that had "Issac Wakefield" written all over it. She was a pawn to him, at least in the beginning. He would have had no problem toying with her life, and even admitted he might one day get her killed.

The video continued to play and she pretended to watch, her mind spinning with possibilities and adamant denials.

A brilliant plan, maybe, but Issac wouldn't do that to her. Never once did he insinuate it could be anyone other than the CRF who tried to poison her.

But the video was incriminating.

And he had been there when she arrived that afternoon. The Tuesday night date had been his idea as well. An odd choice.

Did he set it all up?

She recalled Doctor Fitzgerald's concern when she mentioned the shots after her medical exam. His shock was believable. That was not a man who ordered her assassination. She wondered at the time if Doctor Patel worked on her own and somehow knew about her fledgling status. Because Issac told her?

No. He wouldn't do that to me.

This had to be a scheme, a way to turn her against Issac. The man who dropped her off today was not someone who wished her ill will; he'd even advocated against all of this. He wanted her safe. Protected. His.

It may have been a charade in the beginning, but not anymore.

He cared about her.

And she cared about him.

"You asked me to trust you, Aya. Now it's your turn to do the same." His words from the car played through her thoughts, vibrating in her heart.

She couldn't fail him now.

He didn't do this.

"I'm sorry," Doctor Fitzgerald murmured. "Are you familiar with Nizari poison and why it's used?"

Her spine tingled.

The rune.

Someone nearby was using an Ichorian gift.

Was it Doctor Fitzgerald? She'd never asked Issac what he could do.

She frowned. "I'm sorry. Can you repeat that? I'm still a bit, uh, well, shocked."

He smiled gently. "Of course, dear. I understand. It's all a bit harsh to hear, and I'm very sorry to be the bearer of bad news."

I just bet you are, she thought back at him. Oh, he sounded genuine enough.

Even looked apologetic. A master manipulator, the man behind the mask. *Who are you really?*

"I asked, 'Are you familiar with Nizari poison and why it's used?'"

More tingling.

She cleared her throat, focusing. Instinct told her to lie. "Uh, no, I'm not familiar with it."

"It's used to kill Ichorian offspring. Permanently. My guess is Issac wanted to test your mortality. When you didn't react, he knew you were human and therefore a viable candidate for him to pursue."

"Viable candidate?" she repeated, her brow furrowing. *What the fuck is he talking about?*

"Yes. I think he intends to turn you." His gaze went to her neck again. "After he's done reaping the benefits of your mortality, anyway." A deliberately cold statement that made her shiver. He couldn't be more wrong on that assessment. Not that she could correct him. "He doesn't have any female progeny yet. It seems you've caught his fancy. He must sense something unusual about you that will benefit him."

"You seem to know a lot about him," she noted, uneasy with the turn in conversation. Issac told her his attentions would intrigue Doctor Fitzgerald, but now her mentor wanted to know more about *why* the renowned billionaire Ichorian had chosen her. She did not want to go down that path of speculation.

"I do. I've never seen him so interested in a woman. It's made me wonder if perhaps his interest is also tied to your employment, or maybe your relationship with me. Any ideas?"

She pretended to consider and shrugged. "He hasn't mentioned anything." *But it's fascinating that you would make that assumption. And also somewhat incriminating.*

"Interesting." He scratched his chin in a thoughtful manner. "You know, we've never had a female Sentinel. This could be a unique opportunity. As you're already aware of the world, it's an obvious next step. Of course, if you prefer to continue working in marketing, that's perfectly acceptable. The pay won't be as good, or the benefits, really, but I'll understand."

Wait… "Are you offering me a job?" Because that was not at all what she expected from this conversation. Hell, she still hadn't even called Human Resources back.

"It's a win-win in my book. You learn more about the supernatural world, we keep you safe and train you how to defend yourself, and we groom our first female Sentinel. Of course, I'm just thinking on my feet here. I would have to run it by the team first."

Okay, uh, what? "But I'm not military."

"No, but you're young and in decent shape. Stark or Tom will handle the rest. It'll be a lot of hard work and long hours. You would also have to end whatever you have going on with Issac, though I doubt that'll be much of an issue after what I revealed today."

And that's the catch, what he desired.

To take her away from Issac.

"How—"

The door flew open with a bang. Tom stood just outside, his face contorted in rage.

"I need a minute with you. *Now.*" The words were spoken through clenched teeth and directed at his father.

Doctor Fitzgerald sighed, standing. "Stas, will you excuse me? My son seems to have lost his manners."

By the look on Tom's face, those were the wrong words to say. What the hell had gotten into him? He looked ready to commit murder. *And is that blood on his hand?*

"Yeah, sure," she murmured at the closing door.

What the fuck? Tom hadn't even looked at her. She wasn't used to seeing him angry, let alone disheveled.

The screen of the computer was still facing her with Doctor Patel's face frozen in a smile that made her stomach churn.

She nearly turned the screen off again when it dawned on her that she was alone in Doctor Fitzgerald's office.

The card. She stood and pretended to stretch while searching for any signs of surveillance. There weren't any, but that didn't mean there wasn't something obscure observing her.

Plucking the card from her pocket, she pretended to read the contact details and the note on the back. Then, acting as though she was annoyed, she flicked the card onto the desk, sending it across the space toward Doctor Fitzgerald's laptop.

Anyone watching would assume the item offended her.

And after that video, they'd know why. Because it had Issac's name and handwriting on it.

With a feigned huff, she stared up at the ceiling.

What the hell had set Tom off? she wondered. Clearly, there was something going on here.

She glanced at the still-closed door. Were they having a conversation in the hall? She stepped casually closer, hearing nothing.

Hmm.

Maybe she could open it and say she needed to use the restroom? Give her a chance to wander with the camera on her chest?

Seemed practical enough.

She cracked open the door, prepared to voice her excuse, except the hallway was vacant.

With a frown, she stepped into the corridor. No sign of life. Silent. But the entryway to the room Doctor Fitzgerald had occupied earlier was slightly ajar.

Had they ventured in there?

She could just wander and knock, right? Voice her excuse politely?

On impulse, or perhaps due to a moment of stupidity, she crept forward.

Curiosity killed the cat, her helpful conscious reminded.

Good thing I'm not a fucking cat.

She stopped outside the room, listening for voices. Nothing. Weird. Where did they go? Stas took a step, when a soft humming caught her attention, the sound hypnotizing.

"Do it again, Mommy!"

Her mother's laugh tickled the air around her as she reappeared, joy radiating in her features. "Oh, my darling, you are truly my little angel."

"Teasing our daughter again?" Daddy came up behind Mommy and wrapped her in his arms, his lips against her neck.

Astasiya scrunched up her nose. "Gross."

He chuckled. "One day, little angel, you may disagree."

Her mother snorted. "Are you kidding? You'll kill anyone who touches her."

"Well, that's true," he agreed, nuzzling her.

"Mist again," Astasiya said, pleading with her mom. "Please. Please mist again!"

Her mother smiled and disappeared, the sound of wings humming through the air as she fluttered her invisible feathers.

A tear rolled down Stas's cheek at the vivid memory, one she'd forgotten for nearly twenty years. Was it real? Did that actually happen? Or was it a dream?

That whisper of a sound drew her gaze back to the room, the soft purr forcing her forward.

She pushed open the door to find a woman crumpled in the corner, her face hidden beneath a curtain of brown hair.

Not her mother.

Not even close.

A whimper escaped the female, her pain palpable and visible from the metal cuff digging into her ankle.

Oh, fuck. Stas rushed forward and came to an abrupt stop when the frail woman lifted her head. Clear, sapphire eyes met hers.

"Well, this is new," she said, her voice stronger than Stas would have expected. "What game is Jonathan playing at now?"

Stas gaped at the woman, her striking features and British lilt familiar. But it was the eyes she recognized most. They were the spitting image of Issac's.

"Amelia," she breathed. "You're alive."

And, oh God, he can see this…

"For today, anyway." Amelia stretched an arm over her head and winced. Bruises and welts littered her skin, while her face remained unmarred. Someone had recently delivered a beating. A bad one. *Jonathan…*

"I've got to get you out of here." Stas checked the hallway for surveillance. No visible cameras anywhere in this area, unlike the others.

She frowned. Okay, but how would she be able to get Amelia past security?

And the elevator only moved for Tom's key card, not hers.

And that shackle around Amelia's very swollen ankle appeared to be locked on tightly.

Stas eyed the thin silver collar around the woman's neck, as well as the tiny blinking light at the center. *Definitely not your typical accessory.* Was it a remote-activated device? Would it sound an alarm if she left the building?

"That's rich, love." Amelia extended her legs, revealing more bruising that painted her skin in shades of purple and blue.

"*Jesus.*" She looked nothing like the beautiful woman in Owen's photos. "What the hell did he do to you?"

Her long, dark lashes blinked once. "He beat me, of course. Are you here to do the same?"

"No!" Realizing she yelled that, she glanced at the door again and waited to hear voices.

Still nothing.

Thank God.

She didn't have much time and she needed to think. Except she had no physical way to help Amelia escape.

Is Issac already on his way here?

He had to see the footage, right? Assuming the camera was working?

What if it's not? The thought chilled her. He'd never believe this without seeing it.

"Issac thinks you're dead." The words sort of spilled from her mouth unceremoniously.

"Oh, this again? Yes, as I told Jonathan months ago, or maybe that was years ago. Time is a weird thing here. But yes, I have finally come to that conclusion as well. Are we done?"

"No, I mean he might not believe me when I tell him you're alive." She really, really hoped the camera was working. Except that would also mean he'd just seen his sister in this state. "I need to give him something only you would know."

Those perceptive blue eyes that were too much like her brother's looked her up and down. "This is a terrible game. Obviously, I'm not going to fall for this." She rested her head against the wall and closed her eyes. "Can we get back to the healing bit now?"

An odd request, one Stas didn't have time to clarify. "Look, I don't know how much time I have."

Amelia appeared unfazed, simply rolling her forehead against the wall and groaning to herself. This woman was as stubborn as her brother.

Shit.

Okay.

She needed to give her proof. What had he told her about Amelia that not everyone would know? "Uh, you taught him to dance because it's the way to win a woman's heart, but he always told you he had no interest in it."

Amelia snapped upright and took Stas's measure again. "What have you done to my brother?"

"Nothing. He's, uh, we're sort of… No, that's not important." She glanced again at the door, terrified they would get caught. "Give me something to tell him."

Amelia's gaze flickered to the wall beside the door. "This is quite dull."

Stas grabbed the back of her neck, her limbs shaking from the possibility that someone may catch her here. And then what?

No.

She had to make this quick, get out, and tell Issac.

"I'm risking my life right now standing here. Give me something, Amelia. I'm begging you."

The first signs of uncertainty filtered through Amelia's features, her lips curling down as she tilted her head in an eerie way. "Issac sent you?"

"It's complicated and I don't have time to explain."

"Mmm, and he's all right?" she asked.

"Yes."

Amelia bit her cheek, her gaze falling to the floor before lifting again. "I miss his blue butterflies, you know." She traced indistinguishable designs on the wall with her finger, a tear licking a path down her cheek that she didn't seem to notice. "I dream of them sometimes. Maybe I'll dream of them again tonight." She sighed, closing her eyes. "I'm wary of this madness, you see. So very wary."

Fuck, what had Jonathan been doing to her all these years? She was so utterly broken. So… fragile.

Stas resisted the urge to console the woman and instead checked the hallway. Still clear. But she doubted it would be for long. The blue-butterfly line would have to be enough.

"I have to go," she told Amelia. "But he'll come for you. Even if it means burning this place to the ground."

"I used to believe that," Amelia murmured, still drawing aimlessly on the wall. "Then I learned hope only equates to pain."

Chapter Twenty-Nine

The First Female Sentinel

Stas sprinted back to the office, Amelia's parting words a shadow on her soul. *Hope only equates to pain.* Stas had wanted proof of Issac's claims; now she more than had it.

Doctor Fitzgerald was a monster. She may not have seen him beat Amelia, but he'd clearly been the last one in her room.

Was that why Tom wanted a word? Why he'd been so furious?

The handle twisted, Doctor Fitzgerald entering with an apologetic smile. "Sorry about that. Minor issue regarding asset management." He softly closed the door, Tom nowhere to be seen.

"It's okay," Stas managed to say, her throat as dry as the Sahara.

He smoothed his hand down his dress shirt and sat across from her, his eyes deceptively kind. "Where were we?"

Her heart jumped, an entirely different question popping into her mind while he spoke. *Where were you?*

Does he know I just found Amelia?

Are there hidden cameras that caught me?

She swallowed, wiping her palms against her pant leg. He stared at her expectantly, waiting for a reply. What had he asked? *Where were we?* Right.

"Um." She cleared her throat, her voice slightly hoarse. "I, uh, you were talking about a job, I think."

She knew from his expression she'd given him the correct response. "Indeed I was. What do you think?"

I think you're a sociopath who likes to beat women.

"Well, it's a little overwhelming," she said instead, referring to the job.

Then an idea occurred to her.

One that could ensure he let her leave here alive while also potentially allowing her to return to save Amelia.

Hmm, it was a long shot, but if he agreed, it just might work. She just had to play this right, to stroke his ego and entice him into an arrangement he couldn't refuse. All while not revealing a single emotion or thought.

No pressure.

She cleared her throat again. "But"—Stas forced a smile—"it's also exciting."

Pride radiated from Doctor Fitzgerald's expression. "It is, isn't it?"

Such a masterful façade. Even now, despite everything she knew, a part of her wanted to beam with gratitude, as if he'd trained her to accept and adore his praise.

A larger part of her wanted to throw up all over his desk.

His desk.

Oh, fuck.

The card.

It still sat beside his laptop, Issac's name proudly displayed on the cardstock paper.

"Now, Tom just mentioned you met Osiris," Doctor Fitzgerald continued, curiosity coloring his tone. "I'm afraid that makes it a little more imperative for you to join us. If you become a Sentinel, I can give you certain resources that are not available to civilians—resources that can save your life."

Well, that was unexpected. "You can protect me from Osiris?"

"I can provide you with the ability to guard yourself, yes."

"Like weapons?" she guessed.

"Among other things." He laced his fingers together on the table again, leaning toward her conspiratorially. "I'm sure Issac has promised to keep you safe, but his way would involve taking on immortality. Am I right?"

Not in the way you think, she thought while nodding.

"That's a big decision. Are you ready to make it?"

Well, at least on this she could answer honestly. Because no, she absolutely was not ready for immortality. "No."

His head bobbed as if he expected that response. "Well, joining my team would grant you an opportunity to explore the supernatural world in its entirety before you decide whether or not to join it." He settled back in his chair. "With the added bonuses of learning how to defend yourself with weapons and via other supernatural means."

Runes, she realized. *He's talking about runes.*

"You know, since the first day I met you, I suspected you were destined for greatness," he added, his charisma on full display. "That's why I recommended you to Brandon down in marketing. But now, I'll admit, I'm keener to have you on my team. Assuming you're up for it, of course."

A clever way of pretending she had a choice in the matter when they both knew she didn't. Stas suspected refusing would result in something uncomfortable, such as her death.

Yet, looking at her mentor now, she'd never suspect it. He had an air of eagerness and sincerity to him that masked the evil lurking beneath his skin. Because only a sadistic bastard could leave Amelia in that condition down the hall.

"What do you think?" he prompted when she remained quiet for too long.

"When would I start?" she asked, needing time to work out her plan. It would take the right wording, a way for him to think it was his own idea all along.

"Well, given the Osiris situation, I would say as soon as possible. I can talk to the marketing team on your behalf, save you from any hard feelings."

Yes, her boss would be slightly disappointed. Not that she'd been an all-star employee this last week, what with forgetting to call Human Resources back and all that.

"I would appreciate that," she admitted. After everything she'd learned, she never wanted to work with the CRF again, but that didn't mean she disliked her boss. Chances were he had no clue of the company's sinister purpose.

"Then it's settled? I mean, assuming my team approves, but I don't see why they wouldn't agree."

She forced herself to hold his gaze. "There's just one thing."

"Oh?"

She pursed her lips, needing to phrase this the right way without sounding too eager or conniving. "I don't want to end things with Issac."

That sent both of Doctor Fitzgerald's eyebrows into his hairline. "You care about him more than this opportunity? Even after the video?"

"God no, nothing like that." A blatant lie. "But I think there might be an opportunity here."

He studied her for a long moment, his thumb stroking the stubble dotting his jaw. "What kind of opportunity?"

Curiosity piqued? Check.

"Well, he already took me to a Conclave, right? Imagine what else he might show me. Unless you already have someone on the inside of Ichorian society feeding you information?"

"You want to be a double agent," he translated.

More like a triple agent. "Maybe. I don't think I'm phrasing this right." She pretended to consider, needing him to speak the idea for himself. "I'm just wondering if we could somehow recruit him, or if I could use my connection to him to somehow further the CRF. Honestly, I don't know what all you need, so feel free to tell me I'm way off base." *But I know I'm not.*

He continued rubbing his chin, his interest evident. "This could place you in a precarious situation."

She snorted. "I'm already in one, thanks to Issac."

He flashed her a knowing grin. "Thirsty for revenge?"

"You have no idea." Vengeance for Amelia, possibly for Owen. *Fuck, the card.* How was she going to get that back without Doctor Fitzgerald noticing?

He considered. "Do you really think he could be of use to us?"

"Issac?" she asked. "Yes. Yes, I do." Another idea formed, an impulsive one that she jumped on without considering the alternatives. "Look at that." She glanced pointedly at the card.

Doctor Fitzgerald frowned at the item, picking it up to study it. "Where did this come from?"

"Uh…" She feigned a sheepish look, twisting her lips to the side and clasping her hands in her lap. "Yeah, I may have tossed that at your desk while you were gone. He gave it to me earlier, telling me to use it after our meeting. And, well, after seeing the video, I was a little annoyed. There wasn't anything else of his to throw, so…" She trailed off with a shrug.

He gave her a look before turning over the card to read Issac's scrawl. "What's the code for?"

"His security alarm." One Issac would need to change after today. "He wants me to meet him back at his condo."

Doctor Fitzgerald's eyebrows shot up again. "His personal residence off Chambers Street, or one of his guest suites on the same floor?"

"He has guest suites?" she asked, actually curious. "I think I've only stayed in his penthouse." As far as she knew, anyway. All his suits and books were there. That made it his personal space, right?

"Did it have a formal dining area? Balconies overlooking the Hudson?"

She nodded. "It's, uh, impressive, yes." Understatement.

"That's his condo, not one of the guest suites." He whistled and set the card down. "He really is quite taken with you, isn't he?"

"Sure. Enough to try to poison me, apparently."

Doctor Fitzgerald chuckled. "I'm guessing he just wanted to test your bloodline before investing the time." He shrugged, his entire demeanor changing. "Honestly, it's pretty common practice, if a bit archaic."

Uh-huh. "Well, regardless, I'm not all that pleased with him at the moment. Still, I think he could be useful." She dangled the bait and waited, hoping he would bite.

Stas couldn't save Amelia on her own, but Issac might be able to with access to the right resources. This would hopefully open the door he needed to proceed, or a way around the runes.

And she would help him every step of the way.

"Do you think he might be interested in working with us?" Doctor Fitzgerald asked, his voice sending a tingle down her spine.

Someone is using a gift.

She frowned, unnerved by the sensation. It had to be him. But what was he trying to do? *Why didn't I ask Issac about Jonathan's talent?*

Swallowing, she focused on his query and how to reply. "With the right motivation, I think we could convince him. But it won't be something he accepts overnight."

"And you think you can convince him?"

"I'd like to try," she replied. "When he explained the CRF to me, he wasn't negative. If anything, he sounded impressed." In a dark "I want to kill Jonathan" sort of way, but she didn't mention that part.

"Did he?" Doctor Fitzgerald sounded surprised. "I've just assumed him to be uninterested all these years."

"Perhaps he wasn't presented with the right opportunity," she suggested. *Such as the motive to kill you and free his sister.*

Her former mentor nodded, his gaze taking on a dreamlike quality. "He could bring a lot to the table."

Blood.

Torture.

Murder.

Death.

Yep.

"All right, Stas. You've intrigued me. The relationship can remain for now while you either siphon information from Issac or potentially recruit him." He smiled. "These things take time, so as long as you're up for the task, I see no problems with it."

"Oh, I'm up for it," she assured. And hopefully, Issac would be, too. Unless, of course, Mateo gathered everything he needed from the hard drive. Were the immortals on their way here now?

What if they want me to stall?

~*~

Several Minutes Earlier

"I'm in," Mateo announced, his fingers flying across the keyboard.

"Thank fuck for that," Issac replied, running his fingers through his hair. They were all standing in his study, where Mateo had set up shop about an hour ago.

Aidan stood beside the oversized desk, his hands tucked into his pockets, gaze vibrant, while Tristan entertained Clara and Anya in the living area. Nadia lounged on a corner chaise, her long legs crossed at the ankles, her attention on her phone rather than the task at hand.

Rows of data scrolled before them, too fast for Issac to catch, but Aidan seemed to be reading it all with ease, his brow furrowing with each passing second.

"What is it?" Issac asked, recognizing the lines of concern etching a path into his maker's features.

"The files appear truncated." He continued reading, his brow furrowing. "It's like someone placed a bunch of file names with cover sheets in the system while removing the bulk. Do you see that, Mateo?"

"I'm still downloading," he replied, focused on the computer. "But yeah, it feels incomplete."

"Meaning your plan didn't work?" Issac couldn't help the note of censure in his tone, his concern for Astasiya's well-being fraying his nerves. However, their last glimpse from her camera showed her safe and sound. He took it as a good sign that Jonathan hadn't immediately apprehended her.

"Oh, my plan worked. The files just appear to be incomplete." Mateo frowned, shaking his head. "It's like someone keyed the names of all the projects, provided high-level detail, and erased all the metadata."

"There's no reference to additional files, either," Aidan added, his expression rivaling Mateo's. "The entire server is a smoke screen."

"So it would seem. Maybe they're saved to his local drive." Mateo flipped monitors, showing an interrogation room of sorts with three frozen expressions.

"What's that?" Issac peered over his shoulder for a better look. "Are they in another room? Where's Astasiya?"

"That's Jonathan's desktop," Mateo replied. "It's the video he showed Stas before leaving the room."

Ah yes. They'd not been able to hear it. "Can you play it?" Issac requested, curious about the contents. The visual was much clearer now, showing Jonathan, Agent Stark, and Doctor Patel.

"Sure." Mateo pushed a few keys and pulled the image to his other monitor, pressing Play.

Issac's lips thinned as he watched the footage. "Clever," he muttered as they neared the end. "And clearly rehearsed."

"Did you warn Stas about Jonathan's affinity for the truth?" Nadia asked, her ebony gaze on the screen.

"I didn't mention it," Issac admitted, regretting the oversight. "Fortunately, she's immune."

Jonathan's ability to compel the truth out of a person was why Agent Stark played the interrogator in that video. Had it been Jonathan, Doctor Patel would have been forced to answer truthfully, which would have defeated the purpose of the entire charade.

"Will Stas believe any of this?" Aidan scanned the words flowing over Mateo's other monitor while he spoke. "The video, I mean."

"She knows me better than that by now," Issac replied, certain. "Jonathan would have to do a lot better than that to convince her to distrust me at this point." If anything, the CRF's CEO had just proven Issac's accusations to be true.

Jonathan Fitzgerald was an evil son of a bitch.

"Where's Aya now?" Issac wondered, needing to see her again to confirm she was still all right.

Mateo touched a few keys to bring up her video feed.

Issac studied the viewpoint, his brow creasing. "What the hell are we looking at?" he demanded, his chest cracking. "What the fuck is that, Mateo?"

"The v-view from her blouse," Mateo breathed. "That can't be…" He enlarged the live stream on his bigger screen, Amelia's face bright beneath the harsh lighting of the room.

The image blurred as Astasiya moved, a white wall coming into view. And then Amelia's face appeared again.

Issac grabbed the monitor, his knees weak.

Amelia.

She sat crumpled in a corner, wearing a filthy shirt that hardly covered her thighs. Thick clumps of dark hair hung around her gaunt face, hiding her aristocratic features and the blue of her eyes.

But he'd recognize his sister anywhere.

Bruises littered her body, her ankle was twisted at the wrong angle, and a metal collar circled the thin column of her throat.

"Oh my God," Nadia whispered.

Clara, Anya and Tristan were at the doorway a second later, a gasp coming from one of them.

"Is this real?" Aidan sounded hoarse. "Is this *real?*"

Mateo started typing, the sound drifting into the background behind Issac's thundering heart. The video rewound to Jonathan's office, then crept forward as Astasiya stepped into the hallway.

And the room appeared again.

Fast-forwarded to the present, where Amelia remained on the floor.

Alive.

"Amelia," he whispered, his eyes glued to the screen, time ceasing to exist. "That bastard has Amelia."

He shook his head. "How is this possible?" They found records of a crematorium visit near the Hamptons estate. Eli had been found holding her ashes. "Is it a trick?" But no, it couldn't be. Astasiya wore the camera. She wouldn't allow Jonathan to play such a cruel joke, clearly didn't believe it herself by the way she kept moving around the room.

And she appeared to be speaking to Amelia.

Why wasn't there sound attached to the recording?

Would he hear the agony in her voice? Would it match her broken body?

"Can you zoom in on her neck?" Aidan asked, his tone one of reason and practicality and not at all similar to the voice rioting in Issac's head.

Amelia's battered face and neck appeared, black-and-blue marks marring her pale skin. Aidan said something about her collar, his words drowning behind a volcano of fury erupting inside Issac's head.

He couldn't concentrate on anything beyond the image on the screen.

Amelia is alive.

Fuck.

How is this possible?

Eli had been holding her ashes that day. Her rings were in the urn.

But Jonathan had staged it all.

The sick fuck had kept Amelia in the CRF underground for the last six years while Issac focused on his plans for revenge rather than saving his sister.

Because he thought she was dead the entire time.

Oh God, Amelia…

Would she ever forgive him?

"We need to get her out of there," he breathed, interrupting whatever the others were saying. "We need to go now."

He started moving, only to have Aidan step into his path, his hands landing on Issac's shoulders. More words were spoken, a whisper of sound that Issac couldn't understand over the water rushing through his ears.

"We need to go," he repeated, his hands fisting at his sides. "We need to get her the fuck out of there!"

She was alone.

Hurt.

Beaten.

"I'm going to kill that son of a bitch," he growled, picturing Jonathan's smug face. Fuck, he'd kept this from Issac for over six years. Kept his sister prisoner after killing Eli. And pretended to be his *friend.*

Lava poured through Issac's veins, fueling him to push against the wall blocking his way. He wanted to throttle Jonathan, rip him apart, burn the remains, and force the man to watch the entire time.

"…protective wards," someone said.

"…be smart about this."

"Issac, this isn't…"

"You're not… clearly."

"Stop."

The words hardly registered, only one thought driving him forward. *Save Amelia.*

Agony struck his chest, sending a blast of energy and pain through his limbs. His head spun, his hands still fisted at his sides.

The world trembled around him.

Darkness prickled his vision.

A cloud of thoughts all drenched in agony.

My sister is alive.

And I left her there…

Tortured.

Alone.

Scared.

I failed her.

He had to make amends, to fix—

A loud clap thundered through his mind, yanking him from his thoughts. The ceiling appeared above him, followed by Aidan's furrowed brow and a very concerned Tristan.

"Did it work?" Lucian's voice came from the left, startling Issac.

The Hydraians had all returned to Hydria this morning.

Yet all four Elders stood inside Issac's study. In his condo. In New York City.

What the hell…?

"He's back," Balthazar said, voice low, his expression concerned.

Back? Issac repeated. *Back from what?*

"We need a plan." Aidan's voice held a note of urgency in it. "I want her back as badly as you do, trust me. But if we go in there now with our emotions high, we'll die. Or worse."

Issac frowned as he sat up, his head throbbing. *How did I end up on the couch?* His desk sat several feet away, unoccupied. Everyone else stood around him.

"You were hell-bent on saving Amelia," Balthazar explained. "You wouldn't listen to reason."

"I don't…" Issac blinked at the now-black screen—the same one he'd held only moments ago. "Turn it back on."

"We need a plan," Aidan repeated.

"I get that," Issac replied shortly, having heard him the first time. "Now turn on the bloody computer."

"Stas already left." Lucian moved in front of the desk, his imposing body taking on an intimidating stance. "She's on her way here, hopefully with helpful information."

Issac shook his head as if to clear it. "On her way back? She was just in that bloody room with Amelia."

A room he needed to save her from.

He started to stand, only to have Balthazar push him back down. "Take a deep breath, Wakefield. We all want to get her back, but it has to be the right way."

"How are you even here?" Issac demanded, confused and irritated. "And where's Astasiya?"

Aidan handed him a bottle of water. "Drink that. It'll help."

Issac narrowed his gaze. "Tell me what happened." Because he'd clearly lost time somehow. It was the only explanation for the miraculous appearance of the Elders and for him waking up on the couch. He took a sip to appease his maker, demonstrating he was calm despite the insanity surrounding him.

Aidan blew out a breath, taking a step back. "You became fixated on Amelia and wouldn't listen to reason, so—"

"I subdued you," Nadia finished with a grimace. She stood just inside the doorway with Clara acting as a shield in front of her. Both women appeared wary of his reaction.

Understanding tightened Issac's shoulders. Nadia possessed the ability to knock a person out by delivering a psychic blow. The agony he felt hadn't been from emotions but from *her*.

"Why?" he demanded.

"To stop you from doing something stupid," she replied, sounding only slightly apologetic. "You can't just storm in there, Issac. You'll die, or worse."

"We all want her back, but we need to approach this strategically," Aidan added. "Now, we've already begun analyzing the device on her neck, as well as mapping out the underground from Stas's video surveillance."

"The artillery room will be an issue." Lucian folded his thick forearms. "We'll be at an extreme disadvantage, even if we enter armed."

Aidan nodded. "I agree. Have you found anything else that may be of use, Mateo?"

"Still searching for records on the device," Issac's progeny called from another room. "From what I've gathered so far, it's an explosive collar of some kind." He appeared in the doorway with his laptop, his uneasy gaze landing on Issac. "It'll detonate if she leaves the CRF by force."

Fuck.

Issac ran his fingers through his hair, his throat working as he tried to digest all the information. Saving her had been his only thought, his only priority. But now that his initial shock had dissipated, logic overrode his mind.

"Can the device be removed without detonation?" he asked, his voice hoarse.

Mateo shook his head. "The files are all truncated, even on Jonathan's hard drive. I can only find high-level details, like one-sentence or two-sentence summaries in each log. It's almost as if he's reporting the information to a superior—perhaps the benefactor—while keeping the full files on his own personal device. Not his laptop, because I checked that, but something else."

"I wonder—"

"Issac!" Astasiya's yell interrupted Aidan's reply, her voice holding a touch of panic that pierced Issac's heart.

His legs were moving before he registered the action, heading down the hallway into the main room of his condo to find Astasiya panting in the living area. Her wild gaze met his, tears streaking down her cheeks. She dropped her bag and collapsed into his open arms. He held her tight, his lips brushing her forehead, her hair, her temple.

"W-when you didn't answer… I thought… Oh God, I thought you were on your way to the CRF. I tried to stall, but… I couldn't stay there. When he let me leave, I taxied straight here." She shuddered violently, her shoulders hunched over in a way that hurt his heart. "A-Amelia… Issac, she's alive. Jonathan i-is… *Fuck*."

"It's all right, love," Issac whispered, his palm sliding over her back. "You're all right." Just murmuring those words helped heal a part of him he hadn't realized was wounded. Despite the revelation about his sister, he felt oddly whole again, as if Astasiya's presence had soothed him somehow.

My other half.

"We have to get her out of there." Astasiya gripped the lapels of his jacket, tugging as she pulled back to meet his gaze. "You saw her, right? You saw her?"

Issac swallowed and nodded. "Yes. We saw her."

Astasiya sagged against him again. "I was so worried you might go after her, but the runes… the guns… the Sentinels…" She shook her head. "I couldn't help her, Issac. I wanted to, but I couldn't. I didn't know *how*."

"You did the right thing," Aidan replied, joining them in the living area. "Had you attempted to save her, Jonathan would have placed you in a similar predicament, or worse."

"He's right." Issac continued rubbing her back, his heart thudding in his chest. "We can't react emotionally." Even if all he wanted was to march into that building and rip Jonathan's head from his body.

I will kill him.

But it would be the right way.

With planning.

Because they needed to play this smart.

Once they had Amelia back, Issac would destroy Jonathan and everything the man had ever created. Starting with the CRF.

"I…" Astasiya cleared her throat. "I… I might have a suggestion."

CHAPTER THIRTY

What is Elizabeth Watkins?

Issac listened intently while Astasiya detailed her discussion with Jonathan, telling them everything from the video—which she didn't believe—to the job offer.

"So that's why I suggested we recruit Issac," she concluded from her seat beside him on the couch. "Because it might give him access to something that can help us free Amelia."

"I still vote we just storm the place and torch it to the ground," Alik said with a shrug. "Not many would consider it a loss."

"Too many innocent lives," Lucian replied casually. "It would also attract Osiris's attention, something I'd prefer to avoid."

Yes, and the only way to take on the CRF as a collective unit would be to involve the Hydraians. Which could be perceived as an attack since the Ichorians considered New York City to be their home.

Issac ran his palm over his face and blew out a breath. "It was a smart move, Aya," he admitted. "It'll grant me closer access to Jonathan and his organization, which we can use appropriately." Not only to free Amelia, but to demolish the CRF empire.

Aidan nodded from the chair across from him, his hands clasped in his lap. "If you can earn his trust, we might be able to locate the device with the missing files and find out more about his mysterious benefactor."

"It also serves as a way to protect Stas while she's undercover as a Sentinel," Lucian added. "Which I consider to be a requirement."

"A requirement?" she repeated.

"Yes. You are a future Hydraian, and if you're going to risk your very valuable life by playing double agent in a city full of Ichorians, then I am entitled to several requirements for your stay. The first being your protection."

Astasiya's eyebrows lifted. "I'm not property, Luc."

"No, but you are a powerful fledgling and a future asset to Hydria. I take that very seriously, as should you." The not-so-subtle reprimand in his voice had Astasiya's shoulders tensing.

"We can work through the semantics at a later point," Issac interjected, his arm tightening around her shoulders. "For now, let's review our options. How do we free Amelia?"

Lucian crossed his ankle over his opposite knee, the chair beneath him resembling a throne more than a recliner. "If we storm the CRF tonight, we have a thirty percent chance of saving Amelia. That's a success rate that does not account for the collar that may or may not detonate upon exit. Not to mention the external consequences involving the Conclave, as well as giving up a valuable playing card—Stas's double agent status."

"It's not the most strategic response," Aidan agreed. "We need additional information on the device, plus a more detailed layout of the CRF's underground. The video footage only accounts for maybe a tenth of the estimated square footage beneath the building."

"Meaning we require more surveillance to establish a better plan," Lucian translated. "As much as it pains me to say this, rescuing Amelia tonight would not be in her best interest or ours."

Issac's chest ached, his instincts warring with reason.

He'd left his sister there for too long already and continued to fail her every second he remained here. Yet, it would not help her if he were captured, or worse, killed.

I'm going to slaughter Jonathan for this.

Losing Amelia had been the worst experience of Issac's life.

Knowing that she was alive and he couldn't save her was worse.

Astasiya flinched beside him, reminding Issac that he held her hand.

"Sorry," he whispered.

"I understand," she replied. "I want revenge, too."

"Well, you're really going to want to kill him now," Mateo announced as he entered the room with his laptop, his expression grim. "I was sorting through the files, looking for anything that might be able to help us, and I found something you all need to see." He set his computer on the table, the image on his screen one Issac recognized immediately.

Astasiya's intake of breath confirmed she did as well. "That's Owen."

Mateo nodded and brought up a file with a handful of words on it, starting with the date of Owen's murder.

Order executed by JF at 00:00.

Assignment completed by GS at 04:00. Visual confirmation attached.

"That confirms Jonathan ordered his death, but not why," Aidan said, studying the document.

"Yes." Mateo clicked another button. "But I found this, too. From about a week before."

JF: It's been brought to my attention that Owen Angelton is not only residing in New York City but has also befriended the roommate of a valuable CRF asset. We believe he is using her for access to information. Suggested action is termination.

GS: Assigned project to Sentinel Charlie.

CC: Suspicions confirmed. Owen Angelton is too close to the asset and requires termination.

GS: Task to be handled personally.

Astasiya's hand was at her mouth. "The date at the top is the day I mentioned inviting Owen to dinner after graduation."

"Which would imply they hadn't known of his existence in the city until then," Issac deduced. "Then who funded the bar?"

"An excellent query." Aidan stared thoughtfully at the screen. "It's potentially a bogus file, but I can't determine a purpose for it. Have you found anything else on him?"

Mateo shook his head. "These are the only two referencing his name. I also searched for the bar, dates corresponding to when Owen befriended Stas, anything on Stas and Elizabeth living together, and a variety of other items, and these are my only findings thus far."

"Confirming this to be a crime of circumstance and not related to a history of working together." Lucian's lips flattened. "That's both comforting and disappointing. What have you found on Elizabeth?"

"Nothing." Mateo sounded frustrated. "Not even a file name."

"Why would there be information on Lizzie?" Astasiya asked.

Right. Issac hadn't covered that topic with her yet. "We suspect Elizabeth is a product of the CRF. Likely a failed experiment, or perhaps a successful one. We don't actually know."

"A *what*?" She pulled away from him, her eyes wide. "You think my best friend is an experiment? And you didn't think to tell me that until *now*?"

"As Issac said, we don't know for certain." Aidan used a soothing tone that did nothing to dispel the fury radiating from Astasiya.

"I've had my plate full with explaining our world, and to be honest, this detail escaped me." Along with surely another dozen or so items. Alas, this particular one was something he should have told her. "For what it's worth, Elizabeth is completely unaware of everything. From the way she behaves, it's clear she considers herself human. And maybe she is. The only thing we know with certainty is she is in no way biologically related to Lillian and George Watkins. Until roughly seven years ago, they didn't have a daughter. She merely showed up one day."

Astasiya's mouth opened, then closed, then opened again, and she just shook her head. "I need a drink." She pushed away from him and headed toward the kitchen.

Issac sighed, standing. "I'll fix it."

"Allow me," Balthazar said with a look that had Issac pausing midstep. *Trust me*, his brown eyes implored. *Please.*

Issac studied him for a long moment before giving a nod. *I'll give you ten minutes.*

He returned the nod, his lips twitching in gratitude.

Balthazar could grate on even a saint's nerves, but when it came down to matters of the heart, he was a loyal friend. Issac trusted him. And most importantly, he trusted Astasiya.

~*~

Lizzie is a CRF experiment.

A simple statement, easily voiced, yet completely forgotten.

How?

Stas shook her head and started looking through cabinets for liquor. Preferably, something a hundred proof or higher. The stronger, the better.

"There's a wet bar in the living area, but as I imagine you need a few minutes to yourself, may I interest you in a glass of wine instead?" Balthazar's warm tones flowed through the kitchen, causing her to bolt upright from her crouched position by the island. "Or there might be some bourbon in one of the guest suites across the hall, if you prefer."

She frowned. "Guest suites?"

"Where Issac usually entertains his conquests," Balthazar murmured, a twinkle in his gaze. "Only family and close friends are allowed in his actual penthouse." He found a bottle in the fridge and showed it to her. "A white from Northern Italy? It's one of Issac's favorites."

"You know a lot about him," she observed, folding her arms. Yet, they bickered like rivals. Issac's distaste for the mind reader was palpable.

He chuckled as he found a corkscrew on his first try. "It's a brotherly relationship, I assure you. I care quite a bit about him, which is the reason I'm risking my life in his condo at present. Has he told you about my other gift yet?"

She shook her head.

"Can you grab two glasses from the cabinet behind you?" He nodded with his chin toward the wood door in question.

Stas plucked two crystal wineglasses from the shelf and set them on the island.

"I control emotion," he said while pouring her a small amount. "Taste this and let me know if it suits."

"You control emotion?" she repeated, taking the glass.

He nodded. "I do. The extent of it matches my ability to read minds, meaning I can hear and control for several miles."

That's overwhelming, she thought as she sipped the cold liquid. *Mmm, citrusy.*

"I hear approval," he murmured, smiling. He filled himself a glass before topping off hers and sliding it back across the marble. "And yes, it can be overwhelming, especially when someone I care about is distraught or conflicted." He glanced pointedly at her. "Would you like to know how Issac feels now?"

She wrinkled her nose. "Seems an invasion of privacy, doesn't it?" If Issac wanted her to know how he felt about something, he'd tell her.

"Sometimes we need a little nudge to express our emotions, Stas. Especially when we're not accustomed to them." Balthazar leaned on the island with one forearm resting across the marble countertop, his opposite hand swirling his wine. "I've known Wakefield for several centuries, and would you like to know how many women he's let into his personal quarters?"

She swallowed a healthy sip of her wine, unsure if she wanted the answer. Issac's reputation as a playboy didn't bother her, nor did it really thrill her. But she couldn't hold his past against him.

"One," Balthazar said, even though she never replied. "You, Stas. Which is why you can imagine my surprise when he took you to his bed, rather than to one of the other suites on this floor, after your Nizari poison incident. This relationship between the two of you has been unique from the beginning."

Stas set down her now-empty glass and leveled him with a look. "Why are you telling me all this?"

"Because I want you to understand how special this is, Stas. What you have with Issac is unlike anything he's ever experienced, and he's going to make mistakes, such as not telling you about Lizzie up front. But he's giving it his best effort and he adores you. Try not to be too angry with him for it. You've both had an emotionally draining day. I suggest you work it off in an active manner rather than a negatively reactive one." He finished his wine and collected their glasses, placing them in the sink.

Issac entered, his expression sheltered as he took in the bottle on the counter. "Aidan and Lucian are going through all the files Mateo downloaded to memorize and sort through the details."

"Yes, I hear them," Balthazar said, his lips curling down. "Some of the project names are disturbingly cryptic. Aidan is toying with anagrams in his head, which makes it worse."

"Most days, I do not envy your talent," Issac admitted, a hint of a grin glimmering in his sapphire eyes.

Balthazar shrugged. "No worse than seeing the fantasies of a million people at once, I imagine. Speaking of…" Sin danced through his features, causing Issac to growl low in his throat.

"Continue down that path and I'll turn it into a nightmare you won't soon forget." He glanced pointedly at a set of knives on the counter.

"That's just cruel."

"You thinking I'd ever let you top me is wicked, too."

Stas blinked, the image forming behind her eyes unbidden. The two of them in bed together would be—

"Explosive," Balthazar finished for her. "And next time I'll imagine you topping me, Wakefield. Just for fun." He winked before sauntering out of the kitchen, completely unfazed by the glower Issac sent after him.

"Is he, uh, serious?" Stas couldn't help asking.

"Balthazar never jokes about sex," Issac muttered. "So, unfortunately, yes. And he's been suggesting it for nearly three centuries now."

Her lips parted. "That long?" *And it's never happened?*

"He knows it's an impossibility, which only makes it more fun for him." Issac sighed and ran his fingers through his hair before meeting her gaze again. A beat passed between them, and a hint of wariness settled across his features. "I'm sorry, Aya. I should have told you about Elizabeth earlier. With everything else requiring an explanation, I didn't think about it. And now with Amelia…" Pain flickered in the depths of his gaze, sending an arrow through her heart.

His sister wasn't just alive, but was being held captive by the man he despised. Issac must feel so angry and guilty for not searching for her, for not saving his sister. And that was all made worse now by his inability to go after her.

Because as much as everyone hated to wait, Aidan and Luc were right. They needed a plan founded on strategy, not emotion.

"I'm sorry," Issac repeated softly. "I didn't mean to keep it from you."

Oh, Issac. He mistook her silence for anger. But she didn't have it in her to be mad at him. Not after everything they'd been through.

She moved past the counter and wrapped her arms around him, choosing actions over words. Because he looked like he needed a hug, and the way he clung to her in response proved it. His lips fell to her neck, his nose buried against her skin as he held her tightly.

"Aya," he breathed.

"I'm not upset," she whispered. "I understand."

"I should have told you."

"Yes," she agreed. "But I know now. And it only fuels my decision to go after Jonathan. He's taken too much from us. He won't take Lizzie, too." Her roommate might be an experiment, as they called her, but she was still Stas's best friend. "I won't let him hurt her."

Issac remained quiet for a long moment, his arms a protective band across her lower back, his mouth heated against her neck. "You want to take the job."

"I do." It was the only logical course. She would learn more about the CRF Sentinel program, the underground, and the experiments and feed all the details back to the others. "Those files are somewhere," she added. "If Jonathan lets me get close enough, I'll find them." And Mateo would equip her with the means necessary to do it. "We'll destroy him, Issac. And we'll find the information we need to save those we care about. It's our best move."

His exhale scattered goose bumps down her neck. It was long, low, and hot.

"You're so strong, my Aya." He kissed her pulse and lifted to press his forehead to hers. "This won't be easy."

"I know." It would be the hardest task of her life. Even harder than saying goodbye to her parents. "But we don't have a choice." She needed to do this for Owen, for Lizzie, and for Amelia. And she knew Issac felt the same. "It's the right decision."

"Yes," he whispered, his exhale a breath against her lips. "We're in this together."

"Always," she agreed.

"Always," he repeated, brushing his mouth against hers. Electricity hummed across her skin, his kiss sealing an unspoken promise between their souls. He repeated the action, sending a jolt through her bloodstream. And again, this one harsher, more urgent.

"*Issac.*" His name was part plea, part vow. She didn't know what she wanted, but it translated to a desperate sound in the back of her throat that he silenced with his tongue.

His fingers knotted in her hair to angle her head to where he desired, his kiss intense. Hard. Thorough. Possessive. He put everything he owned into their embrace, and she returned every emotion with one of her own.

Pain.

Sadness.

Heartache.

Confusion.

Joy.

Because while she'd experienced hell over the last few weeks, she'd also been introduced to a passion unlike any she'd ever known.

"I need you," he whispered, lifting her onto the counter and stepping between her legs. "Fuck, I need you, Aya." His hands were on her pants, his thumb on the button. "Distract me, please. I can't think anymore. It's driving me to insanity."

The beseeching quality in his voice said everything.

Issac wanted to lose himself in passion, to forget the present, to forget the hopelessness of Amelia's situation, to forget his inability to help his sister escape.

And he'd chosen Stas to help him through it.

To provide him with the release he needed from reality.

She would never deny him. Somehow, at some point, he'd become a part of her, adhering himself to her heart and soul and binding them for eternity. Their future didn't matter in the present.

All that mattered was the here and now, the heavy emotion flourishing between them, and the passion only he could unleash in her.

She kissed him again, her fingers threading through his hair as she answered him without words.

Take me.
Use me.
Love me.
I'm yours.

Chapter Thirty-One

Blood Vows

Issac lost himself in Astasiya's mouth, her tongue doing things to him that he could hardly comprehend, let alone describe.

He felt possessed.

Adored.

It was exactly the distraction he craved. She was his cure to the madness lurking in his thoughts. The only one keeping him grounded. His rock.

It terrified him.

Floored him.

Left him vulnerable in a way he'd never experienced.

Yet, she also strengthened him.

The convoluted combination drugged him, shadowing his mind and soothing his soul. All he could do was enjoy the afterglow and take what she readily gave, to sink into her body and connect them on a level that shouldn't exist.

Mine.

The impossibility of their relationship no longer mattered. Issac adored a challenge. They would figure this out. Somehow, someway, they would make this work.

He led her to his room, not caring at all that they still had company in the living area, and ordered her to strip beside his bed. Her blouse and bra fell to the floor. Her boots, socks, and pants followed. Then her lace thong, an item he should have removed with his teeth, fell to the top of the pile, leaving her naked and flushed before him.

Perfection.

Curved in all the right places.

Confident.

Legs for days.

His ideal woman, his partner, his Aya.

"On the bed, darling," he murmured, his gaze running over her in a heated wave.

That she obeyed him thrilled him all the more. Her stiff nipples and quivering thighs said she returned the sentiment.

Her blonde hair spilled over Issac's pillows, her gaze hooded as she watched him loosen his tie. He considered binding her wrists to his headboard, knowing it would leave her open and exposed to his touch.

But he needed her hands on him tonight. Her lips. Her tongue. Everything she had to offer.

He tossed his tie onto the ground beside her clothes and began unfastening his cuff links. Astasiya's green eyes flared with desire as she watched, her tongue dampening her swollen lower lip.

"Spread your legs," he demanded, needing to see her aroused flesh.

She complied on a moan that went straight to his cock. He adored that sound, enjoyed even more the damp haven between her thighs.

Issac slowly unbuttoned his shirt, prolonging the anticipation and admiring the flush creeping over her skin. She'd not balked as he strode her past the others in the living area, fully trusting him to shield their presence from everyone in the room. He hadn't even needed to explain; she merely knew.

Their connection only intensified the intimacy flowing between them, her faith in him fueling his need to fuck her.

Mmm, no, not quite the right word. He was craving something slower, more thorough, and underlined in passion.

Her gorgeous eyes danced appreciatively over his chest and abdomen, his shirt falling to the floor behind him. Followed by his belt, pants, and boxer briefs. His shoes and socks were long forgotten, leaving him naked as he knelt on the bed.

Astasiya reached for him as he crawled over her. He took her mouth in a kiss meant to brand, to own, to possess, his tongue demanding reciprocation and devotion. She conceded on a groan, her nails digging into his shoulders, her legs wrapping around his waist. Slick, wet heat met his erection, her body more than ready to take him despite their minimal foreplay. And as much as he wanted to take his time, he also needed to feel her, to take her, to claim her.

She cried out as he slid into her on a harsh thrust, her back bowing off the bed. "Issac," she breathed, her body trembling beneath him. "*Fuck.*"

"Too much?" he murmured, his lips tracing her jaw.

"Not enough." She pressed into him, forcing him deeper, her heels digging into his ass. "More."

"Mmm." He drew his nose across her cheek, his mouth tasting her skin as he went. "What if I prefer slow?" He demonstrated with his hips.

She growled in response. "Don't hold back on me now."

"Maybe I want to worship you." He continued the unhurried motion, driving them both mad and loving every minute.

"Liar," she accused, breathless. "Gentle isn't in your nature."

"Care to test that theory?" he asked softly.

He swallowed her responding groan, his tongue parting her lips to engage her in a passionate dance between their mouths.

Fuck, he adored kissing this woman. It satisfied him on a level he didn't know existed until her. And the way her hand curled around the back of his neck, holding him in place, suggested she felt the same.

He palmed her cheek, his fingers sliding into her hair. She tasted like mint, her tongue determined against his. Her nails against his nape spurred him on, her hips rising and lowering to meet his measured movements.

No rushing.

No fucking.

Just adoration.

Every touch, nip, and lick was his way of cherishing her. He'd never done anything like this with a woman, had no idea he would enjoy it, but with Astasiya, it came to him naturally. She would be the only one he'd ever indulge in this manner—the only one he'd ever revere.

So thorough, tender, and mind-melting.

His heart pounded in time with hers, sweat trickling between them not from the physical strain but from the thriving emotional connection.

"What are you doing to me?" she whispered, her lips brushing his with each word. "God, Issac, I feel… I feel like I'm on fire."

"Mmm, it's addictive," he agreed, his cock throbbing for release inside her despite the leisurely penetration. "Kiss me."

"I am." Her tongue followed her words, entering his mouth and dueling once again with his, lighting him up from within. His fingers curled in her hair, tugging. She reciprocated in kind, competing with him and proving herself his equal even while submitting to his assault below.

My Aya.

He sank his teeth into her lower lip as she unleashed a delicious moan. He fucking loved that sound. His hips drove into hers, the pace deliberate and right, his lips curling as she moaned again.

Glorious.

He felt every quake, every squeeze, every groan as he brought her closer and closer to orgasm. The intensity nearly undid him, his skin slick with the force of their lovemaking.

"I'm close," she whispered.

"I know," he mouthed, keeping his movements steady and complete. "Say my name when you come."

Her nails scored his back, her slick walls tightening around his shaft. It felt amazing, perfect, exactly the way it should.

"Take me with you, love," he murmured, thrusting deep and hard. "Come with me."

"Issac..." She froze for one tantalizing second, her muscles cementing around him, and then released on a wave of quivers that shook him to his very being.

Her name left his lips on a guttural growl that rumbled between them as they dove headfirst into a cloud of ecstasy and wonder together.

The power of it shocked him, sending trembles through every limb as he spasmed inside her, marking Astasiya as his in the most masculine of ways. She clamped down around him, her body forbidding him to leave, her nails firmly embedded into his back, and everything about it felt *right*. A mutual claiming. Their bodies joining as one while their souls bonded on a plane of their own existence.

And Issac wouldn't have it any other way.

"You're mine," he whispered, his mouth tracing the words against her throat. "I'm never letting you go." His incisors pierced her skin, pulling her essence into his mouth and solidifying the pact on instinct alone.

She writhed beneath him, her lower half reacting to the endorphins pumping through her bloodstream and sending her into another orgasm. His name rent the air on waves of her passion, telling the world who owned her.

"More," she begged. "Everything, Issac. Give me everything."

He gave in to the urge to fuck her—hard—his cock seeking the heaven of her tight sheath and blissful warmth. Each stroke drove them to oblivion, her blood euphoric on his tongue. They were lost in each other, in the moment, in how they felt together.

Time became obsolete. Thought no longer processed. Only sensation and emotion ruled them now.

Rapture masked the pain of the past.

Agony melted into sensual bliss.

Their moans mingled intimately, their hearts beating as one.

And sometime, a long time later, they finally paused to breathe, his forehead touching hers, their bodies a tangled mess beneath the sheet. Somehow they'd ended up on their sides facing one another, Astasiya's leg strewn over his hip, his cock lodged deep inside. She panted against him, sweat glistening across them both, her lips pulled up into a drowsy smile.

The lack of sound and visuals in his condo said they had long been left alone, something he would thank his friends and family for later. Because he needed that—*this*—with Astasiya. She grounded him, healed him, strengthened him.

"What was my life before you?" he sighed, his arms going around her.

A laugh escaped her, the sound hoarse and tired. "I think I should be the one asking that. A month ago, graduation was all I cared about. Now…"

"Your life is forever changed," he finished for her, his fingers running through her hair and twisting the strands behind her ear. "How are you faring, darling?" he asked softly. So much had happened over the last few weeks between finding out her future path, Jonathan's intentions, the truth about Owen's murder. *My sister being alive.*

"I'm overwhelmed," she admitted, her green eyes glistening with sincerity. "I'm also furious, like I want to break something or someone." She studied him for a long moment, a serious quality overtaking her features. "I understand your desire for revenge, how you could justify using another for the sake of vengeance."

He ran his thumb over her bottom lip. "Mmm, yes, my perfect pawn." He met her gaze again. "But you know this relationship between us is no longer a charade, that these emotions run far deeper, yes?"

She nodded. "I do, but I'm still the right tool in this equation. Jonathan offered me the job, Issac. All I have to do is formally accept it, and I'm in. You wanted to destroy him from the inside. We now have the opportunity to do so, with you at my side."

His fingertips lightly traced her jaw, the shapely lines alluring and strong, just like her. "You're certain this is the path you prefer? Because it will be a dangerous one, especially with you residing in the city near Osiris."

"Is there another choice?" she asked, her voice low. "You felt the impact of the runes, Issac. And you saw the artillery room. That's only the beginning of our obstacles. To free Amelia, we need more reconnaissance. What better way to gather information than by playing alongside the enemy?"

"Not to mention the ability to destroy his organization from within," Issac added, his shoulders falling. "But it means leaving Amelia with him." Just saying the words battered his heart, sending an ache to his gut. "I don't know if I can do it, Aya." Even now, knowing the risk, part of him *needed* to rescue his sister.

She cupped his cheek. "We'll save her, Issac. I promise. But it has to be the right way. You will be of no use to her dead."

He swallowed, knowing she was right and hating it all the same. Issac rolled to his back and Astasiya followed, her chin resting on his chest, her thigh draped over his. "How did she seem?" He wasn't sure he really wanted the answer, but needed it all the same. "Was she…?" He swallowed the rest of the words, his throat thick with emotion.

"She dreams of blue butterflies," Aya whispered. "And she seemed… strong."

He glanced down at her. "Strong?"

Astasiya nodded. "She thought I was another of Jonathan's games, whatever that meant. But she didn't feel like playing. She said a few odd things, but mostly, she came off as empowered."

His breath shuddered out of him, a weight lifting from his shoulders. "She's not broken."

"No," she replied. "But she was wounded."

"I saw the bruises." He'd memorized them as well so he could inflict the same ones on Jonathan, only with deeper coloring and blood. "I'm going to kill him."

"I know." She cupped his jaw, her gaze meeting his. "And I'll help you." Promise radiated from her irises. "We can do this, Issac. We'll save her. Together. And then Jonathan will pay for everything he's done to those we care about. To Amelia, to Lizzie, to Owen." Her voice cracked on the last name, but her expression never wavered. "I need to find out what he's done to Lizzie, to avenge Owen's death. Just as you need to destroy him for what he's done to your sister and everyone else. Let's beat him at his own game."

"You want to be the queen on my board," he murmured.

"An upgrade from a pawn."

"Indeed." He pushed her onto her back, hovering above her on his elbows. "Does that make me your king or a knight?"

She cupped his cheek. "It makes you my partner and fellow mastermind on the playing field. My very own demon." The latter was said with a twinkle in her gaze. "You're mine, too, you know."

"Am I?" he asked, amused.

She nodded. "You—"

An urgent knock on his bedroom door cut off her words, the unexpected intrusion causing Issac's gift to engage throughout the building.

Mateo.

Aidan.

Jacque.

"They've found something," Issac said, his jaw tightening. "That's the only reason they'd return." And from the image he was reading from Mateo's mind, he understood the urgency of their interruption. With Astasiya's assistance today with the card trick, Mateo had been able to build a back door into Jonathan's system through the hacking connection. Despite her taking the device home, his presence in the CRF network remained.

"What is it?" Aya asked, sitting up as Issac rolled off her.

Asset Seven. Based on Aidan's analysis, that classification applied to Amelia, something he conveyed with a series of images to Issac.

"My sister," he said, his tongue suddenly too thick for his mouth. "There's a new file with today's date."

The color drained from Aya's face, her hands automatically bringing the sheets up to cover her chest. "Oh no… What does it say?"

Issac swallowed thickly, his heart fracturing in his chest. "The orders are to move her."

"To where?"

"We don't know," Aidan said, entering the room. "Which means there's no other option. You need to accept the job. And Issac will be working with you."

EPILOGUE

Gabriel

"You realize this would be easier if we just told her the truth, yes?" Ezekiel asked, a glass of amber liquid in his hand. He'd ordered a second for Gabriel that remained untouched on the bar countertop.

"Not yet," he replied. "Not until she's grown into her gifts."

"You Seraphim sure enjoy the long game, hmm?" Ezekiel took a sip, his leather jacket and long, dark hair drawing notice from the females at the bar. Not that he noticed or cared. The former Nizari assassin would sooner kill the gawkers than fuck them. "At least Issac will be helping us guard her with Owen's untimely retirement."

"I'll be assisting as well through the CRF," Gabriel replied.

"Assuming she takes the job."

"She will." He was certain of it. "Jonathan just issued orders to move Amelia to somewhere remote."

"Why do I suspect that was your idea?"

"Actually, his son suggested it under the guise of hiding her from Stas." Gabriel had been impressed. It demonstrated that the younger Fitzgerald may have a future yet. "Jonathan wasn't too keen on it originally, so I may have urged him to reconsider."

"You always harbored a soft spot for Amelia," Ezekiel mused. "Not that I blame you. She's lovely, from what I recall. Pity what Jonathan has done to her."

"You're missing the point entirely. I didn't do this for Amelia." *Not directly, anyway.* Gabriel hid his grimace by taking a sip of his drink, allowing the burn to etch a path down his throat. *I've been around humans far too long.* He was losing his grip on practicality. "The reason I pushed the suggestion was because it will entice Stas to join the CRF, and it also frees me up to be more involved in her training."

"Providing additional security."

"Precisely." He finished the amber liquid in his glass and signaled for another. "But yes, I admit that it also gives Amelia a break from the torment." No one should endure the type of treatment Jonathan had inflicted on Amelia. If Gabriel didn't need the Ichorian alive, he'd have killed the bastard years ago.

"Who did Jonathan assign to babysitting duty?"

Gabriel's lips actually curled, a feat considering they rarely moved, aside from being used to speak. "Have I mentioned that being my favorite part of the whole plan?" He rarely deviated from the course, but this, well, *this* he rather enjoyed contriving.

Ezekiel cocked a brow. "Who did you set up?"

He met the assassin's gaze, brief amusement touching his chest. "Tom Fitzgerald." It served as a way for the CRF's CEO to punish his son for his recent "untoward" behavior and presented Tom with a unique opportunity. One Gabriel hoped he would accept. If Tom was the man Gabriel suspected him to be, then Amelia would be in far better hands.

Ezekiel chuckled, devious energy rolling off him in waves. "Oh, I bet he loved that."

"On the contrary, he's quite displeased. But of all the Sentinels, I trust him with her the most. He's the only one with a heart." And the only one with potential to prosper beyond the darkness. This would prove to be a test of sorts, to see how Tom handled it. Gabriel wished him luck. Because if he failed, Gabriel would have no choice but to kill the man.

"Brilliant," Ezekiel replied. "And I told you—you're soft on her."

Gabriel snorted. "I'm not soft." But, all right, maybe he wanted Amelia to escape. Just a little bit.

"Not even for Stas?"

A young girl flashed through his mind, one with big green eyes radiating pain and sorrow over the loss of her parents. Sethios and Caro.

Soon, he vowed, closing his eyes briefly. *I'll tell you everything soon.*

"Definitely soft," Ezekiel said, understanding darkening his gaze. He picked up one of the new drinks as they were delivered and raised it. "To fate."

Gabriel snorted. "Fuck fate." He clicked his glass against Ezekiel's. "To Skye's prophecy."

May it come to fruition, and soon.

Forbidden Bonds

Book Two

A Soldier is Born

15 Years Ago...

Blood.

Death.

Unspeakable things.

Shades of red and black coated the walls, pictures, and toys, but none of that compared to the gory mess on Tom's bed. His mother's lifeless eyes stared back at him as he cowered in the corner. He tried not to cry, but the treacherous tears leaked down his cheeks, rolling over his trembling lips to the soiled ground below.

"Come here, son." His dad engulfed Tom in a hug, holding him tightly as they grieved in silence. Father and son. A bond forged in birth and strengthened by death.

"Now you understand our purpose," his dad whispered. "Why we must fight."

Tom nodded. The monsters who did this were evil. They deserved to die.

"Your training won't get any easier," his dad continued, voice broken. "It will be brutal, and I will be hard on you, but I want you to be strong enough so that this never happens to you. I can't lose you, son. And there's only one way I can protect you."

By training to become the perfect soldier. A walking weapon designed to kill immortals. To seek vengeance for his mother's brutal murder. And to protect humanity from the evil on Earth.

Tom never understood his purpose before, why his father constantly pushed him away, but seeing his mother's mutilated corpse changed everything. It shattered his heart and left rage brewing in its wake. He would channel that emotion, sharpen it into a weapon for immortals to fear, and become a man who would make his father proud.

"I'm ready, sir. Teach me everything."

Chapter One

Welcome Home

Tom Fitzgerald hated this place. Memories hung in the air as he searched each room for suspicious items or objects. He held his pistol low with both hands, ready to shoot anything that moved. People were always trying to kill him—an occupational hazard. And his fledgling bloodline didn't help matters.

The phone in his pocket buzzed. He knew who it was without looking. That detour he took to grab a few things from the store hadn't gone unnoticed. Fucking GPS tracker.

He holstered his weapon after clearing the guest suite. It no longer resembled the childhood bedroom he remembered due to the renovations completed after his mother's murder. His aunt stopped by weekly to keep the place up and running, which was a waste of time. No one lived here. Tom owned the family property and wanted nothing to do with it. Too many raw emotions were floating about, and no amount of redecorating would fix that. If it were up to him, he'd sell the place, but his father forbade it.

Tom hit the speed dial on his phone as he walked toward the front of the cabin. His dad, who also happened to be his boss, picked up on the first ring and didn't bother with a greeting.

"Your report is late."

The days when Tom enjoyed his father's brief calls were long gone. A consequence of their last few months together.

"I didn't realize I was on a deadline," Tom drawled. "Maybe you should have been clearer." He suppressed the urge to add *asshole* to that statement.

"My directions were more than clear, Sentinel. Has the asset been moved to the appropriate quarters?" Of course his father would want to know this first. He was obsessed with the *asset.* Tom eyed the sedan parked in the gravel driveway through the front window. *The asset is contained and unconscious, sir.*

"Is this how this is going to go?" Tom wondered. "With you checking up on me every ten minutes? Because we both know I'm more than capable of handling this job."

"Like how you handled the Stas situation?"

The reminder of why his father sent him on this mission made him cringe. All Tom wanted was to show Stas the truth about her blood-sucking boyfriend, but that plan backfired big-time. He doubted she would ever trust him again, and now he was stuck in the middle of Upstate New York on a babysitting mission. *At least* she *is safe here…*

"The asset and I are on site. What other information do you require, sir?" Tom learned a long time ago that formality was the best way to placate his father. And he wanted nothing more than to end this conversation and go about his business. The sooner he completed this mission, the sooner he could go back to preparing for the inevitable.

"Is the asset secure?"

Tom looked at the black car outside. "Yes." *Just not in the way you want.* The unconscious woman didn't need to be restrained, which was why he removed the handcuffs the second they crossed the New York City limits. And fuck the idea of keeping her in a cage as his father wanted. This mission would operate according to Tom's plans, and that did not include locking a female up like an animal.

"Why did you stop at the pharmacy?" his father asked.

Ah, and now we get to the real reason you called me. "I needed a few things."

"Such as?"

Tom recognized that steely tone. John Fitzgerald's innate ability to force the truth out of others only worked in person, but that didn't stop him from attempting it over the phone. *Nice try, Dad.*

"What, you want a list? Toothpaste, shampoo, deodorant, some painkillers for the headache I know you're going to give me. Oh, and I got some cereal for tomorrow because I didn't realize Rosalie was going to stock the fridge for me." He'd noticed the abundance of food when he cleared the kitchen area. It brought a brief smile to his face. He hadn't seen his aunt in over a year. As his mother's only sibling, she felt obligated to take care of this cabin even though he told her not to. But family could be insistent.

"You'll need to keep her away from the asset, Sentinel." The "or else" part of the statement hung unsaid at the end of that sentence. Tom already knew what his punishment would be should he fail: assassinate the civilian. His father wouldn't care that Rosalie was family. If anything, he'd consider it the perfect reprimand.

"Understood." Tom had no intention of anyone meeting his charge. If his aunt insisted on visiting, he would join her in town for a meal. He walked outside toward the car. "Anything else, sir?"

"Nothing for now, but I expect a detailed report every evening until I say otherwise. Also, Anita will likely be in touch regarding a visit. She needs more samples."

Tom eyed the female sleeping in the backseat of his sedan. He knew what "samples" meant, and it made his stomach roll. Arguing would accomplish nothing, and the relationship with his father couldn't be more tenuous lately. Tom needed to lie low and follow orders if he wanted his freedom back.

"I'll await her call, sir." A few blood samples never killed anyone. Besides, he'd be there to monitor the situation. All good.

"Excellent. Do try to behave, son."

He refrained from rolling his eyes. "Yes, sir."

His father hung up without a goodbye. *Typical.* Tom pocketed the phone and opened the back door. Amelia's dark hair hung in unkempt ringlets over her face, and her threadbare shirt hit her midthigh. No pants, shorts, or anything underneath.

"Un-fucking-believable," he muttered not for the first time since this nightmare started. He was thankful for the exclusivity of their location as he gathered the woman in his arms. His father suggested keeping her in the basement, but Tom had other ideas.

He laid her slender form on the double bed in the guest room, then went outside to retrieve his belongings from the car. Agent Stark said Amelia would be unconscious for a while but failed to give a stringent timeline. Tom hoped she woke sooner rather than later, because the girl needed a shower. His father preferred she live in her own filth, but that treatment ended now. Hence his detour to the store.

Back inside, he opened his suitcase in the master bedroom and pulled out a T-shirt and a pair of gym shorts. He held them up and frowned. *Too big.* The woman needed to eat more. He swapped the shorts for a pair of boxers and added *buy her some clothes* to his mental to-do list. Grabbing the shirt and plastic bag of bathroom essentials, he ventured into the guest room and froze.

She was gone.

He dropped the items on the bed and checked the window. *Locked.* With the exception of a few boxes, the closet was empty as well. *What the hell?* The tiny cabin consisted of two bedrooms and a single bathroom. How had she escaped without his notice? He walked into the hallway, noted the unoccupied restroom and checked the living area. The front door hung ajar. So not only did she get up without him hearing her, but she also walked outside. That's what he got for staying up all night to drive here.

"I don't have the patience for this shit," he muttered as he headed outside. Amelia didn't have proper clothes or shoes, so she wouldn't make it far in the woods. The closest neighbor lived over three miles away, and the nearest city was a half-hour drive. *Secluded* didn't begin to cover it.

Keys in hand, he started toward the car. She most likely ventured down the long gravel driveway, hoping to find the road. The rocks against her bare feet would slow her down. And if she went into the grass, he'd see her from…

Movement in his peripheral vision gave him pause at the car door. He squinted and frowned. Wisps of dark brown hair danced in the warm breeze as his charge twirled in a circle near the lake about fifty yards from the side of the cabin. What was she planning to do, swim to her freedom? Because she would be in for a surprise when she realized it only led deeper into the wilderness.

Tom pocketed his keys and moved toward her. She didn't seem to notice his approach, too lost in the bliss of the sun shining down on her. Her smile made him hesitate.

There was no question. Despite her frail condition, Amelia Wakefield was a gorgeous woman. Her long legs, subtle curves, and angelic face gave her an otherworldly appeal any man could appreciate. He suspected that was the reason his father withheld shower privileges and forced her to wear that hideous shirt. All the Sentinels were male, which posed a risk around an alluring female. Especially one considered to be the CRF's greatest asset. Not that any of the men would necessarily act on it, but better to avoid the situation than to welcome it.

The girl paused mid-twirl to stare up at the sky and laughed. The broken sound echoed with disuse and went straight to his gut. *What the hell have I gotten myself into?*

~*~

Amelia Wakefield loved this dream. It was nothing like her usual trips into the darkness. First, she woke in a real bed, and now, she stood outside. *Fascinating.*

The sun warmed her hair and face and felt so real. It had to be the drugs. Agent Stark mentioned they were different than the normal pills he smuggled in for her during the healing process. She hadn't really cared when she swallowed them. Anything to get rid of the pain. *Then that strange girl came in, talking about my brother…* A hallucination like this one? Her mental faculties usually recovered at unnatural speeds, just as her body did, a perk of being immortal, but maybe Jonathan's beating had jarred her worse than she originally thought.

Amelia shook her head and spun around again. She didn't care to think about what anything meant. This moment meant too much to her. When was the last time she experienced the outside world? Years, maybe? Decades? Time was an elusive concept in her cement prison.

She stopped her dancing to fondle a leaf. The lifelike texture made her grin. *Beautiful.* She needed to ask Stark to give her these drugs again. It would make her next beating worthwhile.

"Amelia."

She jumped at the unexpected voice and whirled around. Of all the men she expected to visit her in this dream, Tom Fitzgerald was not one of them. But it didn't truly surprise her. Amelia thought of the man often, a side effect of him being the only decent person in her life at present. He brought her things in captivity, like food and water. She recognized his role as the good cop to his father's bad cop. Another game, no doubt. But she enjoyed playing along. It wasn't like she had anything else to do.

"Hello, Tom." Her voice came out softer than she expected and hurt a little. Almost as if she hadn't spoken in days. *Could this dream get any more realistic?*

"What are you doing?"

"Enjoying the fresh air." She twirled, wishing her shirt would transform into a sundress. One would think she would have more control over her dreams. Maybe she could build a bonfire and burn the offending fabric.

"When do you suppose I'll wake this time?" she wondered aloud. "Stark warned me the drugs were laced with a sedative. Perhaps I'll sleep longer than expected?"

Tom's hands were in the pockets of his jeans as he studied her with those intense brown eyes. *So much like his father.* But the cruelty in his father's gaze didn't linger in Tom's dark depths.

"Stark gave you drugs?" he asked with an arched brow.

"Mmm," she murmured and faced the sun again. "He always gives me something, but this is definitely the best. It feels so real." She knelt to touch the lake again. The water was cool against her palm. "I want to stay here forever and never wake up."

Silence met her reply, making her wonder if Tom disappeared. Then his boots appeared beside her at the water's edge. He crouched down and rested strong forearms on his knees. The gray shirt he wore stretched across his broad chest and strained over impressive biceps. If he wasn't the son of a monster, she might call him handsome. As it was, she would kill him—and all the others—at her first opportunity.

She touched the metal choker around her neck and grumbled, "This bloody thing follows me even into my dreams." If she ever got it off, she'd make Jonathan Fitzgerald eat it.

"Amelia," his deep voice rumbled, "this isn't a dream."

"What?"

"You're not dreaming."

She smiled and shook her head. Of course she was dreaming. What else could this be? There was water, sunshine, and trees. "I wish for you to go now." No need for the handsome Sentinel to spoil her temporary reprieve from reality.

"I wish I could, but I'm stuck here for the foreseeable future." Tom rose to his full height beside her and held out a hand. "Let's get back to the cabin. You need a shower, and I need to get some sleep."

She frowned at his long, masculine fingers. He wiggled them once in an impatient gesture that matched the tick in his square jaw. When she stood up, she found the top of her head barely met his chin. The heat radiating from his broad chest felt very real, so real that she pinched her thigh to test his theory. A slight pain radiated up her side, making her eyes widen. "I'm not dreaming?"

He gave her a small smile. "No, Amelia. You're very much awake."

She stumbled back and nearly lost her footing over a rock near the pond's edge. *What is this?* A new CRF illusion? A simulation of some kind? She scanned their surroundings for a clue but saw none. Where were all the researchers and Sentinels?

"What game are we playing?" Because this was obviously another one of Jonathan's tricks. A manipulation meant to drive her insane. That seemed to be his favorite pastime of late.

Realizing she had no intention of taking his hand, he dropped it to his side. It drew attention to the pistol on his hip. "Not a game, Amelia. Just a new location."

She peered up at him. "A new location?" What did that mean? She was no longer in the CRF basement? *Impossible.*

He palmed the back of his neck and blew out a breath. "Yeah, it's a long story, but in summary, we're staying here for a while."

"In the middle of the woods," she added. Where serial killers took their victims to dispose of them. Had Jonathan finally gotten what he wanted through all those tests? Was she no longer of use to them? *Am I here to die?*

She stared into those dark eyes that gave nothing away. Tom looked so much like his father, but more muscular, and taller. She took a careful step back, which had him raising a blond brow.

"I'm not going to hurt you, Amelia."

Said the wolf to the lamb. She had trusted Jonathan once, and he'd done unspeakable things to her. Why would Tom be any different? They were in the middle of nowhere, where no one could hear her scream. She moved another step back while evaluating her options. If they were indeed away from the CRF, that meant she had a chance of escape. She just needed to take down the armed Sentinel in front of her. *Easier said than done.*

"I can see what you're thinking, and…"

She didn't wait to hear the rest of Tom's statement, but took off in the opposite direction through the woods. Her bare feet screamed as she stumbled over rocks and uneven terrain, around the lake and toward whatever was on the other side of all those trees. She ducked and swerved to avoid branches and heard Tom's muttered curses following her in the wind as she moved aimlessly through the wilderness.

He was too close for comfort, making her push harder and faster. Her lungs screamed for air as she tore through the underbrush as fast as her body would allow. Her size was an advantage, allowing her to move between the trees at an angle he couldn't. *I'm finally escaping. Maybe this is a dream after all? Why else—*

Her thought was cut off as she slammed into the trunk of a tree. She started to fall, but a pair of sturdy hands caught her before she could hit the ground.

"Ow," she mumbled as she massaged her bruised nose. Peeking between her fingers, she realized it wasn't a tree at all, but Tom's muscular chest. He'd somehow gotten in front of her.

"Are you done?" he asked, his voice patient.

Amelia's breaths came in heaves from the mad dash through the woods, and he wasn't even panting. He hadn't even broken a sweat. Realizing her body was pressed far too close to his, she pushed away with a huff and stumbled when he let her go.

"Don't…" She paused for a necessary inhale and started again. "Don't touch me."

"You ran into me, sweetheart."

"Because you… you… teleported or something." She waved a hand like that explained it all.

"You were running in circles around a group of trees, Amelia. No teleportation required." His condescending tone made her want to hit something. *Like his face.* Deciding that sounded like a solid backup plan, she launched herself at him. If she could get ahold of his gun, she could shoot him. It didn't matter that she'd never used one before. How hard could it be? She attempted to slap him but found both of her wrists caught in one of his sturdy hands.

"Seriously? Who taught you how to fight? The Three Stooges?"

She had no idea who or what that was but sensed he was making fun of her. She brought her knee up as hard as she could and hit his thigh. It felt like kneeing a steel wall, but the abrupt shift of his legs to protect his sensitive parts doubled as a distraction. Twisting a wrist free from his grasp, she curled her hand into a fist and aimed for his defined cheekbone. It connected with a hard thunk that sent pain shooting up her forearm.

"Christ, Amelia!" He grabbed her again, but this time he pressed her up against a tree with his legs braced on either side of hers and both of her hands in one of his. Despite the aggressive hold, he maintained a gentle touch as he examined her throbbing knuckles. The pain was minor compared to what Jonathan had done to her over the last few years, but her ego was bruised. Here she was, bleeding, broken, and out of breath, and Tom wasn't even fazed. She wanted to crawl into a hole and hide. *I'm hopeless.*

"Doesn't look broken," he murmured after moving the thumb of her right hand. It was the one she used to punch him. *Unsuccessfully.* "Next time, curl your fingers like this, and put your thumb on the outside." He demonstrated with his free hand. "If you were stronger, you would have sprained or broken your thumb doing that. Now, are you done?"

She glowered up at him. It wasn't like she could move with his big body pressing her up against the tree. What choice did she have?

"Look, even if you get away from me—which you won't—that metal collar around your neck is tied to an object in the cabin. You get more than two miles away and it explodes. And don't get any ideas about me taking it off of you. It's not going to happen." He pushed away from her with those final words and dropped her hands. "Now, do you prefer to walk or be carried?"

She eyed the pistol on his hip again, making him smile.

He folded his arms and cocked a brow. "Try it. See what happens, sweetheart."

"Stop calling me that."

Tom chuckled and turned away from her with a shake of his head. "Suit yourself, *asset*. I'll be making breakfast."

She stared at his muscular back as he walked toward the cabin. It was still within sight, which meant she hadn't run nearly as far as she thought she had. A glance down at her bloody feet told her maybe he was right about running in circles. Could anyone blame her? She'd been a lab rat for who knew how long in a tiny room without windows. Exercise hadn't been part of her daily regimen.

Why am I here? Why move me now? She wondered if it had anything to do with the blonde woman who visited her cell after Jonathan's beating.

"*He'll come for you. Even if it means burning this place to the ground.*" Were those words real? Did Issac know she was alive? She pressed her palm over her aching heart. Was her brother finally coming for her after all this time? Jonathan showed her articles and photos of Issac, a way of confirming that her brother had moved on and no longer mourned her. It hurt at first, filled her with both fury and hopelessness, but she understood. Everyone thought she was dead. She couldn't blame them for moving on with their lives. But what if that woman hadn't been a hallucination? Did her brother know the truth? Would he save her from this hell?

The hope blossoming in her chest hurt. She didn't want to trust it. But why else would Jonathan move her if not to hide her? If she was here to die, surely Tom would have killed her already. *Unless he wants me to suffer…*

She stared after his retreating form as he entered the cabin. He hadn't bothered to turn around once. Whatever his purpose, he was confident she would follow.

The damn choker. She pressed her fingers to the cold, abnormal metal around her neck and sighed. She didn't doubt for a second the truth of his statement. The CRF's technology was far superior to anything she had ever seen, and the simple metal necklace repressed her immortal gifts. She couldn't shift while wearing it. She couldn't even impart wisdom.

The tears welling up behind her eyes disappeared with a blink. One gift Jonathan had given her was the ability to hide her emotions. She was an expert at deception, something that could be a benefit in this situation. Fighting Tom physically wouldn't get her anywhere, but mentally? She was up to that challenge. And if they were truly alone out here, that gave her an advantage.

Issac's searching for me. She could feel it. All she needed was to gain Tom's trust, and then she could use it to garner her freedom. Men were easy to manipulate, especially when it came to sex. She shivered. Seduction was a weapon she never contemplated in captivity, but with Tom? She could consider it. He was the only thing on this planet Jonathan cared about other than himself, which made him an ideal candidate. She would use Tom to escape and exact some semblance of revenge on the man who ruined her life. It wouldn't be easy, nor would she enjoy it, but it would be worth it to escape this hell.

She gazed at the sky, hidden above the cloud of trees, and closed her eyes. *Eli.* He would understand this sacrifice and forgive her this sin. He had to. She didn't have a choice. Then she could avenge him properly by murdering Jonathan.

Decided, she started toward the house and stubbed her toe on a rock. The pain reminded her that she was not dressed to impress in the ratty old shirt and bloody feet.

"All right, so I'll shower." She regarded her scrawny legs and thin arms and pursed her lips. If her limbs looked like that, what did her face look like? She hadn't seen a mirror in, well, forever. But her hair was tangled, not smooth, and her skin felt dry and chapped.

Good thing Tom said they were here for the unforeseeable future, because she would need some time to ready herself for this task. Not only to improve her appearance, but also to figure out how to entice the Sentinel. All of her experiences were tied to Eli, but she'd seen other women seduce men. How hard could it be?

CHAPTER TWO

Doctor's Call

Tom's white lie about Amelia's collar worked like a charm. It contained no explosive, only a mechanism that disabled her psychic abilities. Was it a kind lie? No, but he preferred it over locking the woman in her room. And it ceased her foolish escape attempts. She needed some serious training, and the last thing he wanted to do was accidentally hurt her.

They fell into a quiet routine during their first week together, which suited Tom. He preferred solitary work, and he suspected Amelia wanted her space. They only spoke when necessary, and mostly during meals. The first few times he gave her food, she watched him eat his half before tentatively nibbling on hers. By day four, she started eating like a normal person, which he took as a sign that she was somewhat trusting their situation. Tonight, she opted to dine with him on the couch while he enjoyed a baseball game.

He wasn't sure how to react to the change in her pattern. She usually ran back to her room after finishing dinner, but she set the dishes in the sink and joined him in the living area instead.

Having a woman dressed in his shirt and boxers played tricks on his mind and made it difficult to focus on the game. Her dark hair held a healthier tint, thanks to the daily showers and the brush he had given her, and she had it piled in luscious waves over one shoulder. He swallowed thickly as she curled her finger around the strand dangling against the side of her breast. The innocent gesture provoked all manner of inappropriate thoughts, making him regret not locking her in the guest room.

This mission better end soon. And not just because of the alluring woman beside him.

Tom finished his beer and went to the fridge to retrieve another. He'd offered one to Amelia their second day together, and she gave him a look of such grave offense that he didn't bother again. Apparently, she wasn't a beer girl.

"I don't understand the purpose of this sport," she said as he returned to the couch. He intentionally put an extra foot between them. Attractive she might be, but she was still an asset, and dangerous. "At least football has a defined timeline of two halves. This nonsense goes on and on, and nothing interesting happens. How are you not bored to tears?"

Her English accent was sexy, but the same could not be said about her words.

"Okay, first? We call it 'soccer' here." He took a swig of beer before continuing. "Second, have you not heard of the Yankees? Nothing boring about them, sweetheart." He inwardly cringed. *Why do I keep calling her that?* The endearment just seemed to roll off his tongue every time she walked into the room, and he couldn't seem to stop it. The look she gave him said she liked it about as much as he did.

"I told you not to call me that."

Yes, and I told myself not to call you that, either, but you see how well that worked out. Clearly, his mouth had a mind of its own.

"Yes, ma'am," Tom replied. He gave her a mock salute with his bottle to loosen his tense muscles and went back to enjoying the game. Or tried to, anyway. He loved baseball, but her presence absorbed his focus. Feeling her eyes on him, he glanced sideways at her. "Yes?"

"You never answered my question."

"Regarding?"

"How are you not bored by this? It's mind-numbing."

He set his bottle down on the end table and turned toward her. "What would you prefer to watch, Amelia?" Not that he would change the channel. The one benefit to this new assignment was all the free time, and he planned to use it appropriately.

"Hmm, let's see. I haven't had the opportunity to watch a television in, honestly, I have no idea how long. But there has to be something better than this."

"You realize you're insulting one of New York's proudest accomplishments, right?"

"Should that matter to me?"

He snorted. *It was so much nicer when she stayed in her room.* He opened his mouth to say just that, when his pocket buzzed. Time for the evening check-in with dear old Dad. Picking up the controller, he muted the television and answered the phone with a "Yo."

"Very professional, son."

Tom grinned. "You know, Dad, I try. I really do." Amelia tensed beside him, her blue eyes going round at the device in his hand. Yeah, he could imagine she wasn't very fond of his father. *Join the club, sweetheart.* "To what do I owe the pleasure, *sir*?" He couldn't help the sarcasm on that last word.

These nightly conversations only seemed to further drive the wedge between them. His father used to call when Tom had done something to impress him, but now he only phoned to remind him how much he'd fucked up. It hurt to an extent, but it also pissed him off. Hence his attitude. The sooner his father disconnected, the sooner he could continue his discussion with Amelia. Someone needed a lesson in why insulting the Yankees was poor form.

"Have you been drinking?" his father asked.

"What, no status update first? The asset is fine, by the way. And, yes, I am enjoying an adult beverage. Anything else before I hang up?"

The silence on the other end of the line told him he'd overstepped. He envisioned his dad's expression turning darker by the minute. The familiar look used to terrify him, but now it only served to irritate him.

When Tom returned from the Special Forces to work for the CRF, his father had been so proud and excited to show him the ropes. They worked well as a team at first, managing the Sentinel unit and discussing future plans. As they delved into his father's pet projects and the company's secrets, however, Tom's respect and admiration dwindled. Then he discovered Amelia in the research wing, and everything changed.

Her kinship to his biggest enemy didn't detract from the fact that she was an innocent woman in captivity. He'd made his feelings known that day and openly disagreed with his dad for the first time ever in his life. The heated argument fractured their father-son bond, and their relationship had yet to recover.

His stomach hurt with the memory as his blood boiled. The convoluted response left him unsure how to feel—furious or guilty. He spent his every waking moment trying to please the only person in his life who loved him, and he betrayed that over a disagreement. But looking at Amelia now, with her wide eyes staring at the phone by his ear, he couldn't help but feel a tiny bit of pride for sticking up for her. Not that it had done any good. Here she sat, a prisoner in a new outfit, awaiting her fate.

He ran a hand through his hair and blew out a breath. *Time to play ball,* he thought. If his father pulled him from this mission out of anger, he would send him somewhere worse, and he didn't want to know what mindfuck his father would throw at him next. Tom intended to survive, with or without his father's help, but his contingency plan wasn't ready yet. He needed freedom to complete it, which meant he had to obey. For now.

"I'm watching the Yankees game," he said, voice devoid of humor. "And enjoying a beer, yes. Sorry, sir."

"I see." His father fell silent for too long. *Something bad is coming.* "Please be advised that Doctor Patel and her team are five minutes out. Prep the asset and await further instructions." The line went dead.

He stared at the phone. "Well, shit." An hour warning would have been great. "Yeah, I'm going to need you to follow me to the guest room."

Her eyebrows shot up. "Excuse me?"

"Doctor Patel is coming for samples, and I doubt she'll approve of you hanging out with me in the living room."

The indignation in Amelia's expression fled as her face paled. "Anita's coming?" Her soft voice sounded nothing like the stern woman of ten minutes ago.

"Yeah, and she'll be here any minute." He made a shooing motion toward the hallway. "Come on. I need to ensure the guest room looks unlived in."

Some of the color returned to her cheeks as she puzzled over his statement. "What? Why?"

"Because I'm supposed to be keeping you in a cage in the basement," he muttered as he started toward her room.

"There's a basement?" she asked as she followed.

"*That's* your question? Seriously?" He took in the guest room's immaculate appearance, then glanced around for anything personal. Their clothing routine consisted of him leaving fresh shirts and boxers in the bathroom, and Amelia leaving folded laundry in its place. "Nothing incriminating. Go ahead and sit on the bed."

He didn't wait to see if she obeyed, but went into the bathroom to stow the feminine items, like her brush and deodorant, under the sink. If Anita's team noticed them, he would say they belonged to his aunt. Then he would take on his father's persona and ask why they were snooping. Sometimes it paid to remind CRF employees who he was destined to become.

Grabbing the laundry basket and Amelia's towel, he moved into the master bedroom and tossed everything in the closet. The telltale sound of tires over gravel greeted him as he returned to the living area. Rocky driveways were a good warning system. He flipped off the television, picked up his beer, and relaxed against the wall with one ankle crossed over the other. His favorite pistol rested in its permanent spot on his hip, and there was a knife hidden in his left sock. Just in case. He only disarmed when he was naked, and even then, he had a weapon within arm's reach.

Agent Stark entered first in his trademark jeans and T-shirt.

"Thanks for knocking," Tom drawled. He should have known his father's favorite Sentinel would lead Doctor Patel's entourage. "Aren't you supposed to be training Stas?" That was the whole point of this babysitting assignment. Tom guarded the asset while Stark trained the CRF's first female Sentinel. Another punishment from his father, because he knew Tom wanted to manage his friend's training. He loved the woman like a sister, and it hurt not to be there to help her.

"I gave her the night off. She has to maintain her cover with Wakefield."

"Ah." Tom sipped his beer to hide his grimace. Issac Wakefield made him want to play target practice with his favorite handgun. "And how's the training going?"

"I didn't come here to chat, Fitzgerald. Where's the asset?"

Stark stopped two paces in front of him and lifted a blond brow. They were similar in size and stature, but the stoic man lacked a sense of humor. Something was very wrong with the Sentinel, his ability to heal with touch notwithstanding. Whatever he was, he wasn't human.

"Why the late-night visit?" Tom wondered. "Why not wait until tomorrow?"

"Because I was in the middle of a case study when your father decided to move my asset," Anita Patel announced from the doorway. The tiny woman boasted a no-bullshit attitude. Tom supposed she had to be that way to lead the CRF's research wing. She managed multiple assets at headquarters, most of which were rogue immortals who committed heinous acts. Amelia was the anomaly, a victim of circumstance.

"Doctor Patel." He nodded a greeting to the dark-haired woman. Two male researchers entered behind her with bags and averted their gazes. Typical behavior for CRF employees. Not only was Tom a Sentinel, but he was also their future CEO.

"Hello, Tom." The doctor bowed her head in a gesture of respect, something she also did with his father. "Where's my test subject?"

His hand tightened around the beer bottle—a bizarre reaction to an innocent question, as was the knot forming in his gut. Playing warden meant guarding the asset from potential escape and discovery. It did not mean protecting her. But his fingers twitched like they wanted to caress his favorite gun. *Not a good sign.*

"What are you planning to do with her?" It wasn't like him to pry, but he couldn't help himself. Anita clasped her hands in front of her and pursed her lips. She didn't seem to care much for his interest. *Well, too fucking bad.* "I only ask because this cabin isn't exactly built for extensive lab research, and I don't have a lot of supplies on hand."

Understanding brightened her dark gaze, and she gave an approving nod. "Of course. I have all the supplies I need to run my routine tests and obtain a few samples. But it may take a little longer than usual, so I'd like to get started."

"Right." Tom shrugged to loosen his stiff shoulders. What she said seemed legit, but something about this situation didn't sit well with him. Ignoring the strange vibe, he gestured to the hallway behind him. Better to get this over with as soon as possible. "She's in the guest room." At Anita's raised eyebrow, he added, "I didn't think you'd want to do this in the basement. Bad lighting." Growing up around a human lie detector made him skilled at telling half-truths.

The doctor nodded, pleased. "Excellent. We'll let you know if we need anything." She snapped her fingers at the researchers, who trailed after her like obedient dogs.

Stark didn't follow, his expression void of emotion. Tom eyed the man over his bottle as he took another swig. *Yeah, definitely not mortal.* Not Hydraian or Ichorian, either. He suspected Stark was one of Anita's pet projects. That would explain his ability to heal through touch and his bizarre demeanor.

"Are you providing protective detail for Doctor Patel and crew?" Tom asked.

"No." Flat response with no elaboration.

"Okay, then." He finished his beer and tossed it into the trash bin in the kitchen.

He paused near the hallway to listen for any signs of struggle coming from Amelia's room but heard nothing. Doctor Patel administered his medical exam last year and was a complete professional, but something about her always struck him as dangerous. Morbid curiosity lurked in that woman's gaze, which was a typical trait for a researcher, but it rubbed him the wrong way sometimes. And tonight was one of those occasions.

The instinct to grab his firearm hit him again. Hard. "Any idea how long this is going to take?" he asked, ignoring the sensation. *What the hell is wrong with me?*

"Why?" Stark's light green eyes flicked toward him. "Do you have somewhere to go?"

Tom gaped at him. "Did you just make a joke?"

"Some might refer to it as a taunt."

"Or a joke."

Stark shrugged. "Sure. I'm going for a run."

"A run?"

"Yes. We're going to be here a while, and it was a long drive." He rolled his neck and shoulders while he spoke. "And I'm bored."

Because that's normal. "Okay. Have fun."

Those eerie eyes looked Tom up and down. "You know these woods better than me. Show me around, and I'll tell you how the training with your friend is going. And maybe we can talk about what I have planned."

Tom started. "You want me to go running with you?"

"That's what I said, isn't it?"

If it was any other Sentinel, he wouldn't have batted an eye. But Stark, the lone wolf on the team, asking him to go running? He never expected that. Maybe he really was bored.

Or maybe he's up to something.

His instincts warred. Leaving Amelia alone with the researchers felt wrong, which was ridiculous. His father was the one who enjoyed beating the shit out of her, not the researchers. She was safe here, away from the lunatic CEO of the CRF. And so far he hadn't heard any sounds coming from her room to indicate distress.

I'm overthinking this. A run would be good for him, and he wanted to know what Stark had planned for Stas. She might be pissed at him, but that didn't keep him from caring about her.

"Yeah, okay." The June heat would be hot as hell in jeans, but if Stark wasn't putting on jogging shorts, neither would he. Part of their conditioning was to train under unnatural circumstances. Sounded like they would do just that tonight. Together. He laced his tennis shoes and met Stark by the door. "After you, Agent."

~*~

Sadistic bitch.

Whatever nerve agent Anita stuck in Amelia's arm made it impossible to move or utter a sound. But she felt every single poke and prod as they explored her nude body with cold instruments.

The doctor loved testing the limits of Amelia's immortality. Pain management didn't exist in their sessions. It was all about seeing how much she could take before passing out, and she was on the verge of it now. Hence the smelling salts beneath her nose.

Time eluded her.

Minutes, hours, days…

Everything hurt.

The burning sensation crawling up her spine consumed her and fractured her thoughts into incomprehensible pieces. She wasn't sure how much longer she could win this battle against insanity.

Darkness loomed, waiting to take her to that place where she stopped feeling. She created it for moments like this where the pain became too much.

Her own personal drug.

Addicting.

Sating.

One day, her mind would go there and never return.

Would that be so bad? she wondered.

Yes… Jonathan can't win.

Anita's stern voice floated from above. Something about containers. Amelia couldn't be sure.

She screamed internally as someone inserted a knife between her ribs. Tears fell of their own accord from her unblinking eyes. This was what Anita wanted, and knowing that made her sick to her stomach.

One of these days, Amelia would kill her. She wondered what Eli and Issac would think of her violent fantasies. Kindness and formality were traits of her past. They wouldn't recognize the woman she'd become through this experience.

Ice hit her chest, followed by fire, as one of the research minions shoved a needle into her heart. She both craved and hated this part. It hurt like hell, but it meant her torment was coming to an end, and she would be able to move soon. Then the vomiting would start, followed by brief rest, and the inevitable mental countdown of when this would all start again.

She thought being in the cabin meant she would have a break from this torture. But no. Just hope playing another evil trick. She hated that tormenting emotion.

"Three, two…" Anita's voice grew louder with each number. "One."

Amelia gasped, taking in a much-needed breath, and shuddered against the plastic sheet beneath her.

"There, that wasn't so bad, right, dear?" Anita's smile was pure evil.

A litany of curses lined up in Amelia's mind, but her mouth refused to expel them. If she ever got her hands on the sadistic doctor, she would paralyze her, then pump her heart full of adrenaline and see how she handled it. A cough worked its way up her burning lungs to her throat, and the researchers rolled her to the side as she expelled the contents of her dinner.

No mortal could survive this treatment. As an immortal, she barely did. Amelia hated her mind's ability to heal in a fraction of a second. It held her on the edge of insanity during Anita's sessions, while keeping her lucid.

Unless I venture into the darkness…

Not tonight.

"Go fetch Agent Stark," Anita said after several agonizing minutes. The command was unexpected. Usually, she requested Stark's presence later in the process. Maybe Amelia needed to be healed before they began another round of testing?

"Ma'am." Stark's deep voice soothed her on a deep level. She craved his healing touch more than she wanted to breathe.

"I assume you've distracted Tom?" Anita asked.

"Yes, ma'am. He's on the phone outside talking to Stas."

"Good. Take the asset into the bathroom and clean her up. We'll take care of this mess."

So clinical and detached. *I hate you.*

A sturdy arm slid under her knees while another wrapped around her shoulders. She didn't look at the man as he carried her into the bathroom, nor did she meet his eyes as he set her in the bathtub. He kicked the door closed before kneeling beside her with a bland expression.

"Here." He held out one of his famous pills, and she opened her mouth without question. This was their routine, though she suspected he wasn't supposed to give her pain medication. There were a lot of things Stark seemed to do that he wasn't supposed to do. Like disappear into mist. He did that during their last healing session, much to her shock. She knew he could heal, but had no idea he could disappear. Or was that a hallucination?

He grabbed a cup from the counter, filled it with water, and then brought it to her parched lips. "Drink."

She swallowed the cool liquid and the pill before closing her eyes. Her immortal genetics healed her mind faster than her body, but Stark's touch would help the latter along. It would hurt, but she welcomed the eventual reprieve. Unless Anita planned to start all over again, in which case, this would be a long night.

Heat enveloped her as Stark pressed his palm to her shoulder. The energy exchange always tingled at first, then grew into an inferno that had her crying out on instinct. He pressed his opposite hand over her mouth to quiet the screams as he poured his power over her. Last time, it knocked her out, but her injuries weren't as substantial this round. Jonathan enjoyed inflicting internal damage. Anita preferred exterior pain. The woman loved to make Amelia bleed.

"Almost done, Amelia." His deep voice was a sweet caress, despite its lack of emotion. She couldn't figure him out. He did things that seemed counterintuitive to the CRF's goals, like letting that girl walk out of her room the other day. Assuming that conversation was real.

It had to be. Issac's coming for you… The conversation in her cement prison was bizarre, to say the least, starting with the way Stark vanished into thin air just before the blonde woman opened the door. Then all that talk about her brother romancing the girl with a dance? That sounded very unlike the Issac she knew, though the speech was right. But if the woman meant what she said about breaking her out of the CRF basement, why did Stark not intervene?

Unless…

Her eyes flew open as she met his glowing green gaze. "You're—" She couldn't speak because of his hand. *You're the reason I'm here*, she accused with a look. But why hide her in a cabin? Surely it would be easier to dispose of the girl who found her.

"Not everything is black and white" was his cryptic reply. "Go ahead and shower when you feel up to standing. I'll find your clothes."

He closed the shower curtain before she could say a word.

CHAPTER THREE

Target Practice

Tom hung up the phone as the researchers walked out of the cabin. They were grinning about something, but their mirth died upon seeing him. He rolled his eyes when they averted their gazes and scurried over to the car with a set of containers. *Blood samples. Gross.*

Stark exited next with their equipment bags. It didn't escape Tom's notice that it took two men to carry all that in originally. The assistants weren't big guys, but they weren't scrawny, either.

"The asset is taking a shower" was all Stark said as he passed him. He tossed the bags into the trunk like they weighed nothing before leaning against the massive jeep with his arms folded. The bulky man had changed his shirt. It was black before, and now it was red.

Why? They hadn't worked up that much of a sweat on their five-mile run. Instincts prickling, Tom started toward the cabin but stopped when Anita walked out. That fucked-up gleam was back in her gaze, making his gut churn.

"The asset is ready to be returned to her cell. Do you mind taking over from here? We need to get these samples back to the lab, and the clock is ticking."

"Sure." He kept his stance casual as his mind raced.

The run had done little to dispel his nerves, though his conversation with Stas had given him a temporary reprieve. He hated to admit it, but he felt an inkling of admiration for Stark. The stoic Sentinel had created a masterful training plan, and Stas sounded happy about it.

He didn't call her often, but this situation warranted a verbal update. She thought he was on a mission overseas, something he didn't bother correcting. Then her roommate stole the phone to give him a piece of her mind.

Lizzie Watkins was a close family friend and daughter of a CRF employee. She launched into a tirade about Stas becoming a Sentinel, of which she did not approve, and then lectured him about being safe while abroad. He had hung up with a grin and a shake of his head. She had no idea that immortals existed, and he intended to keep it that way.

"Fitzgerald." Stark gave him a nod. His version of a goodbye.

"Stark." He returned the nod, and the team disappeared into the jeep.

A wave of loneliness hit him as the headlights disappeared down the driveway. He considered calling the girls back for a longer chat but decided against it.

As much as his friends cared, they didn't truly know him and never would. A man with his background wouldn't be around long enough to experience such connections. Death loomed at every corner and haunted every dream, and every person in his life was a liability.

I should have stayed in the Middle East. At least there he had a true purpose. Just a man, a rifle, and his target. Peace.

With a sigh, he walked back inside. The bathroom was empty, and the guest room door was shut. He knocked and waited for a reply but heard none.

"Amelia?" He didn't like the way his arm hair stood on end. Violent memories tormented this cabin, and he suspected some fresh ones were made here tonight. When she didn't reply, he knocked again and cracked open the door.

"Are you all right?" He realized the stupidity of that question the second it left his mouth. Of course she wasn't okay. The woman was a prisoner of war.

His father kidnapped her as an act of revenge, but rather than use her to bring their real enemy to justice, he kept her in the research ward.

"You have to see that she is useful, son," his father had argued after Tom first discovered her. "Think of what we could do with her genetics."

"This is wrong," Tom had replied. "You have to know this is wrong."

The CRF wanted to replicate her unique gifts. The heated debated ended with a promise that Amelia was well cared for, despite the way she might appear. That lie crashed and burned when Tom found her beaten to a pulp earlier last week. When he confronted his father about it, he was reminded yet again that he didn't have any choice but to go along with it.

"Where would you go, son? The Ichorians want you dead, and the Hydraians won't protect you. Not after everything you've done. We're all you have. I suggest you play ball."

Shoving the vile words from his head, he pushed open the door to find Amelia curled in a ball in the corner of the room. Her damp hair sprawled around her frail frame and clung to her shirt. He wondered if Stark or Anita noticed she wore his clothes. If they did, he would no doubt hear about it from his father later.

A spot on the floor near the foot of the bed caused him to frown. He knelt to get a closer look, and his heart skipped a beat.

Fresh blood.

Flipping on the overhead lights, he investigated the room and found more blood on the furniture and walls. They resembled tiny specs to the untrained eye, but Tom recognized them for what they were. *It's even on the ceiling…*

"What the hell did they do to you?" The anger in his voice couldn't be helped. Seeing blood—in this room, of all rooms—made his head spin.

His mother's mutilated body sprawled out on his childhood bed.

Screams that he later realized belonged to him.

"Fuck." He staggered backward out the door and into the hallway wall. With his hands on his knees, he took several deep breaths to calm the nightmarish images. This was why he refused to visit this place. Hell lived here.

He stumbled into the kitchen to grab a bottle of water and guzzled it. With each gulp, the memories subsided, and reality resurfaced.

A friend once told him he had unresolved issues surrounding his mother's untimely demise.

No shit.

There was a reason he hunted rogue Ichorians, but his father wouldn't let him take out the one responsible. Issac Wakefield was too valuable alive, so his dad settled on taking Amelia instead. It seemed unfair to punish the woman for her brother's sins, but here they were.

Exchanging his bottle for a fresh one, he headed back toward the guest room with renewed purpose. His charge hadn't moved from the corner, but her blue eyes were bright with curiosity when he reentered the room.

He sat beside her and held out the water without a word. She accepted it with a suspicious look and examined the seal. Finding it unbroken, she opened it and took a sip. He leaned his head against the wall and closed his eyes. It'd been a long fucking day, and he was exhausted.

"For what it's worth, I'm sorry." He wasn't sure what else to say.

Who knew what horrors this woman had endured at the hands of his father?

Tom used to idolize the man, but he wasn't sure how to feel anymore. The man he grew up loving and admiring did awful things behind closed doors for reasons that remained unknown. Like beating the shit out of a female hostage. His father never justified his actions and instead reacted by assigning Tom as Amelia's babysitter. A test of loyalty? Punishment for disobeying orders? Only his dad knew the answer.

Amelia shifted beside him. Her leg brushed his, making him hyperaware of her actions. He could tell what she was planning before she moved. Eyes still shut, he caught her wrist an inch away from his firearm. "Even if you got ahold of it, would you know how to use it?"

"Maybe."

That's a no. He peeked at her through one eye. "First rule of firearm safety: make sure you know how to handle a weapon before you play with one."

Her frown was cute. It puckered between her brow and gave her an innocent appeal. "How hard can it be?"

He pulled the firearm off his belt and held it out for her. *I'm so going to regret this.* But it would be a fun diversion. Maybe.

"Show me what you would do with it." She stared at him like he'd grown three heads. *An accurate assessment.* He had no idea why he was showing her this, but it seemed the least he could do considering their situation. "Go on. Show me."

"Is this a trick?"

"No trick. Show me how you would use it."

"You're not worried I'll shoot you with it?"

"I know you won't." And even if by some miraculous measure she did, it wouldn't matter. His immortal genetics would kick in after he died, and he'd wake up tomorrow as a Hydraian. She had to know that.

Long, slender fingers slid over the metal in his hand as she gingerly took what he offered. He made no move to stop her, even when she moved back and pointed the pistol in his direction. By his calculations, if she pulled the trigger, the bullet would graze his ear and hit the wall. And that was only if she managed to hold the handgun steady, which she wasn't.

"What's next?" he wondered.

"You tell me where the device is that controls my metal collar."

He smiled. "No."

"Then I'll have to shoot you."

"Works for me." He rested his head back against the wall and closed his eyes again. "Let me know when you're done playing, sweetheart." There's that word again. A slip of the tongue. He never called anyone *sweetheart*, but it suited her.

Cold steel met his temple. "I told you *not* to call me that."

"And there's mistake number one," he replied.

"Excuse me?"

He grabbed her wrist in one hand and the barrel with the other and disarmed her in a swift move, all with his eyes closed. *Child's play.*

"Never get within arm's reach of someone who knows how to handle a gun, especially when you yourself don't know how to use one." He held out the sidearm in his open palm. "Try again." She snatched it from him and scooted away. He stretched out his legs and crossed them at the ankles. This was an excellent distraction from the memories threatening to overwhelm him in this room.

He heard her try to pull the trigger and grinned.

"As I mentioned earlier, know how to use a weapon before you try to take one. Which, coincidentally, would be mistake number two. While you're trying to figure out how to shoot me, I'd be disarming you."

He paused for a dramatic yawn.

"Oh, and if you managed to shoot me, you still wouldn't have the device to remove your collar." Not that there was one for her to find. "Which means you'd have to wait for me to wake up tomorrow, and I probably wouldn't be too thrilled with you."

A low noise emanated from her throat, causing him to peek at her. "Did you just growl at me?"

Her next move was not one he expected. Instead of aiming the firearm at him again, she threw it at his head. He caught it reflexively with one hand and gaped at her. "Well done."

"Oh, let me guess, *mistake number three.*" She did a poor representation of his voice. "Giving the predator back his weapon. You're a right arse, you know that?"

"A right…?" He trailed off on a laugh. She looked so indignant, glowering at him like that. What a pair they made, sitting in a room full of horrors where she'd undergone God knew what in the last few hours. He shook his head and holstered his favorite toy.

"For the record, throwing the gun at me was your smartest move because it was what I least expected. And since you couldn't use it for its intended purpose, you might as well create a weapon out of it. I'll consider this lesson a successful one." He pushed off the ground and started toward the door. Then he paused and met her blue eyes over his shoulder. "Everyone should know how to use a firearm. If you're interested, I'll show you tomorrow."

Probably not the wisest move on his part, but who the fuck cared anymore? This mission was a joke. He might as well have a little fun with it. And if he died in the process, it wouldn't be the end of the world. He'd just wake up immortal the next day.

~*~

Amelia studied the woman in the mirror. The bone structure was right, if a little hollow, but the eyes were all wrong. They looked haunted and darker.

She finished combing her damp hair and used a rubber band she found to pull it up into a ponytail. It felt good to have it off her back. The researchers occasionally cut her hair, but they were not proper hairdressers.

She slipped on the shirt and shorts Tom left for her on the sink and eyed the socks and shoes.

Those were new.

Did he intend for her to meet him outside? She recalled his offer from last night and frowned. Was he serious about teaching her how to fire a weapon? Why would he do such a thing?

The Elders never let her near the armory on Hydria, and Eli's weaponry in the house was off-limits. No, that wasn't quite right. They would have let her in if she asked, but she never had a need. She was surrounded by some of the most powerful immortals in the world. Why would she learn how to fight? No one expected a close family friend to betray them, least of all her.

She slipped on the socks and shoes and was surprised to find that they fit. The sneakers definitely didn't belong to Tom. No way would his over-six-foot frame fit in these tiny things. She hopped once and half grinned. Stilettos had been her go-to footwear in the old days, but she could get used to these. Even if they did look a little worse for wear.

Stepping into the hallway, she moved toward the music playing in the living area. It sounded grungy with a heady base and growly voices. Not her preference. She meant to continue her journey to the fridge to grab a bottle of water and a snack but froze upon spotting a shirtless Tom in the main room.

Oh, wow…

She didn't know bodies could move like that. It was some bizarre variation of a push-up that involved clapping behind his back and moving from side to side in rapid succession. When he popped up into a standing position, she assumed it was because he noticed her watching. She was wrong. He grabbed hold of a bar hanging over the doorway and lifted himself with ease into a pull-up. Amelia stood hypnotized by the muscles flexing along his back.

Eli had been a sight to behold in his own right but had a burlier frame. Tom's athletic form was leaner, more refined. *A human weapon.* He went back to the floor again to begin another series of exercises that left her mind boggled. She couldn't keep up with his reps or positions, but she enjoyed the way his body moved. No wonder he disarmed her so quickly. His reflexes weren't human.

After another set with the bar, Tom switched off the music and picked up his water. He turned toward her with the bottle in hand and paused mid-drink. Surprise flitted over his features at finding an audience. She tried to look away, but his rippled abdomen was even more impressive than his back. Her throat went dry as he squirted water in his mouth and swallowed. Oh, this wasn't good.

You cannot be attracted to him. Ever. But what woman in her right mind wouldn't fancy a man built like Tom? *A woman being held in captivity against her will.* Right, well, there was that. She'd blame the drugs Stark had given her last night for her lapse in judgment, but those wore off hours ago.

Giving herself a mental head shake, she forced her feet toward the kitchen. She grabbed a bottle on autopilot and noted the sandwiches in the fridge.

One plate each.

She chose the closest one and made to go back to her room with it, but a half-naked Tom stood right behind her. His skin glistened with fresh sweat, making her lick her lips.

All right, no. No, no, no.

She would not be attracted to him. Gorgeous he may be, but he was Jonathan's son. And her guard, for crying out loud.

I will not be tempted by this… this… god of a man. Especially not less than twenty-four hours after Anita's torture session.

So wrong.

"I see the shoes fit."

"Hmm?" She followed his gaze to her feet. "Oh, yes. Thank you."

He shrugged and reached around her to open the fridge. "I think they belong to Rosalie. She's about your height and occasionally stays here." His arm brushed hers as he snagged the other plate.

"Rosalie?" she repeated, ignoring the butterflies fluttering in her stomach.

"Yeah, she maintains the cabin for me." He shut the fridge behind her. "That's where the food came from, but I'll need to run into town to get more." He paused to study her. "If you give me your measurements, I can get you some clothes, too."

"Measurements?"

His gaze went to her breasts. "Yeah, for whatever." He hesitated a moment too long and turned around. "Just let me know what you need."

She followed him to the couch. "Are you offering to buy me essentials?"

"Essentials?" he repeated as he sat down. "Is that a fancy word for undergarments?"

"Like knickers?" She had a fetish for silk in her previous life but doubted she would fancy it now. It would be too soft.

His gaze darkened as he looked her over again. "Maybe it would be easier to let you shop online and have it delivered to town." He focused on devouring his lunch while she considered his statement.

Shop online? What did that entail? She had shopped in a store, but never online. "Do you mean the World Wide Web?" she asked after taking a few bites of her own sandwich. It was turkey and cheese, and much better than anything the CRF ever gave her.

"Uh, yeah. The internet."

"You can shop online for clothes?"

The look he gave her was a mixture of shock and pity. "Yes."

"But how do you try them on?"

"You don't. You shop based on your size."

"Size, like measurements." She gestured to her breasts on instinct, which made him choke on his food.

He took a long swig of water and stared up at the ceiling. "Yes."

"I have no idea what my American sizes would be, and I doubt my English sizes are still accurate." She regarded her scrawny form with a frown. She missed her natural curves.

"Exercise."

She blinked. "Pardon?"

"We'll exercise together. It'll help you put on a few pounds, and you'll feel better." He suggested it so easily, like it was the most natural decision in the world. "As for the sizing, I'm sure there's some measuring tape lying around somewhere. You can use it and order some clothes."

"With a computer."

He finished off his sandwich and cast her a sideways glance. "Yes, with me sitting beside you."

She almost laughed. If he thought she was going to reach out to someone using his machine, he was crazy. She barely knew how to type. "You'll have to show me how it works," she warned.

"Sure. But first, I'm teaching you how to use a firearm." He snagged their empty plates and took them to the kitchen. She ate the rest of her sandwich and trailed after him.

"You mean you were serious about teaching me how to operate your weapon?"

"Yes." He finished loading the dishwasher and grabbed another bottle of water. She supposed he needed it after all that working out.

"Not that I'm ungrateful, but why would you do that?" It seemed counterintuitive to keeping her here. Although, she couldn't shoot him until he removed the device. Was that the reason for his confidence?

He shrugged. "Because we have nothing better to do, and maybe I'm up for a challenge. Besides, it's not like you'll ever get the chance to shoot me, right?"

Arrogant arse. "Care to test that theory?"

His smirk said he wasn't worried. "I'm ready when you are, sweetheart."

"Now sounds good."

"Then I better teach you how to shoot to even the odds a little."

Her eyes narrowed. If her Hydraian gift for imparting knowledge could work in reverse, she'd steal all of Tom's gun skills and use them against him. Oh, and she would use her other gift for shifting and choose a huge male humanoid form to kick his arse. Brilliant.

Even if that was possible, you'd need to remove the collar first, her unhelpful conscious reminded her. *And there's also that tiny matter of not being able to shift anymore.*

That day when Anita blocked her ability to shift without the collar would forever haunt her.

No. I will not think about this right now.

Eventually…

No.

"Let's go before I change my mind," Tom said, interrupting her mental gymnastics.

Yes, let's do that instead. Thankful for the diversion, she nodded. If he wanted to teach her self-defense, she wouldn't stop him. Even if she did find it a bit odd.

Grabbing his shirt from the back of a chair, he tugged it on, picked up a bag by the door, and led the way outside. Distracted by all the muscle on display, she hadn't noticed the handgun strapped to his side. *Did the man ever go without it?*

"We'll start with the basics," he said as they walked. "The safety."

"Rule one: know how to use a weapon before you handle it," she parroted. That's what he told her yesterday.

Tom's warm chuckle provoked a shiver from deep within. *Oh, that's…*

pleasant.

"Right, but that's not what I meant." He stopped under the shade of a tree, dropped his backpack, and removed the pistol from his side. "You remember how you tried to pull the trigger last night and failed?"

Her cheeks warmed at the memory. His eyes had been closed when she tried to use his weapon, so he didn't know that she'd aimed away from him when she pulled the trigger. "Yeah, it didn't do anything."

"Right. Because the safety was on. Here, see this?" He pointed to a tiny switch-looking thing toward the top of the handle. "Switched this way means it's on. If you switch it this way, it's off."

"So you're saying I could have killed you if I switched it off."

"Sure. If your aim was right."

She folded her arms. "I was three feet away from you."

"Yes, and holding the firearm with one shaky hand. Had you hit me, it wouldn't have been fatal. But it would have hurt like a son of a bitch."

The cocky arse made her want to try shooting him again. And this time she would use proper aim. "Go on."

"Let's master rule one first." He handed her the gun. "Turn the safety off and back on."

She did as he asked with very careful fingers and kept the barrel pointed away from them. "Next."

He grinned. "Rule two: always aim the firearm at the ground unless you intend to shoot something."

Pointing the metal at the ground, she raised an eyebrow. "Better?"

"Yes. Let's talk about stance. Do you see that tree over there with the bull's-eye set up?"

She followed his gaze to the circles in question. Apparently, he'd prepped for their training while she'd slept. Intriguing. "Yes."

"Okay, I want you to put your left foot forward with your toe pointed down the range or, in this case, toward that tree. Good. Now bring your right foot back and angle it a bit. Uh, not so much." He kneeled to grab her ankle and moved it where he wanted it. "Do you feel stable like this?"

She swallowed as she met his gaze. The sincerity in those brown depths unnerved her. How could she hate him when he looked at her like that? That didn't make her feel stable at all, but she nodded anyway. "Sure."

He stood and eyed her form. "Uh, right. This would be easier if I can position your arms. Do you mind?"

He's asking permission to touch me? She couldn't remember the last time someone had given her the choice. Her heart fluttered in response, and she gave him a nod. *All right.*

A woodsy scent assaulted her senses as he wrapped his arms around her from behind and took hold of her wrists. This was not at all how she expected a man to smell or feel after exercising without a shower. The earthy undertone was actually quite pleasant, if a little distracting.

"Gun in your right hand. Good. Now you're going to lock your right arm like this." He demonstrated by pulling it straight and locking her elbow. "Lower your head a little so your line of sight is focused on the target." He slid a hand to her bicep on the other side. "Left arm, not as tight. You want a slight bend in your elbow. Your right arm will control the recoil."

"Recoil?" she repeated as he pressed his body tight against her back. *Why does that feel so good?*

"You'll understand in a minute." He curled her finger around the trigger and swiveled her hips a bit to the right. "Do you see the target there? Down the center of the barrel?" His breath was hot against her ear, making her shiver.

It took more effort than it should to focus on the bull's-eye. "I see it." Hitting it would be another matter.

"Okay. Don't move." He let go and bent to retrieve something from his bag. "Rule three: ear protection."

A pair of earmuffs appeared in her peripheral vision as he slid them over her head. If he put on a pair himself, she didn't notice because he wrapped himself around her again. Those nimble fingers of his flicked off the safety before gliding over her hands to help her readjust her aim.

"Focus on the target," he said, voice softened by the earmuffs, "and forget everything else. When you're ready, take a deep breath in, hold it for a beat, and squeeze the trigger."

Amelia couldn't believe she was about to do this, and with Tom, of all people. She tried not to think about how secure she felt in his arms. It wasn't appropriate or relevant. All that mattered was that bull's-eye and learning how to fire this weapon. Because one day soon it would be him at the other end of this barrel, and she'd need to know how to aim.

She took several deep breaths, preparing herself for the inevitable, and pulled the trigger.

CHAPTER FOUR

Unwanted Emotions

Amelia woke to an empty cabin. She didn't think much of it at first. Tom went on an early morning run before breakfast every day, so she didn't expect today to be any different. But when the clock switched to the afternoon hour, she grew uneasy and finally glanced outside. That's when she noticed the car was gone.

Tom isn't here. A chill skittered down her spine. When he went grocery shopping last week, he reminded her not to run because of the collar. But this time he didn't mention leaving. *Why?*

Had he left her here for good? Was the CRF finally moving into the next phase of this game? By her estimation, they'd been stuck in this cabin together for three weeks, and Jonathan loved his diversions. It would be just like him to change the rules after letting her get used to this new environment. That was part of the reason she slept on the floor every night instead of the bed. She refused to allow herself the comfort when it could so easily be ripped out from under her.

She searched for any cameras that might be observing her reactions. Nothing obvious. Perhaps the replacements were on their way? They knew she couldn't run because of the explosive around her neck. She traced the metal with the pad of her finger and frowned. The device that controlled it was somewhere in this cabin. She considered looking for it the last time Tom left her alone but didn't want to risk him catching her in the act.

What if he's not coming back this time? If she found the device before his replacement arrived, she could escape.

And go where?

Semantics.

She hunted for anything that resembled a remote in the living area. Aside from the two that controlled the television, she found nothing. Other than a few knives, the kitchen was useless. She bypassed the bathroom and paused at Tom's door. Her tummy did a funny little somersault at the notion of entering his private quarters. Ignoring the fluttering, she turned the knob and paused on the threshold.

Bold, masculine colors decorated the bedroom, and the sweet cedar scent she associated with him dusted the air. The deep brown quilt was haphazardly strewn across the bed, almost as if Tom had left in a hurry. And one of his dresser drawers hung open. She peeked inside and frowned when she found it empty. She threw open the closet beside it and discovered several moving boxes. No clothes. Her heart skipped a beat. This confirmed her suspicions.

Tom's gone.

Fear-inducing panic settled across her shoulders, forcing her into action. She had to find that remote before the next phase of this madness began. The boxes were all taped shut, making them impossible to search, so she went through all the drawers instead and paused when she opened the nightstand. A gun.

She danced her fingers along the cool metal. It wasn't what she hoped to find, but it was better than nothing. She carried it with her to the kitchen to search for a knife. Those sealed boxes were about to become unsealed.

Her hand was on the drawer handle when the front door opened. The galley kitchen wall hid her from view, giving her just enough time to lean against the counter and hide the illegal item behind her back.

Tom entered the kitchen with two paper bags and gave her a lopsided grin. "Sorry, grocery shopping and laundry took a little longer than I expected. But we needed food."

"Uh, right." She tried to clear the cotton balls from her throat and failed. *He's back.* Why did that make her feel so light, and safe? "Yes, I was trying to find something for lunch." Complete farce, but it explained her presence in the kitchen. Now she just needed him to walk away so she could slip out and hide the weapon. *Did I remember to close his door?*

His dark chocolate gaze slid over her in a quick assessment, making her want to squirm. She held her breath when he paused on her hips and again on her breasts. "I need to get the other things from the car." Was it her imagination, or did his voice drop an octave? And what happened to the handsome grin?

"Okay."

He gave her another cursory glance and stepped backward out of the kitchen. The second she heard the front door swing shut, she sprinted for the bedrooms. Closing all the drawers and the closet took priority, then his door. She was on her way to the kitchen when she remembered the pistol in her hand.

Tom turned the corner with a laundry basket before she could fix the problem, forcing her to tuck the gun behind her back.

I'm so dead. The smile she forced felt like plastic against her lips.

"Uh, the clothes you ordered finally arrived." His sharp gaze went to her free hand and then to her opposite arm. When he met her gaze again, amusement danced in his dark depths. Maybe he thought she was a loon? She was certainly acting like one. "I went ahead and washed these with my clothes at the laundromat in town. Here." He held the basket out for her. "I hope they fit."

She considered the basket and then his cheeky grin. "Are you making fun of me?"

"Me?" The look on his face was overly innocent. "Never."

"No, I think you're teasing me."

"Or I'm genuinely hoping these fit so we don't have to go through the online shopping experience again."

That made her scowl. "It's not my fault they make it so bloody difficult."

"You have to be the only woman I've ever met who finds shopping online difficult, especially when it's under someone else's credit card."

She folded her arms and glowered up at him. "I didn't ask for clothes or to be forced to order them online. That was all your idea, Sentinel."

"Yes, one I thought you might appreciate, *asset*, but I learned my lesson. Hopefully, these fit so we don't have to do it again."

They spent several hours last week trying to order clothes. Technology and Amelia were not friends. Firing a handgun had been easier than shopping online. She frowned at the offending object in his hands. A basket full of shorts and tank tops. If Eli could see her now, he'd die of a heart attack. His precious little flower wearing street clothes? Never. Except, when given the option to buy anything she wanted, these were the outfits she chose. The Amelia who loved dressing up died a long time ago.

"Fine." She gestured to her room in an *after you* manner that had him raising his blond eyebrows.

"Is that your way of politely asking me to set this in your room?"

"If you're looking for a *please* and *thank you*, trust me when I say you'll be waiting for a very long time."

"Ouch. I probably deserve that, but ouch." He shook all that glorious hair and flashed her a dimpled smile. "After you, sweetheart."

"What?"

"Lead the way."

"Oh, er, okay." She started to turn and stopped. *The gun. Damn it.* She did an awkward skip to the side to keep the wall at her back and felt the metal slip in her clammy hand. *Okay, so no jumps or the evidence will fall to my feet.*

Tom cocked an eyebrow at her bizarre behavior but didn't say anything as she moved down the hallway to her door. She kept her front to him while turning the knob with her free hand and stepped inside backward. Heat caressed her cheeks when she bumped into the bed behind her. Tom set the basket on the ground beside the door and shocked her by kicking it closed.

"Easy way or hard way? Lady's choice."

Her pulse leapt. She had to clear her throat twice to speak. "Excuse me?" *He couldn't mean…*

"Hard way it is." He stepped forward and caught her hip before she could scramble to the side.

"What—" The words froze in her throat when his opposite hand snaked around her back to the illicit item in her palm.

He tsked. "Someone was in my room. Find anything else interesting while snooping?"

She bristled at that. "I was not snooping." *Liar.*

"No?" He removed the weapon and threw it on the bed. Instead of moving away, he turned his hand to her lower back and pulled her closer. Her palms flattened against his chest to maintain a slight gap between them. It did nothing to ease the flutter in her lower belly or dispel the heat at the back of her neck.

"So the gun from my nightstand magically appeared behind your back? That's a neat trick, sweetheart."

"Stop calling me that." She bloody hated the way his endearment made her heart race. It was hard enough having his body pressed up against hers. Did the man have to be so hard? Eli had a bulky, muscular build, but Tom's athletic form felt sharper, more lethal.

"What else did you find, Amelia?"

"Nothing." *Because I wasted too much time this morning waiting for you to come back from your run.* A mistake she would not make again in the future.

All traces of amusement fled as he narrowed his gaze. "Did you go through the boxes?"

"Is that where you hid the remote?" She kicked herself for the hope in her voice. If it was where he hid the remote, it would be moved now.

His chuckle vibrated through her hands and went straight to her gut. Why was that sound so charming? "So, what was your plan? You shoot me, and then what? I wake up a pissed-off immortal tomorrow, and you ask me nicely for the remote?"

She blinked. Shooting Tom hadn't been a part of her plan at all. Did she suspect it might come to that in the future? Yes. But not today. "I thought Jonathan was moving into phase two of this game and sending a replacement."

He stared down at her with intense brown eyes so much like his father's, and yet so very different. Jonathan's vapid gaze held no soul, while Tom's was a richer brown and underlined in candor.

"So you intended to shoot my replacement?" he asked.

"I intended to defend myself."

"With my second favorite Smith & Wesson. Nice."

She had no idea who Smith was but assumed he meant the item she found in his drawer.

"No, I intended to defend myself with the weapon I found in your *empty* room," she corrected.

The hand on her back felt like a brand through her shirt. She wondered if he realized his thumb was tracing the top of her shorts or if he understood how close they were standing. The heat radiating from his muscular chest seemed to be melting into her veins, making all sorts of strange things happen throughout her body. Maybe it was time to revisit her earlier plan of seducing him? If she could get him to tell her where he hid the remote, she could use it to free herself.

And how will you get away from him?

One step at a time.

"My room is not empty," Tom countered. "There are boxes, a bed, and a dresser, but you know all that since you snooped through my things."

"Your clothes were gone."

"Because I took them to the laundromat."

"Yes, well, I didn't know that."

"And then you stole the gun to shoot my replacement." He shook his head and tsked again. "We need to work on your planning skills, sweetheart."

"I swear you want me to hit you." It came out as a growl, which only seemed to amuse him, if his responding smile was anything to go by. *There are those damn dimples again…*

"You tried that already and failed." He lowered his lips to her ear. "But feel free to give it another go," he whispered.

Taunting arse.

She shifted to meet his gaze and ended up way too close to his face because he hadn't lifted his head yet. The retort died in her throat. His breath feathered over her parted lips, making her shiver. She flattened her palms against his chest again and slid them up to his strong shoulders. What would he do if she closed the gap between them? Could she do this? Seduce him into helping her escape, and then kill him? *Yes.* She would do anything to survive, even if it meant—

Tom took a step backward, causing her hands to drop to her sides. The unexpected move left her feeling cold. It took her a moment to realize the temperature difference stemmed from him releasing his hold when he moved away. She preferred his natural heat over the cool air.

"Right." He cleared his throat and palmed the back of his neck. "I, uh, need to put the groceries away. You should try these on and make sure they fit." His tone lacked the humor from earlier when he gestured to the clothing basket. He definitely wasn't teasing this time.

Her tongue felt thick in her mouth, making a vocal response impossible. She gave a wobbly nod instead. *I almost kissed him.* Why did he move away?

"Okay." He turned to leave and paused at the door. That strong hand of his was still wrapped around the back of his neck, making her fingers twitch. She wanted to touch him again, to finish what she started. *Who am I?*

"If you try to use that on me, you'll regret it." There was nothing funny about his tone or the way his dark gaze pinned her to the spot. A threat lingered between them, a threat underlined with challenge.

"You're letting me keep the gun?" That was the only object in the room he could be talking about, and he'd left it lying on the bed behind her.

"For now." He walked out of her room, leaving her gaping at the doorway.

~*~

What the hell is wrong with me? Tom's father would kill him if he found out about this. He let the asset keep a .38 caliber Smith & Wesson. It didn't matter the age of that particular piece, because it was loaded and could be used against him at any moment. But he couldn't bring himself to walk over to the bed to grab it, not with her standing so close.

Clearly, he had a death wish. Or maybe he wanted a challenge, or something to do, or a way to distract himself from this passion radiating between them. Either way, it was a stupid move. Especially considering how well her aim had improved over the last two weeks of training. It filled him with pride to watch her shoot, but also unnerved him.

Her brother brutally murdered your mother.

True, but how is that her *fault?*

You're playing a dangerous game by teaching her how to shoot, encouraging her to exercise, and giving her a gun…

"I've officially lost my damn mind," he muttered to himself in the kitchen. Not only had he given his charge a lethal toy, but he'd almost kissed her also. Both were entirely inappropriate. Amelia was his ward. She wouldn't have a choice but to respond, and no way would he take something that wasn't willingly given. John Fitzgerald may have raised him with unscrupulous morals, but he'd never force himself on a woman. Ever.

"Fuck." He gripped the counter beside the refrigerator and strove for control. This wasn't him. He didn't crave women he couldn't touch. But Amelia was far from the average female. Three weeks of eating right and regular activity had given her a healthy glow. Not to mention, it was filling out all those natural curves of hers. He didn't follow the scientific nuances of immortal genetics, but he understood the high-level benefits of being a Hydraian or an Ichorian. Unnatural healing, immunity to disease, and body regeneration at fast speeds. Because Amelia no longer had that emaciated look, but was turning into a healthy woman with lethal curves.

Grocery shopping felt too much like playing house. He kept wondering what food she would prefer and debating what meals to prepare. She didn't appear to be picky when it came to eating, but he suspected that was a result of living in captivity for six years. He wanted to make something special for her, which was utterly fucked up considering their situation. They weren't dating. And Tom didn't woo women. His wealthy background and appearance afforded him an array of willing bed partners. The words *Special Forces* brought them to their knees, and he knew it. Somehow, he suspected those two words wouldn't work so effectively on Amelia.

Enough. Not going to happen.

He slammed the door on his wayward thoughts and focused on putting the groceries away before they went bad. With that task completed too soon, he grabbed a few items for sandwiches and slapped something together for lunch. Amelia walked in just as he finished, and his jaw almost hit the floor. She looked hot in his clothes, but this? *Holy shit.*

"Seems like the clothes fit," he managed through his dry mouth. How did the woman manage to look like a knockout in a tank top and shorts? Her dark hair was piled up into a haphazard ponytail that hung past her exposed shoulders. Not the sort of outfit that should draw the eye, but with her shapely legs and subtle curves? Oh, it definitely grabbed his attention. *I need to get laid.*

Amelia's brow creased as she glanced down at her new tennis shoes. "I suppose, but it feels strange being in real clothing."

The way she said it sent an arrow through his heart. *This is wrong.* He should have fought harder when he discovered her in the CRF basement, but even now, he knew there wasn't a damn thing he could do other than be decent to her. Because helping her escape equated to a death sentence. No one would help him, and everyone would hunt him. And his contingency plans weren't robust enough yet.

"I made you a sandwich." *Yes, that's a fantastic apology for ruining her life.*

"Thank you."

Her puzzled expression had him quirking an eyebrow. "Not a fan of turkey and cheese?" Most of their meals were quick due to his lack of skill in the kitchen, but this was the first time she eyed his offerings with confusion.

She blinked big blue eyes up at him. "No, I actually quite like your sandwiches. I was just thinking about how much I used to adore being in the kitchen, but I can't for the life of me remember why." Her fingers danced over the stove to the counter beside it. "I find I have no desire to cook. Is that odd?"

He snorted. "Not to me, but there's a reason our fridge is packed full of easy meals to prep." Minus the lasagna ingredients he bought. Why he decided that sounded like a good idea was beyond him. Part of the whole wanting-to-please-her thing. As if that were possible in this situation.

Picking up the sandwich, she gave him a small smile. "Cheers."

He grinned at her adorable English accent. It seemed thicker at times than others, almost as if she had been around Americans too long. Perhaps it was an age thing? Based on her appearance, Tom guessed Amelia was in her midtwenties when she became a Hydraian. Her actual birth date remained a mystery to him, but it had to be at least three centuries ago. Maybe closer to four. That type of thing would shock most humans, but having an immortal father born over a thousand years ago lessened the impact.

Amelia led the way to the living area and folded herself gracefully onto the couch. All those lean, elegant lines were far too tempting in those fitted clothes, so he settled himself a few feet away and focused on his sandwich.

It dawned on him when he finished that the television wasn't on and they'd eaten in companionable silence. Most women required constant conversation, but not Amelia. He wondered if she always preferred quiet or if her years with the CRF had something to do with it. His military academy upbringing and sniper experience altered him on a fundamental level. The boy his mother once loved became a man she would never recognize. Or maybe she would. He'd become an adult version of his father, but with a conscience.

"Tom?" Amelia turned to him with a determined gleam in her eyes that made him nervous. Nothing good ever happened as a result of that expression on a woman's face. He set his empty plate on the table and cocked an eyebrow in expectation. "Will you—"

The ringing of his phone cut her off. He pulled it out of his pocket and fought a growl. Of course his father would call now. *Fucking GPS.* His next assignment better be overseas, or he might kill the man who helped create him.

"Hi, Dad. Didn't we just chat last night?" Like they did every night. "I had no idea you missed me so much. Maybe we should grab dinner later this week?" Amelia frowned at his sugary tone. He'd played the role of obedient soldier for last two weeks, yet his father still monitored his every move. Tom was more than over this game, and his tone implied that.

"Why did you leave the asset unattended?"

"Because I needed food, and you specifically told me not to have Rosalie over. So I went out to get groceries, just like last week and the week before."

"And the detour to the post office?"

Tom didn't miss a beat. "I wanted to send you a postcard, but they didn't have any with the greeting I wanted. Apparently, 'Fuck You' isn't a common card. Who knew?"

Silence answered his sarcasm. It should have unnerved him, but he had no patience for this shit anymore. What was his father going to do? Disown him for a little back talk? Not likely. The threats got old after a while. Would he die without his father's protection? Maybe, maybe not. All those years of training had paid off, and Tom had the means to take care of himself. At least for a little while.

"So look, are we done here?" he continued when his father said nothing. "I'm doing my job, just as I've been doing it for the last twenty-one, almost twenty-two, days. We don't need the daily briefings. If I have something important to report, I will, but how about we not talk until that happens?"

"Am I being dismissed?"

"No, I'm suggesting you use your time more wisely. You don't need to babysit the babysitter. I know what I'm doing, and if you don't trust me to do it, send someone else." He didn't really mean it. The idea of another Sentinel watching Amelia made his skin crawl.

"I don't need you to advise me on how to use my time. I'll continue to monitor the situation as I see fit."

"Sure. Then we'll chat again in five or so hours, unless there was something else?"

"I would like an update on the asset's condition."

He glanced at the woman in question. Her current condition? *Gorgeous.* "She's secure," he said instead.

"Good."

The phone line went dead, making Tom roll his eyes. "Bye to you, too, Dad." He pocketed the phone and turned back to Amelia. "Sorry, what were you asking me before?"

Her brow drew downward as she studied him. "Your relationship with Jonathan is curious. I thought you were close."

We used to be. "I don't want to talk about him. What did you want to know?"

"Oh." She wrung her hands in her lap and licked her lips. "I, er, I was wondering if you could show me how you did that gun trick. You know, the one where you took it from me after…?"

Her voice trailed off, but he knew what she meant to say. *After Anita's visit.* That was the only time he disarmed her, other than today, which didn't count.

"You want me to teach you how to disarm someone," he murmured. Because that wasn't walking a dangerous line at all. *Oh, like you haven't already leapt over that line.* His conscious was an ass.

She bit her lip and nodded. "I don't plan to use it on you. I'm just… curious."

The woman was a terrible liar. Guilt dilated her pupils and settled on her stiff shoulders. *What are you planning, little asset?* Why did evening the stakes between them sound fun? He almost wanted her to fight him, just to see how far she could get. Too bad her request couldn't be summed up in a single lesson.

"All right, give me your hand." She did as requested without hesitation. A sign of trust? He placed his fingers against a pressure point just above her thumb. "Okay, see what happens when I press down?"

"It forces my hand to move."

"Right. If I tug this way, you have to move." He demonstrated by pulling her closer. She went up on her knees beside him in response and stared at her hand in fascination. "I can control you with two fingers now."

"That's brilliant." Her excitement was palpable, making him grin.

"Sure. There are several pressure points all over the human body. Each one can be used to a disadvantage."

"And you use them to disarm someone?"

"You can, or you can use it for simple defense. Pressure points can bring a man twice your size to his knees, if you know how to do it right." He showed her several more points, each one making her smile wider. She tried a few on him, and each touch went straight to his gut. By the end, she was gazing at him with a reverence that discomforted him. Mostly because all the touching had excited his hormones. All he wanted to do was lay her out on the couch and introduce her to more pleasurable points.

"Okay, but none of that tells me how to take the gun away from someone," she murmured when they were done.

"No, because disarming a person depends on a variety of factors. Their weight, height, angle, strength, type of firearm, the way it's being held, and several other things. I can't teach you that in a day"—*or even a month*, he thought—"so we started with self-defense basics."

"Oh." Her hands dropped to her lap only scant inches from him. How had they managed to get so close? He swore he kept putting room between them, but their bodies seemed to gravitate to one another. She tugged her plump bottom lip between her teeth and nibbled. Amelia Wakefield was a gorgeous woman, but her innocent gestures made her all the more alluring.

I've got to get out of here before I do something stupid. Because kissing her would be wrong on so many levels.

Tom stood and took a step away from the hypnotic brunette. He could busy himself with cleaning their dishes, but what he really needed was some fresh air.

"I'm going to go for a run." *Again.* He went for one this morning before the sun rose. Maybe he would enjoy some target practice as well. And do some bodyweight exercises. That should keep him busy for a few hours and take his mind off of sex. Hopefully.

"Oh, so no more self-defense basics?" Those guileless blue eyes were going to get him killed.

"I can show you a few helpful things tomorrow." He'd already stepped way over the boundaries on this assignment, so why not push the envelope a little more? "Outside," he added. Because inside wasn't working, and her floral scent was intoxicating enough. At least outside he would have other sights and sounds to distract him. "Right. Be back in a bit."

He didn't bother to change into workout clothes. Jeans, boots, and a T-shirt would make for an uncomfortable run. But it couldn't be worse than having a hot, unattainable woman within arm's reach and not be able to touch her.

CHAPTER FIVE

Unwelcome Visitors

"Okay, straddle me again."

This woman is trying to kill me, Tom thought.

The first few days of training were a breeze because they kept the touching to a minimum. He taught Amelia the weak points on the shin, how to properly form a punch, and general self-defense basics. Today, they graduated to full-body contact.

Why am I doing this to myself? he wondered—not for the first time—as he straddled Amelia's hips. This had gone beyond a death wish and firmly into torture territory. What had started as a fun way to pass the time had escalated to a risky activity that required too much skin-on-skin contact.

"Hold me down like you mean it," Amelia chided when he gently placed his hands on her shoulders. "No going easy on me."

How about you go easy on me, then? "If I use all my strength, you won't be able to push me off."

Her brow puckered. "Then what's the point?"

What's the point, indeed…? "To teach you how to escape in a normal situation. I'm the opposite of a normal opponent."

"Then take this collar off so we can play fair."

Nice try. "Make your move, sweetheart." He purposely used the nickname she loathed to get her moving, and it worked. She slid her right arm between them, hooked her leg over his ankle, then rotated her body in an attempt to roll him off of her. The mediocre defense maneuver might shift an aggressor with the right angle and force, but he knew how to roll with it. Literally. He rotated with her and used the momentum to carry them in a full circle so her back hit the ground again.

Her resulting growl went straight to his groin. *All right, maybe that was a bad idea.* But it was oh-so fun.

"Something wrong, sweetheart?" he asked, feigning innocence.

Blue fire glared up at him. "I would like to shoot you now."

The threat was so unexpected and said with such venom that he couldn't help but laugh. "I'd love to see you try."

"I'll more than try." She sounded so confident. Too bad she didn't stand a chance.

"Hmm." He settled more heavily on her by stretching his legs alongside hers and going to his elbows on either side of her head. Danger instincts flared through his brain while heat licked through his veins. "And then what?"

Her glare cooled as her gaze dropped to his lips. "I would run." Some of her earlier confidence seemed to have disappeared. *Smart woman.*

He toyed with the loose strand of her hair lying beside his hand. "Probably a good idea considering you'd miss and I'd be chasing you. Can you do me a favor, though?"

She blinked up at him. "What?"

"Try not to run in circles. It takes the fun out of things."

"Arse." The slap to his shoulder barely registered. He enjoyed having her beneath him too much to notice. A soft, pliant female with spirit was his favorite kind of woman. Too bad he couldn't have this one. Getting laid might cure the itch, but heading into town for a one-night stand didn't appeal to him. So working out had taken priority, as had training Amelia. He secretly hoped she would use her new skills on his father someday. Not to kill the man, just to hurt him a little. Tom would pay good money to see the look on the old man's face after she hit him.

I really do have a death wish.

"Okay, teach me how to get out of this position." Amelia started to squirm beneath him, making his decision to lie over her a bad one. If she kept doing that, his cock would never forgive him. *Down, boy.*

"You have to gain the upper hand," he managed. Not that he had any desire to help her do that. He rather liked being in charge and on top of her.

"And how do I do that?"

"What do I keep telling you about the element of surprise?"

"Right." Her plump bottom lip disappeared between her teeth. It made him want to close the gap between them and take a nibble himself, but that would be inappropriate.

Right, because you haven't already run a mile over that line…

Warm hands ran up his back to the nape of his neck, making him shiver. Her expression gave little away as her long fingers wove into his hair. A slight tug had him lowering his head toward hers, only to be yanked back violently by her fist.

Fuck. As far as defensive maneuvers went, it was effective, but pain was an old friend. He wrapped his hands around her wrists and pressed them to the ground beside her head. She started wiggling again as a result, which intrigued the lower half of his body. If this went much further, he would end up doing something they would both regret.

"Bloody hell. I have no arms, no legs, and your big body is impossible to move. Now what?"

"It's all about surprise, sweetheart. In this situation, you roll with whatever your aggressor is doing and look for an opening. The more comfortable they are with you, the more likely they are to lessen their guard. That's when you attack."

"But you'll never lower your guard."

"Then I guess you're stuck with me." He gave her a grin he knew was cocky and pushed away from her. After getting to his feet, he held out a hand to help her up. She accepted it with a grimace.

"There are worse people to be stuck with," she muttered as she wiped the grass off her jean shorts and bare legs. He suspected that wasn't a compliment.

"I think that's enough for today." Because he couldn't handle any more. A long run, some bodyweight exercises, and a cold shower were on his afternoon agenda. He started toward the house and paused when something hard hit the center of his back. A look at the ground near his feet indicated the culprit. "Did you just throw a rock at me?"

"Surprised?" was her snarky reply.

He turned around and took in her empty hands and open stance. *Someone wants to play. Okay.* "Next time try a smaller stone you can actually throw."

Her brows shot up. "Excuse me? I nailed you in the back."

"And it felt like a raindrop." Not true, but it had his desired impact. Those blue eyes of hers lit up like liquid fire, and a faint pink tinted her pretty face. He leaned against the tree beside him and hooked one ankle over the other while keeping his arms loose at his sides. "Go ahead and try again."

"I'd rather use your head for target practice."

"Well, you do have my Smith & Wesson." *Against my better judgment.*

"Smith and…? Oh, right. You mean the gun. Well, it's not on me."

"That sounds like a *you* problem." He caressed the sidearm at his hip. "I always carry mine."

She rolled her eyes. "We both know you would just take it from me."

He smirked. "Oh, I'd more than take it from you, sweetheart."

"Arse."

"Asset."

The glower she shot him inspired all sorts of sordid thoughts. Oh, how he'd love to kiss that mouth of hers into submission. Bickering with Amelia had become his secret indulgence. Her quiet demeanor from the first week was long gone, and he didn't miss it. This feisty side was far more attractive and fun. He winked at her and resumed his trek toward the cabin.

~*~

"One of these days, you'll regret turning your back on me," Amelia muttered.

"Sounds fun" was all the arse said as he continued moving in those confident strides of his through the woods. The man was all lean, muscular lines, and it was bloody distracting. He felt far too tempting when straddling her, which was why Amelia demanded he do it again. If she stood any chance of taking him down, she needed to master this ridiculous attraction. Too bad he made it worse by sprawling over her like some big, lazy predatory cat.

She should have tried to seduce him while he had her pinned, but her oxygen-deprived brain refused to function. That's what happened when one forgot how to breathe, and it seemed to occur every time Tom touched her. It bothered her on a deep level because the last person to affect her that way was Eli, when they first met all those centuries ago. One glance from him and her world stopped. She never expected to feel that way about anyone ever again. Especially not the son of her enemy.

Maybe I'm on the verge of having a fit. Wouldn't Jonathan love that? A hysterical laugh bubbled in her chest and died on an exhale as Tom shoved her up against a tree. He moved so fast she didn't realize he was there until his hands were on her shoulders and her back hit the uneven bark.

"Is this another lesson in surprise?" she asked on a harsh breath. Because that would not be fair. He said they were done training today and hadn't seemed at all fazed by her attempt with the rock. She opened her mouth to say more but stilled upon catching the panic in his dark eyes. This was not another lesson. "What's wrong?"

"There's someone in the driveway."

Ice crept through her veins, going straight to her heart. "Anita?" It felt like forever had passed since her last visit. Amelia was no doubt due for another round of experimentation. It bothered her more than it should, an indication that she'd grown too comfortable in this situation. Was that part of Jonathan's plan all along? For Tom to gain her trust just to squash it?

The man in question gave her a concerned look, almost as if he could read her thoughts. But she knew mind reading did not run in his genes.

"No, it's Rosalie. My aunt."

Pardon? "Your aunt?" He mentioned a Rosalie before but never indicated a familial relation.

"Yes. She's the one who maintains the cabin when I'm not here."

She processed his words. *Oh*… "You mean Anna's sister." Because Jonathan didn't have any siblings. None that were alive, anyway. That made this woman an aunt on his mother's side of the family.

He frowned. "You knew my mother?"

"Not well, but yes. We met once a few decades ago." Tom had told Amelia the date last week. Six years in captivity had felt more like six centuries.

"You met my mom?" Tom seemed bothered by that. Well, too bad. She couldn't change her history any more than he could.

"She came over for a dinner party once with Jonathan before you were born." *Back when I trusted him and considered him a friend.* "She was a lovely woman." Or at least appeared that way on the surface. Issac knew her better than Amelia did and only had pleasant things to say about her.

It seemed like Tom wanted to ask her something, but he changed the subject instead. "Okay, I know you don't owe me anything, and this is a lot to ask. But can you stay here while I get Rosalie away from the cabin?"

What an odd request, almost as if… "You don't want her to see me." Because Rosalie could help her escape? Maybe go to the authorities? Or maybe get a message to someone on her behalf?

"No, your thoughts are written all over your face. Please, I'll beg if I have to. I need you to stay here."

Oh, she liked this. What a conundrum for him indeed. "And if I decide not to?"

His heavy sigh settled over her shoulders in a wave of sadness. "If Rosalie discovers you, I'll have to kill her. My father will require it."

Okay, maybe this wasn't as fun as she originally thought. "What do you mean 'require it'?" What happened to free will?

"He'll consider it my punishment for fucking up."

"And if you refuse?"

"I can't." He made it sound so simple. Black and white. No gray.

"Everyone has a choice."

"Not me. I'm a fledgling with no allies and hundreds of enemies." He peered around the tree and grimaced. "Look, she's already gone into the cabin. I need you to stay here. I'll get her away by taking her to an early dinner in town, and then you can go inside. Please. I'm begging you, Amelia. Don't make me kill her."

She wanted to argue that last point about making him kill someone. Jonathan was the culprit here, but she understood the implication. If she created a scene, he wouldn't have a choice, at least from what he said. And from what she'd gathered, the freedom he afforded her wasn't standard. She overheard several of the conversations with his father where they discussed the *asset in the basement.* It could all still be part of a simulation to gain her trust, but it seemed too long of a game for Jonathan to play. He'd be bored by now. And why teach her about self-defense?

"Amelia." The urgency in Tom's voice snapped her back to the present. "She's back outside. Please, will you stay here?"

She met his pleading gaze and felt a little piece of her heart break at the hopelessness she found there. Maybe she wasn't the only prisoner here… An interesting twist to their situation.

"All right," she agreed. "I'll stay here until you leave."

Tom seemed to sense the sincerity in her tone because relief filled his handsome face, making her heart race. She'd done something to please him. Why did that realization warm her all over?

"Thank you," he whispered and pressed his forehead to hers. "I'll be back soon. I promise." A dangerous word that sent a shiver down her spine.

"All right," she whispered, unable to say anything else. The moment was over too quickly as he pushed away and jogged down the path toward the cabin. She peeked out from behind the tree and watched him embrace his aunt in a familial hug on the gravel driveway. Rosalie's back was to Amelia—something Tom no doubt did on purpose—as they spoke. It didn't take him long to get his aunt into her car. Then he disappeared into the house and reappeared with what she guessed were keys because he started his own car and followed Rosalie down the driveway.

Amelia waited a few minutes before heading toward the cabin and considered Tom's comments. *I'm a fledgling with no allies and hundreds of enemies.* Why would he believe such a thing? Surely Lucian and the Elders would accept him into Hydria. Fledglings were so rare, thanks to the infamous Nizari who specialized in slaughtering Ichorian offspring. She couldn't remember the last time she met a fledgling. Maybe over a century ago? That was why her brother and the Elders had helped Jonathan keep Tom safe throughout his youth.

Why would he think the Elders wouldn't help him now? Because of his kinship? He couldn't be charged for the sins of his father. Lucian was a fair leader. He would understand Tom's innocence. Besides, it was Jonathan who deserved retribution for murdering Eli and taking her hostage, not Tom.

She muttered an expletive under her breath and laughed at how ridiculous it sounded. Her former self cringed somewhere deep inside at the vulgarity of it. Amelia never cursed. Not in her past life, anyway. But this new version of herself enjoyed the words very much. Hence her pet name for Tom. *Arse* had a lovely ring to it and fit the man to perfection.

"Because he has quite the backside as well," she said to herself with a smile as she entered her bedroom. Maybe she would take a hot shower and think more about her captor. The man was a puzzle she intended to solve, and she had nothing better to do.

That's not true, her conscious muttered. She could search for the device that controlled her collar. *By checking the boxes in Tom's room…*

That's what he questioned her about first the other day. She frowned. Could she snoop again? It felt oddly wrong to invade his privacy, especially knowing he didn't want her to search his closet. But what if she found her freedom? *And where would you go?* An excellent question, one she would answer after she got away.

Her feet moved of their own accord, but she paused outside his door. Her stomach revolted at the idea of going farther. *Why?* This was what she wanted. To escape. Why did it suddenly feel so wrong to get away?

Because you'll never see Tom again. And why should that bother her? He was a means to an end. Surely he understood that as well as she did. He taught her a few defense moves, of which she was thankful, but she needed to go home.

And where is that, exactly?

"I really am on the verge of a fit," she decided. Might as well make it worse.

She pushed open the door and enjoyed the subtle hint of pine floating in the air. Either Tom wore a woodsy cologne or all that running outside had given him a natural foresty scent. Her nose approved. She went straight for the closet and found it in the same state as the other day. Empty, except for a few sealed boxes.

"Seems an odd place for a device, but let's see." She picked up the first one and carried it over to the bed. It was lighter than she expected, but taped shut. After a quick wander to the kitchen, she retrieved a knife and sliced it opened. What lay inside was not what she expected to find.

"Oh." Little toy soldiers stared up at her. She grabbed another box. More childhood items. It wasn't until she pulled the final box that she found something more interesting. Photos, jewelry, and a set of delicate scarves. Her gaze caught on a photograph of a young Tom clinging to Anna's pant leg. It warmed her heart in a way it shouldn't have, but she couldn't help it. The love and adoration in the woman's face reminded Amelia of her own mother. She turned over the photo to look for a date and froze. The back was splattered with dark brown stains.

"No…" She recognized dried blood all too well. And it decorated all the items sitting beside the photographs. Nightmares lived in this box. She closed it on a whim and shoved it back in the closet. But it was already too late. Invisible spiders crawled up her legs, along her spine, and down her arms. Death lived here. In this cabin. Was this where his mother died? She couldn't remember. Issac mentioned it once, saying they didn't get there in time to save her. But she never pressed for details. Polite Amelia never involved herself in derogatory affairs. That was for the men in her life. But now she wanted to know. What happened to Anna Fitzgerald?

A sound outside had her freezing in the middle of Tom's room.

Was that a car door?

The dimming sun peeking through the curtains surprised her. Surely she hadn't been sorting through his personal effects for that long. But then again, time always seemed to elude her.

She grabbed the boxes of toys from the bed and shoved them into the closet. Not that it would help. He'd clearly see the broken seals. She would have to try to sneak back in here later to fix it somehow, or deal with the consequences. Tom would not be pleased, but he wouldn't physically punish her. Not in the way Jonathan would, anyway.

You trust him. Her conscious truly grated on her last nerves, but she did not have time to argue. There was definitely someone here, and the only person it could be was Tom. She tucked the kitchen knife into the back of her jean shorts as the front door of the cabin opened. Masking her expression into one of innocence, she moved toward the living area and froze.

Three people in lab coats. None of them were Tom.

"Well. It seems I'll have quite the report for John when I get back." Anita Patel's voice reminded Amelia of nails on a chalkboard, but it was the maniacal grin that made her want to crawl inside herself and die.

Oh, this is going to hurt.

Her blood ran cold at the bags in Anita Patel's hands. Amelia's initial thought was one of submission, but the cold blade at her back suggested an alternative. *Fight*, it whispered.

"I'd ask if you managed to escape, but your clean clothes and healthy state suggest otherwise." Anita's evil gaze slid over Amelia in a chilling manner, making her heart race. The doctor pursed her lips. "I had such high hopes for Tom, but it seems he's like most men and follows his dick instead of his head. His father is going to be so disappointed. Maybe he'll let me be your new warden?"

If Amelia had any inclination left that this was all one of Jonathan's games, it died with that threat. No way would he keep Anita in the dark. They enjoyed playing together too much to maintain such a charade. Which meant Tom taught her self-defense because he wanted to, not because of his role as good cop. *But why?*

"Well, we can get to the reporting in a bit. I have a few samples I need. Then I'll talk to John about taking ownership here. It'll take away from some of my other research, but I'm sure we'll have fun together."

Fun. Yes. That's exactly what you'll be having.

A tiny fire brewed at the center of Amelia's chest, spreading warmth to her frozen limbs. The idea of spending any alone time with this sadistic woman, with no supervision or Stark to heal her, did not appeal to her. She wondered if the infamous healer stood outside, guarding.

"Shall we move to the bedroom?" Anita continued. "I would hate to ruin any of the furnishings out here."

She motioned to her minions to get moving.

Amelia shifted backward to keep the knife concealed and walked sideways toward the room. The doctor was too caught up in her internal scheming to notice. Amelia could see the plans running through those beady eyes as the petite woman considered her favorite torture methods.

Not this time, a small voice whispered. If she could get to the gun tucked between her mattresses, she could end this. *Unless there's a Sentinel outside.* But would it matter? Dr. Patel would be dead before they reached her.

She backed up to the other side of the bed to allow room for the researchers. They unzipped their bags, and the one with frail shoulders and a balding head pulled out a plastic sheet. If he draped it over the bed before she got ahold of the weapon, it would ruin everything.

"Go ahead and undress," Anita said dismissively as she started assembling needles on the nightstand.

Amelia gave the woman an obedient glance and pretended to bend down to unlace her shoes. But instead of untying them, she slid her hand between the mattresses at her side and wrapped her fingers around the cool metal handle of the gun. She checked the location daily, so she knew it would be there, because for whatever reason, her warden let her keep it. And it was loaded. Slipping it from the bed, she held it loosely at her side and considered her options.

It's all about surprise. Tom's deep tones rolled through her mind, making her shiver. *Make them comfortable. Lower their guard. Attack.*

They seemed content at the moment, and preoccupied. Like they would never suspect her of retaliating. Because the old Amelia would never dare. She wouldn't know how. For years, she did whatever they told her to do and allowed unspeakable things to happen to her body due to hopelessness and a lack of a choice. But the metal in her hand afforded her an opportunity she didn't have before.

It's now or never, sweetheart. She swore his voice took on a taunting edge to force her into action. Not that it was real. The smooth tones in her head were of her own making. *Because I'm losing my mind.* And she had no doubt the mad doctor would officially break her psyche if she became Amelia's warden. She refused to sit by and let that happen.

Anita pulled out her torture toys as the researchers finished covering the bed with plastic. Seeing the bone saw churned Amelia's stomach. Her last encounter with that tool had not ended well. Anita had used it to saw open her chest, right through the center of her sternum. The pain had thrown her into a dark state, so close to death, that she'd wondered if her eyes would ever open again. Unfortunately, they did.

I can't go through that again. Not here.

You can do this, Amelia. Tom's warm tones flooded her body with a confidence she didn't know existed. *Now shoot before they notice you.*

She lifted the gun and aimed it at the head of the researcher closest to her, flicked the safety off, and fired.

Chapter Six

Sentinel Code

"I swear, you're just like your father," Rosalie said with a shake of her head.

Tom forced a smile. "Not sure that's a compliment," he responded with a light tone, but deep down, he meant it. Being told he was like John Fitzgerald used to please him. He idolized the man growing up and wanted to be him most of his life. But now all he did was cringe. *I don't want to be like him anymore.*

All those subtle threats about having nowhere to go hadn't fazed him much as a youth because the only place he wanted to be was by his father's side. All the training, military experience, and college education suddenly took on a new meaning when he started working as a Sentinel.

His father had bred his own private soldier, a man he expected to carry out missions without any questions. A man who would remain loyal without fault. Tom was slowly proving not to be that man. Did that make him more or less like his father? He wasn't sure, but he hoped it made him better.

Rosalie's laugh stabbed him through the heart. She sounded so much like his mother. It hurt to be around her, which was why he avoided her. They saw each other once a year or so, if that. Her petite frame and near-black hair was a stark contrast to his mother's blonde bob and svelte figure, but her almond-shaped eyes were the same shade as his mother's. Every time he met his aunt's gaze, his stomach churned. There were too many memories lurking in those brown depths.

"You know it's a compliment," she chided, bringing him back to the present.

"Your father is a successful man, powerful, too."

Don't remind me. "I'm sure he'd love to see you." A complete lie. His dad had no interest in his mother's side of the family. Hell, he hadn't shown much of an interest in the woman herself.

She came over for a dinner party once with Jonathan before you were born. Amelia's words from earlier didn't match his memories of his dad's relationship with his mother at all. The John he knew left his son with Anna in that cabin for a decade, visiting once in a blue moon to check on his future toy soldier. That didn't strike Tom as a man who cared enough about his wife to take her out to a dinner party. The only time they ever ate as a family was on his tenth birthday when his father had stopped by with a surprise announcement. Military school.

That was the last day he saw his mother alive.

Tom finished his beer and considered ordering another. If Amelia wasn't waiting for him back at the cabin, he probably would have, but as it was, he needed to drive home. Sober. Or he might end up doing something stupid when he got there. Not to mention, he wasn't the type to drive drunk.

"I've missed you," Rosalie said, her voice taking on a melancholy tone. "You realize you're the only family I have that I actually like, right?"

He chuckled, thinking of his mother's extended family. His grandparents were long dead on that side, but she had a few cousins who were still alive.

"I'll try to come around more." He refrained from making that a promise because he knew he wouldn't keep it. Shit, with the way he was going, he'd end up in hiding soon anyway. This might be the last time they ever saw each other. It bothered him a little that he wouldn't be around to keep her safe, but she was far from being on his father's radar. His aunt had no immortal ancestry. She was a nurse, and very human.

"No, you won't." She sounded sad but gave him a smile. "You forget I know you, Tom. You're too busy for an old lady like me."

"You're not old, Aunt Rosalie."

"Oh, don't let the hair fool you, kid. I have an excellent hairdresser who hides all the gray."

He rolled his eyes. "You're only forty-seven." His mother would have been fifty-two if she were still alive.

"Yeah, I'm half-dead."

"Bullshit. Don't talk like that."

"Just trying to put it into perspective that I'm getting old and you need to visit more."

"And I said I would."

"Uh-huh. You said that two years ago, which was the last time I saw you. And the only reason I'm seeing you today is because I hunted you down at that cabin of yours. How many more weeks were you going to live there before reaching out?"

Uh, a lot. "I was busy."

Her gaze narrowed, making him distinctly uncomfortable. His mother used to give him that look just before scolding him as a boy. Sometimes it unnerved him how much Rosalie resembled her, but they were sisters.

"I know what you're going to say," he started, only to be cut off by his phone vibrating on the bar table. A glance down had his insides turning cold.

Oh, shit.

"I've gotta go," he said, standing. The code scrawling across the display was a Sentinel distress signal, and the coordinates matched his cabin. *Fuck.*

~*~

Amelia stared at the dark blood coating her hands. *What have I done?* The ringing in her ears from using the gun had yet to subside. No wonder Tom insisted on ear protection during training. She swore the entire world heard the shots fired in the small bedroom.

"He'll… kill… you." Anita's raspy threat floated up in a cloud from the floor. Amelia almost forgot about the woman beneath her. She'd been too consumed in the blood dripping from her fingers. The kitchen knife sat idle in her palm. After the shots went off, Anita had lunged at her and knocked the pistol from her hands. But not before Amelia had managed to send a bullet into the woman's stomach. It brought the doctor to her knees, while the other two researchers lay dead on the other side of the room.

Five shots in total, two of them misses. At least that's what Amelia remembered. It all happened so fast before her brain could process the repercussions of her actions. She had straddled Doctor Patel and pressed the blade to her slender throat—poised to kill—when she realized she needed the woman alive. For now.

"Deactivate my collar," Amelia demanded again.

Being the torturer was a new experience for her.

Years of suffering as the victim had taught her a few things, but she didn't much care for this role. She thought killing her aggressors would help her feel some sort of justice or relief, but all she felt was empty as she stared down at the woman quivering beneath her.

Amelia pressed the sharp point to the tender place beneath Anita's eye and repeated her demand a third time.

No Sentinels had arrived yet to investigate the thunderous gunshots, which told her the trio had arrived alone. But she knew a few of them were on the way, thanks to the doctor. She mentioned backup with one of those evil grins, her black eyes smiling with triumph. Amelia didn't care because she planned to be long gone by the time they arrived, which required someone to deactivate the device around her neck.

"Do you remember that time you removed my eyes to see how long it took them to regenerate? I wonder what would happen if I did that to you. I bet I can remove them before the Sentinels arrive. Want to see?" Amelia loathed every word coming out of her mouth, but she needed her enemy to cooperate.

And recalling one of the worst days of her existence in this cruel woman's custody helped ground her resolve. If anyone deserved this treatment, it was the monster beneath her.

"Remove this device from my neck, or say goodbye to your right eye." She pressed the blade hard enough to draw blood.

"Stop!" Anita cried, her head thrashing to the side. An idiotic move on her part considering her position. The blade sliced open her cheek and potentially something worse, causing the woman to shriek in pain.

Amelia almost lost the knife to a cringe, but Tom's voice in her head held her steady. She had the upper hand here; she just needed to finish the job.

A bloody hand flew up to cover the wounded eye. The woman didn't have much time before she bled out on the floor. That gunshot to her abdomen had hit something vital, if all the blood was something to go by.

Amelia tried to feel remorse for it but couldn't manage it. Anita Patel deserved her fate, and worse.

Amelia started to cut her again, but the doctor squealed.

"I can't! I f-fucking can't!" Those words seemed to take everything out of her as she deflated on a shaky exhale.

"Then how do I deactivate the explosive?" she wondered, more to herself than to Anita.

If she couldn't remove the collar, Amelia was a dead woman. Decapitation killed immortals, which explained why Jonathan installed the safety measure.

She wasn't ready to give in to death. Not when she was this close to freedom.

"E-explosive?" The doctor couldn't seem to decide which injury she wanted to guard more as her palm went from her eye to the wound at her stomach. Anita's opposite arm lay limp at her side. "Wh-what explosive?" Her shaky words unnerved Amelia.

I did this to her.

And I killed two people.

How was that possible?

Who am I? The blade trembled in her hand. *I don't want to be this person.*

Torture didn't suit.

She liked the confidence of knowing how to handle a gun but didn't enjoy using it to hurt someone.

It emboldened her and weakened her at the same time.

She expected her revenge to be empowering, to be a sort of cathartic experience, but it didn't have that impact at all. If anything, she felt evil, like Anita and Jonathan.

I can't do this.

She set the knife on the bed and stood on shaky legs. It didn't matter how much this woman deserved a dose of her own medicine. Amelia wasn't the one to do it.

"D-don't." Anita held up her only working hand for a split second before clasping her abdomen. "I-I can't. E-explosive?" The uptick in her voice was unexpected. Why did she sound so confused?

"Yes, the one in my collar." Amelia pointed to her neck for reference. "Tom said it's tied to a device in the house. Do you know what it looks like?"

Anita blinked one eye up at her and grimaced. Or maybe that was supposed to be a laugh? She couldn't tell through the haze of blood and gore. *Had I really been about to remove her eye?*

"Th-that's why," the doctor rasped. An odd choking sound came from her throat, followed by a violent cough. Blood seeped from the edge of her mouth. Amelia often suspected the woman might experiment on herself with immortal blood. If she did, it wasn't working in her favor. *She's going to die.*

"That's why what?"

"Why… h-aven't r-run… threat." Several words were cut off by a horrid hacking that had Amelia taking a step back.

"I don't understand."

Anita's chest rose and fell in quick succession as her single eye drooped. "T-Tom," she whispered. "L-lied. No ex…" The silence that followed was deafening. It seemed to stretch on and on.

Her chest isn't moving.

Because she's dead.

And I'm the one who killed her.

Dizziness hit Amelia hard and fast, making her stumble backward into the wall beside the bed. She finally did it.

"Anita's gone," she whispered to the quiet room. Why didn't she feel elated? Triumphant? Free?

Tom lied about the explosive.

She could run…

Or was that Anita's final form of torture? Making Amelia question everything and debate escaping over waiting for someone who could remove her collar?

What a terrible conundrum indeed. But there'd been shock in the woman's expression when Amelia mentioned the explosive, then an odd form of respectful understanding, almost as if she were amused by the joke. Did Tom lie to keep her from running? From what she'd learned about the man, it seemed like something he would do. A way to keep her pliant without locking her up.

"Bloody hell." She couldn't believe she fell for it. The clever arse had duped her.

She couldn't wait to give him a piece of her mind later.

Or maybe not.

No way would he approve of the events in this room.

Blood splatter, bullet holes, and three very dead CRF employees. He wouldn't have a choice but to report it, and then he'd end up having to kill her, or worse. Just this afternoon he spoke about having to do whatever his father wanted, which meant he would carry out the orders dealt.

And Jonathan's form of punishment would not be pleasant.

"I need to get out of here." She stripped the soiled clothes from her body, scrubbed the filth from her skin as best she could in a quick shower, and re-dressed in clean shorts and a tank top. Her shoes were speckled with blood, but there wasn't anything she could do about it now. They were her only option, and she'd need them to escape.

Might need this, too, she thought as she picked up the handgun. It felt heavier in her hands than it should.

I killed three people with this little thing.

Don't think about that right now.

She could lose herself to the emotions racing through her mind later. Right now, she had Sentinels to worry about, and having a weapon made sense. The knife could stay on the bed.

Flicking on the safety, she tucked the cold metal into the back of her jean shorts and headed outside. That's when she noticed the car. As far as escape methods went, *that* would be the fastest.

How hard could it be to drive a car? Automobiles didn't exist in Hydria, and Eli did all the driving when they traveled. But surely she could figure this out. All she needed were keys.

Heading back to the massacre, she searched everyone and eventually found what she needed in Anita's lab coat. She pocketed the keys and started toward the living area again but froze upon hearing the crunch of gravel beneath boots. It was a good thing she left the front door open, or she may not have heard them until it was too late. She darted into Tom's room and unlocked the back window. It was just the right size for her to squeeze out, and she didn't bother shutting it. No time.

Amelia snuck around the side of the cabin, hoping to steal the car while the new arrivals were inside, and nearly ran into a Sentinel.

CHAPTER SEVEN

A Sentinel's Betrayal

"Well, well." Sentinel Blake stood a good foot over her, with shoulders twice the size of hers. If that wasn't bad enough, he had his pistol drawn and aimed at her head.

She gulped. "Erm, hello." What else could she say?

"You're not where you should be, Asset Seven."

She hated when they called her that. Like she was property, not a person. Although Tom seemed to use it as an endearment, sort of like when she called him an arse in jest. *Now isn't the time to think about him.* Right. Because there was a gun pointed in her direction.

"Where should I be?" she asked, feigning confusion. If she could get him to drop his guard, she might be able to shoot him like she did the researchers. He stood close enough that she wouldn't miss, but his training rivaled Tom's, making it unlikely for her to take him down with one shot. And from what she had observed of Blake in her holding cell at the CRF, he didn't distract easily.

"How did you get out?" His silver-blue eyes danced over her in amusement, but his aim never wavered. "And where did you get these clothes?"

She fidgeted with the hem of her tank top. Should she answer truthfully or lie? "I found them." *Online,* she added to herself. *There. Not a lie.*

He snorted. "Right. Yo, Scott! I've got her!"

Ice slid down her spine at the familiar name. Sentinel Scott had a tendency to eye her with a little too much interest during his guard shifts. She didn't know

Blake as well, but he kept their brief meetings professional. *Although, that look in his eyes right now isn't very proper…*

A stout man jogged around the corner and came to a stop beside his much taller counterpart. It must have reassured Blake, because he holstered the sidearm and folded his thick arms over his wide chest.

Good news, no more bullets pointed my way. Bad news, two pissed-off Sentinels.

"Anita's dead" was the stocky man's greeting. He stood half a head shorter than Blake but had twice as much muscle.

"No shit?" Blake frowned. "Where the hell is Fitzgerald?"

"No sign of him. Did you check the asset?" Scott took in the other man's curious expression and snorted. "I'm going to take that as a no." His charcoal gaze landed squarely on her, making her take a step back into the side of the cabin. No way could she pull the handgun in time and hit them both. Not without suffering injury herself, or worse.

Blake aimed his firearm at her again as his bulky partner approached. Grubby hands patted her sides, down and up both legs, then settled on her hips to turn her around. His tsk made her cringe. She knew he'd find the weapon, but having him remove it left her feeling deflated. Escape had tasted so refreshing, if just for a moment. And now it was gone. She should have known better than to ever believe in hope.

Scott tucked the metal into the band of his jeans and continued his pat-down. Bile rose in her throat as he spent a little too long examining her breasts. It worsened when those fingers went to the waist of her shorts and dipped inside for a feel along her underwear.

"I doubt she's hiding anything there," Blake said, voice bland.

"Can never be so sure after what I just saw."

The taller man whistled. "That bad?"

"All three of them are dead, and Anita had some weird cuts to her face," Scott explained as he continued his search on the outside of her jean shorts. Her stomach revolted when his palm slid between her thighs and pressed to her most private area. It was a good thing she hadn't eaten in a while, or she was sure the contents would be on the ground at her feet.

"See, man, I told you we should have stayed here instead of going to grab a bite to eat. It didn't feel right with Fitzgerald's car being gone."

"Anita told us to leave." Those thick fingers moved to her backside again, exploring every bit of her covered by the jeans, and again up her back over the tank top. Fire licked at her face, making her want to hide even more than she already did. That, coupled with the nausea, and she was surprised she could still stand.

"We should have ignored her, and, dude, I think you got the only weapon. It's not like she's wearing much."

"Oh, I know. I'm just enjoying these new curves she's put on." He gave her ass a slap, making Amelia yelp. Rough hands on her waist flipped her around so her back was to the cabin again.

"You're terrible." Blake holstered his sidearm again and cocked a brow. "What are we going to do with her?"

"I can think of a few things I'd like to do" was the licentious reply as his head dropped a little too close to her face. "How did you manage to kill them all, asset?"

The rumble of a car coming up the driveway saved her from having to answer. Scott's arm snaked around her waist as he moved her in front of him. A metal barrel appeared in her peripheral vision as he used her as a shield for whoever had just arrived. *How chivalrous.* A nod to his partner sent him out to investigate.

Could this get any worse? Her answer sauntered around the corner a minute later with a scowling Blake at his side. *Yes.*

"I leave for three hours and you two juggernauts fuck this up. How?" Tom sounded furious as he addressed the two Sentinels. He planted his feet in a wide stance, arms folded, and glowered at the man holding her. The metal disappeared from her peripheral vision as Scott holstered the firearm.

"Explain. Now." Tom's authoritative tone reminded her so much of his father's.

This was the man groomed by Jonathan to take over the CRF. Had she been wrong about him? Did Tom take on the compassionate role just to put her at ease? Was all the training a trust-building exercise? If the ache in her heart was anything to go by, it worked like a charm. Because seeing him like this broke something inside of her. She'd felt hope for the first time in six years, and he'd snatched it away in an instant. Breathing became laborious as her insides crumbled into a pile of self-pity. She knew better than to trust him—she did—but somehow, he'd gotten under her skin.

"Someone better start talking." His smoldering gaze went to the taller Sentinel since the one at her back hadn't muttered a word.

Blake rubbed his bald head and scratched his jaw. "Well, see, Anita told us not to bother guarding since we're in the middle of nowhere, so we went to grab dinner…" He cleared his throat and cocked a blond brow at the man holding her.

"Right, well, Anita sent out the distress call, and we came back," Scott said, his meaty arm tight around her waist. He continued by outlining everything they'd done upon returning to the cabin and included a vague description of the murder scene inside. It was enough to make her skin crawl.

I killed three people. Getting caught by the Sentinels seemed a fitting punishment. No amount of cruelty warranted her actions. The research technicians only did as they were told. They didn't deserve to die. Anita's death could at least be somewhat justified, but the torture…

She shivered. No. No one deserved to be tortured.

Those researchers tortured you, her conscious reminded her. *They got what they deserved.*

At what cost? she wondered. *Maybe I don't want to be that woman.*

Maybe you already are.

"Did you search the asset?" Tom asked, interrupting her thoughts.

"Yes," Scott replied and released her long enough to hand over the item he confiscated earlier. Then his tree trunk of an arm settled around her again. When he pulled her back more firmly against him, her butt met his groin, and he pressed back. She felt it then, his desire to do more than just fondle. Acid crept up the back of her throat, making her once again thank the heavens for skipping lunch.

Would this be her punishment? Jonathan forced her through countless forms of pain, but never rape. Everything else was fair game, but defilement remained out of bounds. She never understood why. He allowed all sorts of unspeakable things to be done to her, but never that. Had he reserved sexual torture for a moment such as this? She would prefer death over that fate.

"And where's Stark?" Tom asked as he slid the pistol into the waistband of his jeans. He scanned the woods as if he expected the blond Sentinel to appear out of thin air. It wouldn't surprise Amelia. She'd seen the inhuman healer pull that trick more than once in her cell.

"He's busy with Stas." Scott sounded annoyed by that. "Why did he get to train the hot Sentinel?"

Tom gave the man a droll look and changed the subject. "Have you reported in yet?"

Blake shook his head. "Not yet. We haven't finished assessing the scene, and we were in the process of securing the asset when you arrived."

Those dark brown eyes finally met hers, but only briefly. "Yes, I see that. Have you requested backup yet?"

"No need. Headquarters was notified when Anita hit the panic button on her watch." Blake's summary explained the doctor's comment regarding backup. Amelia hadn't doubted her but wondered how she knew.

Tom gave a nod and focused those angry eyes on her. If there wasn't a solid wall of male behind her, she'd have taken a step back. "You checked her thoroughly?"

"Well, I didn't have her strip if that's what you mean." Scott's smug tones sent a tornado of unease through her stomach. "But I'd say I was pretty thorough." His hand splayed along the side of her abdomen as he spoke, and his thumb traced the underwire of her bra.

"I see. Mind if I check her again?" The smirk Tom paired with the request squeezed her heart. *This is it. The charade is done.* Why did she ever trust him? Amazing what a little kindness could do for a woman in her condition. She'd probably put faith in a goat at this point.

"I'd take that as an insult, but I don't blame you for wanting to check this one out yourself. She's a gorgeous little thing." The palm against her abdomen lifted to her breast as Scott spoke. He gave it a firm squeeze before releasing her into Tom's custody.

"Blake, why don't you call in an update? I'm sure Scott can cover me."

Familiar hands grabbed her hips and pushed her up against the wall.

"Got it, boss," Blake said as he presumably pulled out his phone. Her vision was obscured by the fuming Sentinel in front of her.

"Keep your legs spread, arms above your head." Tom's commanding tone showered goosebumps down her limbs, and not the good kind. She met his cool gaze with one of her own and lifted her arms as requested. His betrayal hurt, but she wouldn't give him the satisfaction of knowing that.

Warmth spread up her side as his palms ran from her waist to the sides of her breasts. Unlike Scott, he didn't take any liberties but kept it light and professional. His fingers trailed down the center of her sternum to her abdomen before running over the front of her thighs.

She shivered when he told her to face the house. The heat from his body confused her senses, as did the seductive hint of pine teasing her nostrils. *I cannot still be attracted to him. Not after everything.*

"Remember what I told you?" His words were a breath against her ear, so low she barely heard him. "Element of surprise, sweetheart."

Her eyes widened. *He's helping me? Or is this another trick?*

His belt brushed her backside as he crowded her personal space. Strong fingers wrapped around her wrists as he placed her hands against the wall over her head, then traced her arms down to her shoulders and lower. When he paused at her lower back, she trembled.

What is he doing?

Then she felt it.

The subtle sensation of metal glided against her spine as he returned her weapon. Of all the things she anticipated him doing to her, this was not it.

"Hard to let go, isn't it?" Scott's voice left a bad taste in her mouth.

Tom's tension radiated through her for a split second but was dispelled by a deep laugh of his own. It reminded her of fresh hot chocolate, dangerously tempting.

Take a sip too soon, and you'll get burned.

"Oh, you have no idea what I want to do right now." The dark humor in his tone made her pulse race. His actions probably appeared indecent to their Sentinel audience, but his hands never strayed out of bounds.

He's making them comfortable.

"I'm pretty sure I do," Scott replied.

Gripping her hips, Tom turned her around and slid a thigh between her legs. She clutched his shoulders and stared up into his molten chocolate eyes.

If looks could kill…

"Don't move" was the only warning he gave before spinning into action.

She thought the events in the bedroom moved quickly, but they were nothing compared to this.

One shot sent Scott to his knees in a howl of pain, and a second caused Blake to the drop the phone and pull a gun of his own. But the tall Sentinel wasn't fast enough.

Tom slammed his pistol into the side of Scott's skull before grabbing Blake's arm and twisting it at an awkward angle with one hand to confiscate the firearm. He threw it at Amelia's feet, followed by a blade he pulled from the Sentinel's belt and a second flash of metal.

"What are you doing?" Blake gritted between his teeth.

Scott remained motionless on the ground. He was either dead or knocked out. Amelia couldn't tell.

"Not killing you," Tom replied while countering Blake's attempt at a struggle. "Look, I didn't hit anything vital, so you'll live. But keep fighting me, and you'll lose your only good arm."

Right. Because the other shoulder had a bullet put through it. Blood pooled from the wound, soiling the Sentinel's T-shirt.

Amelia gaped at them.

Blake's tall, muscular physique made him the obvious winner in this duel, but Tom controlled the bigger man with one hand around his wrist.

Fascinating.

"What the fuck, man? What's wrong with you?"

~*~

"So many things," Tom replied. "Walk with me."

"Dude, she's in your head. Think about what you're doing."

He grunted. *Oh, trust me, thinking is all I'm doing right now.* "Let's go." Using the leverage he had on Blake's arm, Tom maneuvered his friend toward the front of the house.

He felt mildly better after putting a bullet through Scott's kneecap and pistol-whipping him upside the head. Maybe it would knock some fucking sense into the bastard. It took all Tom's willpower not to shoot the asshole on the spot when he rounded the corner. Years of training held him in check until the time was right to make his move. And now that he'd pulled the trigger, he had no choice but to follow through.

"Seriously, I know you, man. This isn't you." Blake's deep voice had taken on the trained tone of a negotiator. Too bad Tom knew all the tricks.

"Maybe, maybe not." He stopped at the trunk of his sedan and used the remote in his pocket to pop it open. "Any idea why I wasn't notified of this surprise visit?" he wondered as he grabbed a handful of rope.

After receiving the page, Tom tried to call headquarters, but no one answered. He knew then that his father had played him. Why else would he send the cavalry in without warning? *A test.* One he undoubtedly failed. Who knew what Anita reported back after discovering Amelia walking freely about the cabin?

"I don't know, dude. I just did as I was told."

"Which is exactly why I'm not going to kill you for it." Tom nudged the big guy toward the other sedan in the driveway. "Where are your keys?"

"Fuck, man. What the fuck is wrong with you?"

Not an answer, and he had no desire to search the man's pockets.

All right, inside then. Probably a safer place than the trunk, and if he tied the ropes right, Blake would be able to free himself. He forced the guy into the living area and bound him to the only chair in the room. All the while, Blake pleaded with Tom to *snap out of it.* He wished he could. This all felt like a nightmare come to life.

For twenty-seven years, Tom anticipated the day his father would take him under his wing and teach him more about the family legacy. Oh, he knew all along that the CRF humanitarian wing was a front for hunting and killing rogue immortals. And he approved of it because he knew firsthand the things those beings were capable of doing. But Amelia? She could hardly hurt a fly. Her captivity never felt right, but finding her beaten to a pulp had taken his distaste to a whole new level. What kind of a man could do that to a defenseless woman? Especially one as beautiful and charming as Amelia Wakefield?

John Fitzgerald wasn't a hero. He was a manipulative bastard with self-serving goals and principles that he expected Tom to follow blindly. And he did for a while because that's what he was raised to do. But then he started to question things, and the disagreements began. The most recent one regarding Stas had forced him to take action behind his father's back, which drove an even deeper wedge between them. And now, with everything he'd learned about Amelia? He had no respect left for his father.

Sending Anita to the cabin behind his back spoke of a level of distrust that could not be repaired. His father loved games, but he rarely played them with Tom. Not like this. He clearly wanted to give Anita privacy, which meant he authorized whatever she planned to do. And it couldn't have been good if it forced Amelia to kill three people.

Their father-son bond was officially severed. And any notion of repairing that bond shattered when Tom pulled the trigger on his own men. He had chosen Amelia and his freedom over the Sentinels.

There would be no coming back from this decision.

So I'll make my own path. He had the necessary resources to survive, at least for a little while.

"I need you to give my dad a message," Tom said as he tied the final knot around the man's ankles. The strategic combination should take the trained Sentinel twenty minutes to dismantle. Fifteen if he pushed through the pain in his right arm. The bullet had severed his tendon. A necessary move to weaken Blake's shot. The man had killer aim.

"That you've lost your motherfucking mind?" he guessed, voice flat.

Tom snorted. "Tell him I quit."

Blake shook his head. "You've fucking lost it, man."

He patted the big man's uninjured shoulder. "Just two words. 'I quit.' Got it?"

Tom didn't wait for confirmation. No time. By his calculations, the backup unit would arrive in thirty minutes, maybe sooner, and Scott would wake up any minute. The Sentinel wouldn't be able to do much with his shattered kneecap, unless he crawled. *Likely.* He probably should have disarmed him, but Blake was the bigger threat.

Time to run.

Tom grabbed his go-bag from his bedroom and paused outside the door of Amelia's room. The bloody scene unsettled his stomach. Dead bodies didn't bother him, but blood in that particular space did. An onslaught of gruesome memories threatened to overwhelm him, but he forced them away and focused on Anita Patel's corpse instead. A bullet to the stomach appeared to be the cause of death. Too easy. If what he suspected about the woman was true, then she deserved far worse. Her assistants suffered even easier fates, with one of them dying instantly from a bullet to the brain.

Nice aim. His chest warmed. Amelia defended herself because of the tools he gave her. It seemed those lessons were worthwhile after all.

Pulling the bag over one shoulder, he headed outside to find Amelia waiting for him with a perplexed expression near the driveway. Surely she'd figured this out by now.

"We need to get moving."

Amelia blinked those beautiful blue eyes at him. "Excuse me?"

"We have about thirty minutes at best before backup arrives, so we need to move." He demonstrated by walking toward to the car, and she followed.

"And go where?"

He put his bag in the trunk before replying, "Right, I just knocked out a Sentinel and tied another one up in the living room, and from what I understand, you killed my father's favorite researcher. We can't stand here chatting. I need you to either trust me right now or not. Up to you, but I can't wait forever. If you need anything from your room, I suggest you get it now."

Pulling a pocketknife from his jeans, he knelt to deal with the GPS locator. He knew his father used it to track him earlier. Once he saw Tom's location, he sent in the crew to assess Amelia. Which meant his dad suspected foul play. *Probably shouldn't have antagonized him so much over the phone.* Not like he could change that now.

"I don't understand," Amelia said as he located the tracker above the tire.

"Not sure how to make this any clearer," he muttered. The damn locator did not want to part ways with his car. "We're running."

"From who?"

"My father and the CRF."

"But why?"

Tom sighed and glanced up at her. "Look, this place is going to be swarming with Sentinels soon, and I don't have enough ammo or heart to take them all down. Just give me a second to remove this GPS tracker, and we'll go."

He went back to his task. *Almost there.*

"Oh, you arse!" She kicked his shoe as hard as she could, making him flinch.

"Anita told me about your lie. There's no explosive."

He paused to cock an eyebrow. "Seriously? *That* is what you want to talk about right now? A white lie that kept me from having to lock you up?"

"I could have escaped weeks ago!"

"And gone where, Amelia? To the woods? Maybe for a swim in the lake?" He snorted and finished removing the device.

"That's not the point."

"It's entirely the point," he countered as he pushed off from the ground and wiped his hands on his jeans. "Look, you need to decide what you want to do. Come with me or stay. Up to you, but I'm getting the hell out of here with or without you. And honestly, without you would make it a hell of a lot easier to disappear." He added that last part to piss her off. If he got her riled up enough, maybe she'd stop thinking and do the logical thing, which would be to go with him.

Amelia gasped. "Oh! You… You… you… arse!"

Tom smirked and set the GPS on the car in front of him. He turned just in time to catch her fist. "I'm trying to help you," he reminded her as he lowered her arm.

She snorted. "And why should I believe you?"

Why indeed? "How about a gesture of good faith?"

Her fury dimmed a fraction as suspicion leaked into her gaze. "What do you mean?"

"Here." He showed her his palms before gently clasping her neck and pressing his right thumb to the side of her metal collar. Her pupils dilated as a pretty flush touched her cheeks. He wasn't sure how to interpret that. Arousal or fear? Likely the latter, so he explained why he had his hands on her. "It's genetically modified to unlock for certain biometrics at a very specific point."

Tom had researched the device after he found Amelia in the basement. The technology intrigued him, and the cautious side of him wanted to know how it worked in case he ever found himself wearing one. None of the technicians batted an eye when he requested his credentials be added to the biometrics code. A perk to being Jonathan Fitzgerald's only son.

The metal separated with a gentle hiss that made Amelia stiffen. He carefully removed the collar from her neck and handed it to her. A faint red line marked her skin, the only indicator of the choker. He suspected it would disappear in minutes, given her immortal genes.

"You're free, Amelia. The decision is yours."

"Why?" Amelia whispered as she studied the item in her hands. He expected her to throw it or try to rip the thing apart, but she didn't. "Why are you helping me?"

"Maybe I'm helping myself." *Maybe you gave me the push I needed to finally break free.* He'd thought about it more and more over the last few months. A nagging idea in the back of his mind to run away from it all, but he didn't know where to go. *Well, I'm about to figure that out.*

"We both know I'm your best bet to get out of here." He tucked a piece of her silky hair behind her ear before cupping her cheek with one hand. "But I won't force you to come with me."

A river of emotion swam in those deep blue irises, each one pricking at his heart. He'd given up everything today for a woman he barely knew, a woman who despised his existence. Yet, despite knowing she would never trust him or care for him in any way, he didn't regret the decision. It was the right thing to do. She deserved his sacrifice, and so much more.

"If you're determined to part ways, then I suggest taking one of the cars, because you won't stand a chance on foot in these woods. When you can get to town, ditch the car and shift forms to blend in with the locals. That's the best advice I can give you." He gave her one last, searching look and sighed. "Good luck, Amelia."

He dropped his hand and got in the car.

"Wait." She grabbed the door before he could close it. Her bottom lip disappeared between her teeth, and she let it go with a huff and tossed her collar to the ground. "All right, I'll go with you" was all she said. No explanation as to why or an ultimatum. But he could see in her eyes that she had a plan. Or at least the beginning of one. And he had a feeling it involved turning against him in some way.

Oh, this should be fun.

Game on, sweetheart.

CHAPTER EIGHT

Diversions

"What are you doing?" Amelia asked, confused. They were standing in the middle of a cinema car park after leaving their vehicle at a restaurant several blocks away.

Tom snorted. "What does it look like I'm doing?"

"Playing with wires?" she guessed.

"It's called hot-wiring, sweetheart."

Heat crept up her neck at the now-familiar endearment. *I like that far too much.* And if she was honest with herself, she'd always enjoyed it. Terms of affection were commonplace in her former life, but not this new one. Only Tom called her *sweetheart*, and the way he said it made her feel cherished and a teensy bit girlish. Something she never expected to experience again. It suggested that maybe not all of her personality had been erased during her six years of torment.

When he removed that collar from her neck…

No. She refused to think about how his touch had burned her in all the right ways. Completely inappropriate and never going to happen. Tom was a means to an end. She'd use him until the opportunity struck, and she'd escape. For good.

She cleared her throat and pinched her lips to the side. "This appears to be entirely too complicated. Why not use a key or go and get the car you left in the other car park?"

Molten chocolate peered up at her. "First, I don't have a key. Second, it's called a parking lot. And third, we're switching cars."

Her brow creased. "Why? Your car is in perfectly good condition."

"Yes, and owned by the CRF. Which means they'll have all electronic surveillance on this side of the continent searching…" His gaze narrowed on her breasts, then widened. "Down!" he shouted as he leapt from the car and tackled her to the ground.

Pain shot up her spine, making her limbs tingle, and her head spun. *What in the world just happened?* She blinked against Tom's shoulder. He held her tightly beneath him with his palm cradling the back of her skull. She couldn't see a damn thing from this angle, but her ears worked. Shattering glass and a sharp thud against the car beside them had followed his tackle. A low growl rumbled in Tom's chest as he moved above her. Those dark eyes searched her in a quick, efficient wave.

"Are you all right?" The concern in his voice made her heart flutter. She hadn't heard a tone like that directed at her in years.

She swallowed and gave a short nod. Her backside ached, but otherwise, she felt fine.

"Keep your head down," he advised as he lifted his arm. A soft crack sounded as he took out a nearby light with a bullet. Shadows fell over them as he shot out two more. She frowned as he holstered the weapon. The gunfire was nothing like the ones from earlier. These shots were nearly silent. Or were they really loud and she'd lost her hearing?

"Your white top is too bright." He went to his knees and removed his leather jacket. After shaking the glass from it, he handed it to her. "Put this on."

The command in his tone sent a shiver down her spine. She liked that voice. It oozed confidence and left her feeling safe. Which was insane considering someone had clearly been shooting at them.

Tom's position over her made shrugging into the coat difficult, but she managed. He dusted off the bag beside them and put it on his back. "I need you to do exactly what I say."

She didn't hesitate. "Okay."

He went into a crouch beside her and motioned for her to do the same. "The sniper no doubt has night vision, so we're going to need to do some clever maneuvering and hope there are no Sentinels on foot lurking around yet." He outlined the path, pointing to the cars she could see that created a route to the cinema doors. It seemed an odd plan, but he'd been right about most everything so far.

"I want you on my left, got it?" He paused, waited for her nod, then continued. "If they shoot me, keep moving. Ignore everything. Just get to that theater, shift, and blend in. Good?"

Easier said than done. But she didn't tell him that. He wouldn't understand. "Okay," she repeated.

He removed the pistol from his hip and gave her a nod. "On my count. Three, two, one." He moved.

She went with him, keeping low as he did and matching his confident strides. Glass shattered in her wake, and something zipped too close to her shoulder, but she kept pace with Tom, trusting him to lead the way.

They reached the cinema as a group of people walked out, causing her to pause until Tom wrapped a sturdy arm around her lower back and pulled her into the middle of the throng. She took in his empty hand and then the missing holster on his hip and frowned. Where did he hide the gun? He hadn't removed the bag from his back during their run, and his gray cotton shirt was practically glued to his muscular chest and abdomen. Did he specialize in invisibility?

He didn't give her time to ask but maneuvered her up to the clerk and requested movie tickets. His charming grin made the blonde woman blush. Amelia's heart beat an erratic rhythm in her chest as she fought to catch her breath while he appeared unfazed and casual. How did he do that?

The red-faced attendant exchanged Tom's paper money for tickets without giving Amelia a second glance. *Probably a good thing since I feel like hell turned over.*

"Shh." Tom pressed his lips to her temple in a date-like gesture that sent butterflies dancing about in her lower belly. "Blend, Amelia. Just breathe." The words were a breath against her ear as he guided her to an unpopulated area in the cinema and through a door marked "Staff Only."

He turned on the light to what appeared to be a storage room and locked the door. Slipping the backpack from his shoulders, he shuffled through it and pulled out a slender electronic device.

"Frequency jammer," he explained as he flipped a switch and slipped it into his pocket. "It'll buy us some time while I figure out where they hid a tracker on you."

Her eyebrows shot up. "What? Like the one you removed from the car?"

"Exactly like that, only it'll be smaller." He pulled out a pocketknife and handed it to her. "It should be close to the surface and, if we're lucky, protruding just enough for me to feel. Take off the jacket."

She did as he requested and was surprised by how heavy the coat felt. Tom pulled the holster and gun from one of the pockets and reattached them to his hip before dropping the leather garment over his bag. Oh, well, that explained his arm around her waist. Clever man.

"Okay, so I didn't realize the CRF tagged their assets. Any idea where they put the tracker before I get started?" he wondered, eyeing her exposed arms and legs in a clinical manner.

She swallowed and shook her head. "It could be anywhere."

"Right." He kneeled and started with her left ankle. The pads of his fingers worked over her skin in tender, sure strokes, all the way up to her jean shorts. Goosebumps danced along her calves and thighs as heat pooled in her lower belly.

It'd been a long time since a man touched her with such care. His strong hands were so different from Eli's soft caresses. He was always afraid he might break her, a side effect of his inherent ability to kill through touch. Eli could never lose control around her, or he risked her life.

Tom didn't have that problem. He handled her with self-assurance and didn't seem at all fearful of hurting her. She wondered how that type of boldness would be applied in the bedroom. Would he allow her to explore him? To lick him? She always craved that with Eli, but his gift required ultimate control, and he never let her touch him as she wanted. Would it be like that with Tom, or would he control her in a different way?

Warmth crept up her neck and into her cheeks. How inappropriate could she be? Men outside were trying to kill her or, worse, capture her alive. And they were surrounded by bathroom essentials. Nothing about this situation could be defined as sexy or even remotely appealing, apart from the hands sliding up her side. Tom stayed on his knees before her as he lifted the hem of her shirt to explore the lower half of her stomach. He went to her hips on both sides, then turned her around to repeat the action on her lower back.

Foreign sensations built between her thighs, making her want to squirm. His thorough touch did things to her she hadn't felt in a very long time, things she never expected to ever feel again. *I'm obviously on the verge of a fit.*

He stood behind her and slid her shirt upward to examine her spine, then lowered the fabric before moving on to her shoulder blades. Would he fondle her breasts next? Butterflies danced in her belly, making her flush hotter. Strong hands slid up her bare arms to her neck and paused at the base of her scalp. His thumb pressed something that tingled. "Should have gone from top to bottom." He held out his palm for the pocketknife, and she gave it to him. "This is going to sting."

Her subtle nod urged him to continue. A minor slice of the blade wouldn't compare to Anita's version. He wrapped his fingers around the front of her neck and puffed out a breath that tickled her exposed shoulders. The sharp point pierced her tender skin below her hairline and was gone quicker than she expected. Tom blew on the abrasion, as if would remove the pain.

"I'd give you a Band-Aid, but I know you'll heal in a minute." The palm against her throat tightened in a tender way before he let go. She turned as he shrugged on his jacket and a baseball cap from the bag. The tracker must have gone into the pocket of his jeans.

"Can you shift clothes or just, uh, skin?" he asked as he pulled on his backpack.

"Humanoid appearance," she corrected. "And no, clothes are not part of the process."

"Right." He rubbed the back of his neck and stared at his shoes. "Okay, the sniper means a full unit hasn't arrived yet but is close. My guess is Greg jumped the gun, because he's the only one I know incapable of handling a rifle. Which means we're about to be surrounded. So we put the tracker on someone else and wait it out. They might anticipate that, but they'll also expect us to run. Staying here is the worst idea, and therefore, it's the one thing they won't consider."

She gathered from his conversational tone that he was conversing with himself and not her, so she remained silent.

"Right. Let's find a movie to watch." He held out his hand, and she eyed it with curiosity. "We're on a date, sweetheart. Act the part."

~*~

Tom expected Amelia to shift forms at the earliest opportunity and leave him to handle the Sentinels alone. He wouldn't blame her. It's what he would do in her situation. But she stayed by his side, holding his hand, and went into the nearest theater without comment. He left her there with his bag and went into the busy lobby area to deal with the locator.

Weekend nights at the movie theater yielded large crowds, something he worked to his advantage as he identified the appropriate target. Someone with a similar build to Amelia, but surrounded by a lot of people. He didn't want to get the person hurt and knew the Sentinels wouldn't attack a crowd. Especially a large group of females.

There, a brunette with shapely legs and a tiny waist. She would do and seemed to be on a girls' night out. Their proximity to the bathroom near the exit indicated they were getting ready to leave as well. *Excellent.* He scanned the room for faces he recognized and, finding none, approached the target.

"Carol?" He tapped the woman on the shoulder and feigned an apologetic expression when she turned around. Her bag bumped his leg, giving him the opportunity to drop the tracker inside. "Oh, I'm so sorry. I thought you were this girl I used to date in college, which isn't awkward at all, is it?" He gave a little chuckle that he knew women found endearing and shook his head. "Sorry to interrupt, ladies."

Giggles broke out at the smile he flashed them, and a few of them flushed. He gave them all a charming grin and turned before anyone could engage him in conversation. Once he reached the hallway, he flipped the frequency jammer off and searched for any lurking Sentinels. *Still alone.* It proved his suspicion that Greg operated without thinking through his actions. Tom never thought he'd be thankful for the idiot's career aspirations. His superiors would be pissed when they found out. *Poor bastard.*

Tom opened the door to the theater and found Amelia where he left her in the third row from the back. *Why hasn't she shifted yet?* It seemed the most reasonable defense mechanism and would help her hide. The CRF would never find her without the locator. He slid into the chair on her right side—a position where he could see the door best—and returned the jammer to his bag. The pack had all his favorite toys and remained ready at all times. A man in his position never knew when he'd have to run, like he did today. But it would only last them a few days, which was why they needed a car.

He slid an arm around Amelia's shoulders and pressed his lips to her ear. "Tracker is placed, and no sign of anyone yet. How's the movie?" It appeared to be a romantic comedy of sorts, but his pseudo date didn't seem very amused.

"I've been too busy wondering whether or not you'd be back to focus on it."

He grinned against her neck. "Aww, you were worried about me. That's sweet."

"Arse." She elbowed his side, but his leather jacket acted as a cushion and took the brunt of her move. Some of the tension tightening her limbs seemed to disappear with the playful jab, making her relax a little into the chair beside him. "What now?" she whispered.

"We wait and hope this movie lasts another sixty minutes or so." Otherwise, they would be hopping theaters, and that would appear suspicious on security feeds. Baseball caps weren't the best disguise—even if this one was for a team he would never be caught dead supporting. And his leather jacket looked out of place in the summer heat, but he needed it to conceal his firearm. At least Amelia could change her physical appearance. He doubted they would think twice about her white tank top and jean shorts.

Light seeped in from the hall as someone opened the door and stepped inside. A lone male without a date in this particular theater stuck out like a sore thumb. That was why Tom chose it, so he would have ample warning.

"I need you to shift, Amelia. Right now." He should have told her to do that the second he sat down. Hell, he should have recommended it as soon as they entered the theater.

She blinked at him. "What?"

"Change your hair, or something. Now."

"I… I… Why?"

The Sentinel at the back of the theater started forward, eyes scanning. *Fuck.* Not enough time to explain why or push the point. Tom did the only thing he could think to do and kissed her. Hard.

She tried to pull back, but he tightened his hold on her shoulders and fisted his hand in her hair to keep her in place. Making a scene would get them both caught, and he had no intention of letting that happen. He wrapped his free hand around one of her wrists and placed it on his upper arm. When he moved to grab the other, she surprised him by pressing it to his stomach beneath his coat. If her goal was to find his firearm and shoot him with it, then she had the wrong side. But he'd let her figure that out for herself.

He angled her head to give him a better view of the walkway. The tall man—definitely a Sentinel—stood a few rows in front of them. *Excellent.* Public displays of affection made people uncomfortable. They never wanted to get caught staring, so their natural reaction to kissing couples was to turn away. In this case, it worked like a charm. Tom just had to maintain the charade. He kept his body relaxed and his eyes mostly closed, but remained alert. Then Amelia returned the kiss and blasted his plan to hell.

Her lips softened beneath his as a soft moan slipped from her mouth. And damn if that wasn't the sexiest sound he'd ever heard. Fuck. If this was her idea of playing along, she needed to tone it down a bit, because he couldn't focus with her reacting like that. She derailed his resolve by running her hand up his arm to the back of his neck. Exploring her body in the closet without misbehaving had been hard enough. Her caressing him while they kissed? He considered himself a good man, but even that would tempt a saint to sin.

The palm on his abdomen slid to his hip as Amelia shifted closer. He should have put the armrest down before putting his arm around her earlier. But no way could he have anticipated her doing this. Her breasts felt like heaven against his chest, and her hand was far too close to his groin. *Shit.* He needed to regain control of the situation, because if she got any closer, she'd be straddling him, and he couldn't be held liable for his response to that.

He grabbed her shoulder to force her back, when her tongue slipped into his mouth. *So tentative and sweet…* He had half a brain to check the aisle again just as the Sentinel left the theater. *Thank fuck for that.* With what little remained of his restraint, he pulled a hairsbreadth away and swallowed his tongue. The bright arousal in her gaze slammed into his gut and pulled everything tight down below. It had to be a trick of the lighting in the theater. No way she desired him. Not after everything she'd be through.

"The, uh, Sentinel is gone," he managed in a whisper.

"Sentinel?" she repeated.

"Yeah, he's gone."

She blinked again. "Oh. That's why…?"

"Yeah, sorry. You wouldn't shift, so I, uh, yeah." He cleared his throat. Talk about awkward. "Sorry," he repeated, looking away.

"I don't understand."

Right. It seemed like a natural course of action to him, but wouldn't to a person without field training. He pressed his lips to her ear and kept his voice low to avoid any unwanted attention. "Most people avoid public displays of affection because they don't want to get caught staring. Kissing you kept him from studying us long enough to recognize us."

When she didn't say anything, he pulled back to examine her expression. A blank expression replaced the earlier arousal, which confirmed his thought that the light in here had tricked him. *Damn.*

"Then next time I'll shift."

"Good. That would be easier." *And far less enticing.*

She gave him a stiff nod and focused on the movie ahead. "Right. Let me know when we're allowed to leave."

Her flat tone prickled at his conscience. He'd hurt her somehow. Because he kissed her? He shouldn't have done that, but what choice did he have? At least he held his passion in check. Even now with his arm around her stiff shoulders, he felt a pull to take her. Fire licked through his veins as a deep-seated need settled in his lower abdomen. His attraction had gotten worse, not better, and he knew he didn't deserve her. Not after everything she'd been through.

He vowed to get her to safety, even if it killed him, because he owed her that much. Allowing his father to continue her captivity after discovering her was unacceptable. He should have put a stop to it, but he ignored his instincts. And now he'd kissed her. *I'm an asshole.* She wouldn't want him, not after everything, and he'd practically forced himself on her. An apology wouldn't cut it.

He ran a hand over his face and tried to focus on the movie but couldn't. Shooting something would help get his mind off of it. Maybe he should go out and play with some Sentinels. But no, those were his colleagues. Or rather, his former friends. He couldn't shoot to kill any of them without due cause. The majority of them were just doing their jobs. Even Scott, though Tom would argue he more than deserved that pistol whip to the head.

I'm a fucking mess.

Understatement of the century. Whatever. He'd keep his shit together long enough to get Amelia to Hydria. Then he'd let fate take over.

The movie flashed by in a blur neither of them seemed to enjoy. A hazard of knowing what waited for them outside. By the time it ended, Tom had formulated a plan of action. He estimated a fifty percent success rate at that, and it hinged on the Sentinels having split up to follow the tracker.

"We're going to move with that group," he whispered, gesturing to a large crowd in the middle that had started walking up the aisle. "And if you can at least change your hair color, that would be great."

She glared at him. "It's not as easy as flipping a switch, you know."

It's not? His father's abilities triggered automatically. Amelia should be able to shift on demand as well, but maybe it took more energy? "Okay, can you put it in a bun or something?"

Her movements were stiff as she refashioned her ponytail into a messy array of brown curls. Somehow it was more alluring like this and not the least bit inconspicuous. "Blonde would be better." Or a duller color. Her dark, luscious waves were too memorable.

She narrowed her gaze. "I'm not going to change on command just because you prefer blonde hair."

Stubborn woman. He preferred her hair, but that was neither here nor there. The passing group meant they didn't have time to argue. He wrapped his arm around her shoulders to pull her forward without a word.

"Loosen up," he murmured against her temple. It felt like walking with a robot, and they needed to resemble a couple on a date. If anything, his words caused her to stiffen more. This wasn't going to work. They'd stand out in a crowd moving like this, and her beauty already made her more noticeable than the average woman. At the next theater, he pulled her inside the door and thanked heaven above for the vacant room. The lights were low, but not off, and commercials scrolled silently over the large screen. Given the late hour, he doubted a new movie would be showing in this theater anytime soon.

"Amelia, I need you to calm down, or we're never going to get out of here."

As it was, he already needed to formulate a new plan because the crowd was long gone. Maybe they could wait until another theater released in a few minutes? The emergency exit door at the back would be their last resort. He had no idea if it would trip an alarm, not to mention the Sentinels waiting outside. That'd be the first place he'd put a man on a stakeout.

"Talk to me," he murmured when she said nothing. "What's wrong?"

"I can't shift." Big blue eyes met his, and what he saw nearly broke his heart. Terror mingled with something darker in those oceanic depths, causing his stomach to flip over with unease.

"What do you mean?"

"I… The last time… I couldn't." She nibbled her bottom lip and dropped her gaze. "Anita," she whispered. "She did something to keep me from shifting, and it worked."

His hands fisted at his sides as the urge to hit someone overwhelmed all reason. His father had allowed this type of experimentation? A way to block Hydraian and Ichorian genetics beyond the metal collar? What the fuck was he thinking? He had to know how that would bite everyone in the ass, himself included. *Did they ever do something to me without my knowledge?* There wasn't time to think about that. This was about Amelia.

"Is it permanent?" He kept his voice low to hide the fury boiling beneath the surface.

"I don't know, but I'm afraid to try." Her soft, defeated tones killed a part of him. How had he let this happen?

"How long?" he wondered. "How long did it go on?"

"What do you mean?" Confusion trickled in to replace the sadness in her gaze.

"The experiments. How long did they go on?"

She blinked. "The entire time."

"Why didn't you say anything?" The question tumbled out of him without thought. Even if she had said something to him, what could he have done? His father would have waved him off with a reminder about staying in line. It'd been a miracle Tom had been able to convince him to let Amelia go to the cabin, and even then, it'd been Stark's input his dad had listened to most.

"Say anything?" she repeated, her brow furrowed. "I wouldn't give Jonathan the satisfaction of a response of any kind. He'd only use it against me."

"What did Anita do to you at the cabin?" he wondered and regretted it the second he saw the horror trickle back into her expression. *Nothing good.* "Actually, don't answer that. We don't have time and we need to get out of here. Can you relax a little and follow my lead?"

The fear melted as she studied him with an intensity that set his soul on fire. He liked this look so much more than the wounded one. The wheels ticked behind those sapphire eyes as she formulated some sort of plan. It intrigued him.

What are you plotting now, sweetheart? He liked a good challenge, and he had a feeling Amelia would provide him with just that.

"All right," she murmured. "Tell me what to do."

Gladly.

Official Resignation

Amelia's heart raced. She couldn't believe she'd told Tom about her inability to shift. The last time she tried left her feeling empty inside, like a key part of her was missing. She couldn't go through that again without breaking. To be able to do something for centuries and have that ripped away from her was like forgetting how to breathe.

His arm felt solid against her shoulders as he maneuvered into a hallway crowd. They'd waited for the theater beside them to open before blending into the throng. Tom's presence kept her moving. He seemed so self-assured that she couldn't help but trust him in this situation.

On her own, she wouldn't last a day. She had no phone, no identity, no money, and no way to contact anyone. In Hydria, she used supernatural resources to reach out to friends and family. If she wanted to see her brother or father, she asked Jacque to teleport her to them. Now she had no way of phoning anyone because she didn't know their numbers. And she couldn't tell Jacque where to find her because she didn't know her location.

Never had she felt so hopeless and idiotic in her life. She could finally escape but didn't have the means or wherewithal to do so. How childlike could she be? Here she was, centuries old and unable to fend for herself. Tom had taught her more about defense in the last few weeks than her family and friends did in a lifetime. Her prim and proper former self didn't need to learn such things. How the new Amelia longed to knock some sense into her previous version. *You dolt, how could you go through life so blind?*

"This way." Tom's lips against her ear sent a shiver down her spine. He'd kissed her with that mouth, and it had melted her down to her toes. Too bad it hadn't meant a damn thing to him. A simple diversion to keep them hidden. She wanted to thank him for that, but her palm itched to slap him.

That kiss had unraveled her. Eli never touched her like that. He treated her like a vase he might break, while Tom ravaged her. He handled her with the confidence of a man who took what he wanted when he wanted it. And to know that it had all been for show both angered and intrigued her. If his controlled touch could do that to her, then what would it be like to truly kiss him?

She trembled at the thought. It was best she didn't find out, or she may never be able to carry out her plans. He had to remain a means to an end, or she might never return home. Because she had a feeling the woman she'd become wouldn't belong there. She belonged with him.

The crowd started to dissipate around them as they reached the car park. Tom veered them to the left with two other couples and kept an easy smile on his face that warmed her inside. If the grin met his chocolate eyes, then she'd be in trouble. They paused as one of the couples said good night. It seemed a strange place to lurk, but she liked the way Tom pulled her into a hug and kissed her temple. He massaged the back of her neck and slid his lips to her cheek and then back to her ear.

"Don't scream," he whispered.

She had no idea what he had planned until his hand swung into the neck of the guy in front of them. Amelia's hand flew to her mouth as a tiny yelp of surprise darted out. Thankfully, it was too soft for his date to hear; she had already walked out of sight. The guy rocked backward, and Tom caught him with his free arm to ease his fall to the ground.

"He'll wake up with a headache later, but he'll be fine," he whispered as he fished a set of keys from the guy's jeans. "Sorry, buddy." He clicked one of the remote buttons and smiled when the car beside them lit up. "Okay, I don't feel as bad since he didn't bother walking his date to her car. Bad form, kid."

Amelia gaped at him. "Seriously?"

"What? I can be chivalrous when I want to be."

She sputtered. "You're going to give an unconscious man dating advice whilst stealing his car?"

He shrugged those big shoulders and set his bag in the backseat. "Well, someone had to do it. Hop in, sweetheart. I'll even close the door for you."

She eyed the messy interior and scrunched her nose. The old Amelia would never agree to this. The new one, however, recognized they didn't have a lot of options. She brushed some stray crumbs off the seat and climbed in, then watched in the rearview mirror as Tom carried the blond kid to the sidewalk near the building. He set him down with a tenderness Amelia hadn't expected from him and started to jog back toward her but stopped at a car one aisle over. Had he forgotten where he left her?

She put her hand on the door but froze when glass shattered beside Tom. *Oh, God.* Her eyes darted left to where he stood a second ago.

He was gone.

~*~

Tom knew their exit had gone too smoothly. He felt eyes on him the second he hit the sidewalk. It didn't appear that they'd seen the car he dropped Amelia in, which was his only saving grace. Protecting her while trying not to kill his former colleagues would be nearly impossible. At least this way she remained safe while he dealt with three—make that four—Sentinels.

His instincts flared a second before the glass shattered beside him. The shot barely missed his shoulder when he ducked. He picked up the bullet shell and snorted. Apparently, it was shoot first, ask questions later. His father knew killing him wouldn't be permanent, but his teammates didn't know that. Tom had kept his fledgling status a secret from the majority of the unit, but maybe his dad had let the cat out of the bag. Or his teammates wanted to assassinate him for betraying the cause. Either way, not good.

He rolled to his side to get between the row of cars and chose a new set farther away from Amelia to duck between. He hoped like hell she stayed in the car. If she got out, this would go south fast. With a pistol in one hand, he crept forward and ducked around the hood to put himself closer to the sidewalk again. The quad were no doubt trying to surround his last position, which meant he needed to get outside of the circle.

Subtle movement near the van at his right forced him to pause. Blake's hulking shoulders appeared as he zeroed in on Tom's original location. Whoever shot at him probably thought he'd made contact and sent the tall man to confirm. Or, knowing Blake, he volunteered for the job. The bastard should be in a hospital room recovering, not performing reconnaissance with a bum shoulder. *Stubborn ass.*

Tom slipped around the opposite side of the oversized vehicle and swept out his leg to take down the top-heavy Sentinel. Blake went down with a surprised "Oomph" but came up fighting. Tom anticipated his moves and snagged the tall man in a choke hold from behind on the ground. He locked his legs around the Sentinel's waist to keep him still and bear-hugged the shit out of him.

"Sorry, man," he murmured as Blake tried futilely to knock him off his back. Tom took a few elbows to the side, but his high pain tolerance kept him from flinching. His rib would be bruised later, which was the least he deserved for this. His friend tried a final jab, but the effect lacked passion. It was his final move before passing out. Tom checked the Sentinel's pulse, felt it slowing, and let go.

Snagging the handcuffs from his unconscious buddy's belt, he secured one end to the big guy's wrist and the other to his opposite ankle. That would keep him busy for a bit when he woke up. But just in case, Tom robbed the man of his guns and knife and added them to his personal collection. He might need them to take out the other three. His final move was to steal the man's earpiece and microphone.

"Gentleman," Tom greeted after assembling the communication unit. "Blake sends his regards. Who wants to dance next?" Knowing his words would reveal his location, he moved deeper into the parking lot on the other side, away from the sidewalk and farther from Amelia. He really hoped she'd been smart enough to hide in the car and not try to find him.

"Hello, son," his father replied. "You mind telling me what the fuck you're doing?"

John Fitzgerald using curse words brought a smile to Tom's face. He'd thoroughly pissed off the CRF's CEO enough that he had lost his cool over the communication channel. Nice. How far could he push him?

"Right now?" Tom asked, voice low. "I'm taking out your unit. Or did you mean in general?" A flash of metal grabbed his attention. Sentinel Charlie was in a crouch position thirty feet to his left and facing the wrong direction.

Tom shook his head. How many times had he told the man to watch his six? *Idiot.* He took a detour around a few cars to sneak up on his former teammate while John spoke.

"The asset is messing with your head, son. You need to come in so we can fix the issue."

Tom suppressed a snort at that plan. *Fixing the issue* no doubt equated to torture and eventual death by brainwashing techniques. Because Tom was built not to break, and his father knew that better than anyone.

He slammed his pistol into the back of Charlie's skull and sighed as the man went down. "Well, that wasn't even any fun," he said. "You really ought to send Charlie back to training, John. He still hasn't mastered surveillance."

He purposely used his father's first name instead of "Dad" or "sir" because he knew it would piss the man off. The pause on the other end told him it worked. He pictured his old man sitting behind his massive desk at headquarters, pinching the bridge of his nose while taking steadying breaths. All those years of creating the devoted father-son charade down the drain. *Too bad, so sad.*

"Think about what you're doing, Thomas."

"Oh, trust me, that's all I'm doing." He heard the shuffle behind him just in time to turn and block the fist coming at his head. "Seriously, Justin. Shoot me next time." Because he would have taken Tom down, but instead, the younger man had let his emotions drive him into a hand-to-hand fight he would never win.

The juvenile Sentinel went for a kick next. Tom caught the foot one-handed and twisted it hard to the left to expose his teammate's back. He slammed his palm into the center of the kid's spine and brought his knee up to connect with Justin's face when he keeled over. He had the guy in a headlock position a second later.

"Assss," Justin hissed as he clawed at the forearm around his throat.

"I love you, too, buddy," Tom murmured as the man lost consciousness. He handcuffed him in a similar fashion to Blake and sighed. "Did you leave all the trainees at the theater, John? Should I expect to see Stas next?" Because that would be rich. He had no idea what his father planned to tell the new female Sentinel about this.

And Lizzie…

Oh, fuck. He hadn't even thought about the girl he loved like a sister. Tom rubbed his chest on reflex. All of his decisions today were made in such haste that he hadn't considered the repercussions for his friends and family. What would John tell them? That Tom died overseas while on a humanitarian mission? Oh, he'd no doubt enjoy reaping the benefits and rewards that resulted in news like that. Scholarship funds and memorial services would be enacted in his son's honor, granting him unlimited access to money he did not need.

Tom shook his head and started hunting the fourth Sentinel. He knew at least four searched for him, because he'd seen them while leaving. They'd looked right over him, or so he thought. Obviously, someone had recognized him since the unit had relocated to the parking lot. Which told him there might be a fifth man out here. Had he seen Amelia? If yes, they would have snagged her from the car already, and knowing John, he'd have said something about it. So she must be safe. For now. Too bad telepathy wasn't one of her abilities.

A fresh surge of fury lit his blood on fire at the reminder of her immortal talents and how Anita had taken away her ability to shift. He bit his tongue to keep from saying something to the man who no doubt authorized that experiment. Did his father know the results? If yes, then he knew Amelia couldn't change her appearance. But he sent some of his men after the tracker, which indicated uncertainty. Maybe the research wasn't permanent?

The crack of a bullet several yards away had him ducking on instinct. Two more shots followed in quick succession as Greg's deep voice rumbled over the line. "Asset Seven is down."

Tom's heart stopped. No. *No.* He left her in a safe place. Why the hell did she move? What was she thinking? The direction of the gunfire made no logical sense from their position. Running toward the crowds and the movie theater was a safer bet than going to the back of the lot near the road. She'd be an open target there, even with her trademark circle running.

He frowned. *Circles.* Several weeks together had taught him a few things about Amelia, specifically in regard to her movements. She wouldn't have gone that way. He knew in his gut that she would have crossed over to the opposite line of cars and headed north, not south. But the Sentinels wouldn't know that. They could only guess where Tom left her, and in this case, they'd guessed wrong. He'd purposely picked a car near her, knowing his former team would assume he'd run in the opposite direction of her to keep her safe. Hence, the location they chose for *shooting* her. Clever bastards.

"She better not be dead," he growled, pretending to play into his father's trap. If they thought he was heading toward the murder scene, that left his path to Amelia open. Assuming she still sat in the car.

"Don't tell me you care about her and that's what all this is about." His father sounded so disappointed. That voice used to eat at Tom's conscience. Now it only pissed him off. Why he ever admired this man was beyond him.

"Tell me, John. Are all your Sentinels aware of the experiments you're running on them to enhance their genetics? Or did they all volunteer for that?" He knew the answer but wanted the old man to squirm a little.

"I don't know what you're talking about."

"No? Shall I refresh your memory, then?" He approached the car he left Amelia in and felt a surge of relief when a pair of blue eyes gazed up from inside. She'd squeezed herself between the glove box and the passenger seat. Smart girl. He pressed a finger to his lips as he slid into the driver's seat and motioned for her to stay put. If one of them caught sight of him driving off, he didn't want them to know Amelia was with him.

"All those vaccines you force everyone to get. Some of them are genetic enhancers, right? Things your little lab technicians developed from Hydraian and Ichorian DNA. I'm going to take your silence as recollection or, perhaps, shock that I know about it. You know, there are benefits to being John Fitzgerald's son. You'd be surprised what the technicians were willing to talk about in my presence."

Although they never answered his questions about what they did to Lizzie Watkins, something he had hoped to research more prior to tendering his resignation. But it seemed that wouldn't be happening. Helping his childhood friend would be his number one priority after he finished assisting Amelia. From what little he knew about Lizzie's involvement with the CRF, they considered her important and had no plans to harm her. Yet.

He pressed a button to mute his microphone. Let his father mull over that for a moment while he escaped. He threw his cap into the backseat with his leather jacket and dug around for anything that would act as a disguise. Sunglasses, no. What appeared to be a few day-old leftovers, yuck. Then he spotted a beanie. It pained him to pull the thing over his head because God knew where it had been, but the hipster guise would help. He paired it with the fake, blocky glasses he found in the door's cup holder. If Amelia's expression was anything to go by, he looked like a fool. Good.

He un-muted the line long enough to ask, "Speechless, John?" and turned on the car.

"Is that why you're acting out? Because of something a technician told you? I'm disappointed. I thought we were closer than that."

Tom snorted. *Right.* He was a toy soldier in his father's game, one who had grown a brain of his own and started to misbehave. Their relationship was irreparable at this point.

"Come on, son. If you give yourself up now, we can talk about this and clear up whatever misunderstandings there are between us. I shouldn't have put you on this babysitting mission. That's clear to me now, and I apologize."

He pressed the button and asked, "Yeah, and what about Amelia? Why did you kill her?" The car idled quietly enough that they wouldn't be able to hear the engine while he spoke, but he had to keep it muted otherwise. Which he did.

Tom pulled out of the parking spot with a casual ease and headed toward the exit. There would no doubt be Sentinels in place, but the majority of them would be waiting near the trap. He deepened his voice when he mentioned Amelia to indicate his displeasure over her supposed murder. Let them think he was on his way to investigate and seek retribution.

"They used normal bullets, not the incendiary kind. She's fine, but your unnecessary concern for her is disconcerting, son. Have you forgotten our history with the Wakefields?"

She's not her brother, Tom wanted to say. But he needed to focus on getting out of the parking lot without notice. He pushed the glasses up the bridge of his nose and slouched in the bucket seat. Snagging a cigarette from the pack on the dash, he put it in his mouth unlit and drove the car single-handed. Amelia's snort of disgust amused him. Good to know she approved of his disguise.

"I hope your silence means you're reconsidering whatever foolishness you have planned," his father continued. "We both know the CRF is your home. Where else would you go?"

He tightened his hand on the steering wheel. This line of bullshit had haunted him since childhood. As a kid, he believed every word and had nightmares about the bad men hunting him. But his father always saved him because he loved Tom more than anything and vowed to keep him safe from the evil in this world. No one else would ever want him because of his Ichorian genetics.

If anyone excelled at brainwashing, it was John Fitzgerald. And to an extent, his impact on Tom still held true today. Because he knew deep down that Hydria would turn him away and the Conclave would murder him on sight. He had nowhere to go, but that didn't make the CRF home, either.

Tom exited the parking lot without incident and kept an eye on his mirrors for anyone tailing him. *So far, so good.*

"If she told you Hydria would welcome you, she's lying," John added after a tense moment of silence. "Lucian will kill you on sight just for being a Sentinel, and if he doesn't get to you first, one of the Elders will do it for him. You won't be accepted there."

He pressed the button and murmured, "I'm not naive, John. Amelia didn't promise me anything."

"Then you agree we should have a conversation about this, and that what you've done is wrong."

"No, unfortunately, we don't agree, John. We don't agree at all. But you know, something's been bugging me, actually. Mind if we chat about that instead?"

"Sure." *Oh, one-word answers.* John Fitzgerald must be on the verge of a meltdown. Tom wondered if he was sitting in his office at corporate or in the car en route to the theater. Either way, he felt certain his father wasn't in the theater parking lot. There would have been a lot more Sentinels. And senior ones, like Stark.

"Greg, you mentioned the asset was down. Just curious, what did she look like? Because I put Amelia on a bus to the airport two hours ago, so I'm thinking you got the wrong girl. You might want to check that out." Let them stew on that for a bit. Of course, once they pulled the security feeds at the cinema, they would figure out the lie. But it would buy them a few hours' head start, and by then, he'd be finished with this car.

"Oh, I'm sorry," he continued after a moment of silence. "You all probably thought I was on my way to investigate the scene for myself. My bad, truly. I just didn't feel like hanging around. This has all been enlightening, though, guys. I think I might miss this a little. Or maybe not." He rolled down the window to his left as he maneuvered onto the freeway and unsnapped the communication unit from his ear.

"Oh, hey, *Dad*, one final thing," he said into the microphone. "Not sure whether or not Blake gave you my message, so I'll go ahead and repeat it now. Consider this my formal resignation." He tossed the equipment out the window and smiled. "I quit."

CHAPTER TEN

Waterworks

"We're sleeping here?" Amelia didn't mind the hotel room's crude furnishings or the questionable carpet, but she did mind the single bed. How would she explain her preference for the floor?

"I know it's a dump, but the good places require a credit card, and all mine are flagged at the moment," Tom replied.

He dropped his leather jacket and bag onto an old chair and stretched his arms over his head. The gray T-shirt lifted to reveal a sliver of his toned abdomen. Amelia tried not to stare but couldn't help herself. His body was a work of art. And she had to share a room with him. At least she knew the attraction wasn't mutual. He kissed her earlier as a diversion, not because he wanted to.

Why am I even thinking about this? There was no future between them. For six years, she craved her freedom and to be reunited with her family. That was what she needed to worry about, not how Tom felt or what happened at the cinema.

He's just a means to an end.

Keep telling yourself that.

"Here." Tom pulled a shirt from his bag with a pair of boxer shorts and set them on the bed. "We'll get more clothes and supplies tomorrow. For now, we need to sleep."

The clock agreed with him. Was it just this morning that they were training outside by the lake? It felt like a lifetime ago.

I killed three people less than twenty-four hours ago. Ice trickled through her veins. She'd been so consumed with escaping that she'd pushed this afternoon's events from her mind. But now that they were settling down to rest, the emotions came back with a force that left her queasy.

She grabbed the clothes from the bed and headed to the washroom without a word. Her insides heaved as she closed the door. She had a split-second thought to turn on the shower to mask the noise before emptying her stomach into the toilet. A deep ache settled in her gut as she slid down the wall behind her. Now that the adrenaline had worn off, everything hit her at once.

For years, she fantasized about killing Anita Patel. That woman had done unfathomable things to her. There was no question that the doctor deserved her fate. But pulling the trigger today had changed Amelia on a fundamental level. She despised weapons in her former life and had chastised Eli about his fondness for them on multiple occasions. And today she used one to kill not one but three people.

"Who am I?" she whispered. Maybe Jonathan had broken her after all, because the woman she used to be wouldn't recognize the person she'd become. A killer.

Her insides heaved again, but nothing was left in her stomach. She leaned over the porcelain siding of the bath to turn the shower to a cooler setting and disrobed on the ground. Part of her acknowledged the filthy surroundings, but it was the fate she deserved. She crawled into the tub and curled into a ball while icy pellets rained over her. It did little to calm her heated skin but helped dispel the nausea.

Not for the first time, she questioned her sanity. How did this become her life? Freedom tasted so sweet yet so incredibly bitter. Home seemed a forbidden dream. Everyone would expect the old Amelia, not this new, hideous version of herself. What would Issac think? Lucian? Her heart ached at the thought of their disapproval. They would loathe her actions.

Amelia, the murderer, her subconscious whispered. That's what they would call her. Pity and disgust would color their expressions and destroy what little was left of her heart.

She hiccupped and shuddered. The tears wouldn't stop, and the ache deep inside consumed her very being. A black hole appeared above her, swallowed her whole, and refused to let go. She wasn't sure that she cared. It seemed a long time coming. Why not take her now?

Reality mingled with another plane of being. She'd found this place long ago during one of Anita's more infamous visits. It took her deep within her soul where no one and nothing could harm her and pain no longer existed. Darkness swirled around her here, but she embraced it. Loved it, even.

The nothingness made her feel numb.

Alone.

Fearless.

She curled deeper into the safe place, determined to hide forever. *Finally.*

A hot brand replaced the cold droplets on her shoulder, making her tremble in confusion. Warmth didn't exist here, or it shouldn't. Her frozen haven seemed to thaw around the edges as twinges of light threatened at the corners of her conscious.

No.

She clawed desperately at the dark space, begging it to let her stay.

I'm not ready to leave yet.

To not feel after years of excruciating pain…

I can't go back to that.

Don't make me feel again.

"Amelia." Her name drifted in and out of her thoughts. "You're okay," the deep voice told her. Oh, she liked that voice. It soothed her. She settled deeper into her safe place as he continued talking, telling her over and over again that everything would be all right.

You're safe, he repeated. *I'm here.*

Eli? she wondered. No. That didn't feel right.

Tom…

Heat enveloped her, as did a calming woodsy scent she rather enjoyed. Amelia nuzzled into the warmth and felt hard bands tighten around her.

A sense of security washed over her, making her sigh.

Another dream, no doubt.

She had a lot of those and always woke to the horrors of her life.

Except this time, she couldn't recall falling asleep.

Her brow creased. She couldn't remember falling into bed, either, which explained the hard tile beneath her. But that didn't account for the water.

"Amelia," the deep voice murmured. "Come on, sweetheart. Talk to me."

Fingers combed through her hair, tracing a line down her bare spine and back up her arm. When the palm cupped her cheek, she leaned into the welcoming warmth. It'd been too long since someone had touched her in a gentle way that she wasn't sure how to respond other than to embrace it.

Eli used to treat her like porcelain that might break, while the other men in her life held her on this invisible pedestal that she never quite understood. The male holding her in the tub gripped her with a foreign ferocity that made her feel secure and cherished.

She blinked at the absurdity of it all and found herself staring at a gray shirt. A warm palm held the back of her head to a hard chest, and a pair of wet jeans were beneath her. The water had gone from cold to hot and fell over them in a refreshing wave that thawed the chill from her limbs. She relaxed into the comfort of Tom's arms until understanding kick-started her heart. *I'm naked.*

"Shh," Tom pressed his lips to her temple and tightened his hold when she tried to leap out of the tub. "I'm not trying to hurt you, sweetheart. But you scared the shit out of me."

Her limbs locked around her knees in an effort to keep everything hidden, but he had to have seen an eyeful already. Not to mention, he wasn't the first

Sentinel to see her nude.

Supervised showers.

She slammed a door shut on those memories and buried her head in Tom's neck. His hand resumed that caress up and down her back, his touch mysteriously peaceful. She melted against him, accepting his support.

Don't let go…

"Talk to me," he whispered.

She swallowed and winced.

Had she screamed?

Or was the ache in her throat a result of being sick?

She couldn't remember, which sent a terrifying chill down her spine. That happened a few times before, usually when Anita's psychological trauma became too hard to contain. But no one had hurt her this time, so what sent her to the dark place?

"I…" She paused to allow some water from above to fall into her mouth and soothe her raw throat.

Tom curled his hand around the back of her neck and massaged the tender area beneath her ear with his thumb. All the tension fled her body as she relaxed into his magical touch.

Exhaustion took over, making her eyes droop and her limbs heavy.

She didn't want to ever move, but Tom seemed to have other ideas as he reached over to turn off the shower and wrapped her in a towel.

It all happened in a daze. She barely registered him carrying her to the bed but recognized his familiar warmth when he returned. His wet clothes were gone and replaced by a dry shirt and boxers. She rolled toward him on instinct and sighed when his arms settled around her.

"I'm so going to hell," he muttered.

"I'll welcome the company," she replied with a yawn. Hell was her reality for the last six or so years. If he wanted to join her, she wouldn't turn him away.

He snorted. "Get some sleep, Amelia."

For the first time in a very long time, sleep sounded pleasant. Maybe she would do that for a while and escape the tortures of her mind. With Tom's comforting strength surrounding her, she closed her eyes and allowed the exhaustion to take over.

~*~

Waking up next to a naked woman in his bed had never been so uncomfortable. Amelia had one shapely leg draped over Tom's thigh, and her exposed breasts were pressed firmly into his side.

But that wasn't the worst part.

Her palm felt like an invitation against his lower abdomen. If she shifted those fingertips another half an inch, she'd be caressing the head of his cock. And then all hell would break loose.

Tom had firmly earned his saint badge last night by cuddling a gorgeous woman in the shower, and again in bed, without any inappropriate touching. But if she shifted downward, his lower half would take over and ruin everything.

Sex had to be the last thing on her mind, especially after whatever the fuck happened in that bathroom.

He'd heard her throw up through the too-thin walls and debated whether or not to intervene. But once the hysteria started, she'd left him no choice. The agony in her cries pierced his heart and sent him running into the other room. What he saw made his blood run cold. Her skin had turned blue from the icy water pouring over her. He didn't hesitate to reheat her, but then she went catatonic in his arms, which scared the ever-living shit out of him.

If he needed proof that she'd undergone trauma in his father's care, he more than had it. She had post-traumatic stress syndrome written all over her, and he'd done the only thing he knew how to do. He'd offered comfort and warmth, and given her current relaxed state, he'd say it worked. For now.

But something had set her off last night, and he was determined to figure out what. It could be her inability to shift. Ichorians and Hydraians operated their gifts with a natural ease, similar to the way a mortal might wave a hand or blink. To have something like that taken away… Well, he couldn't imagine how that felt, but *devastated* came to mind.

Amelia stirred beside him, then relaxed with a moan that went straight to his balls.

Jesus.

Talk about mind over matter.

His brain knew better, but his body sensed the warm, pliant woman beside him and reacted on instinct. And he swore that hand of hers just went a centimeter south. God, if she woke up and found his hard dick in her hands, she'd lose it. And that would be the end of any semblance of trust he had established between them.

If he shifted a little, he could reach the towel she'd lost overnight and re-cover her. That would shield his view, but of course, her fantastic curves would forever be engraved in his memory. Something to consider while alone in the shower later. Though, he doubted any amount of jerking off would help in this situation. His attraction to her had reached lethal levels over the last twenty-four hours, and not just physically.

Hysterical women terrified him and usually sent him in the opposite direction. But when he heard Amelia's cries, he ran to her side without a second thought. He couldn't recall a single moment in his life where that had ever happened to him. Even Lizzie's tears caused him to scurry away like a frightened animal, and he loved that girl like his own flesh and blood.

Amelia's pain called out to him on a fundamental level, and he'd reacted without thought. Holding her felt right, too right.

This bond forming between them wasn't healthy.

He couldn't keep her.

She belonged in Hydria, and he belonged in hell.

Not the ideal match by a long shot.

Tom served as a constant reminder of what the CRF had done to her. No amount of helping Amelia or saving her would erase that history between them. He may not have been the one to hurt her, but his presence would forever remind her of the man who did.

My father.

A buzz on his wrist had him cringing. He forgot all about the alarm he'd set, and of course, it was the arm wrapped around Amelia.

She jolted awake and flew upward in a panic.

Great.

He thought having her breasts pressed against him was bad. This was worse—much worse. Because now they were on full display for his viewing pleasure. No amount of recited baseball stats could compete with that.

Perfection.

That sole word described Amelia to a tee.

The woman had the body of a goddess, and she deserved to be worshipped.

But not by me.

He cleared his throat and used what remained of his self-control to roll off the bed.

"Morning. I'm going to take a shower." *With cold fucking water.*

He didn't wait for a reply—he couldn't or he'd end up back on that bed with Amelia beneath him.

His hands shook with a deep-seated need as he peeled off his shirt and boxers and climbed into the shower. The cold water pellets from the showerhead did nothing to dispel the steam rolling off his body as he recalled the feel of Amelia's breasts against his side.

He leaned back against the tile wall and fought the urge to stroke his shaft. Kissing her yesterday—platonic as it was—had stoked the fire in his veins to an overwhelming fury. He wanted her more than he wanted to breathe, and knowing it was forbidden only made matters worse.

This is so wrong.

The last time he stood here, she was naked and catatonic in his arms. But the images in his head were of a vivacious woman with lips meant for sin, and oh, how he wanted to feel her mouth wrapped around his cock.

"Fuck," he muttered and turned to bang his head against the wall.

His common sense had disappeared down the drain with what was left of his dignity. What harm could a little fantasy cause? She'd never know, and he'd feel a hell of a lot better afterward. His guilty conscience would be worth the sweet relief.

Amelia's deep blue eyes flashed through his mind, and he recalled their vacant look from the night before. That woman had gone through enough. She didn't deserve to have his sordid thoughts on top of it.

He fisted a hand at his side and bit off a curse. The sooner he got her back to Hydria, the better. Then he would take care of the ache in his balls. Until then, he'd behave. Even if it killed him.

His jeans were still damp from the night before, but he put them on anyway. It was that or boxers, and he needed pants. He used the shirt he slept in and towel-dried his hair.

He'd need another shower later when he had proper soap and shampoo, but this would do for now.

Amelia sat waiting for him on the bed, her dark hair tousled with sleep and a sheet pulled over her chest. The image almost sent him back into the bathroom to take care of business. He had to get rid of her, and soon.

"Bathroom's free if you want to use it." He cleared his throat. "We'll, uh, do some shopping for clothes this afternoon."

They had to make a pit stop first and dispose of the stolen car at a nearby restaurant. Or maybe they would leave the car here and walk. His escape plan wasn't far, hence the reason he chose this motel.

Tom walked over to the window to check the lot. Nothing out of the ordinary. It appeared his evasion techniques had worked to fool the CRF. They wouldn't work forever, and he had no doubt the Sentinels would be crawling all over this small town by nightfall, if not sooner.

The bathroom door closed with a snick, indicating Amelia had left the bed. He hoped she held it together this time because his heart could not handle another breakdown, not when he didn't know for certain what caused the first one. As much as he wanted to know what happened, he wouldn't push her to talk to him. If she confided in him, it would be because she wanted to, not because he demanded it.

Her hair was pulled back into a damp ponytail when she stepped out of the bathroom in her shorts and tank top from yesterday. Those full lips of hers were curled down at the edges, making his heart hurt. He preferred curious Amelia over this sad version, but he wasn't sure how to fix it.

Pulling on his jacket and backpack, he stepped over to the door and opened it for her. She hurried under his arm and paused on the sidewalk.

Yeah, this wasn't going to work today. He needed a confident partner to pull all this off, and this meek version wouldn't cut it.

"I hope you're up for a jog, because we're leaving the car here." Nothing like a little competition to get her blood pumping.

Her gaze darted up to his. "What?"

"You heard me. Let's go for a run."

Some of the uncertainty was replaced by incredulity. "Now?"

"Yeah, why not?" His body could certainly use the exercise. Maybe it would redirect the blood flow away from his groin.

She took in their surroundings with a frown. "We're in the middle of nowhere."

Not exactly true. The cabin they stayed in was more remote than this place, but the population of this town topped out around a thousand. A good place to buy a small storage unit under a false name and hide some things no one would ever think to look twice at for his escape plan. The national park nearby attracted a lot of tourists, especially those from the city, which meant the locals were used to new faces, which was why he selected this area three months ago.

He zipped up his jacket. The run would hurt in this heat, but he'd take the painful distraction over the ache down below. "Ready?"

The last bits of her wariness fled as she gaped at him. "You're serious."

"Always."

"And apparently, you've lost your bloody mind."

After everything that happened yesterday? "A possibility, sure." At a minimum, he had a death wish. "Shall we?"

"Do I have a choice?"

Technically, she did, but a pissed-off Amelia trumped a depressed one. So… "No. Let's go." He rolled back onto the balls of his feet and took off at a pace he knew she could hold.

"Arse," she growled as she fought to catch up to him.

"Asset," he returned with a grin he knew she would find cocky. She'd probably kill him after this three-mile stint, but if it kept her grounded in reality, he'd consider it a win.

They arrived at the storage locker forty minutes later, which had to be a record for him in terms of slowness. But he didn't tell Amelia that. He spent half the run jogging backward to taunt her into keeping up. The blue fire in her eyes served as an amusement and a turn-on. She threatened to shoot him several times, but he had all the guns. A good thing, too, because he suspected she was serious this time. She bent over, arms on her knees, outside the garage door, sputtering colorful phrases. As she kept repeating *arse*, he knew they were all directed at him.

"And…" She gulped in a lungful of air and blew a strand of hair from her eyes. "You're not… even… sweating."

True. The jog had felt more like a light walk to him. A good thing considering the heavy leather jacket and bag. Not to mention the damp jeans.

"I live for this shit," he told her as he pulled off his pack. The key he needed peered up from the outside pocket. Snagging it, he headed toward the unit under his alias with a panting Amelia trailing behind him. He wondered how exhausted she would be after a night in his bed. With how fiercely he wanted her, he'd leave her breathless and replete, over and over again.

"What is this place?" Amelia asked as he unfastened the padlock. Her pink cheeks and parted lips taunted his devious side. She looked freshly fucked, but not in the way he preferred. So much for that run helping to dissuade his arousal. If anything, it had gotten worse. *I need to get her away from me as soon as possible.* Which meant he'd need to expedite his plans. Not a problem.

He pulled the garage door upward to reveal a ten-by-twelve room. Seeing Amelia's expression, he realized he never replied to her inquiry. His brain had been temporarily distracted by the member in his pants.

"I've suspected for a few months now that this choice might be inevitable," he explained, turning on the light overhead. "Of course, I didn't expect my exile to happen this soon, so I don't have everything in place yet, but I have enough to get started."

Various weapons littered the walls, and boxes cluttered the floor. But it was the safe in the corner he went to first. His fingers rotated the dial using the appropriate code, and it sprung open.

Two passports sat inside, one American, the second Canadian. Both were aliases the CRF knew nothing about. Beneath them was a wallet filled with credit cards tied to bank accounts in each name, and large bills from various countries. All those humanitarian trips around the world made collecting foreign currency easy. It also aided in his ability to transfer his inheritance around without his father noticing. By the time John's analysts tracked the money, Tom would be long gone and using another identity on the opposite side of the world. Or that was the idea, anyway.

He set the passports and money on top of the safe, then bent to pull a set of dry clothes from a box near his feet. He knew these would come in handy one day. Dropping his bag and coat, he tugged off the dirty shirt and threw it to the ground. A tiny gasp from the other side of the unit reminded him that he wasn't alone. Right. Wide eyes were glued to his chest as he turned.

"I need to change out of these wet jeans." They were chafing his groin, which ached enough already. His hand went to the button of his jeans, as did her gaze. "You might want to turn around because I'm swapping the boxers, too."

Amelia licked her lips and gave him a strange look, like she wanted to say something. She must have thought better of it because she turned around to stare at his favorite sniper rifle instead. Too bad it wouldn't be going with them. He'd have to return for it later.

Losing his shoes, jeans, and damp boxers, he pulled on the dry clothes and re-laced his boots. He put the passports in one pocket and the wallet in another before closing the safe. A burner phone sat in a box on one of his shelves. He slipped that into his jacket pocket and started swapping items from his bag. Certain weapons would be required for where they were headed, not the standard ones in his pack. Amelia, realizing he was clothed, turned to observe with a curious expression.

When he finished, he walked out of the garage to the unit across from them and used the same key to open it. Inside sat his favorite toy. He bought it two months ago and drove it once. Here. Now he could have some fun with it.

"Are you going to do that wire thing again?"

He chuckled at the irritation in Amelia's tone. Apparently, she didn't enjoy their last hot-wiring experience. "Don't worry. This one has keys inside."

Tom opened the door to the beautiful machine and popped the trunk. His bag went in first, followed by a few additional firearms from the other unit and, lastly, a box of clothes. He'd need to procure a suitcase today for their stuff so the hotel didn't question them later. Minor detail.

After locking the other unit, he walked over to open the passenger-side door. "Ladies first."

"How gentlemanly of you." She didn't sound all that impressed with him.

"You'd prefer to stay here?"

Those gorgeous eyes narrowed. "Are you going to force me to run again?"

"Probably."

She snorted. "Arse."

"Asset."

All the teasing today was worth it to see her responding grin. He could tell she didn't want to be amused but couldn't help it. And he loved that. He'd made her happy, in a backward, fucked-up way.

"Tell me where we're going first."

"I could just leave you here," he replied, smiling. Not that he would. She didn't know it, but he'd promised her something last night after she fell asleep. And he intended to see it through, even if it killed him.

"Yes, or you could be a *gentleman* and tell me."

Oh, he liked that. Using his words against him. "Okay, sweetheart." He folded his arms on top of the open door and leaned over as if to let her in on a secret. She moved closer, expression curious. He loved that look on her and couldn't wait for it to mold to shock. "We're going back to New York City."

She didn't disappoint. Those luscious lips parted on a gasp, and her eyebrows shot up to her hairline. "What? Why the bloody hell would we do that?"

"Because it's the last place they'd ever expect us to go."

Chapter Eleven

A Moment of Hesitation

Amelia couldn't believe it. Of all the hotels in New York City, Tom chose The Pierre for the night. The Treaty of 1747 kept her from ever staying here, or anywhere in the city limits for that matter, but she knew of this place through her brother. He loved this hotel.

She wondered how far it was from Wakefield Pharmaceuticals. Jonathan had told her Issac had taken a more active role in his company after her supposed death. He used it as proof that her brother had moved on and would never come for her. She didn't let it break her spirit, not entirely, anyway. Because she knew deep down her brother might believe she was dead, but he'd never forget her.

"Shall we, darlin'?" Tom drawled. He looked ridiculous in a pale pink polo shirt, khaki slacks, glasses, and a flat cap. Not that she appeared any better in her floppy hat and sundress. They were dressed for a croquet match, not a classy New York City hotel, but he insisted on the disguise.

She wrapped her gloved arm around his offered one and followed along. Her English accent couldn't be molded into a Southern drawl, so she played the part of silent type at his side while he chatted with the bellman in the elevator.

Their room on the thirty-eighth floor boasted a splendid night view of Manhattan. Amelia almost felt bad that she wouldn't be sticking around to enjoy it. Being this close to freedom and her brother left her little choice but to flee, but she needed a few things from Tom first. *Money and a weapon.*

It sickened her stomach to think about touching a gun again, but she knew the necessary evil would come in handy. Hydraians like herself were not welcome in this city, and Ichorians lurked at every corner. Her father being one of the eldest of his kind made her recognizable to most immortal beings, especially the more dangerous ones. She'd be shot on sight if anyone recognized her. Thankfully, the immortal world presumed her to be dead already.

"Amelia?" Tom called from the living area. She had wandered into the suite bedroom while he finished his discussion with the bellman. His lack of a drawl told her the hotel employee had left.

She turned away from the window to join him. He stood beside the couch with a book in his hand. "What do you want to eat?" he asked while reading.

Food was the last thing on her mind, but her stomach rumbled at the question. A quick meal before she ran away might be a good thing. It would help keep her energy levels high, something she suspected would be needed. She peered over his shoulder to review the room service menu and pointed to a random salad with chicken.

He snorted and faced her. "We haven't eaten since that crappy meal at the mall, and not a whole hell of a lot before that. You need more than a salad."

She folded her arms and raised an eyebrow at him. "Well, if you know what I should be eating, then why don't you order for me?"

"You know, I think I will." He picked up the phone while holding her gaze. "Evenin', darlin'. My fiancée and I are starving. Uh-huh, yup. Okay, well, we'd like the shrimp starter and two bowls of lobster bisque. And for the main course, we'll take two filet mignons with some baked potatoes and string beans." He grinned at whatever the lady said to him. "Yes, ma'am, green beans are just fine. And yessum, medium rare. As for dessert, the sundae bar with all the sides and some warm chocolate chip cookies oughta do. Thank ya much, darlin'. You, too."

"I hope you're hungry, because that's a lot of food, *darlin'*," she said with a horrible accent. While he sounded sexy as sin, she came off as ridiculous. At least she wasn't wearing that stupid flat cap. *Though even I have to admit the arse pulls it off nicely.* The man could wear a trash bin and still be handsome.

Her attraction to him had worsened over the last twenty-four hours. Falling asleep in his arms after he pulled her away from the darkness had been refreshing. She couldn't think of a better word for it. After overcoming the shock of waking up naked beside him, she'd realized it'd been the best night of sleep for as long as she could remember. Part of her wanted to blame the bed, a luxury she hadn't experienced in over six years, but that would be a lie. She'd felt safe, and that terrified her. Any deeper and she'd be in trouble.

Which was why she needed to leave. She considered asking Tom to release her, but she didn't know how he would react. Escaping seemed easier.

A coward's approach, her conscious chided.

Maybe.

But if she didn't run tonight, she risked losing her heart to this man. She refused to rely on another person to take care of her, to save her. Not after what happened last time she fell into that trap. Amelia owed it to herself to follow through with her original plans of running away and finding her brother. She'd steal some money and a gun and ask the hotel concierge to send her to Wakefield Pharmaceuticals. Issac wouldn't be working at this late hour, but she'd find someone there who could help her contact him.

"What are you thinking so hard about, Amelia?" Tom asked, eyes narrowed in suspicion.

Oops. She tried to recall what they'd just been discussing and came up blank. "I don't remember." Not a lie because she couldn't recall their conversation.

"Uh-huh." He folded his arms and cocked his head to the side. "Well, dinner will be here in thirty minutes. Why don't you go freshen up and take off that hideous hat? Your new clothes are in that suitcase."

She ignored his gesture to the bags by the bedroom door. "You're calling my hat hideous? Have you tried looking in a mirror?"

He flashed her a cocky grin. "Lose the hat, sweetheart."

"You're an arse."

"Yes, we've established that, little asset," he murmured with a wink. "I'm going to catch up on the news while you change." He plopped down on the couch beside them, kicked up his feet, and turned on the TV.

She wanted to stomp her foot at him for assuming she would do as he requested, but truthfully, she couldn't wait to get out of this hat and dress. Her former self lived for this brand of fashion, but the new Amelia preferred denim and tank tops. And maybe pajama pants. She'd bought a pair on a whim and decided those might do for dinner tonight. *With the food he ordered for you.* That's what they'd been going on about before her mind took a detour.

"What if I don't fancy a steak?" she asked, arms still folded.

He smirked. "Then I guess I get two filet mignons, and yes, I know. I'm an arse. Go change."

She wanted to smack him. Or worse. Kiss him. A light flutter stirred in her lower belly at the thought. What would he do if she sat on his lap, wrapped her arms around his neck, and pressed her mouth against his? *He'd push you away,* her conscious grated. Just like he did this morning when she woke up naked beside him. He moved so fast it was as if her skin burned him. Not the sign of a man who wanted her attentions. So slapping him would be the better option of the two, then. Too bad he'd catch her hand before it reached his cheek.

With a huff, she grabbed the suitcase and rolled it into the bedroom. If he wanted her to change, then she would do just that, and take a shower. Might as well refresh before her escape later tonight.

The marble washroom came equipped with a bath and shower. After spending far too long beneath the hot spray, she pulled on her knickers, a pair of soft gray flannels, and a creamy tank top. She went braless beneath, because, why not? Tom had already seen her naked, and from his reaction, he clearly wasn't impressed. Might as well be comfortable, then. She ran a comb through her clean hair and left it down to dry before returning to the living area.

Her nose twitched at the savory aroma filling the room. Tom sat at a small dining table of two chairs, waiting for her to join him. The stupid cap sat on the floor, as did his polo and khakis. In their place were a pair of sweatpants and a white shirt that clung to his biceps. She swallowed her tongue and forgot whatever witty comment she'd been planning to say.

His eyes went to her breasts and darkened, making her wonder if she'd been wrong about his feelings toward her. Then his gaze dropped to the table, and the moment passed. Of course he wouldn't want her. And she shouldn't want him.

He cleared his throat and gestured to the chair across from him. "Let's eat."

Her growling stomach agreed, so she sat and devoured her meal. Filet mignon had never tasted so good, and the bisque was a treat to her taste buds. She felt positively spoiled when they were done, which caused her chest to ache. Despite their situation, Tom had been good to her, but she had no choice except to betray him. If she learned anything over the last decade, it was to watch out for herself first and foremost. And staying with him for any longer endangered not only her sanity but also her emotional well-being. She couldn't risk falling any deeper down the rabbit hole.

"Uh, you can take the bed," Tom said after cleaning up their dishes and placing them in the hallway. "I'll stay on the couch."

"I can sleep on the couch," she replied without thinking. At his speculative expression, she backtracked to better explain. "I mean, you should get the bed since you paid for the room." *And I want to be closer to the door.*

Tom shook his head. "I'm on the couch; you're on the bed. It's not up for debate."

She bristled at his dismissive tone. "And why not? What if I fancy sleeping on the couch?"

"We're in the middle of Ichorian and Sentinel territory, Amelia. I think we fooled the cameras, but one wrong glance is all it takes for facial recognition software to find us. And you better believe my dad is using every resource in his power to track us down. So if you don't mind, I'd like to sleep on the couch to keep guard while you sleep in the bedroom."

She blinked. Right. No way to argue with that logic. "I'll sleep in the other room, then."

"Good." He blew out a breath. "You can take the bathroom first. Just let me know when you're done."

Which implied he would require the washroom next, but for how long? If he took a shower, she would have plenty of time to steal a weapon from his bag and some money. But she doubted he planned to do that. Still, it could work if she moved quickly.

I can escape. Her heart kicked up a beat, then sank to her stomach when she realized it also meant she would never see Tom again. *He's a means to an end.* But was she ready to end it now?

"You all right?" he asked, frowning. "You look a little pale."

She swallowed. Hard. "Yes, I just— I need some sleep." A lie. Thanks to last night, she'd never felt so well rested. Why did that make her feel like a horrible person?

"Right." He palmed the back of his neck as concern furrowed his brow. "I'm here if you need me."

A spike went through the center of her chest. He mistook her fretting for thoughts of last night, which she had been able to avoid all day, thanks to his cheekiness and commanding attitude. Running had been the last thing she wanted to do this morning, but even she had to admit it distracted her from the darkness.

"You're a good man," she blurted out. Her version of goodbye, and thank you?

He snorted. "Yeah, I don't know about that."

"You are, though. You're nothing like Jonathan." Despite looking like a young version of him.

Tom's eyes darkened to a luscious brown. She liked when they smoldered like that. It made things low in her belly tighten in a way she hadn't experienced in a very long time.

"Thank you," he murmured and cleared his throat. "I'm, uh, going to get the couch ready."

"All right." She gave a nod and wandered to the washroom to freshen up. Escaping while he readied himself for bed meant she wouldn't have time to change, so she pulled on a bra beneath her tank top and stuffed a pair of socks in her pocket. She'd grab her shoes on the way out and put them on in the elevator. Her hair went up in a ponytail, and she brushed her teeth and gave herself a stern look in the mirror.

You can do this, she repeated to herself as she walked back to the living area. But what she found there had her freezing in the doorway.

"What the bloody hell did you do?" she asked, shocked.

Tom glanced up from his makeshift bed on the floor. His muscular arms were tucked behind his head, and his bare feet were crossed at the ankles. "As I mentioned earlier, we're in renowned Sentinel and Ichorian territory."

"So you put the couch in front of the door?"

"Yes." A simple answer. No explanation.

"And you moved the cushions to the floor because…?"

"Because if someone comes for us and they try the door, they'll shoot there first." He pointed to the seating area of the couch. "And I'd prefer to avoid that."

"Right." Hysteria bubbled deep inside. How did she keep coming this close to fleeing, only to have it yanked out from beneath her every bloody time? Someone up there found her misery humorous.

Tom popped up to his feet in that agile way of his and gave her a nod. "Be right back."

"Right," she repeated, her gaze on the obstacle. No way could she move that without making a ton of noise and attracting his attention. Not to mention, she didn't have time.

Plan B.

Which would be?

"Oh, I almost forgot." Tom stood in the doorway holding a gun. The sight of it made her stomach turn over. "I'm putting this in the nightstand, just in case. Try not to shoot me with it, okay?"

He didn't wait for her reply, which was good because she didn't have one. Her limbs went numb as her insides crumpled.

What the bloody hell am I going to do? She had a weapon, which meant little to her now that she couldn't leave.

Unless I use it to disable him…

No. No way could she consider hurting him in that way. Killing Anita had been one thing, but Tom? That would break her on a different level.

But he'll wake up just fine in the morning. A mortal death would trigger his immortal genetics, and he'd become a full-blooded Hydraian in the morning. Just like her.

No.

The idea was unacceptable.

But logical.

She covered her ears with her palms in an attempt to shut up the devil in her mind, but it wouldn't stop.

He's a fledgling. Being reborn a Hydraian is his destiny. You'll just be helping him along.

What if he isn't a fledgling, though?

Don't be daft. You know he is. He's the spitting image of his father, who is one hundred percent Ichorian.

She couldn't believe the debate happening in her head. Was she really considering this? Shooting Tom to temporarily disable him long enough to run away?

"My God," she whispered, appalled. He saved her life, and this was how she intended to repay him?

"All done," he said from behind her. She'd been staring at the couch the entire time, debating his fate.

I'm going to hell.

No, you're escaping it.

"I'm going to bed," she announced, moving past him without looking up. He didn't try to stop her or say anything when she closed the door to the bedroom. Thank goodness for that because she didn't trust her mouth.

Flopping onto the bed, she pulled a pillow over her head and willed the voices to stop. She'd never felt so conflicted in her entire life. Her goal only a few weeks ago had been to take him down, but now everything had changed.

She liked him. At some point, the arse had gotten inside of her heart and made her care. He taught her things no one else had ever considered teaching her and treated her as an equal. The men in her life told her she didn't need to know this or that because it would never be an issue. No. That wasn't entirely fair. Issac tried to show her a few things, but Eli always brushed him off with an "I've got it." Well, he didn't have it. He had died.

Amelia rubbed her chest. Not for the first time, she blamed her former love for putting her in this situation. Oh, he never meant to, and she knew it, but had he just showed her a few tricks, maybe things would have been different in the end. Or maybe not. They both trusted Jonathan, and neither saw his betrayal coming until it was too late.

Sort of like how Tom won't predict you using the firearm…

She groaned. The logical part of her agreed shooting him was a sound plan. He'd wake up tomorrow pissed off, but alive, and she'd be one step closer to her brother. Really, she'd be doing Tom a favor by removing herself from his life. He obviously had the means and knowledge to take care of himself, while she functioned as unwieldy baggage. He said so himself at the cabin that going on without her would be the easier route. She could help him out with that and assist herself in the process. A win-win.

Her head hurt by the time she decided what to do, and a glance at the clock said it had taken her long enough. No light trickled from under the door, indicating Tom had gone to bed.

It was now or never.

She retrieved the gun from the nightstand as quietly as she could and crept over to the threshold. Pausing with her hand on the knob, she listened and heard nothing from the other side. With a deep, calming breath, she twisted and pulled and gazed into the near-black room. Tom had drawn the curtains, but a soft glow between the cracks illuminated her path to him on the floor. He slept on his back, with one arm tucked behind his head, and the other sprawled at his side.

He really is a beautiful man. High cheekbones, long lashes, a solid jaw, and a slightly bent nose. She'd miss his face. She'd miss him.

Her hand trembled as she aimed at his chest.

Pull the trigger, the sensible part of her urged. *Before he wakes up.*

Amelia hesitated, her stomach rolling in turmoil. She thought her mind was made up in the bedroom, but seeing him lying there so innocently had her backtracking. How could she do this to him after everything they'd been through? Captor or not, he never harmed her. And it seemed he never wanted to hold her hostage to begin with; it was all his father. Punishing him for Jonathan's sins felt wrong.

She fell to her knees beside him as her legs gave out. Her aim never wavered, though, as the gun remained pointed at his heart.

"Do it," Tom whispered, startling her. She met his wary gaze and felt a piece of her heart break. Witnessing the resignation in his gaze was too much. When he grabbed her shoulder to draw her closer, she went because she couldn't fight him. Not like this. His opposite hand wrapped around her wrist, but instead of disarming her, he guided the barrel to his rib cage.

"Shoot me," he urged. "If it's what you need to do, then do it."

A tear found its way to the corner of her eye and rolled down her cheek. She couldn't remember the last time she cried; she thought Jonathan had beaten it out of her.

The palm on her shoulder slid to the back of her neck as Tom pulled her down the rest of the way and rolled her beneath him. His grip on her wrist never faltered as he kept the gun aimed at his chest. She shuddered as his hips settled between her legs, and closed her eyes when his lips brushed hers.

"I'll understand, Amelia. I know it's what I deserve."

But he didn't. Not at all. And she knew that deep down. It's why she couldn't kill him.

He balanced on his elbow beside her head but kept his mouth a hairsbreadth away from hers. The quiver in her belly went lower and evolved into something hotter. Another tear slipped from her eye, a direct conflict to the sensations building deep inside. Darkness returned, but it held a different allure this time. A passionate one that tempted her to do things she never dreamed of doing with a man other than Eli.

Her fingers tried to slip from the weapon between them, but his grasp remained firm.

"Don't," he whispered. "Or I'll do something I shouldn't."

She shivered. "Like what?"

"This." His mouth captured hers in an unforgiving kiss that left her breathless beneath him. Their embrace in the theater had been a preview to what he did to her now. All his focus and confidence flowed from his lips to hers as he provoked her deepest desires.

She couldn't move, couldn't think, couldn't breathe…

He consumed her very being, leaving her in a puddle on the floor.

All she wanted was him.

Her tongue yearned for his, but he demanded control, and she gave it to him. The fingers around her wrist tightened as his hips pressed intimately into hers. His arousal was thick and hot between her thighs.

My God…

"Tell me to stop," he whispered against her lips. "Make me stop."

No.

She closed the gap between them and tried again to move her hand away from the weapon. If she accidentally shot him, she'd never forgive herself. But his grip remained as he possessed her mouth.

When his tongue parted her lips, she moaned and lost all semblance of control. No man had ever kissed her this way.

Tom treated her like a woman, not a girl, and he didn't hold back. His hips met hers again, and all hell broke loose. The gun disappeared as he set it on the floor away from them, and his palm went to her breast. She grabbed the back of his neck and arched into him with a force she didn't realize she possessed.

What is he doing to me?

Everything felt so foreign, so good.

"Amelia," he breathed. "Fuck, I want you."

His hand slid to her neck, holding her in place as he devoured her once more. She wrapped both arms around his shoulders and threaded her fingers through his hair.

Approval vibrated deep in his chest, making her squirm. She liked that low growl. The nerves in her lower belly tingled in anticipation at the sound, and it sent a fresh surge of desire to the apex between her thighs.

I'm turned on, she realized with a start. *Well and truly turned on.*

Did she ever expect to experience this again? With a man other than Eli?

Thinking of her former lover should have ruined the moment, but all it did was reinforce it. The emotions Tom inspired in her were unlike anything she'd ever experienced. She was a new woman in his arms, cherished and protected, yet revered and respected. The way he dominated her with his body was just what she needed. An escape from reality, similar to the darkness, but so much better. Here she could feel and be and enjoy.

The palm on her neck went to her breast and down to the hem of her tank top. Heat met her bare skin as he ran his hand up her side.

She quivered beneath him and luxuriated in the feel of pleasurable contact.

It'd been so long…

"Tell me you want this," he breathed. "I need to know you want this, sweetheart." Her heart fluttered in response to the endearment. She loved the way it rolled off his lips onto hers.

Amelia tried to capture his mouth again, only to be held down by the palm between her breasts. His eyes smoldered with an intensity that caused her pulse to race. Arousal never looked so good on a man. And she thought he didn't want her. *What was I thinking?*

"Kiss me," she pleaded. "I need you to kiss me."

"I want to do a lot more than kiss you, Amelia." The warning in his voice made her shiver.

She swallowed. "Then do it."

"One word, and I stop. Say no, and it all stops."

Never. "Kiss me," she repeated. "Please."

"I want to taste every inch of you," he whispered against her lips. He led with his tongue, taking her mouth with a possessiveness that left her breathless. A fire blossomed in her lower belly and spread heat to all her nerve endings. Her clothes were suffocating. She needed them off and moved to lift her tank top higher, but Tom caught both hands in one of his and stretched them over her head. His lips trailed down the column of her neck to her collarbone, where he nibbled her delicate skin.

She squirmed beneath him, desperate for more, but he prolonged the sensual torture by licking the swell of her breasts. When he dipped down to her bra and back up, she thought she might die with want.

Too long had she gone without these sensations brewing in her abdomen. And the way he touched her was unlike anything she'd ever felt.

No fear or hesitation, and all confidence.

This man understood how to handle a woman and knew what he wanted and how he wanted it.

Bunching her top in his free hand, he lifted it over her head and let it rest against her elbows while he flicked open her bra.

"Perfection," he murmured, making her hotter.

One nipple disappeared between his lips as he sucked deep, and her body bowed off the makeshift bed beneath her. The heavy thickness of his arousal hit her right where she wanted it as his hips pushed her back down.

Spasms shot down her legs, making her shake with need.

He switched breasts to take her opposite peak deep into his mouth.

Pain mingled with pleasure, sending a sharp sensation to her lower abdomen.

"Tom…" Her hoarse voice barely registered to her own ears, but he seemed to hear her.

He shifted downward, kissing and nipping her abdomen, before hooking his thumbs in the soft cotton of her panties beneath her pajama bottoms. His eyes held hers as he pulled the fabric, pants and all, over her thighs, knees, and ankles, leaving her completely naked before him.

His gaze drifted over her in lazy sweeps as he admired every inch of her exposed body. Hunger dilated his pupils, making her thighs clench.

"Your blush is very pretty, sweetheart. I wonder how red I can make you," he mused as he crawled over her, fully clothed, and stopped at the juncture between her legs.

She opened her mouth to reply, but he nuzzled her core, and all coherent thought spiraled to a puddle at her feet.

His hands ran up her thighs to spread her wider as his mouth settled over her clit.

No warning or teasing, but direct, straightforward, and amazing.

She whimpered at the onslaught of sensation, and goosebumps rained down her arms.

Pleasure overwhelmed her being, shutting down all thought of anything other than Tom's tongue against her damp flesh. He gave her a deep lick that made her toes curl and pulled her sensitive bud between his teeth.

Time stopped as an incredible surge of ecstasy swept through her, starting at her center and bursting to every cell in her body. A scream ripped through her throat as her body convulsed beneath him. Tom's hand against her abdomen kept her grounded as he drew out the sensations with his tongue.

Lights flashed behind her eyes, making her dizzy, as he climbed over her. His grin was all satisfied male when she finally focused on him.

"This is a good look on you," he murmured against her lips. "Red, dazed, and thoroughly pleasured. I want to see it again with my cock deep inside of you." A fresh surge of arousal hit her lower belly at the taste of her own pleasure on his tongue. He kissed her hard, leaving his mark on her soul.

"Do you want me to stop, Amelia?" It was a breath against her ear. "Or do you want more?"

Her mouth went dry. "More," she whispered. "So much more."

Chapter Twelve

Killing Isn't Easy

Those three words went straight to Tom's groin. His balls tightened to a painful degree as his cock twitched. Control resided in his blood, but even he had a limit. Amelia's irises deepened to an oceanic blue as desire enflamed her pupils. He knew that expression well, had seen it on countless women throughout the years, but on her, it felt brand new. A gift meant for only him to unwrap, and he had every intention of finding the prize inside.

He pulled his shirt over his head and grinned when she tried to lift her hands to touch him. Her tank top looked so pretty around her forearms. She didn't realize he'd hooked it to the button of the cushion beneath her. A spur of the moment twist of his fingers that kept her bound prettily for his viewing pleasure. Of course, he kept it loose enough for her to wiggle out if she wanted. A hard yank would set her free as well, but she appeared too mesmerized by his abdomen to try.

Her hot gaze went to his sweatpants as he pulled the tie loose. Stripping for her had its merits. To see a gorgeous woman sprawled out before him flushed with desire as he revealed his body never got old. But Amelia amplified it tenfold. Her eyes glinted as he set his cock free and shed the rest of his clothes, and her hands twitched. He leaned over to yank the top off her arms to see what she would do. Featherlight fingertips flitted over his arms and pectorals and then down his stomach to stop above the place he wanted her most.

"Touch me." The request sounded more like a demand due to the desire deepening his tone. He wanted her more than he could remember wanting any woman, but it would always be on her terms. "Please," he managed.

"Where?"

The innocent word gave him pause. It should be obvious, but he wouldn't push. "Anywhere you want."

Her eyebrows rose, and excitement touched her lips. "Anywhere?" she repeated. "Truly?"

Amelia couldn't possibly be a virgin. She and Eli had been lovers for centuries, and no way the former Elder hadn't taken her to bed. Unless his lethal touch prevented him from loving her properly. An image formed behind his eyes, making him growl low in his throat. The thought of anyone else worshipping this woman painted Tom's vision red. *No.* He would erase all those who came before him and make it impossible for her to forget him.

"Wherever you want, Amelia," he whispered and shifted to lie beside her on the bed of couch pillows and blankets.

She went to her elbow and licked her lips. "I can taste you?"

Fuck. Those words alone nearly pushed him over the edge. He was known for his restraint, yet this woman could undo it with a few innocent phrases.

"Yes." It came out rough, and her expression suggested she liked it.

That mouth of hers was designed for sin, but that smile? Oh, he loved that smile. It made his dick throb in anticipation and his balls pull tight. Her nails traced the ridges of his abdomen, hesitant. When she reached his happy trail, his eyes fell shut on a groan he couldn't contain, and her hand disappeared.

"If you're trying to kill me, sweetheart, it's working."

"You like it?"

He peeked at her. "I'd like you to do a hell of a lot more." Preferably before he came apart at the seams, pinned her down, and fucked her. If her comfort didn't mean so much to him, he'd do exactly that.

"More?" She pressed her palm to the area above his groin. "I like the idea of more." Her silky strands danced against his chest as she lowered her mouth to his sternum. He laced his fingers through her hair in encouragement as she licked a path down the center of his torso to where her hand rested, and lower. His breath caught when she took his cock between her lips without warning.

Shit. The wet heat proved almost too much to bear, but he couldn't pull her away. Especially not as she took him deeper, her lips caressing every inch as a soft hum of approval sounded in the back of her throat.

Her fingers wrapped around the base of his shaft as she swirled her tongue around the tip. His hips flexed upward as he hissed a curse.

She paused, as if startled by the sound, and he glanced down to find her watching him.

"Fuck," he growled. *So fucking hot.*

Arousal shone bright in her eyes, making it impossible to look away as she took more of him between her lips and sucked. Hard. Another move like that would send him over the edge, and he wasn't ready to come in her mouth.

Not tonight.

Not after the weeks of tension and abstaining.

He needed to be inside of her. With his fist in her hair, he pulled her off of him and rolled her beneath him. His hard length settled against her wet heat, sending electricity through his veins.

"I wasn't done." Her admonishment lacked fervor.

"You can taste me thoroughly later," he whispered and captured her lips in a punishing kiss. Her responding moan set his blood on fire. "I need you, Amelia. I need you now."

"Take me." The two words against his mouth sent him over the edge, pushing his hips forward.

Her tight sheath fit him like a glove and made everything tighten down below, but he didn't like the way she stiffened. In his eagerness to be inside her, he'd moved too fast, and her body wasn't ready for a man his size. Rookie mistake.

Tom dropped his mouth to her neck as she acclimated to his intrusion. He placed soft, soothing kisses along the column of her throat, her chin, and up to her ear. "Sorry, sweetheart."

"I'm all right." She relaxed and eventually started to move against him. When her nails dug into his shoulders, he tried a shallow thrust, and she groaned his name. Her grip on him tightened when he shifted again, and her legs wrapped around his waist to allow for deeper access.

Tom let his control slip a notch and pushed harder. She rewarded him with a guttural sound that went straight to his balls. He explored and learned her body and cravings through varying degrees of penetration and found that hard and rough seemed to be a pace she enjoyed most. Her nails scored his skin as he pushed himself to the hilt, and her legs trembled around him.

His mouth found hers, and he ravaged her with his tongue. She felt perfect beneath him, as if destined to be there, and he worshipped her with each thrust. When he felt her slick walls tighten around him, he slid his thumb down to the center of her pleasure and jolted as she came around him. He moved with her, prolonging her orgasm, and bit off a curse as he followed her over the edge.

Ecstasy shot from his groin to every nerve ending as he emptied himself inside of her. All that bullshit about delayed gratification had merit, because this was unlike anything he'd ever experienced. His limbs shook from the impact, but he remained hard and ready inside her for another round. The earth-shattering explosion wasn't enough. He needed more. So much more.

Her legs loosened from his waist, but her arms remained around his neck as he kissed her with a ferocity he couldn't control. His tongue memorized every inch of her mouth before pulling back. She gazed up at him through hooded eyes and flashed an impish grin that excited his cock.

He brushed his lips against hers and moved lazily against her, luxuriating in the feel of their intimate connection. She surprised him by mimicking his thrust with one of her own.

"Careful, sweetheart, or I'll take that as an invitation."

"Maybe you should," she whispered. But the way her body strained beneath him confirmed she needed a break. He pushed deep one final time and gently pulled away before desire overrode reason.

"I want to hold you for a while first." He rolled to his side and wrapped an arm around her waist to cuddle her against him. It placed her curvy ass against his groin, but it was her giggle that pleased him most. She'd laughed around him a few times, but never quite like that.

He smiled against her hair and kissed the top of her head. What a pair they made on the floor, beside the couch, sprawled out over cushions and blankets. He'd carry her to the bed once his arousal died. If he carried her now, he'd end up taking her again, and she wasn't ready for what he had in mind.

Her body stiffened, putting him on alert. Then he followed her gaze to the gun a few feet away and relaxed. He'd heard her creep into the living area and hadn't been shocked by the weapon in her hands. His reaction to it, however, surprised him.

Rather than find amusement in the situation, he had felt resigned. If she had needed to kill him in retribution, he wouldn't have stopped her. As Jonathan's son, he was the perfect person for her to punish for the sins leveled against her. He understood that better than anyone, even if it broke his heart to see that weapon in her hands and pointed at him. But now that he knew the truth about her feelings, he wouldn't let her go without a fight, and he certainly wouldn't offer up his life again. She deserved better than that.

Tightening his arm around her, he pressed his lips to the pulse at her neck. "If you're thinking about shooting me now, think again, little asset. I might be aroused as hell, but my reflexes work just as well while I'm naked as they do when I'm clothed."

Her responding tremble took the teasing right out of him. He eased her onto her back to stare down into her wide, wet eyes. Sorrow replaced the beautiful arousal deep in their depths. He wanted to destroy whatever caused her such grief.

"Talk to me, Amelia." He brushed the hair from her face and tucked it behind her ear before cupping her cheek. "What's wrong?"

She shuddered and whispered, "I don't know who I am anymore."

He frowned. "Why?"

"I… I shot people, threatened you with a gun, wear jeans and tank tops, and hate silk. And I don't know what any of that means. I don't know if anyone will recognize me." Tears were streaming down her cheeks by the end, which was not at all how he intended their evening to end. Then the first thing she said kicked him in the gut.

Of course.

"Yesterday was your first time killing someone." That explained her breakdown. He hadn't even considered it as a cause, because his first time happened so long ago. But of course that impacted her. It was never easy to pull the trigger, especially for a civilian.

"I didn't even think," she whispered. "I just reacted."

"Anita got what she deserved, Amelia." He brushed away her tears with his thumbs and kissed her. "I don't know what happened in the labs, but I've gathered it was bad. And if she showed up behind my back, I have no doubt she had a horrible session planned. You acted in self-defense."

"She threatened to call Jonathan and become my new guard."

"Because she found you roaming about freely?"

Amelia nodded and buried her head against his chest. He folded his arms around her and kissed the top of her head. This emotional breakdown seemed less intense than last night, which relieved him to an extent. Maybe talking it through would help her feel better.

"Why do you hate silk?" he wondered, starting off on a lighter topic.

She didn't reply right away, as if startled by his change in subject. "It's too soft," she finally said. "But I used to love it."

"And you don't anymore?"

She shook her head. "I also used to love skirts and dresses and never wore jeans. But softer fabrics don't feel right to me anymore. I prefer rougher, durable cloth."

"Well, jeans are more practical, but maybe you'll come around when you see your old clothes again." His words caused her to stiffen. "You do still want to go home, right?"

~*~

Do I? Amelia wasn't sure. "I'm worried they won't recognize me or want me anymore."

Tom's arms tightened around her in a protective gesture that melted her heart. Seeing the gun on the floor brought back her earlier plans, and guilt washed over her. She'd been about to shoot him. *Who have I become?*

"Of course they'll want you, Amelia. They'd be crazy not to."

"But I'm not who I used to be." He couldn't possibly understand. The old her thrived in Hydria, acting as a party planner and social butterfly. Throwing a dinner party with friends no longer held the same appeal.

"Maybe, maybe not." He pressed his cheek to the top of her head and sighed. "You're a gorgeous, strong, intelligent woman who has survived unspeakable things. If they can't love this version of you, then they're not worthy of you."

"Strong?" she repeated. No one had ever called her that before. "You think I'm strong?"

"I do." He pulled back to stare down at her. "You amaze me more every day."

Despite the fresh tears gathering in her eyes, she smiled. "Thank you."

"See? You're gorgeous." His lips touched hers, sending a flutter of excitement to her lower belly. Making love to him had been unlike anything she'd ever experienced with Eli. Tom's authority more than translated to the bedroom, and his domineering control set her blood on fire. She loved the way he handled her, never fearing for a minute that she might break. It was refreshing and hot and oh-so good.

"Mmm," he murmured. "Not yet. We're not done talking. You're afraid they won't recognize you, but haven't mentioned the elephant in the room."

She frowned. "Elephant?" What the bloody hell did an animal have to do with anything?

"Your ability to shift, Amelia."

Her blood ran cold. "I don't want to talk about that."

"What about your secondary gift? It has something to do with intelligence, right?"

She frowned.

All Hydraians inherited a gift from each parent, and she was no different.

Her father, Aidan, passed on an intellectual ability, but no one ever asked her about it because her talent paled in comparison to what he could do. Being an Ichorian with several millennia of life, most considered him omniscient. Her half brother Luc inherited the same talent, making them the perfect father-son duo for strategy. It left her feeling inadequate since all she could do was impart wisdom, while they functioned as all-knowing gods.

"What about it?" she wondered.

"You gift knowledge through touch, right?"

"Sort of. If it's something I know, like a language, I can gift it to someone. But I have to know it first, which makes it a useless talent. If I had Luc and Aidan's brain power? Now that would be worth discussing."

He went onto his elbow beside her, and she fell to her back to stare up at him.

"What languages do you speak?"

Not the question she expected. "English, French, and Greek. Some Spanish and German, too, but not well. Why?"

"Hmm." His palm felt hot against her hip as he slid one leg between hers. "Greek, I learned for obvious reasons, but never French."

"Did Jonathan teach you Greek?"

"No, it was one of the many curriculums assigned to me as a child. I didn't exactly have a standard upbringing." He spoke with a nonchalance that didn't match the turmoil in his gaze.

"Tell me about it."

"I'd rather you teach me French."

His deflection made her smile. "Truly? French?" Eli found it useless, but few things fascinated him. Being several millennia old did that to a man. He'd experienced so much, while she experienced so little. Perhaps that was why he never taught her practical things, like how to defend herself.

"Why not?" Tom replied. "I speak half a dozen other languages and only a little bit of French. Let's add it to my knowledge base."

"If I teach you French, then you have to tell me more about your upbringing." Because she wanted to know everything about him, to better understand why he chose to help her instead of stay by his father's side.

His gaze darkened and dropped to her lips. "You teach me French, and I'll tell you how I learned Greek."

"No, you already told me it was a curriculum. I want something more substantial."

"Hmm." He brushed his mouth over hers in a lingering kiss and grinned. "There isn't much to tell. My dad sent me to a military school when I turned ten"—another kiss—"and paid someone to act as my guardian while he busied himself with the CRF. I didn't see him much, and when I did, it was usually during one of my exams."

"Jonathan monitored your examinations?" That sounded like the man she knew. He monitored more than a few of her own exams.

"Teach me French, and I'll tell you more."

"Tease," she accused. But she had to smile. His sly negotiation tactics matched the man she'd come to enjoy. "Okay, fine."

Amelia palmed his cheek and closed her eyes to concentrate. Transferring knowledge took minimal effort on the psychic plane, but she hadn't engaged this part of herself in a very long time. Sort of like riding a bicycle after a decade of sitting down. She murmured a few key phrases in French to herself and smiled as the tendril of knowledge flowed to the forefront of her mind.

"This might tingle," she warned as she strung the mental threads together.

"Tingle away, sweetheart."

With a smile, she released the psychic thread from her fingertips and guided it into his essence. It took less than a minute for the transfer to hold. *Like fitting a piece into a complicated puzzle.* Her heart fluttered at the awe in Tom's expression as she pulled her hand away.

"C'est génial," he murmured. *That's amazing. "Ça dure combien de temps?" How long does it last?*

"Forever, if I will it." Which she did in this case. What would be the point in making a foreign language temporary?

"So you can gift someone knowledge temporarily?"

"Yes, but I've only done it once or twice. On the off chance someone asks for something, it's usually long-term."

"I take it you don't use it often, then?"

"Well, no, it's not like I have the knowledge base of Luc and Aidan. I can only gift things I know, which isn't very much when surrounded by Hydraians two or three times my age."

Plus, she spent most of her time with the Elders, who had several millennia on her three centuries. Learning something as simple as French didn't compare to ancient Greek or Coptic.

Tom nuzzled her chin and placed a kiss against her neck. "I don't think you realize how powerful of a gift this is, Amelia. Knowledge isn't power. Personal experience is, and you have a lot of it."

She frowned. Why would she ever pass her history on to someone else? Her most recent experiences at the CRF, especially. No one would be interested in understanding those memories.

"But more importantly…" He pulled back to meet her gaze. "You just used one of your Hydraian talents, which suggests you can use them both, as they are genetically related."

She blinked, not understanding. Then it hit her squarely in the chest. He tricked her into using her ability to test whether or not it worked. Heat washed over her, and not the good kind.

"You bastard." What if it hadn't worked? Did he realize what that would have done to her?

"Yes, but now you know—"

"No! You don't get to decide that for me!" She tried to push him off her, but he didn't budge. His leg between her thighs kept her from squirming out from beneath him.

"Amelia—"

"You don't get it!" Tears gathered in her eyes as she fought futilely to get away from him. "You bast—"

His firm mouth sealed over hers, stealing the breath from her lungs.

She bit his lower lip, hard, and dug her nails into his shoulders, all in an attempt to avoid the arousal thickening her blood.

But that only turned his kiss more demanding.

Damn the attractive man and his skilled tongue.

He cupped her cheeks and angled her head to better take her mouth.

She shuddered beneath him, defeated. This sensation felt so much better than climbing into her black hole of nothingness. He helped her forget everything with a few seductive caresses.

"I was trying to help," he breathed against her lips. "I'm sorry."

He kissed her again before she could reply, wooing her into submission. His hips settled between hers as his elbows caged her in above, and she couldn't help but wrap her arms around his back and pull him closer.

She'd gone so long without physical comfort, and Tom's touch set her veins on fire. He was an arse for tricking her, even if he meant well. She needed him to understand why it hurt, why she hated that he tricked her, so he would never do it again.

"My powers are part of who I am. Imagine for a minute that someone cut off your legs and forced you to walk." The words clawed at her throat, but she forced them out. "Not once, not twice, but over and over again. And no matter how hard you tried, you couldn't do it anymore. That part of you was gone and all you had left was a constant reminder that you're less than what you were. Would you ever want to stand again?"

"Jesus, Amelia." Darkness swirled in his gaze as he stared down at her. "Why didn't you ever say anything to me?"

"What would I have said?" He worked for the monster in charge of her captivity. Why would she ever expect him to help her?

"I didn't know, but I suspected. That's why I kept checking on you."

All the bottles of water. She didn't trust them at first, but dehydration proved a powerful motivator, and one day she caved. When it didn't affect her negatively, she accepted the others but always wondered why he visited. He never said much, except on his last visit. "You were so angry that last time in my cell. Why?"

"Why?" Both his eyebrows lifted. "Are you seriously asking me that?"

She frowned. "Well, yes. All your other visits were cordial, but you were positively incensed that last time."

"Because I found you lying on the floor, vomiting blood."

"Right. Jonathan hated that, too." He used to make her lick it up afterward. A punishment for daring to bleed in his presence. The blood of a Hydraian was toxic to an Ichorian, something she knew very well and fantasized about daily. If only she could get him to ingest it...

"I was furious because my father beat you for no fucking reason, not that there is ever a reason to hurt a woman." His lips flattened. "Why do you think we ended up in a cabin upstate? My dad was livid with me already and decided babysitting you was the perfect punishment, especially since moving you was my suggestion."

Her brow furrowed. "I thought Stark suggested it." He implied as much during their last healing session, didn't he?

"No, he agreed with my idea, which is why... Wait, how did you know that?"

"He told me."

"Stark told you moving to the cabin was his idea?"

"In a way, yes. He mentioned things not being black and white." Her memory was a bit fuzzy due to the drugs he administered, but she thought that's what he said. "He's a strange man." *With strange powers.*

"Well, it was my idea, but my father only agreed because Stark approved of it. And it gave my dad a way to punish me. Bet he's regretting that right about now." Amusement danced in his eyes, making her curious.

"Tell me more about the examinations." That was part of their deal before he distracted her with hot kisses and infuriating tricks.

Some of the amusement died at her request. "I suppose that's only fair." He blew out a long breath and shook his head. "My dad used to administer certain exams. Not the academic kind, but the practical kind."

"I'm not quite sure I understand. What is a practical test?"

"When I was thirteen, he dropped me off a block away from the Arcadia on the night of a Conclave, handed me a gun with eight incendiary bullets, and told me to fight my way home."

Amelia's lips parted. She'd never attended a Conclave but knew of them.

And placing a fledgling so close to all those Ichorians? Especially one as infamous as Tom? That was a death sentence. "That's horrid."

"I survived, barely, and he rewarded me by sending me back to school the same night. My private martial arts training took on a brutal twist the following week because my father wasn't impressed with my time." He shrugged. "As I said, my upbringing wasn't exactly normal, but if it taught me one thing, it's that sometimes you have to pull the trigger to survive."

"I had no idea." Jonathan always brimmed with pride when he talked about Tom. Another act, or something else entirely?

"Well, that makes two of us, then, because I didn't realize how bad it was for you until, well, recently." His expression darkened. "What you did to Anita was a mercy compared to what I would have done to her, Amelia. Killing someone is never easy, and having a conscience about it is what keeps us humane." The intensity in his stare almost undid her. "You aren't a bad person for pulling the trigger, sweetheart. It's when you start enjoying the kill that you have something to be concerned about."

She swallowed, unnerved by the veracity of his words. "I don't want to think about this anymore."

His gaze dropped to her lips. "I can assist with that."

"Make me forget, Tom." Her fingers wove through his hair, pulling him closer. "Help me forget everything."

He nibbled on her lower lip and shifted his hips to align with hers. Despite the troubling conversation and frustration boiling through her, she remained ready for him. Something that became all the more obvious as he slid his erection through her damp folds. This man did something to her. Whether healthy or not, she wasn't quite sure, but she liked it. His ability to take her away from reality to a land of pleasure where only they existed was a place she could get used to going.

"Kiss me," she whispered.

His mouth captured hers in an addicting kiss. So much control, passion, and heat radiated from him, making her melt beneath him.

A moan escaped her as he palmed her breast and tweaked her nipple. She loved how he handled her, so confident and commanding, yet gentle and attentive. With every stroke and caress, reality fled and pleasure overtook her being until all she could think about was him.

Yes, this is what I want. Always.

When he slid inside her again, she sighed.

His slow, loving pace was what she craved. It created a fire in her lower belly that grew with each deep thrust until the fierce sensations rolled through her limbs, making her shake with uncontrollable lust.

Tom's hand slipped between them, going straight to where she needed him most, and sent her over the edge with one flick to her clit.

She cried out as she came around him, her nails scoring his back, and his name a benediction on her tongue. He didn't come with her but kept his lazy pace and kissed her like a man who had all the time in the world.

"Again," she begged, needing more.

Dark brown eyes held hers as amusement flirted across his luscious lips. "I can do this all night, sweetheart."

Arrogant arse. "Prove it."

His grin was all self-assured male. "A dangerous request, but as you wish."

Chapter Thirteen

Incendiary Bullets

"Isn't it a bit hot for that?" Amelia wondered, eyeing Tom's leather jacket.

"I lived in the desert for three years. Trust me, I can endure a New York City summer dressed like this. Besides, it hides my guns." He flashed her the weapons at his sides, making her grimace.

"Are all those necessary?" They were going to her brother's office, not the Arcadia.

"Yes." Flat, no room for negotiation.

"Issac isn't going to hurt you." She wouldn't let him. Not after everything Tom had done for her.

"It's not your brother I'm worried about."

Right. They were in a city filled with Ichorians and Sentinels, and Tom wasn't wearing a disguise. Nor did he ask her to shift, something she thanked him for silently. It appeared their discussion last night had the desired effect. She might be able to shift, but she wasn't ready to try yet.

Amelia winced as she pulled on her jeans. The man wasn't kidding about going all night. When she woke up this afternoon with his head between her thighs, she didn't think it possible to come again, but he proved her wrong before taking her hard and fast in the shower. *Impressive* didn't begin to cover it. She could still feel him between her legs. The satisfaction in his gaze when she buttoned her jeans suggested he knew. *Cocky arse.*

"Keep staring at me like that, and I'll postpone our plans another day or two." His deep voice sent a shiver down her spine.

She batted her eyes in an innocent gesture that belied the heat blooming below. "I'm sure I don't know what you're talking about."

"No?"

Oh, that look can only mean… She scrambled backward as he came after her, but hit the wall with her back. Pressing her palms to his chest, she said, "Okay, but—"

He silenced her with a scorching kiss that left her shaking. "Did that clarify things for you?" he whispered darkly against her lips.

She had to clear her throat to speak. "Maybe a little."

"Good. Are we staying or leaving, sweetheart?"

Tom had asked her what she wanted to do today after their lovemaking in the shower. Finding Issac had been at the top of her list and still was, but Tom provided an alluring alternative.

He licked her lower lip. "Mmm, I'd prefer to stay here another week or so, order room service, and lose myself in you for hours at a time." His words showered goosebumps down her arms. The good kind. "But that would be selfish of me and goes against all my training. We need to keep moving, and your brother is the one best positioned to help you survive."

"You mean us," she corrected. Issac would help them both.

"Sure."

The sarcasm in his tone wasn't lost on her, but she didn't argue. Her brother would prove Tom wrong, and then she'd say, *I told you so.*

He let her go with a tender kiss and went to fuss over his bag while she put on a shirt and shoes. Her hair went up into a ponytail that she strung through the back of the ball cap he gave her to wear. He wore a matching one and sunglasses.

"I wish I had a camera," he murmured. "You're cute in Yankees garb."

She rolled her eyes. "If this is your idea of payback, I'm not amused."

"It's the heart of baseball season, and we're in New York City. Just trying to help you blend in."

"Yes, I'm sure that's what this is."

She followed Tom's lead as they left the hotel, averting her gaze when he did and avoiding the cameras in the elevator and reception area. Once outside, he linked his fingers with hers and kept her close. He commented on the sights and weather as they walked, acting as if they were on a date. But despite his casual demeanor and relaxed posture, she knew he was hyperaware of his surroundings and taking in every detail. When they entered the subway, he handed her a ticket and reminded her to keep her head down.

"There are cameras all over the place," he murmured. "And the CRF has access to everything in this city."

By the time they exited the subway, her stomach was in knots. Their destination stood a few blocks away. Her feet felt like lead with every step as she wondered what to say to Issac. Would he be able to accept the new her, or would he expect her to revert to her old self?

"How do you feel about a quick lunch?" Tom asked, surprising her. They had room service shortly before leaving the hotel. How could he be hungry already? "Maybe here?" He picked a pizza place on their left and opened the door. "Ladies first."

"All right." Has he lost his mind?

"Let's sit and peruse the menu." He grabbed a stack of menus from the ordering counter, chose a table at the back, and gestured for her to scoot into the corner. His bag went between them as he settled beside her.

"Why are we…?" Her voice trailed off as the bell over the door announced the arrival of two broad-shouldered men wearing curious expressions. Tom gave them a little wave from the booth and wrapped his arm around Amelia's shoulders.

"You know them?" she whispered, frowning. They weren't Sentinels she recognized.

"Gentlemen." He greeted the pair with a grin. "Care for a bite to eat?"

"A Sentinel loose in the city during broad daylight? Never thought I'd see the day," the one with darker hair said.

Amelia's blood chilled. *Ichorians.* The hungry gleam in their eyes was a dead giveaway, especially when they focused on her. Rumor had it Hydraian blood acted as an aphrodisiac to their kind. A natural seduction to lure them to their deaths. Issac never seemed bothered by it, but her brother wasn't one to succumb to weakness easily.

"Now, boys, you wouldn't be looking to cause any trouble in a public place, would you?" Tom tsked. "Bad form."

"How about you walk outside quietly, and we let the pretty brunette live." This came from the shorter of the two. His blond waves were lush and tousled and didn't at all match the mean expression on his round face.

"You know, I think I'll pass. I promised her the full New York City experience, and that includes pizza. But hey, if you want to wait a bit, I might be able to accommodate in, oh, say, never? Does that work for you?"

"You're just as cocky as they say, but I don't see what has everyone so scared." The bulkier one folded his arms. "Maybe we should take them back for our Mistress to play with. Alive."

"Who do you think she'd set on fire first?"

"The girl, definitely. And force him to watch."

"That would be fun."

Tom's expression turned bored as they continued to discuss their fate. How long would it take the Ichorians to recognize her? Most immortals did immediately, but perhaps her new fashion sense kept her incognito. Also the fact that they thought she was dead would help.

"I'm thinking pepperoni," Tom murmured to her. "Extra sauce?"

Have you gone mad? she asked with a look.

He shrugged. "Okay, okay. We'll go half cheese." He drummed his fingers over the menu. "Boys, would you like anything before we get started?"

"I'm one hundred and eighteen," Mister Bulky replied. "Hardly a boy."

"Congratulations," Tom drawled. "I'm twenty-seven, but my birthday isn't for another few months. Want an invite to the party?"

"Can you believe this guy?" Bulky asked.

The blond shook his head in disbelief. "Unbelievable."

Tom pushed off the booth to come face-to-face with both men. "Now, just remember, I did offer to buy you lunch first."

"Are you—"

Tom slammed his fist into the bulky one's jaw, cutting off whatever he'd been about to say, and nailed the other Ichorian with a knee to the groin. A flash of metal appeared as one of them drew a blade, but Tom snagged it in a move too fast for her eyes to catch.

Amelia worried one of the restaurant patrons might call the cops or try to break up the fight, but the employee only looked on with a concerned expression while the couple by the windows watched with mild curiosity.

She jumped as the bulky one crashed into her table. His eyes rolled into the back of his head as he lost consciousness, and the blond fell beside him to the floor a few seconds later.

"Bag," Tom said without breaking his stride and held out his hand. "We've gotta go. Now."

She pushed the heavy pack toward the edge of the booth, and he snagged it. "Are they dead?" she asked as she stood on shaky legs.

"No, just unconscious." He pulled the straps over his shoulders and stepped over their hulking forms.

"Hey, y-you're not g-going anywhere," the employee stuttered, blocking their path with a phone in his hand. His scrawny build and curly hair suggested he was no older than twenty.

Tom sighed. "Look, kid, those two dickheads followed us for the last two blocks and said some not-so-pleasant things to my girl here. I'm sorry for the mess, but they had it coming."

The young man frowned, then considered Amelia. "Is that true?"

She nodded. *Technically, yes.* The couple in the corner nodded along with her. She suspected they only did that because they wanted to be on Tom's side. Who wouldn't after a performance like that?

"I dunno man. I should probably call the cops," the employee murmured, scratching his head.

"You should," Tom agreed. "And while you're at it, have these two asshats arrested. Meanwhile, I'm getting her out of here." His tone brooked no argument, and as he stepped forward, the clerk jumped out of his way. "For the mess and trouble," her Sentinel added as he slapped a few bills on the counter. She ducked under his arm out the door and accepted his hand.

"We need to move quickly," he said as he tugged her down the sidewalk. "Dumb and Dumber called for backup before entering the restaurant."

"How do you know that?" she wondered, baffled. He hadn't even hinted at them being followed until pulling her into the pizza place.

"Because I saw them."

"Where?"

"On the subway. It's why I chose this stop instead of the one closer to your brother's office."

She hadn't even noticed. New York City's geography was foreign to her.

"We're moving on to plan B," Tom said as he took a left down an alley. "It won't take long for word to get back to the CRF that I'm in the city, so we need get the hell out and don't have time to go back to The Pierre."

"Okay." She kept his brisk pace and came to an abrupt stop as a short woman with brown spikes stepped in front of them. A sharp blade played through her fingers as she twirled it with a casual ease and looked them over.

"Ya know, I never liked Bobby. Always thought he was an idiot and didn't understand why Lucinda kept him around, but Sam is a friend." The stranger's expression darkened on that final word. "And you just knocked him out."

Another Ichorian. There was a reason the treaty stated Hydraians entered New York City at their own risk. Hydria posed the same threat, just the other way around. What Amelia wouldn't give to be home on the island right about now.

"With a blow to the head," a voice from behind rumbled. Amelia jumped, while Tom didn't react, probably because he already sensed the second party. The man behind them stood well over six feet, broad shouldered with a belly that suggested one too many American treats, and a beard. Oh, and he was glowering menacingly at them. Good. Just what they needed. Why had Tom suggested New York City, again? Because no one would expect them to come here? She was beginning to understand why; only those who courted death would visit this city.

"She smells sweet. Too sweet," the girl murmured.

"Hydraian sweet," the male replied.

The brunette cocked her head in a birdlike manner and blinked. "Yes. I think you might be right, Steve."

A chill skittered down Amelia's spine. Once they recognized her, all hell would break loose. Aidan's progeny were infamous. As one of the oldest Ichorians in existence, he held a certain reverence over his kind, which meant they would have to take her to the Conclave, alive. Then Osiris would likely kill her for sport because he was a sadistic bastard who enjoyed torture, but it would be even worse for her family. Aidan and Issac would be forced to watch.

One rule: stay out of New York City.

Oops.

~*~

Being discovered on the subway by two of Lucinda's favorite pets had not been part of the plan. They'd no doubt been drawn to Amelia's looks and maybe even her scent, but had settled their challenging gaze on Tom not a second later. And then the game of chess began with Tom moving his queen to safety and the pawns falling into the king's trap. Except he hadn't counted on two more knights showing up so quickly. Good thing he packed more than one gun for this mission.

The petite woman displayed a quiet confidence that identified her as the leader of this ambush. Two or three more were likely on their way, and perhaps Lucinda herself. If she showed up, he was a dead man. No amount of reflexes and guns would help him out of that predicament, which meant he needed to get this dance over with as soon as possible. He had no desire to become that sadistic bitch's new plaything. She had an affinity for fire and blood, and not necessarily in that order.

He took a step sideways toward Amelia, which forced her to back up into the wall beside them, and put his back to her chest so he could see both players.

"I have this thing about hurting women," he explained to the brunette, "so if you want to walk away, I'll wait."

Her hazel eyes lit with a fire, suggesting he'd struck a nerve. *Just trying to do the chivalrous thing here.* Okay, nope, he took that back. She threw her blade with a precision he would have admired had it not been aimed at his chest. Reflexes were all that saved his heart. He swiveled to the side and barely had enough time to take Amelia with him. She fell to the ground with an "Oomph." He dropped a gun in her lap before engaging the tiny girl in hand-to-hand combat. Size could be deceiving, because the chick had a powerful punch that hit him square in the jaw and made him see stars.

Fuck, this woman is fast. He wondered if that was her gift as he ducked to sweep her legs out from under her. She jumped and attempted a kick to his face, which had him backing up a step with his hands raised.

"Low blow," he admonished. Facial injuries crossed the line, but Ichorians weren't known to play fair. Killing a woman didn't sit well with him, but as he said to Amelia last night, he either pulled the trigger or risked harm to himself and maybe even her. The coldness in the woman's gaze helped his decision, as did her connection to Lucinda. Anyone who worked with or for that bitch deserved a lethal fate.

He blocked another blow and twisted out of reach as she went for his family jewels. *Oh, hell no.* On her next kick, he whipped out the gun from beneath his jacket and fired a round between her dead eyes. The standard bullet was enough to knock her out, but not kill her. Something he might regret later, but for now, mission accomplished.

The fight felt like it had gone on for minutes, when in reality, it was more like fifteen seconds. Amelia was rocking back and forth on the ground as the bearded dude stared down at her. Whatever psychic gift he'd engaged to hold her there couldn't be that strong if he had to focus that hard. Tom gave the Ichorian a solid kick to the back to snap his concentration and went to fire his weapon, when Amelia beat him to the punch. She let lose a round into the man's chest and screamed as she did it. His brow rose at the colorful display of words leaving her lips. He had no idea she could curse like that.

"That bloody hurt!" She punctuated the statement with another bullet to the man's brain, making Tom cringe. Those incendiary bullets were not cheap, nor could he find them at any regular store, and she'd just used five or six of them on one very dead Ichorian.

He held out a hand to still her when she took aim again. "He's dead, sweetheart. Very, very dead."

She growled and stomped her foot. "He did something with wind that bloody hurt my ears."

"An elemental," Tom mused. "But a shitty one if all he could do was mess with your hearing." Her glower told him that was the wrong thing to say. "You showed him, though. Nicely done, sweetheart."

She eyed the man on the ground, frowned down at the pistol in her hand, and looked back at Tom. "He's dead?"

"Yeah, and we're going to be, too, if we don't get moving. There's more coming." He suspected this was the B-team, and he didn't want to wait around for the A-team.

"But only fire and Hydraian blood can kill an Ichorian, other than a beheading I mean."

"Yes. That's not your average gun." The CRF engineered it to hold bullets that ignited on contact. Hence the sizzle and smoke coming from the bearded dude. One of those babies to the heart set the bloodstream on fire and killed Ichorians instantly.

"This is the gun you gave me last night."

"Right, in case we were attacked by Ichorians. Can we get moving?"

Blue fire swirled in her irises as she stalked toward him. That look froze him in his tracks. She resembled a pissed-off goddess.

"I almost shot you with this gun." She shook it in his face.

Fuck. "Are we going to do this now?" Because they really didn't have time for it.

"I almost *shot* you. I thought you'd wake up, but with these bullets? You would have *died.* For good!"

"True, but—" Her palm connected with his cheek so hard he couldn't speak. His face was not having a good day. "Amelia—"

"No! I almost killed you! Like really, truly killed you!" Tears gathered in her eyes, making his chest ache.

"I didn't…" He cleared his throat and tried again. "I wasn't going to stand in your way if you wanted to leave, Amelia."

When he saw that gun in her hands, all the excitement of a challenge fled, and grief settled in its place. Maybe it was exhaustion, but it felt a whole hell of a lot more like resignation. Death had knocked at his door more times than he could count. It caused him to be cavalier with his life and perhaps a tiny bit suicidal.

"You're a bloody arse for doing that to me. I couldn't. I wouldn't…" She slapped his shoulder, but it lacked heat. When she hit his sternum, he wrapped his arms around her, and she buried her head in his chest. Standing in this alley made them the perfect Ichorian bait, but she was useless to him like this. He needed her to calm down and fight with him later.

"I hate you," she whispered.

The words vibrated through his heart, leaving a stroke of pain he didn't expect. She wasn't the first woman to say those words to him, but she was the first to leave an imprint. He kissed her hair and held her close. "Why would you do that to me, Tom? Why?"

"I thought it was what you needed," he admitted. "For retribution against my father. A way of seeking punishment for the sins leveled against you. Who better to kill than the son of the man who tortured you?" It sounded ridiculous now after everything he'd learned, but a part of it still rang true. Tom *was* her best option for revenge, if she wanted it. She had the power to destroy him because he would never fight her. Ever.

Amelia remained quiet for too long. "I considered it once. In the beginning, I mean. But I could never…" She trembled and clung to him tighter.

"Shh, it's okay. I expected you to hate me, Amelia. I mean, I'm John's son, and all the things the CRF did to you…" He paused to breathe deeply through his nose. *Not going there right now.* "I never would have put you in that situation last night had I known. I'm sorry. I thought it would help."

"Never." She implored him with her eyes. "That would *never* help."

"I know that now."

"Do you? Because if you do that to me again, I will shoot you. Just with a normal gun and a lot of normal bullets."

He couldn't help his grin. "Is that a promise?"

"No, don't you smile at me like that. I'm not done being mad at you."

"I know. But can you be mad at me later?" he asked softly. "After we get out of the city alive?"

"You wouldn't be alive if I had shot you," she grumbled. "But you're right. I don't want to die."

"Neither do I." He brushed his lips against hers and felt a smidgen of relief when she returned the kiss. "Can we go?"

She nodded against him and pulled away. He took the gun she offered and returned it to his holster, then linked his fingers with hers to start a brisk walk down the alley. One perk of his job? He knew the city inside and out and had an escape plan ready. He took a left onto a busier street, then a right, and found his target.

"What are we doing?" she asked as they entered a parking garage.

"I'm going to need you to do me a favor," he replied. "See that guy over there?" He gestured to the valet station, where a man sat behind the desk. "I'm going to need you to distract him."

"Distract him?" she repeated. "By what, shooting him?"

He chuckled as they walked. "Well, that would certainly be a distraction, but no. I was thinking you saunter over there and be your charming self while I snag a pair of keys. Unless you prefer to watch me hot-wire a car again?"

She blinked. "You wish for me to flirt with him?"

"Yes." He stopped a few yards away and ducked behind a pillar. "Act like you're lost and trying to figure out how to retrieve your car from the valet. When he asks for your ticket, pretend you lost it and stall."

She gaped at him. "You can't be serious."

"You prefer the hot-wiring?"

Her frown was cute. "Oh, all right, but you better be quick."

"On my honor," he murmured with a smile.

She shook her head. "Right. I'm still mad at you."

"Good. Now go distract him."

"Yes, sir." Sarcasm be damned, he liked the way that sounded on her lips. *Something to consider later.*

He watched as she strolled up to the valet and engaged the grinning man in conversation. The dude folded his arms on the counter and leaned toward Amelia while she pretended to search her pockets. *Worked like a charm.*

Tom crept toward the cabinet of keys behind them and selected a few for shopping purposes. Ducking into the staircase, he headed to the parking decks belowground and clicked the various buttons to find an appropriate ride. He stopped when a sleek motorcycle caught his eye.

"Well, hello, beautiful." He swapped his baseball cap for the helmet hanging from the handle and grabbed another from a nearby bike for Amelia. Then he settled over the sporty seat, tested the key, and gave the bike a good rev. "Oh, yeah. You'll do."

The garage had a self-park level in addition to the valet, making it easy to drive out without notice. Just needed to pick up his woman and go. He maneuvered the new ride to the valet desk where he left her and stopped by the curb. Amelia's gaze widened when she caught sight of him, and her lips parted.

"You cannot possibly expect me to get on that thing," she blurted out as the man behind the desk watched with a wrinkly brow.

Just stealing a bike, kid. Nothing to see here.

"I do," Tom replied. "Hop on."

Her head swung back and forth. "Absolutely not."

"Seriously? After everything we've gone through, a bike is what you take issue with?" Didn't they just agree not to bicker until they were safe?

"It's a death trap."

"And standing here arguing while a horde of Ichorians are searching for us isn't?" he asked, baffled.

She bit her lip and shook her head again.

Stubborn woman. "Here." Tom held out the helmet, and she cocked a challenging brow in response. They didn't have time for this. "Put this on, and get on the bike. We've gotta go. Now."

"I'd prefer a car" was her succinct reply.

"And I'd prefer to get the hell out of here. Put on the damn helmet, Amelia."

"You know this guy?" The lanky valet guy went for the hero card and failed. One glance put the kid back in his place and allowed Tom to refocus on his rebellious asset.

"I'm not asking again, sweetheart."

Amelia shot him a glare and yanked the helmet from his hand. She seemed to take great pleasure in throwing her Yankees cap to the ground. *Vixen.*

"We're so having a talk about this later." The growl in her voice made him smile.

"I look forward to it."

"Arse," she muttered as she threw a leg over the bike.

"Hold on, asset." He waited for her arms to settle around his waist before maneuvering out of the garage. The valet would realize Tom had stolen the bike whenever they found all the missing keys, which he suspected would take them a few hours tops. By then he'd be well out of the city and on his way to plan B: the Hamptons.

* * *

Tom's last visit to Wakefield Manor had been one of desperation. Heading down the long driveway after pressing the call button felt much the same, if not worse.

Coming here was a risk for multiple reasons. The CRF would consider it a potential escape option, but his father's pride would come into play. John Fitzgerald would expect Tom to exhaust all his options before seeking help from their biggest enemy. In this case, his dad would fail to consider just how far Tom would go to protect Amelia. It turned out he would risk his life because it was very likely Issac Wakefield would kill him on sight.

Like mother, like son.

Amelia's tension behind him broke his heart. He understood her hesitation all too well, because he felt the same way every time he returned to the cabin.

Death roams here.

Tom's father betrayed Amelia in the darkest of ways on these grounds. He murdered her lover, Eli, before taking her hostage. The two unforgivable sins no doubt weighed on her thoughts now.

"This was the best alternative to your brother's office," he said, feeling like an asshole. She couldn't possibly want to be here any more than he did, let alone with a Fitzgerald. Didn't matter that he played no part in the crime; his blood made him guilty by association.

She nodded against his back and laid her head against his shoulder. He placed his hand over hers and squeezed as he came to a stop by the guesthouse. A round man with a curious glint in his kind eyes walked out with an elderly woman by his side.

"How can we help you?" He sounded so cordial, yet he had to recognize the name Tom gave him at the security gate. No way did he work for the Wakefields this long and not have a clue as to Issac's immortality.

"Not me." He removed the helmet from his head and shook out his hair. "Her."

Amelia's arms were cement around his waist, so he gave her hand another gentle squeeze. "You can do this, sweetheart," he murmured low for her ears alone. "I'm here if you need me."

Another nod against his back, and her grasp loosened a fraction. He hung the helmet over the bars and ran his fingers over her hands and forearms, willing her to relax. The couple watched with concerned expressions, and he noted the phone in the older man's hand. Someone with immortal genes would be along shortly because no way did he call the cops. If not her brother, one of the Hydraians. They had a notorious teleporter with unimaginable skills. *Talk about a fun talent.*

"I can do this," she whispered.

"Yes."

"Okay." Her palms slid along his abdomen to his sides as she used him to climb off the bike. She unlatched the helmet and pulled it off slowly before handing it to him. The sunglasses went next, and the couple gasped loudly.

"Amelia?" the man asked with a hand at his mouth.

"Hi, Robert. Cherie."

"Oh my God…"

CHAPTER FOURTEEN

A Sleepy Homecoming

Amelia refused to go in the main house. It held too many memories, good and bad, and her heart couldn't handle it. She sat by the swimming pool, nibbling on a sandwich Cherie had brought her, while Tom paced a few feet away. Robert said Issac would be here soon, something that should have pleased her, but this manor made happiness impossible.

The low-hanging moon reminded her of that night—a dinner that started between friends and ended between enemies. Inviting Jonathan over for an evening of food and drinks had been second nature. She'd known him her entire life, likened him to an uncle due to his relationship with her father, and never expected his treachery. His familial charade burned to the ground when he pulled out that gun and shot Eli in the chest without blinking an eye.

She shivered despite the sultry summer heat. Tom's hands on her shoulders had her meeting his dark gaze. Kindness and concern with a touch of comfort stared down at her. Just what she needed at precisely the right moment. She stood and wrapped her arms around his neck as he folded his around her back. He pressed a kiss to her hair, then rested his cheek on her head.

"It's going to be okay, sweetheart."

"I know," she whispered. "But this place… I can't stay here tonight."

"The history haunts you."

She pressed her chin to his chest and gazed up at him. "Did he tell you…?"

She trailed off, unable to finish. Of course Jonathan told his son about that night. He considered it one of his biggest victories, taking down Eli the Elder, one of the strongest Hydraians in existence, with a bullet to the chest.

"I know enough of it, but that's not what I meant. That weight in your chest lessens over time, but I don't know if it ever goes away. Mine hasn't. Not completely, anyway."

She considered his meaning, wondering what memory he could be referring to, when realization washed over her. The way he reacted in the room after Anita's first visit to the cabin, how he cursed and fled from the room as if he'd seen a ghost, and the blood on the photos in his closet. Of course. Anna's murder. It happened at the cabin. She had a vague memory of Issac calling to tell her about helping Jonathan and being too late.

"Why do you keep the cabin?" she wondered.

"My mother left it in my name, and my father insisted on keeping it. I want nothing to do with it, so my aunt essentially maintains it in my absence."

"And sending you there with me?"

"Served as a punishment of sorts."

Tom mentioned that last night but never explained himself. "Punishment for what?"

He blew out a breath. "That's a long story, but in a nutshell, I went behind my dad's back to show a friend the truth about Ichorians, and she nearly died. Of course, he's reaping the benefits now because he's turning her into a fucking Sentinel."

"A female Sentinel?"

"Yeah, and about that. She's also sort of your brother's girlfriend, which is why—"

"Hold on." Her hands fell to her sides as she peered up at him. "My brother has a girlfriend?" No bloody way. Issac didn't go beyond a first date. Ever.

"Apparently."

"My brother, as in Issac?" The man who refused every woman she ever introduced him to? Who had no interest in relationships that lasted more than one night? *Monogamy might work for you and Eli, love, but it does not suit me.* How many times did he say that to her? "Are you certain we're talking about the same man?"

"Unfortunately, yeah. Definitely the same guy."

She didn't know how to process that. How many decades did she spend playing matchmaker with him and failing?

Tom went rigid against her, his hands fisting at her back as he squeezed his eyes shut. She studied him in alarm as his cheeks went white.

"Are you all right?"

"Your brother." He spoke through clenched teeth and grimaced. "He's here."

She spun around as his arms fell, and took in the empty patio. Strands of soft lights illuminated the area without moonlight, while a soft glow emanated from the pool. "I don't see him."

"Trust me," he growled, posture stiff. "He's nearby."

Her brow furrowed, then lifted as she caught on. "He's in your head." Issac could manipulate vision on a psychic level, similar and yet so different from Amelia's ability to shift humanoid appearance. They inherited their imagery skills from their mother. If her brother could tap into Tom, then he could also tap into her thoughts. She searched for a memory of their mum from childhood and painted a vivid picture of the woman lecturing them about how to properly treat guests. A blue butterfly fluttered through the image mid-lecture, making her heart race.

"He's here," she whispered. Tears filled her eyes, and for once, they weren't the sad kind. She pressed her hands to her mouth and spun to face Tom. "My brother is really, truly here."

"Yeah, and he's a dick." Tom muttered, glowering at the patio. He didn't appear to be in pain anymore, but he did look ready to commit murder.

"What did he do?"

He shook his head. "Let's just say it wasn't a thank-you."

"My apologies, Thomas. Do I owe you a thank-you?" Her brother's voice floated over the night air and showered goosebumps down her arms. She would recognize those cool tones anywhere.

He's here. Amelia turned and watched him saunter around the side of the manor with Tristan at his side. They resembled dark-haired angels in suits and wore matching warrior-like expressions. She pinched her side, a habit formed from nights of dreaming about this moment only to wake to an empty room. When Issac didn't disappear, her knees wobbled.

Could it be?

"You're here," she whispered. "I can't believe you're here." A sob caught in her throat as the fantasy she never thought would become a reality came to life before her eyes.

Issac's strong arms went around her as he pulled her into an unforgiving hug. *Is this real?* She inhaled the fresh linen of his crisp dress shirt and sighed at its familiarity. *My brother.* Tears rolled down her cheeks as his love and devotion washed over her in heady waves. She didn't need an emotive ability to feel it; his warmth and strength was enough.

"You're alive," he breathed, holding her impossibly tighter. "I'm so sorry, Amelia. I'm so fucking sorry."

She held him with the same ferocity and sobbed into his sturdy chest. God, how she missed him. The last two or three years had dulled her to the emptiness inside, but being near him again rekindled all those old feelings of dashed hope and resignation. At some point, she stopped believing in him, and that moment hurt the most.

But he's here. He's real. She clung to him for support as her legs threatened to buckle beneath her.

I'm finally free.

"I thought you were gone." His voice cracked on the words as he buried his face in her hair. "I would have come for you, Amelia. I'm so fucking sorry I didn't." The pain in his words broke her heart. Of course he would blame himself. Her brother had a knight complex, always wanting to protect her from the evils of the world. If she learned one thing during her captivity, it was that villains existed in all forms. *And so do heroes,* her heart whispered, thinking of Tom. He stood silent behind her, a wall of protection and warmth that soothed her soul.

"Finding your ashes was the worst day of my life," her brother continued. "God, Amelia, I missed you so fucking much." His agony trembled through her and ripped her chest wide open. Her brother, who rarely showed emotion, was falling apart in her arms. And he blamed himself for something he had no control over.

"I forgive you," she whispered, knowing he needed to hear it. *I don't blame you, dear brother. I could never blame you.* "Jonathan fooled us all."

Issac stiffened as his trademark armor snapped into place, and resolve straightened his spine. *There's the brother I know and adore.* Further proof that this was indeed not a hallucination. How many days and nights had she dreamed of this moment? Perhaps not with Tom as a witness, but his presence felt right here. *I'm home.*

"I'll execute him for this." A promise underlined with a conviction only her brother could convey. Ichorians were notorious for their grotesque murder scenes, and Issac had participated in more than a few of them. There was a reason his kind held him in high regard. They feared him.

"If anyone has earned the right to seek vengeance against my father, it's Amelia. Not you." Challenge replaced the usual playfulness in Tom's tone, making her wonder what history she had missed between him and her brother. Or was he still sour over the vision game?

"Shall I silence him, Issac?" Tristan asked.

"That won't be necessary. Not yet, anyway." Issac kept his arm around her shoulders, tucking her into his side as he turned to face Tom with a bland expression. Her brother always could turn off his emotions in the blink of an eye. "Tell me why I shouldn't kill you, Thomas."

Amelia gasped. "Issac!"

"You probably should," Tom replied with a shrug.

"Okay, no, not this again." Amelia threw her brother's arm off of her shoulders and moved to stand in front of her suicidal lover. "If you hurt him, I'll never forgive you, Issac."

Her brother's brow hit his hairline. He glanced at Tristan, who appeared just as shocked. The old Amelia would never talk back in this manner unless they'd committed a social faux pas. Which, really, she could argue threatening to murder a houseguest was a major infraction, but that belied the point.

"Amelia, I'm…" Issac's voice trailed off as his phone started to ring. He put the device to his ear. "Yes, Mateo?" He nodded. "Very good. Yes, please." He pocketed the mobile and trained his gaze on the man behind her. "Sentinel chatter indicates they're on their way here for a scouting mission. Care to elaborate?"

"Sure. Knowing my father, he's covering his bases. Wakefield Manor is the last place he would expect me to go, but it's not like I've let that stop me before, so he's sending men to watch your property. My guess is, he's more worried about you discovering that Amelia's alive than he is with catching me."

"Because it would ruin the illusion," Issac murmured with a nod. His sapphire gaze softened as it lowered to her. "Jacque is on his way. Do you wish to change before we go?"

She fingered the Yankees shirt. "Are my clothes still here?"

"Yes." No elaboration. Typical Issac.

"You didn't refashion the suite for yourself?"

"This is my second time to the estate since your, er, departure."

Her eyes widened. "You've only been here two times since…?"

His intense look unsettled her stomach almost as much as her unfinished question. She knew before he spoke that his words were going to hurt. "Jonathan left Eli in the ballroom with a vase holding your ashes. To say this place gives me nightmares is an understatement."

His blatant depiction weakened her knees. She fell back into Tom, and his arms came around her automatically. If he was intimidated by the death glare her brother flashed him, he didn't show it. He held her while she trembled and offered the support she so desperately needed. That night flashed through her mind as if it were yesterday. Jonathan had pointed the gun at her after shooting Eli and gave her a choice. *Comply or die.* She chose to comply at the time but hadn't realized what that would mean in the end. Oh, how she selected the wrong option that night.

"I'll destroy him," Issac bit out, obviously seeing the scenes tumbling through her thoughts. She tried to stop them but couldn't. This place overwhelmed her. All the memories of her life with Eli were tainted by that single night and what happened next. She turned in Tom's arms and buried her head against his chest to breathe in his masculine scent. Darkness loomed, threatening to consume her being, but his strength cocooned her, protecting her when she needed it most.

"We need to get her away from here," she heard him say. "It's too much."

"So now you're the expert when it comes to my sister?"

"Yes." Flat, no room for argument.

"We'll see about that." Issac's cool tones floated over her in a dreamy wave.

Oh no. She recognized this sensation, the one of drowsiness right before falling asleep. Except there was nothing natural about it, not right now. She didn't want to leave Tom's warmth, but Issac gave her no choice. His gift for vision manipulation extended to the dream world, something he activated and flowed over her. He meant well, he always did, but the Amelia who accepted his comfort in the past wasn't here now. She craved a different type of escape, one that involved a certain blond Sentinel.

Her lips parted in protest, but no sound escaped. Heaviness settled over her shoulders and back and ventured downward. Tom's hold was all that kept her from falling as her legs gave out. His responding curse sounded so far away.

We'll be chatting about this later, dear brother.

* * *

Silky sheets twined through Amelia's thighs as she rolled over on the too-soft bed. She woke with a start, blinking into the fading sun outside her windows. The ocean lay beyond it with waves rolling over black sand.

Oh my God. Her hand flew to her mouth. *I'm trapped in a dream.*

This happened so often lately, especially after one of Jonathan's beatings. Memories tortured her every time she closed her eyes. Usually, she woke up just as she started to believe they were real, and then the crushing pain of reality fell on her, making it difficult to breathe.

No. Never again.

She tore off her flimsy tank top and shorts, refusing to let something so delicate ever touch her skin again, and was in the process of ripping the silk sheets from the bed when a male cleared his throat. Standing in nothing but a thong, she met a pair of chocolate eyes that only existed in her distant memories.

It's about time Balthazar visited me in a dream.

"You mean to tell me I don't visit them often?" he asked with a devilish grin. "I'm wounded, truly."

Oh, good, his mind-reading ability works here, too. Of course, it was her dream, so she could take it away. But what would be the fun in that?

Amelia sat on the pillow-top mattress and studied him. No one would blame her. Balthazar was a god among men, and he knew it. Square jaw, perfect nose, high cheekbones, dark eyelashes women would kill for, and a chiseled body made for sin. She'd seen him shirtless countless times, yet he wore jeans and a T-shirt. Too bad he couldn't show up in her head dressed to seduce. She could use a little escape.

A frown creased her brow. No. Pleasure wasn't what she desired right now. Not with him, anyway. She craved a certain blond Sentinel, one who chased away the darkness…

"Oh, bollocks." Heat swam up her neck. "I'm not dreaming."

"No, you're very much awake and also very naked."

She grabbed the sheet and pulled it around her like a dress as memories overwhelmed her. They ended with Issac putting her to sleep for what felt like days.

I'm finally, really, truly home. So why did it feel so foreign and wrong? She sat down on the mattress and flinched. *Too soft.*

Balthazar pushed off the door frame and placed a mug on the nightstand before settling his big body beside her on the bed. The man could seduce a woman with a single look, but concern deepened his eyes and tugged at the edges of his full lips. "Come here, love."

She went willingly into his arms and rested her head against his chest. As an Elder, and one of her oldest friends, he knew her well. At least in her former life.

"God, it feels so good to hold you," he whispered. "When Issac told us you were alive, it was hard to believe."

"I missed you, too, B." His nickname rolled off her tongue but didn't feel quite right. None of this did. The bed was too comforting, the home too warm, and the setting sun was too bright.

He combed his fingers through her hair and sighed. "I can help."

She knew exactly what he meant but couldn't bear it. "Don't."

"I'd never force it."

"And that's why I love you." She meant it. He might come off as arrogant and brazen, but deep down, he cared. His abilities to control emotion and read minds made him a master manipulator. He could drown out all her concerns and cocoon her in a sea of bliss, but it wouldn't be real. She needed to feel, to remember, or she'd become a shell of nothingness. The darkness would be a better alternative. When it became too much, she knew whom to turn to, unless…

Panic settled in her chest, forcing her to pull away from her old friend. "Where's Tom?" She fell asleep in his arms, but Jacque had obviously teleported her here. What about Tom? Did he leave without saying goodbye? Was he still in New York? And where was her brother? They needed to have a discussion about his actions.

Balthazar's mouth curled down into an uncharacteristic scowl. "The Sentinel's here."

"In Hydria?"

"Yes."

Her shoulders sagged in relief as her heart gave a little flutter. He hadn't left her. "Is he here now?" She suspected he wasn't, or he would be in the room, not Balthazar. Unless the Elders had him occupied. They were a bit chatty on occasion, especially with visitors. And Tom's fledgling status would have Luc wanting to learn all about him.

"No."

She frowned at Balthazar's one-word response. The man's notorious wit seemed to have disappeared behind a fog of frustration. "What aren't you telling me?" she wondered.

"He's indisposed at the moment."

"What the bloody hell does that mean, *indisposed*? Tell me what's going on."

He looked her up and down and smirked. "I'm liking this new feisty side of you, Amelia. It's kind of hot."

"Don't change the subject or distract me with sex. Where's Tom?"

All teasing fled his features, and the Elder in him peeked out from beneath the surface. "I'm not going to pretend I haven't figured out what happened between the two of you, but trust me when I say it's done."

She bristled. All the Elders, except Eli, treated her like their kid sister, and she could see that hadn't changed in her absence. Usually, she felt special, but not today. "Excuse me, but that's not your decision to make."

"You're right. It's Luc's, and his word is law." He stood up and ran his fingers through his dark hair. "I know you think this is harsh, and I'm sorry for that, but we're doing what's best for you. That man is in your head, and not in a healthy way."

"Unbelievable." She stood to be on his level and didn't care for a second how ridiculous she looked dressed in a silky sheet. "You have no idea what he's done for me or what I've been through or why you couldn't be more wrong."

Tom never mistreated her or caused her to feel inferior. If anything, he treated her as an equal, taught her how to defend herself, and centered her when she needed it. Like the other night in the bathtub and again when she couldn't pull the trigger.

She thought back to his first visit in her cell, the surprise in his gaze she mistook for a game when he asked if she was okay. At the time, she called him the good cop, but he meant it. He genuinely cared. All those water bottles and sporadic visits were his way of checking up on her, which she understood now. And the grief in his eyes when he realized Anita's visit to the cabin hadn't been pleasant, that was real, too. What they had was unique and new and not something anyone would stop her from pursuing, because she needed him. And from what little she'd gathered over the last few days, he needed her, too. Because the man clearly had a death wish.

Curiosity colored Balthazar's expression, indicating he'd eavesdropped on her thoughts. He might not control emotion on a whim, but he always listened. Even when he shouldn't.

"He's locked up, but alive. That's all I can give you."

"Locked up?" she repeated, incredulous. "Why on earth would Luc lock him up? He's a fledgling, one of us."

"That Sentinel is *not* one of us, Amelia. He's spent his short existence slaughtering immortals, and that includes Hydraians. He's about as welcome here as his father."

Amelia's mouth fell open. "You cannot compare him to Jonathan."

"Oh, yes, I can. You don't know him like we do."

"And likewise!" She hadn't meant to shout at him, but locking Tom up after everything he had done for her was madness. They should be welcoming him with open arms. Fledglings weren't common, and a man with his skills could be exceptionally useful. "You know nothing about him," she added in a normal tone.

"If that's true, we're about to know a hell of a lot more."

Her blood ran cold. "What are you doing to him?"

He blew out a breath and palmed the back of his neck. "Nothing. Yet."

Her brow crinkled at the irritation in his reply. It didn't appear to be directed toward her, but toward someone else. "Tell me what's going on, B."

"No." All playing left his stance and expression, telling her he wouldn't budge. The Elder, not her big brother or friend, stared at her now. Her lips trembled at the feeling of being an outsider, but she expected this. She wasn't the woman they once adored, and Balthazar would see that better than anyone.

"I'll always love you, Amelia," he murmured, his veneer cracking. "Don't ever think otherwise." She knew he meant that literally since he could read her thoughts.

"Why won't you tell me what's happening to him?"

"Give us some time to figure this out, okay?"

She nibbled her lip, considering. If Balthazar wouldn't talk to her, no one would, except maybe Issac. And she doubted even he would say anything in this situation after the way he treated Tom last night. They meant well and wanted to keep her safe, but ignorance wasn't always bliss. Her friends and family remembered the Amelia who would bow down and do nothing. She'd introduce them to the new her soon, but not yet. "Fine."

Balthazar narrowed his eyes, obviously having heard that last thought, but didn't press her. Knowing him, he'd prefer to find out by observing. He looked her up and down and folded his arms. "I'll have you know those are not cheap sheets you tried to destroy, and last I knew, you loved silk. That's why I put them on the bed for you."

His words had her glancing around. She hadn't thought much of the warm tones, masculine furniture, or the colossal bed until he pointed it out. "Why am I at your house?"

"Because your home was repurposed after the incident and turned into a guesthouse for fledglings. Luc thought it was the best way to honor your memory."

She shivered. *Honoring my memory*. Because they all thought she was dead. Such a surreal feeling, though she agreed that refashioning her home for fledglings was a fitting tribute. Amelia served as a mother hen to several future Hydraians, teaching them about immortal life on the island and serving as a social coordinator. Would she ever be that woman again? Just thinking about it made her sick to her stomach. How could she serve as a role model in her current mental state?

"Hey," Balthazar murmured, his hand settling on her bare shoulder. "Don't worry yourself about the future. Just focus on the now. And remember, you're not alone. We're going to love you no matter what, Amelia. There are no expectations. Do you understand?"

She bit her lip. He meant well, but he couldn't understand just how different she'd become, how her experience shaped her. Six years to an immortal his age meant little to nothing, but to her, it redefined her existence. Jonathan stole her innocence, destroyed her faith, and removed all aspect of hope. How did she even begin to describe that?

He did the same thing to Tom, her conscious whispered. Which explained her bond with him. Of all the people she knew, Tom was the only one who understood how it felt to be manipulated and destroyed by a loved one. Neither of them had a choice; they were just held in different cages. And now he was in a cell somewhere on the island. She intended to do something about that.

"I need clothes," she told Balthazar. "And preferably not a dress." Who would have thought she'd rather wear Tom's boxers and shirts right about now? They suited her more than her old clothes.

Balthazar's brow rose. "I'm not sure whether to address that little plan of yours, or the words you just said out loud. But by the look on your face, I won't say anything about either item." Amusement danced through his gaze as he took her measure again. "Oh, I do like this new side of you. Luc is in for a treat. Wakefield, too."

"Clothes."

"Yes, ma'am." He walked over to one of his dressers to muddle through the drawers. His gaze was wicked as he turned around and handed her a pair of boxers and a shirt. "Mine might be a bit bigger than the Sentinel's, but they'll do. Just do me a solid and let me be there when Issac sees you in these, yeah?"

Some things never changed. "Are you two still bickering like little boys?"

He pressed a hand to his chest. "Me? Never."

"Right. I'm surprised Issac even let me stay here with you." Her brother and Balthazar had a tedious relationship underlined in begrudging trust. It seemed more logical for her to wake up at Luc's house than Balthazar's, but she wasn't complaining.

"Your brothers are preoccupied with another issue at the moment." Humor danced in his gaze, making her curious.

"What other issue?"

"Oh, I'll let them explain that one to you."

"Okay." She pulled the shirt over her head while he watched and dropped the sheet to put on the shorts.

"You do remember that I have a full bath complete with all the toiletries a man or woman could possibly want, right?"

"Yes." His notorious hospitality pleased more than a few bedmates. The man was insatiable, but he treated his partners with respect and made them all feel like gods. Or so she'd been told. As good of friends as they were, they'd never crossed that line, and they never would. Eli meant too much to them to ever even consider it.

"I miss him," Balthazar murmured, hearing her thoughts. His sad smile tugged at her heartstrings. "This new you would shock the hell out of him, but in a good way."

Her stomach knotted at his words, as a feeling of unease crept over her. "I'm not the woman he loved, B."

"Maybe not," he agreed. "But he would have loved this you, too. That man was crazy about you."

Guilt weighed on her conscience as Eli's face flashed behind her eyes. Every time she thought of him, another detail went missing. This time, it was the dark shade of his irises, a unique gray that didn't quite hold the same appeal they once did. A luscious brown stared back at her instead.

Amelia couldn't love Eli like she once did, not after everything. He would always hold a special place in her heart, but she needed someone who regarded her as a partner, not a princess, and her Eli would never be that man. Not because he was dead. Because he would insist on putting her on a pedestal, where she no longer belonged. And it killed her to realize that, but the foundation of their relationship was built on her inexperience and purity, which she no longer had. Jonathan had destroyed that part of her and created a new woman. One she wasn't sure Eli could adore, at least not in the way he once did.

"Eli would want you to be happy," Balthazar murmured.

I know. And that only depressed her more. He was such a good man, who deserved better. But the part of her soul that forever loved him died with him that day, leaving behind a void she never thought to fill. Until Tom. He'd wormed his way inside and planted seeds of hope, suggesting that she may one day be able to love again. Assuming she got to him in time.

"Before you go gallivanting about the island, I should warn you there's a party tonight. And you're the woman of the hour."

Dread pooled in her belly, making her feel ill. "A party?"

"As that used to be your favorite pastime, the others thought it would be a good way to welcome you home. Jacque and Lara are in charge."

She sat on the bed again, hands in her lap. "What time does it start?"

"In an hour. That's hot chocolate, by the way." He gestured at the nightstand. "I even added little marshmallows."

That used to be her favorite drink, and he always prepared it from scratch with dark cocoa. A taste wouldn't kill her and might help her feel a bit better. She picked up the mug and let the rich aroma tease her nose.

"You're trying to distract me with deliciousness." Which wouldn't work. Not for long, anyway.

"We're not going to decide anything on the Sentinel tonight," he added, voice low. She knew the *we* referred to the Elders, which included Balthazar. "Let us love on you tonight, Amelia. We need it almost as badly as you do."

Maybe immersing herself in her former life would help bring old parts of her to the surface. She owed it to her friends and family to try, didn't she? And Balthazar was right. She craved their love and acceptance, especially now, because she needed to know they still cared about her despite everything she'd been through and done. All she wanted for the last six years was to return home. She needed to embrace it.

"He's safe?" she asked, referring to Tom.

"Yes, and unharmed."

Balthazar never lied. He valued trust and transparency too much for it. She took a sip of the hot chocolate and moaned into the cup. It tasted like heaven and sin and flowed with purpose to her empty stomach. Issac had knocked her out for at least twelve hours; of that she was certain.

"All right, I'll go to the party, but I need proper clothing and a meal first." *And to see Tom for myself.* The challenge would be finding him and circumventing whatever security measures the Elders had put in place.

Amusement danced through his gaze and curled his lips. If he heard her thoughts, he didn't comment. "Well, you go freshen up, and I'll take care of the rest." They used to cook together all the time, so she had no doubt he would prepare something outlandish.

She set the mug aside, stood, and pressed a kiss to his cheek. "Thank you."

He wrapped an arm around her lower back to hold her to him. "Don't thank me, Amelia. We should have come for you, and I don't think any of us will ever be able to forgive ourselves for believing you were dead all these years."

"I don't blame you," she whispered.

"You don't have to, love. We blame ourselves." He kissed her hair and rested his cheek there. "I can't begin to understand what you went through, but I'm here when you're ready to talk about it."

She swallowed. "I'm not ready yet." *And I probably never will be.* Some horrors were better left buried.

CHAPTER FIFTEEN

Welcome to Hydria

Tom leaned against the cement wall, hands in his pockets and legs crossed at the ankles. A group of Hydraians were having a heated argument out in the hallway beyond his locked door, but he'd given up on eavesdropping a while ago.

They'd taken his guns and knives and left him in a tiny room with one chair, a table, some food, and a bottle of water. Being as all he cared about was Amelia's well-being, he hadn't touched any of the items and stood waiting for someone to give him an update. No one seemed all that willing to talk to him, which he expected. It wasn't like he made a lot of immortal friends as a Sentinel.

When a female's voice rose outside the door, his attention piqued. Not Amelia, but she sounded familiar—and furious. The knob jiggled, but stayed shut, and something loud hit the wood. He pushed off the wall and paced to the side as the thing crashed open. A familiar blonde appeared a second later, making his mouth drop.

"Stas? What the hell are you doing here?" he asked, dumbfounded.

"I told you he was fine." Wakefield's cool tones preceded him as he stepped into the room behind Stas. Her fiery green eyes narrowed at the haughty Ichorian before fixing on Tom. She gave him a once-over and seemed relieved at finding him in one piece. He returned the favor, noting her toned arms and legs, and received a warning glare from the jackass at her side. *Possessive much?* The woman was best friends with Lizzie and therefore like a sister to him. He'd never be able to view her outside the platonic filter. The same could not be said about Amelia.

"I want a minute alone with him," Stas murmured.

"No."

"I wasn't asking, Issac."

"And I wasn't debating, Astasiya."

She folded her arms and glowered up at the well-dressed man. Even in Hydria, he sported a suit. *Pompous ass.*

"Do you need me to persuade you to leave?" Stas asked.

Wakefield tilted his head to the side as a smile played over his lips. The adoration in his gaze was apparent as he considered her, surprising Tom. He had no idea the Ichorian had it in him to care about a woman for longer than a few hours. No wonder John wanted Stas to become a Sentinel. She was in a prime position to function as a double agent, which made her very dangerous in this situation. If she reported back to the CRF that Amelia and Tom were here, shit would hit the fan. Not that he cared, really; his father deserved to be punished for his sins. He worried more about Stas becoming collateral damage, but she became that the moment she agreed to play spy with the Ichorians.

"Hmm," Wakefield murmured. He palmed her cheek and brushed a thumb over her lips. "You win this round, little complication of mine. But I plan to repay the favor later."

Stas flushed, making it clear what her boyfriend meant by that threat. Not that Tom wouldn't have inferred it by the tone. He rolled his eyes at the obvious display of possession as Wakefield kissed her to punctuate his point. *News flash, man. It's* your *sister I'm into, not the girl I love like a sister.*

"Thomas," Wakefield said when his lips were half an inch away from Stas's mouth. "Your death is already imminent, but I will ensure it is very painful if you so much as think about hurting my Aya. Understood?"

Stas slapped her boyfriend's arm before Tom could reply to that unveiled threat. "His death is *not* imminent."

"Whatever you say, love." He stepped backward before she could hit him again and ducked out of the room with a playful grin.

The man has lost his mind over a woman. Sort of like how Tom had lost his over Amelia. *Well, fuck.* He never thought he'd see the day when he and Wakefield would have something in common. Other than the death of Tom's mother, of course. He never did ask Amelia about it. He didn't want to see her reaction. What if she knew about Wakefield's involvement in the murder? What would she say?

Stas interrupted his thoughts by slamming the door shut behind the Ichorian.

Tom cocked a brow. "I assume you're *Aya*?" *Great first question, buddy.* It was a weird nickname, though. He preferred Stas.

"Apparently," she grumbled before blowing out a long breath. Concern trickled into her gaze as she looked him over. "Are you okay?"

"Never been better. Why?" he asked, feigning innocence.

Her hands went to her hips, and her gaze narrowed. "Seriously? There are a bunch of pissed-off Hydraians out there who want to murder you in various ways, and you're going to be all nonchalant about it?"

"Sounds about right." He figured they would want him dead. It didn't matter that he had never hurt a Hydraian or that his father called all the shots; he was guilty by association. He wondered what Amelia thought of his death sentence. Did she know? Would she care? His chest hurt at the thought of her brushing him off, but he wouldn't think less of her for it. Someone deserved to pay for his father's sins, and he seemed the prime candidate in this situation. But only to an extent. He would fight if he had to.

"Are you even listening to me?" Stas asked, interrupting his thoughts.

No. "Of course. Does my dad know you're here?"

"Yes."

Shit. "So you've told him about me and Amelia." Not a question, but a statement.

"I came in here to ask questions, not the other way around."

He waved her on. "Ask away, Sentinel Stas."

It pained him a little to be such an asshole to her, but he knew the purpose of this chat. She didn't want him to tell the others about her double agent status. If he did, they'd kill her. The fact that she felt the need to even ask him to keep quiet pissed him off. If she didn't realize how much he cared about her by now, she'd never understand. He would never put her at risk like that, but he would advise her to go home and stop this nonsense before she ended up in a body bag. The Hydraians allowing her this close to their nest meant they trusted her or, at a minimum, trusted Issac's judgment. If she didn't stop this charade soon, she'd get herself killed, or worse.

"Why did Doctor Fitzgerald move Amelia from the CRF basement?"

He blinked. That was not at all what he expected her to say. "What?" How the hell did she even know that? Did Amelia tell her?

"You heard me. Why did he move her?"

If Amelia told the Hydraians about being moved, she would have told them why, too. Which meant Stas's knowledge was based on something else. "How do you know she was moved?"

Her lips flattened. "Remember that day Issac dropped me off at the CRF? To meet with your dad?"

"Of course I do." It was a few days after he'd made one of the biggest mistakes of his life—sending Stas to the Arcadia.

"Do you remember how you stormed into your dad's office all pissed off and he walked out with you to have a chat?"

Tom went rigid at the memory. "Yes." He had wanted to kill his father that day. The bastard had taken his frustration out on Amelia and left her broken on the floor. And it was technically Tom's fault his dad was pissed to begin with, something that worsened the situation.

"I found Amelia while you two were talking. Is that why he moved her?"

He gaped at her. "So wait, you knew about Amelia?" Why didn't she say anything?

"I just said I did. Now answer my question."

"My dad moved her so you wouldn't find out about her."

Stas's gaze widened. "What?"

He dragged a hand over his face and started pacing to burn off some of his excess energy. Thinking about that night provoked his desire to punch someone, mainly his father. "After you accepted the Sentinel position, I suggested we move Amelia so you wouldn't find her. I didn't think you'd react well to it." But apparently, he'd been wrong, because she hadn't cared at all.

"And you brought her to Issac?" she asked, incredulous.

He blew out a breath and gave a humorous laugh. "Yeah, well, that wasn't part of the mission at all, something you no doubt know all about."

Stas frowned at that. "Actually, I don't know anything about it. Doctor Fitzgerald—sorry, your *dad*—told me you were overseas on a covert mission, and Stark has kept me otherwise occupied." She said the latter with a scowl that told him just how much she enjoyed that.

"We were in Upstate New York at my mother's cabin, but wait." He turned to study her, watching for any sign of a lie. "If you weren't briefed, then you haven't reported back that I'm here."

She held his gaze. "Doctor Fitzgerald thinks I've run off for a romantic weekend with Issac."

"Why would you lie to him?" Or was she saying that to maintain her cover? Could the Hydraians hear their conversation?

"Because I despise him." The venom in her tone was new. He'd never heard Stas speak like that, and his expression must have shown it. "Why did you bring Amelia to Issac?"

He palmed the back of his neck and considered how to answer that. Speaking the truth during an interrogation went against all his training, but this wasn't a typical situation. "I don't have an easy answer to that."

At some point, he had developed feelings for Amelia. How deep they went remained a mystery he was too afraid to solve. If he admitted loving her, he risked having his heart ripped from his chest. So he settled on caring about her, to an unknown extent. It felt safer that way.

"Want to know why I stormed into my dad's office that day?" he asked, changing the subject to something he could answer.

She studied him with an incredulous expression. "Yes."

"Because of what I found in Amelia's room. You claim to have seen her, so you must understand why that infuriated me. He beat the shit out of her because of what I did to you."

Her frown deepened. "I don't follow."

"The Arcadia, Stas. He was furious that I sent you there and thought I'd gotten you killed. While I was out checking on you, he was taking his frustration out on her, and I had no idea. When I found her like that . . ." He had to pause to swallow the growl forming in his throat. "Well, let's just say I lost my shit. Then you accepted his job offer, and I jumped at the chance of getting her away from him. I suggested he move her, Stark agreed, and my dad sent me along as the babysitter. It was my punishment for telling you about Ichorians."

Her lips parted in shock, a tell that all of this information was new to her. So Amelia hadn't talked to anyone, yet. Interesting detail. *Where are you, sweetheart?* he wondered not for the first time. Being apart from her bothered him more than he wanted to admit. Having been attached at the hip for weeks had left an imprint. He missed her.

"Now tell me something," he continued, curious. "If you saw her that day, why didn't you say anything? It didn't bother you that the CRF had a female prisoner? Let alone one beaten to a pulp by the company's CEO only minutes before you arrived?" He couldn't help the hint of anger that infiltrated his tone. She hadn't reacted at all, and that puzzled him. He expected better of her.

"Oh, it bothered me a hell of a lot. And I didn't say anything because I didn't want to end up in a cell."

He blinked. "My father would never do that to you."

"Really? Considering everything he's done to me, I think he would. You know, with murdering Owen, trying to kill me with the Nizari poison, oh, and let's not forget him trying to blame that last part on Issac to manipulate me against him."

Tom gaped at her. Information overload. "Owen?" He racked his brain for a memory and frowned. "Your friend that was murdered right before graduation?"

"Yes, he was also a Hydraian."

His gaze widened. "Seriously? What the fuck was he doing in New York City?" Talk about seeking a death sentence.

"You didn't know?"

"How the hell would I know that?"

"Because your dad had him killed."

He blinked. "Back up. When, how, and why?" And did she say something about the Nizari poison almost killing her? That only harmed fledglings like himself, not mortals. And no way was Stas anything but human.

"I was hoping you could tell me that."

"I have no idea. Owen wasn't causing any trouble or hurting anyone, right? The CRF only goes after rogue immortals who have harmed humans in some way. Stark should have explained that by now."

"He did, but regardless, your father had Owen killed. Because of me."

"I don't understand." What did she have to do with anything? "Why would he murder someone on your behalf?"

"I imagine it was for the same reason he gave me the Nizari poison. To test me."

"Test you," he repeated. "To see if you were a fledgling?" he guessed. His dad never mentioned anything about suspecting Stas of being a fledgling, but maybe he tested all the new recruits?

"Maybe." She chewed her lip for a second and sighed. "You didn't know anything about it, did you?"

"Of course not. You think I'd let him deliberately hurt you like that?"

"Honestly? I wasn't sure."

"Wow." He laughed humorously and shook his head. "I've got nothing to say back to that, Stas. I really don't." Man, it seemed that all the women in his life had little faith in him. Awesome. He had no idea he came off as such an asshole.

"It's hard to know who to trust," she murmured. "You have no idea who I really am or what—"

The door opened, cutting off their conversation.

A man he knew all about, but had never seen in person, stepped through the threshold with his hands behind his back. His emerald gaze settled on Stas first, then Tom. With it came a wave of discomfort. *Old* didn't even begin to describe the Hydraian King. Oh, he resembled a thirty-five-year-old man, with his short blond hair and muscular physique, but the intelligence radiating from his gaze was positively ancient.

Lucian, otherwise known as Luc.

Tom admired him as a leader, unlike Amelia's other brother. Wakefield was a pompous ass who killed for sport, while Luc was an honorable man known for his fairness. The latter were traits Tom couldn't help but respect, even if they wouldn't work in his favor today.

"Tom," the Hydraian King greeted. "Could you give us a minute, Stas?"

Her gaze narrowed, but the look Luc leveled her silenced whatever she was about to say.

"I know what you want to do, and I strongly advise against such recourse. For there will be consequences if you do."

"Fine," she gritted out. "But faith goes both ways, Luc. If you ever want me to join you willingly, I suggest you consider this situation very carefully."

Tom's brow rose at her boldness. Did she not realize who stood before her? He could have her killed with the flick of a wrist, and no one would argue otherwise because of her Sentinel status. Dating Wakefield had certainly bolstered her confidence, and perhaps not in a healthy way.

"I'm always analyzing the pros and cons in every situation" was Luc's curt reply. "This is no different. Amelia might be my half sister, but logic outweighs familial obligation. I believe you're familiar with the concept."

Okay, I've clearly missed something.

Was this not Stas's first trip to Hydria? Did no one care about her working for the CRF? Oh, and speaking of them, why was she working for them if she hated his father? Especially as a Sentinel. Her actions were illogical.

Unless she's just a fantastic actress?

"Fine," Stas replied. "I'll go for a walk."

"Thank you." He studied Tom while Stas escorted herself out and softly closed the door. "I think it's time you and I had a chat, fledgling."

~*~

Balthazar found Amelia a pair of jeans and a tank top, as well as underwear. She didn't know where they came from or how he knew her sizes without asking, but the clothes fit perfectly. Nothing surprised her when it came to B, and she found herself smiling as she left his house. She missed him more than she realized, and it gave her hope that seeing the others would bring more joy. But she wanted to see her brothers first.

Unlike Balthazar's home, Luc's house sat up on a hill away from the beach. He could see every inch of the small island from up here, something she knew he enjoyed and preferred. It was also in a secluded area, giving him necessary space from the others. As the leader of their race, he rarely had a moment to himself.

Warmth tightened her chest when Issac opened the door before she could knock. Relief brightened his gaze as a boyish grin curled his lips. All her frustration from the night before melted at that look. She never could stay angry with him for long, even when he deserved it.

I'm truly home.

She fantasized about this moment so many times over the years, always dreaming of the day Issac would rescue her. She had willed him to sense her, to come for her, but he never did.

Because he thought she was dead.

But he's here now.

Whether her savior or not, he would always be her big brother, and she adored him.

"You're breaking my heart all over again, love," he whispered as he pulled her into his arms. She'd obviously telegraphed some of what she felt on her face or in her thoughts.

"Sorry." She hugged him back and closed her eyes. "I just… I never thought I would see you again."

His arms tightened. "I'm here. I'll never let anyone hurt you ever again. I promise."

Amelia considered his words and frowned. Although she appreciated his intentions, she didn't want to rely on him to keep her safe. That was how she ended up in this predicament with Jonathan to begin with—by counting on the men in her life to protect her. This experience taught her the flaws in that logic.

She stepped back and held his gaze. "I'm learning how to defend myself."

Tom started the process, and she wanted to continue it.

Thinking of him made her heart ache. She longed to see him but knew no one would let her.

And that was part of the problem. Everyone wanted to keep her sheltered and make all the decisions for her. She couldn't blame them, because the old Amelia preferred it that way. But that had to change. She needed them to train her, to teach her how to be independent, so a monster like Jonathan never captured her again.

I'd rather die fighting than suffer his treatment again.

Issac gave her a long, hard look and nodded. "All right."

"All right?" she repeated, startled. She'd expected an argument or at least a bit of pushback, not easy acceptance.

He grinned and cupped her cheek with his palm. "Amelia, love, I spent decades trying to teach you practical defense moves, but Eli always said there wasn't a need, and you always agreed. Remember?"

Because Eli treated me like a delicate damsel.

She would never hate him for that, as she understood. He came from an era where a man took care of his wife, and although they never married formally, they were monogamous for centuries. Eli considered it his duty to protect her always and never wanted her to be bothered by such things. As a daughter of a duchess, it hadn't been a difficult life to accept.

But… "I've had a change of heart."

"I can see that." His eyes crinkled. "And I have the perfect sparring partner for you."

"You do?"

"I do." He turned as a blonde woman threw open the back door with a huff and slammed it.

"You'll never believe what Luc just said…" The newcomer's voice trailed off upon spotting them in the living area. "Oh."

Amelia's fingers fluttered to her mouth as she gasped in recognition. She *knew* her, and not because she was a fellow Hydraian.

This woman had visited her in a dream.

Or what she thought was a dream, anyway.

"You're real."

If she existed, then that means Stark truly did disappear into mist. She frowned. *Why didn't he mention her conversation with the blonde to anyone? Or did he tell Jonathan?*

Was that the real reason they moved her to the cabin? She opened her mouth to ask the newcomer, but Issac's behavior put all of Amelia's thoughts on hold.

Adoration poured from his blue eyes as he greeted the blonde with a kiss, followed by some whispered words that made the girl blush. When he nuzzled her neck and grinned, Amelia's lips parted in wonder.

Who is this man, and what did he do to my brother?

This must be the woman Tom mentioned.

The one Issac had seen beyond a first date.

How did this happen?

Tears pricked her eyes as a wave of conflicting emotions settled over her. Happiness that her brother had finally found someone, sadness that it had happened during her absence, and confusion as to why he had chosen a woman under Jonathan's employ.

"Amelia, this is my Aya," Issac murmured. "But she prefers to be called Stas."

The blonde smiled up at him. "I don't think I've ever heard you use my nickname."

"That's because Aya is your nickname," he replied as he brushed his knuckles over her jaw.

"You gave her a nickname?" Amelia asked, bewildered. "You don't even call Luc by his preferred name, and he's your brother." That alone told her how he felt about this woman.

Love.

My brother is in love.

"I believe you met briefly at the CRF," Issac continued, his expression darkening. "Aya wore a camera that day. That's how I knew you were alive."

Stas cleared her throat, looking uncomfortable. "Yeah, I agreed to work as a Sentinel in hopes of finding a way to help you, but you see how well that turned out."

Amelia blinked. "You became a Sentinel to help me?" That explained the bit about Issac accepting Stas's employment situation.

Issac hugged Stas to his side and kissed her temple. "Aya's amazing, if a little reckless." The blonde elbowed him, making him grin.

Amelia swallowed, unsure what to say. *Amazing* didn't seem to cover it. "Thank you," she murmured, though it seemed underwhelming given the circumstances. *This woman put her life at risk for me.* She owed her more than two words, but what more could she give?

Stas snorted. "It's not like I did much. John moved you before I had a chance to even talk to you again."

Amelia nodded. "Yes, on Tom's recommendation."

"So it's true, then? He helped you?" Hope lined the woman's voice, making Amelia wonder at her history with Tom.

"Yes, in more ways than one." She looked to her brother. "You put me to sleep before I had a chance to explain last night." And then he kept her in that state for nearly twenty-four hours. No wonder she woke in a daze and thought Hydria was a dream. She'd slept too long. "Which reminds me, never do that again without my express permission."

His eyebrows rose. "You've always enjoyed my dreams, Amelia."

"Yes." Which was why she could forgive him for last night. "But I need you to request permission going forward." The notion of anyone manipulating her vision after so many years of hallucinations and torment made her queasy. Issac would never harm her, and she knew that, but she needed her space. For now.

He studied her with an intense expression, then slowly nodded. "Of course."

"Thank you. Now, I want to see Tom," she said, feeling stronger. "B already explained that you won't allow it, which is why I came here to talk to Luc."

"He's temporarily indisposed," Issac replied in that haughty way of his.

"And Balthazar is correct. We will all deny your request."

"She has a right to see him," Stas argued.

"Just this morning you agreed that he should be removed."

The girl narrowed her green eyes. "No, I said he should be given a choice of staying or leaving. Nice try, though."

He shrugged. "So the edict remains."

"It does."

"Brilliant." His sarcasm was not lost on Amelia.

"What are you two going on about? And what do you mean by *removed*?"

"Execution," Issac answered simply. "But my little complication here used her fledgling gift of verbal persuasion on the Elders and myself, making a sentence impossible."

Amelia's gaze widened. "Fledgling?"

"Yes," he replied.

Oh, Issac.

Her brother had fallen in love with a woman he could never have, not truly. Once she died, she would be reborn a Hydraian, and a relationship between them would be rendered impossible. Politics aside, they could never physically be together. One drop of ingested blood would kill him. The risk would be too great.

Her heart splintered as she struggled for what to say. He flashed her a look that said he knew exactly where her thoughts had gone and to not comment. Did his Stas not realize the extent of this complication? Or were they both in denial?

"I won't be taking it back," Stas stated. "No one on this island can touch him."

"The Elders are waiting to see how long your compulsion lasts, specifically Lucian. You're lucky he's more fascinated by it than displeased." The light admonishment in his voice prompted the blonde to grin.

"I wanted to hear his side of the story first."

"And did you?"

"Yes, and he had nothing to do with Owen."

"Owen?" Amelia repeated. "Our Owen?"

Issac's gaze turned troubled, and he cleared his throat. "Yes. I'm not sure how to tell you this other than to be blunt… Jonathan had him killed a few weeks ago in New York City."

"What? Good heavens, why? He couldn't possibly have been a threat." She knew the Hydraian well. His infectious laugh and general joviality added to his role as a social butterfly on the island. Everyone loved him.

"To test me," Stas whispered.

"Aya and Owen were close friends," Issac added. "His murder scene is actually how we met. Not exactly the most romantic of tales, is it?"

Amelia's vision started to darken at the edges. *What else have I missed all these years?* She stumbled over to the table to sit down before her legs gave out beneath her. This was too much. She rubbed the ache in her chest and considered resting her head against the table to cool it. Owen did not deserve his fate. Another mark on Jonathan's dark record.

A glass of water appeared in front of her as her brother took the seat across from her. "I know it's a lot, love," he murmured. "I'm sorry. We're going to get through this."

She nodded numbly. "Who else have we lost?" she asked, though she wasn't sure she really wanted the answer.

"Only Eli," he whispered.

She closed her eyes and breathed in slowly through her nose. That news she could handle. Her heart didn't ache the way it used to when she thought about him. Now her heart hurt for a different reason. *Tom.* They had formed a bond over these last few weeks that felt tenuous yet strong. She wanted to explore it further, but too many obstacles had sprung up in her path. The first of which being her brothers.

"What did Tom do that has you all so displeased with him?" she wondered.

"You mean aside from being Jonathan's progeny?"

"You, better than anyone, know not to fault a man for his parentage, Issac." It would be akin to condemning a Hydraian for the sins of his or her Ichorian father. And so many of them were immortals who lacked any semblance of humanity. A consequence of their age and customs. Her father managed to avoid it by creating a support network of family and friends that kept him grounded. But sometimes she saw that faraway glint in Aidan's eyes, a hint of insanity creeping in from too much experience. Luc possessed it as well. She wondered if it had gotten worse during her absence.

"He's his father's son, Amelia. Jonathan has molded him into a walking puppet with excellent aim."

"That's rather harsh." Even if a little accurate. Tom said himself that he had no choice but to do what his father told him to do, but he went against Jonathan's wishes by taking her to Issac. "Tell me why you suspected him of murdering Owen." She used the past tense since Stas stated he wasn't involved, but she wondered why Issac would even consider accusing him of it.

"Because he's craved his father's love and affection his entire life. Thomas would die for that man, which, coincidentally, he might."

She shook her head. "You should have heard the way he spoke to him these last few weeks, Issac. That wasn't a boy seeking love, but a man rebelling."

"Or…" Issac reached for her hand and squeezed it while holding her gaze. "Or it's a man playing a game with a woman in a fragile state. A man trying to gain trust, to be invited to a place like Hydria, where he can operate as a spy and report back to his father." He let that sink in before continuing. "He's the perfect soldier for the job, darling. A fledgling with no home, nowhere to go except here, and with your approval, he might be allowed to stay."

"A game," she whispered.

No.

This could not be another of Jonathan's tricks.

Except, how many times did she wonder when the charade would end? How often did she question Tom's intentions? Almost daily for weeks, until he risked his life to save her. She hadn't doubted him since that afternoon at the cabin, which was only a few days ago…

No.

She shook her head, denying the possibility.

I know *him.*

But did she? The man excelled at deception and nonchalance. Would he hurt her like this?

He held me that night. Also part of the illusion? A way to gain her trust? It worked liked a charm.

But what about the gun? She could have killed him.

Unless…

She never checked it for bullets.

Had he removed them prior to leaving it on the nightstand? A clever stunt, indeed. And it landed her in his bed.

Issac swiped a tear away from her cheek with his thumb and cradled her face with his palm. "I'm speculating, but you need to be prepared, love."

She bit her lip to keep it from trembling. The possibility that it was all no more than a game to Tom made her heart hurt. Had she fallen for a master manipulator? It seemed like something Jonathan would do. He always did want to break her, and this was the perfect way to do it. Send his son in to woo her, become her confidant and lover, and betray her in the most hurtful of ways.

Another tear fell, but this one she swiped away. "If it's true," she whispered, "I want a say in his punishment." Because even if Tom was guilty, she refused to let the Elders execute him. She could never hurt him, not like that. She'd demand his safe release instead.

"But it's not true," Stas put in, frowning. "I've known him for almost seven years, Issac. He's not a bad man, and he had no idea his father killed Owen. I saw his expression today. He wasn't lying."

Issac considered the woman with a seriousness Amelia had never seen in him. *He respects her opinion*, she realized. How interesting. It usually took decades to acquire that sort of trust with her brother, but Stas had managed to secure it during their brief acquaintance.

"Perhaps," he murmured. "A decision will not be reached tonight. I can't believe I'm about to suggest this, but let's head down to the beach. I think being around your family will help, and I would prefer to avoid having Jacque flash up here with one of his expectant looks."

Amelia wished so badly to smile at that, but the pain in her chest made it difficult. An evening at a beach party did not appeal to her at all, but she owed it to her family to try. And maybe she would feel better after surrounding herself with love and support. There was only one way to find out, and later, she could think more about Tom and his potential betrayal.

He wouldn't do that to you, her conscious whispered. *He chases away the darkness.*

She shuddered. *I have to talk to him.* It would be the only way to know for sure whether or not this was all a ruse, and mentally debating it would accomplish nothing. She was finally free, and she didn't want to spend it wallowing. Jonathan would not win. Never again.

"Let's go."

CHAPTER SIXTEEN

New Cravings

What started as a calm affair exploded into a rave once all the formalities were finished. Amelia appreciated the diversion because it shifted the focus from her to the festivities. Jacque managed the music with Stas at his side. He appeared to be teaching her how to do something with the controls while Issac looked on with amusement.

"It's weird, isn't it?" Jayson murmured as he roasted a marshmallow over the bonfire in front of them. She'd opted to sit with the Elders instead of joining the dancers on the beach. There were too many of them, and she wanted her space. Her brother had offered to join her, but she didn't want to take him away from his new love.

"He's happy," Amelia said, smiling as her brother wrapped his arms around Stas from behind.

"It won't end well." Alik's matter-of-fact tone matched his bored expression. He sat next to Jayson with his back to the party. Typical. He did greet her with a smile earlier, though—a rarity for the Elder, and one that meant a great deal to her.

"You're doing it wrong," Luc muttered as he collapsed into a chair across from them. She'd seen him dancing with Mya and Lara a few minutes ago, his expression one of contentment, but now his narrow focus was on Jayson's marshmallow. "It's going to catch fire."

"And that's how I like it," Jayson replied as the fluff went up in flames.

Luc shook his head. "Blasphemy. Ruined a perfectly good cylinder."

"You would only care about the shape and not the taste." Jayson leaned forward to sandwich the now-black marshmallow between a graham cracker and a bar of chocolate. Not the healthiest of desserts, but the man didn't have an ounce of fat on him. None of the Elders did.

Alik was the smallest of the trio with his lean athleticism, while Luc and Jayson reminded her of rugby players. All height and muscle, short hair, and handsome faces. These were Eli's best friends, the men he loved like brothers and had known most of his life. They also happened to be the oldest of her race, hence their nickname. It felt good sitting beside them, if a little surreal.

She had thought of them often, but the little details had never left her, like Jayson's adorable dimples, the constant crease between Luc's brows, and Alik's trademark scowl. Amazing how she could recall all those traits, but the color of Eli's eyes eluded her. All she could see now was a luscious brown she knew didn't belong to him.

Tom.

Jayson handed her the marshmallow skewer, and she passed it to Luc. The thought of dessert turned her stomach. Despite her best intentions, Tom kept popping into her thoughts. Random comments and memories from their time together haunted her heart and mind. The way he held her after she broke down, his intoxicating kiss and addictive touch, but most of all, the sincerity in his gaze. Every time she closed her eyes, he stared back at her with that concerned look that melted her. All his actions and words didn't add up to a traitor, but Issac's comments held a touch of logic she couldn't refute.

A piece of chocolate appeared beneath her nose, pulling her back to reality. Jayson cocked a brow and waggled the treat at her. "I know you want it, Amelia," he taunted. "Dark chocolate, fresh from Argentina. Your favorite."

She smiled at his playfulness and snagged the sweet. "You haven't changed at all, Jay."

"And I never plan to, A."

The Elders had a thing about nicknames. It drove Issac mad, but she loved it. "I missed you guys," she admitted, which earned her a side hug from Jay and an air-kiss from Luc. Alik's dark gaze met hers briefly in a moment of understanding before he went back to staring at the fire.

She nibbled the chocolate and fought a moan. It was the same kind Balthazar used in his hot cocoa earlier. These men knew her too well, and yet, part of her felt like an outsider despite their warmth and comfort.

You don't feel that way around Tom.

The chocolate soured in her mouth. Sitting here enjoying herself while he sat God knew where felt wrong. He had been there for her in a moment when she needed him most, and she sat out here while he suffered. It wasn't fair.

A hand settled on her shoulder from behind, making her jump until she realized whom it belonged to. Balthazar stared down at her with a question in his eyes. "Want to take a walk?" he asked. "Catch up a little?"

You've been playing in my mind, B.

The sadness in his expression answered her thought. He brushed his thumb against her neck in a soothing gesture that made it hard to refuse him. "All right," she murmured and stood.

"Don't go too far, A." The emotion in her brother's voice tugged at her heart. Her relationship with him differed from what she had with Issac, mostly because she didn't grow up with Luc, but she loved him. Even when she disagreed with a decision, such as keeping Tom locked up. He stood as she walked over to him and engulfed her in a hug.

"I'm not going anywhere," she whispered.

"I know." He kissed her hair and held her a little longer than he used to, as if he feared she might disappear on him again. "Let's talk in the morning. I'll make waffles."

Balthazar snorted beside them. "Rubbish."

"Ignore him," Luc replied as he let her go. "Pancakes are flat and shapeless, while waffles are geometrically delicious."

Amelia smiled at the familiar debate. "Good to know not everything has changed around here."

"Pancakes can hold a variety of shapes," Balthazar argued.

"But do they form pockets for the maple syrup?"

"Not all of us are obsessed with even servings."

Luc arched a haughty brow. "That's not an answer."

"Jesus Christ," Alik muttered. "Make it stop."

Jayson chuckled and shook his head. "B, I thought you were going on a walk, man."

"Right." Balthazar extended his arm to her. "Walk with me, and I'll explain why pancakes are the superior breakfast food along the way."

She slid her arm through his and grinned. "You realize I've heard this debate a thousand times, yes?"

He looked at Luc and addressed him instead of her. "I've proven you wrong a dozen times on that front." His gaze narrowed. "You're on. Next weekend. I choose Brazil. Fine. Yes, maple syrup is allowed. Whipped cream as well. All the toppings, Luc. That, too, and yes, I pick Jay. Deal."

"What kinky challenge did I just agree to?" Jayson asked.

"Luc will fill you in while Amelia and I take a walk."

She snorted. "You act as though I'm a blushing bride." She knew Balthazar and Luc were constantly engaged in a battle of wits, and it usually involved sexual escapades of some sort. Seemed this one involved breakfast, Brazilian women, and teams. *I don't want to know.*

"One day I'll corrupt you, love." Balthazar grinned. "Don't you worry."

"Uh-huh." He'd been saying that for centuries but never followed through. His relationship with Eli made her off-limits, which suited her fine. She adored the man but didn't want to cross the line.

They strolled arm in arm along the beach, away from the raging techno music and raving immortals and toward a quieter section of the island near the docks. Tourists sometimes stopped by for day visits from Athens, but there were no hotels for them to stay overnight, and the last ferry left before dinner each evening.

Automobiles and motorbikes were prohibited on the island, a way to keep the air clean, according to Luc, but bicycles were available for rent. The Hydraians also sold artwork and manned two cafés for tourists who needed a bite to eat during their visit. It helped with some of the living costs in Hydria, but most of the cash flow came from those who worked full-time.

Luc had a whole system in place, and everyone played their part. Her role used to involve mentoring younger Hydraians and playing hostess as needed for a variety of parties. She wondered what use she would be to her people now.

Tom would be useful, she thought. If Luc would give the man a chance.

"You know, I remember the day you met Eli," Balthazar murmured, cutting into her thoughts.

"Yeah?" she asked with a small grin. Amelia remembered that day, too. Her eighteenth birthday, the day she met all the Elders, including her brother Luc, for the first time. Advanced technology and global transportation hadn't been invented yet. Jacque didn't exist yet, either, but more than that, Aidan wanted to keep her hidden from the supernatural world. The immortals were on the cusp of war as tensions between Ichorians and Hydraians rose. So he resided in England with Issac and their mother, a wealthy, widowed duchess, and kept her safe until the day he handed her over to the Elders.

"It was love at first sight for him," Balthazar mused. "That man would have moved the earth just to see you smile."

And there it was, the purpose for this walk. She didn't have two older brothers. She had five, and they all adored Eli. Dating anyone else would never be acceptable to any of them, especially not a man they already hated.

"It shocked the hell out of me at first, but I'm glad he found you," he continued. "You gave him three centuries of joy, Amelia. He would have wanted more time, as we all would, but I know with certainty he wouldn't want to hold you back from finding happiness." He stepped in front of her, stopping her in midstep, and stared down at her with an intent expression that caused her pulse to jump.

"Eli was your first love and every bit the man you needed once upon a time, but people change. Experiences shape our outlooks, our dreams, our cravings..." His chocolate eyes twinkled with that last part, making her snort. He never could be serious for long.

"What are you trying to tell me, B?" Because it sounded like he was hitting on her, but despite his incessant flirting, she knew he would never be interested in her that way.

"Sometimes what we need evolves into something, or someone, we least expect. Eli was your perfect match. You made each other happy and lived a full life together. But he's gone and never coming back, and even if he did, I'm not sure he would be the right man for you today. He'd lock you in a room and kill anyone who tried to walk inside without his permission, but that's not what you need." His smile was sad as he looked at her. "I've been listening, Amelia, to everything. I might not like it, but Tom is the one for you, at least for the moment. Which is why I'm going to help you."

She gaped at him. Of all the things she expected him to say, this was not one of them. "Truly?"

"Yes. He's in there." Balthazar pointed to a small utility hut off the beach, making her jaw drop. That little box was half the size of her cement prison at the CRF. Her feet were moving before she could think better of it, and Balthazar grabbed her shoulder. "Ash is in there."

Amelia froze. "You left him alone with a fire elemental?" The woman's pyrokinetic talents made her one of Hydria's greatest assets, and also terrifying.

"She's under strict orders not to kill him, and you know she takes her job seriously."

Oh, she knew all right. The woman was part of Luc's personal guard whenever he left Hydria, and redefined the meaning of protection. "She'll never leave her post."

Balthazar waggled his brows and grinned. "You know how much I love a good challenge, A. Leave it to me." So much arrogance for one man, but if anyone deserved it, he did. Ash wouldn't stand a chance under his sensual assault.

"Right. Cheers, then." Because what else was there to say?

"Stay out of sight until we leave. I'll ensure the door is unlocked. Go inside, head down the stairs, and he's in the room on the left."

Her eyebrows jumped. That little shack resembled a gardening shed, not a home with rooms. "How new is this little whatever-it-is of yours?"

"Luc built it when we founded the island. It's a prison of sorts, and before you ask, you were kept in the dark because 'a lady doesn't need to know those things.'"

"I do not sound like that." Though, it did sound like something she would say, at least about this aspect of Hydraian life. A prison, or the things done in a dungeon, would never appeal to her.

"Oh, but you do, love." He kissed her cheek. "The guards are scheduled to change shifts in three hours. I suggest you leave before that happens."

~ * ~

Tom paced the tiny room, hands in his pockets. *Antsy* didn't begin to cover his current state.

Stas is a fledgling. More than that, she could bend others to her will. How the hell had he missed that little detail? It didn't bode well for him that Luc had given him that information. The words came off more as a threat.

"*Once her compulsion ends, we'll decide your fate. Until then, please enjoy our hospitality.*"

The Hydraian King left him with a plate of food, another bottle of water, a stack of blankets, and a pillow. Sleeping on the floor he could do, but not here. Not when his life hung in the balance. Escape seemed the logical option, but leaving Amelia felt wrong. She was perfectly safe here, yet he felt an idiotic need to stay for her.

A giggle sounded from the hallway, followed by a deep, masculine voice and a thump.

What the hell?

Jesus. Are they?

Oh, yeah.

Some Hydraians were about to get it on outside his door. Ridiculous. If he wanted to escape, now would be the perfect time. The door hinges were solid, but a kick at the right angle would do the job, and his guards would be too distracted to react right away. All he needed was a weapon, and they'd be toast. Of course, then he would be trapped on an island inhabited by immortals with various unworldly powers.

Nice. Talk about a challenge.

Except it didn't appeal to him as much as it should. He used to live for this shit, but Amelia changed everything. His trademark "love 'em and leave 'em" mentality didn't apply to her. She was under his skin and deep in his head, dictating all his decisions and actions. Such as the one to willingly come here. Because he could have knocked Issac and Tristan out with a pair of bullets while they were distracted by Amelia at the manor, but he chose not to. He wanted to go with her and disregarded the consequences.

A female yelped, making his eyes roll. The Hydraian guards needed better training if this was the shit they pulled during their shifts. It would be so easy to teach the immortals a lesson, but Tom refrained. The Elders already wanted him dead, no reason to further that along.

I told you so, son, his father's voice taunted. *Should have played ball.*

His hand curled into a fist.

Tom didn't regret his decision to help Amelia but did feel sorry for allowing hope into his heart. Somewhere along the line, doubt had crept in, and he'd wondered just what the Hydraians would do to him. Fledglings were rare, and his unique skill set could prove useful, but Luc made it clear today that he was not welcome here.

The knob wiggled, drawing him from his thoughts.

He moved to the opposite side of the room to lean against the cement wall, hands in his pockets, and feigned a look of boredom as someone undid the dead bolt. The door cracked open, and Amelia's head popped through. Relief illuminated her gaze when she spotted him.

"Tom." His name on her lips brightened his entire day. Hell, it brightened his existence. It took all his effort not to walk over, wrap her in his arms, and take her against the wall. But he knew she wasn't alone. No way the Elders or her brothers would let her visit unsupervised.

"Hi, sweetheart."

"Hi." She slipped inside, closed the door, leaned back against it, and nibbled her lower lip. "I needed to see that you were all right." Interesting phrasing considering she didn't appear to be looking at him so much as the floor.

"I'm okay."

She nodded. "Good."

The silence between them felt heavy and uncomfortable. What happened to his confident Amelia, the one who questioned everything and loved to bicker over silly things like baseball and motorcycles? He pushed off the wall and frowned when she stiffened.

"What's wrong, Amelia?" When she didn't respond, he stepped closer and crowded her against the door. He expected it to fly open and be greeted by an irate Hydraian, but nothing happened. "Talk to me, sweetheart."

Gorgeous blue eyes peeked up at him through thick lashes. "They think you're playing a game with me," she whispered. "They think Jonathan sent you on a mission to infiltrate Hydria as a fledgling, and you're using me to do it."

"A logical assessment." He rested a forearm over her head and placed his opposite palm against the wall beside her hip. Her shiver encouraged him. "And what do you think, Amelia?" he whispered. "Am I a spy?"

"Are you?" she asked, those guileless eyes blinking up at him. "Are you playing with me?"

Oh, I'm definitely playing with you. Partly because he was furious that she could even ask him that, and partly because it hurt. Her words could kill him, but he wouldn't let it show. If the experiences they had shared weren't enough for her to believe in him, then they were doomed to fail. Nothing he could do would ever change her mind. He would forever be Jonathan Fitzgerald's son and share the burden of another man's sins. *Thanks, Dad.*

"What do you think, Amelia?" Because if she had to ask, she didn't trust him, and no amount of talking would fix that. "Was everything between us a lie?"

Her gaze dropped to his mouth. "I wouldn't…"

"You wouldn't what?" he prompted, his voice low.

"I wouldn't be here if I didn't trust you."

"Then why ask?"

"Because Jonathan always wanted to break me and failed. But if this is all a charade?" Her gaze flicked up to his, and the look there cut him deep. "It'll destroy me."

"You think I could do that to you?"

"I used to," she admitted. "I thought everything was a game, all the training, you giving me a weapon, the teasing… And I think it was to an extent, but not because of Jonathan. You use cheekiness to protect yourself, but deep down, you're lonely. You don't feel like you belong anywhere because the man you admired most filled your head with lies."

Not all of them were lies, he thought numbly. The Hydraians really did hate him.

She palmed his cheek and sighed. "Jonathan altered us both irrevocably, but what he did to you was worse."

"I beg to differ—" Her thumb over his lips silenced him.

"Let me finish."

"Okay," he mouthed as she dropped her hand.

"I promised myself if I ever got out of that hell, I would never rely on another person for anything ever again. But you're the only one who brings me a sense of peace and comfort, and that terrifies me. I don't want to rely on you, Tom. But I can't seem to help myself."

Her words both warmed and chilled him.

He removed his hand from the wall near her hip to palm her cheek and felt some of the chill dissipate when she pressed into his touch.

"Leaning on someone for comfort doesn't mean you're weak, sweetheart. But I understand where you're coming from; you want to be able to protect yourself."

He felt the same way, which was why these feelings for her confused him. Whenever he considered leaving the CRF, he only thought about how to look after himself, but she changed everything. A life of loneliness no longer appealed to him.

"You also make me feel strong," she told him. "In addition to the peace and comfort, I mean."

"Yeah?"

She nodded. "And you teach me things. It may have been a diversion at first, but I think you enjoyed training me."

His grin was automatic. "Oh, I more than enjoyed it." He fucking loved it.

"What did you enjoy most?" she asked, a smile in her voice. So much better than the sadness lurking there before. He liked playing with flirtatious Amelia.

"Everything." From the gun stance lessons to rolling around with her on the ground, he enjoyed every minute. If he died soon, those would be the memories he'd miss most. And their one explosive night together.

"All right, but what did you like teaching me most?"

He ran his thumb over her bottom lip. "Defensive moves, even though you about killed me."

"How's that?" Her mouth curled down at the edges, and he traced it with his thumb.

"'Straddle me again,'" he quoted. "Ever say that to me again, and I'll well and truly straddle you."

Arousal darkened her gaze. "I think I'd like that."

"Your brothers wouldn't." And he didn't need to piss them off any more than he already had. Though, it might be worth it in this case.

"They don't need to know, and Balthazar won't tell them."

"Balthazar?" he repeated, frowning.

"He distracted the guard for me."

"Really?" An Elder helped her get to him? "Why would he do that?"

"Because he thinks you're good for me, even though he doesn't like it."

He didn't know how to interpret that. Luc made it sound like his death was imminent, but that could have been his interrogation technique. Tom hadn't spilled all his knowledge, but he'd provided enough to indicate his worth. He never mentioned Stas's double agent status, though he now suspected she was a triple agent and reporting CRF details to Issac. An interesting twist of events.

Amelia brushed her lips over his in an impatient gesture that amused him. "Did you come here to check on me or because you need me to help you forget again?"

"Can't it be both?" Her impish expression made it difficult to remember why her suggestion was a bad idea.

"This isn't a very romantic venue." *There's gotta be a better reason.*

"I don't want romance." She hooked her thumb in his belt loop and gave it a tug. "I need you." Those words on her lips were pure sin.

"Careful, sweetheart." *Or I'll be tempted to take you up on what you're offering.* This might be his last night alive. Might as well enjoy it.

"I don't want careful, either."

"What do you want?" he whispered, needing to hear her say it. There could be no misunderstandings between them. Only truths. She pressed her mouth against his, and he pulled back. "Tell me what you want, Amelia."

"Kiss me."

"Is that all you want?" He spoke the words against her lips.

She shivered and tugged on his jeans again. "No. I want to well and truly straddle you. Without clothes."

He palmed the back of her neck and pulled her in for a kiss filled with pent-up heat and yearning. It'd been a long fucking day, and he wanted nothing more than to lose himself in her. But he needed her to know what that meant.

This wouldn't be like the other night, and he demonstrated that with his tongue. He memorized every inch of her mouth in dominating sweeps, and she melted.

Oh, she'd straddle him all right, but not in the way she thought.

"This is going to be hard and fast, Amelia." It came out in a harsh whisper against her neck. He punctuated the warning with a tender bite at the base of her throat, and she responded by arching into him. He grinned against her soft skin. It seemed she liked that. Good. Because there would be no slow burn tonight. They didn't have time.

He fisted his hand in the hem of her tank top, while his opposite palm tightened around her neck to force her attention up to him. "You still want to straddle me, sweetheart?"

"Oh, yes." Her flushed cheeks and thoroughly kissed lips nearly undid him. But it was her words that sent him over the edge. He ripped her top over her head and flicked her bra to the floor.

Her fingertips danced along the top of his pants, beneath his shirt, and he swore electricity trailed her every move.

His cock hardened against his zipper, begging her to go a little lower and give it a stroke, but she kept her touch light and taunting.

He paid her back by taking her nipple into his mouth and sucking. Hard. Her hands flew to his hair, his jeans forgotten. He gave the abused peak a little nibble, and her head flew backward against the door on a deep moan.

"Take off my pants, Amelia." He followed the order with another bite before taking her other nipple into his mouth.

She tossed her head back and forth, her hands trembling and tightening in his hair rather than going where he wanted them.

He grinned against her breast.

This wasn't defiance, but a woman too lost in pleasure to think clearly. He took hold of her wrist and lowered her palm to his upper thigh and then up the center of his jeans. Some of the lust-induced fog must have cleared because she grabbed the denim and held on. He rewarded her with a lick that made her groan his name.

His balls tightened as she went for his zipper first, then popped off the button, and pushed the fabric down to his knees. He finished the job and kicked it away as he pulled off his shirt.

She eyed the bulge in his boxer shorts and licked her lips. "I really want to taste you again."

"Fuck." Tom fisted his hand in her hair and kissed her sinful lips into submission.

He needed to be deep inside her, to memorize every inch of her slick heat with his cock. Then they could taste each other. Her jeans disappeared, followed by her panties and his boxers, all while he fucked her mouth with his tongue.

She locked her arms around his shoulders and held him as if she couldn't get close enough. Clingy women usually turned him off, but he loved Amelia's desperation because it rivaled his own.

He adored this woman, would give up his life for her, and very likely was by staying here when she'd offered him the perfect chance to escape. But all he wanted was her. She intoxicated him on a level he didn't know existed, and he loved it. Maybe even loved her.

He grabbed her hips and lifted her up against the wall. Her legs wrapped around his waist as he settled his hard length against her damp center.

This was how he wanted her to straddle him.

Always.

He slid his palm to her ass and shifted back before thrusting into her waiting heat.

"Harder," she demanded and dug her nails into his shoulders to encourage him.

He wrapped his free hand around her nape and placed a bruising kiss on her lips. She nipped back at him, making him grin. "What happened to my sweet, compliant Amelia?"

"She met you."

Oh, he liked that. "I wouldn't have it any other way."

"Good. Now start moving."

"Yes, ma'am." He drove deep and captured her mouth as she screamed.

Her wet, eager body hugged him, sending electricity zipping up and down his spine. If she kept moving like that, he wouldn't be able to last long despite his unworldly control. Amelia undid him with her strong spirit and feisty energy, and all he could do was lose himself in her. Her screams turned to cries of approval as he increased the pace and swiveled his hips in a way that stimulated her clit.

When her legs started to tremble, he knew she was close and gave her one final, deep thrust to send her over the edge into bliss.

She convulsed around him, squeezing his cock in the most amazing way, leaving him no choice but to follow her into ecstasy. His knees shook from the force of his orgasm, making him lean harder into her against the wall and intensify his hold.

"Amelia," he breathed, burying his head in her neck.

She hugged him back with a ferocity that completed him. No one had ever held him with so much adoration and care. Not that he'd ever let anyone get this close, but Amelia was different.

One look from her was all it took to get under his skin. He thought of her often and chalked it up to worrying about her treatment.

But it went so much deeper than that.

Her soul spoke to his.

Suggesting that his father move her had nothing to do with Stas and everything to do with keeping Amelia safe. He hadn't wanted to babysit her because he feared their inherent connection. And all the training was a way of making her stronger because he craved an equal.

He pressed a kiss to her throat and slid his hands to her waist to pull her away from the door. His pile of blankets would have to do, because he wanted to love on her for hours.

Tom went to his knees with her legs still wrapped around him and lay over her on the bed of blankets without breaking contact between their hips.

She met his lazy kiss with a sensuous one of her own, tracing his lips with her tongue and sliding it in his mouth for a luxuriating taste.

He cradled her face between his palms and moved slowly inside her, cherishing their deep connection.

Her lips curled into a smile but froze when a flourish of footsteps came from the hallway.

Oh, shit.

He pulled away and threw a blanket over her just as the door crashed open.

Chapter Seventeen

Kiss of Death

Tom stayed on his knees, with his hands folded in his lap, naked.

Well, this isn't awkward at all.

Three sets of eyes stared down at him, only one of them making him truly uncomfortable. "Stas," he greeted.

Her wide gaze swung back and forth between him and Amelia. Then understanding colored her expression, and she jumped in front of her fuming boyfriend. "Issac, don't."

"As if I could," Wakefield seethed. "This is not cute, Amelia."

Tom frowned at his harsh tone. "Don't talk to her like that," he said at the same time someone else said something very similar in his voice. He glanced to his left and met the gaze of his identical twin. *Holy shit.* "You shifted."

"Nice try, sweetheart," Amelia replied in a voice that sounded exactly like his own. "She doesn't need to see this, Wakefield. Take her away."

Tom gaped at her, then realized what she was doing. "Oh, hell no. She's lying."

His identical twin rolled his eyes. *Note to self: never roll my eyes again because I look like an idiot.* "Give me a gun, and I'll prove who's lying."

Wakefield tried to step forward, just to be forced back by Stas. "Don't touch or hurt him, Issac."

"Trust me when I say you do not want to do this to me, Astasiya. Not right now."

Stas remained in place, hands on his chest, and acted as a barrier between them. To Wakefield's credit, he didn't try to remove her, though every line of his suit-clad body was tense and ready to fight.

The third member of their party leaned against the wall with his arms crossed, his green eyes darting between the two Toms with a curious expression. Seemed the Hydraian King was mildly amused. *No doubt planning my colorful execution.* Except there were two Toms to choose from, which put Amelia's life in serious danger. No fucking way would he let her suffer for him.

"Okay, that's enough." Tom grabbed a blanket, wrapped it around his waist, and stood to meet Wakefield's gaze. "I'll prove it's me." And vividly recalled the night he accidentally sent Stas to the Conclave. Her face had resembled a white sheet as she left the Arcadia. He'd wanted to approach her, but the Ichorian at her side had made that impossible.

Wakefield narrowed his gaze, then nodded. "He's Tom."

"What? No. I'm Tom."

"Nice try, sweetheart," the real Tom murmured, echoing her words from a few minutes prior. "I'm glad to see your gift works again, though."

Amelia shifted back to herself with a sigh and hugged the blankets to her chest while staying on the ground. "Please don't hurt him. I made my own bed. Quite literally, I suppose."

"Don't hurt him?" Wakefield repeated. "Dear sister, this man—and I use that term lightly—has fantasized about murdering me several times in my presence. Why am I not to return the favor?"

Tom snorted. "Might as well finish what you started, right, Wakefield?"

He gave him an affronted look. "And what the bloody hell is that supposed to mean?"

"You know damn well what it means." And it pissed him off that the Ichorian pretended otherwise.

"I assure you, I do not." He folded his arms and cocked a brow. "Do enlighten me, Sentinel."

"Oh, you want to talk about it?" Because he sure as shit didn't. That night haunted him. He'd wanted to go home for months, to seek the comfort of his mother's arms and beg her not to send him back to that awful place, only to find her slaughtered on his bed. The image flashed behind his eyes of its own accord, and his hands curled into fists. Only a handful of Ichorians knew about Anna, one of whom was standing before him, pretending not to have a damn clue about that night.

"Why are you showing me this?" Wakefield asked, his brow furrowed.

"Ring any bells?" he forced out through clenched teeth. "Or did that night mean nothing to you?" Just another merciless killing for no fucking reason. That was why he hated Ichorians. They lacked humanity and heart.

Surprise lit Wakefield's features. "You think I did this?"

"I know you did."

"Do you? And how is that, Thomas? Were you there?"

"No, but I saw what you did afterward."

"I see. And Jonathan named me as the culprit. How fitting."

Tom took a step forward and froze when Luc pushed off the wall. Right. Two on one, unarmed and naked, not a fair fight. Time to rein in the emotions a bit. "You're right to want to kill me, Wakefield. Because if you don't, I'll kill you."

Amelia's gasp struck him like an arrow through the heart. He never had a chance to explain his side or tell her why her brother deserved to die, and now he'd leave her without answers. Because the glower Wakefield leveled at him was one he'd seen countless times. His minutes were numbered.

"Would you like to know how I recall the events of that evening, or would you prefer to die with your ignorance?"

Amelia jumped up and placed herself between them. "I'm begging you not to do this, Issac. He's not working for his father. I know he's not."

"Alik" was Wakefield's reply.

A chill slithered down Tom's spine as the shorter Elder sauntered into the room. The Hydraian was a legend. He could bring a room of people to their knees with a single thought and not blink an eye. Tom had never seen a photo of the infamous immortal but recognized his dark traits and placid expression. Death would be preferable over an evening with this guy, but it seemed Wakefield had other plans.

"Amelia," Alik murmured. "Would you mind accompanying me into the hallway?"

"I'm not going anywhere."

Alik sighed and stepped forward to take hold of her arm, making Tom want to intervene, but one glance from the man told him that would be the wrong move.

"I said no," Amelia argued.

"I heard you," Alik replied as he gently nudged her over a few paces. "So we'll stay here while Wakefield and the Sentinel continue their chat."

"You can't do this," Amelia whispered. "I'll never forgive any of you."

"Time forgives all transgressions," Luc stated. "Trust me."

Tears filled her eyes, breaking Tom's heart. As if the woman hadn't been through enough, now she had to watch his trial? No. He wouldn't allow it. "Just get whatever it is you plan to do over with," he said, focusing on Wakefield. "For her."

Stas's shoulders stiffened. "Issac, don't—"

"Thomas, for the record, I did not kill your mother. I was on the opposite side of the state at a military school, saving the life of a young fledgling who was the spitting image of his father. Perhaps you'll dream of it."

The crack of a bullet and Amelia's scream preceded the pain. He always wondered what it would feel like to die.

It turns out you don't feel anything at all.

His eyes closed on that thought, and the world fell silent around him.

~*~

Amelia collapsed, her hands at her mouth, and her heart shattering in her chest. Watching Tom fall to a lifeless heap on the floor was worse than anything Jonathan or Anita had ever done to her. It hurt more than Eli's death. He at least lived a full life, but Tom? His life had been cut short by the man she called her brother.

How could you, Luc? I trusted you.

Her body shook in a way she knew too well. Darkness was calling, and this time she'd let it consume her. What was the point? Her so-called family had betrayed her in the cruelest of ways. It appeared Jonathan would win after all.

I'm broken.

The conversation floated around her, but she felt too numb to care. Their words meant nothing to her.

They would never understand.

They never cared.

Revenge won every time.

"It seems Stas's command wore off," Luc remarked. His voice made her cringe. She didn't want to hear him ever again. When she saw the gun in his hands, she tried to jump in the way, but Alik held her back.

I hate them.

"Why are you glaring at me like that?" Luc asked.

"This is not what we agreed on," Issac replied flatly. "You quite literally jumped the gun."

"Stas commanded you not to hurt him again, which left me as the viable option. Or have you forgotten that Amelia is my sister as well? Also, logic dictates that as the Hydraian King, it's my duty to handle fledgling issues as I see fit. And so I did."

Amelia wanted to cry but couldn't. It took too much energy to call on tears.

All she needed was to crawl into the dark place and never come out.

She created it all those years ago and hid there often during experiments. It seemed she'd crafted a forever home for her conscious.

Maybe it would kill her.

She wasn't sure she cared.

A sad reality considering how hard she'd fought these last few years.

Tom wouldn't want you to do this, her conscious chided.

Well, he's not here to care, is he?

She shivered, feeling so cold and alone.

Tom's warmth was a million miles away. Her heart ached without him.

I'm so weak.

All that talk about making her stronger had been a lie. She promised never to rely on another person again, but he'd anchored her in inexplicable ways.

All the ghosts his presence chased away came roaring back, badgering around in her head and pulling her deeper into that hole of nothingness.

"Jesus Christ!" A deep voice crashed through the waves of her mind.

She swam farther away while the conversation flowed above the dark water.

"What the fuck were you thinking shooting him in front of her?"

Warmth flowed over her, but it felt foreign and wrong.

Not Tom.

She struggled to get away, but something strong wrapped around her and flooded heat through her veins. It hurt, yet numbed at the same time.

Amelia fought like hell to push it away, but the power broke through and forced her back into reality.

Her eyelids felt heavy as they opened, her mouth dry.

Eventually, her focus returned, and Balthazar's worried expression filled her view.

How did I get in his lap?

Then it hit her like a punch to the chest. "*No.*"

"Oh, yes. Sorry, love, but you needed me."

She tried to slap him, but her arms refused to move. "Bloody bastard," she settled on saying instead, despising that he'd used his gift for emotional manipulation on her. "I hate you."

"I know." He looked contrite as he brushed a lock of sweaty hair from her forehead. "He's going to be okay, Amelia."

"He's dead," she replied, her voice flat.

Inside, she wanted to scream, but Balthazar had muted everything on the surface. It was like sitting inside a dense fog of foreign emotion with all her true feelings locked up inside a vault. And she didn't have the key.

"He's a fledgling, A. He's going to wake up in twelve hours with a headache and a new set of immortal genes."

Luc peered down at her over Balthazar's shoulder. "We didn't behead him or set him on fire, and I used a normal bullet, Amelia. A direct shot to the head provides the least amount of pain. He'll wake up Hydraian tomorrow."

She glowered at the Hydraian King. "You're a right bastard."

"One who just did his baby sister a huge favor. A mortal death was the sentence we agreed upon. When he wakes up, he'll be one of us. A useful addition, if I do say so myself."

"You should have fucking explained that to her prior to pulling the trigger," Balthazar growled in a voice she didn't usually associate with him. When those chocolate eyes met hers, they were filled with fear and understanding. He knew how close she'd been to crossing a line she wouldn't have come back from.

"Yes, well, the plan was for me to kill him. Not Lucian." Issac crouched beside her and brushed his knuckles over her cheek. "I'm sorry, love. I still don't care much for him, and likely never will, but I would never intentionally hurt you or Aya."

"I'm still fucking pissed at you." Stas's voice came from the other side of the room, and she sounded furious. "All of you. Except B."

Balthazar smirked. "Hear that, Wakefield? Your competition is the only one she likes right now. Should I use that to my advantage?" He waggled his eyebrows at Issac, making Amelia groan. She did not want to be in the middle of this discussion. Balthazar let her go as she squirmed away to lie beside Tom's lifeless form. He seemed peaceful enough, and someone had placed a pillow beneath his head.

"Lucian, may I borrow your firearm?" Issac asked. "I would like to give Balthazar a headache."

"No," Stas said, arms folded. "No more guns. No more shooting. No more *anything*."

Issac sighed, "Aya—"

"No. You just killed my friend. Sorry, not you, but Luc. But don't you see? Tom didn't get a choice in becoming a Hydraian. You took that from him, and that's not okay. If you *ever* do that to me, any of you, I promise you will live to regret it. Life is not something you just take on a whim or for some idiotic form of punishment. It's not a game. Especially not to me." She stormed out of the room without a backward glance.

"Fuck," Issac muttered, palming the back of his neck.

Balthazar whistled. "Yeah, good luck fixing that."

"As always, your commentary is not helpful." Issac started after Stas but stopped to study Amelia. The pain radiating from his sapphire gaze made her feel a little better. He should feel bad, because if Luc hadn't pulled the trigger, he would have done it. But she hated the conflict in his gaze. He didn't know whom to choose. She would never stand in the way of love, especially for him.

"Go after her," she told him. "I'll be okay." And she wouldn't stay angry with him. Something told her Stas would punish him enough for it.

He stared at Balthazar, and the Elder gave him a nod. Then Issac disappeared out the door. They had such a bizarre relationship, bickering one minute and friends the next.

A hand settled on her shoulder, making her flinch. Luc stared down at her with a mixture of emotions in his eyes. "When Tom wakes in the morning, ask him what we talked about today. Then let me know if what I did was truly as wrong as you and Stas seem to think it was." With that, he left. Alik, who had stood silently in the corner, followed her brothers without a word.

"Right, then. Leave me to clean everything up." Balthazar stood and wiped his palms on his trousers. "Let's move Tom to my guest room. He'll be more comfortable there in the morning, and you can stay with him."

"Did you know what they planned to do?" she asked.

"Yes." He held out a hand to help her stand, and she accepted.

"Why didn't you tell me?"

"You know why, Amelia."

Elder business. They rarely made decisions for Hydraians, but when they did, their edicts stayed private unless otherwise appropriate. "But you helped me sneak in here to see him."

"Yes, to give him an opportunity to choose his fate, and he chose you."

She didn't understand. "What?"

"Think about it, love. You being here gave him the perfect chance to escape, but he didn't. And why didn't he? Because he wanted to be with you more than he wanted his freedom. Some might call that love."

She gaped at him. "It was all a test?"

"No, it was a choice. Had he chosen to escape, we would have let him leave. But he chose to stay, so Luc made him immortal. Now, can we head back to my house? Digging into your emotional psyche was exhausting, and I'd like to get some sleep."

Oh. She worried her lower lip. "About what you saw…"

"Don't. You're not ready to go there yet, A." He palmed her cheek. "But when you are, I'm here, okay?"

She nodded. "All right."

"Let's get him to my house, rest, and regroup in the morning over breakfast. I'll make pancakes, too. You can flaunt them in front of Luc as revenge."

"I'd like to do a lot more than throw pancakes at my big brother right now."

"Take his advice and talk to Tom tomorrow. You might be more forgiving afterward."

"Doubtful."

He shrugged. "Then you can take Luc a plate of pancakes and force him to eat them."

She shook her head, bemused. "You and your breakfast food."

"He's the one obsessed with waffles."

"Uh-huh."

Balthazar secured the blanket around Tom before lifting him with a gentleness she didn't expect.

He didn't appear dead so much as asleep.

A good thing because it implied Luc had told the truth about the bullet.

Tom's body still functioned on a psychic level, keeping his organs and bodily functions intact, while his immortal genes took over. There were those who swore the heart still beat a little during the process. She might have to listen for it later.

Balthazar cast her an amused glance. "Not that I mind, but can you maybe throw on some clothes before we walk out of here? Don't want to cause too much of a scene between you and the dead fledgling."

She took in her bare legs and realized someone had dressed her in Tom's shirt at some point.

Right.

Because she'd been naked in a blanket when they walked into the room. Her years as a laboratory rat kept her from feeling too embarrassed by that fact. It was the lovemaking fresh between her thighs that made her face heat.

No way any of them had missed that detail.

Especially Balthazar.

Not wanting to wear her own clothes, she pulled on Tom's boxers, gathered their trousers and other items, and followed B out the door.

At least he's alive.

~*~

Tom squinted into the semidarkness and willed the truck parked on his head to move, but it refused. The weight centered between his eyes and spread in agonizing lines through the rest of his skull.

Shit. Talk about a hangover. Except he couldn't remember the last time he overindulged in alcohol. Intoxication could get him killed in his line of work.

He frowned.

Killed.

He shot straight up out of the bed and regretted it the moment his head started to spin.

"Fuck," he muttered, touching the middle of his forehead. Smooth skin met his inspection, but he could swear something had hit him there.

"Tom?" Amelia's husky voice went straight to his balls. She yawned and stretched on the bed he'd just jumped out of, and blinked sleepy eyes up at him.

What the hell happened last night? Because the sun outside told him it was late morning. He fought to remember, but a thick haze filled his memory. Something about fucking her against the wall and wanting to make love to her on the pile of blankets in a room that did not resemble this one in the slightest.

Dark wood furniture, a four-poster bed, and a balcony with a beach view stared back at him.

"What the hell happened last night?" he asked.

Amelia cleared her throat. "Er, you don't remember?"

He examined the pajama pants covering his legs. "Whose pants am I wearing?" Because they sure as hell didn't belong to him.

"Balthazar procured them for you. We're in his guest room. Apparently, a woman named Eliza is staying in my old home." His cock stirred at the sight of her stretching her arms over head. Her breasts looked fantastic in that thin tank top.

"I don't really mind, though," she continued. "It would be weird to stay there, and from what I understand, she needs it more than I do."

He touched his forehead again and grimaced. Did he hit it against something? Maybe that's what woke him. No. Adrenaline woke him with an odd jolt, and the headache followed. He caught Amelia admiring him and cocked a brow.

"You've seen me shirtless before, sweetheart. Not that I mind you gawking, of course."

She grinned. "You have no idea, do you?"

"Mmm, no idea about what?" he murmured as he crawled over her on the bed. A different part of him was starting to ache, and he had the perfect solution.

Mischief lit her blue gaze. "Oh, this is quite fun."

"Is it?" He settled his hips between her legs and allowed her to feel the full weight of his arousal.

"You know," a deep voice intruded, "I'm all for exhibitionism. Voyeurism, too, of course, but I'm afraid not everyone in the house right now shares my liberal views."

Tom glanced over his shoulder to find Balthazar leaning against the door with his arms crossed. He met the Elder before the Hydraian King's interrogation. *Was that yesterday? Why is everything so damn foggy?*

"Because Luc shot you in the head," the mind reader replied. "Welcome to Hydria—officially, I mean. The pancakes are ready." He pushed off the doorjamb and left with a wicked gleam in his eyes. Tom stared at the empty space for a solid minute before returning his focus to Amelia.

"I'm a Hydraian?" He didn't feel any different. Just well rested with a killer headache.

"Are you mad?" she whispered.

"Mad?" he replied. "Why would I be mad?"

"Because my brother took away your mortality without asking?"

"Not exactly." He frowned. "He asked me for my opinions on becoming a Hydraian during his interrogation. I thought he wanted to know about my feelings toward his kind, not because he planned to turn me. What does this mean? Why am I not dead?"

And why don't I feel any different? He should have two supernatural talents, like Amelia's shifting and knowledge transfer. But he didn't sense anything unique. *Am I broken?*

"Luc said your mortal death was your punishment, though I still don't know why he needed to punish you to begin with, and he considers you a Hydraian. A useful one, if I remember correctly."

That made him grin. Tom had mentioned his potential to the Hydraian King several times during their discussion. Not to beg for his life, but to give the practical reasons why the Elders shouldn't kill him. He gave up a few CRF details but kept the important ones close to his chest. Some of the memories from last night tumbled through his thoughts, making his eyes widen. "You shifted."

Amelia's cheeks flushed a pretty pink. "I did."

"Into my twin."

She nodded, biting her lip. "Your trick the other night, although cruel, worked. I didn't even think twice about it. I just shifted."

His lips curled. "So I helped?"

"Maybe," she conceded, her pupils dilating. "Want to help me…?" Her voice trailed off into a frown. "Never mind. Issac's here. He's filling my head with butterflies."

"Do I even want to know what that means?"

"I believe he's apologizing for last night. Which reminds me"—her gaze narrowed—"when were you going to tell me about your intentions toward my brother? Who, by the way, did *not* kill your mother."

His blood ran cold, and whatever was left of his erection died. He didn't want to talk about this. Not with her. She would never understand.

He rolled off the bed. "Is my shirt lying around somewhere? Or one that I can borrow?"

"Seriously? You're going to change the subject and walk away?" She jumped out of the covers to stand in front of him with her hands on her hips. "We need to talk about this."

"Why?"

"Because you wrongly think my brother killed your mum, and never bothered to mention it."

He folded his arms. "Yeah? And when would have been a good time to bring it up?"

"You had the last several weeks to do it."

"To what point? So I could see the same self-righteous look you're giving me now? No, thank you." He tried to walk around her, but she stepped into his path.

"He's my brother, so of course I'll defend him, but in this case, it's because he's innocent. He said as much last night." She placed her palm over his heart. "But this isn't so much about him as it is about us, Tom. This will never work if we don't talk to each other."

Us. What a strange and amazing word. Tom had nothing against monogamy or relationships but never considered having one due to his line of work. There was the occasional girlfriend in college, though they all stopped coming around after realizing his career aspirations were his first and only love. But with Amelia, he liked the sound of *us.*

"Is that what we are? A couple?" he wondered, his voice soft. "Is that what you want?"

She studied him for a moment, silent.

Then swallowed.

"When Luc shot you, I..." She paused to clear her throat. "I didn't handle it well. You told me leaning on someone doesn't mean I'm weak, but I was last night. This bond, or whatever this is, terrifies me." Her lids lowered as she peered up at him. "But losing you terrifies me more. I stayed with you all night, worrying that you may never wake up even though I knew you would. How do you define that?"

You don't.

There were no words for it, only feelings.

He wrapped his hand around her nape and pulled her in for a long, devastating kiss. Her arms went around his shoulders as she lifted onto her toes to get closer to him. He left her panting against him when he pulled back to stare down into her gorgeous eyes.

"You were right the other night," he admitted. "I've always been alone. I'm not used to having someone I can confide in or trust. This isn't going to be easy, sweetheart."

"Nothing worth having ever is," she whispered.

He nuzzled her nose. "I want this—you—more than anything I've ever wanted. And it terrifies me, too. That's why I didn't mention your brother. I didn't want to lose you."

"You won't," she promised. "But you do need to talk to him."

He groaned. "I knew you were going to say that." Tom would rather have all his teeth pulled than talk to Wakefield.

"Tell me why you think he killed your mum?"

"Because Jonathan told him I did," a cultured voice said from the doorway. Apparently, the bedrooms in Balthazar's home weren't considered private. "Amelia, could you give Thomas and me a moment?"

Oh, good. Looks like we'll have that chat now, then. If his supernatural talents could appear now, he would love that. They might come in handy while talking to Amelia's big brother.

Will you be okay? Amelia's eyes seemed to ask.

He sighed. What choice did he have? Amelia's comments about last night had brought back his memory of Wakefield's final words.

"I was on the opposite side of the state at a military school, saving the life of a young fledgling who was the spitting image of his father."

That night forever haunted him.

The phone call from his mother telling him to run, being cornered by a horde of Ichorians who wanted him dead, and a man saving him from the shadows.

His father claimed to be the savior, but Tom never understood why he couldn't picture his face clearly.

Everything else was so vivid, except the one who saved him.

He'd been in shock, his father said. That was also how he explained the memory gap between leaving the school and arriving at the cabin too late to save his mom.

Hearing Wakefield's words made him wonder if it hadn't been shock so much as someone fucking with his vision.

"Tom?" Amelia whispered, waiting for an answer to her unspoken question.

He let her go with a nod and stepped out onto the stone-paved balcony. The humid air did little for the heat climbing up his neck, though the pants-wearing Ichorian beside him seemed perfectly fine.

"Do you not own shorts or something?" Tom wondered.

Wakefield eyed his khaki slacks and polo shirt. "This is acceptable island attire."

"If you say so, buddy." He folded his arms onto the railing and admired the Aegean Sea.

The clear water rolled in smooth waves over the black sand beach below, giving the scene a peaceful atmosphere that appealed to his tormented soul.

He could see why the Hydraians chose to stay in this place. It might not be economically sound, but something could be said about its tranquility.

"I used to admire your father a great deal, Thomas. Aidan considered him part of the family, despite being sired by a different Ichorian."

Tom knew the story. His father had been reborn too weak, according to his maker, and he'd left him for dead. Being able to force truths from people wasn't exactly a competitive skill among the Ichorian community, but Aidan took him in anyway and gave him the means to defend himself.

"As a result, I considered him family. Amelia did, too," Wakefield continued. "So when he called me that day and requested my assistance to save his son, I agreed without question." He leaned against the railing, his back to the ocean and his gaze on Tom. "Imagine my surprise when I found a twelve-year-old soldier fending off Ichorians twice his size. They would have won, of course, though today I think you'd put up a good fight."

"Careful, Wakefield, that almost sounds like a compliment."

He smirked. "It is. I don't have to like a man to admire his skill. But my point is, my only dealing with Anna's death was delivering you to her cabin that night. Your father was the one covered in her blood, presumably after trying to save her life, but I always wondered as to the veracity of his retelling. And I find it particularly convenient that he blamed her death on me. If you want my opinion, I'd say he was trying to drive a wedge between you and the only allies you could ever potentially depend upon."

To leave me forever alone and dependent on him.

A perfect manipulation.

How many other lies had his father told throughout the years? Luc's acceptance of him in Hydria proved one of the biggest threats false, and now this?

Tom shook his head. *What a mindfuck.*

A commotion from inside the house drew his attention. "What's going on?"

Issac frowned, his gaze distant. "I'm not quite sure. They appear to be crowded around the television and watching a news report. Something about a foiled terrorist attack in Upstate New York at what appears to be a hospital."

Ice dripped through his veins. "What part of New York?"

He said the name and blinked. "Is that your mother's hometown? It's near the cabin."

"No. That's where my aunt lives, and that hospital is where she works. I need a phone."

Chapter Eighteen

Family Bonds

"Two hours and fifty-seven minutes? I'm disappointed, son. Have you forgotten your training already?"

Tom ignored his father's jibe and got to the point. "What have you done?"

John tsked. "Now, Tom, it's not about what I've done, but what I'm going to do. Unless you cooperate."

His hands fisted, but he kept his voice calm. "What do you want?"

"The asset, of course."

The tension in the room was palpable as all eyes fell on the phone in the center of the dining room table. Tom had put his father on speakerphone, not because anyone requested it, but because he wanted to be transparent. Trust was earned, and he had a lot of making up to do. Allowing the Elders, Stas, and Amelia to hear this conversation was just the beginning. Everyone stood in a circle around the table, but no one spoke except Tom.

"Yeah, that's not going to happen, John," he said, replying to his father's request. "She's gone."

Silence. Then he asked, "And where did she go?"

"Home."

"If that were true, I would have received, at a minimum, a call from at least one of her brothers—or perhaps her father. Try again."

Wakefield and Luc both shrugged as if to say, *Man's got a point.* Which he did, but he failed to factor in that they cared more about seeing Amelia than they did revenge. And from what Tom had gathered about both men, they were the type to think things through before reacting. Otherwise, they would have killed Tom without a second thought.

A moan sounded over the line, followed by a crack. "Quiet," his father snapped. "Can't you see I'm having a conversation? Though I must say, Rosalie, it's not going in your favor. Seems Tom prefers his new plaything over you."

Cold rage replaced his nonchalant demeanor. "Rosalie has nothing to do with this."

"Well, it was her or Lizzie, and the latter would upset Stas. But really, son, this is your doing. Had you just gotten this fling out of your system and returned home, none of this would have been necessary. Alas, here we are."

"You're a dead man," Tom seethed, meaning every word.

"Ah, there it is! I wondered when the real you would come out to play. Excellent. Shall we get to the point, then?"

Prick. He wanted to get to the point ten minutes ago. "Yes."

"Sorry, what was that? I didn't quite hear you."

I'm going to fucking kill you. "Yes, sir."

Tom pictured his father's triumphant grin and fought not to break something. "Very good, then. I propose an exchange: your only living relative on your mother's side for the asset."

A bullet through the heart would hurt less, but he refused to let it show. John loved a good game of chess, and he'd trained his son to be a master. "All you want is the asset for Rosalie? Fine. Done. But I get my freedom."

Luc smirked, clearly catching on to his strategy, while Issac cocked a brow and Amelia flashed him an affronted look. He tucked her closer to his side and kissed the concerned lines of her forehead. As if he'd ever give her up.

"So you admit she's with you?" Arrogance underlined John's tone.

"Where else would she be?"

"You said she was home."

"I lied. I can do that over the phone, you know." His father's powers only worked in person, a fact he seemed hell-bent to change despite it being that way for over a millennium. He may have created a small army, but Ichorian gifts didn't evolve over time. Not naturally, anyway. Tom wouldn't be surprised if some of the CRF's research was devoted to enhancing immortal gifts.

"When and where do you want the asset?" he asked, his voice bored.

"You're willing to trade?"

"Yes." He kept the answer simple and flat on purpose to inspire curiosity.

"I expected more of a fight," John replied, his disappointment clear.

"The asset for Rosalie and my freedom. You're giving me the better end of the deal, so why would I argue with that?"

He pictured his father frowning as he considered. "And where will you go?"

"Well now, John, that's the whole point of having my freedom. I won't have to answer to you or anyone ever again."

Silence. "I see."

"So we have a deal, then?" Tom prompted.

"No."

He grinned. "No?"

"I'll release Rosalie if you agree to come home and undergo rehabilitation. Willingly."

Checkmate. "But you just said—"

"I know what I said, and I changed my mind. Your willing rehabilitation and the asset for your aunt's release, or no deal."

"So you want me and the asset? That seems a hefty price for one relative." It killed him to say it, especially knowing she could hear him. But he had to play this part, or John would bulldoze him. "Especially a relative who will die in a few years while I live for eternity."

"Fair point," John conceded. "I guess I need to sweeten the deal by throwing in a person I know you care about with immortal genetics, then. Like, say, Lizzie? Of course, I don't know how immortal she is, but I'm sure the scientists would enjoy testing her limits, don't you think?"

Ice coated his spine, making him freeze. Stas met his gaze with a look of fury and horror, all mixed into one. He had to clear the cotton from his throat to speak. "You have my attention."

"Do I? Good." The smile in his father's voice made him want to shoot something. "So I leave Lizzie alone, for now, and release your aunt—"

"Unharmed," Tom amended.

"Sure, no more harmed than she already is," John continued, "and you turn yourself and the asset in. I think that sounds like a splendid trade."

Tom stared at the phone, unsure of what to do. So much for his checkmate. A motion in his peripheral vision brought his attention to Luc, who gave him a nod.

Yes to what? The deal?

Luc nodded again, clearly reading the questions from his eyes. He followed it with a *hurry up* motion, and Balthazar mimicked it beside him.

You want me to agree? he asked the mind reader.

He moved his head in the affirmative.

I'm not handing her over.

Balthazar gave him a look that said, *No shit,* and gestured impatiently at the phone.

"Have I lost you, son?" Jonathan asked, victory evident in his tone. "Or would you like to hear a demonstration of what I intend to do to Lizzie? Your aunt probably won't survive it, but you don't seem to care anyway."

Fucking prick. "I'll do it."

"Sorry, what was that?"

Oh, he would rip his father apart when he saw him. "I agree to your terms, sir."

"Very good. Now how far away are you from your mother's cabin?"

Luc held up the number seven and mouthed, *Hours.*

"I need at least seven hours to get there."

"You have six. Bring the asset, and come alone."

"Who the hell would I bring?"

His father laughed. "Fair point. See you soon, son."

Tom pressed the End button with a little too much force, picked up the phone, and threw it at the wall. It shattered into a dozen pieces.

"You know, untraceable mobiles are not cheap," Jayson said conversationally from his position in the kitchen. "And I happened to like that particular model."

"Because you don't have ten more just like it at your house," Balthazar replied.

"I was talking about quality, not quantity, and it's the principle of the thing. You don't break other people's stuff. It's impolite."

"Yeah, and how many beds have—"

"Enough." The authority in Luc's voice captured everyone's attention. "Tom, tell me about Lizzie."

"Yes, what he said," Stas echoed, her expression dark.

"Right." He cleared his throat. "I don't know a lot. My father implied once, about a decade ago, that she could be biologically related to me when he found us in a rather compromising position." At Stas's raised eyebrows, he clarified. "She tried to kiss me. Nothing happened."

She nodded for him to continue.

"Anyway, I assumed he had an affair with Lillian until I found some CRF files on Lizzie a few months back. I didn't realize it was her at first, just someone called 'Test Subject Four-Seven,' but one of the researchers slipped her name. When I asked my dad about it, he told me it wasn't anything to worry about, that he would keep me apprised of any developments." *Whatever the fuck that meant.* "All I gathered is she has immortal genetics of some kind inside of her, and I don't think they were put there through normal means."

"That confirms what we've suspected," Wakefield murmured. "Elizabeth resembles neither of her parents, and she appeared out of nowhere about seven years ago."

"Were there any files on Test Subject Four-Seven in Mateo's records?" Stas asked.

"Only a cover page denoting her genotype as nonhuman." Luc's gaze took on a faraway gleam while he spoke. "The project name was *Rebirth.*"

Her green eyes widened. "So are you saying Lizzie—my best friend—definitely isn't human?"

"She's something other than mortal, and I'm pretty sure the CRF is still experimenting on her despite her not being in the lab." Tom palmed the back of his neck, unease trickling down his spine. "My father mentioned something about her needing the monthly dose once to George. I didn't think much of it at the time, but now I wonder if he meant a medical treatment of some kind."

Luc scratched his chin. "Interesting. Any idea how many people are aware of the study?"

"Knowing my dad, he's the only one with all the knowledge and he's only given pieces to others." John never divulged enough to give up his position, a power play to keep himself in charge. "He wouldn't even tell me about it, and he considered me his heir." Her records were all classified at the highest level, above what Tom's used to be, and the technicians refused to talk about her files. He tried a few times with no luck.

Luc nodded. "An intelligent strategy that makes him more useful alive, and also coincides with our file discoveries. Mateo hacked the CRF a few months ago, but all the information is superficial and high level."

"Sounds like something my dad would do," Tom muttered. "He doesn't trust anyone." Not even his own son.

"Hmm, yes, well the question becomes, how valuable is Lizzie Watkins?" Luc wondered, his expressive features suggesting he was already compiling a list of pros and cons.

Tom bristled. "If you think I'll sit by and let her suffer in John's hands, then think again. She might not mean anything to you, and I might be a shitty friend, but I love that woman like my own flesh and blood, and I will not sacrifice her life for my freedom."

"What he said," Stas growled.

"Easy, love," Wakefield murmured as he wrapped an arm around her shoulders. "I believe Lucian is trying to determine whether or not the Hydraians should look into Elizabeth's case."

"Correct. And from what I'm hearing, she's valuable to Tom and Stas, making her of interest to me. I would offer her asylum, but Tom's comments regarding her monthly dose concern me. Until we learn more, I can't help her."

"What do you propose?" Wakefield asked, his eyes narrowing.

"We keep Stas in play at the CRF while someone else infiltrates Lizzie's life in a more intimate capacity."

"Uh, hello?" Stas waved her hand. "I'm her roommate and best friend."

"You're also not staying on as a Sentinel. Given recent events, it's too dangerous," Wakefield added.

Tom nodded his agreement. *Stole the words right out of my mouth, buddy.*

"She's my best friend, Issac. It's my decision."

"Did you hear what Jonathan threatened to do to Elizabeth just now? He'll do worse to you, Aya. Especially if he thinks it will control me or Thomas to do his bidding. With Amelia being home, the environment is too unstable. Jonathan—"

"I have an idea regarding that," Luc cut in. "A solution that keeps Stas safe, or at least as safe as she's been, and protects Amelia and Tom. Also, it'll keep Jonathan alive, for now."

Tom frowned. "Why do you want to keep him alive?" He assumed they would want to slaughter him. Brutally. Or at least torture the man for what he did. The boy in him who once loved his father unconditionally ached at the thought, but the man he'd become understood John deserved to be punished. Even if it hurt.

"I want to know who Jonathan is working for," Luc replied.

"My father works for himself." He was too egotistical and arrogant to report to anyone else.

"Really? So how did your father acquire the wealth to build the Catastrophic Relief Foundation?" Luc paused for effect before continuing. "He went from relying on Aidan's financial assistance to opening his own humanitarian organization in less than a year. Then he miraculously created a secret army of superhuman soldiers to fight Ichorians and Hydraians overnight. That's quite an achievement for a man whose only gift is to force truths. I'd like to know how he managed that."

The CRF was created prior to Tom's birth, so he didn't know much about it. "I thought Aidan loaned him the funds for it, like he did Wakefield."

Wakefield snorted. "Is that how he explained my history as an entrepreneur? How quaint."

Another lie, then? Fantastic. "Okay, but my father never mentioned working for anyone other than himself."

"Which is why I sadly still need him alive," Luc replied. "And I need him comfortable, so he keeps his guard down."

Okay, I'll bite. "You obviously have a plan in mind. So what do you suggest?"

Luc grinned. "I thought you'd never ask. Let's start by talking about your new Hydraian gifts and how to use them."

* * *

The cabin hadn't changed. Tranquil, secluded, and haunted by memories. Tom shivered at the thought of stepping inside. He wanted to burn the place to the ground and never return. And if Luc's plan worked, he would be allowed to do just that.

"You okay?" Amelia whispered.

He swallowed and nodded. She stood beside him in jeans and a tank top, while he wore his favorite leather jacket to hide all his weapons. His father would ask him to hand them over, but by then, it would be too late.

Wakefield leaned against a tree about a hundred yards away, hands in his slacks. He would disappear when his father arrived, as would Tristan, Mateo, and the Hydraians who opted to join their mission. Jacque had teleported everyone in without breaking a sweat. A true testament to his potential. Tom caught him walking along the roof and admiring the night sky.

His entire sense of time was fucked up, thanks to his immortal rebirth and all the traveling. But he felt more alive than he'd ever been, especially now that he understood his abilities. Amelia's analogy the other night proved to be accurate. Using his gifts were as natural as walking, except without the toddler learning curve. He hadn't noticed them earlier, because they were second nature to him and just enhancements of skills he already owned as a human. The plan hinged on his new gifts, which should have unnerved him, but didn't.

Tom only had one concern: wards.

Wards, or cryptic symbols, were what kept the CRF headquarters safe in a city of Ichorians, though he never did understand how they worked or where they came from. All he knew was they blocked supernatural gifts and kept immortals from entering the CRF compound without being invited. His father's researchers were trying to figure out how to apply the wards in a mobile capacity but hadn't solved that puzzle yet. At least, Tom hoped that was still the case, because if they had discovered how to apply wards to a person rather than a building, then this entire plan would fail.

When Tom mentioned it to Luc, the big man had shrugged and said, "Then we'll move on to plan B." But they didn't have time to discuss what that actually meant.

"Alik says they're coming," Amelia murmured, breaking into his thoughts.

"I had no idea he was a telepath until Luc explained his plan today." Tom knew about the whole mental torture thing but never looked into his other power. It didn't really matter when compared to his ability to take out a room full of people with one thought.

"He doesn't use it unless he has to."

"Well, that's good, I suppose. So what can Jayson do? Aside from control metal, I mean." He seemed to be the carefree one of the Elders but held an unmistakable air of danger around him. There was a reason the four Hydraians had lived so long and were considered royalty among their kind. Each of them carried deadly gifts that made them difficult to kill. But of all the Elders, Jayson's records at the CRF held the least information, and Tom always wondered why.

She grinned. "You don't know?"

"There are not a lot of records on him, other than he's old and has an affinity for metal. His appearance varies in all the notes as well."

"And there's a reason for that. He can alter visual perception and memory, which is why no one can recall what he looks like, unless he allows it."

Tom frowned. "So his gift is similar to your brother's?"

"Not really. Jayson only controls the visual memory of his own physical appearance, not the surroundings. He more or less influences how someone remembers him, but doesn't change the surroundings or where they met."

"In other words, he's the perfect spy," Tom mused.

"Yes, he—" Tires rolling over gravel cut off the rest of Amelia's reply. Three four-wheelers headed down the drive toward them. Tom kept his stance loose with his hands in his pockets, while Amelia shifted from foot to foot beside him.

"You ready?" he asked.

"Yep." Confidence underlined that single word, making pride blossom in his chest.

"I so want to kiss you right now."

"And do you want to straddle me as well?"

Minx. He swallowed his grin. The last thing he wanted was to appear amused as his father approached. John would expect repentance and submission, not excitement. The flirtation in Amelia's voice didn't show in her expression, only determination. His father would interpret it as defiance, which worked well for their plans.

"Hello, son," John greeted as he strolled up the drive in one of his signature suits. Half a dozen Sentinels flanked him on each side, all of them former friends. Stark was notably missing, which meant Stas's role in their plan had worked.

"Sir," Tom replied. *I see your arrogance has taken over the unit.* None of them had their weapons drawn. His father must have told them it wouldn't be necessary. *Mistake number one.*

"Ah, I'm almost disappointed to see the cocky demeanor go, but it is the first step in your rehabilitation."

Fucking prick. He couldn't wait to begin their charade, but he needed to see his aunt first. "Where's Rosalie?"

"Right. Our trade." John motioned over his shoulder, and Blake broke rank to return to one of the four-wheelers. His blue eyes flicked to Tom before opening the back door. Rosalie's appearance sent a jolt of shock to his system. He expected her in a similar state to Amelia, but instead, she was dolled up for a date, with her black dress, heels, and stylish updo.

Something isn't right here…

She sauntered up to his father's side and placed a hand on his shoulder. "Hello, Tom." His stomach turned over at the smile she flashed him. So familiar, yet with a touch of cruelty. Did his father engineer an identical twin to take her place? This sophisticated woman didn't resemble the down-to-earth aunt he knew.

"What is this? We had a deal, my life and the asset for Rosalie." And this look-alike was clearly not his aunt.

"And I'm upholding that deal to an extent. We agreed on her release, of which she's free, but choosing to stand by my side." John gazed at the stranger beside him. "Would you like to tell him, or shall I?" he asked.

"Oh, I think you should. You're his father, after all." Her voice sent a chill down Tom's spine. *She sounds like Rosalie.*

"Indeed." Dark brown eyes, the same color as his own, locked on Tom. "Rosalie and I have an understanding of sorts. It started around the time I met your mother and has continued, well, through today, obviously. She's helped me keep an eye on you, and before you, your mother."

Tom couldn't speak but maintained a studiously blank expression. Clearly, John wanted to tell a story, and the evil glint in his eyes implied he wanted it to hurt. A form of punishment, no doubt.

"You know, I liked your mother. Sweet woman, and gorgeous, too, but she decided to do something I didn't quite agree with. She planned to give you to the Hydraians, which, for obvious reasons, was not in your best interest, and I therefore had to deal with the issue."

Tom's jaw hurt from squeezing it so tightly. There were no words. His father hadn't finished yet, but the purpose of this lecture was clear. He wanted to explain how Anna died. The real story. And it seemed Tom's aunt was involved, which would force him to change the part of the plan where he saved Rosalie's life. She might be his blood relative, but if she willingly worked with his father in any capacity against his mother, he would have no choice but to leave her in John's hands.

Please tell me he's lying, Rosalie. Tell me this is all a cruel joke. But the adoration on her face as she listened to John's retelling lent truth to his words. Was this really his aunt? The woman he trusted? The woman he considered giving his life up for only hours before?

What a fool I've been.

"You were too young to understand at the time," John continued, "but I'm sure you see now why she had to die. As for Rosalie, she was the one who informed me of your mother's plans and helped me fix the problem. It was perfect, really, as she took over the motherly role in your life but remained loyal to me. The perfect way to keep you in line until this most recent mission. I suspected something was going on with the asset, of course. That's why I had Rosalie arrange dinner with you. Had I realized all hell would break lose, I would have gone about it in a different way."

"Not your fault, darling," his aunt cooed. "We both underestimated his loyalty."

Tom couldn't decide whom he wanted to shoot more—John or Rosalie. The smile in her eyes made her the ideal candidate for a bullet to the head, not that he had the heart to follow through. But Jesus Christ, he wanted to do damage. She voluntarily distracted him so Amelia could be tortured? And she betrayed her own sister to his father? Those sins alone were unforgivable. Fuck trying to save her. She dug her own grave with John and, from the looks of it, was quite happy about it.

Jesus. How had he missed the obvious connection between his aunt and his father? Every time he saw her, she commented about how alike he was to John. He didn't even realize they'd stayed in touch, let alone knew each other well. But she mentioned him every time they spoke. Like a hypnotic chant reminding him to stay in line, but in a different way from his dad.

Fuck.

It took all his energy not to react and keep his breathing even. Inside, a beast raged, but outside, he maintained his calm demeanor. The same could not be said about Amelia, who he could see bristling in his peripheral vision. His father must have noticed as well because he switched focus to her.

"You cost me a brilliant researcher, Amelia. Now we'll have to find someone else for the position, but we can offer you for their employee orientation. I wonder if Anita's replacement will think of any new tests? Hmm, this actually might be a good thing, a fresh pair of eyes is just what we need on your case. I would apologize for your future pain, but really, dear, you only have yourself to blame."

Amelia smiled. "I mean this sincerely when I say, go fuck yourself, Jonathan."

In all their time together, Tom had only heard her use "arse" and "bloody hell." Never "fuck." She said it with such arrogance and vigor that he couldn't help but feel a trickle of satisfaction.

That's my woman. And she'd just stood up to his father's threats instead of cowering. It provided the distraction he needed to regather his focus. Reacting to his father's reveal would do nothing to move their plan forward, and he needed Amelia safe once and for all. He could digest the reality of his mother's death later and, one day, seek his revenge. But today was not that day. There were too many other players in this game for him to call checkmate now.

"So the threat against Rosalie was a lure to bring me home. Well played, sir." Tom kept his voice calm, with a touch of boredom.

"I appreciate the sentiment, though, Tom." Rosalie gave him an indulgent smile, the same she gave him as a teenager when he confided in her about his studies. "I care about you, too, you know. We're just trying to do what's best for you here."

He couldn't respond to her. The betrayal was too new, too deep, and it threatened his focus. He leaned on his inherent ability to ignore his inner turmoil, something his father had beat into him as a child. *Good job, John. You trained me well.*

"As to my mother," Tom continued, "you were probably right. The Hydraians would never accept me." He put a little power behind those words, focusing them on John, and willed for him to believe his sincerity. "No one would. That's why I'm here, Dad. You're the only one who cares about me. I have nowhere to go."

He stressed the helplessness while weaving in notes of persuasion.

Trust my words.

It seemed all those years of finding ways to lie had turned into a unique talent, one Luc found particularly useful in this scenario. Tom's gift wasn't so much the same as Stas's ability to compel as it was a way to twist lies into words others mistook for truths.

"There's just one thing," Tom continued. "I don't think we need Amelia. She can't shift anymore, and she's pretty fucking unstable. I considered delivering her back to her brother for fun, but obviously, I decided against it. So, instead, I suggest we dispose of her properly and be done with the mess. It solves the problem of Stas ever finding out, and Wakefield as well."

The words nearly killed him, but they were part of the plan. He put his compulsion behind each statement, encouraging John to accept the veracity of his sentiments.

The Sentinels and Rosalie were included in the web of lies, while he exempted all the others in their vicinity. Those in the cars couldn't hear him, and he didn't want to mistakenly set off one of the immortals.

It amazed him how easy the gift came to him; all he had to do was think about it, and the psychic threads snapped into place.

"So none of the immortals are aware she's alive?" John asked.

A pointed question, which meant Tom couldn't lie. But he could evade. "What immortals would I have told, sir? And would any of them have allowed me to return with the asset in exchange for my mortal aunt?"

His talent naturally weaved through each word, setting the statements in stone. *I speak the truth, John.*

His father nodded. "Yes, where would you go? I'm glad you've come to your senses, son. Of course, rehabilitation will still be required, and there are those in your unit who would see you punished."

"Of course." *I'd like to see them try.* "Can I shoot her now?"

Surprise filtered through John's features. "You want to kill her?"

Another direct query that required evasion. "Why not? Wouldn't it be a good way to start my therapy or, at a minimum, serve as a punishment for fucking up again?"

Say yes, John.

"Tom…" The plea in Amelia's voice made him cringe. It was part of the act, but did she have to sound so hurt? She stared at his profile, while he refused to acknowledge her.

His father scratched his chin, thoughtful, as he studied them. "It could be a reasonable start, yes. Tell me, how would you feel about killing her?"

Ah, finally something I can answer honestly. "The very thought of hurting her makes me want to tear my heart from my chest and burn it."

"She's well and truly in your head, son. How did that happen?"

"We spent a lot of time together." *And I loved every fucking minute, even when she insulted my precious Yankees.* "I developed feelings for her as a result."

"And you realize those feelings are wrong now?" his father asked, curiosity evident in his expression.

This would be tricky. "I've realized what needs to be done about them, yes."

"You don't mean that," Amelia implored, playing her role. "Please look at me."

He folded his arms and cocked a brow at his father. "We need to end this, sir. And I need to be the one to take her down. It's the only way I'll be able to prove my worth and rejoin your ranks."

Compliance was his father's weakness. He wanted everyone to bow down and call him master, and Tom did just that both with his words and his body language. It lowered the asshole's defenses and allowed Tom's gift for lie manipulation to settle in and take effect.

"You have all the samples you need to further your research. Keeping her alive is a waste of space and resources, sir. Let me kill her and prove my loyalty once and for all."

"It would be a good lesson in loyalty," John replied, considering. "And it would help with the Stas issue and enable me to pursue a business deal with Issac. But I've always been hesitant with having Amelia in custody. Hmm." He stepped forward and waved off the Sentinels who tried to follow. "Do you have anything to add, dear? Care to beg for your life?"

"What kind of life would it be?" Amelia's broken voice sounded so different from her confidence of minutes ago that Tom almost risked a glance at her. But he knew if he did, he wouldn't be able to pull this off. Aiming a gun at her would be hard enough without meeting her gaze.

"A painful one." John almost sounded contrite, but then he smiled. "I don't think I'm ready to give her up yet, even if it is the logical thing to do."

Check, Tom thought as his father took another step forward. He lifted his hand to cup Amelia's cheek in a false act of tenderness. "But Tom does bring up an excellent point about loyalty. Maybe I can replace you with another Hydraian?"

"I hope you burn in hell," Amelia seethed, her entire demeanor changing as she grabbed the hand against her cheek and let loose her secondary gift. Just like they planned.

John had expected her to be defenseless without her ability to shift, but Tom had reminded her before they arrived that experience was a powerful weapon. And she unleashed it on his father now, pushing six years of pain and suffering into one forceful tendril of information.

It brought the CEO to his knees with an agonized shriek, and the Sentinels reacted. They leapt forward to pull John to safety while Tom drew his weapon, aimed it at Amelia, and pulled the trigger.

Twice.

One bullet to the head and a second to the heart.

Or at least that's what everyone else would see, thanks to Wakefield's intervention.

In reality, both bullets went into a nearby tree, the sound muted by Tristan. Having two Ichorians on standby with sensory gifts was certainly useful, as was Tom's new gift for perfect aim. It hadn't surprised him to learn that his secondary Hydraian talent revolved around his ability to shoot. All he had to do was focus on his target, and he'd never miss. He couldn't wait to explore that one more later, as Luc suggested it went beyond guns. *You could throw a knife with perfect accuracy every time as well.*

Shrugging off the possibilities, Tom holstered the weapon and went to his knees beside his wheezing father.

"Dad? Talk to me." He allowed a semblance of panic to enter his voice, despite feeling victorious inside.

"What the fuck, man?" Blake cried after realizing Tom had shot Amelia. She lay off to the side, staring blankly into space. Her brother had agreed that sending her into a temporary comatose state would help with the charade.

"Shit, man," Charlie added. "You used incendiary bullets."

"Did you not see her trying to kill John?" Tom asked, irritated as he watched the CEO slowly recover. *You deserve so much worse for your sins.* "What the fuck was I supposed to do?"

"Use normal bullets like the rest of us?" Blake suggested, his tone incredulous. "You *killed* her."

"I did what needed to be done," Tom argued as he studied his father's expression.

Awe and understanding had entered his dead eyes. He lifted his hand to weakly touch Tom's arm and gave it a soft pat before letting it fall to the ground.

Amelia obviously hadn't given him the full dose of knowledge because he seemed to be recovering quickly.

Not nearly enough suffering.

"Welcome home, son," his father managed on a wheeze.

And there it is. Checkmate.

Hello, Death, My Old Friend

"Well done, son." The satisfaction in his father's gaze when he looked up from Amelia's presumed corpse confirmed that Wakefield's manipulation had worked. An invisible weight fell from Tom's shoulders.

Step one was complete, which meant no wards were in play.

Good.

On to step two.

All the Sentinels and Rosalie wore similar expressions to his father's, except Blake. His old friend's lips were flat and his shoulders tense. Hopefully, the Sentinel kept his feelings to himself, because the plan hinged on all the pawns moving to the right spaces on the board.

"Let's put her in the cabin and burn it," Tom suggested.

"Eager to be rid of your past, son?"

"Yes." *And that includes you, asshole.*

Pride curled the edges of his father's mouth. "Excellent. Yes, the cabin will do."

"You're going to burn it?" Rosalie asked, hesitation leaking into her expression for the first time. *About fucking time.* Would have been nice if she hesitated like that the night his mother died, but something told him she didn't. His father had clearly seduced her, which—yuck. Thinking about their relationship, whatever it entailed, made Tom want to hurl. Better to divert his focus.

"I can manage the asset," he said and lifted Amelia with ease.

"Let's put her in your old room," John suggested, a taunt in his voice. The bastard knew how much Tom hated that room, and to add a dead body to it would only make it worse.

He swallowed the growl growing in his throat and managed a "Yes, sir."

"Wait, we can't burn it down," Rosalie was saying as Tom moved toward the cabin. John followed with Sentinels Blake and Charlie at his back. The others remained outside to guard the perimeter, and what excellent scouts they were proving to be, what with being surrounded by immortals.

The fact that not a single one of the CRF's men detected the dozen or so Hydraians and Ichorians lurking outside said a lot about their training and technology. Of course, Wakefield had his progeny Mateo to take care of the latter. Apparently, the Ichorian had an affinity for cybernetics and could hack into anything, with or without a computer. Fascinating talent.

Tom didn't look around as he walked through the cabin. He felt fine until he entered the bedroom and noticed the blood-stained floors. The bodies were gone, but their murder scene remained. His grip on Amelia tightened as his mother's death came roaring back and smacked him between the eyes.

Dad covered in blood.

Mom ripped to shreds on my bed.

Toys coated in red.

Ruined photos.

An expression of horror in Mom's eyes.

Something isn't quite right with Dad.

He shuddered. Everything was so vivid, so clear, so real. That moment changed him irrevocably. It haunted his essence, reminding him every day of the dangers in this world. Except that night was a lie. Another story his father told him to strike fear in his heart and mold his outlook to match his own. And he used this place to taunt him. Another form of manipulation to keep him under control and obedient.

John Fitzgerald redefined the meaning of *monster*. He told him the Hydraians would shun him, but they welcomed him. He cited Wakefield as Anna's executioner but more or less admitted tonight that he lied. He vowed that Amelia would remain unharmed but beat her when Wakefield pissed him off. He sent Tom on hundreds of missions, both as a child and an adult, all of which could have gotten him killed, and never batted an eye.

I'm the queen on his chessboard, Tom realized. A powerful piece for him to dictate about, but sacrifice as needed. There was no love between them, only a history of violence. And John considered himself the king.

Tom laid Amelia on the bed and pulled a blanket over her head to hide the missing wound before turning to meet his father's amused gaze. Another manipulative game of torment meant to add fractures to his son's psyche, but for the first time, Tom saw the scene clearly. His mother's death had been a mercy, a way for her to escape this world. And Tom's death would be the same.

"You can't burn this place down," Rosalie repeated from the doorway beside John. "This is my family's cabin."

"Actually, it belongs to Tom," his father corrected. "And this place holds no value, right, son?"

"No value at all," Tom agreed, realizing he meant it. The cabin's dark hold over his past morphed into a new strength, one founded on truth. He spent years fighting the wrong demons, when the real one stood in front of him all along. His father.

"Don't I get a say in any of this?" Rosalie asked.

John's lips flattened as he refocused on her. "No, I'm afraid you don't, my dear." He cupped her face in a loving gesture that made Tom's stomach turn over. "You've been so useful to me all these years, but Tom and I are about to enter a new era of our lives that doesn't quite apply to you. Tom no longer requires a mother figure, and I suspect he'll have no interest in confiding in you now that he knows your role in Anna's death, so you're rather worthless to me, aren't you?"

"What are you saying?" she asked, eyes wide.

John's sigh was all hot air. "You see, dear, this is why I have no patience for mortal women. It doesn't matter how I say it; you'll never understand. Give Anna my regards." The crack of the gun startled Tom. He'd been so focused on his aunt that he missed the weapon at his father's waist. Blood pooled from Rosalie's torso as a single tear fell from her wide eyes. She crumpled to the floor with a gurgling sound that must have irritated his father because he promptly shot her in the head.

Bile rose in Tom's throat at the sight, and it took all his effort to maintain his nonchalance. He focused his breathing in the same way he did when sighting a target through his scope and forced his limbs to still. Breaking now would ruin everything, and he was so close to succeeding. Rosalie chose her fate by getting in bed with his father, and she'd paid the ultimate price.

"I believe our deal was for you to release Rosalie, sir." The words felt foreign in his mouth and tasted bitter on his tongue. He wanted to rant and rave and knock the shit out of his father. But Luc's reminder that they needed him alive shouted in the forefront of his mind. It took him a minute to realize the voice he heard belonged to Alik, not himself. As if he needed the reminder.

"Well, yes, and I did. She's been released from her mortality." John exchanged his weapon for a handkerchief and wiped a spot of blood on his shirt. "Well, that's ruined. Sentinel Charlie, can you go start a fire in the kitchen?"

"Yes, sir." The young blond man scampered off to do his master's bidding.

John dropped the soiled handkerchief on Rosalie's corpse and focused on Tom. "Shall we go, then?"

"If I may, *sir,* when did we start assassinating women?" Sentinel Blake asked, expression livid. Tom tried to warn him with a glare that he ignored. Not good. "Because I didn't sign on for this shit. The asset I can let go, because you put her out of her misery, but the mortal? That's over the line."

John fixed his tie before turning to address the Sentinel in the doorway. "I'm not sure I like your tone, Sentinel. Have you forgotten who you're speaking to?"

The final part of the plan required Tom to make it to the front door without incident, and it seemed his old friend Blake was about to throw a wrench in it.

"Not someone I respect, that's for damn sure." The Sentinel narrowed his gaze at Tom. "You know, man, I had a begrudging respect for you standing up for your beliefs, but you crawling home with your tail between your legs has got to be one of the most pathetic things I've ever seen. You killed the asset without batting an eye. I've never been so disgusted in my life."

Okay, ouch. "Just doing what I was created to do, Sentinel." *Now, if you could start moving and stop talking before you fuck all this up, that'd be awesome.*

His father nodded in agreement. "Sentinel Blake, if you have an issue with how things operate here, I'll be happy to entertain your resignation."

Oh, shit. "Let's—"

"You have it," Sentinel Blake said, cutting Tom off.

Fuck. Time to improvise. Tom drew his weapon and aimed it at Blake. He made sure it was the same one he used earlier on Amelia so everyone would know it held incendiary bullets. All part of the original plan that appeared to be taking a trip to hell in a handbasket.

"How about we go outside and talk about this, Sentinel. Preferably before the house burns down." *Because I need to get to the front door.*

Blake pointed his gun at Tom's head. "I'm fine here."

"Gentlemen," his father chided, "we're wasting precious time."

"Why? You have another woman to kill?" Blake sneered. Tom understood the man's anger, but he'd seriously chosen the wrong time to display it.

Sentinel Charlie whistled from the hallway. "Yo! Fire's going. Let's go!"

Tom raised his brows. "Sentinel, do you really want to die like this?"

"It's here or outside. We both know that's the only way out." A hint of sadness echoed in Blake's gaze.

He opened his mouth to reply, when all hell broke loose. Gunfire broke out, not in the bedroom but in the hallway, and Blake reacted. John shouted just as a bullet hit Tom square in the chest. It fucking burned and knocked him into the bed. He dropped his pistol in shock and clutched his jacket.

Jesus Christ, it hurt. His blood was on fire, burning a path from his heart outward and shooting pain to his limbs. A scream lodged in his throat, but refused to escape, as his vision blurred. His father's face appeared, stark horror filling his expression.

"Thomas!" he shouted, but it sounded so distant. Like a faraway dream.

I'm dying, Tom realized. *I'm truly fucking dying.* And he hadn't had a chance to tell Amelia how he felt. Her eyes filled his vision, those gorgeous blue irises, blinking innocently down at him as a smile curled her full lips. God, he would miss that expression. His biggest regret would be never seeing it again.

"Son, my son," his father's voice echoed in his mind. The sadness lingering there would haunt him in the afterlife, because for a brief moment, it made him wonder if it was possible. *Does John Fitzgerald actually care?*

Darkness swallowed him, leaving him with his last cognizant thoughts of a man he vowed to hate, who may have loved him after all.

One Week Later…

Amelia floated on her back in the pool with her eyes on the stars, wearing a wistful expression. This was her new favorite spot. She said it gave her a sense of peace that reminded her of the dark place, but with bright spots to keep her grounded.

"Still pissed at me?" a snarky voice asked from the pool deck.

Tom scowled. "Yes."

Alik shrugged and snagged the chair beside him. "Good thing we have eternity to fix that."

"If you tell me it was the only way one more fucking time, I'm going to shoot you. And we both know I won't miss."

"I'll have you on your knees before you can even think to grab your gun," Alik returned. "But seriously, consider it an initiation. We've all fucked with each other at one point or another. You just got tag-teamed by three of us at once."

Wakefield, Tristan, and Alik. One screwed with his vision, the second obscured his hearing, and Alik set his insides on fire. All to make him and everyone else in the cabin think he'd actually been shot by an incendiary bullet. If the cabin hadn't been on fire, the trick may not have worked, but his father and the Sentinels didn't have time to examine him too closely. Then Jacque had popped in, grabbed Tom and Amelia, and whisked them to Hydria.

"We needed them to think it was real," Wakefield had explained the next morning. Tom would have believed him if it wasn't for the smirk at the end.

"You improvised, so we improvised" was Tristan's version of an apology. Alik had just said, "Welcome to Hydria."

"I had the situation handled," Tom said now, not for the first time.

"Probably," Alik agreed. He sat forward, legs splayed, and braced his forearms on his thighs. "But here's the thing. You're one of us now, and we take care of our own. That's the beauty of being a Hydraian. We watch out for each other, which means we'll never just drop you off in the middle of a fight and expect you to figure it out on your own. Same goes for a flaming cabin in the middle of the woods. You're not alone anymore, kid. Deal with it."

Tom arched an eyebrow and focused on the part he felt comfortable commenting on. "I'm not a kid."

"You are to me," he replied, then nodded at the beauty in the pool. "But maybe not to her."

Tom met Amelia's glittering gaze with a smile. *Definitely not to her.*

Alik hopped up, took a step, and paused. "Oh, by the way…"

"Yes?" Tom asked, meeting the Elder's burning stare.

"Hurt her, and what we did to you last week will feel like a happy dream. You understand?"

Well, that makes four. The other Elders had threatened him earlier in the week, in a variety of ways. All about Amelia. "She's lucky to have so many people who care about her," Tom replied. "I wouldn't have it any other way."

Alik tilted his head in acknowledgment and left.

"He likes you," Amelia said as she folded her elbows on the side of the pool.

"He has a funny way of showing it," he muttered.

"Alik doesn't talk a lot, but he just gave you a lecture about family and what it means here. That means he likes you."

"So you missed the threat before he left?"

She smiled. "Oh, no, I heard that, too. Another sign that he likes you since he cares enough to let you know."

"Right, because that's exactly how I took it." *Not.*

Amelia pulled herself out of the pool and straddled him over the chair. Water pooled between them, but he didn't care. She could get him wet anytime, anywhere she liked. He brushed her damp strands from her face and palmed her cheek.

"I'm not used to this," he admitted. Not the half-naked woman on his lap or the arousal straining the zipper of his jeans, but the feeling of family. Of love. "I don't know how to accept it or, really, how to allow it." Relying on others to help him out of situations felt so foreign to him. He understood Alik's lecture on principle, but applying it took a strength Tom wasn't sure he possessed.

"We'll learn together." Amelia brushed her lips against his. "You're not the only one who has trouble trusting, Tom."

"I trust you," he admitted. She was the reason he stayed in Hydria, because fending for himself would never be an issue. But he didn't want to leave her.

She smiled. "You can say 'love,' you know. I won't shy away."

He chuckled and grabbed her ribs to give them a tickle. "That's where my arrogance went. I wondered who stole it."

She squirmed and squealed. "Tom!"

He didn't stop tickling her until she was under him on the lounge chair and he had her straddling him the way he wanted. Settling between her bare thighs was heaven personified. Until a cough broke the moment. He glanced over to find Wakefield and Stas standing on the pool deck, dressed in black.

"Oh, good, this will make five threats," he muttered as he pushed off Amelia and helped her stand. She fixed her blue string bikini before picking up a towel to wrap around herself.

"Hi," Amelia greeted, her cheeks flushed. She opened her mouth to say more but paused when Stas threw her arms around Tom's neck and buried her face in his shoulder. He returned the hug while flashing a *What the fuck?* look at Wakefield.

"We've just come from your memorial service," he explained. "I think it felt a little too real."

Stas nodded, her shoulders shaking.

"My memorial service?" Tom asked. He supposed a funeral wouldn't work without a proper body to mourn. "Bet John had fun milking that."

"Oh, he's opening several Fitzgerald funds in your honor." Wakefield smirked. "And he's requested an official business partnership with Wakefield Pharmaceuticals."

"No, shit. What did you say?"

"I agreed under the pretense of trying to please Aya, which it is to an extent, as I intend to use my resources to dig into Elizabeth's welfare. If Jonathan truly is experimenting on her, then I imagine he may be interested in acquiring certain inoculations or medications, of which I own several."

Stas pulled back to stare into Tom's eyes. Her concern unnerved him. "I really am fine, Stas."

"I know. Yes, I know." She shook her head and finally let him go, taking a step back. Wakefield draped his arm around her as she sniffled. "But Lizzie doesn't… And I can't help her. No one will let me bring her here."

It broke a piece of him to see Stas so upset, but Lizzie mourning him was what really took a toll on his heart. He wished there was another way, but they had to keep her in the dark to keep her safe. For now.

"She thinks you died overseas. John made up this whole crazy story, and he included Blake in it. Said you both were true heroes." She bit her lip and shook her head. "He's a fucking bastard."

"Blake is undergoing rehabilitation," Wakefield added. "Your father is making an example out of him, claiming he set you up and then killed you."

Tom's hands curled into fists at his sides. "You could have saved him."

"Not without announcing our presence, and you know that. We needed Jonathan to believe you and Amelia were dead for this to work. Blake is a sacrifice."

"He doesn't deserve it."

"Perhaps not, but blaming ourselves is counterproductive. Jonathan is the one to blame here, and he will pay." The promise underlining Wakefield's voice did little to dispel the tension lining Tom's shoulders.

"Sometimes I think killing the bastard would be easier," he growled.

"Absolutely it would, but waiting will make his death more meaningful. We need to know who is pulling his strings and what he did to Elizabeth."

"And that's where I come in," Jayson announced as he stepped onto the pool deck with a suitcase. He dropped the luggage and folded his arms.

Wakefield gave him the man nod. "How was Brazil?"

"Fabulous." Jayson's satisfied expression was one all men recognized. *Someone had a good time.*

"Who won the challenge?" Amelia asked.

"Come now, A. You know I don't kiss and tell."

Amelia rolled her eyes. "Fine. Be that way."

Jayson blew her a kiss before looking at Tom. "Any questions about the house before I head to New York?" He'd offered to let them borrow his home, which came equipped with the swimming pool, while he was out of town. It served as the perfect housing solution while they built their own place down the beach, but that didn't mean Tom approved of the reason behind it.

The notion of relying on someone else to protect his oldest friend grated his nerves. But he didn't have a choice. It was this or announce his reincarnation, which would spoil everything. And as Luc noted, Jayson's abilities made him the best man for the job.

"Trust," Amelia whispered, wrapping her arm around him. "Jay knows what he's doing."

The Elder slid on a pair of shades despite the late hour and resembled a fallen angel in his suit and tie and disheveled hair. "Don't worry, kid," he said to Tom. "Miss Watkins is in good hands."

"Are they all going to call me that?" Tom muttered, referring to the "kid" part.

Amelia smiled. "Consider it an endearment."

"Like 'arse'?"

"Yes, exactly like that."

"Whatever you say, asset." He kissed her temple and hugged her close.

Wakefield pulled a few items from his jacket pocket and handed them to the Elder. "Mateo set it all up, including your new residence in her building."

Jayson flipped through the documents and grinned. "Jayson Masters. Indeed, I am."

"The other items you requested are already in the flat, including the knives."

The Elder nodded. "Then I'm all set." He regarded Amelia and Tom. "Stay out of my bedroom. You two aren't ready for that level of experimentation yet." With that sound advice, he picked up his bags and disappeared.

"Okay, never mind. That's where my arrogance went," Tom remarked, playing on his earlier statement.

Amelia shook her head. "Jay redefines arrogance."

"Are you sure about this?" Stas asked, her gaze on her Ichorian. "He seems a bit much for Lizzie, don't you think?"

"Oh, I'm certain Elizabeth can hold her own. In fact, I'm looking forward to it." He shifted focus to Amelia. "On a similar topic of amusement, I hear Aidan is scheduled to visit tomorrow. Do you plan to introduce him to the Sentinel?"

Tom pictured shooting Wakefield in the face and smiled when the Ichorian flinched. *Thanks for that reminder, jackass.* Meeting a lover's father was hard enough with normal people, let alone an ancient Ichorian with the gift for omniscience. Talk about nerve-racking.

"Yes, he mentioned something about Osiris being preoccupied and it being a good time to visit." Amelia's excitement was palpable. She had spoken to her father a few times over the last week but hadn't seen him yet. "I can't wait to see him, and he promised to bring Clara with him."

Stas scowled at the name, making Wakefield chuckle. "Don't worry, Aya. We won't be here."

"I didn't say anything."

"No, but you did turn a lovely shade of green," he teased.

She attempted to push the Ichorian into the pool, but he lifted her into his arms on a laugh as she struggled.

"This suit would not fare well in the chlorine, darling."

"I beg to differ." She used an impressive move that almost sent them both into the water, but Wakefield countered it and wrapped his arms around her in an impenetrable hold. Tom felt a begrudging surge of respect for the man. Those moves weren't luck on either part, which indicated Wakefield had an understanding of martial arts. Interesting.

He nuzzled Stas's neck and hugged her close. "When do you to return to work, love?"

"In about twelve hours," she muttered, still squirming.

"Brilliant. How about a jaunt down the beach and a quick dip?"

"I would like that." Stas's smile was unlike any Tom had ever seen from her. *He really makes her happy. How did I miss that before?*

"I want to have a conversation with you when I return, Thomas. Don't go anywhere."

And just like that, he didn't care how happy the Ichorian made his friend and went back to hating the bastard.

"Oh, I'm looking forward to it," he replied, his voice thick with sarcasm. Wakefield responded by blacking out his vision for a split second as he and Stas left. "Your brother's an ass, and I don't mean that endearingly."

Amelia giggled and slipped her arms around his waist. "You'll change your mind someday."

"Doubtful."

"You changed your mind about me."

"Did I?" He smiled down at her. "And what did I change my mind about?"

"You trust me."

"And I didn't trust you before?"

"You didn't trust *anyone* before."

"Hmm…" She had him there. "You know what else I didn't feel before you?"

She shook her head. "No. What?"

He nibbled her earlobe and whispered, "Love."

"And you feel that now?"

He nodded. "For you, I do."

Her smile took his breath away. "Truly?"

"Truly," he repeated with a grin.Her accent amused him, especially when she used odd words like *truly*.

He tucked a damp strand behind her ear and allowed some seriousness to leak through.

Actions were his preference over spoken endearments, but there were some moments that required words, and this was one of them.

"You make me feel, Amelia. You're my home." There was no other way to describe it. He never had a sanctuary or a place he felt safe, until her.

She went onto her toes to kiss him and sighed against his lips. "You're my home, too."

"I know."

She smacked his arm with a laugh and rolled her eyes. "I see your arrogance is back."

"It never left, sweetheart."

"Yeah?" She pulled back to look him up and down. "Straddle me again."

His gaze narrowed. "Are you asking me to spar with you while wearing nothing but a towel and a skimpy bikini?" Because he definitely approved of that idea.

"Maybe."

"Be certain, Amelia."

She bit her lip and grinned. The minx. "You'll have to catch me first."

"A chase, followed by sparring?" God clearly invented this woman for him, and only him.

"Only if you think you're up for it." She dropped the towel and jumped into the pool with an excited squeal that went straight to his groin.

"Oh, game on, sweetheart."

BLOOD HEART

BOOK THREE

TOP SECRET
(SECURITY CLASSIFICATION)

ASSET FILE 4-7

HANDLE VIA

CRYPTO-VARIUM

CHANNELS

ACCESS RESTRICTED

CATASTROPHIC RELIEF FOUNDATION LEVEL 9

ASSET FILE: 4-7
GENOTYPE: NONHUMAN
PROJECT NAME: REBIRTH

WARNING NOTICE

TOP SECRET EYES ONLY

GLOBAL SECURITY INFORMATION

UNAUTHORIZED DISCLOSURE SUBJECT TO CRIMINAL SANCTIONS

TOP SECRET
(SECURITY CLASSIFICATION)

CHAPTER ONE

Pepperoni Pizza Party

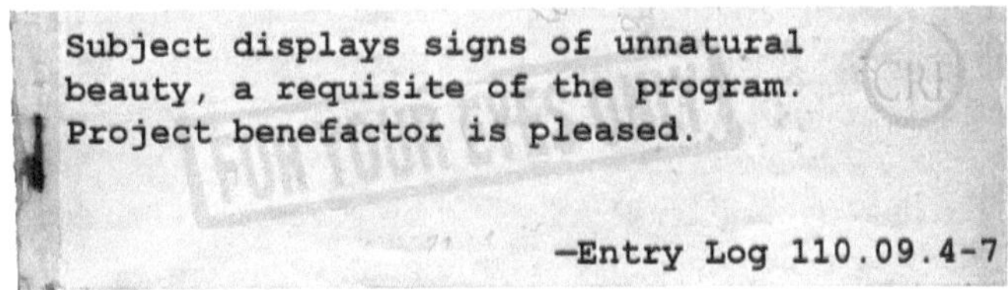

Subject displays signs of unnatural beauty, a requisite of the program. Project benefactor is pleased.

—Entry Log 110.09.4-7

Bang.

Bang, bang.

Lizzie Watkins glared at the ceiling. Reviewing spelling tests for first graders was a daunting enough task without the gladiator theatrics going on above her.

She blew a raspberry. Clearly, the new owner on the third floor had finished moving into his condo. Lizzie hadn't even known her upstairs neighbors had moved out until she saw the relocation company carrying boxes through the lobby for the new resident.

Crash.

She set the papers aside with a huff and climbed to her feet. Normally, she welcomed new tenants with cookies, but this one had touched her last nerve.

Thud.

"For crying out loud!" She slid on a pair of pumps by the door, grabbed her keys, and stomped off toward the stairwell.

One flight of stairs later, she stood outside the new tenant's home and waited for the horrid song to change over before introducing her fist to his door. Repeatedly.

"Just a second!" The male voice sounded deep and masculine.

She tapped her foot while waiting, arms folded, eyebrow quirked, mouth ready.

"Sorry," the voice continued as the door opened. "Had to finish my set."

Abs.

That was the first thought that registered.

Because the man had greeted her shirtless.

A pair of navy gym shorts sat low on his lean hips, leaving his muscular physique on full display. The trail of moisture licking a path over his chiseled chest suggested he'd been working out. At least that explained the clanking and banging.

"Um…" Lizzie met a pair of soft brown eyes and faltered.

Milk chocolate, her cook's brain supplied.

I don't care what color they are, she snapped back.

Or that his gaze appeared to be roaming shamelessly over her body right now.

No.

Focus.

We're here to yell.

Right.

She cleared her throat and leveled the attractive man with a look she used on her misbehaving students. "I live in the condo beneath yours, and your—uh—workout, is, well, it's distracting me from my work."

Yes, Liz. That's a wonderful lecture.

"Is it?" He didn't sound apologetic, and his gaze had yet to return to hers. He seemed fascinated by her breasts. Damn man.

"Yes, it is." She inserted a little more force into her tone, which only seemed to amuse him.

"Hmm, I'll try to keep it down," he murmured. "And I would apologize, but there wouldn't be much truth in it."

She gaped at him. "Excuse me?"

"Well, I can hardly feel bad about attracting you to my door, especially dressed like that." He waved a hand over her body, causing Lizzie to consider her attire.

Black pumps, tiny blue sleep shorts, and a rose-colored tank top with no bra underneath. With her roommate out for the night, Lizzie had slipped on her pajamas before starting on her paperwork. And she hadn't bothered to change before scurrying upstairs.

"Oh." Her cheeks burned from mortification. Even her hair was a tousled mess. If her mother caught her out in public like this, she'd throw a fit. "Right. Uh, thanks for keeping it down. Nice to meet you."

She turned to walk away, quickly, and cringed as his chuckle followed her down the hall. He probably thought she was nuts. Great. Well, she didn't like him much, either, with all that racket.

"I'll try to keep it down," she scoffed, doing a poor impersonation of his deep voice.

She slammed her front door with more force than necessary, kicked off her shoes and wandered to the master bathroom.

"Awesome." As she suspected, her makeup was fine, but the long auburn strands she always wore styled in public were a hot mess on top of her head. And her pink camisole top left nothing to the imagination thanks to her oversized boobs. No wonder he'd been so enthralled.

"At least we're even," she muttered. He'd given her an eyeful of his perfectly sculpted chest as well. "Can't complain about that."

Feeling naked, she pulled on her favorite New York University sweatshirt and tromped into the large kitchen to search for something to eat. Her parents had gifted her this condo on the Upper East Side after college graduation. She suspected it was a way to keep her at a distance. As if she would move back in with them.

Although, with her roommate working all day and spending almost every night with her new boyfriend, Lizzie felt lonelier than ever. She wanted to be happy for Stas, but she didn't trust the Catastrophic Relief Foundation (CRF). The world-renowned humanitarian organization always struck her as wrong, and after Tom died on one of their missions—

Knock. Knock.

She blinked. "What now?"

Closing the refrigerator, she wandered over to the front door and groaned upon peering through the peephole. A now-clothed muscular giant stood in the hallway. She pressed her forehead against the wood and grumbled under her breath before calmly twisting the handle.

"Yes?" Not her most eloquent greeting, but the circumstances weren't exactly favorable.

A pair of adorable dimples flashed at her as the man braced his forearms on the door frame over her head. "Do you like pepperoni?"

"Excuse me?" Apparently, that was her go-to phrase in this guy's presence.

"Pep-per-oni," he repeated slowly and arched a brow. "Well?"

"Who doesn't like pepperoni?" she asked, flabbergasted. *And why the hell are you asking me about it?*

"My thoughts exactly," he replied as he breezed past her into the condo like he owned the place. He kicked off his sneakers onto the mat beside the door before glancing around her living area. A couch, two big chairs, a coffee table, and an entertainment system. Nothing too extraordinary, but she liked it.

He seemed to focus on her curtains as he murmured, "It's a little pink for my tastes, but otherwise nice."

"Glad you approve," she replied from the still-open door, startled. "Is there something I can help you with?"

Before I call the cops, she added to herself. Lizzie had half a mind to scream, but her manners kept her in check. He was a neighbor, after all, in an exclusive condo building with security downstairs. Still a stranger, but not quite, given their residential situation.

"Do you frequently barge into other people's homes like this?" she demanded.

"Yes." His dimples flashed as his eyes crinkled. "Do you have any beer or wine?" he asked as he started in the general direction of the kitchen. His navy shorts and white shirt looked very out of place as he crossed through her formal dining room.

Lizzie kicked the door closed as she chased after him. "What are you doing?"

"You're not very observant, are you?" He grinned over his shoulder before opening her fridge. "Wine coolers." He shut it with a shudder. "No, thank you."

Her brain started working again as he went through her cabinets.

"Okay, mister, I don't recall inviting you inside, nor do I even know you. So, if you could kindly leave…"

His responding chuckle silenced her. From anyone else, she might have enjoyed that sound, but she didn't like it from *him*. She should have felt afraid, not irritated. But he kept using those dimples and chuckling.

Ridiculous charmer.

"I think we know each other well enough, Red."

She bristled at the unoriginal nickname. All her life people had commented on her red hair and lack of freckles. "You can go now."

"Don't be like that," he murmured as he found her wine stash. "Finally. I was beginning to think I lived above a puritan." He pulled out a bottle of her favorite cabernet and set it on the counter. "Perfect."

"Are you going to make me call security?" Because she would. The doorman downstairs was a good friend thanks to her obsession with baking. Lizzie brought him cookies at least once a week.

"Sure." He selected two wine glasses from her cabinet. "I like Dennis."

Great. Maybe I'll invite him up here to drag your butt home.

Her gaze dropped to said butt. Pure muscle, as were his long legs. He had to be close to six and a half feet tall. Poor Dennis didn't really stand a chance. Which should have terrified her, but didn't.

It's his smile.

A ridiculous reason to trust a muscular giant in the kitchen.

Fair point.

Okay, plan B.

"How do you feel about the cops?"

"Depends on the district," he replied flippantly as he uncorked the bottle. "Are you a half-glass or full-glass kind of girl?" His chocolate gaze danced over her bare legs and sweatshirt. "Definitely a full glass."

Her phone buzzed before she could bite off a response to that.

Where are you, Elizabeth? Her mother's condescending tone underlined the text message. Tonight was the CRF's annual gala. Her family went every year due to her father holding one of the highest positions within the organization, but Lizzie couldn't stomach attending tonight. She used to look forward to the event because it meant seeing Tom.

Her heart ached with the sensation of loss.

No.

She refused to think about him or the organization he devoted his life to. Literally. Or the fact that Stas was currently attending the event in misguided support.

Fruity notes touched her nose as the stranger wafted the glass beneath her chin. His eyes grinned down at her, clearly oblivious to the turmoil stirring inside of her.

"Thanks," she managed to say and took a healthy sip. Then she remembered that this was *her* wine in *her* glass in *her* condo. She shook her head and slammed the stem down on the marble countertop. "Okay, buddy, just who do you think you are?"

"Jayson Masters," he replied without missing a beat. "And you?"

She blinked, taken aback. This… this… *man* acted like no other person she'd ever met. He was rude, arrogant, and pushy, gave her one hell of a headache… and was smiling at her with the most charming expression she'd ever seen.

She shook her head again. "You need to go."

"Why?" he asked. "Do you have plans for the evening?"

"Well, no, but—"

"Are you expecting someone?"

"No, but that's—"

"Have you eaten?"

She frowned. "No, you interrupted me while I was trying to find something to cook."

"Then my timing is perfect. Dinner should be here in about"—he checked the clock over the stove—"twenty minutes, give or take. Hopefully, you like San Dinos. I've heard good things, but it's my first time."

"You've never had San Dinos's pizza before?" It was one of the best places in Manhattan. Everyone loved their New York style of thin crust, cheese, and light sauce.

"I've only been in the city six weeks, Red, and I've spent most of that time working." He sipped his wine and murmured, "This isn't bad."

"It's fantastic," she corrected. "And stop calling me Red. It's unoriginal."

"Give me something else to call you and I'll consider it," he countered, reminding her that they didn't know each other.

"I'm sorry, but why are you here, again?"

"Dinner," he drawled. "It's this activity where two people enjoy decent drinks and food and sometimes socialize. Perhaps you've heard of it?"

"Of course I have, but why are *we* having dinner?" She gestured between them as if *we* needed a definition.

"Consider it my way of apologizing for being too loud." He winked and turned toward the dining area again, bottle and glass in hand. "Can you grab some plates and napkins? We'll need them."

She gaped after him. How had her quiet night alone turned into a meal with a stranger who lacked boundaries?

Her phone vibrated again on the counter.

You're late, Elizabeth. You know how I feel about tardiness.

Lizzie snorted. That was the understatement of the decade. She picked up the device and typed out a message.

Something has come up. I can't make it.

She turned off the power and tossed the phone into the breadbox. Her mother would call incessantly for the next hour at least, and then the messages would start. Lizzie would delete them all tomorrow.

The television flickered to life in the other room.

"Seriously, no boundaries," she grumbled as she started toward the living area. Suddenly, she thought better of it and grabbed the plates and napkins he requested—as well as her wine—and found him sprawled out on her leather couch.

"Favorite movie genre?" he asked.

She set all the items on the coffee table in front of him, folded her arms, and considered tapping her foot again. "You seem to enjoy choosing things for me, so why don't you pick?"

He flipped to her movie history and cringed. "Chick flicks. Given all the pink decor, I should have known."

"Romantic comedies," she corrected, irritated. Stas liked to remark on all the rosy room accents as well, but Lizzie thought it brightened the overly modern condo. No one would ever convince her otherwise. "And that genre sounds perfect," she added for good measure.

His disheartened expression almost pulled a smile from her. *Almost.*

"Hmm." He looked her over, considering. "Okay. We'll watch a 'romantic comedy,' but only if you tell me your name."

"Oh, now you want to get to formalities? After taking over my condo?"

"I did ask earlier, and I introduced myself." He pointed to his chest. "Jayson, remember? And you are…?" The twinkle in his gaze matched the playfulness in his voice, causing her exterior to crumble slightly.

He's actually pretty cute.

Hot, her hormones corrected. *Off-the-charts hot.*

And possibly crazy, her brain pointed out.

Can't have it all.

With a shake of her head, she finally gave in to him. "Lizzie."

"There. That wasn't so hard, was it?" He started surfing through the options as he added, "Most women prefer giving their name before showing up at my place half-dressed, but I think I prefer your method."

She sputtered. "You're one to talk, answering the door shirtless." *Yes, great comeback, Liz.*

God, was it her, or had the temperature in her condo gone up ten degrees? Rather than turn on the air conditioning—something that should not be needed in late September—she walked across the room to switch on the overhead ceiling fan in an attempt to hide her discomfort.

"True, but at least I was inside my own condo." Jayson selected a film before continuing. "You were wandering the halls with your assets on display for the neighborhood to see. Not that I'm complaining. You're obviously gorgeous."

Her tongue forgot how to function.

How did she even begin to reply to that?

And "gorgeous"?

Please.

Sure, she had an okay figure and her skin rarely blemished, but she was far from being anything extraordinary. Something her parents reminded her of daily. She looked nothing like them, which they considered her fault.

Familiar music started on the television as the film rolled to life. Of all the movies in her library, he'd somehow picked her favorite.

Jayson patted the cushion beside him, distracting her from analyzing that coincidence too deeply. "Come relax with me, Lizzie."

She wanted to ask whether or not he'd showered after working out, but the jibe felt childish.

Besides, he didn't smell all that bad. If anything, he smelled quite nice. Not that she'd noticed the underlying hint of cedar he'd introduced to her apartment or the fact that, despite having just worked out, his thick brown hair looked perfectly tousled.

Nope. She didn't acknowledge any of those things.

With a sigh, she settled onto the cushion she'd vacated earlier and curled her legs beneath her.

"For the record, I'm only agreeing to this very bizarre dinner because you ordered from my favorite pizza place. Turning down San Dinos would be a sin, and I consider myself a good New Yorker."

His laugh lines crinkled, suggesting he smiled often. "Whatever you say, Lizzie."

She picked up the papers from earlier and sifted through them. Might as well get some work done in the process. Or try to, anyway.

~*~

I'm in.

Jayson typed the two words into his phone and hit Send while pretending to focus on the television. He'd waited until after the pizza arrived to inform the team of his progress. It seemed only fair to spend some time with the woman he had been admiring these last six weeks before having to bail.

Not that Lizzie Watkins had spoken much while pretending to work and eat. She had traded her half-eaten slice of pizza for some paperwork, but she didn't seem to be making much progress.

She pinched her lips to the side while she focused on the same sheet of paper she had pulled out ten minutes ago. Jayson suppressed a smile.

The woman had surprised him with her fiery response earlier tonight. Lizzie came off as politely sweet during all his observations, especially when volunteering with the youth center in the Bronx. She was a female of means with a heart of gold, and Jayson found his respect for her growing every day.

But he didn't enjoy her movie preferences.

He'd selected the boring romance because his notes indicated this to be her favorite. That's also why he chose San Dinos. The pizza wasn't bad, but not the best he'd tried either. Granted, his experience vastly outweighed the woman beside him, in more ways than one.

Mateo's reply flashed on the screen. *Brilliant. Engage in sixty seconds.*

Jayson eyed the clock and started counting. On the minute mark, he flicked the trigger on his watch. Now the fun would begin.

He finished his wine and set it on the table before relaxing into the couch.

When he volunteered for this assignment, he hadn't expected to enjoy it. Babysitting a spoiled rich girl sounded about as fun as spending a month in an Ichorian den. But Lizzie Watkins continued to surprise him.

Six weeks of observing her taught him a lot about her habits, gentle mannerisms, and innate innocence. The request to officially infiltrate her life came two days ago after several failures to understand Lizzie's genetics.

She wasn't human; that much they knew based on the CRF's obsession. But she also didn't appear to be an Ichorian or a fledgling and definitely not a Hydraian or a Seraphim.

Whatever she was, the CRF considered her an important asset.

Hence today's little test.

How fast would they react to the blocking mechanism radiating from Jayson's wrist?

Lizzie Watkins's condo was under constant electronic surveillance, but he didn't know how strictly the CRF monitored her or who had been assigned to her personal detail. Jayson suspected the amount had increased now that her roommate was dating a renowned Ichorian. They were very careful not to discuss anything pertinent in the condo as a result.

This experiment, however, would provide them some interesting answers.

"Are you going to eat that?" Jayson asked, nodding to her plate.

Lizzie blinked alluring brown eyes up at him. "Yes. I'm just trying to finish grading this homework."

"What grade do you teach?" He knew the answer already but liked her voice.

"First grade," she murmured.

"Yeah? Do you like it?" Kids weren't his thing, but his observations of Lizzie suggested she enjoyed mini-humans.

"Well…" She nibbled her lip again. Such a sexy little quirk, not that she seemed to realize it. "I like it so far, but it's only my third week. I graduated with a master's degree in education from NYU a few months ago." All things he read about her, but they sounded far more interesting now.

"Congratulations," he murmured, meaning it. He saw how hard she worked despite having everything handed to her on a silver platter. Lizzie Watkins was blessed with a good heart, one he knew would be devastated when she learned the truth someday. Fortunately, he wouldn't be the one responsible for that part. He was here for information-gathering purposes only.

"What do you do for a living?" she asked. "Other than create a lot of noise and break in to your neighbors' apartments, I mean?"

He smirked at her little jibes.

Jayson had decided the best way to establish contact with the asset was to force her to come to him, so he had thrown some weights around to grab her attention. He never in his wildest dreams imagined she would show up at his doorstep in that revealing tank top and shorts, but he harbored no complaints. The woman possessed the body of a lingerie model and the face of a goddess.

Too bad she was strictly off-limits or he would consider acquainting himself with her more intimately.

"I work in acquisitions," he replied vaguely. His usual cover when on assignment. "It's not very exciting." *Unless hot redheads are involved.*

"I wouldn't call teaching exciting, but I do find it rewarding," Lizzie murmured as she swapped her paperwork for her plate. "Thank you for dinner, by the way." Even after barging into her apartment like a Neanderthal, she still thanked him. That alone said so much about her.

"My pleasure." And he meant it.

The phone lit up again. *Jackpot. Three Sentinels en route.*

Jayson slid the metal into his pocket and stood to stretch his arms over his head.

"I should probably get going." They were only an hour into the movie, but he needed to work. "We should do this again, Red. I like spending time with you."

She laughed. "Yeah? You don't even know me."

Oh, if only you knew, sweetheart. "Maybe I'd like to."

Her humor subsided as a splash of pink brightened her cheeks. "Oh, uh… I…"

Most women jumped at the chance to follow him up on an offer like that. It intrigued him that she didn't. Jayson knew what he had to offer both in the looks department and in bed, and she'd had more than an eyeful of his assets.

And likewise.

He cleared his throat. "We're neighbors, and neighbors hang out. You know, as friends."

"You're really not from the city, are you?" She smiled and shook her head. "Where did you move from?"

He bent to lace up his tennis shoes before replying, "I'm from all over." Considering his three-thousand-plus years on Earth, that wasn't necessarily a lie. "But work brought me to the city."

"Oh, okay."

He stood upright, shoes in place. "So, dinner again? As neighborly friends?"

"Sure." She shrugged. "Just, you know, maybe ask to come inside next time."

His phone vibrated again. A final warning.

"What would be the fun in that?" he teased as he walked over to the door. "Make sure you lock up, Red. You never know what other crazy neighbor might barge in here and demand a pizza date." He said it in jest but meant every word. Especially about the locking-up part. She needed to be careful, not that she understood that yet. One day, she would.

"Funny." Her brown gaze held a touch of happiness that warmed his heart. Watching her grieve these last few weeks had been an uncomfortable experience. She hid it well in public, even within herself, but she wore the sorrow in her eyes.

If only she knew the truth.

"Anyway, I'm sure I'll be seeing you, Red." He gave her a salute rather than a handshake and showed himself out.

"Not if you keep calling me Red," she retorted.

He waggled his brows. "It'll grow on you."

"Doubtful."

"We'll see, won't we?" Because he couldn't stop calling her that. She probably assumed the nickname referred to her hair, but it didn't. Those rosy cheeks of hers had turned a delicious red after realizing her lack of attire in the hallway, and the image would remain etched into his memory for a long time.

Jayson loved women of all kinds, but a gorgeous redhead was his kryptonite. And Lizzie Watkins definitely hit the mark.

He winked at her before starting toward the stairwell. "Lock up, Lizzie," he reminded, knowing full well she'd watched him move down the corridor. "Good night."

She muttered something before closing her door, and he paused to listen for the latch. When he heard it, he continued his mission, heading down the stairs instead of up. He wanted to be seen leaving the building. It would coincide with the release of the electronic interference in her condo.

Jayson engaged his gift for concealing his physical appearance as he hit the lobby and strolled past the Sentinel waiting for him.

Pretending to get the mail. Could you be more conspicuous?

The CRF needed to improve their training.

Two more Sentinels stood twenty feet down the sidewalk outside, pretending to chat like old friends. Their open stances and vigilant behavior proved that to be a lie. They could have at least feigned having a smoke or something.

Jayson continued shifting his facial traits as he moved past them. He kept his stride casual while searching 79th Street for anything else out of the ordinary. The last thing he needed was to invite a hunting Ichorian to the party.

As per the Treaty of 1747, Hydraians who entered New York City did so at their own risk. Considering the place was overrun with Ichorians and home to the CRF headquarters, most of Jayson's kind weren't keen on paying a visit. But he could alter the perception of his physical appearance. For that reason, Luc had assigned this mission to him. The Sentinels could see and pursue him, but once he lost them, they would remember his traits differently.

Hence his ability to blend in, in a city overrun by his enemies.

He turned the corner onto Columbus Avenue and sensed the two juveniles from outside following. As much as he would enjoy killing them, he couldn't. He needed the CRF to think the interference was a fluke and maybe send in a technician to review all the connections. Nothing more.

Jayson paused beside the American Museum of Natural History. He pretended not to see his stalkers as he stretched out each of his quads. *Just going for a run, boys.*

He glanced at his watch.

One hour until his rendezvous with Mateo and Tristan.

That gave Jayson twenty minutes to play.

Let's see just how good of shape you Sentinels are really in.

He rolled his neck and shoulders, jumped up and down a few times, and took off at a light jog toward Central Park.

Game. On.

Chapter Two

Bloody Good Times

Subject's intelligence levels are above average, but sympathy for humanity is abnormally high.

—Entry Log 114.1.4-7

Friends.

Lizzie leaned against the door, considering the term as the movie continued.

She had several *friends*, most of whom she rarely saw anymore because of her current hermit status, but all of them were female. Stas, Cam, Kristin, and now… Jayson?

She shook her head.

What a weird evening. Most of her neighbors were friendly, but not like Jayson Masters. A hello or a wave about covered the camaraderie of the building.

"*We're neighbors, and neighbors hang out.*"

Lizzie giggled. "Definitely not from here."

She settled back into the couch and finished her slice of pizza. Her stomach hadn't allowed her to eat much with Jayson sitting so close. His presence seemed to consume the entire room, something she noticed as the evening progressed.

The man had entered as a decent-looking irritant and left as a hot-as-hell "friend." That's what he called this, anyway.

"He must be really lonely," she half joked. Lizzie made friends easily, but didn't usually befriend gorgeous men. Except for Tom, but he didn't count.

She grimaced at the unwanted reminder, and a sense of deep longing soured her good mood. His untimely demise haunted her every thought. It didn't help that the details of his death were classified by his employer, the damn CRF.

When she asked his father for information, he'd just given her a sad smile and said Tom died a hero overseas. No comment as to where or how, just a one-sentence story that meant nothing. Stas's similar response firmly placed Lizzie on the outside. She didn't even qualify as need-to-know.

The wine disappeared from her glass as she inhaled every last drop. Then she poured herself a fresh one. She took another healthy sip and cringed as someone knocked on her door.

"Seriously?" Just as the tears started, too.

The knocking turned to pounding.

Okay. She enjoyed dinner with Jayson, but he couldn't just keep coming down here and demanding entrance into her personal space.

Her blood heated as the man jiggled her knob.

Too far.

She stomped over to the door and threw it open. "Now, you listen—Oh!" She cleared her throat. "Uh, hi, Charlie."

"Miss Watkins," the Sentinel replied, all business. "Sorry for the intrusion, but your father requested I stop by to check on you."

Charlie worked for the CRF's paramilitary unit. They specialized in saving people in complex situations all over the world and, apparently, sidelined as errand boys for her parents. She knew him reasonably well as a result.

"You mean my mother told him to send someone." She shook her head and started toward the bread box to find her phone. Oh, her mother wasn't so much worried as pissed. The Sentinel at her door served as a warning that Lizzie had stepped out of line by refusing to attend the gala.

Well, screw her.

She powered up the mobile and snorted at the myriad of messages filling the screen.

Ridiculous.

Sending a babysitter to check up on her like she was ten years old and not twenty-four.

Delete, delete, delete.

She didn't even bother reading a single one. They would all say variants of the same thing.

We're so disappointed in you. Why can't you be a better daughter? Is this because you can't fit into the dress I sent you? I told you to start dieting.

Blah, blah, blah.

She turned to find Charlie leaning against the entry to her kitchen, blocking her path to the dining area. His familiarity and ease with entering her condo created a stir of unease inside—different from Jayson, who merely irritated her. The Sentinel boasted a presumptuous air that left a sour taste in her mouth.

"Everything okay, ma'am?" he asked in that professional tone.

All the Sentinels addressed her in this manner.

Well, except Tom. He always teased her the way an older brother would, but that had to do with them being raised together.

As for the others, she suspected her dad had something to do with it. Or maybe Tom's father, John—who was their boss and the CRF's CEO—had told the Sentinels to address her formally. The man treated her like a daughter, a habit formed out of being best friends with her father.

"I'm fine," she replied. "Thank you for stopping by." Years of practice in being polite kept her tone even and calm, despite her innate need to scream. It wasn't his fault her parents sent him here to check up on her.

She escorted him back to the foyer where he had closed and locked the door, but he paused upon seeing the pizza boxes and wine on her table.

"Do you have company, ma'am?"

"I really hate when you all call me that," she grumbled. "It makes me feel old."

He didn't smile or react but continued to stare at her while waiting for an answer. The professional act felt cold and sterile. She could be naked and he'd probably still address her the same way.

"I had a friend over, but he left," she finally said. "Do you want to take some of the pizza with you?" Jayson had ordered two boxes, one of which he finished himself and the other still had seven of the eight pieces left.

"No, but thank you, ma'am. What was the friend's name?"

She blinked. "What does it matter?"

"Just trying to provide a full report back to Mister Watkins."

Uh-huh. Her father couldn't care less. This had her mother's touch all over it.

"Well, you can tell my father that if he wants my friend's name, he can call me himself." She opened the door while speaking and cast a saccharine smile at Charlie. "Since you don't want any food, I imagine you'll be going now."

The Sentinel cast an uneasy glance around the condo. "Is your friend still here?"

"Do you see him here?" she countered, irritated.

"Right." He tipped his blond head at her and exited. "My apologies for the interruption, ma'am."

"You're forgiven, *sir*," she retorted as she closed and locked the door.

Now her mother would get an earful on Lizzie's lack of manners. Her parents could add it to their pile of her shortcomings.

And they could add this text message as well.

You can call off the CRF lackeys, Mother, she typed. *I'm fine.*

The reply came five minutes later, indicating Charlie had already delivered his report.

What male friend did you have over?

Of course her mother wanted that information. *No one you know.*

Clearly, no one I want to know if he felt you need to indulge in pizza. That is not a solution to being unable to wear your dress, Elizabeth. I'll schedule an appointment with Doctor Schwartz next week.

The nutritionist.

Great.

Have a good night, Mother.

Lizzie threw her phone onto the table, grabbed a pillow, and screamed. She hadn't bothered to try on the size four dress because she knew the damn thing wouldn't fit her boobs.

Lizzie wore a solid six. It had been that way since high school, much to her willowy mother's chagrin. Over a decade of ballet and strict eating hadn't stopped her curves from flaring, and the last five years of eating how she wanted hadn't added to her body, either.

"Cheers." She toasted her mother with a slice of pizza from the table and enjoyed it with more wine.

So much for her productive evening.

~*~

Fifteen minutes.

That's how long the Sentinels lasted at Jayson's pace through the park. He ran in circles for another half hour before exiting near *The Pierre*—a favorite meeting place over the last century.

Jayson nodded to the doorman at the Fifth Avenue entrance before skipping up the checkered stairs to the first-floor lobby. He wandered through the plush seating area and found Tristan waiting in the elevator bay with a female hotel employee.

Always flirting, Jayson thought, grinning.

"Ah, here's my friend now," the Ichorian murmured with a wink to the blonde beside him. "Thank you, lovely, for keeping me company. Perhaps we'll meet again?"

The woman simpered, as they always did in Tristan's presence. His Irish lilt, seductive charm, and rich demeanor embodied the female dream, and his reasonably good looks, athletic form, and dimpled smile helped, too. What his conquests failed to notice was the incredibly lethal nature lurking behind those forest-green eyes.

Or maybe they did realize it and enjoyed the potential challenge of taming the predator.

Her reply was lost to the arriving elevator. Jayson gave the lady a nod while Tristan brushed a kiss against her wrist—an intentional move to test her pulse.

"Hungry?" Jayson joked as the doors closed.

"Starved," Tristan replied. "But I'll handle my appetite later."

"Well, she certainly seems willing."

"Most of them are," the Ichorian replied as the doors opened to the 17th floor. "How was your run?"

Jayson shrugged. "Uneventful."

"Pity." Ichorians loved blood, but Tristan thrived on violence. Still, Jayson trusted the Ichorian despite his proclivities and immortal race, because of ancient family ties.

But that didn't mean he always liked the sadistic leech.

Mateo opened the door before they could knock, and let them inside. Luc and Balthazar stood near the windows, observing the skyline, while Jacque relaxed on the bed and flipped through channels on the television.

Jayson grinned at his best friends, happy to see them after six weeks of living in solitude above Lizzie Watkins's condo. All their planning sessions and conversations were over the phone due to the danger of them visiting in person, something they clearly ignored tonight.

"You need to get laid," was Balthazar's greeting. Typical. The notorious god of deviance probably pitied Jayson's temporary vow of chastity. But he couldn't afford any distractions, women included.

"I'm missing Brazil right about now," Jayson admitted.

Balthazar nodded solemnly. "I'm already planning your return party."

"Excellent." Jayson focused on Luc and folded his arms. "*You* shouldn't be here."

As the leader and king of the Hydraian race, venturing into New York City was a serious risk. Ichorians would love a reason to kill Luc—not that he would ever give them one—but his presence here put several lives at risk. Specifically, Mateo's and Tristan's.

Ichorians had strict laws about fraternizing with Hydraians. Just being in this room sentenced Mateo and Tristan to death, not that they seemed bothered.

Centuries of skirting the rules and meeting in private bolstered their confidence, but chatter in the immortal community suggested Ichorians were falling under harsher scrutiny by their governing power, the Conclave.

But what concerned Jayson more were the rumors about immortals actively looking for ways to break the tenuous balance of power between Ichorians and Hydraians. Killing Luc, the leader of his kind, would be an excellent way to ignite chaos and start a war. Something everyone in this room preferred to avoid.

"Next time, send Jacque to collect me and we'll meet somewhere safer," Jayson continued. "For all our sakes."

"A hundred bucks," Jacque boasted from the bed, his silver gaze on Mateo.

"I didn't accept your bet," the blond Ichorian replied flatly. "I owe you nothing."

"Jacque guessed you would demand that," Luc explained. "And I'm perfectly safe at the moment." The stubborn brute crossed his strong arms and narrowed his emerald orbs at Jayson. "I'm here to reiterate that although you've established contact with the subject, you can't fuck her."

"Seriously?" Jayson was almost offended. He glanced at the more reasonable of the two. "It's like he doesn't trust me, B."

Balthazar shrugged. "I've told him it's a ridiculous edict, but you know how inflexible he gets."

"True. Maybe he's the one who needs to get laid?" Jayson suggested.

"An accurate assessment," his friend agreed. "By a certain dark-haired fledgling, maybe?"

Jayson's eyebrows inched upward. *Eliza?* he asked silently, knowing his mind-reading friend would hear him.

Balthazar nodded in confirmation.

Interesting. All of the exchanges Jayson had witnessed between Luc and Eliza were heated debates where she questioned his authority.

It surprised them all, considering her experience with a hoard of sadistic Ichorians and her less-than-pleasant attendance at a recent Conclave, but the woman possessed an ironclad will to survive. Her personality started to resurface after a few weeks of feeling safe in Hydria. Some of it was a result of Balthazar using his gift for emotions to assist her in the healing process, but most of it stemmed from her innate strength.

I'm sorry to be missing the fireworks, Jayson admitted.

"It's quite a show," Balthazar replied, grinning. "I'll send you updates."

Please do.

"Are you two done acting like children?" Luc asked, his emerald gaze flickering with irritation. "And I already told you that's never happening. Eliza's a child." He turned to the blond Ichorian in the corner. "What are our next steps?"

And back to business already.

Mateo glanced up from his phone. "I want to check our surveillance in her condo since we put it there over six weeks ago—I know the CRF hasn't detected it, but it never hurts to refresh the equipment. And I'd suggest you all use it as an opportunity to look for anything related to the serum."

Ah, the reason for all of this. Whisking Lizzie off to Hydria and telling her the truth would make all this easier, but the Hydraian Elders, Jayson included, had voted to withhold the information from her while they assessed the situation.

Tom, the son of the CRF's CEO, was a recently acquired ally with a wealth of helpful information. Part of his debrief included information regarding Lizzie. She required some sort of medication to stay alive, but no one knew what or how the organization administered it. Hence Jayson's purpose in New York City.

He had observed her for six weeks to no avail, and their contact on the inside hadn't gathered anything useful. Luc opted to escalate the plan because time was running short. They needed answers—and fast—before they could decide how to proceed with Miss Watkins.

"When?" Luc pressed, his focus still on the blond.

"Issac suggested Tuesday," Mateo replied. "Something about Stas working late with Stark and Jonathan."

"Excellent." Luc turned his intelligent gaze on Jayson. "We'll need you to distract Elizabeth while Stas handles CRF interference."

"Oh, I'll distract her plenty." *And enjoy every minute.* "But you can't search her condo, Luc. Send someone else." Luc might be his leader and king, but on this, Jayson would not falter. "It's too dangerous."

In a rare moment of seriousness, Balthazar said, "I agree. We'll send Grace and Ash with Jacque." His brown gaze met and held Luc's as a one-sided debate ensued between them. "We'll send Alik with them, too." Silence. A nod. "She'll say yes, and you know it."

Those final words helped Jayson follow the debate. "Grace is ready," he said. "Saying otherwise is an insult to her training." Which he took personally, since he'd been the one to provide it.

Sparkling green eyes met his and narrowed. "I refuse to risk one so young."

"Nine hundred is hardly young, Luc." Jayson shook his head. "You can't do everything, and I'm confident she'll handle it. Besides, her ability to read the history of objects will come in handy."

Balthazar ran his fingers through his dark hair and shook his head at whatever Luc was thinking. "I'll work on him, Jay. For now, we need to get moving."

Luc refocused the discussion. "Anything else to report on?"

Always so serious.

"He does need to relax more," Balthazar agreed. The mind reader never gave anyone any privacy, something that used to irritate the hell out of Jayson, but after three thousand years of knowing the bastard, he was used to it. Besides, his ability to hear thoughts made him the best wingman imaginable. "I love you, too, Jay."

Jayson grinned before recalling Luc's question. "I'm good for now."

Luc nodded his blond head as if he expected as much. "I wish we could stay longer, Jay, but…"

"You shouldn't have come to begin with," Jayson finished for him. "Get going before the bloodsuckers track you down."

"I take offense to that," Tristan murmured, speaking for the first time since entering the room.

"Says the one thinking about his meal downstairs," Balthazar remarked, amused. "She sounds delectable."

"Oh, she will be." Tristan grinned. "Does that mean I'm dismissed to enjoy my evening?"

Mateo rolled his eyes. "Sure. I'll report to Issac on your behalf."

"Brilliant. I'll escort Jayson downstairs before I seduce my snack."

"How gentlemanly of you," Jayson joked before nodding at Balthazar and

Luc. "Go home."

They returned the nod while Jacque hopped off the bed. "Teleporter at your service." He gave a mock bow before extending his hands. "Nice to see you, Jay."

"Likewise," he replied as the three of them disappeared into thin air.

Bye, old friends.

A touch of envy caressed his chest.

He didn't so much miss home as his people.

And his own bed. And his pool. And the food.

He sighed. The sooner he solved this case, the better.

Jayson faced the Ichorians. Tristan stood ready, his expression bored, while his counterpart remained focused on his phone.

"We're all set for Tuesday," Mateo said as he typed something onto the screen. "Issac says to have Lizzie out by six in the evening."

"It's a date," Jayson replied. "Shall we?"

"Indeed." Tristan fixed his already immaculate suit jacket and tie and led the way.

With nods to each other, they parted from the elevator, and Jayson left the Ichorian to his evening of seduction.

Jayson walked most of the way home, his eyes vigilant as he moved through the park. He was almost disappointed to find no Sentinels waiting for him on 79th Street.

Another early night for me.

He nodded to the night doorman, wondering only briefly how the Sentinel had gotten past him to enter. Probably a show of identification, or perhaps the man was on a guest list of sorts. He'd check that later.

Three flights of stairs later, he was at his door and paused.

A shift in the air provided him a millisecond of warning before someone fired a bullet.

From inside his condo.

In the direction of his head.

Jayson engaged his affinity for metal as he fell to a crouch.

"Fuck," he muttered as he caught the succession of bullets too late. They pelted his door with soft thuds, denting the wood. "Damn it."

At least it wasn't CRF issued. Those fuckers would have exploded into flames. Incendiary bullets were the organization's deadliest invention yet, and Jayson hated them.

But that meant a non-Sentinel was in his condo.

And the bastard had deadly aim.

Jayson located the source of the mayhem and bent the gun with his mind as he entered his condo and dove into the dining room. Two knives graced his palms as he found them beneath the table, and he threw them at the source.

But the asshole caught them in midair with one hand and paused to examine the craftsmanship. "Beautiful," the Ichorian murmured. "I'll be keeping these since you just destroyed my favorite pistol."

"Perhaps you shouldn't have fired it at me," Jayson growled.

The uninvited visitor stood to his full height. "I had to ensure you were still a worthy opponent, and you proved as qualified as ever, Jedrick."

God, that name. Jayson hadn't heard it in over a millennium. "I go by Jayson now, or Jay."

The black-haired immortal shut the front door before leaning against it and folding his lean arms. "Really? Why?"

"You don't ever change your name, *Ezekiel*?"

He laughed. "Actually, it's Kiel right now."

"Kiel," Jayson repeated. "Like *kill*?"

"A brilliant play on words, no? Can't say the same about Jayson. A bit boring, if you ask me."

"I wasn't asking." Jayson pushed off the floor and wiped his hands on his shorts. "And I preferred Zeke," he admitted, referring to an old nickname. Though Kiel suited the Nizari assassin well. "What are you doing here?"

"Ah, now isn't *that* the question of the night?" Ezekiel shrugged out of his leather jacket and hung it on the door. All-black clothes lurked beneath, befitting the immortal's profession of choice. He was one of the most renowned fledgling assassins in history and Jayson's notorious rival, yet the two of them had a strange camaraderie, as well; an unspoken agreement that should one of them die it would be by the other's hand.

"You know, I amuse myself in the oddest of ways," the immortal continued. "Like stalking Sentinels for sport. I followed three here earlier tonight. Imagine my surprise upon sensing you, a Hydraian Elder, leaving the building shortly after." The Ichorian cocked his head to the side. "Blood laws dictate I kill you now, but I say, what would be the fun in that? I'd much prefer to know what has you so intrigued by the alluring redhead downstairs that you're willing to risk your existence so openly."

Ice drilled through Jayson's veins. Not because Ezekiel knew about Lizzie, but that her condo had attracted his attention. A fledgling lived there.

Stas.

The moment an Ichorian learned about Stas's existence—and, more importantly, her abilities—she would become the target of the immortal world. Something she knew and refused to acknowledge, ergo her insistence on staying with the CRF and trying to learn more about Lizzie.

Jayson would admire her courage if her choices weren't so suicidal.

"Now…" Ezekiel relaxed into one of Jayson's oversized chairs and crossed his long legs in an elegant way that belied his words. "I'm already aware of Elizabeth's relation to George Watkins and that her intriguing roommate is a Sentinel—who is also romantically involved with Issac—but why are the Hydraians so interested?"

If you know about the inhabitants, then I doubt you were following the Sentinels for sport, old friend, Jayson thought. *How very informative of you.* Meaning the assassin had given him the intelligence for a reason. Ezekiel never did anything without thinking five steps ahead.

Does he already know about Stas?

Jayson crossed his arms and cocked a hip against the dining table, feigning a boredom he didn't feel. "I'm sure you have a theory, Zeke." *Tell me more.*

"Oh, I have several." Ezekiel smiled, and it was positively lethal. "Elizabeth Watkins looks nothing like her parents. I'm sure you've noticed? Oh, I can see you have. She's gorgeous, isn't she?"

"Get to the point." *Before I kick your ass.*

"Don't worry, old friend, she's not my type," Ezekiel purred. "But I can see she's definitely yours."

Jayson didn't take the bait, but a fire brewed inside—one created by a protective instinct he hadn't felt in a long, long time. He feigned a yawn to hide his sudden drive to throw a blade at the Ichorian's head. "Sorry, I'm bored. What do you want, Zeke?"

The assassin smiled. "Nothing yet. I'm too curious."

That sounded ominous, especially coming from Ezekiel. He was the notorious right-hand man of Osiris, the head of the Conclave and the leader of the Ichorian race. Except Ezekiel had been off the radar for the last century or so.

"I thought you were dead," Jayson remarked. "Where the hell have you been?"

"Oh, here and there," he replied flippantly with a wave of his hand. "Off seeing the world and all that jazz."

"Right." Jayson believed that about as much as he believed Ezekiel had a heart. "So you dropped by to say hi? Reminisce about old times?" *By trying to shoot me.*

"Sure." Ezekiel stood and smoothed his button-down shirt. "I also wanted confirmation."

"Of?"

"Your feelings for the girl below," he replied as he retrieved his jacket. "I'm looking forward to our new game, Jedrick. It's been too long." He slipped on his coat and pulled his long, dark hair from the collar to lay it over his back. Ezekiel clearly hadn't received the fashion guides for this century, or perhaps he enjoyed the old "vampy" style. His pale skin and black, gold-flecked eyes only added to the nefarious appearance.

"What if I don't want to play?" Jayson asked, wary.

"Oh, but we've already started." He held up the blades. "Thanks for these. I'll be putting them to good use." He opened the door and grinned over his shoulder. "See you soon, old friend."

I certainly hope not. "Try to work on your aim in the interim," Jayson suggested.

Amusement flickered in Ezekiel's eyes. "And you work on keeping that poor girl safe. It would be such a shame if she fell into the wrong hands, Jedrick."

He disappeared into the corridor before Jayson could reply. Mostly because his throat had clogged with an emotion he didn't feel often.

Fear.

It paralyzed him inside while pissing him off at the same time. Jayson lived through more horror than most immortals his age, and yet this minute detail gave him pause? Unacceptable.

She was just a girl.

A beautiful, smart, tenderhearted one who may or may not be human.

Most likely not human, anyway.

"God damn it," he muttered.

Lizzie, through her connection to Jayson, had just earned herself a lethal admirer. One with a propensity for killing brutally.

Not exactly true. Ezekiel already knew about her through her connection to George Watkins and the CRF itself. But he hadn't been *interested* until Jayson arrived.

And that put Stas in danger too.

Fuck.

Jayson closed the door and dialed a number from memory.

A cool British accent came over the line two rings later. "One moment."

Loud music and conversation flowed over the line while Jayson waited, and the dimming suggested Issac was walking away from the source of the commotion. "Is Elizabeth all right?" he asked.

"She's fine, but an old friend just dropped by uninvited."

"Who?"

"Ezekiel."

Silence met that proclamation.

"He suspects I'm here for Lizzie, and he's intrigued," Jayson added. "And he mentioned Stas. He knows she's a Sentinel and commented on your relationship with her."

"I see," Issac replied, voice devoid of emotion. "Does he suspect her heritage?"

"His history of tracking and slaughtering fledglings suggests that, if he doesn't yet, it's only a matter of time before he does. Especially now that he's fascinated." Which meant Stas needed to get the hell out of New York City. Now.

"Issac?" Stas's voice flowed in the background, as did the click-clacking of heels. Jayson pictured her walking toward the suit-clad Ichorian. Their relationship concerned him, mostly because it would only end in heartache. Not that it was his place to comment.

"What's going on?" she asked, voice concerned. "Is Lizzie okay?"

"Jayson has just had a visit from a renowned Nizari assassin."

"What?" Her voice held a touch of fear. As it should. "I thought you said they didn't exist anymore."

"Their purpose is moot due to a lack of known fledglings," Issac clarified.

"But some of them are very much alive, and the one who visited Jayson is the deadliest of them all. And he knows about you."

More silence. Jayson guessed they were either embracing or staring each other down.

Issac proved it to be the latter as he said, "It's time, Aya. We need to get you out of the city."

"Absolutely not." Stas's tone was resolute and brooked no argument. Not that it stopped Issac.

"It's not safe for you here."

"You've been saying that for months, and while I agree with you, there is no way in hell I'm leaving Lizzie behind. Or you."

"Stubborn woman," Jayson muttered. Because he understood and admired that level of loyalty. It was why he agreed to venture to New York City despite it being a likely death sentence. He had a responsibility to his kind to investigate and help Lizzie, especially if it meant bringing her in as an ally. The Hydraians needed all the help they could get.

"Aya…" Issac sighed. "Jayson, keep an eye on Elizabeth."

The line went dead.

"Well, that went as expected." He shook his head and dialed Luc.

It was going to be a long night.

Chapter Three

A Blood Promise

Subject's roommate has engaged in a sexual relationship with a renowned Ichorian. Benefactor is not concerned.

—Entry Log 124.06.4-7

"Aya," Issac repeated, this time with a little more force in his tone.

Astasiya stopped near the stairwell, her spine rigid. "I'm not debating this."

He caught her hip and pressed his chest against her exposed back. Her sapphire gown hugged her curves in all the right places, giving him quite the uncomfortable evening. But now was not the time for such indulgences.

"I may not be well versed in relationships, but I believe communication to be a fundamental point. Yes?" His lips brushed her ear with every word.

She melted against him on a groan. "I hate when you do that."

He grinned. "On the contrary, love, I think you quite enjoy it." He nipped her pulse and slid his palm to her lower abdomen to stop her from moving away from him again. "We're discussing this, Aya. You promised me you would relocate to Hydria at the first sign of danger."

Not that she seemed all that enthused with upholding her end of the bargain. He had tried to convince her to leave the CRF once they saved his sister from

Jonathan's clutches, but Astasiya used her roommate as an excuse to stay. Her arguments were sound, therefore, he didn't press his opinion, but every moment she spent in this city, he worried. Endlessly. Never had he cared so much for a woman other than his next of kin, and it hurt on a level he didn't know existed.

Astasiya turned in his arms and placed her hands on his shoulders as he grasped her waist, holding her flush against him.

"Okay, a Nizari assassin told Jayson he knows about me, but he hasn't done anything yet. Is it because he doesn't suspect me, or is it something else?"

"Ezekiel's intentions are cryptic at best, but he's notorious for playing with his food." The Ichorian was renowned for his cruelty and lethal intelligence. His ability to track by blood type increased his notoriety. He was part of the short list of beings Issac considered to be a true threat.

"But he hasn't come after me yet," she repeated.

He arched a brow. "And so you would prefer to wait for such a moment?"

"No, but I'm prepared to deal with one."

"Your training with Agent Stark may be far superior than I anticipated, but that does not qualify you to handle an assassin of Ezekiel's caliber."

Astasiya's eyes widened. "I'm pretty sure that entire sentence was an insult."

"No, it was a rational statement. You are still new to this world and do not know Ezekiel like I do, nor are you prepared to fight him. He will win, you will die, and I do not accept that outcome." His grip unintentionally tightened, but he couldn't seem to loosen it. She was here and real, and he refused to let go. Life without her… "I can't lose you, Aya."

Her serious mask crumpled as she wrapped her arms around him and buried her face in his chest. "You won't."

A lie. They both knew he would lose her eventually. She couldn't remain a fledgling forever, but he would rather her live an immortal life without him than lose her forever.

"It's time," he said again. "You know it's time."

She shook her head against him. "She's my best friend, Issac. I won't leave her behind."

He threaded his fingers through Astasiya's beautiful blonde hair as he returned her embrace. His lips found her forehead as he suppressed the urge to sigh. He could never deny her, even when he needed to.

"She's well-guarded by Jayson," he murmured. "And I'll be here too."

"How would you explain my disappearance to John?" She pulled back enough to meet his gaze. "And Osiris?"

Two excellent questions. "I'm not concerned about Osiris." Not in the way she mentioned, anyway. The ancient Ichorian showed an uncanny interest in Astasiya during the Conclave but had yet to reach out to inquire as to her immortal status. If he thought of her at all, it could be months or years down the line. Time passed in a unique way for immortals of his age.

"And John?" she pressed.

"Would likely inquire about your disappearance and perhaps cause a nuisance, but I'll handle it."

Her eyes expressed admonishment. "You're allowed to be cavalier about your life, but I'm not at liberty to risk mine." She cocked her head to the side. "This is a relationship, Issac, where we both care for each other. If you stay, I stay."

"Oh? And if I opt to move to Hydria, will you come with me?"

"Do you want to move to Hydria?"

"That belies the point. Would you move?"

She stared him down, as if contemplating his sincerity, and he let her see the truth in his gaze. He truly wanted to know. Would she follow him?

"Issac…" She closed her eyes and sighed, long and slow. "I know you're worried, and I am too, but she's my family. Would you leave Amelia?"

His chest ached with memory as he forced himself to answer honestly, "No." Issac had left his sister once, though not intentionally. He had thought she was dead, only to find out Jonathan had played him for a fool. "If I had known she was alive at the CRF, I never would have left her there."

"That's how I feel about Lizzie," Astasiya replied, opening those enchanting eyes once more. "I know your bond is by blood, but she's my person. I love her, Issac. And I won't leave if I can help her."

"But can you help her?" he countered.

"Could you have helped Amelia?" she tossed back, eliciting a growl from him.

"Aya—"

"No, listen to me. Those runes at the headquarters would strip your gift for illusion, yet you would have tried everything to breach them to save her, even if it cost your life. That's how I feel about Lizzie, but unlike you, I'm in a position where I can help her. I just need more time."

"To do what? You're not any closer now than you were six weeks ago." He pulled away to run his fingers through his hair. "This is madness, Aya. An assassin was in your building tonight. Does that hold no bearing on your thought process?"

She bristled. "Don't talk to me like I'm a child."

"Then stop acting like one," he retorted. "This is your life we are discussing, not some Sentinel mission or game."

"This is Lizzie's life too." Liquid fire lit her green eyes, stirring arousal deep inside him. Not a fantastic time to react, but she resembled a goddess in these moments, and his soul yearned to take her in every way. *Mine.*

"I understand the risk," she continued. "But it is my decision. And yes, perhaps I'm not equipped to handle an assassin in combat *yet*, but he's never faced a fledgling like me. All I need is my voice."

Power underlined her tone, exciting him more. She'd grown beautifully in the last few months, not just in physical strength but in mental ability, as well.

"I know you all think I'm being selfish and immature," she added. "Your centuries of experience trump mine, and I respect that, but I cannot ignore my instincts, Issac. Asking me to flee is not in my nature. To stay is ridiculous and dangerous, and I understand all that, but I can't be put in time-out while everyone else risks their lives for my best friend. That's not who I am."

The air thickened as her words lingered between them. So strong and courageous, the embodiment of a warrior. He admired her for it, even as he yearned for her safety and for her to see reason.

She failed to realize this wasn't solely her decision since it impacted him just as much. If Ezekiel discovered her secret, it would be Issac's life on the line as well. He didn't fear the Conclave, but he did worry about how far he would go to protect her.

But she was right. Asking her to sit on the sidelines would break a fundamental part of her. And Issac could never be the one to extinguish the light that burned so fiercely inside her.

"Can we compromise?" he asked softly.

"It depends on your terms." She sounded so regal but seemed unaware of it. This was the cause of Luc's intrigue—he saw the potential for her to lead. And her ability to compel only enhanced that interest.

Issac pushed the thought aside and forced himself to live in the present, to enjoy what time he had left with this incredible woman. For the time being, she belonged to him, as he did to her. And he refused to let the future intrude.

Time for a little game of persuasion.

"My terms," he murmured as he advanced on her. She stepped backward, causing the predator in him to grin. He cornered her in the nook beside the stairwell door, placing them out of sight for anyone who chose to enter this vacant corridor of the hotel.

"I will agree to you staying in New York," he said as he aligned his body with hers, trapping her against the wall. "If you promise to spend every night with me. Whether it be at your place or mine, I want to know that outside the CRF, you are safe."

She swallowed. "Using seduction to distract me isn't fair, Issac."

"You use your gifts; I will use mine." He ran his hands up her sides. "I love this dress. Tell me what you're wearing beneath it."

"That's not relevant… to… our negotiation," she whispered as she arched into him. He loved how her body responded to his every touch as if trained specifically for his brand of pleasure.

Issac caught her lip between his teeth and nibbled. "On the contrary, I find it very relevant." He started pulling the fabric up her legs. "I want to know what I'll be removing later when you come home with me."

She shuddered against him as he exposed her thighs. "Issac…"

"Aya," he replied, his mouth at her neck. He traced her pulse with his tongue. "Tell me you agree, love."

Her nails dug into his shoulders. "You're not playing fair."

"Never with you," he whispered. She meant too much to him. He would break every rule to keep her safe, and he would concede to her wishes if it meant keeping her happy. But he needed this in return. "Please, Aya."

She softened in his arms, her head falling back against the wall. "I need at least one girls' night with Lizzie."

He grinned against her neck. "Granted, so long as I can sneak in after she goes to bed."

"How very teenage boy of you," she teased. "But I concede that point."

He tasted her sensitive skin. "Then we have a deal?"

"Are we making a blood vow?" The taunt in her voice teased his baser instincts.

"Mmm." He sunk his canines into her neck and luxuriated in the sweet essence beneath the skin. Her blood hit the back of his throat, and a growl he couldn't contain slipped out as she clung to him. After two shallow pulls, he released her from his bite and whispered, "Careful what you wish for, Aya."

"Issac…" She shook against him as the endorphins from his lethal kiss worked their way through her system. "Fuck." Another convulsion of hers vibrated his body. "Fine. Yes. I agree to your terms, not that it's a hardship."

His lips curled. "Oh, I think you'll find it to be quite a bit of work, love." He nuzzled her throat and reaffirmed his grip on her dress by inching the fabric upward to expose more of her thighs. "Fancy a preview?"

"Does it involve you biting me again?" she asked, her voice whisper-soft and drowsy with gratification.

He licked the still-open wound. "Yes."

"Then yes, please." She arched her neck. "Take me, Issac."

"Always." He soothed the mark on her tender skin with his tongue before dropping to his knees.

She knotted her fingers in his hair, forcing him to meet her gaze. "Wh-what are you doing?"

He grinned as he revealed her midnight-blue panties. "You did not express where you wished to be bitten, Aya."

"Oh, God…"

"Hold on to that thought, love. You'll be needing it again soon."

CHAPTER FOUR

"Not a Date" Is a Date, Except When It's Not

> **Subject appears reliant on familial approval. Habitat and accommodations should be revisited in future iterations.**
>
> **—Entry Log 118.05.4-7**

Lizzie pressed sweaty palms against her navy-blue shift dress and checked her appearance once more in the mirror.

"You're being ridiculous," she whispered. "It's not even a date."

Yet she had tousled her hair into perfect auburn waves. Her eyes popped with the eyeliner, and a sheen of cherry lip gloss graced her lips.

Her sorority sisters, especially Cam and Kristin, would approve. Stas, however, would laugh at her.

And that's why Lizzie considered her the closer friend.

She grinned at the thought as she sent a text off to Stas.

I'm grabbing dinner with that new neighbor I told you about.

Jayson had slid a note under her door Sunday night asking if she wanted to grab dinner tonight. He'd left his number at the bottom, and like an idiot, she'd programmed it into her phone and sent him a confirmation via text message.

A really stupid decision.

Lizzie didn't go out on Tuesdays, or any weeknights, because of work. But her lesson plans were already done for the month due to all her evenings alone.

Try to behave, Stas teased. Lizzie had given her the full description of their overbearing man upstairs. *I'll be home around ten tonight. Stark is forcing me to work late again.*

You should kick his ass.

Oh, believe me, I'm trying.

See you in the morning for breakfast? Lizzie asked.

They used to eat with each other every day, but things had changed over the last few months with Stas working so much. Tom's funeral hadn't helped, either. It was probably in Lizzie's head, but her friendship with Stas felt stilted. Cold, even.

Her phone dinged with the reply, *Coffee? :)*

Lizzie grinned. Caffeine was the way to Stas's heart. *Obviously*, she replied.

Count me in.

See you then.

It's a girls' date, Stas promised.

Lizzie smiled. *Sounds great.*

She loved that her best friend had finally found happiness, but missed their girl time together. They used to enjoy pizza once a week and binge-watch chick flicks, but now Stas spent most weekends with Issac. Lizzie couldn't fault her for it; her best friend deserved happiness and more.

And yeah, a tiny part of her also hoped Issac might be able to convince Stas to leave the CRF and pursue other opportunities.

Which, of course, made Lizzie a horrible person.

Her hatred of the organization stemmed from an irrational sensation of fear that increased every time she neared the corporate headquarters. She visited her father a handful of times in his top-floor office, mostly when he needed her to sign something. The last time had been some paperwork for her trust fund.

For whatever reason, he preferred to do everything at the CRF instead of at home. Probably because he rarely left his desk unless it involved doing something for work. As the Chief of International Affairs, he traveled often. As a kid, she rarely saw him, which probably contributed to her dislike of the organization. Killing Tom and stealing her best friend didn't improve matters.

There went Lizzie's happy mood. Just in time for the knock on her door.

Six o'clock on the dot.

Lizzie liked a punctual man.

Not that this was a date.

Friends, she reminded herself.

That didn't stop her heart from fluttering upon opening the door. Because, wow, Jayson cleaned up nicely.

Designer jeans, a deep-red sweater, artfully styled dark hair, and grinning chocolate eyes, all wrapped up in a muscular package most women only dreamed about.

Not a date.

Just neighbors.

A man like him wouldn't be interested in you anyway.

That last voice sounded a little too much like her mother.

And I've been staring at his chest for two solid seconds.

"Hi," she managed.

Those adorable dimples peeked at her. "Hi," he returned. "Ready?"

"Yep." She grabbed her purse from the table in the foyer and slipped on her heels. They added three inches to her five-foot, six-inch height, leaving her forehead around his lips.

Stop thinking about his mouth.

Right.

She followed him down the hall to the stairs and said nothing as he led her outside.

Lizzie didn't have a lot of experience with men outside her small social circle. She dated occasionally, but it never blossomed into anything. A few kisses here, some touches there, all of which led to nothing memorable. Only one man ever tempted her to go beyond light petting.

Tom Fitzgerald.

Her crush began at the ripe age of thirteen and continued through the years, though it waned a little in college. She watched him with other women and started to realize he would never see her as anything other than a sister. All hope she harbored of him wanting her died the day of his funeral.

Jayson tugged on the loose strand of hair hanging by her face. "Long day, Red?"

God, they were already a block away from their building and hadn't said more than four words to each other. Instead, she'd trod down a melancholy path that had no place in their evening plans.

Lizzie cleared her throat and forced a smile. "It's been a long few weeks." No sense in lying about it. "But I'm managing."

"Want to talk about it?"

"Not really."

He shrugged. "All right, let's talk about dinner instead. I know you love San Dinos, but I've heard rumors of a better pizza place."

Her eyebrows sprang upward. "That's blasphemy!"

Jayson laughed. "I say we test it and decide for ourselves."

She narrowed her eyes. "What's the name of this supposed restaurant?"

"It's a real restaurant," he replied. "And I think it's called Magilinos or something."

She'd never heard of it. "Where is it?"

"Uh, it's in Brooklyn." He gave her a sheepish smile. "I hope you like the train."

~*~

Lizzie Watkins was trying to kill him.

First, she wore a dress that ended midthigh, revealing those sexy-as-hell legs to the world.

Second, she added fuck-me heels and handled them like a runway model.

And now she sat across from him, moaning.

Oh, he knew the pizza here totally kicked San Dinos's ass, but he hadn't expected his *friend* to react with sexy little noises after each bite.

Luc's unnecessary reminder about keeping the relationship professional with Lizzie didn't help. Jayson knew his job and respected it, but a growing part of him started to see this assignment as a challenge. One he wanted to see naked in his bed.

Not. Going. To. Happen.

"Okay," Lizzie said after polishing off her third slice. "I was skeptical, but you win. That was amazing."

Mmm, he certainly enjoyed those words rolling off her plump lips. Too bad the context was all wrong. The woman maintained the innocence of an angel, and that only increased the allure. Her every move seemed to radiate erotic appeal without even trying. Anywhere else, and any other time, he would seduce her out of the dress, leave on the heels, and give her a night to remember.

Alas, he had work to do, as the buzzing against his thigh constantly reminded him.

We need at least another hour, the last message had read.

Sixty minutes of small talk ought to do it. He could handle that.

"So, you've never heard of this place?" he asked, feigning surprise. Lizzie's high-society upbringing sheltered her from the simple pleasures in life, such as finding off-the-beaten-path pizza pubs.

"I have now," she replied cheekily. "Not that I'll get out here much with that forty-five-minute train ride."

He chuckled, remembering her expression when he mentioned their destination earlier. Shock had mingled with horror at the idea of leaving her cocoon in Manhattan, but she'd been a good sport about it.

"It was worth it." He referred to both her initial reaction and the subtle jibe at their long journey. "Okay, so far I've learned you're a teacher who enjoys decent pizza and rarely leaves Manhattan. Oh, and you dislike loud music—can't forget that bit." He folded his arms on the small table, leaning toward her. "Tell me more. How long have you been in the city?"

"First," she said, holding up a finger. "I have no problem with loud music, just neighbors who like to throw weights onto the floor above my head. Music and I happen to get along just fine, thank you very much."

"Yeah? I bet you listen to pop crap."

She snorted. "And you clearly enjoy men screaming at unfashionable levels while banging on drums."

"There is nothing wrong with metal, Red."

"Says the man who has to throw his weights around just to be heard above the commotion."

He could apparently add witty to her long list of positive traits. The smile on his face actually hurt. It'd been there most of the evening because of her. "I guess I need to cross 'attend a concert' off the idea list for future neighborly activities."

She giggled. "Most New Yorkers consider waving to be the extent of activities that should occur between neighbors. Where did you say you were from, again?"

"Now hold on, I believe I asked you that first." He needed this conversation to be about her, not him. Because although he could lie, he didn't want to, and there were only so many ways to twist the truth. "How long have you lived in the city?"

"All my life," she replied. "Born and raised in Manhattan, attended Columbia for undergrad and NYU for grad school. And you know where I live now."

"So, your family lives in the city too?" He phrased it as a guess but already knew the truth. "Any siblings?"

He kept it light to appear politely interested, but inside, he was dying to know more about her relationship with George and Lillian Watkins. Stas had provided some of the sordid details, but maybe Lizzie could give him some minute detail that would help crack this case. Doubtful, but worth a shot.

Some of the amusement left Lizzie's expression, but her tone remained pleasant. "I'm an only child, but yes, my parents live in Manhattan."

"Do you see them a lot?" A natural follow-up question.

She pinched her lips to the side, considering. He caught the moment she decided to say what she wanted rather than the polite response.

"I do," she admitted. "Usually often, but not very much lately. We're not really getting along right now, but I have to see them this Sunday. It's tradition."

"Tradition?" he repeated, curious.

"Yeah, it's this monthly brunch, except it actually happens every four weeks, so it's technically thirteen times a year, not that it matters." A delectable pink caressed her cheeks, endearing her to him even more. "Sorry. It's silly. It's just a late breakfast with my parents and my dad's best friend."

"And you can't skip it?"

"Uh, I mean, I could, maybe. I've never actually tried. The Sunday brunch fell over Christmas one year, and we all still went." She laughed without humor. "Pretty sure my mom would kill me if I ever skipped."

"And you always go to the same restaurant? Even the time you went on Christmas?" He tried to maintain an innocent curiosity in his tone, but her revelation floored him.

This has to be related to the CRF somehow.

Lizzie nodded. "Yep. I don't know how my parents managed it, but the restaurant opened just for us. It couldn't have been cheap, not that money would ever stop them." Her crimson cheeks darkened deliciously, solidifying her nickname. "You probably think I'm some spoiled rich kid now, don't you? Living in a condo I obviously couldn't afford on my own and telling tales about my parents buying out restaurants."

Her gaze fell to where her hands were clasped in her lap. A telling gesture that confirmed his suspicions regarding her fragile confidence.

"I'm not in the habit of judging people based on their familial relations, Lizzie." Otherwise, they wouldn't be having this dinner. "I mean, my father is a dick." Understatement of the millennium. "And my mother passed a long time ago." Because his Ichorian sperm donor killed her for sport. "But I'm my own person, and I don't associate who I am today with either of them." *And haven't done so for about three thousand years, to be precise.*

"I'm so sorry," she said, meeting his gaze. "About your mom, I mean."

Her apology surprised him. He hadn't thought of his mother in ages, but of course Lizzie wouldn't realize that. His facial appearance, which he didn't bother altering in her presence, likened him to a thirty-year-old man, maybe even younger. She would assume his mother passed in the last decade or so.

"I've long reconciled with her passing," he answered carefully. "But thank you." Time to switch it back or she might ask how his mother died, and wouldn't that be a fun conversation? "So, why every four weeks?"

"The brunch?"

"Yeah."

"Uh, it's always been that way. My father's best friend is also his boss, John Fitzgerald. Do you know anything about the CRF?"

He forced a confused expression. "The humanitarian organization?"

"That'd be the one." A note of sarcasm underlined her words, amusing him. It seemed she wasn't a fan. Something they definitely had in common. "Anyway, John is the CEO. My dad works for him."

"And they always go to brunch together, huh?" Stas had mentioned something about this, but no one thought much of it. A mistake on their part.

"Every four weeks," she replied. "You're welcome to join me Sunday if you like uncomfortable conversation and salad." That blush worked its way up her neck again. "Oh, that sounded like an invitation to meet my parents, and that's so not what I meant. I know we're just friends, that this isn't anything, obviously, and… and yeah, I'm going to shut up now."

She hid behind a glass of water and drank it with a little too much vigor while he chuckled.

The woman was adorable.

And charming.

And very off-limits.

Damn it, Luc.

"Actually, I think I'd enjoy going with you." Just to see the look on Jonathan Fitzgerald's face. "But I'm leaving for a work trip on Sunday."

The first blatant lie of the evening. Oh, he would be working, but in New

York City. And very likely at her brunch. Because his curiosity was piqued.

Every four weeks.

That couldn't be a coincidence.

The records Tom—Jonathan's son—found stated she needed some sort of serum to stay alive. What Jayson hadn't deduced yet was *how* the CRF gave it to her, because in the last six, almost seven, weeks of watching her, he had yet to see them intervene in her life other than Friday night after he blacked out their surveillance.

But maybe it was simpler than that and didn't require her visiting headquarters.

Just a brunch.

"Oh, are you off to somewhere fun?" Lizzie asked, referring to his trip.

"No, definitely not." Anything dealing with the CRF could not be classified as enjoyable. "But I won't be gone for long. A few days maybe." More like hours.

Relief touched her expression, and it warmed him that she didn't bother to hide it. Or maybe she couldn't. "A few days of peace and quiet? I can handle that."

Oh, the little minx! "Darling Red, I do believe you're asking for trouble now."

"Me?" She batted innocent eyes at him. "Never."

"You know what? I think our next date will be at a concert after all. One of my choosing."

"That's a *date* I'll turn down," she tossed back.

"Yeah?"

She nodded, her expression underlined in certainty.

A sense of challenge swept over him.

Okay. He couldn't bed her, but a little flirtation never killed anyone.

Her triumphant grin faltered as he stood and walked to her side of the table. By the time she realized his intentions, he was already behind her, hands on her chair, and leaning down to whisper in her ear. "You can resist me that easily, can you?"

Her chest rose and fell in quick succession as her pulse beat an unhealthy rhythm beneath his chin. Mmm, not so unaffected after all, it seemed. Not that he was any better. Being this close to her felt too right for his liking. Not to mention she smelled far too sweet for his taste. He suddenly had a desire to indulge in a new fantasy—and the forbidden undertone was not helping.

She swallowed and tried to catch his gaze by looking sideways. "I might be persuaded," she admitted. "If you promise to bring me earplugs." As unnerved as he clearly made her, she still managed to maintain an air of wit.

It was fascinating, and he loved it.

And he wanted to push it one step further.

He nuzzled her neck and luxuriated in her sharp intake of air. It lifted her ample breasts for his viewing pleasure, something his lower half enjoyed far more than it should.

His fingers itched to knot in her hair and introduce his mouth to hers—just for a second—but the buzzing against his thigh reminded him of his purpose.

Attractive or not, she was still an assignment.

And he had better control than this, not that his hardening member downstairs seemed to accept that.

Damn.

"Consider it a future neighborly date," he whispered, unable to resist. And straightened to check his phone.

Never mind. There's nothing useful in the condo. We'll be done in about thirty minutes. Sorry to disappoint you. Grace's defeated tone bled through the text. He would have to call her later to let her know it was fine. Jayson never expected her to find anything, only hoped. But he'd gotten what he needed through the art of old-fashioned conversation, and then some.

~*~

Lizzie fought to breathe.

What just happened?

Jayson had leaned so close she could almost taste his woodsy aftershave. Now he stood just behind her as he typed something into his phone. She glanced up to see him grinning—not at her but at his screen.

Another woman, maybe?

He could easily be a player. She knew little about him other than he enjoyed barging into his neighbor's condo and demanding pizza dates. But his easy candor and smooth lines suggested a comfort level with women that required a lot of practice. Pair that with his gorgeous exterior, and yeah, he likely slept around a lot.

Not that it mattered.

They were friends on a *neighborly date*, as he had called it.

And so what if his lips grazed her ear while he spoke? That could hardly be considered romantic. Even if it did set off a flurry of butterflies in her lower belly.

"We should probably start heading back," he said, his focus still on the phone in his hand. "It's getting late, and we both have work in the morning."

Right. He went from flirting with her to wanting to leave. Either she'd misread the signals or she had done something wrong. Maybe a mixture of both?

Irritated with herself for overanalyzing a very straightforward situation, she shoved her chair back into Jayson's legs.

"Oh!" She rotated to look up at him and cringed at his pained expression. "I'm *so* sorry!"

He cleared his throat and took a step back to allow her to stand. "No problem." Except it certainly *sounded* like a problem. She had pushed back with more force than necessary, but it shouldn't have hurt that much.

Unless the chair had connected with more than his legs…

What a typical way to end an otherwise decent evening. With Lizzie being a klutz.

Heat overwhelmed her cheeks and neck, even her breasts, as she wished teleportation existed so she could pop herself home and hide under her bed.

"I'm sorry," she said again, helpless.

His warm gaze met hers. "I think I'll live, Red."

She couldn't even argue the use of that dreadful nickname. Although it did come off as more of an endearment when he said it. Or maybe that was just her imagination.

He picked up her purse and slipped it over her arm. "You just caught me by surprise, which was my fault for focusing on my phone." His fingers danced down her wrist, and then he linked his hand with hers. "Shall we?"

So casual.

Like holding her hand was the most natural and platonic thing in the world.

He led her outside and toward the nearest station.

The temperature had dropped, cascading goose bumps down her exposed arms and legs. Her dress's short sleeves were enough to keep her comfortable in the restaurant and during the early hours of the evening, but they had stayed out later than she anticipated.

"Sweater or arm?"

Lizzie blinked up at the strange man. "Excuse me?" *There's that awesome phrase again.*

"Shall I choose?"

Uh… "Sure?"

"Excellent." Jayson's hand left hers as he draped his arm over her shoulders and pulled her close.

Oh, well, this is nice.

His body felt strong and warm against hers. And who knew cedar smelled so good?

"Better?" he asked as his hand ran up and down her arm.

Her mouth forgot how to form words, so she nodded instead.

Friends were allowed to keep each other warm, right?

Yes.

Okay.

This wasn't date territory at all. Just a friendly gesture to keep Lizzie from freezing her ass off. Stas would do the same and had done so on several occasions, because Lizzie had a penchant for dresses, even in winter.

Tom would have done it, too, her heart helpfully reminded.

She shoved that thought in a closet and kicked it closed. No sense letting the past ruin a mostly enjoyable evening with a new friend.

Jayson's touch left all too soon as they settled into a pair of seats on the train. They made small talk for a bit until he asked Lizzie why she chose teaching as a profession. Her standard reply about liking kids seemed to stick in her throat, not because of nerves, but because, for some inexplicable reason, she wanted to give him more.

The truth.

"Children are so impressionable at that age," she murmured. "I think having a positive influence means everything, and I want to provide that since one wasn't provided to me."

He stretched his arm along the back of their seats and shifted slightly to face her. It caused their knees to touch, but he didn't seem to mind. "Did you have bad teachers while growing up?"

His tone held a note of incredulity. Obviously, he assumed her wealthy parents had provided her with a reasonable education, and they did. But that's not what she meant.

"I attended private school, and my teachers were all exemplary, but when money is involved, they tend to look the other way." And they did. All the time. "Like when a student misses classes to attend beauty pageants or is spending more hours taking ballet lessons than studying, you would think a teacher might intervene, right?"

"They didn't?"

"Nope." The word popped in her mouth, but he didn't smile.

"I assume the ballet and beauty pageants refer to you?"

She nodded. "It was a constant in my life until college."

And even then, her mother had tried to force her into the adult pageants. However, after Lizzie turned eighteen, she exercised her legal right to refuse. But she never quit dancing. Not completely, anyway. She attended classes for fun now whenever she had time, which wasn't much lately.

His brown gaze roamed over her, and he smiled. "I bet you won often."

She didn't return his amusement. "Occasionally." And when she didn't, her mother never let her hear the end of it. She studied her hands and sighed. "I went into teaching to help children like me, to help those who might be suffering from emotional or physical abuse." Because that's what it was, even if her mother would never admit it.

He lifted her chin with his thumb and stared deep into her eyes. "I think that's very admirable, Elizabeth. And I'm sorry."

She blinked. "For what?"

"For making a joke of something that clearly pains you so deeply, and that you had to go through that. Childhood is the time for fun and games, though I know from experience that's not always the case." He traced her jaw with his fingertip before extending his arm behind her again and relaxing. "My parents, or rather, my father, had certain expectations for me as well. Needless to say, I didn't abide by his wishes."

"But you're obviously doing well for yourself," Lizzie replied. If he could afford a condo in her building, then he wasn't horribly off. Unless his father bought it for him, too, something she highly doubted.

"Oh, I'm definitely doing okay without him, perhaps even in spite of him."

Jayson chuckled to himself and shook his head. "Hmm, I believe this is our stop?"

Lizzie smiled. "Still acclimating yourself?"

"It's a huge city."

"Uh-huh, and you still haven't told me where you're from originally."

He stood and held out his hand for hers, tugging her upward. "I think I'll keep it a secret for now, Red." He waggled his brows. "Gotta give you a reason to hang out with me again."

"Oh? You mean I'll have a choice?" she teased as they ascended the stairs. Next time they went out, she would remember her cardigan.

"You had a choice tonight," he reminded.

"I only agreed so you wouldn't barge into my condo again."

His arm fell over her shoulders as he yanked her into his side. Her palm went to his abdomen to keep from falling. His chuckle vibrated the arm she wrapped around his waist to steady herself. "I see the thanks I get for buying you pizza. Twice."

She tried really hard to focus on his words and not the rock-hard muscles bunching beneath her fingertips. Seeing them was one thing, but feeling them? Quite another.

He kept walking, and she hobbled along with him as she searched for her brain.

"Thank you?" She thought that's what he wanted her to say. Maybe. She really didn't know. Being this close to such a fine specimen of male short-circuited her thoughts. It was a miracle she didn't fall on her ass with these heels.

At least she wasn't cold anymore.

"That almost sounded believable, Red."

"Sorry?"

He laughed again and led the way to their building while she focused on remembering how to walk.

What the heck is wrong with me?

Stas always called Lizzie boy crazy because of her obsession with boyfriends and marriage, but a lot of it was said in jest. Lizzie wanted her best friend to be happy, while never really considering her own happiness because she always wanted Tom. Or she thought she did.

But Jayson left her questioning everything; the way she felt around him was decidedly different. Not love drunk, but happy and protected. And warm.

She barely acknowledged the night doorman and navigated the stairs in silence with Jayson right behind her. When she stopped at her floor, he waved her on, and she laughed.

"Oh, this is the part where you demand entry for dessert."

He grinned. "No, this is the part where I ensure you're safe before I go upstairs."

"Well, that's good, because I haven't baked in days."

"You bake?"

She turned to relax against her door and stared up at him. "I'll neither confirm nor deny my hobbies until you tell me where you're from."

"I see what you're doing." He leaned his forearm over her head, caging her between the door and his solid form. "If you bake me cookies, I'll tell you more about all the places I've lived."

"Why cookies?"

"Because Dennis tells me they're amazing."

Damn it. The doorman was giving away her secrets but she had to laugh. "He loves chocolate."

"I do too," Jayson murmured, holding her gaze. "But then again, I like a lot of things."

She swallowed, unsure how to respond to that. The innuendo in his tone left her breathless. Most men who stood this close to her only left her uncomfortable—including the ones who had kissed her—but something about Jayson was different. She experienced happiness with him, an emotion few people had ever evoked from her.

"I had fun tonight, Red."

"Me too." She swore her pulse was louder than her voice right now. It sounded like a drum in her ears.

Thud, thud, thud.

And she'd thought his music was obnoxious. Ha! She couldn't even think over this pounding.

"I'll text you after I get back from my trip next week, and we'll plan that concert. Or maybe a movie."

She nodded on autopilot, unsure what she was saying yes to exactly, but agreeing nonetheless.

His chuckle tickled her lips, sending tingles through every limb.

"Friends can kiss good night, right?" he asked as he brushed his mouth over hers.

Another nod, because no way could she argue with that logic.

His opposite hand lifted to cradle her cheek as he pressed his lips to hers in a firm but chaste kiss. He stepped back all too soon, leaving her dying for more, and his smoldering gaze suggested the feeling was mutual.

"Good night, Lizzie," he murmured. "Don't forget to lock up."

Right.

Door.

Somehow she managed to open it and mumble, "Good night."

That kiss left her quivering long after Jayson left.

She sat on the couch, staring at nothing and feeling everything.

It was as if he'd imprinted himself on her soul, which sounded ridiculous even to Lizzie. But his presence melted into her blood, leaving her a trembling mess of uncomfortable need.

Over a single kiss!

Not even Tom's hugs had made her stomach twist like this, nor had any of her previous experiences.

Friends can kiss good night, right?

Not like that, they don't.

I'm in so much trouble.

Chapter Five

A Game of Cups

> **Day eight without human food and subject's vitals fall within adequate levels. Next phase will include blood ingestion.**
>
> **—Entry Log 105.02.4-7**

Lizzie's skin crawled as she stepped into the elevator of the last building she wanted to be in right now. She much preferred her silent condo on a Sunday morning, but her mother would kill her if she skipped brunch.

Stas's hand found hers and gave it a gentle squeeze. "It's going to be okay, Liz."

"The last brunch wasn't," Lizzie muttered. Tom skipped several family brunches while he was deployed, but this one he had missed for an entirely different reason. One his father and her parents refused to talk about during their last brunch because it contradicted her mother's etiquette rules.

"Well, this one will be different," Stas promised. "Because I won't put up with the Evil Bitch's shit."

Lizzie's lips twitched. Her best friend had given her mother that nickname after their first meeting. "How did you convince Issac to come to this?" They had been an item for a few months, but he never attended previously.

"Doctor Fitzgerald asked him to attend."

"He did?"

"Yep. So you have at least two of us on your side, Liz. Because Issac won't tolerate Lillian's bullshit, either."

The elevator announced their arrival before Lizzie could reply. Issac Wakefield stood just outside the door, waiting for them in the lobby in one of his hand-tailored suits. Black on black today, which paired nicely with his dark chestnut hair and striking blue eyes. He didn't smile as they exited, but his gaze glimmered with satisfaction as it slid over Stas's navy dress and matching heels.

"Aya," he murmured as he tugged on one of her blonde strands of hair. "I missed you this morning." Stas brushed a kiss against his cheek and whispered something in his ear that caused his lips to curl upward.

They weren't outwardly touchy-feely, but a genuine love radiated between them. Not the fuzzy, quick-and-easy kind, but the soul-destroying, heart-wrenching kind. It almost hurt to watch. A connection like that didn't exist between normal people, and it certainly didn't apply to the older couple watching the exchange from the reception desk.

Lizzie's happiness died upon spotting her mother's overly done profile. The woman needed to loosen a few brown curls and maybe stop using eyeliner altogether. It seemed to have permanently damaged her face. Or maybe that was from the frown lines.

She appeared positively petite next to Lizzie's well-fed father. He wasn't necessarily overweight, just a little chubby in the belly, especially when compared to the lithe, blond male beside him.

Her chest ached to behold him. He resembled his son in every way, and it didn't help that he didn't look a day over forty despite having to be in his midfifties by now.

"Hello, Elizabeth," Issac greeted. His English accent gave her name a sexy appeal she didn't hear often. "How are you, love?"

She forced a smile. "I'm okay. You?"

"Eager to get this over with," he admitted quietly. "Shall we?"

His honesty was refreshing and just what she needed. She nodded.

Stas looped her arm through Lizzie's and took on the role of bodyguard as they approached the waiting party. Formal greetings followed despite everyone already knowing each other very well before they claimed their usual table near the windows.

Let the countdown to two o'clock begin.

~*~

Jayson's heart ached for Lizzie. Discomfort and sadness radiated from her as her mother whispered in her ear again.

Verbal poison.

Stas sat to her right, irritating Jayson even more. The woman should be in

Hydria, not at a brunch in the middle of Manhattan. Apparently, she'd worked out some sort of arrangement with Issac that Luc had begrudgingly approved.

But she seemed to be the only one keeping Lizzie from crying and also appeared to be as pissed off as Jayson. Her eyes were narrowed, and Issac's hand had disappeared beneath the table ten minutes ago in an attempt to either calm her down or, more likely, to prevent Stas from leaping over Lizzie and kicking Lillian's ass.

The two other men at the table seemed oblivious, or perhaps didn't care.

Jackasses.

Jayson wanted to introduce Lillian to the oversized windows by tossing her through the glass. Alas, he had work to do in the kitchen.

Issac's admirable ability to manipulate vision worked well in situations such as this. He could tap into everyone's visual receptors and alter reality, and he easily manipulated hundreds of people at a time. The Ichorian once likened it to a row of televisions, saying he merely selected the channel he wanted everyone to watch.

Centuries of experience had only perfected his craft.

Right now, it allowed Jayson to move freely through the dining room without anyone noticing him, including Lizzie.

The only one immune to the manipulation was Stas. She was marked with a rune of sorts that blocked Ichorian gifts. Whoever put it there and why remained a mystery, but it served as the reason the two lovebirds initially met.

Jayson slipped into the kitchen and followed the blonde waitress who had just taken the drink orders from Lizzie's table. He had arrived thirty minutes early with Issac to investigate the restaurant but found nothing useful. They decided on plan B, which included Jayson supervising every second of the meal and looking for anything out of the ordinary.

So far, nothing.

But their brunch had just begun.

The short waitress punched all the meals into the system, including Lizzie's green salad with no dressing and dry chicken breast.

That sounds horrible.

What happened to his pizza-loving redhead who enjoyed greasy pepperonis as much as he did?

Stas ordered two pasta dishes with extra garlic bread.

Nice.

Issac had chosen well.

Not that they had a future, but that wasn't for Jayson to worry about.

He trailed after the petite waitress to the refreshment station, where she poured five drinks. She pulled a phone from her pocket and typed one word.

Ready.

The response was immediate. *Here.*

She left the drinks unattended and wandered to the back entrance with an empty glass in hand. The solitary service elevator held her focus. Jayson hoped

Issac was seeing all this; otherwise, his cover would be blown as soon as the door opened.

He leaned his hip against the wall and left his hands loose in case he needed to fight. His affinity for metal would help, as would the knives tucked into his suit jacket.

The gentle *bing* sounded a second before the metal slates slid open to reveal a blond male with broad shoulders and a bored expression.

Sentinel Stark, Jayson recognized. He was Stas's primary trainer at the CRF.

The man's light green eyes flickered Jayson's way, but his lack of an outward reaction confirmed Issac's interventions.

Stark stepped forward with a glass of water in his hand.

"Hi, Stark," the waitress greeted.

"Bridget," he returned as they swapped items. "Your assistance is appreciated, as always."

She smiled. "It's not a very hard job."

He didn't return the smile as he moved backward into the still-open elevator. "See you in four weeks."

Jayson wanted to kick himself for missing this obvious connection. Stas had mentioned the brunches, but no one thought a damn thing of it.

He was still shaking his head when the blonde turned around, shrieked, and dropped the glass. It shattered into a bazillion pieces between them.

Apparently, Issac had decided now would be a good time to drop the visual charade.

Jackass, Jayson thought. His lack of a warning caused their best lead to explode all over the fucking floor. And now he had to deal with a hysterical woman. Because no way could he pretend to just be wandering around the employee-only area.

His instincts fired.

He grabbed her, placed his hand over her mouth, and pulled her into a corner mere seconds before two other employees rushed into the back area.

"What the hell?" A stocky male in a chef's hat eyed the broken glass and surroundings with annoyance. "Seriously, what the fuck?"

The brunette beside him scratched her long nose and glanced in Jayson's direction. Her lack of a reaction set his body at ease.

Thanks, Issac, he thought. Not that the Ichorian could hear him.

"Get a broom," the chef said. "Clean it up."

He didn't wait for a response as he left the back area.

"Asshole," the brunette muttered as she grabbed a mop and broom and proceeded to take her sweet-ass time picking up the sharp pieces.

All the while, the waitress in his arms tried futilely to escape, but Jayson wasn't a rookie at restraining a woman. He kept one arm locked around her middle, trapping her arms to her sides, and used his other hand to cover her mouth. Her legs flailed uselessly as he held her off the floor. She managed a few decent back heel kicks, but pain was an old friend.

By the time the pseudo janitor finished cleaning, the blonde was exhausted.

He waited a full minute before pushing out of the corner and carrying his ward with him to the door, where he closed and locked it quietly.

"Now." He rotated the blonde to face him and read the absolute terror etched into her expression. "I'm not going to hurt you, but I do need you to do me a favor."

Her eyebrows shot upward as tears streamed down her cheeks.

"Okay, let's get one thing straight," he continued. "Screaming will just result in my holding you captive again, and as you've, hopefully, already deduced, your coworkers won't see us. So I recommend you stay quiet and hear me out. Then you can scream later to your little heart's content. All right?"

He had her pinned up against the door with one forearm across her abdomen and the opposite keeping her silent with his palm. But she didn't appear to be fighting anymore. He took that as a good sign.

The horror radiating from her blue eyes, however, would remain for a while.

Humans didn't take well to learning about the supernatural. Her mind would supply her with a multitude of excuses for what just happened, none of which would be the obvious. Her reaction, though, answered at least one burning question.

She had no idea that Ichorians and Hydraians existed.

Which meant she knew nothing about the true nature of the CRF.

He slowly removed his palm from her mouth and waited for her to react. When she didn't scream, he dropped his hand and loosened his hold on her.

"Thank you," he said quietly, meaning it. She was obviously terrified, but intelligent as well. He could respect that. "Now, about my favor. I need you to call the man from the elevator and tell him you need another glass of whatever it is he brings you."

Her eyebrows inched upwards. "You… What?"

"Do you have any idea what's in that glass he gives you?"

She shook her head slowly.

"But you give it to the redhead, right? Every four weeks?"

Some of the color returned to her cheeks as she nodded.

"I assume they pay you," he continued.

Another nod.

"Great. I need you to text him and tell him you accidentally dropped the glass. And I want you to do it on speakerphone so I can listen."

"I… I…"

"Look, I don't exactly have a lot of time. And all I need is that simple phone call. Then I'll disappear." Afterward, she could tell whomever she wanted about him. With him distorting his features, she wouldn't be able to describe him, and the security feeds were already altered thanks to Mateo's intervention. All avenues were covered.

She swallowed but otherwise didn't move.

He took back his assessment regarding her astuteness. The shock had clearly fried some brain cells.

"Unlock your phone and hand it to me." He held out his palm, waiting.

Her hand shook as she complied.

Jayson scrolled through her text messages from Stark and reviewed some of their previous exchanges to understand their usual cadence. Short and to the point. He could do that.

I accidentally dropped the glass. What should I do?

"I suspect he's going to call." And likely not be very pleasant. "I need you to talk to him. Mention me, and you won't like the consequences. Understood?"

She gave him a short nod as the color drained from her cheeks again.

Jayson knew he could evoke fear when he wanted to, but this was just ridiculous. Aside from holding her still, he'd done nothing menacing. It was the Sentinel she should worry about.

The phone rang within seconds, flashing with the name: Agent Stark.

Well, here we go.

Either she helped or she didn't.

Jayson selected the Talk button and raised an eyebrow at her.

"H-hello?" Her nerves were expected and appropriate. Stark would assume she was startled by dropping the glass and worried about his reaction.

"You dropped the glass," he repeated emotionlessly.

"I… I tr-tripped."

"Indeed."

"I-I'm sorry."

"That I believe," Stark replied. "Obviously, you won't be paid this month."

Tears welled in her eyes. "C-can't you just b-bring me another one?"

"No." His flat reply reverberated through the room and was followed by a click as Stark ended the call.

Bridget cast big doe eyes up at Jayson. Clearly, she expected the worst from him and he couldn't necessarily blame her.

"Excellent. See, that wasn't so hard, right?" He pushed away from her and waved a hand at the door. "You're welcome to go."

"Th-that's it?"

"I told you I just wanted a favor."

She frowned. "You meant it?"

"I try to keep my word when I can," he replied as he punched the service elevator button. "Oh, but a piece of advice. Find a new job and change your number."

"What? Why?"

"Because Stark? He's bad news. When he grows tired of you, you'll be replaced. And I don't mean fired." He stepped into the elevator as it opened. "Have a good afternoon." He gave her a salute before pressing the button to take him down to the ground floor.

His phone slipped into his hand as the doors closed, and he had it at his ear a second later.

Jacque answered on the first ring. "'Sup?"

Jayson loved military technology, and that adoration extended to telecommunications.

Hence his perfect signal inside the metal box.

"I need a teleport," he said.

"From the coordinates you sent me?"

"Yep." Jayson anticipated something might go wrong, and it never hurt to have a backup plan.

"Peace." The phone went dead.

Jayson shot a text off to Issac while he waited for the elevator to continue descending. *Heading to Hydria for a debrief.*

Regroup at 16:30, was the reply as the doors opened.

Jacque stood in the building's lobby, leaning against a column with his hands in his jeans. His rock band shirt and floppy black hair brought a smile to Jayson's face.

Home.

~*~

Lizzie looked at the clock for the thousandth time.

Brunch should have ended thirty minutes ago, but thanks to their waitress's disappearing act, they had just finished eating.

Lizzie handed her half-eaten salad off to their replacement waiter and folded her hands in her lap. Her mother had commented three times so far on Lizzie's choice to wear black.

Such an unflattering color on you.

Why would you wear black with your red hair, considering that it's so close to Halloween?

Really, Elizabeth, it's like you're in mourning.

Lizzie wanted nothing more than to shove a fork down her mother's throat.

But she remained proper, quiet, and hyperfocused on the flower arrangement in the middle of the table.

Stas squeezed her thigh, grabbing her attention. "How do you feel about Friday night, Lizzie?"

Uh… "As in this Friday?"

Stas nodded. "Is that enough time to prepare for a dinner party?"

Lizzie's eyebrows inched up. She'd clearly missed an important conversation. "Depends on what you want to eat." *And who I'm feeding?*

"I've always enjoyed your cooking," Doctor Fitzgerald replied.

"Likewise," Issac murmured. "Is there anything your Sentinel won't eat?"

Which Sentinel?

Doctor Fitzgerald shrugged. "I'm certain whatever Lizzie decides will satisfy him."

"Sentinel Stark," Stas whispered while Issac and Doctor Fitzgerald discussed a time. "They want to come over for dinner Friday."

"Why?" Lizzie whispered back.

Stas shrugged. "I don't know. Doctor Fitzgerald received a call and inquired about dinner afterward, saying Stark wants to meet you."

"Why?" Lizzie repeated.

"Probably because I've told him so much about you, or maybe he wants to come over and beat me some more," Stas muttered.

"It's quite rude to whisper at the table when dining with company," Lizzie's mother stated loudly.

"Really? Because you seem quite fond of whispering things in Lizzie's ear," Stas snapped back.

Oh no.

Her mother locked gazes with Stas, but before she could say a word, Issac spoke up.

"Does seven work for you, Elizabeth? Or will you require more time for a party of five?"

So my parents won't be attending. Good. Not that she really wanted company anyway, but she could tolerate an evening with Stas and her coworkers.

"Seven is fine," she replied.

Lizzie loved to cook, but lately, she hadn't wanted to be anywhere near her kitchen. Even to bake cookies. Which was the primary reason she had yet to deliver chocolate sweets to Jayson.

That and the fact that he hadn't bothered to text her once since their non-date five days ago. And now he was traveling, so who knew when or if she'd see him again.

Just friends, she repeated for the millionth time.

He owed her nothing, and she barely even liked him anyway.

So what if she had dreamt of him every night this week.

She was just lonely.

That kiss hadn't meant much, either. Her lips may have tingled for an hour afterward, but that was because she hadn't kissed anyone in over a year. Of course she reacted to it.

"Lizzie," Stas murmured. "Is everything okay?"

"I'm fine." The phrase rolled easily off her tongue, just as it did every time someone asked how she was feeling.

Because it was the expected reply.

The man I've been in love with for most of my life just died, but I'm fine.

My mother enjoys battering my self-confidence, but I'm fine.

You just invited the man who resembles the dead love of my life over to dinner Friday night, but I'm fine.

My best friend has decided to work for the very company that ruined my childhood and killed Tom, but I'm fine.

Our new neighbor kissed me and never called me afterward, but I'm fine.

Fine.

A lie.

Lizzie most definitely wasn't fine.
And she hadn't been for a very long time.
"I'm fine," she repeated for good measure.
Because if she said it enough, she'd believe it.
Someday.

Chapter Six

When a Ghost Invites Himself to Coffee

> The benefactor's associate who supervised today's experiment suggested the subject's social training be expanded. We're taking it under advisement.
>
> —Entry Log 109.04.4-7

He missed her.

He shouldn't.

It was ridiculous.

But he did.

Jayson flipped his phone around a few times in his hand, debating. What could it hurt to pay her a short visit? Say hello?

They were neighbors.

Friends, even.

I kissed her.

Though he could hardly call it a kiss. B would send him to sexual therapy for considering it anything other than a platonic gesture.

Jayson didn't chastely kiss women. He devoured them.

So this hardly counted. No rules broken; forbidden ribbon intact.

One week since he'd last spoken to Lizzie. He protected her every day, but she didn't know, nor did she have a clue he'd been at the restaurant two days ago.

Her forlorn expression that morning still killed him. He usually ran in the opposite direction at the first sign of emotion from males and females, but her heartache called to him on a level he didn't know existed.

"Shit," he muttered, standing.

He needed a good run.

Or a fuck.

Maybe both.

The celibacy was screwing with his head. He never went long without sex. Jayson enjoyed all varieties, types, positions, and kink. Had even shared women with men and vice versa.

Three thousand years was a long time to be alive not to vary it up every now and then.

A knock at his door had him springing up off the couch, hopeful that a certain redhead had come up to say hello. Instead, he found Ezekiel leaning against his doorjamb, looking bored. He didn't ask to come inside. He just stood there, legs crossed casually at the ankles, black eyes gleaming.

"You want to get a drink?" he asked, surprising the shit out of Jayson.

"Is that an innuendo for something?"

Ezekiel flashed a row of perfect teeth at him in his version of a smile. "No, not tonight."

"Let me change." Jayson left the door open while he retreated to the bedroom to don a pair of jeans, a sweater, and several knives. When he returned, he found Ezekiel in the same spot by the door. "If you try to kill me, you'll fail."

The Ichorian shrugged as if to say, *Perhaps.*

Jayson locked up his condo and followed the leather-jacket-wearing assassin down the hall and stairs. The fact that he presented his back to Jayson was a sign of trust, a way of returning the favor for agreeing to the impromptu drink rather than slamming the door in the man's face.

"How is your wooing of the sexy redhead going?" Ezekiel asked casually as they walked.

"I'm not wooing her."

"Oh, I agree it's not going as expected," the Ichorian replied, nodding. "A pity after that pizza date in Brooklyn went so well. Perhaps you should try calling the woman more? I hear they like that."

Jayson resisted the sudden urge to drive a blade down the other man's throat and focused on keeping his voice calm. "I had no idea you were so bored, Zeke." *Or that you followed us to Brooklyn.*

How could he keep Lizzie safe if he didn't even sense a lethal assassin trailing their every move?

"More like *curious.*" Ezekiel flashed another one of those terrifying grins. "Still, what gives? Why woo her one night and ignore her the next? That sounds like a woman's game."

"I'm not trying to woo her," Jayson said again.

"Right you are, Jay. Because you're doing a shit job of it." Ezekiel shook his head as he stopped in front of a coffee place only a few blocks from the condo. "Shall I show you how it's done?"

Over my dead body.

Jayson swallowed his desire to throttle Zeke and redirected the conversation. "When you said you wanted a drink, I thought you meant at a bar."

"This is a bar of sorts. They just happen to serve coffee."

Suspicion tightened his chest. He may have lost touch with the Ichorian over the centuries, but he knew the assassin's proclivities did not include relaxing in casual locations.

"What are we really doing here, Zeke?"

"Playing," he replied as he opened the door. "After you."

This isn't going to end well.

And that thought was confirmed when he spied Stas and Lizzie sitting on a couch across from the entrance. Big brown eyes met his, widened, then narrowed.

"Ah yes, she's sour with you indeed." Ezekiel nudged Jayson's arm. "Let's see if I can't help fix it?" The Ichorian started toward the duo with a confident swagger.

Fuck.

He knew Ezekiel had a game in mind, but he didn't expect this one. It took all manner of control to keep a straight face as he trailed behind the sadistic assassin. Lizzie's glower didn't help, and neither did the concerned expression on Stas's face as she glanced up from her coffee mug.

"Jayson?" Lizzie asked, her expression confused and tinged with hurt. "I thought you were traveling on business."

"We were," Ezekiel replied before Jayson could utter a word. "We just returned this evening and were searching for a place to have a drink when Jayson saw you inside." He gestured to the giant glass windows overlooking Broadway.

Well, at least he didn't call me Jedrick.

Lizzie peered at Ezekiel, her eyebrows inching up slightly. "You're coworkers?"

"More like business rivals," the assassin replied smoothly and extended a hand. "I'm Kiel, by the way."

She pinched her lips to the side, but manners won as she accepted his gesture and shook his hand. "Lizzie."

"I know," Ezekiel replied. "Jayson won't stop talking about you."

Wow.

If Jayson didn't want to kill him before, he did now.

"When he saw you from outside, he suggested we ask to join you, but now he's being shy." He tsked. "It's very unlike him. I daresay your beauty has tied him up in knots. Scared him speechless, hmm?"

Oh, for fuck's sake. He'd painted Jayson as a pansy. A knife between those black eyes would make for a fantastic facial ornament. Maybe he'd add another to the man's groin. Ezekiel always did fancy metal decor, hence the random lip piercing.

"What Kiel is trying to say is that we're here for a cup of coffee and will be leaving you alone in a minute." Jayson gestured to the counter, but of course, Zeke didn't move.

"Oh, but you've told me so much about her. I want to learn more. You wouldn't mind if we joined you for a bit, would you?" Ezekiel's placating tone made Jayson's skin crawl.

Damn it.

Say no, Red.

"Uh…" Lizzie looked to Stas for approval, but the blonde was focused on Ezekiel's profile. "I mean… I think that's okay?" She seemed to be waiting for Stas to speak up, but her lips were firmly closed, her attention on the leather-clad Ichorian.

Could she sense the lethal air surrounding Ezekiel?

All the Hydraian Elders wanted Stas out of the city. It was dangerous, but she ignored their wishes. Would this finally force her to see reason? Not exactly his preferred method, but fear could be one hell of a motivator.

"Excellent," Ezekiel murmured. He relaxed onto the couch cushion catty-cornered to Lizzie. "Get us a round, yeah?"

Jayson folded his arms, unamused. "It's not a pub, Kiel."

"Right. I'll take a cappuccino."

His eyebrows inched upward. "And I'm paying?"

"Obviously." Ezekiel turned to Lizzie and Stas. "Would you ladies like anything?" He eyed Stas's mug. "Perhaps another latte, darling?"

Her knuckles went white around the ceramic as she met his gaze. And all the color drained from her face.

No response.

Lizzie frowned at her friend before gazing up at Jayson. "I'm okay, thank you."

"I say, are you all right?" Ezekiel asked, his tone holding a touch of amusement as he studied Stas. "You look like you've seen a ghost."

She cleared her throat. "No. Sorry." She stood suddenly. "I'm just going to grab a water."

"Jayson can do that for you," Ezekiel offered.

"I'm good," Stas said, waving him off. "I'll be right back."

Lizzie frowned after Stas as she walked stiffly over to the counter.

"You should go with her, Jay," Ezekiel encouraged. "Order our drinks."

Jayson narrowed his gaze. *If you touch her, I will kill you.*

Isn't this fun? Ezekiel seemed to reply. "Go ahead. I promise not to bite or misbehave while you're away." He flashed a conspiratorial glance at Lizzie. "He's terribly overprotective."

Funny, Jayson thought, irritated. "I'll be right over there." He spoke the words for Lizzie alone. One scream and he would be here.

"Okay," she replied, her brow furrowed. She likely thought he was insane. Not for the first time, Jayson wished Lizzie knew the truth.

He kept her in his periphery as he moved through the coffee shop and flinched when Ezekiel made her laugh.

No way would this end well.

Nails bit into his bicep through his sweater, distracting him from his mission, and he met a pair of terrified green eyes. His arm slipped around Stas's shoulders on instinct as he maneuvered her out of sight of Lizzie and Ezekiel.

"What's wrong?" he whispered.

She clutched her phone to her chest as if it were her only armor.

"Talk to me, sweetheart," he said, voice low. No one had noticed the strange embrace yet, but it was only a matter of time.

"He… That man…" She shuddered and pressed her forehead to his chest. If Lizzie saw this, their cover would be blown. Jayson wasn't supposed to know Stas.

Ezekiel oozed a lethal air that she'd obviously picked up on, and he was particularly deadly to her as a Nizari assassin. "You recognize him."

She nodded vigorously.

"Because Issac gave you his description, or is it a sense?" he asked, curious. Fledglings were so rare these days that their innate abilities remained a bit of a mystery, and Stas was far from typical.

"No." The single word sounded so broken he had to pull her away to study her face.

Tears, horror, and such deep sorrow.

"Okay, I really need you to talk to me, Stas." This woman had faced other immortals with similar dispositions without reacting like this. She had survived a Conclave, for crying out loud. A Nizari assassin should scare her, but this went beyond fear.

She hiccuped. "Jay…" She squeezed her eyes closed and took a deep breath. "That…" Another breath. "That's the Ichorian who killed my parents."

~*~

"So, you work in acquisitions?" Lizzie asked, curious. Kiel's long black hair, lip piercing, and leather jacket appeared more rocker than businessman.

He smirked. "I do, yes. For a rival company of sorts."

"But you're friends?"

"Yes, I suppose we are, in a manner of speaking." He crossed one leg over the other and relaxed against the arm of the couch. "You could say we have a long history."

"Did you go to school together?" she asked.

"We trained together, yes."

That was an odd way to phrase it, but most of his mannerisms and phrases were different. So was his accent. "Where are you from?"

He chuckled. "That's a complicated question. Define *from*."

"Uh, like where you were born?"

"Babylon," he replied, not missing a beat.

She blinked at the too-familiar name. "Like the ancient city?"

"The very one. And you?"

"Okay, but hold on, are you saying you're from the actual city of Babylon, as in the area from, what was it, the Mesopotamia period?" Lizzie didn't major in history, but that sounded right. "Or do you mean a city called Babylon?"

He leaned closer to her, his black eyes smoldering with gold embers. "What do you think?"

"That you clearly mean a city named after Babylon." His pale skin suggested northern roots, and no one would refer to that area in the Middle East as Babylon. They would call it Iraq, or whatever city it was now called in that country.

"Sure." He smiled. "And where were you born?"

"New York City."

"Are you sure about that?" he asked.

She stared at him. "Yes."

He nodded. "I see. Fascinating. And you've lived here your very short life?"

Another odd phrase, but she went with it. "Yes, in Manhattan."

"Do you ever tire of it?" he asked, those hypnotic eyes captivating hers. She wouldn't call him handsome as she would Jayson, but sexy, in a very dark way.

"Sometimes," she admitted, recalling his question. "But I don't know where else I would live."

"Greece, I imagine." Another quick reply that left her baffled.

Of all places to mention… "Why Greece?"

His Cheshire-cat grin reminded her of the devil. Alluring, yet evil. But whatever he planned to say was silenced by Jayson setting a tray of cups down rather loudly on the end table between their couches.

"Cappuccino," he said flatly.

"Brilliant. Thanks, mate." Kiel plucked it off the tray and took a sip. His nose wrinkled, but he didn't comment.

Lizzie glanced at the counter for Stas but didn't see her.

"Your friend is making a phone call," Jayson explained as he took Stas's vacated seat beside Lizzie. "She introduced herself then asked me to let you know. Something about work."

Of course. The CRF owned her best friend's soul now. "I see. Kiel was just telling me I should move to Greece."

"Was he?" Jayson murmured. "Well, it is a beautiful country with fantastic weather and the islands are nice, but I'm not sure why Kiel would recommend it. I don't believe he's been there often."

His friend peeked at them over his coffee cup. "Oh, I've been there more than you realize."

"I bet." Jayson reached over Lizzie for his own coffee mug, brushing her breasts in the process.

A surge of heat crept up her neck, stemming from her hardening nipples.

Crap. Her thin, lacy bra and violet dress wouldn't hide the reaction well. *Maybe he will think I'm cold.*

Or not notice at all.

He didn't show any outward reaction as he balanced the mug against his thigh with one hand. "How was your week, Red?"

"Uh, fine." *Boring. Long. Sad. Lonely.* When did it get so hot in here? She cleared her throat and searched for a safe topic. "How was your business trip?"

"There was a minor break in the plan, but I think we're close to finishing up our project."

Kiel leaned forward with interest. "And what project is that, Jay?"

"None of your business, Kiel."

"Oh, if only that were true," he replied with a twist of his lips. He finished his cappuccino and set it on the table. "That was mediocre at best."

"Grabbing a drink was your idea."

"Yes, yes, it was." The lean man stood and stretched long arms over his head before sighing. "I think I may go scout for a proper drink elsewhere. I assume you would prefer to stay here?"

"The company is significantly better," Jayson replied. "So, yes."

"You wound me, old friend." Kiel didn't appear wounded at all, just amused. "Please tell your friend I'm sorry we didn't get to properly meet. Perhaps next time. I'll try not to appear so ghostly."

Lizzie's brow furrowed. "I'm not clear on what that was about, but I'm sure she'll be happy to meet you at some point." Not that she had any idea when that would be or if she would ever see this eccentric man again.

"Oh, I doubt that, but time will tell," he replied cryptically. "Jay, as always, a pleasure. Stay sharp, yeah?"

Jayson rested his arm across the back of the couch, behind Lizzie's head, and gave his friend a meaningful look that she couldn't interpret.

"Likewise, Z," Jayson said.

"Cheers, Jay," Kiel murmured. "Lovely to meet you, Lizzie. I'll see you again soon."

"Uh, nice to meet you too." *And when*?

He winked and sauntered toward the exit without a backward glance.

"Jay," Lizzie repeated after the man disappeared through the door. "Is that your nickname?"

"Yeah, most people call me Jay." With one hand, he swirled the coffee in his mug against his thigh while his other arm remained stretched out behind her head. "Of all my friends for you to meet, that's not the one I would have chosen to introduce you to first, or even last."

"Why not?"

Jayson focused on his cup as if it held all the answers. "Let's just say, he's bad news."

She nodded in understanding. That much she had gathered from his demeanor, though there was a charm to him as well. "He's certainly different."

"That's an understatement." He sipped his coffee with a grimace and set it on the table. "I hate to agree with Kiel, but that's crap."

Lizzie grinned. "Is the coffee in Greece better?"

"It is."

"Which you know because you've lived there?" She kept the question light and innocent, not letting on to how much she truly wanted the answer.

But he saw right through it.

"Oh, Red." His arm fell to her shoulders as he leaned into her personal space. "I believe you owe me cookies first."

"I didn't know when you would be back." A sad excuse since she never intended to bake them anyway, but he didn't know that.

"Uh-huh. You could have called to ask."

"And you could have texted me at any point to say hello, but you didn't."

His chuckle was low and sexy, and far too intimate. "So what you're saying is, if I want cookies, I need to message you?"

She swallowed, her mouth dry. Somehow this man had turned baking into a seductive topic. Visions of him drizzled in chocolate swept through her mind. *Yes, please.*

But the clearing of a throat interrupted the moment.

Issac stood in front of them with his arm around Stas. They both wore matching expressions of disapproval.

"Uh, hi, Issac."

"Elizabeth," he returned. "Introduce me to your friend."

She bristled at the demand in his tone. "Introduce yourself."

"Fine." He stared straight at Jayson. "Issac Wakefield."

"Jayson Masters," her *friend* replied with an easy smile. He didn't remove his arm from her shoulders but did shift slightly to give her more space. "You seem uptight. Maybe you need to sit down."

"Funny," Issac replied. "I was about to escort Aya back to her flat. You should join us."

Jayson chuckled. "Yes, sir."

"What if we're not ready to leave?" Lizzie snapped, irritated. She didn't know what the hell had gotten into Issac or why her best friend wasn't calling him on his bullshit, but Lizzie wouldn't stand for it. Billionaire or not, he couldn't tell her what to do.

"It's okay, Red," Jayson murmured. "We can go."

"Please, Liz," Stas said. "Can we hang out at the condo? I need something stronger than a coffee."

Lizzie noted the puffy circles beneath her best friend's eyes and the slight redness to her cheeks. Almost as if she'd been crying. "Did something happen?"

"Nothing I can't handle, but I would feel better at home." Stas gave her a pleading look, one she rarely used.

Girl code took over.

If Stas needed to go home, for whatever reason, Lizzie would agree. And she wouldn't ask questions. She learned a long time ago that they rolled right off Stas. Her best friend was the type to open up, but only when ready.

"Sure," Lizzie said. "Yeah, we can go."

Jayson stood first and held out his hand for Lizzie to help her up. She didn't really need it, but she accepted anyway. When he didn't let go and linked their fingers together, her heart skipped a beat. Issac's glower at the obvious display of affection only worsened the effect.

They were friends.

But not.

Or more?

Would he kiss her again?

Probably not with Issac giving him that glower.

Just stop.

Jayson squeezed her hand as they walked in silence, and she looked up to find him grinning. "You still owe me cookies."

She returned the smile. "Only if you tell me about Greece."

"Deal."

Stas halted on the sidewalk in front of them but didn't turn around. "What about Greece?" she asked, her voice thick with emotion.

Lizzie frowned. "Uh, Jayson used to live there. Even though he won't admit it."

"Kiel, an old associate of mine, implied it, but I've neither confirmed nor denied it."

"He used to live there," Lizzie confirmed. "He's just playing hard to get because he wants me to bake for him."

Jayson dropped her hand and wrapped his arm around her shoulders, pulling her close. "You're trouble, Red."

"You both are," Issac interjected. "In trouble, I mean."

"You really need to relax, Wakefield." Jayson gave him a pointed look. "Keep walking. We're right behind you."

"Leave it alone." Stas nudged Issac onward. "It'll work itself out."

"Oh, something will be worked out," Issac replied, causing Jayson to chuckle.

"I don't know why he's acting like that," Lizzie whispered up at him. "He's usually a lot more pleasant."

"He's protective," Jayson whispered back. "But don't worry, Red. He doesn't scare me." His easy smile left in the next moment as he tripped and let out a curse.

Issac caught Jayson by the arm as he started to fall. "Easy there, mate," he said, his voice holding an edge to it. "Pavement can be tricky."

"You know what else is tricky?" Jayson breathed. "Metal."

Issac flinched. "Noted."

"Escort us home," Stas demanded. "Now."

Issac's resulting smile reached his eyes. "Certainly, Aya."

Jayson didn't seem to be nearly as amused, but he laid his arm across Lizzie's shoulders and started walking again. It felt colder and less intimate, and he didn't look at her again.

His behavior baffled her. He seemed to be attracted to her, or so her minimal experience with men suggested, but he also treated her as only a friend. Like Tom did.

But Tom never kissed her on the lips, only on the cheeks.

Except Jayson hadn't truly kissed her, either, not in the passionate way a man who desired a woman would, anyway.

It was chaste and friendly.

Why is this so complicated?

The doorman of the building greeted them all by name. Lizzie smiled but said nothing as Jayson led her to the stairwell and up to their door.

"I think Issac and Stas can take it from here," he said softly.

"You don't need to go." The needy note in her voice left a sour taste in her stomach. Was she that starved for attention that she had to beg? Ouch.

"It's okay, Red. We'll catch up later over cookies." He brushed a kiss against her temple. "Chocolate, please." He pulled back with a wink. "Talk to you soon, Liz."

"Chocolate," she repeated. Right. She swallowed the lump in her throat. "Okay. Night."

His leaving shouldn't have bothered her as much as it did, but she had finally enjoyed herself a little, only to have it ripped away like everything else in her life. A few stolen moments of flirtatious words and laughs

Was that all she could expect? Or would there ever be more?

As he walked off toward the stairs, she worried she would never know.

A melancholy thought, but if she had learned anything over the last few months, it was that life was short.

The next time she saw Jayson, she would tell him how she felt because she refused to make the same mistake with him as she had with Tom. He died not knowing she loved him, and though she may not love Jayson yet, she didn't want to risk not telling him that she liked him. Perhaps even more than a friend.

She stepped through the open door and locked it behind her.

"I'll be in my room if you need me," she said to the couple standing inside the foyer.

"Liz…"

"It's okay, Stas. Enjoy your time with Issac." She gave them both a small smile before leaving them to their own devices. At least her best friend was happy. She deserved it more than anyone Lizzie knew, even herself.

CHAPTER SEVEN

Secrets and Lies

> **Subject has formed an emotional attachment with her new roommate in a very brief period, suggesting future memory protocols may require minor altering.**
>
> **—Entry Log 118.10.4-7**

Stas collapsed against Issac, her heart breaking for so many reasons.

"Not here," he whispered against her ear, reminding her of the surveillance in the condo. He led her into the hallway without a word, guiding her to who knew where. She barely registered him locking the door.

She hated everything.

The CRF.

This world.

Fate.

The monster who killed her parents.

Issac's arms held her upright as her legs buckled beneath her. Just as he'd done outside the coffeehouse. He'd arrived within minutes of her call, indicating his nearby presence. It should have infuriated her that he felt the need to babysit her, but she'd never been more thankful for his unwavering protection than she was tonight.

And he was right. Staying in the city was a suicide mission. But she couldn't leave Lizzie. Especially not with an assassin lurking around the corner.

She shuddered. It'd taken all her strength to walk back into that coffeehouse for Lizzie. But by the time they returned, the man who stalked Stas's memories was gone. She'd tried to put on a smile for Lizzie's sake, but it felt false. Wrong.

He's real.

And he was not only the villain of her past but also the one who wanted to destroy her future.

"Aya," Issac murmured, bringing her to the present. They were standing in the stairwell, locked in an embrace she never wanted to leave. Ever. "Lucian has requested a meeting."

"About...?" She couldn't finish, couldn't say *his* name.

Understanding flashed in his midnight gaze. "Ezekiel."

She swallowed and forced a nod.

"In Hydria," he added. "Jacque is coming to retrieve us."

She nodded again, unable to speak. The terror she felt tonight... She shivered and hugged Issac tighter.

He'd been right.

She was no match for the assassin. He would rip her to shreds, and enjoy it.

That smile... Oh God, that smile...

Issac pressed his lips to her temple and rubbed her back. She knew what he wanted to say. *It's time.*

She agreed but couldn't leave Lizzie behind. "What about Liz?" They couldn't run off to Hydria and leave her unprotected.

"Jayson has requested one of his Guardians watch over her while we are meeting with Luc. Jacque is dropping her off right now."

"Oh."

From what Stas understood, the strongest Hydraians were part of the Elders' personal security teams. Jayson had requested his remain in Greece due to the threat of Ichorians in the city and him being the only one capable of concealing his identity. That he and the others felt it necessary to send someone in his absence spoke volumes about how they perceived Lizzie. They wanted to protect her too.

That small insight helped calm some of her nerves.

They really do care.

"'Sup," a deep voice greeted from behind them. Stas had gotten to know the teleporter well over the last few months and usually grinned upon seeing him. But not tonight.

"Hello, Jacque," Issac murmured as one of his hands left her back. "Thank you for the lift."

"Anytime."

The world shifted around them, churning Stas's stomach as her scenery changed. Issac released her from his hold, allowing her to gain her own footing. Then she turned to face several familiar immortals, all of whom were seated at a long wooden table. No drinks or food. No games. Only stern expressions, a whiteboard, several computers at the back wall, and a basket of phones.

It seemed to be the Hydraians' equivalent of a war room.

"Stas. Wakefield," Luc greeted from the head of the table. "Have a seat."

"Lucian," Issac replied as he pulled out a chair for Stas. "Have you called Aidan?" He settled into the seat beside her and laid an arm over her shoulders. So casual, yet so meaningful. A sign of partnership and care, and one she desperately needed right now.

"Yes, I conferred with him earlier," Luc said. "He feels Ezekiel is playing a game of strategy and is very much aware of Stas's bloodline."

"That is my opinion as well," Issac murmured, his thumb drawing a pattern against her upper arm. "Did he have a recommendation?"

~*~

"He thinks we should play along," Jayson informed them, irritated. Aidan had clearly lost his damn mind. Engaging Ezekiel in a game was the last thing any sane person would ever do. "I happen to disagree."

"What were Aidan's reasons?" Issac asked, his expression blank.

"Put simply, we need more information." Luc scratched his jaw. "Our best course of action is to continue gathering intelligence while Elizabeth remains ignorant, and as it seems Ezekiel has no intention to harm her—"

"Yet," Jayson added, unable to help himself. He understood the assassin better than anyone at this table, not that they were listening to him.

Luc blinked those all-knowing eyes at him, an indication that he was in full omniscient mode. "Ezekiel's penchant for violence is renowned, yet he chose to carry on a conversation with Elizabeth instead of killing her for sport. I would love to know why, wouldn't you?"

Stas cleared her throat. "Honestly, no, I don't really want to know why." Her voice seemed softer than normal, almost hoarse, but her spine straightened with every word. "But I would like my best friend relocated and protected."

"We cannot protect her properly without the serum," Luc pointed out. "And without it, we risk killing her."

Stas's shoulders fell, causing Issac to pull her closer. His sapphire eyes went to Luc, communicating something only the two men seemed to understand. They shared a father, in a manner of speaking, anyway, which created a brotherly bond between them a few centuries back. It didn't quite rival the one Jayson, Luc, Alik, and Balthazar had formed over their thousands of years together, but the connection between Luc and Issac was one of loyalty, love, and family. And it showed now.

"We can't help Lizzie until we know what the CRF—my father—did to her," Tom said, his voice quiet. Normally, new Hydraians weren't allowed in these sorts of conversations, but his knowledge on the subject qualified him to be here.

Issac gave the man a measuring look and nodded. "I agree with Thomas. Taking Elizabeth now could put her at risk. We need more information regarding her origin before we proceed."

Jayson cursed inwardly.

Logic.

He knew that.

But their flawless reasoning did little to dispel his inner turmoil over the events of tonight. Although he agreed that they needed more details before liberating Lizzie from her situation, a growing part of him longed to tell her the truth.

The hurt in her gaze when he left her standing in the hallway nagged at him all the way upstairs. Had Jacque not been waiting in his condo, Jayson very likely would have ended up back at Lizzie's door, begging for a good-night kiss.

What the fuck is wrong with me?

Jayson didn't pine after women. He dated sporadically, but most of his dalliances were for a night or two only.

Yet this redhead had him all tied up in knots.

It was her innate goodness. After six weeks of observing her tender treatment of others less fortunate—like the homeless man she gave her lunch to that one day on the subway—Jayson couldn't help but feel a little for her.

And the nurturing relationships she'd formed with her students; even from afar, he could see their affection for her. Children were excellent judges of characters, and they adored her.

Because she's genuine.

He ran his fingers through his hair and looked at the ceiling as the memories rolled through his thoughts. All those beaming expressions directed at a woman who never expected them.

Fuck.

Lizzie deserved so much better than this.

He actually felt guilty for doing his job, which made little sense. It wasn't his responsibility to tell her the truth. That task belonged to Luc, Stas, and Tom. Jayson's purpose was to observe, report back, and protect as necessary.

Damn it.

Lizzie had to feel alone right now, and they were all to blame. Grace was in Jayson's condo right now, protecting Lizzie from above, but his Red had no way of knowing or understanding that.

But Luc and Issac were right.

They would need a safe place to take Lizzie after she learned the truth, which required a better understanding of her genetic makeup. "We need the serum," he muttered.

"Indeed," Issac agreed. "Which, I believe, is the purpose of our dinner Friday night."

Jayson nodded. Jonathan had requested the gathering at Lizzie's condo shortly after the fiasco at brunch; inviting Stark to tag along only confirmed the plans.

"But that requires Stas to go back to the city," Jayson added. "Where Ezekiel is likely to be very aware of her."

Silence as all eyes turned to the woman in question.

She cleared her throat as she straightened her shoulders again. "It's a necessary risk to help Lizzie. I'll be better prepared the next time I see him." Her tone lacked the usual confidence, indicating that—for the first time—she actually understood the danger she'd put herself in.

She's learning. Finally.

"Forgive my insensitivity," Luc murmured, his gaze on Stas. "But are you certain Ezekiel murdered your parents? I ask because his methods have always been quiet and reserved, not one of passion and mayhem. Yet, from my comprehension, your parents were burned alive. That strikes me as quite different from his usual methods."

She remained quiet, her shoulders and back still. After several beats, she nodded. "I'll never forget the way the flames glowed in his black eyes. It was him. I'm certain of it."

Luc's forehead crinkled in a way Jayson recognized after millennia of knowing one another. *Doubt.* The facts weren't adding up in that omniscient mind of his, leaving him puzzled, but he didn't question her further.

"I'm sorry, Stas. I can imagine this is painful for you, but it is the logical course. We will help Lizzie in due time. You have my word."

Stas would have no way of knowing just how powerful a statement that was coming from the leader of the Hydraian race, but Issac and Jayson understood. Luc had just made a blood vow of sorts, and he took those very seriously.

She said nothing, but Issac answered for her with a subtle nod of gratitude.

"It's settled," Luc murmured. "Dinner Friday night."

Jayson stretched his arms over his head. "Looks like we get to play another game of hide-and-seek, Wakefield."

Issac smirked. "My favorite."

"Try not to drop the charade too quickly this time," Jayson suggested, referring to the part where Issac let the waitress see him on Sunday without any warning.

"Perhaps you should try working on your reaction time," Issac replied.

Jayson shook his head and shifted his focus to Jacque. "I'm ready."

"Stay alive," Luc said as the teleporter appeared at Jayson's side, his hand at the ready.

Jayson nodded once in agreement. "Likewise."

CHAPTER EIGHT

Playing Hide-and-Seek

> **Project benefactor requested additional supplements be added to the subject's regimen. Observation required.**
>
> **—Entry Log 103.11.4-7**

Jayson threw a baseball up in the air, caught it on its way down, and repeated the action.

"Anything new?" he asked as Jacque paced beside the couch. It'd been a few days since they saw each other last.

The teleporter shrugged. "Amelia and Tom broke ground on their home over the weekend."

"Yeah?" Jayson grinned. "That's good. I'd like my house back when I return." It would require a thorough cleaning since the two lovebirds had used it as their own for the last few weeks, but at least they had put it to good use during his time away from the island.

The ball landed in his palm, and he lowered it to his stomach. He'd chosen to lie on the couch while he waited for Issac's call, but his legs were restless. Jonathan and Stark would be over any minute to enjoy Lizzie's company under a false promise of friendship. Similar, he supposed, to him asking her to go to dinner as a way to lure her from her condo. But while they wanted to drug her with some unknown substance, Jayson actually enjoyed her company.

Would she ever understand the difference?

Or would she hate him once she knew the truth?

He didn't want to be bothered by such trivial questions, but the notion of displeasing her unsettled him.

She's just a woman.

An attractive one he wanted to see naked, but that was par for the course with most females he met.

Except this one had gotten under his skin.

It's the guilt, he decided. Jayson prided himself on always telling the truth, and although he hadn't quite lied to her outright, he had withheld pertinent information.

To protect her.

"Okay, what gives?" Jacque demanded.

Jayson stopped throwing the ball. The teleporter stood beside his head, arms folded, silver eyes glinting. His uncharacteristically serious expression kept Jayson from cracking a joke at the man.

"What do you mean?"

"You're seriously distracted, Jay. I'm over here telling you about what Eliza did to Luc, while you're over there in la-la land thinking about fuck knows what." He started pacing again while studying his oversized watch.

"Uh…" Jayson didn't even realize the teleporter was talking. "Sorry." He sat up, planting his feet on the floor, and gave Jacque his undivided attention. "What's up?"

"No, that's my line. What's up with you?" He paused again and cocked his head to the side. "Is it the girl? Has she gotten to you?"

Jayson snorted. "No, nothing has gotten to me. It's an assignment like any other, except with a little added risk." He stretched his arms over his head and relaxed into the cushion behind him. "But I am feeling a little antsy being stuck here all day and night."

He rarely left the building as a safety precaution. If he did, it was to follow Lizzie to work and observe their surroundings. Not the most exciting pastime considering her steadfast routine.

Jacque nodded in understanding. "Why don't you go out tonight? After the task, I mean. Just go let loose for a while and have some fun. Stas can watch the chick downstairs. It's her roommate, after all. Right?"

Jayson rubbed a hand over his face. The thought had crossed his mind more than once to enjoy either a night in Hydria or one on the town. He needed to do something other than sit here in solitude. Working out only expelled so much stress from the body.

"I'll consider it," he muttered. His body craved the freedom—a night of bliss and pleasure, losing himself in a woman, without thinking…

It'd been too long since he felt that sweet relief. A few weeks he could manage, but two months without it was a record of sorts for him. At least in this century.

It would have to be a redhead.

Brown eyes.

Legs for days.

Enough curves to fill his hands.

He would of course think of her.

Wrong.

His fists clenched as a sense of responsibility overrode the desire thickening his blood.

You can't leave Lizzie.

And you can't have her, either.

His job was to learn more about her, but even more than that, he needed to protect her. One night, hell, one minute, could change everything.

Jayson's phone buzzed, giving him the distraction he needed to cease his internal debate. He would decide how to spend his evening after crashing the party downstairs.

"We're up," he said, standing.

The four of them worked out a plan earlier. Jacque would teleport Jayson to Stas's bedroom. Then Jayson would wander around the condo like he did at the restaurant with only Stas and Issac being able to see him. Once he gathered the information they needed, he'd meet Jacque in the bedroom again and return to his condo.

Easy.

He grabbed the teleporter's shoulder and braced himself for the tunneling sensation. It barely registered due to the small distance, unlike his longer trips to Hydria. Those were hell on his stomach. It beat flying any day of the week, though.

Jacque collapsed onto Stas's bed, jean clad legs crossing at the ankles as he pulled out his phone and tucked one arm behind his head. Apparently, that's how he planned to spend the next hour or so.

Jayson smirked and slipped out the partially open bedroom door. Voices trickled down the hall. From the sound of it, Jonathan and Issac were engaged in a conversation regarding the financial market.

Fascinating.

Jayson left those decisions to Luc. He was a mastermind with investment strategy. His funds alone could sustain all of Hydria for centuries, pending any unforeseen disasters.

Such as an Ichorian invasion or an attack from the CRF.

He paused on the threshold of the kitchen. One more step and the party in the dining room would be able to see him.

Wakefield better have brought his A game tonight.

Here goes nothing.

He stepped as quietly as possible onto the marble tile. Lizzie stood near the oven, waiting for the timer to sound, while everyone else was seated at the table.

No one looked at him.

Jonathan kept rambling on about business markets while Issac, Stas, and Stark listened. Jayson eyed the Sentinel dressed in jeans and a button-down.

He knew very little about the man other than Jonathan considered him a leader on the unit and Tom referred to him as a cold son of a bitch. That description seemed apt. Stark appeared neither amused nor interested in his superior's dialogue, but his stiff posture suggested he was alert and very aware of their surroundings.

Jayson lifted his arm up and down, waiting for a reaction.

None.

With a shrug he moved farther into the kitchen and admired Lizzie's bare legs. The dark red dress hugging her gorgeous form left him wishing he was here for other reasons.

She stilled, her nose twitching, as he silently moved behind her. He meant to take another step, but her reaction intrigued him.

"I'm losing it," she whispered to herself, eliciting a grin from Jayson.

She sensed him, or perhaps caught a whiff of his aftershave.

The recognition pleased him immensely, as did her tight dress. It clung to her curves in all the right places. His hands itched to explore every inch of her, but the oven's buzzer had him moving quickly to the counter beside the sink.

Stas started to stand, but Stark waved her off with a gruff "Allow me." He pushed away from the table with an air of authority and strode with purpose into the kitchen.

"How can I help?" he asked, his tone and expression emotionless.

"Umm…" Lizzie tugged that plump lip between her teeth, driving Jayson wild. He longed to complete this mission just so he could have the right to know her mouth. Even if for only a moment.

Dude, what the fuck is wrong with you?

He shook his head. Maybe he could ask Jacque or one of the Hydraian Guards to babysit Lizzie while he sought some necessary relief. Because this pining business needed to end.

Drooling over a woman like a dog over a bone.

Pull it together.

"Can you grab the salad and rolls?" She sounded so sweet and shy, her demeanor almost demure. The dominant in Jayson enjoyed this side of her, while the man in him craved the feisty woman underneath.

Where's my confident Red?

"Sure." Stark picked up the bowl and the basket beside it and took the items to the dining room. Lizzie trailed after him with what appeared to be homemade lasagna.

Jayson glared up at the ceiling.

He didn't believe in a deity, but he had to ask: *Did you create this woman just for me?*

Because, seriously, the woman boasted a body built for sin and enough intelligence to entertain him for days, and she loved food. If he believed in soul mates, he'd consider her his, but his thousands of years of experience kept him logical.

Love existed for very few, and even in those rare cases, it never lasted forever. Most people grew tired of each other after several years, decades if they were lucky. And Jayson's kind lived forever.

Immortals didn't do long-term romance, but he wasn't opposed to repeating sexual encounters. And with someone like Lizzie? Yeah, he could enjoy a few rounds with her.

She set the dish on the table and turned in to Stark's chest.

Jayson moved forward, ready to intervene, but logic froze him on his second step.

What the hell are you going to do? Yank him off of her?

He ran his fingers through his hair.

This mission was fucking with him in a bad way.

At this rate, he'd need Balthazar to take him out for the night. Maybe hit Rio again or jump up to Dublin. He needed a trio of redheads, at a minimum, to help cure this itch.

Shit.

This feeling would only grow worse as the mission continued, and he desperately needed his focus. A woman should not have him reacting against instincts. Ever.

He settled on his perch again and pulled out his phone to text Grace. *I need a night off when this thing with Wakefield is done. Arrange it and tell B.*

After ensuring his sound and vibrate features were off, he returned the device to his pocket and watched as Stark helped Lizzie into her seat. The touching really wasn't necessary. Surely she could manage sitting on her own.

"I haven't gotten the glass—"

"You've already done enough," the Sentinel interrupted. "I'll grab them with the drinks."

Drinks, huh? Jayson thought. *How convenient.*

"This looks amazing," Jonathan murmured, distracting her from replying as Stark pushed in her chair.

"Oh, uh, thank you," Lizzie replied, her attention falling to the notorious Ichorian. She would see the CEO of the CRF. All Jayson saw was a murderous traitor who had murdered Eli, one of Jayson's oldest and closest friends.

I'll kill you someday, Jonathan.

Stark's broad shoulders blocked Jayson's view, reminding him of his purpose. He relaxed his hands and arms, just in case he needed to fight.

The kitchen was large enough for an island but didn't have one. The oversized counters and open bar overlooking the dining area gave it an airy feel, yet Stark's presence consumed the space as he opened the fridge.

Danger poured off him, and not just because of the six metal blades Jayson sensed on him. It was in the way he moved, like he knew he was the most lethal predator in the room.

He retrieved a bottle of white wine from the fridge.

"Where do you keep the glasses?" he asked, his focus on Lizzie.

She pointed to the cabinet on the opposite side of the sink from Jayson. He considered moving but worried that even the slightest rustle of clothing would alert Stark to his presence.

The man seemed too attuned to his surroundings, as if he could feel things he shouldn't. Tom's report mentioned the possibility that Stark may have undergone CRF enhancements. From the way he acted, Jayson had to agree.

A row of wine glasses appeared, followed by Stark uncorking the wine and serving equal portions. Normally, that bit would be done at the table, not beside the sink, but the purpose became obvious when he pulled a vial of clear liquid from his pocket.

And there it is.

Stark poured a quarter of the contents into one of the glasses, closed the small container, and set it on the counter. He swirled the wine twice before picking up a second drink and turning towards the table.

Jayson caught Issac's gaze before slipping off the counter to open the same cabinet Stark had used. Hopefully, Lizzie wouldn't count her crystal stemware later.

He didn't waste time glancing over his shoulder. If someone noticed his antics, he would hear their reaction, but more importantly, he trusted Issac to have his back.

The little jar contained a few ounces at best of the serum. He couldn't take it all without being obvious, so he settled on roughly the same amount Stark had poured into the wine glass and hoped it would be enough. He carefully placed the vial right where he found it and returned to his spot, glass in hand, with a few seconds to spare.

Stark picked up two more drinks, delivered them to the table, and returned for the final one. He slipped the vial into his pocket without looking at the contents.

It occurred to Jayson as the Sentinel walked away that the casual way he had left the item sitting on the counter seemed a bit too convenient. Almost as if he had done it on purpose.

But why would he do that?

Stark had no way of knowing Jayson stood there waiting for such an opportunity. Unless he sensed him.

The Sentinel took his seat without a backward glance, his expression as passive as it was when he poured the wine.

No.

Stark couldn't sense him. If he did, there would be a fight, yet the Sentinel seemed almost bored.

With a shake of his head, Jayson made his way back to Stas's room, where

Jacque waited on the bed. He didn't glance up from his phone as he lifted his elbow in the air. Jayson grabbed it and chuckled as his living room appeared around them. The teleporter managed to land perfectly on the couch, with his legs crossed and phone still in hand, while Jayson stood beside him.

"I remember when you couldn't walk five feet without accidentally shooting off somewhere. You'd return several hours later with this mien of terror on your face."

Jacque shrugged. "I've mastered the craft."

"Clearly." He set the glass carefully on the coffee table before checking his messages from Grace.

You know I love you, but babysitting is not my job. x

He grinned at the joke. All the Elders kept a personal security team of Hydraians with unique abilities. Jayson had five on his protective detail, and one of them was Grace. Jacque primarily served Luc, but his insane skills tied him to everyone.

"Be right ba—" Jacque disappeared before finishing the sentence.

See you soon, G, Jayson typed, knowing Jacque was on his way to retrieve her.

He considered changing out of his jeans and tee in the interim but didn't know what Balthazar would have in mind. Probably a European nightclub given the midnight hour overseas, or maybe they could find something in the States to keep him occupied.

Either way, it would be a fun night of debauchery, as usual.

The smile he anticipated at the thought never came. Instead, a strange sort of ache radiated from his gut.

"This is insane," he muttered.

Because that bizarre pain reminded him of guilt, something he had no business feeling. He owed Lizzie nothing and vice versa.

Except he wanted to owe her something.

A lot of things, really.

It's the forbidden thing, he decided. Jayson loved a challenge, and being told he couldn't have someone only encouraged him to want her more. Paired with Lizzie's innate innocence and alluring features, no wonder he had plummeted down the rabbit hole.

He palmed his neck and glared at the floor. "Fuck."

"Yes, I believe that's exactly what you need," Balthazar murmured from beside him. He'd appeared at the perfect time, as always. "Where to first, Jay?"

~*~

Three glasses of wine did little to dull the headache forming behind Lizzie's eyes.

She tried so hard to smile and enjoy the conversation, but it was difficult when every topic revolved around the CRF and political affairs.

I don't care, she wanted to say more than once.

But this latest topic regarding Stas's training had Lizzie's stomach in knots.

"She's ready for the next stage," Stark was saying. "Shadowing."

"Yeah? You're tired of kicking my ass every day?"

The blond smirked, or at least Lizzie thought he did. From what she had observed, his facial expressions rarely changed. "That'll continue until you beat me. So you should expect that to continue forever."

Stas nudged Issac. "See, I told you he occasionally makes jokes."

"I believe this is the part where I should be disturbed, yes? Discussing another man harming my girlfriend?" Issac asked with a grin that didn't quite reach his striking eyes.

"She defends herself well enough," Stark replied. "Lately, at least. When we first began, I thought she preferred lying on the ground to standing."

"And I've also told you he's a jackass too, right?" Stas added.

Doctor Fitzgerald shook his head with a laugh, while Lizzie concentrated on her wine. This evening would have to end eventually.

She used to love a reason to host a dinner, especially when it involved inviting Tom and his father over, but her interest waned over the last year or so. It started when Stas accepted her internship with the CRF and intensified when she decided to join the organization full-time after graduation. Now she was a Sentinel, just like Tom, and would probably end up in a grave too.

Lizzie's grip on the crystal stem tightened with the thought.

How could no one see the issue here?

They were all blinded by the CRF's innate goodness and ignoring the very real possibility that Stas could end up hurt, or worse.

All of them were chuckling about her painful training and the next step in her shadowing Stark abroad. Like this was some damn comedic play instead of a tragic one.

She shook her head, trying to clear it, but the anger only grew.

Did they feel no remorse at all?

Tom's father sat two seats down, *smiling*. It'd been eight weeks since the funeral, and he seemed completely unfazed, while Lizzie sat here with a broken heart, worrying that everyone she ever loved would die horribly.

And no one cared.

The conversation carried on around her in a vacuum of sound that tunneled through her ears.

All about the CRF.

Nothing regarding Tom's death.

No sadness.

No guilt.

No memories.

Just a general discussion on Stas's future with the organization that consumed Lizzie's father, leaving her to fend for herself with Lillian Watkins.

Endless ballet classes, beauty pageants, and lectures on how to properly behave in society. There was also the encouragement not to eat and the general disapproval over having a future in any profession other than being the perfect housewife.

As a child, Lizzie hated her father for never protecting her and loathed the job that took him away from her.

She understood, as an adult, that it was never really the CRF's fault, but that irrational hatred never left, giving her an uneasy feeling anytime she went near the headquarters.

And then Tom's demise brought it all back, coupled with Stas's employment and her decision to join the very same unit that killed him.

They didn't understand how painful it was to sit here and listen to them all chat about an organization she detested—to be the only one sitting in misery while they laughed and smiled and *enjoyed.*

I hate them.

Such an irrational thought.

She knew that, but it reverberated through her mind over and over until a scream built in her throat. A swallow of wine shoved it back down to where it belonged inside her heart. Her mother taught her how to hide emotion well, one of the only useful gifts from her childhood.

Needing something to do, Lizzie set about cleaning up the dishes without a word. She could feel Stas's worried gaze on her as she moved, but she refused to acknowledge it.

Being angry with her best friend felt wrong, yet right. They used to be so close, confiding in each other over everything and spending quality time together, but lately, Lizzie felt like she was living with a stranger.

Stas rarely came home, and when she did, she brought Issac or stayed for a few minutes before leaving again. Their weekly girls' nights were now monthly and stilted, and always ended early. Lizzie just didn't see a point anymore.

She felt so alone.

A tear threatened, but she swiped it away.

I'm being a child.

Emotional.

Irrational.

She needed a distraction.

And maybe to grow up a little.

Tom always saw her as a child because she behaved like one, and sulking in the kitchen certainly proved him right.

She set the last of the plates in the sink.

This was the part where she hand-washed them meticulously and set them out to dry, but her hands refused the task.

Why do I do this to myself?

Not even nine o'clock on a Friday night and she stood alone in her kitchen, staring at a pile of plates.

A giggle blossomed in her chest at the absurdity of it. *Twenty-four-years-old going on fifty.*

To hell with it.

She would clean the dishes later. Maybe even tomorrow.

The minor change in her routine lifted an invisible weight from her shoulders. All the stress and disappointment of dinner left her on an exhale.

A sense of freedom and bliss overwhelmed her as she realized she could do whatever she wanted.

There were no papers to grade, no work in the morning, and no commitments except for the guests at the table. But none of them were talking to her anyway, so why stay?

Maybe she could call Cam or Kristin. It'd been a while since she saw her sorority sisters. Why not meet them at a bar and let her hair down a little?

Or she could go out alone and meet a stranger. That sounded scandalous. She liked it.

With a smile, she went to her room, freshened up, slid on a pair of stilettos that paired well with her red dress, and grabbed her purse.

The sound of her name stopped Lizzie in the hallway beside the dining room.

"Yes?" she asked, turning.

"What are you doing?"

"I'm going out," Lizzie replied with no destination in mind. Her mother would be furious when she heard about this, but she couldn't bring herself to worry. She more than earned this reprieve from social niceties. "Enjoy your evening."

"Wait, Liz—"

But Lizzie had no intention of waiting for anything or anyone.

She opened the door and let it slam behind her with finality. Her feet were moving in the direction of the stairwell before she realized what her heart had in mind.

Jayson Masters.

Why should he be the only one allowed to stop by unannounced? Lizzie could be spontaneous, too, and if he happened to be out, she'd figure out plan B.

Her lips curled with the challenge.

Yes, this was what she needed to be doing—enjoying life.

She'd start by telling a certain overbearing neighbor how she felt. Not with words, but with her mouth.

CHAPTER NINE

Running Domestic Errands

> **Subject appears ready for human interaction trials. Meeting with moderator tomorrow to discuss parameters and requirements.**
>
> **–Entry Log 117.12.4-7**

"You ready?" Balthazar asked from the bedroom doorway. He'd left with Jacque to deliver the mysterious liquid to Luc's team for research. His delayed return suggested their omniscient friend had several questions. Typical.

"Just about." Jayson fixed the collar of his gray dress shirt, leaving the top button undone, and added a light jacket to the mix. His dark jeans lent a casual feel that suited their destination. Balthazar was dressed similarly, minus the jacket.

"Fewer clothes to take off later," he murmured, responding to Jayson's mental observation.

"That's half the fun, B."

"And see, this is why I've missed you. The others just haven't achieved our level yet." He clapped Jayson on the back. "Let's go have some fun."

"Don't let Luc hear you talk like that." The trio had a history of competition, and Luc more than held his own. "He owned that syrup challenge last year."

Balthazar grinned as they walked toward the living area. "That was an excellent week."

"How he managed to get those two women in that position…" Jayson whistled at the memory. "That was a sight to behold."

"He earned that win," Balthazar agreed. "Hands down."

"Or up, as it were."

Balthazar chuckled. "Indeed."

"I still want to hear about what went down in Brazil," Grace said from the couch. She had her bare feet up on the coffee table and a bowl of popcorn in her lap.

"Jay, several times."

Jayson's eyebrows hit his hairline. "And you didn't?" The whole damn competition started after Balthazar and Luc disagreed—again—about waffles and pancakes. The debauchery that ensued as a result satisfied Jayson for several weeks.

"I assumed that was self-explanatory." B winked at the now-blushing Hydraian on the couch. "Grace knows how I handle women in the bedroom, don't you, sweetheart?"

There were some things Jayson didn't want to know. This was one of those things.

"I think we should go before I lose my interest." *Just need to find Jacque.* The teleporter was probably in the kitchen, stealing his food.

"Mmm, I highly doubt that's about to happen anytime soon," Balthazar replied with a secret smile.

Jayson didn't like that look. He knew what usually followed. "What—"

A knock at his door cut him off.

"You should probably answer that." Balthazar relaxed onto the couch beside Grace. "Might be important."

Lizzie. If it were anyone else, Balthazar would have opened the door himself. A peek into the hallway confirmed it.

He twisted the handle and grinned at his favorite redhead.

She dove right into the conversation without waiting for him to begin.

"I've decided that you're not the only one who can stop by unannounced." The confidence in her voice and lack of a greeting deepened his smile.

"Well, hello to you too, Red."

"Hi," she added as an afterthought. "I don't actually know what I want to do, but I want to do something."

His eyebrows inched upward. "Yeah? Like what?"

"Dancing." She slipped past him as she spoke. "And maybe more drinking…"

Her voice trailed off as she spied the couple on the couch.

"Oh…" That delectable red graced her cheeks and neck as she spun to face him. "I'm so sorry. Oh God. That was so rude of me. I didn't realize you had company, but of course you do. I'll… uh…" She tried to slide past him again, but Jayson blocked her exit.

"Dancing and drinking," he murmured, repeating her requests. "Does that mean you're ready to attend that concert with me?"

She snorted, her gaze meeting his again. "I said I want to dance, not bang my head against a wall."

He covered his heart. "You wound me, Lizzie."

"Somehow I doubt that," she replied with a saucy little grin. "And you never texted me to plan the concert, so I think that means you owe me another movie night instead."

He leaned into her personal space. "I definitely prefer drinking and dancing over that option," he admitted softly. "But if you insist, then it's a date."

"Hmm, I give it a five-point-two," Balthazar murmured as he strolled up next to Lizzie. The words would go over her head, but Jayson understood the implication behind them.

Give me a break, B. She's an innocent. If he laid it on any thicker, she'd run downstairs.

Balthazar's expression said, *Let me show you how this is done.*

"You must be the beautiful neighbor Jay won't stop thinking about." He held out a hand. "I'm Balthazar, Jay's oldest and dearest friend. Lizzie, right?"

"Uh, yeah." She accepted his hand.

"Lovely to meet you." He brought her wrist to his lips.

"Likewise?" Lizzie's breathless voice sizzled over Jayson's skin.

He never cared how women reacted to Balthazar. The man could send lovers to their knees with a look, something that made him the ideal wingman and provided them both with endless entertainment and pleasure. But hearing Lizzie react to his friend in that same way undid something inside of him.

Balthazar released Lizzie's hand far too slowly for Jayson's liking as he asked, "I assume you're staying for the party?"

"Party?" she repeated.

What are you doing?

Shh. I've got this, Jay, his eyes seemed to say.

Oh, I bet you do.

"Jay didn't tell you?" Balthazar tsked. "That's just like him. He doesn't know how to properly host." That last part was whispered conspiratorially at Lizzie, eliciting a giggle from her.

Now you're just being a dick.

Balthazar's gaze glimmered deviously. "Like even now, he still hasn't offered you a drink." He shook his head in mock reproach. "What can I get you, sweetheart? A glass of wine, perhaps?"

Jayson closed the door because, clearly, Lizzie would be staying for the party he had no intention of throwing. It shut a little louder than intended, not that anyone seemed to notice.

"Um." Lizzie licked her lips. "I do like wine."

"Excellent," Balthazar murmured. "You make yourself at home while Jay and I procure the drinks. A beer for you, Grace?"

"Obviously," she replied from the couch. Her legs were still kicked up on the table, but the popcorn had been set to the side.

"Come on, Jay." Balthazar nodded at the kitchen. "Time to play host."

"Sure," Jayson replied. "Lizzie, this is Grace. I promise she's mostly harmless." He winked at his favorite Guardian while he said it and pushed away from the door. "Be back in a minute." *I need to go kick my best friend's ass.*

Balthazar chuckled. "You'll need more than a minute."

"We'll see, won't we?" he muttered while following his friend through the dining room.

They rounded the corner to find Jacque sitting on one of the counters with a pizza box in his lap.

Jayson eyed the now-empty container. "Do they not feed you in Hydria?"

"Your fridge is full of leftovers. I'm just helping you clean it up," the slender teleporter replied around a mouthful of food.

"Charming," Jayson muttered.

"I could say the same about you, Jay. What was that back there?" Balthazar demanded. "Half-assed flirting? I've taught you better than that."

"Come on, like you've taught me anything." Jayson opened his fridge to look for a bottle of wine he knew didn't exist. "We both know I can hold my own just fine, B."

"Did I hear something about a party?" Jacque interrupted. "'Cause you're going to need more liquor."

"And people," Jayson added. "What the fuck were you thinking inviting her to stay for a party?"

"You let me worry about that." Balthazar grinned knowingly. "First things first, we need a bottle of wine. Jacque?"

"On it." He disappeared in a flash.

Jayson palmed the back of his neck and blew out a breath. "So much for a night off." Something he blamed Balthazar for more than Lizzie.

"When have I ever let you down?" his friend asked. "I've got this."

"A new challenge?" Jayson guessed with a laugh. "Do tell."

"Oh, no. This one is personal and all my own, but you'll be thanking me in the morning." The promise in his voice was one earned by centuries of perfected experience.

He shrugged. "All right." When Balthazar set his mind to something, it happened, and on this, Jayson had no complaints.

Assuming it doesn't hurt Lizzie.

He frowned at the thought. Why would it? They didn't owe each other anything. He liked her, sure, but she was forbidden fruit—an asset—that he couldn't touch.

She doesn't know that.

"That's quite a conundrum," Balthazar mused. "She has you tied up in knots, my friend. But don't worry. We'll get it straightened out." He clapped

Jayson on the shoulder just as Jacque reappeared with a bottle of wine in each hand.

"Didn't know what you'd prefer, so I grabbed two from Wakefield's cellar." The teleporter set them on the counter and turned to Balthazar. "I assume we're off to pick up some people and more drinks?"

"We are indeed. Let's start with Maria." He extended a hand as Jayson's mouth fell open.

"You can't be—" But it was too late. Balthazar and Jacque had already disappeared.

Fuck.

Maria specialized in altering short-term memory, which could only mean one thing: Balthazar planned to pick up random humans from bars and teleport them here. To Jayson's condo. In the middle of New York City.

He inwardly groaned at the idiocy of this plan. They might as well post a sign out front welcoming the Ichorians to their party.

"Do you need any help?" Lizzie asked as she rounded the corner. She glanced at the two unopened bottles before eyeing Jayson's position against the counter. He'd leaned against it while lamenting about his situation. "Where did your friend go?"

"He's working out some party details," he replied vaguely.

"Oh, okay. Um, do you want me to help you get ready?" The hopeful note in her voice endeared her to him even more.

"I can open the wine." He went to search for a corkscrew. Mateo and Issac had furnished the condo for him. There had to be one somewhere.

The fridge opened beside him, causing him to look questioningly at Lizzie.

"I'll help," she explained with a sweet smile. The woman seriously had no idea how her beauty affected others. "With the food prep, I mean."

"Food prep?"

"Yeah. You know, like cheese and crackers, fruit…" She trailed off as she eyed his mostly empty shelves. "Or… not." She closed the door and lifted one eyebrow. "How do you expect to throw a party without any food?"

"Uh…" Most of his parties ended in the bedroom, not the dining room.

Both brows rose now. "You don't plan to serve anything other than beer and some wine?"

"Well." He palmed the back of his neck again. "I wasn't exactly…" The fiery glimmer in her eyes sent his thought process south. Would her pupils dilate like that in his bed?

"Jayson Masters," she chastised. "You cannot throw a party without food!" She shook her head. "What time are you expecting people?"

He considered Balthazar's intentions and shrugged. "Thirty minutes or so?"

Lizzie huffed a breath. "Hardly enough time, but we can manage." She set the white wine in the fridge, near his personal beer stash, and left the red on the counter. Jayson knew Balthazar would bring more alcohol, but the amount in there would be enough to at least kick-start the party.

"Let's go." She grabbed his hand and gave him a good tug, forcing him to follow. His dick wanted to go in the opposite direction, toward his room, but it seemed she had other ideas in mind.

"Where are we going?" he asked.

"There's a twenty-four-seven market open on Seventy-seventh and Broadway. Let's go grab a few things." She was already at the door. He spied her purse on the end table, but she made no move to grab it. Good thing he had his wallet—not that he would ever let her pay anyway.

"Have fun." Grace waved, her amusement palpable. "I'll just babysit your place until you get back."

"Cute," he returned.

She flashed him a wide grin. "I try, Jay. I do."

Lizzie yanked him into the hallway before he could reply and guided him down the hall. "Now, how many people are having you over?"

Knowing Balthazar… "At least twenty." And most of them would be women.

"I can work with that."

He watched her ass as she descended the stairs before him. Yeah, he could think of worse pastimes than letting her boss him around. Except in the bedroom. He enjoyed control too much for that.

She listed several "party snack" ideas on their way to the store, and he agreed to each one just for the hell of it. Her definition of entertaining differed significantly from his, but he didn't mind.

All of her formalities reminded him a bit of Amelia, or at least the former version, anyway. The one who returned to Hydria two months ago seemed less enthusiastic about social gatherings. Not that he could blame her. Torture changed a person.

Jayson grabbed a basket at the door and followed Lizzie's commands throughout the market. Then he handed his card over to the cashier, with a bemused smile at the total his redhead had managed to rack up in less than ten minutes of wandering.

"You certainly know how to shop, Red," he murmured.

"Oh, this is nothing," she replied. "You should see me with my sorority sisters."

"Yeah? Tell me more about these sisters." He picked up the reusable bags Lizzie insisted on buying in addition to the food. She claimed they were important for the environment, which he couldn't exactly argue against.

"You want to hear about the lingerie parties and pillow fights, don't you?"

"Absolutely."

"Sorry, but that doesn't happen."

Not true, Red. He'd attended several over his lifetime. "Sounds like a bucket list item that requires checking."

She snorted. "No, thank you."

"Not even with me?" he teased.

Her cheeks flushed. "Uh, I…"

"I'm joking, Red." *Not really.* Her virginal ears weren't ready for his suggestions yet. "Now, tell me, why did I need flour again?"

Her lips curled. "Cookies."

"For me?"

"For your guests."

"Oh, Red, that's not going to work. I never share what's mine." And that applied to more than just cookies. Sure, he'd enjoyed a woman, or several, over the years with both Luc and Balthazar, but never the ones he wanted for himself. Like Lizzie. Not that they were talking about that right now.

"Who said they're *your* cookies?" she taunted, her eyes shining with mirth. This playful side of Lizzie appealed to him on a base level. He would even say he found their banter fun.

"First of all, you promised to bake me cookies," he reminded. "That's the only way I'll tell you more about where I've lived. And secondly, I paid for the ingredients. So they're my cookies, Red."

"You paid for the groceries because this is your party. And technically, you owe me for saving your butt and helping you provide snacks for your guests." A taunt glimmered in her gaze. "Furthermore, maybe I'm no longer interested in learning more about you."

"Oh, we both know you're interested," he countered. "Don't lie to yourself."

"That's not cocky at all."

"Darling Red, you haven't even skimmed the surface of my cockiness, but feel free to explore me more in depth at your leisure."

"How very *neighborly* of you."

"Hey, I try to be hospitable." He showed her the four bags in his hands. "Proof."

She laughed and shook her head. "Do you want me to carry one of those?"

"Now she asks, as we round the corner to our block." He shook his head in mock disappointment. "And she calls me a bad host."

Her mouth opened and closed. "Crap. I should have offered… I'm—"

"I'm joking, Lizzie. Like I would let you carry these for me. I might not be the best host, but I do know how to behave like a gentleman." *Even when all I want to do is drop these bags, shove you against the wall, and fuck the hell out of your mouth.*

She skipped ahead to open the door to the building and flashed Jayson a triumphant grin. "Now I'm being socially acceptable."

"Pretty sure you're always acceptable," he replied with a nod to the doorman, who stood behind Lizzie with a welcoming expression. "Hi, Dennis."

"Evenin', Jayson. Lizzie." He tipped his hat and secured the front area after they walked through it.

Jayson considered giving him a heads-up about the party, but Lizzie was already on her way to the stairwell. Her ballerina legs sure were quick when she wanted to move them.

He trailed after her with a chuckle and took the stairs two at a time to keep up. When they reached his hallway, he sent a prayer above for the silence. Either Balthazar wasn't back yet or he'd recruited fewer people than expected for their little soirée.

"It's probably open," he said as they approached.

Lizzie twisted the handle and froze as sensual music spilled into the corridor. "You said maybe twenty people…"

He peeked over her shoulder. "I said at least twenty." It appeared to be closer to thirty or forty. He recognized several Guardians in the crowd. They were loyal to a fault. As long as they didn't leave the condo, it would be okay. The rest of the attendees were harmless mortals, if a little loud. Not an Ichorian in sight, with the exception of Tristan.

That explains the sound control in the hallway. Clever man.

Lizzie elbowed him. "We need more food, Jayson."

"It'll be fine, Red," he assured. "Jacque can hop out to get us more if needed."

"Jacque?" she repeated.

"'Sup." The teleporter appeared in front of her. Literally. Not that she saw it, because her eyes had been on Jayson.

"Oh." Lizzie took a step backward, pressing her back to Jayson's chest. "Hi."

"Hi," Jacque returned. "You rang?"

Jayson lifted his grocery-laden arms, bracketing Lizzie between them. "Can you please *walk* these over to the kitchen, Jacque?"

His friend grinned cheekily. "Sure, Jay. I'll walk them over." He grabbed the bags and skipped away a little too quickly. His energy levels were through the roof.

"That's Jacque," Jayson murmured as he wrapped his arms around Lizzie's waist. She hadn't stepped away from him, so he interpreted that as an invitation. "He's a good friend who happens to enjoy running errands."

"Oh," she said again, her body warm against his. "Okay."

"We should go inside," he whispered against her ear. A trail of goose bumps stamped a path down the column of her neck, encouraging him to take it a step further. He pressed firmly into her backside as he forced her forward into the foyer and kicked the door closed behind him. The scene before them matched what he anticipated.

Dancing.

Drinking.

Debauchery.

Typical Balthazar. He went by Bacchus once, a few thousand years ago. His legend still haunted mythology books, though Dionysus was the more popular version of the name thanks to the Greeks. He had perfected his party-throwing skills throughout his very long life, and the scene in Jayson's flat proved it.

The music was pitched at just the right volume to allow casual conversation while also encouraging everyone to move to the sensual beat, and the lighting was bright enough to see while also lending an erotic feel to the air. Almost like a nightclub and a lounge combined, but in a residential flat.

Incredible, really.

The notorious god approached with a woman on each side, his expression welcoming in more ways than one. "I hear you left us for some domestic shopping?"

"Lizzie insisted we grab some snacks for the party," Jayson explained as he eyed the two gorgeous brunettes under his friend's arms. *Argentinian?*

Balthazar winked in confirmation before saying, "That was a lovely thought, Lizzie."

"Thank you," she replied, sounding quite pleased with herself. "You were very right about Jayson being a poor host."

Oh, the little minx.

"Careful, Red," Jayson murmured into her ear as he tightened his hold. "Or I'll show you how I usually host a party."

Her cheeks warmed against his nose.

Mmm.

What other parts of her body could he make blush? Her breasts, definitely. And her thighs would redden beautifully beneath his attentions, as would other more intimate parts of her. His cock woke up at the thoughts overriding his brain, and he didn't bother to hide it. What was the point anymore? She had to know he wanted her, even if he couldn't have her.

His hormonal drive tonight proved how badly he needed to get laid, but it seemed only one woman would satisfy the fire Lizzie evoked inside him. Good thing he had that woman in his arms.

"Without food?" she guessed, her voice breathier than when she teased him seconds before. That she was able to focus enough to answer his taunt said he needed to up his game.

He nibbled her ear before whispering, "Depends on the menu." Her responding shiver pleased him immensely.

"Operating at a level six now," Balthazar said, interrupting the moment. "I approve."

You and I both know that I operate at an eleven on your scale of one to ten, but I'm toning it down out of necessity, Jayson replied mentally as he smiled against Lizzie's neck. Her floral scent teased his baser needs and invited him to explore more.

Balthazar merely grinned. "Well, now that you're both back, we can get this party started properly." His sinful gaze fell to the woman at his right. "This is Delfina"—he looked to the left—"and Sofía." Those lips curled into the picture of seduction as he gestured to Jayson. "Ladies, this is the friend I told you about."

Two sets of amorous, light-colored eyes fell on Jayson, which should have triggered all manner of sordid thoughts yet didn't. He smiled but didn't quite feel it. Not the way he did ten minutes ago while bantering with Lizzie, anyway.

"Ladies," he greeted as he openly appraised the women. Their sky-high heels and short dresses suggested Balthazar had picked them up at a nightclub, likely in Buenos Aires. The majority of the humans here appeared to be from various parts of South America. All gorgeous with curves for days and reminiscent of his last trip to the southern continent.

Nice work.

Of course, his friend's eyes replied, cocky as ever.

Jayson murmured a few complimentary words in Spanish that the women returned in kind. He loved a sexy accent, but his focus shifted as the redhead in his arms tried to step away.

"I'll, uh, leave you all to chat while I get the snacks ready," she said when his arms locked around her waist. He'd been going for polite, not interest, which she'd clearly misinterpreted.

This isn't going to work, B. Not with her here.

Or perhaps even then. Only one woman seemed to be tickling his fancy lately, and that was the one trying to escape his unyielding hold.

"Lizzie promised me some cookies." He skimmed his nose over her neck to calm her down. "And I owe her a glass of wine."

"Really, it's okay. I can manage on my own." She tried again to leave, but his arms remained locked around her.

"I hate to break this to you, Red"—he threaded his fingers in her hair and angled her head backward to hover his lips over hers—"but I'm not ready to let you go yet."

Her pupils flared in the way he wanted. Tonight had been about sating his lust with a random female or two, but Lizzie's presence changed everything. The notion of being with another woman no longer appealed to him, which meant he was in for a painful evening. But at least he could satisfy some of his cravings by spending time with his favorite redhead. His fixation would pass once the mission ended and he took some well-deserved time off.

He brushed his mouth over hers and smiled when her breath fluttered over his lips. At least he wasn't the only one fighting the desire between them.

"Wine?" he asked softly.

"O-okay."

"Good." He spoke the word against her mouth and followed it with a gentle kiss because he couldn't help himself. "Let's go, Red."

Jayson righted her and started to say something to Balthazar and his guests, but the trio had melted into the party scene again. His friend stood in a circle of women, including the duo from before, dancing and managing to make each of them feel equally adored.

He lifted his gaze in a way that said, *Enjoy your evening, Jay.*

A show of solidarity, respect, and understanding. Lizzie was forbidden fruit, but if Jayson took her to bed, there would be no judgment from Balthazar. His ability to sense and control emotion, as well as read thoughts, granted him a deeper insight than most.

Jayson acknowledged the acceptance with a nod. Not that he would do anything about it. His steadfast control would serve him well.

But there were other ways to sate his needs.

Maybe he would explore some of those.

CHAPTER TEN

A First Time for Everything

> **Sensation and pleasure are incomprehensible to the subject. Benefactor is displeased and requests hormonal updates. Lab technicians are working on a cocktail to fix the oversight.**
>
> **—Entry Log 116.03.4-7**

Lizzie needed more wine. The three glasses from earlier had worn off after her walk to the store with Jayson, and this new one wasn't enough to dull the insanity spiraling inside her.

Every touch set her blood on fire.

Every seductive glance elicited goose bumps.

And, oh God, the kisses.

She clenched her thighs.

What is he trying to do to me?

Never in her life had a man worked her into a frenzy like this. Not even Tom. She didn't know how to handle it, and the wine seemed to do nothing to cool her off.

"What do you want me to do with these?" Jayson asked, showing her the bag of grapes she'd picked up at the store. Even those simple words seemed underlined in suggestion. She had to be misunderstanding him.

But all the touching… is irrelevant.

A man who craved the kind of relationship Lizzie wanted did not openly flirt with other women in front of his romantic interest. And he'd certainly flirted with those models in the other room. Not that she could blame him—they were gorgeous.

Just friends, she reminded herself and focused on his task.

"We need to wash them and put them in a bowl." She pulled one from the cabinet and handed it to him. "I'll focus on the cheese and crackers." Lizzie had thought wine snacks would be appropriate given his drinks of choice, but his friends didn't seem very interested in food, as they were too busy bumping and grinding.

To each her own, she supposed. Lizzie would set some food out on the table for those interested and leave Jayson to host his party. She doubted he wanted her to stay. These were his friends. She understood that.

Maybe she would call Kristin or Cam. She still owed them a girls' evening out, and it wasn't too late. They were probably out drinking somewhere. Lizzie preferred to join them over returning to her lonely condo. Issac and Stas were probably still there, and after the way she'd left, Lizzie didn't want to see them.

She finished arranging the cheese and found Jayson watching her. "What?"

He stepped into her space and gently pressed his thumb to the area between her eyes and started to massage it in slow circles. "I'm trying to figure out who or what put this frown here. I thought we were having fun."

"We are… No… I mean, it's not." *For crying out loud!* His hands really impacted her ability to form proper sentences. She cleared her throat and tried again. "My mind was wandering."

"Do you need help bringing it back?" His warm fingers plucked the knife from her hand and set it aside as he crowded her against the counter. "Because I'm happy to help with that."

Her heart skipped a beat as she forgot how to breathe. "Okay," she somehow managed.

His lips lightly caressed hers in another one of his infamously chaste kisses. Oh, she enjoyed them, but each one only deepened this feeling of need churning inside her, and she couldn't handle much more. It felt like an inferno—curling, flaring, and dying for an outlet only he could provide.

She slid her hands up his arms, luxuriating in the Italian silk of his blazer. Lizzie adored the sleek and sexy look, and Jayson wore it so well. She traced the collar of his shirt before dragging her nails up his neck and into his luscious hair.

All their previous kisses were controlled by him, but she desired more.

She locked her fingers in his thick strands and leaned into him.

"Stop teasing and kiss me," she demanded. The voice sounded nothing like hers—so throaty and hot—but it inspired the reaction she wanted.

"Careful what you wish for, Red." He lifted her onto the island counter, yanked her forward, and stepped between her thighs. "You just might get it."

Her body went up in flames as he took her mouth in a kiss meant to devastate her feminine senses.

Oh. My. God.

His tongue… Lizzie didn't know they could move like that.

She fought to keep up, her nails digging into his scalp as he ravaged her inside and out. No way did she regret this request. She'd demanded, and he delivered.

His palms slid up her sides, scattering goose bumps in their wake and hardening her nipples. When he reached her neck, she was putty in his hands, allowing him to do whatever he wanted.

He tilted her head to an angle that allowed deeper entry into her mouth while aligning his lower body with hers.

A jolt of electricity shot up her spine from both shock and something carnal. No man had ever touched her *there*, but she could feel him through the thin barrier of her panties.

Because she was in a dress.

With her legs wrapped around a man.

In his kitchen.

How deliciously wanton.

Never in her wildest dreams did she expect this, yet it felt so right and natural. And positively terrifying at the same time.

The mixture of emotions traveled from her mouth to his as she tried to return his kiss with equal skill. But she knew her experience paled in comparison to his, as was evidenced by the easy way he dominated her mouth and controlled her body with a few practiced moves.

She couldn't bring herself to care, not when it produced this level of euphoria. His fingers knotted in her hair, tugging just enough to keep her grounded while he continued his sensual lesson.

Her legs tightened around his hips as she fought for something she didn't quite understand.

Friction.

Heat.

More.

He broke the kiss with a curse, his breath hot against her lips.

"Come now, don't stop on my account." The unfamiliar voice sent ice cubes dancing down Lizzie's spine.

Jayson's embrace had erased all thought and reason, including the fact that they were very much not alone in his condo. Something she hadn't even considered while he consumed her on the countertop.

And, apparently, they had acquired an audience of at least one.

Jayson combed his fingers through Lizzie's hair before lowering his hands to her sides. She expected him to step away, but he didn't. Part of her wished he would so she could stand up and straighten her dress, while the other part of her felt protected by his possessive stance.

The conundrum left her speechless, if a little mortified at having been caught in the act, but at the same time, hot and bothered. Lizzie never broke etiquette rules—they were ingrained in her after years of training—but Jayson had plowed right through those barriers with his addictive kisses. And she didn't regret it for a second.

"Pity," the voice murmured as he opened the fridge behind her.

"Tristan," Jayson growled. "Is there something I can help you find? The door, maybe?"

"I wanted to top up my wine but found myself distracted by the show." The fridge closed with a snick. "You know how I feel about voyeurism."

Jayson's grip tightened. "Take your kink elsewhere."

"Since when do you mind an audience?" Tristan asked with a slight lilt. *Irish, maybe?*

Glass clinked against granite as the man went about pouring himself wine on the same island Lizzie sat upon. She could feel the coolness of the bottle near her ass, sending a chill down her spine. Or perhaps it was the stranger's proximity that unsettled her.

"I seem to recall you being quite fond of a little exhibitionism," he continued. "Don't tell me you're undergoing a change, as well. I don't think I can handle losing two of my mates to pets. Although, I admit, this one is quite lovely."

A finger trailed down her arm, causing Jayson to yank her closer.

Her hands grasped his shoulders for balance as she finally peered over her shoulder at the tall man behind her.

Vibrant green eyes held her captive.

"Yes, quite lovely." His smile could only be described as wicked. He looked over her at the man between her legs as he added, "But I can see you're not up for sharing, so I'll find a snack elsewhere."

"That would be wise," Jayson replied. "And try not to spill anything."

"Now you're just insulting me, Jay. I know better than to imbibe in your personal space." He returned the wine bottle to the fridge and turned to pick up his glass. "Can I make one suggestion?"

"You're going to anyway."

"I am," Tristan agreed. "Perhaps move this interlude to a more private location if you don't want to invite others. It could confuse those of us who know you well."

Lizzie swallowed and returned her focus to Jayson.

His friend kept referring to sharing and watching, and she inferred he meant in a sexual context. But to what extent?

Her limited experience extended to a male here or there, and never anything below the waist. She couldn't possibly live up to whatever Tristan had just implied.

"Thanks for that," Jayson said, his focus on the other man. "Now go back to being useful in the living area. It's getting loud."

"Oh, I have a feeling it'll be far louder later, old friend." The taunt in Tristan's voice had Jayson's eyes narrowing. "But don't worry. I'll control it for you, because that's the kind of friend I am."

Lizzie had no idea what they were talking about but guessed it was some sort of inside joke between them, though the expression on Jayson's face suggested that might be the wrong term.

"As if you're not getting something out of this," Jayson returned.

"Indeed," Tristan murmured. "Why else would I agree to put my talents to use for such a frivolous affair?"

"Because you're such a good friend?" Jayson suggested.

"I do appreciate your humor, Jay. Enjoy your evening. I know I'll be enjoying mine." He trailed a finger down her arm again, or tried to, anyway. Jayson caught his wrist before Tristan reached her elbow.

"Stop playing," Jayson said, voice low.

Tristan grinned as he twisted his hand free. "Maybe next time." His green eyes glimmered wickedly as they met hers. "Nice to meet you, love. I do so adore a silent woman."

Her lips parted, but by the time she could even formulate a reply, he had left the kitchen with his wine and the bowl of grapes Jayson had prepared.

Warm hands caressed her cheeks, pulling her attention back to the man between her thighs. "I'm sorry, Liz. He's a bit of an ass."

"You have really weird friends," she blurted out. First that coworker, Kiel. Then Balthazar—who wasn't so much weird as impossibly good-looking and far too charming for his own good—and now Tristan. "How do you know them all? And didn't you just move here? Who are all those people? And you speak Spanish?"

She couldn't seem to stop the word vomit—a consequence of being startled, embarrassed, and slightly overwhelmed.

"I need my wine," she decided.

He stopped her from twisting, reached around her to pick up the glass, and handed it to her.

"Balthazar is visiting from where I lived before, and Tristan is an old mutual friend who lives in the city. As for all the others, I recognize a handful, while the rest are Balthazar's acquaintances since he wanted to throw this party, and I speak a lot of languages." He tucked a piece of her hair behind her ear as he smiled. "Did that cover everything?"

She finished what was left of her wine while trying to formulate a response.

"The, uh, sharing thing?" She didn't have the aplomb to clarify that any further, and her face heated just from mentioning it. Or maybe that was the alcohol. "I need more."

She gave him her glass, and he eyed her speculatively. "How much have you had to drink tonight, Red?"

Not the answer she expected. "Are you accusing me of being drunk?"

"No." He set the glass off to the side. "I'm checking because I want you to stay sober."

"Why?" Wasn't drinking the whole point of throwing a party?

He cupped her cheek and forced her to meet his gaze. "Because I need your consent."

She frowned. "For what?"

"For the things I want to do to you." He traced her bottom lip with his thumb. "But we'll determine your limits first."

Her mouth went dry at both his words and the smoldering tenor of his voice. It erased all the awkwardness from Tristan's interruption and rekindled that foreign sensation heating her veins.

"I like you," she said on impulse. "That's why I came up here tonight. To tell you I like you."

Very mature, Liz, she thought with a mental cringe. How old was she? Twelve?

Fortunately, he seemed more amused than annoyed.

"Yeah? I think you've made that clear." He kissed her softly before adding, "The feeling is mutual."

He pulled her off the counter and fixed her dress.

"Follow me, Red."

~*~

Fuck it.

Jayson was going to hell anyway. He might as well enjoy himself on the way there.

He didn't meet Balthazar's gaze as he pulled Lizzie toward his bedroom, but he felt the mind reader's eyes on him. Satisfaction radiated from the man because this had clearly been his plan all along.

When have I ever let you down? He seemed to ask.

Never.

And tonight was no exception.

Fine. Jayson would indulge himself a little. He deserved it after two months of focusing on this mission. If Lizzie didn't want him, he wouldn't touch her, but those little mewls of desperation in the kitchen confirmed all his suspicions.

She hadn't even realized her own reactions or that her body had been on the verge of cresting into orgasm after a few innocent touches.

He bit back a groan at her inexperience. It floored him.

This desire between them was an all-consuming insanity. And something needed to be done about it.

But there would be rules—for him, not her.

Lizzie required a slow introduction into his bed, and he refused to overwhelm her. She deserved better than that.

And he couldn't fuck her the way he wanted to until she knew the truth.

Shit, he shouldn't even be willing to go this far without telling her everything, but his sense of honor had taken a backseat after that interlude in the kitchen.

This would be about making her feel good and nothing more.

She'd forgive him for that, right?

He escorted her into his bedroom and locked the door behind them.

"So, um…" She gazed up at him through her thick lashes as color brightened her cheeks. "You mentioned limits?"

"Yes, I did." He backed her up into the wall, placing his palms against the hard surface on either side of her head. "No sex tonight."

Her jaw hit the floor. "Wh-what?"

"Right. That reaction is exactly why we're not having sex tonight." He traced every inch of her deep-red dress with his eyes before meeting her gaze again. "But I'm open to other options if you are." *Like taking off this dress and exploring the flesh beneath with my tongue.*

That pretty pink tongue darted out to lick her lips, and he wondered idly what it would feel like against his cock.

Not that they would be doing that tonight.

This was about her.

He ran his nose over the blush of her cheeks to her ear. "Let's start with easier questions," he suggested. "How do you feel about me removing your dress?"

She shivered, eliciting a smile from him. "Mmm, you approve, as do I. What else, Red? What else am I allowed to remove?"

He dropped one hand to her waist, sliding it upward to thumb the underside of her breast. "Your bra?" he whispered. Another tremble, followed by a soft little moan, encouraged him to travel downward to where the fabric ended on her leg. He explored the hem before gently prodding the inside of her thigh.

Her breathing escalated, causing him to pause.

"A limit," he murmured. "Mmm, I can work with this."

"I…" She shuddered even as her body tensed. "I-I don't know."

Because she'd never been touched there. He understood.

"That's why we have limits, Red," he said in a soothing tone. He would never force her or any woman into an uncomfortable situation. That went against his personal code.

"I'm not… sure." Another shudder, this one less erotic and more emotional.

He worshiped her neck with his mouth, easing her back into him as he removed his hand from her leg and brought it up to tangle with her hair. "I would be content to kiss you all night, Elizabeth. With or without clothes. It will always be your choice." His lips sealed over her pulse, sucking lightly and coaxing one of those needy noises from her.

That's it, sweetheart. Come back to me.

Her nails dug into his arms, pulling him closer. He pressed his hips to hers, testing another boundary. She reacted by arching into him. His dick ached at the contact, but he shoved his needs aside to focus on her. He could enjoy a long shower afterward.

"Mmm, I think we can begin." He pulled back to capture her gaze. "Tell me if I go too far, Red. One word and I'll stop. Understand?"

Her dazed expression and little nod didn't work for him.

He tightened his hold in her hair and gave it a subtle tug. "Elizabeth, I need to know you'll speak up, or this won't work." He could read all her body cues well enough, but vocal participation was a requirement.

She swallowed, sobering enough through the haze of arousal to focus. "Okay."

"Not good enough." He nipped her jaw. "What will you say if you need me to slow down? If something is too intense?"

She blinked up at him. "To, uh, stop?"

His heart warmed at the genuineness of her response. He would have so much fun training her in the art of seduction and sex. Perhaps even too much fun. "We can start with that if you want, but you may want to word it differently at some point."

Her lips curled downward. "Why?"

He pressed his lips to her ear again. "Because, Red, at some point, your pleasure will be so intense you'll beg me to stop even though it's the last thing you actually want."

~*~

"But we'll explore that later, when you're ready." The words burned against Lizzie's sensitive skin.

Oh. My. God.

He could do that to her?

How?

His hot mouth went to her neck again, sending shivers down her spine. As if it wasn't enough to be caged between him and the wall, he had to add his talented lips to the mix.

I'm in so much trouble.

The best kind, though.

Or so she hoped.

Because, oh God, he was doing those things with his hands again, gently tracing her sides and stopping just beneath her breasts. She wanted to force him higher but didn't know how.

"Turn around," he murmured. "Put your hands on the wall for me."

She didn't know what to think or how to feel but abided the command because she wanted more. Butterflies took flight in her abdomen as he gathered all her hair and pulled it over her shoulder. He traced the line of her zipper from the base to the top, setting her blood on fire.

"Breathe, Red." He pressed a kiss to her nape that scattered goose bumps down her spine. Or maybe that was the result of him exposing her skin inch by inch. She didn't know. Didn't care. Couldn't focus.

He's going to see me naked.

It's just like being in a swimsuit competition.

Totally not the same thing.

God, what underwear had she worn?

Maroon.

Right.

To coordinate with her dress.

Panties, not a thong, and a matching silk bra. Just like a bikini, only with more cleavage. She could handle this.

Her dress fell to the ground.

Oh, God.

Heat flared across her back as he pressed his palms to her bare skin. "You're killing me, Lizzie." He slowly rotated her to face him, and the arousal darkening his gaze knocked her off balance.

She'd never had a man look at her like *that.*

Ravenous.

Hot.

And so incredibly sexy.

It triggered something buried deep inside of her—a confidence she didn't know she owned.

He wants me. She could see it in the way his chocolate eyes roamed over every inch of her skin in unabashed admiration.

Lizzie had no idea what to do with that knowledge, but she wanted to kiss him so badly it hurt. She didn't wait or ask but used her heels to her advantage and pressed her lips to his.

He responded immediately, taking control of the kiss with his tongue and flattening her against the wall. She moaned into his mouth as he parted her legs with one of his.

So good.

She needed more.

That fire was brewing again, so addictive and consuming.

His fingers knotted in her hair once more, tugging her back to the angle he wanted as his opposite hand went to her hips to force her pelvis forward. She jolted as the sweet spot connected with his muscled thigh.

Oh. She liked that.

Jayson awoke something inside of her that she knew very little about. Pleasure and desire were concepts she understood but rarely felt. Even alone at night when she tried, nothing happened. She felt attraction—love, even—but never anything like this.

She kissed him harder, and he returned the embrace in kind, all the while keeping his leg lodged between hers and applying pressure where she desired it most.

What is happening to me?

She felt wanton, dirty, and so very alive.

Her nails dug into his scalp as the sensation mounted, and he grinned against her lips. "What do you need, Red?"

She couldn't articulate a response, because she didn't know.

He cupped her breasts, and she arched on instinct.

Okay, yes, that she wanted. Very much.

"Skin," she managed as fire danced over her senses.

Her bra disappeared, and she moaned as he gave her what she desired. But it still wasn't enough.

"Shh, I've got you," he murmured against her mouth. He lifted her into his arms and carried her over to the mattress, where he laid her down far too gently. His palms slid down her legs to her ankles. He slipped off each of her heels and let them drop to the floor.

Every part of her yearned for more, causing her to squirm uncomfortably on the bed. Jayson watched with a hungry expression while slowly removing his jacket and laying it over the chair in the corner.

She froze when his hand went to the top button of his dress shirt.

Her brain conjured an image of what existed beneath, dampening the space between her thighs.

Oh, yes, please.

He slowly unfastened each button while observing her reactions with that same voracious look.

"What are you doing to me?" she asked with a groan.

"Prolonging the moment," he replied, tilting his head to the side with a knowing smile. "Trust me. You'll thank me for it later."

"Right now, I want to kill you."

"No, sweetheart. You want to fuck me. I can see how you might confuse the two, but they're unrelated." He finished removing his button-down and the fitted shirt beneath, and began loosening his belt.

Her lips fell open at the implication, causing him to pause, but she didn't have it in her to tell him to stop. How could she turn down a naked Jayson?

Whatever he saw in her expression must have appeased him, because he continued and rid himself of his jeans.

Black boxer briefs.

Even mostly naked, the man still had excellent fashion sense. Not in the way of most men who favored suits, but one who enjoyed European fashion. Lizzie more than approved, especially as he strolled toward her with all those muscles flexing and clenching.

Her breathing escalated as he crawled over her.

"You have the most gorgeous breasts," he murmured against a stiffening peak.

His gaze held hers as he slowly took her nipple into the hot cavern of his mouth. She bowed off the bed in response, causing him to chuckle.

"Mmm, you approve." He switched to the other and sucked it harder, eliciting a tortured sound from her throat.

The sensations were too much, yet still not enough. She didn't understand what she needed, just that she *wanted.* Oh God, did she *want.*

He kissed a path down her stomach while she writhed beneath him, and it wasn't until he settled between her thighs that she realized his intention.

Stop was on the tip of her tongue when he did something with his mouth that she never could have predicted.

There, her mind supplied as she dug her nails into the bedding beneath her.

That was what she craved.

Her body shuddered under the onslaught as he tortured her most intimate flesh through the red silk of her panties and applied pressure with his tongue.

Magic.

The man held a mystical touch.

That's what caused all this. Even when she touched herself *there*, it never felt anything like this, nor did she ever enjoy it.

But she *really* enjoyed that twirling thing he was doing right now.

"Jayson," she whispered, uncertain.

He reached out to take her hand, and she squeezed the hell out of it. This feeling hurt so good, and the flames consumed her every thought.

His rhythm, heat, and presence were all she knew.

And the inferno spinning inside her in that secret area she'd never been able to access until now.

It rippled through her and combusted without warning, shooting her soul into the stars as light flashed behind her eyes. Ecstasy reverberated through every inch of her being and poured from her mouth in an endless scream.

She should have been ashamed, but she didn't have the energy. Not after whatever he'd just done to her.

How many times had she tried to achieve the same feeling and failed? She usually gave up before starting, knowing it wouldn't work, but Jayson had played her body like a master. And she'd responded in kind.

Her breath came in pants as he moved over her again. His lips tasted sweet, and she realized with a gasp that it was her essence on his tongue—a sinful treat that thickened her blood and clouded her judgment.

He'd fully and completely corrupted her, and she didn't mind in the slightest. All she wanted was… "More."

"All night, Lizzie." He deepened their kiss and slid a thigh between her legs. "Whatever you need."

She shook her head. "Naked." She wanted to feel his tongue everywhere, not through a silk barrier.

He tsked. "Now, Red, we set limits at the beginning and agreed to keep our underwear on tonight." He nuzzled her neck. "Feel free to renegotiate that next time."

Her blood heated at the thought of the future, and she found herself nodding vigorously. His responding chuckle vibrated her chest in the most amazing way. And then he was kissing her, silencing all her thoughts and using pressure to drive her insane with lust all over again.

All night, he'd said.

Oh, yes.

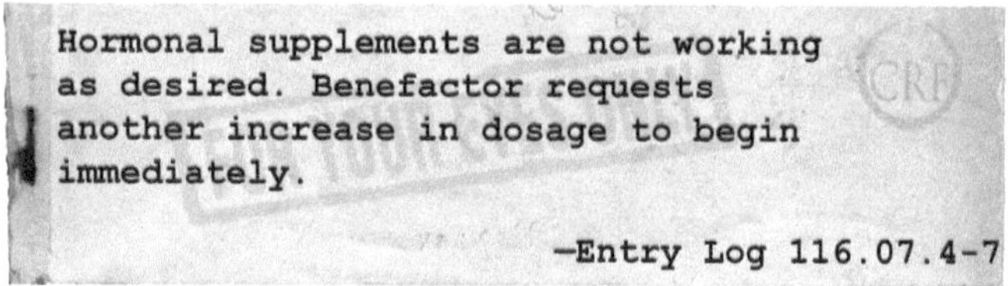
Hormonal supplements are not working as desired. Benefactor requests another increase in dosage to begin immediately.

—Entry Log 116.07.4-7

Jayson's plan backfired.

He thought a night in bed pleasuring Lizzie would help cure this temptation, but it only fortified his craving. Her passion had sprung to life in a way he hadn't expected, driving him all the wilder. Even now, as she snuggled into his side, he could feel the heat radiating from her. The woman had transformed into a sensual goddess under his touch, and he fucking loved it.

He needed more.

So much more.

He palmed his forehead and blew out a breath. This wouldn't end well. He knew that. The second she learned the truth, everything would end, yet he couldn't bring himself to take this any further without her knowing the reality of their situation. It wasn't fair to her.

The conundrum left him with a throbbing headache and a raging hard-on.

He needed a long shower, preferably with the redhead using his shoulder as a pillow.

His steadfast control had never been more important than it was last night when she begged to touch him and reciprocate. It took more energy than it should have to refuse her, mostly because he quieted her requests by exhausting her sexually.

She passed out on top of him around five this morning, hence the early afternoon hour. He'd slept more than he expected and woke with the overwhelming urge to flatten her beneath him and claim her.

Fucking bizarre.

Jayson enjoyed naked women in his bed and usually entertained them with another round of pleasure in the morning, but this desire was unnatural. It went far deeper than a carnal yearning and scared the shit out of him.

He wasn't a "love them and leave them" type but more of a "love them and maybe love them again later" type.

But with Lizzie, he thought he could be a "love her and only her" type. Especially after the way she came apart in his arms. She had responded to his touch like no one else in his long memory.

It has to be a trick.

Something to do with her genetics?

He'd have to ask the others if they felt this strange draw to her. It was messing with his head. Both of them.

Her thigh shifted over his, lifting upward to settle where he wanted her touch most—as if her body knew his needs without asking.

The woman was clearly created to test his control and destroy him.

He bit off a groan as she pressed her ample breasts into his side.

Heaven. That's what she felt like beside him. And every sinful part of him begged to pull her under him and unleash his darkest cravings. But she was nowhere near ready for him, and not just because of all the secrets.

Her leg slipped lower, then higher, and before he could react, Lizzie straddled his hips and stared down at him through hooded eyes.

"Good morning," she murmured in a voice thickened by sleep and lust. It sounded amazing coming from her. And that look? Pure, unadulterated sex.

He settled his palm on her waist. "Good afternoon," he corrected with a smile. "Sleep well?"

"Mm-hmm." She rocked her hips over his erection with the murmur, sending pleasure straight to his aching balls. He tightened his hold to cease her movements, but she rebelled by flattening her chest against his and pressing little kisses to his jaw. "It's a new day, and I'm ready to renegotiate."

Fuck.

"Lizzie…"

She silenced him with a kiss and, with her tongue, unleashed everything he'd taught her last night. It blew his mind how quickly this woman caught on to his preferences. However, she'd neglected to remember one major element to this relationship between them.

He rolled her beneath him and pinned her arms to the mattress on either side of her head. "You're forgetting something important, Red."

Big brown eyes stared up at him as a beautiful flush painted her cheeks. "What's that?" she asked in a breathy voice.

"You're not in charge, sweetheart." He nipped her lip in silent reprimand before pressing his mouth to her ear. "And I say we're not renegotiating yet." He drew his tongue down the column of her neck to her collarbone and farther, until he reached the rosy peak of her breast.

They could test one more limit before breakfast.

Rather than suck the tender nipple into his mouth, he grazed it with his teeth and smiled when she bowed off the bed. A harder pinch elicited a strangled noise of need that sent a jolt of desire straight to his dick.

It seemed Lizzie Watkins wasn't averse to a little bit of pain mingled with her pleasure. He would enjoy evoking more of that at a later time.

He laved her abused breast before placing an open-mouthed kiss to the other and left her alone on the bed.

She blinked up at him in confusion. "Where are you going?"

"Brunch," he replied. "We need to eat." And his gifted nose told him someone was hard at work in the kitchen.

"But…" Her tongue darted out to lick her lips as she ogled at his barely contained cock. He fought the urge to grin. She looked ready to devour him. If only he could allow it.

"That's not on the menu, Red." He selected a pair of boxers from his dresser drawer and a white shirt. "Here."

She ignored the clothes. "I'm not hungry."

"Your eyes say otherwise." He pulled a matching tee over his head before finding a pair of sweatpants. "Get dressed."

The little rebel narrowed her gaze. "Can't we eat after?"

He planted his hands on either side of her head and stared her down. "You're forgetting who is in control again."

She frowned. "I never agreed to that."

"Not true, sweetheart." He brushed his lips against hers. "You agreed the moment you stepped into my bedroom. And"—he pressed his mouth to her ear—"you like my commands." He smiled against her warming neck. "Now get up so we can eat."

If she were lying on her stomach, he would have followed it up with a light swat to her ass. Instead, he gently bit her pulse before standing upright and cocking a brow.

She glowered at him, but her beautiful flush and stiff nipples told him all he needed to know about her aroused state. Lizzie wanted him to finish what he started, but he'd opted to force her to go without—his way of reminding her who called the shots.

And maybe because he wanted her to live through a slight variation of his agony.

Was it fair? Hell no.

Was it necessary? Yes. Because he needed a break before he did something stupid, like fuck her into oblivion.

He would need to talk to Luc today not just about the vial of liquid from last night but about his evolving relationship with Lizzie. This couldn't continue, not with her being kept in the dark. She deserved better.

Jayson immediately regretted his wardrobe choice for Lizzie as she pulled on his clothes. He dressed so many women in this fashion and never cared, yet somehow she captivated him.

His white shirt fell past her hips, ending just above the boxer shorts. The fabric hung loosely on her, but her curves peeked at him in the subtlest of ways. He would definitely be fantasizing about this later. After she left.

"Happy?" she asked.

He threaded his fingers in her hair and allowed a sliver of his arousal to rise to the surface as he kissed the hell out of her. His tongue silenced hers while he unleashed his desire and marked her the way he wanted. Her nails dug into his arms, spurring him on, until he left her panting before him. "I am now," he whispered, responding to her inquiry into his happiness. "Let's eat."

"You're killing me," she breathed.

"Likewise, Red." He swept his tongue over hers once more before sliding his hand into hers and leading her to the door. She followed without argument, her fingers curling around his as he guided her down the hallway and into the kitchen, where Balthazar stood in a pair of boxer briefs and nothing else. He flipped a pancake onto a plate as they entered, and turned to set it on the island.

"A seven-point-six, Jay. Nicely done." Mirth danced in his wicked gaze as he took in Lizzie's disheveled state. "You look famished, sweetheart. Why don't you take the first plate while I finish up the rest?"

Jayson counted the plates on the island while Lizzie stood frozen beside him. Balthazar's physique did that to most women. Men, too, for that matter.

"Are Grace and Jacque still here?" Jayson asked, curious.

"They're in the living area catching up on their American television shows," B replied as he flipped another pancake.

Eight plates, minus the ones for Lizzie, Jay, and the two in the living area, meant that Balthazar had four for himself. *You only took three of them to bed?*

A shrug from the immortal at the stove.

Not the correct assessment. Maybe he wasn't planning to eat. *Four?*

"You need more plates, Jay," Balthazar said as he grabbed one from the counter. "I believe twelve is the standard, but in this case, I need ten."

Five? Jayson grinned. *Nice.* "Yeah, I'll keep that in mind."

"Do." He handed the pancake-layered plate to Jayson. "Luc invited us over for drinks later."

Is he done reviewing the serum? Jayson asked.

Balthazar lifted his chin in the affirmative before saying, "He wants us over as soon as we're free. Does that work for you?"

"Yep." He picked up Lizzie's untouched plate and bumped his hip against hers. "Let's eat, Red."

"Uh, yep." Lizzie picked her jaw up off the floor and managed to follow him to the dining room.

"I clearly didn't do my job right if you find Balthazar more interesting than me," he said as he sat beside her rather than across from her.

"He's practically naked," she whispered.

He selected a set of silverware from the middle of the table—Balthazar seriously thought of everything when it came to the kitchen, and the bedroom for that matter—and handed it to Lizzie.

"Balthazar enjoys all aspects of sexuality, including exhibitionism," he replied. "I'm honestly shocked he bothered to put on boxers at all." He suspected the only reason he wore them was for Lizzie's sake. Everyone else in this condo had seen him naked countless times.

She gaped at him. "So this is normal?"

"For Balthazar? Definitely."

"And for you?" she asked.

He shrugged. "It's not a daily occurrence, but Balthazar has a thing for pancakes."

"No, I meant to throw parties and…" She trailed off as Balthazar left the kitchen with two plates and went in the direction of the bedroom. An array of giggles followed, causing Lizzie to frown. "How do you know all these people, again?"

He told her this last night, but perhaps not with enough detail.

"I don't know most of them," Jayson admitted as he grabbed a knife and fork for himself. "Balthazar is an old friend from Hydria, which is the Greek island I lived on prior to moving here for work." He gave her a pointed look. "You still owe me cookies."

"What about the others?" she pressed rather than agreeing. He'd circle back to the cookies later.

"Jacque and Grace are from Hydria, as well, and are visiting for the weekend with B. Tristan was the only one you met last night from the city."

"And all the women?"

"Balthazar's friends." He found the syrup B had left out for them and grinned at the familiar label. Jacque had clearly procured this from Luc's private stash. Their supreme leader had a thing for pure maple products.

"Do you want any?" he asked, hoping to return her mood to the sexy banter from before.

"Uh, sure."

He drizzled the syrup over her pancakes while she watched before doing the same to his own. "Looks like B decided on chocolate chip today," he mused.

"So, he throws parties like this often?"

Jayson chuckled. "Yeah. I guess you could say it's his specialty."

She didn't return his amusement. "And he usually makes breakfast for everyone the next morning?"

"Sustenance is important after an evening of vigorous exercise," Balthazar replied as he returned to the kitchen to pick up the rest of the plates. "It's the hospitable thing to do," he added as he left for the bedroom again.

Lizzie gaped after him before refocusing on Jayson. "So it's routine for you all to sleep with women and feed them the next morning." Not a question.

"I wouldn't call it routine—"

"But it happens often?"

Jayson palmed the back of his neck. Most of the women he took to his bed understood his no-strings-attached terms, but Lizzie was different for several reasons.

"I don't know about often." As it depended on her definition.

"How many times in New York?"

"This would be the first."

"And in Greece?"

"Depends on the week." He wouldn't lie to her, but he wouldn't elaborate, either.

Her eyes widened as the first ounce of emotion graced her features, and it wasn't one he ever wanted to see on her. *Pain.* "Always with different women or the same ones?"

He sighed. "Lizzie, what are you really trying to ask here? How often I take women to my bed? The last time I was with a woman? What do you want to know?" Because he would tell her, within reason.

Balthazar chose that moment to return again. "The ladies want syrup," he murmured with a wink and sauntered off as Lizzie's eyebrows jumped to her hairline.

"How many women are in there?"

"A few," he replied vaguely. At least they'd switched to Balthazar's sex life as a discussion. That should take some of the heat off Jayson.

"And that's normal?" she asked.

"Yes."

"For you as well?"

"I don't tend to entertain five women in my bed at once, if that's what you're asking." He regretted speaking immediately.

"Five women?" she repeated. "You've had… a… a… 'sixsome' before?"

Fuck. This was not going well at all. "Look—"

She shoved away from the table and out of his reach before he could react. Not that he'd been about to touch her—experience told him that would only make it worse.

"How many, Jayson?"

He knew what she meant—a number of bed partners. "You don't want that answer," he told her honestly.

She wouldn't be able to comprehend it, not without understanding his age and everything else first. And besides, he didn't have a figure to give. He stopped counting a millennia ago.

"Oh God." She blinked rapidly. "Tristan mentioned sharing. He meant…" She covered her mouth while Jayson cursed inwardly.

Fucking Ichorian.

"It's not…" Okay, there was no safe way to answer that. *Not what you think* would be a blatant lie because it was exactly what she thought. "It's not something we will do," he settled on instead. Because he had no interest in sharing Lizzie with anyone.

She shook her head. "I… I…"

The moisture pooling in her eyes broke his heart. "Lizzie—"

"No, I'm not… I don't…" Her lips trembled, and he hated himself a little in that moment. He would never apologize for his past—he didn't regret a second of it—but seeing what it did to her now hurt far more than it should.

"I need to go," she said abruptly and spun toward the foyer.

He hopped to his feet to follow her, but a hand on his shoulder stopped him.

"Give her space," Balthazar whispered, appearing behind him in that uncanny way of his. He'd no doubt heard all the thoughts going through their heads.

"We both know that's the worst thing to do in these situations," Jayson replied as he started after her again.

The grip turned unyielding. "Although I agree, her case is anything but normal. Let her cool off."

"I can't let her leave like that, B."

"And I can't let you go after her."

"What the fuck is that supposed to mean?" He rounded on his oldest friend as the front door slammed. "Since when are you okay with letting a woman suffer on her own?" Balthazar was always the first to provide compassion and understanding, mostly because of his ability to read thoughts and control emotion.

"As I just stated, nothing about this situation applies to the norm," Balthazar replied in that irritatingly calm voice of his. "And you're not in the frame of mind to handle it."

"Excuse me?"

"You want to tell her the truth," Balthazar continued. "And don't deny it, Jay. You've been thinking about it all night, and your emotions right now can't be trusted. You'll break."

Jayson's gut reaction was to punch his best friend in the face, but reason held him in check.

"Fuck…" He rubbed his hand over his face before grabbing the wooden chair beside him and squeezing until it cracked. "Fuck."

"That's exactly what I told you to do last night," Balthazar muttered as he finally let him go. "And with any other woman, you would have done it. But not her. Tell me why that is?"

Jayson shook his head. "It's wrong, and you know it."

"The attraction is mutual, clearly. So how is it wrong, Jay?" Balthazar waited for a response, but Jayson couldn't articulate one fast enough. "Because you're worried she'll never forgive you for it—something you would never concern yourself with for any other woman."

"I'm not an ass."

"And I'm not calling you one," Balthazar countered. "I'm saying you usually wouldn't consider a future with a woman, but you're thinking about one with Lizzie. That's why you won't give in to your desire and also why you can't go after her right now. You're too tempted to tell her everything, and although I can condone sating the needs of you both, I can't allow that. Not without the others agreeing first."

Jayson knew he was right, but fuck if he didn't want to ignore logic and chase after Lizzie.

The hurt in her eyes… He'd put that there. Not because he meant to, but because he hadn't been quick enough to explain.

"I hate this," he admitted. "All of it."

"We'll sort it, Jay," Balthazar murmured. "But first I need thirty minutes to finish up in the bedroom. Afterward, we'll head out to meet Luc."

"Thirty minutes?" Jayson repeated with a half-hearted laugh. He couldn't exactly be amused with Lizzie hurting downstairs, but he tried anyway. "You tired, B?"

"The ladies started without me," Balthazar replied with a shrug. "I gave them an objective, and they're living up to the task."

"Right." Jayson shook his head, irritated. "Not even that appeals to me right now." And it fucking should because he knew syrup was somehow involved. "I'll be here when you're done."

~*~

Lizzie threw her purse onto her mattress and collapsed beside it. She'd been an idiot to leave it unattended on Jayson's foyer table all night and an even bigger idiot for going to bed with him.

Or maybe it was the losing her shit over nothing that qualified her for Idiot of the Year?

A sob tore from her chest as she curled into a ball.

How had her night of bliss and passion ended so horribly? She'd let her insecurities out to play at the worst possible time, but seeing how unfazed he was by his friend's bedroom antics hit a nerve. Their night together—which she more than enjoyed—proved him far more skilled than her, but hearing how experienced he was scared the crap out of her.

Exhibitionism.

Sharing.

Erotic parties ending in ménages of unknown quantities, with breakfast the following morning.

I don't tend *to entertain five women in my bed at once.* Meaning he'd done it before.

Her chest rattled, forcing her to breathe.

How could she ever satisfy a man like that? No wonder he hadn't wanted to renegotiate this morning.

All that talk about the future had given her hope that he wanted more, that he was easing her into their passion out of respect for her inexperience. But his proclivities existed on a level she could never reach, and he surely realized that last night.

Was she just a diversion? The virgin neighbor he wanted to corrupt and deflower?

God, she hoped not. His touch had awakened something foreign in her. And he hadn't hidden how much he wanted her.

Unless he looked at all women that way.

"Damn it," she whispered as more tears fell.

Even if he did want her, she couldn't live up to his expectations. And after the way she'd just acted over breakfast, he surely knew that.

She'd more than overreacted.

But five women at once? That couldn't be normal. What did one even call that? A ménage à six?

And if he didn't *tend* to entertain that many women, how many did he bed on a regular basis?

You don't want that answer.

He was right. She didn't.

Jayson had been the first man to ever really touch her, and she had wanted so much more. She'd ruined that chance by reacting like a prude in his dining room.

Maybe it was for the best. Lizzie never planned to wait until marriage but had never met anyone who tempted her enough for sex. Other than Tom. Except now she wondered if that was true.

The feelings and sensations Jayson had aroused in her over the last few weeks were nothing compared to her past. Tom's hugs gave her girly butterflies, while Jayson's kisses set her on fire.

Her phone dinged, sending a jolt of hope through her heart, followed by a shiver of dread. She'd left her dress and shoes in his room. He probably wanted to drop them off, or worse, needed her to come get them.

Another ping had her groaning and digging through her purse for her phone.

The text on the screen was not what she expected.

OMG! You'll never guess what Cam did!

Oh, and you better be free tonight, Liz. It's been ages since I saw your face, and I need a girls' night.

A second later another message appeared.

Seriously, you need to call me ASAP. I'm dying over here!

Lizzie pressed her face into the bedding and muttered unintelligibly to herself.

She'd been relieved and saddened to find the condo empty. Breaking down in front of Stas would have been mortifying, but also therapeutic. Kristin did not offer the same outlet. She was a fun friend, not a close friend.

Another chime had her peeking at the phone.

Did Kristin tell you about the tickets?

Cam added a bunch of excited emojis afterward, including wicked devil faces and lips. A photo of a fallen angel outfit arrived next, followed by another text.

You still have that outfit from the Alpha B&W party our senior year, right?

Lizzie sat up on her bed, her interest piqued.

Yes, she typed back.

Little dots appeared from Cam seconds before her response popped up on the screen.

Good! Wear it tonight. It's fucking hot, chick.

Lizzie flipped to the conversation with Kristin. She considered texting but decided calling would be easier. After several deep breaths, she cleared her throat and hit dial.

An excited squeal came over the line, forcing her to pull the phone away from her ear.

"Are you sitting down?"

Lizzie cleared her throat again before saying, "Yes."

"Cam scored us tickets to some exclusive Halloween party tonight, and you're totally coming with us. No arguments, Liz. I haven't seen you in like two months, and I know how you feel about dressing up."

Lizzie grimaced. The idea of playing dress-up for anything right now did not appeal to her in the slightest, but she couldn't exactly say that. Not without Kristin requiring a reason and demanding Lizzie go out anyway.

"The fastest way to get over a guy is to get under another one" was one of Kristin's favorite sayings.

"What time?" Lizzie asked.

"Cam says to be at her place by nine, and she wants you to wear that sexilicious costume from that black-and-white party. You know, the one where she hooked up with Dean?" She rattled off some additional details and a comment about her own outfit before ending with, "Any questions?"

"Where's the party being held?" Lizzie didn't really care but thought it might be good information to jot down in case Stas came home later.

"The Arcadia," Kristin replied. "It's supposedly a hot club, though I've never been there, and they throw an annual Halloween party with exclusive clientele. Cam says we should expect celebrities."

Those words would have excited her a few months ago. Now she just wanted to hide. "Sounds good," she managed. "I need to start getting ready."

Kristin would interpret that to mean Lizzie wanted to ready herself physically, but really, she required the time to regroup mentally. Because she couldn't put on a happy face and enjoy an evening out with the girls while moping over Jayson.

"Awesome. Toodles, Liz."

The line went dead.

Lizzie stared at her reflection in the mirror over her dresser.

Maybe this will be good for me, she thought.

She never did anything like this anymore, not since Tom's death, and she so desperately needed to let go of the pain.

Some alcohol and dancing would chase away the shadows beneath her puffy eyes.

A little harmless flirtation could help her forget Jayson temporarily, too.

Hanging out with her old friends would help her feel less lonely. Stas wouldn't like it because she didn't care for Lizzie's sorority sisters.

"But she's not here," Lizzie murmured to herself. "She's never here."

So why not go out and enjoy a little fun? Nothing held her here except herself. Jayson clearly didn't care that she'd run off, or he would have stopped by or called by now. Going out with friends seemed like the natural cure. She already had the outfit and shoes; she just needed the hair and makeup to go with it.

"I can do this," she told herself.

Experiencing a new club wouldn't be a hardship, and if she didn't like it, she'd come home. Easy.

"Now I just need to find that costume."

CHAPTER TWELVE

Angels and Demons at the Costume Ball

College enrollment complete.
Benefactor is eager to see how subject acclimates to the social environment and extracurricular activities.

—Entry Log 118.06.4-7

"Estrogen?" Jayson asked, incredulous. Could that be why he found Lizzie irresistible? He adored women, but something about her drew him in like no one else ever had, which was saying a lot for a man his age. "Are they trying to turn her into a succubus or something?"

Luc leaned against the wall beside him with his hands in his pockets. "She's quite alluring, but I don't think that's the purpose."

"She's a gorgeous woman," Balthazar added. "But I don't find her irresistible." The pointed glance and word choice said he'd been playing in Jayson's thoughts. It was the mind reader's way of confirming that Jayson's feelings were his own and not the result of scientific intervention.

But that didn't mean the serum wasn't at least partly responsible.

"What were the chemical properties?" Anything addictive, perhaps? Because that's how Jayson would describe his desire for Lizzie—an infatuation. He craved her presence and wished he was in New York with her, not here in

Hydria. He'd left her with a guard again, but if she left the condo, the Hydraian wouldn't be able to follow. And that left Jayson antsy and anxious to return.

Luc scratched his jaw, gaze thoughtful. "The solution is primarily composed of estrogen and a few filler ingredients."

"So it's like a birth control pill?" Stas guessed. She stood across from them with Issac at her side.

Neither of them had greeted Jayson favorably, likely because they didn't approve of Lizzie spending the night at his place last night. *Well, too fucking bad.* His only regret was the way she had left this afternoon, something he would rectify as soon as they finished this conversation.

"Not quite," Luc replied. "Nothing in the chemical makeup prevents conception. It's more of a hormonal regimen, but for what, I'm not certain." He shifted his focus to Tom. "I don't see how this serum is keeping her alive."

"I never said it was." Tom folded his tanned arms. The newly turned Hydraian was clearly spending a lot of time near the pool with Amelia. "All I overheard was the mention of a monthly dose, and we all jumped to conclusions that Lizzie required it to live. Your research states otherwise, unless hormones are now required for breathing?"

"It's moot," Luc said. "We can replicate the serum, but I need a blood sample before we go any further."

"From Lizzie?" Stas's tone and expression dared anyone to answer that, but of course, Luc enjoyed a good challenge.

"Yes." Flat, straight to the point, and underlined in authority.

"No," she said immediately. "No. What we do next is tell her the truth. You have her serum. Replicate it, and let's bring her to safety."

"That's not your decision to make," Luc murmured, expression and stance professionally polite. Only those who knew him well would see the tick in his jaw, suggesting his urge to assert dominance.

"Maybe not," Stas agreed. "But I'm not going into her room like some vampire and stealing her blood without permission." She flashed an apologetic look at Issac, who merely shrugged in response. She blew out a breath and refocused on Luc, her expression still contrite but for a different reason.

Luc and Stas had disagreed with one another since day one, mostly because she feared her future and he found her behavior to be selfish. Jayson suspected it would only grow worse once Stas changed into a Hydraian—her innate gift for controlling people undermined Luc's natural sovereignty in Hydria.

"I'm done lying to her, Luc," she said, her tone lacking the confrontation from moments ago. "We agreed that we needed more information about her, and now we have it. Meanwhile, Lizzie's alone in New York with more than one lunatic, and that's unacceptable. It's time to tell her everything and move her somewhere safe before"—she paused to clear her throat, her eyes darkening—"before *Ezekiel* decides on his next move."

Jayson nodded, agreeing with every word but also keeping his mouth shut. His place in this discussion was jeopardized by his selfish reasons for wanting

Lizzie to know the truth. Something Balthazar wouldn't hesitate to point out if it came down to an even vote.

"Stas is right," Tom said, but with a touch more reverence. "We've been searching for two months, and all we've found are some hormone-laced drinks. It's not a lot to go on, but we can gather more details from her once she's in Hydria—where she'll be safe."

Luc remained quiet, considering, and met Issac's gaze. "And you?"

"I do not believe Elizabeth to be a threat to anyone other than herself," he replied. "Informing her of our world and her potential place in it will not go over well, and I worry about her reaction—not for us, but rather, for her."

"He's right," Balthazar murmured. "You'll need me to numb her emotions, or she may do something rash."

"Alik?" Luc asked, his focus shifting to the silent man in the corner of the room.

"I recommended we bring her here two months ago, while you all agreed to send Jayson to play babysitter." Alik unfolded his arms to place his hands in the pockets of his leather jacket. "That should answer your question."

Luc acknowledged the response with a nod before fixing his gaze on Jayson. "And you?"

"Balthazar would tell you that my feelings on this subject prohibit me from offering an unbiased response," he replied honestly. "But I agree with the others that it's time to tell her the truth."

"So you all believe on varying levels that she's ready." Luc's carefully pitched tone suggested he didn't agree but would trust their opinions.

"She's not." Issac wrapped his arm around Stas as she reacted to his frank reply. "But I believe we are at an impasse. We require her cooperation to learn more, and the only way for that to happen is to tell her the truth. And I do not believe waiting for Ezekiel's next play is our smart move."

Jayson agreed with a nod, as did everyone else.

"Well." Luc clasped his hands and shrugged. "I guess that leads us to the next topic of discussion. Who is going to tell her and how?"

~*~

The reason for Cam's request to wear their black and white outfits became clear almost immediately.

Angels and demons.

Not an original Halloween party theme, but a classic nonetheless.

Most of the guests wore sinister outfits with leather and chains, giving the club a gothic feel. The music blaring overhead added to the dark atmosphere, as did the low lighting.

Definitely not Lizzie's usual hangout, but perfect for a spooky evening filled with drinking and dancing.

"Ladies," the bartender murmured as he dropped off their cocktails.

Cam simpered at the handsome man while Kristin handed over her card to start a tab. They alternated nights throughout college, something that had continued after graduation. Lizzie had covered their last girls' night out, and tonight was Kristin's turn.

"You're glowing," Cam said around her straw.

Lizzie grinned. "It's the black light." Her pure-white outfit of a miniskirt, knee-high boots, and a tank top were all glowing a purple color. "If only I had wings." She'd resemble a violet angel.

"Your bra is completely visible," Kristin teased. "We should have worn white too, Cam." They were both wearing black—Cam in a skirt that barely covered her butt and a see-through shirt, revealing her lacy bra, and Kristin in leather pants and a halter top.

Two demons and their pet angel, Lizzie.

"We're too sinful to wear white," Cam replied. "Besides, Liz is the only virgin here."

"Hey! That's not…" Her cheeks flamed as memories of last night rolled through her thoughts. She cleared her voice before finishing with, "True."

"Has something changed in the last two months?" Kristin asked, eyebrows waggling.

"Maybe she's been shacked up with a guy and that's why she's been MIA," Cam said.

"Yes!" That excited Kristin. "I think you might be right. Is she, Liz? Is there a man keeping you busy?"

Lizzie shook her head. "You're both being ridiculous." But thoughts of Jayson crept into her mind, sending another rush of heat down her neck, followed by a chill when she remembered how they left things.

No calls.

No texts.

Nothing.

Not that she should expect it. She'd acted like a crazy person earlier. So what if the man was a little more experienced than her?

Try a lot *more*.

Okay, true, but couldn't that be a good thing?

"Oh my God, Cam's right. You've been hooking up with someone." Kristin set her drink down on the bar and gave Lizzie her full attention. "Spill. Tell us everything."

"Uh, well, I have this new neighbor. It's nothing, really, just, I don't know. He's hot, and we've kissed a few times." She swallowed several pulls from her straw in an attempt to cool off her cheeks, but the alcohol only seemed to warm her more. "It's really not a big deal."

"Jayson would be so disappointed to hear that," a male voice said directly behind her.

She turned in to a muscular chest encased in a leather jacket and lifted her gaze to a pair of ebony eyes tinged with gold flecks.

"Kiel," she breathed. "Hi. I didn't mean, that is, I…" Lizzie cleared her throat as he studied her with an amused expression. He clearly thought she was an idiot, and rightly so.

"Ignore me," she muttered.

"On the contrary, Little Red, I find you impossible to ignore." He curled a long finger through one of her loose pieces of hair and gave it a little tug. "Introduce me to your friends."

"Right, of course." As if she could appear any more incompetent, she'd forgotten her manners. He remained behind her as she rotated to face her gaping friends. "Cam, Kristin, this is Kiel. He, uh, works with the neighbor I just mentioned."

"Hello, ladies," he murmured over her shoulder. "Can I introduce you to some of my friends?"

Cam's eyes brightened even more at the prospect. "Yes, I think you should," she replied in that flirtatious way of hers. Kiel's rocker image didn't fit Kristin's usual type, but Cam rarely discriminated. If the man boasted confidence and good looks, she gave him a chance. And Kiel certainly met both requirements.

"Brilliant." His hand appeared over Lizzie's shoulder as he signaled some friends from one of the booths lining the club's walls. The seating seemed to stretch all around, minus the area where the stairs led to a VIP lounge on the second level, and a dance floor took up most of the middle. The bar near the entrance was where they decided to start after surveying the interior. Kristin liked to begin with a few rounds to help loosen up before chatting with random men, but Cam had no problem initiating conversation while sober, as she did now.

"What do you do for a living, Kiel?" she asked while the two other men approached. Unlike Kiel, they were wearing all-black suits. Lizzie recognized the expensive brand with an inward smile. Kristin would be all over these guys the second she saw them.

"I'm an assassin," Kiel replied in that easy way of his.

Cam and Kristin laughed at his Halloween-inspired joke, while Lizzie shook her head. An assassin didn't really fit the theme, and his leather jacket was the same as the other night. Not all that original, but maybe he didn't enjoy dressing up.

"I'm a devil," Cam replied and used her fingers to form horns over her blonde head.

"Are you?" Kiel sounded impressed. "In the sheets or out, I wonder."

"Why not both?" Cam replied, her expression coquettish.

Kiel's chest was close enough to Lizzie's back that she felt his responding chuckle. "I think you're going to have an enlightening evening, darling," he said as his friends arrived.

"Zach, Lars, meet Cam and Kristin." He curled an arm around Lizzie's waist as he added, "And this is Lizzie, but she's off the market."

Lizzie twisted to stare up at him while the others made their introductions.

"I am?" she asked, incredulous.

"You are," he replied. "Your relationship with Jay is far more important than you realize, young one."

She blinked. "Has he talked to you?" Her tone betrayed a hopeful note she would have preferred to hide, but she couldn't help it.

"Not quite." His gaze danced over her in a curious way. "There is so much you don't know—it's radiating in your innate innocence."

She frowned at his bizarre words. They should have left her feeling uncomfortable, but instead sparked her interest. Nothing about Kiel struck her as normal or safe, yet he didn't strike her as dangerous. He was friends with Jayson—or acquaintances, anyway. Perhaps that's why she trusted him. Knowing her sorority sisters were at her back helped too.

"Would you like to know more, Lizzie?" he asked, tilting his head to the side. "About Jay? About our world?"

"You mean your business?" That didn't sound all that interesting, but she wouldn't mind learning more about what Jayson did every day.

Kiel's lips curled. "What has Jay told you we do?"

"Acquisitions."

"Is that all?" He tsked. "My dear Lizzie, we have so much to discuss."

He nodded at his friends, and she glanced back to see Cam and Kristin being escorted onto the dance floor. So much for girl code. They must have assumed she was safe with Kiel since they already knew each other. Still, they could have asked.

"Do you want to join them?" Kiel asked, his lips at her ear. "Or would you like to know more about our world?"

Our world…

What bizarre phrasing, except it seemed par for the course with Kiel. He was a walking complex—handsome, charming, generally jovial, but with a lethal air, a don't-fuck-with-me vibe, and an accent she couldn't place.

She met his gaze again. "What do you mean by 'world'? "

"Come with me and find out." He let go of her waist and held out a hand. "I promise not to bite."

"All right," she agreed, pressing her palm to his. "But only if we're staying in the club."

His eyes sparkled with a mixture of mirth and secrets. "As the lady requests."

She expected him to maneuver them over to the booth his friends had vacated, but instead, he headed toward the heavily guarded staircase. A nod at the men dressed in black wearing earpieces had them standing aside for the couple to ascend, causing her nerves to sing with unease.

"Where are we going?" she asked, but he didn't hear her over the music. She considered trying again when the electronic beats quieted upstairs, but her new surroundings piqued a stronger curiosity.

Another bar, as well as a variety of more decadent booths with velvet interiors and glass tables, graced the upper balcony. Kiel meandered over to a vacant booth overlooking the dance floor below and gestured for her to slide in first. She did so while he flagged a waitress wearing a string bikini top and chains for a skirt.

Several of the other women up here boasted similar outfits and were all watching Lizzie with curious expressions.

I'm clearly overdressed for this level.

Or perhaps they wanted to know what qualified her to join the VIP lounge.

Lizzie forced a smile, but no one returned it.

"You know what I want," Kiel said. He hadn't taken a seat yet. Rather, he remained standing with his hands in his pockets as the curvy waitress approached. "My friend here would like something fruity, but spike it nicely. She'll need it."

The brunette trailed polished nails up his jacket and grinned. "Anything for you, love."

He caught her fingers and brought her wrist to his mouth. "Anything?"

"Tease." Her tone held a touch of admonishment. "We both know I'm not to your taste."

"Mmm, sadly true." He let her go after nipping the base of her thumb. "But I may need you for a demonstration later."

"Oh?" Her eager gaze went to Lizzie before returning to Kiel. "You let me know when, and I'm your girl."

"Thank you, sweetheart." He kissed her on the cheek before settling on the other side of the booth and fixing his gaze on Lizzie. "We'll begin once Cynthia delivers our drinks. In the interim, what do you think of the Arcadia?"

"Um, it's not my usual scene."

He chuckled. "No, I should think not. You strike me as a country-bar kind of girl, or perhaps a disco?"

"A disco?" she repeated with an ineloquent snort. "I like dancing, but I need something current."

"Disco isn't current?" He frowned as if puzzled by that. "Forgive me, but the decades run together. Hell, sometimes the centuries do as well, though this technology era is quite fascinating."

She gaped at him. "How old are you?" Because he didn't look a day over thirty, but he spoke about time in such a weird manner. Just like everything else.

How is this guy friends with Jay, again? They seemed like very different people.

Kiel smiled. "Oh, we'll get to that very soon, darling. But would you mind terribly if I made a call? It will only be a moment."

"Uh, sure." Lizzie searched for her friends downstairs while he fiddled with his phone.

She could see the throng of gyrating bodies from her perch beside the glass railing, but making out individual faces in the flashing lights was impossible. The booths along the walls were easier to identify, as were the people inside them, but she doubted Cam or Kristin ventured there. At least not yet. Cam worked fast, but not *that* fast.

"Evening, Jedrick," Kiel drawled in a tone that drew Lizzie's attention. It held a sinister feel to it that he hadn't used in her presence before.

"Not a good time? Then I'll make this brief. I have something that belongs to you." He listened, his ebony gaze gleaming with a sinful emotion that unsettled Lizzie's stomach.

The playful charmer from before had been replaced by someone far more wicked.

This was a bad idea.

Too late now, Liz.

"No, not quite." He grinned. "Would you care to say hello to Jay, Little Red?"

~*~

Jayson's blood ran cold as he gripped the phone impossibly tighter. "Lizzie…"

"Jay-Jayson?" Her innocent voice came through the receiver underlined with confusion. "I don't—"

"Listen to me very carefully, Lizzie. You need—"

Ezekiel's tsk came over the line, silencing Jayson's attempt at a warning. "Now that's not a good sport, Jay. I offer you a chance to say hello, or perhaps goodbye in this case, and you try to ruin my fun? Where's the sportsmanship in that, hmm?"

The lamp shattered beside him as he knocked everything off the end table in Balthazar's great room. "If you fucking touch her—"

"You'll what, kill me?" Ezekiel chuckled, his amusement palpable even over the thousands of miles that separated them. "I daresay I underestimated your feelings for the woman. This is going to be quite fun."

Jayson gritted his teeth and forced the words out that he needed to say. "What do you want?"

"To see just how bad you want her back," Ezekiel murmured. "Would you like to know where we are?"

"You know I do," Jayson managed through his aching jaw. *So I can shove a blade between your eyes.*

"The Arcadia," he replied simply. "One of Lizzie's friends managed to procure an invitation to tonight's party, perhaps not by coincidence. But imagine my delight when your gorgeous Red waltzed in wearing a buffet of white. Oh, thank you, Cynthia. That looks lovely. I'll buzz you if we require anything else, such as the demonstration. Thanks, love."

"*What are you doing?*"

Jayson fell to his knees at the terrified note in Lizzie's voice, his will crumbling to his feet. He never should have left her alone. Not with Ezekiel on the loose. What the fuck had he been thinking visiting Hydria while she remained unprotected in New York?

He'd failed her in the worst possible way.

The Arcadia?

Fuck.

What the hell happened to her guard detail?

Ezekiel's cool reply didn't calm his nerves in the slightest. "Trust me, darling, this is for your own protection, as I suspect there will be a great deal of screaming in our near future."

"If you—"

"Hold that thought, Jay." The music died in the background, replaced by a scuffling that suggested a fight—one that ended with a muffled shriek and Ezekiel sighing. "Calm down."

"I won't calm down!" Lizzie snapped. "You just sealed us in a glass bubble!"

"For reasons you'll understand once I hang up the phone. Now sit silently, or I'll be forced to silence you."

A gasp came from Lizzie, filled with shock and fear.

Oh, fuck no.

Jayson would slaughter Ezekiel for this.

His fists clenched as he envisioned ripping the Ichorian limb by limb and burning each piece while forcing the asshole to watch.

Unspoken truce or not, he would end him.

Slowly.

Permanently.

He tried to voice his threats, but words failed him. Agony, fury, and a twinge of helplessness overwhelmed reason, paralyzing him in a shell of fear and loathing.

"I've given you our location. I suggest you act quickly, Jay." The line went dead, and Jayson sent his phone crashing into the wall. It shattered into a million fucking pieces just as Balthazar and Luc ran into the house.

The Arcadia was the one place in the world Jayson couldn't go, and Ezekiel knew it.

"Fuck!" Jayson pounded his fury into the floor, not caring at all for the skin cracking across his knuckles. It would heal in a minute. The same could not be said for Lizzie.

"What the hell is going on?" Luc demanded.

"Jay's losing it," Alik replied from his perch on the couch. "Reminds me of that time in Rome…" His voice trailed off at the glower Jayson flashed him. "Right, you remember."

Alik shrugged and went back to whatever the fuck he was doing on his phone. Jayson had the sudden urge to rip it from his hands and throw it, along with Alik, against the wall in response, but a hand on his shoulder steadied him.

"Talk to me," Balthazar demanded as he knelt beside him.

Jayson still couldn't form a coherent sentence, so he replayed the conversation through his head while clenching and unclenching his fists against the wood.

Violence unlike anything he'd ever experienced lanced his thoughts, slicing his need into two parts. One vied for sanity, while the other craved a suicide mission to New York.

"Ezekiel has Lizzie at the Arcadia," Balthazar translated for those who couldn't hear. "Get Wakefield, and we need to find out what happened to Jennifer."

Jennifer. Lizzie's supposed guard.

Why the fuck didn't she tell me Lizzie went out?

"Already on my way," Luc said as he left the house.

"He won't kill her," Alik said in that irritatingly calm way of his. "There's no entertainment value, and she's worth more alive. He's fucking with you, and winning." He hopped off the couch. "I'll be in the pool if anyone needs me."

Balthazar's hand tightened when Jay considered reacting by tossing a blade at one of his oldest friends. It wouldn't be the first time they fought, or the last, but Alik usually won. His ability to inflict pain mentally far surpassed their own, not to mention his telepathy. Powerful bastard.

"He's trying to redirect your rage," Balthazar murmured after the door slammed.

"It's working."

"Good. Now get up off the floor and act like the warrior I know you are." Balthazar pushed away from him and turned off the television before walking over to the kitchen. Jayson took two deep breaths, forced himself upright, and accepted the water bottle Balthazar handed him on his way to the dining area.

"Alik is right," B said. "Zeke is goading you for fun. He won't kill Lizzie."

"You can't know that for certain. He's a fucking assassin, for crying out loud."

"Who has had multiple opportunities to take her out and hasn't bothered. No, there's something else going on here." Balthazar took another swig of water and focused on the door just before it flew open. Issac and Luc walked in, followed by Stas and Tom.

"Jennifer fell asleep," Luc said flatly.

"She fell asleep?" Jayson repeated, his tone lethally soft.

"Yes, she thought Lizzie was staying in for the night." Luc's expression indicated he was not pleased by that excuse. "I'll deal with Jennifer after we fix this issue."

"Do so. Or I will." And a demotion would be the least of her concerns.

Falling asleep on the job.

Fuck.

If Lizzie dies because of this…

His hands curled into fists at the thought. He'd never forgive Jennifer, or himself.

"What's the plan?" he demanded.

"Mateo and Tristan are already en route," Issac informed. "What do they need to know?"

"Zeke has her in some sort of glass bubble," Jayson growled. "It drowned out all the noise."

Issac nodded. "VIP lounge. All the booths have sound control for purposes I'm sure don't require elaboration. Anything else?"

"He plans to make her scream." Jayson's hands fisted again, this time destroying the plastic bottle in his hand.

Balthazar handed him another one without missing a beat. "That's not going to happen, Stas. Wakefield goes alone." He must have been responding to her thoughts, because her eyes narrowed.

"She's my best friend." The fire in her gaze was admirable, but shadowed by heartache. No way could she go in there and think clearly. Jayson understood because he felt the same. Emotion superseded reason. "And he killed my parents," she reminded them, sounding broken.

"Which is why you won't react rationally when you see him," Balthazar replied softly. "You won't be helpful; you'll be a hindrance."

"The only way Issac will be able to focus enough to get Elizabeth out of there alive is if he knows you're here safe and sound," Luc added, his logic infallible. "Otherwise, you risk never seeing your best friend again."

"Lucian's right," Issac murmured. "You remember the Arcadia, Aya. We barely survived your first trip, and if forced to choose, it will always be you." He cupped her cheek and pulled her close. "I need to do this alone, love. You know that as well as I do, just as you know this is something I'm doing only for you."

"You're also too valuable. I'm all for you making your own decisions, but this would put your life at an unnecessary risk. If you walk in there spouting commands, Ezekiel will slaughter you on sight, and I will not allow that to happen." Luc's voice was uncharacteristically soft, but underlined in authority. He always chose his battles wisely, and this was one he would fight if she demanded it. Jayson would fight with him, as would Balthazar and Alik, if needed.

Stas pressed her forehead to Issac's chest as Balthazar nodded, his way of subtly letting everyone know she'd agreed to Luc's implied edict. Even with her emotions running high, she could perceive and admire logic. The woman would become a fine Hydraian one day, whenever she chose to accept her fate.

"What will you do?" Tom asked with a quiet intensity. "I've read Ezekiel's file. He won't just hand her over to you."

Issac ran his fingers through Stas's hair and kissed her gently on the forehead before taking a step back, his game face firmly in place. "I'm not concerned, Thomas."

Not so much arrogance as well-earned confidence. Issac knew how to handle this type of situation, but it killed a part of Jayson to sit back and wait. He ran a hand over his face and fought the urge to break more shit in Balthazar's house.

This furious reaction was so unlike him. Not even news of Amelia's captivity had impacted him like this, and he'd definitely been angry then. Yet he'd been able to remain levelheaded and calm while thinking through a solution.

Meanwhile, Lizzie had him wanting to go to the Arcadia himself to retrieve her—something he knew defied reason and comprehension. Just seconds ago he'd been commending Stas's ability to remain intelligent in this situation, and now he craved his own version of vengeance all over again.

Something is seriously wrong with me, B.

The nudge against his arm said they would work it out.

If only Jayson believed him. The notion of Issac saving Lizzie on his behalf grated. Walking into the Arcadia would be a suicide mission for any Elder, even one who could distort his appearance. Jayson understood that on a level, but relying on someone else to do it for him—

"Is the smart plan," Balthazar whispered, answering Jayson's thoughts. "You try to go with him, and Alik will knock you out."

"I'd like to see him try," Jayson muttered.

"He's waiting outside," Balthazar informed, voice pitched low for Jayson's ears alone. "That man knows all of us better than he'll ever admit."

"Doesn't make him any less of an asshole."

"Truth," B agreed and took a swig of his water to hide his grin. Leave it to the mind reader to provide amusement under otherwise damning circumstances.

"You rang," Jacque announced as he appeared in the middle of the living area, wearing a pair of pajama bottoms and nothing else.

"Elizabeth decided to visit the Arcadia while we were discussing how to break the news to her tomorrow," Luc explained.

Issac smoothed a hand down his tie as he added, "Yes. It seems I require a lift back to the city."

CHAPTER THIRTEEN

Let's Play a Game of Truth

> **Subject appears to be acclimating to collegiate life as expected. Cataloging all social interactions for future review.**
>
> **—Entry Log 118.10.4-7**

"I'm not going to hurt you," Kiel said as Lizzie paced the small area between their table and the solid glass wall.

It had all happened so fast that she'd barely had a chance to react. Not that she'd gotten far. Kiel's arm had felt like granite around her waist as he yanked her backward into the space she explored now—a rectangular path, measuring/approximately three feet by two feet, beside the booth.

The club goers were all completely unfazed. A few watched her as one might an animal in a zoo, while the others went about their business as if this happened every day.

Because makeshift pods were apparently normal here.

Lizzie rubbed her arms in a poor attempt to warm them and continued exploring her little nook. The glass appeared solid and thick and impenetrable for all intents and purposes. Whatever switch Kiel had used to deploy it remained hidden to her, but if she found it, she could escape.

And then what? Run?

She almost laughed. Kiel had already proven his reflexes far surpassed hers. Lizzie was stuck here until he either let her go or got to the point.

"What do you want?" she demanded, or tried to, anyway. It came out far softer and a little shakier than intended.

"Desire plays no part in why we find ourselves in this situation, darling. I'm merely here to give you information and nothing more."

"Yeah?" She finally looked at him. "Information about what?"

"Let's start with Tom Fitzgerald. He's a friend of yours, yes?"

Goose bumps filed a path down her spine. She didn't want to talk about this with anyone, certainly not with a stranger who had trapped her in a glass box. "Did you know him?"

"Not personally, no." Kiel paused to sip his deep-red drink and gave her a sinister smile. "What would you say if I told you Tom is very much alive and well?"

She frowned. "I'd call you cruel and heartless."

"Both adequate adjectives, I assure you, but in this instance, neither are applicable. Because although you and the rest of the human race were led to believe he died heroically on some mission, I'm here to give you the truth. Would you like that?"

"I'd like you to let me out of this cage," she countered.

He clucked his tongue. "That wasn't what I asked. What if I could provide proof, right now, that Tom is alive? Would you listen to me then?"

She gaped at him. This had to be some sort of twisted joke, but she couldn't see the purpose. He already stated he didn't know Tom, yet he implied he knew about her friendship with him—something she never mentioned to Jayson, and certainly not to Kiel. She barely knew them both, but this man seemed to be insinuating he knew a whole hell of a lot about her.

"Who are you?"

"Ah, now we're getting somewhere." He sounded pleased by that. "But try rephrasing that question using *what* as opposed to *who,* and we'll move along at a far more acceptable speed."

She blinked, more confused than when this all began. Cam and Kristin were off dancing and having the time of their lives, while Lizzie was stuck in a glass container with a madman.

One who was friends with her neighbor.

Whom he called a few minutes ago with their location.

None of this made a lick of sense!

If only she had her purse. Cam had suggested they leave their things at her place since Kristin was on bar tab duty. All Lizzie had brought with her was an ID to enter the club. Not very helpful.

But she hadn't expected to be imprisoned in a soundproof booth with a maniac.

No music sounded through the walls, not even the base. Which meant her screams couldn't be heard, either, something Kiel had implied earlier while speaking to Jayson.

She needed to play this smart and hope like hell her neighbor would come for her or her friends would notice her absence.

Doubtful on both accounts, but she could consider them her backup plan.

Still need a general plan.

Thank you, Captain Obvious.

Maybe if she went along with this asinine game, Kiel would let her go.

Doubtful.

That's unhelpful.

Kiel grinned and sipped his drink, tilting his head slightly as she considered her next move. He was clearly waiting for something. *A question*, she thought.

Who are you? she'd asked.

He'd replied with something about rephrasing.

"What are you?" She couldn't help the uncertainty in her tone, because obviously, he was a man. But Kiel seemed fond of twisting words and sentences into his own strange language.

"Sit down, Lizzie."

"Why?"

"I'm answering your question." He gestured to the seat she vacated when the walls came down. It would put her directly across from him with her back to the balcony, neither offensive nor defensive. If he wanted to harm her, he could just as easily do so with her standing.

Might as well rest her legs in case he gave her a chance to run. Although, that seemed unlikely in their little prison.

She slid into the booth and folded her arms on the table. The waitress had brought a pink, fruity concoction that would usually appeal to Lizzie but didn't tonight.

"My real name is Ezekiel," he murmured. "I've only recently taken on the name Kiel, as I like to switch things up every now and then. Living forever gets boring, you see. It's the small things that keep us entertained."

She nodded. "Sure." *You're insane.*

"Your Jayson went by the name of Jedrick when we first met—that would have been around 1700 BC in Babylon, by the way. We were born in very different circumstances, myself to an impoverished woman raped by a soldier, and Jedrick to a military god. His father, Artemis, wasn't really a god but an Ichorian with a knack for controlling metal and a thirst for blood. But we'll come back to that.

"My mother died of disease when I was nine years old, thus forcing me to learn quickly and efficiently how to take care of myself. To say I had a particular flair for survival would be an understatement. You see, identifying easy prey and assassinating them quietly are strengths, Lizzie, ones I mastered in my youth."

He paused to sip his drink while Lizzie fought the urge to laugh hysterically.

First, he claimed to be from Babylon—the original city.

Second, to be, what, over three thousand years old?

And now he was making up words like "Ichorians," claiming Jayson to be the son of a god, and stating he, Kiel or Ezekiel—whatever he preferred to be called—was an assassin.

The man was a lunatic wrapped in a sane man's skin.

Unbelievable.

"Osiris approached me as a youth," he continued. "You haven't met him properly yet but will someday. Regardless, he appeared to me as a god and stated I was endowed with a unique skill set that suited his needs. He introduced me to his son, Sethios, and encouraged our friendship. Being of similar ages, we bonded quickly, and I essentially found myself in a new home, surrounded by unique principles that did not apply to humanity but to a greater universe."

He smiled, and it chilled her inside and out. "Would you like to know a secret, Lizzie?"

She cleared her throat, but the cobwebs sticking to her vocal cords rendered speech impossible. Probably a good thing, as she couldn't trust herself to speak.

Lizzie nodded, because she suspected a denial would disappoint him, and she had no intention of pissing off a crazy person without having an escape route.

"I have known of your existence for quite some time, even before you met Astasiya. But that's not my secret, actually." He waved a hand and smiled, amused with himself. "What I mean to say is, I arranged for you both to live together your freshman year. It was a result of laziness on my part, but I do believe it worked out for the best, wouldn't you agree?"

The thrumming in Lizzie's ears couldn't be healthy. She never gave him or Jayson Stas's full name.

"Who are you?" she whispered again.

He relaxed into his booth with a sigh. "You're not listening to me at all, are you?"

"I-I am," she stammered. *But you're crafting some sort of fictional tale that holds no relevance in reality.*

Except he knew Stas's full name. "Astasiya" was too specific to be a guess.

"I suspect we're running out of time, so let's try a new angle," Kiel said while spinning his half-finished drink on the table. "Tell me your thoughts on the CRF. Do you ever wonder what their paramilitary unit really does? How a Sentinel like Tom could be killed on a humanitarian operation?"

"He…" She finally gave in and tasted her drink—a strawberry daiquiri. The logical part of her cringed, but she needed something for her throat—it felt stuffed full of cotton balls.

"You work on that, and I'll answer for you, love. The CRF is not what the public thinks it is, which I know won't surprise you. Every time you go near headquarters, your instincts tell you something is wrong. Am I right?"

If he didn't have her attention before, he had it now. Because that feeling he just described was one she'd never told anyone about. Not even Stas.

"How do you know that?" she managed, her voice raspy.

"Because I've seen you in that building countless times over the years and observed the changes in your biology. You're terrified of the CRF, and justifiably so. It's called muscle memory, darling. The things they've done to you are unspeakable, and although you possess no memory of it, your body does."

She swallowed. "Wh-what do you mean?" She rarely visited the headquarters, even as a child. But he was right about her innate reaction. The building horrified her for inexplicable reasons.

"I wish we could go into more detail, but our intimate meeting is nearly over, and we haven't even gone over the basics yet." He captured her gaze and held it. "You asked who I am, and I've told you. Now, as to what I am, I'm an Ichorian, just like Jay's father. Osiris turned me as an eighteenth mortal birthday present, granting me immortality, and before you comment, yes, I do appear to be closer to thirty-five. Mortals these days age far differently from the era I grew up in."

She hadn't been about to say anything at all, but she nodded anyway. Because sure. Why not? He did resemble a man in his thirties, but maybe immortality had something to do with his aging? Or lack thereof…?

Am I really believing any of this?

"I should add that there's one minor caveat to being an Ichorian—we require mortal blood to survive." He passed over his drink. "Have a peek inside and see for yourself."

Lizzie hesitated, especially after his flippant remarks, but did as he suggested, with a frown. "It looks like a Bloody Mary." A strange beverage for a coffee mug, but everything about this place struck her as unordinary.

"No, darling, it's blood from one of my favorite donors in the back. If you don't believe me, take a sip."

She sniffed instead and scrunched her nose as a wave of nausea overwhelmed her.

It certainly didn't smell like vodka and tomato juice.

But he couldn't be serious.

Blood? Gross.

"Like a vampire?" It came out as a squeak.

He chuckled. "A myth, I assure you, but a similar concept. Try not to use that term too loudly outside our glass walls, though, darling. My kind do not take lightly to being compared to vile creatures of the night—our ancestry is much lighter."

Lizzie gripped the edge of her seat. "You're… This is… Impossible. It's not…" She shook her head as she frantically tried to clear it. "I can't…"

Vampires aren't real. The supernatural isn't real.

"I can bring Cynthia in for a demonstration, if you'd like." He sounded so reasonable and normal, like he spoke about immortality and vampires on a daily basis. "Or you could peek over your shoulder into the booth below us near the dance floor, but if you could keep the screaming to a minimum, my ears would thank you for it."

Another sip from that damn bloody mug of his while he waited for her to choose.

If she asked for a demonstration, he would have to lower the glass. In which case, she could escape.

"Your eyes telegraph your thoughts beautifully, Lizzie. If you opt for the live feed, I will restrain you first, and trust me when I say that is more for your protection than anything else. Because a woman of your standard wandering through this club won't last more than five minutes without ending up in one of the booths, whether by choice or not."

She gulped. The way he said that was both unnerving and terrifying. "Why are you telling me all this?"

"Ah, that is an excellent question." He set his mug down with a genuine smile. "My motives are my own, but irritating Jayson is considered quite the bonus."

"He knows about all of this?"

"Of course. As I said, we grew up together. Jay's father, Artemis, is an Ichorian and a close friend of Osiris's, which was how Jay and I eventually met. Our shared proclivities for war and destruction created a competitive bond of sorts that came to a head about five centuries back. You see, my kind realized our progeny, Hydraians, carried lethal bloodlines that could destroy the Ichorian race, and, well, not to go into detail, but a lot of immortals died as a result."

Lizzie couldn't form words. It all sounded so real, yet improbable.

Hydraians?

Did Kiel enjoy making up words?

Except Jayson mentioned a word that sounded similar to that this morning. Hydria, was it? The place Jacque and Grace were visiting from?

Her eyes widened. Could *Hydraian* stem from *Hydria*?

She shook her head. This was all too much. To even believe this hysteria would qualify her for a mental institution.

Yet… Kiel's statements about the CRF and her feelings were spot on, though his casual comment about watching her freaked her out. And he knew things about Stas…

Lizzie gave in to the pull to survey the club, as he recommended, and turned to observe the booths below. Nothing too crazy, just a couple making out.

She squinted as the lights flashed overhead, illuminating their positions.

Is that…?

She covered her mouth with her hand.

A brown head.

There was a man, under the table, between the woman's bare legs with his mouth on her inner thigh. Lizzie expected him to move higher, but he didn't.

The female's body seemed frozen in time as the male beside her shifted his mouth to her neck to lick the trail of blood leaking from her wound.

Lizzie stood, her hands going to the glass, to scream for help when she realized the booth beside them held a similar picture. As did the one beyond it.

"Oh God…" *Cam and Kristin…* She needed to find them, to warn them.

"Your friends will be fine," Kiel murmured. "Zach and Lars may use them for a snack, but I've instructed them to see the girls home safely afterward."

"Why?" *Why would he do that?*

"Consider it my show of good faith," he replied. "Besides, most mortals leave this place with memories of a euphoric evening and nothing more. It's our way of maintaining a healthy food supply, though there are those who would prefer blood farms."

Lizzie turned to see him shrug.

"I see both sides of the argument, but we are digressing again. Shall we talk about Tom now? The friend you buried, who is indeed very much alive?"

Her legs threatened to buckle beneath her, forcing her to return to her seat across from him. Ten minutes ago, she'd called him cruel for even suggesting it. Now, she felt a beacon of hope followed by severe sadness.

Would Tom truly let her mourn his loss while living a life without her?

They were friends.

She loved him.

Why would he do that to her?

"To clarify, Hydraians are the result of an Ichorian father fornicating with a human female. Your friend Tom is the result of his Ichorian father, Jonathan Fitzgerald, coupling with a human woman named Anna."

Kiel draped his arm over the booth, his long fingers drumming a tune she couldn't hear, not with all the blood pumping through her ears.

Tom isn't human? John is an Ichorian?

This… No.

It's ridiculous and not real.

An elaborate story. A ruse.

"Tom staged a scene with several Hydraians and a few Ichorians out in the middle of the woods at his mother's old cabin. His father believes one of the Sentinels shot Tom with an incendiary bullet—thus killing him—but it was all an illusion orchestrated by Issac Wakefield."

"Issac?" she repeated. *He's part of this too*?

"He's an Ichorian—I'll prove that in about a minute—and he helped save your friend's life. I imagine it was a gift for Astasiya, as he is quite fond of the talented woman, but there you have it. Tom is alive, residing in Hydria, and yes, Stas knows as well. Now that brings us full circle, yes? And why they've kept all this from you? I have theories on that, but unfortunately, we are out of time."

"We are?"

"Indeed." He cocked his head toward the bar. "Your rescue is here roughly ten minutes earlier than I anticipated. I'm impressed."

Lizzie followed his gaze to where Issac and two other suit-clad men were walking purposely up the stairs to the VIP section. Issac flashed the bartender a grin that spoke of familiarity and also nodded at several others, who all returned the gesture in kind.

Proof, Kiel had said, that Issac was an Ichorian.

He knew all the members of the club.

She could chalk it up to his billionaire status and say he knew all these people through high society, except Lizzie didn't recognize any of them, and she was very familiar with the elite crowd in New York City.

The Arcadia boasted an opulent air and old wealth, the kind she was raised to recognize. Yet she only knew the man approaching their enclosure.

"Lizzie, if you value your life at all, you'll remain calm throughout this interaction. I may have no intention of harming you, but I cannot speak for the others here. If you cause a scene, they will silence you, and not in a polite manner."

Ice slithered through her veins, freezing her in place as the glass slid upward to its home in the ceiling.

Even if she wanted to scream, she couldn't.

Her airways burned from a lack of oxygen.

Part of her thought this might be a very bad dream, but Ezekiel had remained so calm and collected throughout. The bearer of information, which was expressed in a concise, truthful way, meant to do what? Terrify her? Placate her? Teach her? She didn't know.

As their enclosure disappeared, she shivered not because of the air but because of the loss of protection.

Kiel had told her all of this in a soundproof chamber—he meant to keep her safe in the event that she reacted.

But why?

He clearly didn't care about her.

What was his goal?

To irritate Jayson.

Because Jayson didn't want her to know the truth. No one did, including Issac and Stas.

And Tom.

Her heart ached at the betrayal.

Everyone knew about this except her.

"Evening, Issac," Kiel greeted. "Care to join us for a drink?"

Issac slid into the booth next to Lizzie, his thigh brushing her frozen one. He steepled his fingers on the table, his focus on Kiel.

"I mean no disrespect, Ezekiel, but if you do not release Elizabeth to me right now, I will be forced to react in her best interest."

The quiet lethality lurking beneath his words sent a chill down her spine.

He sounded like a predator.

A villain.

A vampire.

She bit her lip to keep from reacting, but the terror rattling around in her chest begged to be let out.

Because her roommate and best friend was dating a monster, one who seemed completely at ease in this club, where they served blood in mugs and feasted on arteries downstairs.

How could Stas keep this from her?

"Hmm, I believe her best interest requires you not to react at all," Kiel replied as he finished his drink. He set it aside with a smile. "Well, if you don't fancy a drink, then how about a walk?" He glanced at the two men standing guard beside the booth before meeting Issac's gaze again. "Just the three of us ought to do." He smiled at Lizzie. "I imagine you are craving some fresh air right about now, sweetheart. Am I right?"

Her lips formed a response that her voice failed to deliver. If he meant to guide her outside, she wouldn't argue. Anything to leave this horrible place.

"I believe that's her version of acquiescence," Kiel said. "Shall we?"

Issac stood with a nod at his two friends and held out his hand for Lizzie.

Two days ago, she would have accepted.

Maybe even an hour ago.

But now?

No.

Maybe Kiel was a lunatic with a wild imagination.

Maybe she would wake up in five minutes.

Maybe unicorns were real.

She had no idea, but she did know one thing: she didn't trust Issac Wakefield. Or Tom Fitzgerald. Or Jayson Masters. Or Stas Davenport.

I truly am alone.

"What have you done?" Issac demanded, his words directed at Kiel.

"We may have enjoyed story time while you were on your way, but let's continue the discussion outside. I would hate to draw attention from anyone of import."

Issac closed his hand into a fist and dropped it to his side. "Indeed," he growled as he stepped away to give Lizzie a wide berth to exit the booth.

She did so carefully, her legs unsteady beneath her. All those years of dancing failed her tonight. She hobbled about like an old woman with frail limbs caused by years of misuse.

Kiel stood directly beside her, his warmth a comfort in the otherwise freezing club.

What did that say about her sanity?

She trusted the one man she shouldn't, but he'd told her the truth.

He also mentioned being an assassin.

Jesus… She would never move on from this moment.

If it was all true, she'd… How would she…?

Lizzie shuddered.

Where did she go from here?

Kiel had only just begun to talk about the CRF, but even his brief words confirmed her worst fears. Evil lurked there. He implied she had reason to fear them, but didn't elaborate.

No time now.

He led the way down the stairs as she moved on zombie-like feet behind him with Issac at her back.

The bodies gyrating on the dance floor passed in a blur, as did the bar.

She didn't bother looking for Cam and Kristin.

What could she do? Scream about vampires? They would laugh, and she would probably die.

Kiel said they would be safe. She wanted to believe him; he hadn't lied to her yet. Even in the coffeehouse, he'd told the truth.

Babylon.

He meant the real city. The one that existed thousands of years ago.

How was this even believable?

Jayson is the same age, maybe even older…

Her brain couldn't wrap around that logic. It ceased to comprehend. She'd made out with… with… a walking mummy.

Or a god, she thought. Not that it made her feel any better.

The tear ducts behind her eyes attempted to function and failed. Shock rendered her useless.

"Ah, it is a lovely evening for a stroll," Kiel proclaimed as they exited the club. He gazed upward with a grin. "Glorious. Let's meander this way, yes?"

Issac stepped up beside Lizzie, but he refrained from touching her. She followed on autopilot—like a marionette being controlled by an invisible string linked to Kiel.

It took two blocks before Issac finally spoke. "What game are we playing, Ezekiel?"

"Why must everything be for amusement? Perhaps I'm helping you."

"I highly doubt that."

He chuckled. "You might be right, but I'm not the one playing a game here. That would be you, and it's a dangerous one, I might add."

Issac yawned and tucked his hands into his pockets. "Your riddles bore me."

"Do they?" Kiel finally stopped and rotated to lean against the side of a building. "How about a suggestion instead?" He folded one ankle over the other, his gold-flecked eyes serious. "Move Astasiya out of the city before the Conclave discovers her secrets. And I'm not referring to her Sentinel training."

The air chilled between the two men while Lizzie struggled to breathe. This was all too much. The underlying threats, comments on immortality, the realization that everyone she knew had lied to her…

Do I really mean that little to them?

"Why haven't you acted?" Issac asked, his voice quiet but edged with lethality. It trailed goose bumps down Lizzie's arms.

Dangerous.

Predator.

"My reasons are my own," Ezekiel replied as he pushed off the side of the building. He fixed his gaze on Lizzie, eliciting a shiver from deep within.

Run.

But where would I go?

She couldn't trust anyone.

"I'll see you again soon, sweetheart, though I fear our next meeting will be under less favorable circumstances." He managed to sound both contrite and unapologetic at the same time. And she had no idea how to reply to that.

"Have fun fixing this one, Jedrick," he added as he caught something a second before it would have hit his nose. "Another memento. How thoughtful." He slid the metal item into his jacket and disappeared into a shadow.

Literally.

Lizzie gaped at the display of inhuman behavior as her knees buckled beneath her. Issac's arm around her waist kept her from falling, but she spun away on instinct, placing her back to the wall as she tried to locate Kiel.

"Where…? How…?" One moment he was walking, and the next he wrapped a cloak of darkness around himself and vanished into the night.

In the middle of New York City.

On the street.

How was that even possible?

"Lizzie." Stas's voice drew her attention to the left where she approached with Jayson and that Jacque guy from last night.

"Ezekiel has been talking," Issac stated flatly. "How much he revealed, I'm uncertain, but it was clearly enough."

Lizzie stumbled back as Stas reached out to touch her.

"Oh, Liz…"

Lizzie met her best friend's gaze—the woman she'd known for seven years.

Trusted.

Loved.

"Tell me," Lizzie whispered, needing to know. "Tell me that it's not true." She'd just seen a man vanish, for crying out loud. But it had to be an illusion.

All those things Kiel said had to be a lie. Right?

Vampires didn't exist.

"Tell me it's a lie," she repeated, a little more desperate this time. "Tell me he's insane. Please."

Stas glanced at Issac, her lips opening and closing, and Lizzie's heart beat unsteadily in her chest.

Oh God.

Her best friend wouldn't keep something like this, would she?

No.

She couldn't.

But everything Ezekiel said…

"Is Tom alive?" Lizzie's voice held a weird raspy quality to it and sounded foreign to her ears. "Is it true? Is it all true?"

Stas visibly swallowed.

And then nodded.

"He's…" Stas paused and cleared her throat. "Yes. Tom's alive."

"And Issac's a vampire?" It came out on a squeak. "And Jayson…"

God, she couldn't continue.

Insanity.

Complete and utter insanity.

Stas stepped forward. "Liz…"

No!

Lizzie's hand reacted of its own accord, slicing across Stas's cheek with a crack.

It felt so good to hit something, or rather, someone.

She wanted to do it again, only harder.

Everyone had lied to her.

Everyone.

"I deserved that," Stas muttered. "But, Liz—"

Lizzie cut her off with a scream. It'd been building in her chest for hours, days, maybe even months, and exploded in a rush of sound she couldn't contain.

Agony.

Fear.

Fury.

Hurt.

Pain.

They all culminated in that single moment, and she didn't bother to hide it as she collapsed on the sidewalk without any care other than to release it all.

And release she did.

Over and over and over again.

Until she felt a strange sensation surround her.

A whooshing.

It knocked her out of her spell and into a new, dizzying one of dancing light and surreal sound.

Then she landed in a new reality.

On a beach at night with waves rolling in the distance.

"It's okay, Red," Jayson murmured. "You're going to be okay."

What craziness was this? A dream? A shift in dimensions? Her lips parted on a question when a drowsy spell hit her out of nowhere.

"She needs rest," Issac said in response to something. A question, perhaps? Something Jayson… Maybe…

Oh, but sleep sounded nice.

A nightmare. That's all. She'd wake tomorrow.

Everything would be fine.
Yes.
"I've got you," Jayson whispered as warmth wrapped around her.
Floating.
Starless night.
Heaven.

CHAPTER FOURTEEN

Was It a Dream?

```
Subject's collegiate curriculum is not
providing a sufficient challenge. It's
suggested that future iterations
undergo a less rigorous academic
regimen during the development phase.
                     —Entry Log 119.04.4-7
```

"It's going to be okay," Jayson whispered as he tucked Lizzie into his bed. No one had argued about the placement, not even Stas. He tucked a red strand of hair behind Lizzie's ear and pressed his lips to her forehead. They lingered a second longer than needed, but he couldn't help it.

She's safe.

"I'm never leaving you unprotected again," he vowed. She couldn't hear him, but it didn't matter. The promise was more for himself than for her because he suspected when she woke she would want nothing more to do with him.

And that realization hurt a hell of a lot more than he ever would have anticipated.

He brushed his knuckles over her cheek and stepped away reluctantly to join the others in his living room. Amelia and Tom were seated on the love seat, their expressions grim. Stas stood in the corner, her face buried in Issac's chest, and Luc sat in Jayson's favorite recliner, sipping a cup of tea.

Balthazar wandered in with two beers and handed one to Jayson. "Figured you could use this."

Alcohol didn't impact immortals at all, but he accepted the drink anyway. He could use the refreshment.

"She's never going to forgive me," Stas said, her voice pitched low for Issac but reverberating in the eerily quiet room. Even the strongest women required a moment of weakness, and this was it for Stas.

The anger and hurt resonating from Lizzie had been palpable. And that scream… Jayson would have nightmares about that sound. So much agony and pain wrapped up in a piercing shriek meant to wound. He winced at the memory and rubbed his chest on impulse. It did little to ease the foreign ache growing deep inside.

Stas's statement about forgiveness applied to him as well. It was never Jayson's decision to keep Lizzie in the dark, but he had engaged in a relationship with her under false pretenses, which made him a bit of an ass.

"Right. We need to know exactly what Ezekiel told her. Obviously, he mentioned Tom and Issac, but what else?" Luc set his mug aside. "I say we wake her up."

"She'll scream," Jacque warned as he appeared behind the recliner. He must have been listening from the kitchen. "And it's loud," the teleporter added with a shudder.

Luc lifted a shoulder in response. "B has a fix for that."

"We can't," Stas said, her voice lacking its usual confidence. She pulled away from Issac, her green eyes tired as she addressed Luc. "We've taken everything else away from her; we can't take this too. She's earned her pain, and we all deserve to feel it with her."

Jayson rubbed a hand over his face and sighed. Stas was right. Dulling Lizzie's emotions would be taking away yet another choice, and they had already fucked this up enough.

"Regardless, we're solving nothing by keeping her in a coma." Luc glanced questioningly at Issac. "Unless you're speaking to her in her dreams?"

"Given the way she reacted to me at the Arcadia, I believe she would consider that a nightmare rather than a dream," the Ichorian replied.

Silence settled over the living area.

The soft introduction they all agreed on earlier no longer applied. Ezekiel had thrown Lizzie into the deep end without a flotation device and expected her to know how to swim.

Fucking prick. Ezekiel may not have harmed her physically, but he sure as shit hurt her mentally.

"I agree with Luc." The somber note in Tom's words described the atmosphere in the room. "We've hurt her enough. It's time to live with the consequences of our decisions."

"You were protecting her," Amelia murmured, her hand on Tom's chest.

"Perhaps, but she won't see it that way." Tom kissed her on the cheek before standing. "Let's wake her up. I'm ready."

"I'm not," Stas whispered. "You didn't see the way she looked at me."

"My guess is that look will be nothing compared to how she will treat Thomas," Issac said.

"Thanks, buddy," Tom replied with false sincerity.

Issac merely shrugged, unbothered.

"I have an idea," Balthazar said. "One that might make her more agreeable when she wakes up and won't involve any of us taking her choices away. It may also give us some insight into what Ezekiel told her."

Everyone stared at him, waiting for him to elaborate.

"But it will only work if Jayson is up for the challenge," Balthazar added with a gaze Jayson knew all too well.

Anytime Balthazar mentioned a challenge, it always ended favorably, but that wouldn't be the case with Lizzie. This task would be difficult, perhaps even hurt Jayson in the end, and his friend was asking him now with his eyes if he had the heart for it.

Jayson set his beer on the coffee table and raised a brow. "What did you have in mind, B?"

~*~

Lizzie floated in a cloud of cedar, man, and heat. Her legs stretched against the silky sheets as she nuzzled deeper into the muscular pillow beneath her head.

Jayson, she thought with a smile, then frowned as trickles of memories surfaced behind her lids.

The Arcadia, and Kiel telling her stories about immortality and blood. She flew upright and blinked into the darkness.

"Red?" Jayson murmured, his voice thickened with sleep.

Confusion riddled her thoughts.

How had she ended up in his bed again?

Unless…

Was it all a dream?

Lizzie ran her hands over her clothes—boxer shorts and an oversized T-shirt. Her feet were bare. No white clothes or boots.

A warm palm caressed her lower back as Jayson sat up beside her. "You okay?" he asked, his voice low and sexy.

"I…" She licked her lips. "I don't know." It had all felt so real, except that last part with the whooshing and the blackness. The end of a nightmare, maybe?

She turned and placed a hand on his bare chest. Okay, *that* was definitely real. Her fingers danced over the muscular planes to his abs before dropping to her side.

"I had the strangest dream," she admitted. *I think*.

Had it all been a figment of her imagination? Lizzie could come up with a lot of crazy things, but this seemed extreme.

"What was it about?" he asked with a yawn. The hand against her back moved in soothing circles, melting the remains of her tension. She leaned into him, seeking more of that comfort. Her dream had really rattled her nerves.

"You'll think I'm crazy," she said, shaking her head. He slid his palm up to her shoulder and unleashed magic with his fingers. "That feels good."

"Here." He shifted her to relax between his legs and put both hands to work on her upper back. "Now tell me about your strange dream, and I'll decide if you're really crazy."

She groaned at both his words and his skilled touch. Lizzie had no idea she was so tense. The dream must have really worked her up. Maybe talking about it would help.

But not all of it.

She didn't mention the disastrous breakfast conversation or the pancakes and skipped ahead to the part about the Halloween party at the Arcadia.

"It was pretty normal until Kiel showed up," Lizzie murmured. "His friends invited Cam and Kristin to dance. Meanwhile, Kiel asked if I wanted to know more about your world." Such a weird term, one she herself would never use, yet Kiel had used it repeatedly in her dream.

Unless it wasn't a dream at all.

Jayson tugged on a strand of her hair. "Don't leave me hanging here, Red. What did he say about our world?"

Right. A nightmare. Nothing else.

She cleared her throat. "Uh, well, he told me a story about growing up with you in Babylon, as in the original city"—something she obviously pulled from her conversation with Kiel at the coffeehouse—"and he said your dad was a war god. Actually, he called him an 'Ichorian.' I must have made up that term in my head after his original reference and the blood talk because, you know, *ichor* and *Ichorian* sound similar, right?"

Except, was that the order of the conversation? She couldn't remember; it'd all been so insane and—

"You're familiar with ichor?" he asked, his surprise palpable.

"Uh, yeah. I learned about it in school at some point." Why would that shock him?

"Ichor," he repeated, sounding incredulous. "That's something they teach in the New York City private schools?"

"Yeah, in high school, I think." Most of her knowledge came from an ambiguous background, due to all the traveling for beauty pageants and learning on the fly. Lizzie could never recall the specifics of when she learned a subject; she just knew the information, which was all that mattered in the grand scheme of things.

"Anyway, he also said something about knowing me before Stas." Lizzie attributed that bit to the coffeehouse as well since he'd met Stas briefly.

"Afterward, Kiel drank blood in front of me, which was gross." She shuddered at the too-real memory.

"And he called you an immortal 'Hydraian.'" She forced a laugh. "I'm guessing I created that term from your comments about Grace and Jacque being from Hydria…" She trailed off as she thought back to *when* he had said that.

During their disastrous breakfast.

Which never happened…

"I'm not normally this creative," she added, puzzled.

Jayson never mentioned Hydria, but geography was another one of those subjects she just understood. The small island in the Aegean Sea belonged to Greece. But how had she picked that location specifically?

She finally focused on her surroundings, beyond the silky sheets and the sexy man behind her.

Something didn't feel right. Not the temperature or atmosphere. This was definitely Jayson's space, but…

It's too quiet.

"There's no city noise," she realized. "And you have curtains." They went from the ceiling to the floor. Did she miss those before? She'd been a bit preoccupied, but they seemed out of place somehow. As if they were hiding a very large window, something she knew their condo building didn't include.

"Lizzie," Jayson murmured, his hands sliding to her arms. "I need to tell you something."

She focused on the silk curtains and the rustle of cloth at the bottom. *Fresh air?* Impossible.

His fingers went to her chin, tilting her head back to meet his gaze. They resembled mysterious orbs in the dark room. "I'm sorry."

Her gut twisted with those two morose words. "Why?" she managed, her mouth dry.

"Because it wasn't a dream," he replied. "And from what you've said so far, Ezekiel told you the truth."

She blinked. His words were clear but didn't fully register. "So you're…" She couldn't finish. Because no. He must have misunderstood.

"I'm a Hydraian, and we're in my room. In Hydria."

She pushed away from him, and he let her, his hands dropping away. She went to her knees and faced him on the bed.

"In Greece." She couldn't help the incredulity in her voice. "You knocked me out and flew me to Greece?" Because airport officials wouldn't frown upon an unconscious woman being flown across international borders at all. Not one bit.

"Jacque teleported you here. He's a Hydraian, too, as are Balthazar and Grace."

"Turn on the lights," she demanded, requiring proof.

The silk sheets swooshed as he moved, and a lamp popped on beside them. Rich, cream walls and mahogany furniture tumbled into view with a vivid blue curtain, blowing in the night breeze.

"It's a balcony," he murmured. "Overlooking the Aegean Sea."

Lizzie slid off the mattress and padded over to the door, needing to see it for herself.

The doors were open beyond the curtain, revealing a star-filled sky hanging over a rolling ocean. She grabbed the ledge for stability as her knees threatened to buckle again, and Jayson moved in behind her.

"You're… this…" She swallowed. The fingers of her free hand lifted to prod her neck as an image of the booths at the Arcadia soured her thoughts. "Y-you drink blood?"

"No," he murmured. "Hydraians don't require the mortal essence to remain alive. It's one of the many things Ichorians hate about us." He moved to rest his elbows on the balcony, his shoulders falling as he gazed out over the night. "The only time I've ever lied to you was about my job, Lizzie. Otherwise, I've always been truthful, just not very forthcoming. Keeping everything from you wasn't my decision, which sounds like an excuse, but it's merely the truth."

"I-I don't understand. Why? How?" All of Ezekiel's claims settled over her at once, forcing her to squeeze the door hinge hard to stay upright. She didn't know whether to cry, scream, run, or jump. Every emotion rattled inside her at once.

"We're not a threat to you," he said as if sensing her rising fear. "Quite the opposite, actually. I was sent to New York City to protect you."

"Protect me?" she squeaked. "From what?"

"The CRF." He twisted to face her and leaned against the balcony. His bare chest glowed in the starry night, giving him a regal flair she would have admired in a better situation.

"I've spent the last two months trying to determine what it is they've done to you, as has Stas, and our discoveries are minimal at best. We planned to tell you this week, to include you in the research, but Ezekiel had his own plans in mind."

"Research?" she repeated.

"Into whatever the CRF did to you as a child," Jayson replied, his voice low. "Did Ezekiel explain the true nature of a Sentinel?"

Lizzie shook her head, both at his comment about her childhood and at the mention of the prominent paramilitary unit.

"The humanitarian missions are a cover for something far more sinister and deadly. Sentinels are trained to hunt and kill rogue immortals, both Hydraians and Ichorians. It's Jonathan Fitzgerald's pet project."

"Kiel said he's an Ichorian," Lizzie whispered. "Issac, too."

"Both statements are true, but while Jonathan is a monster, Issac is an ally. He's been working with Stas to gain more information about you—or at least, he's tried."

Lizzie finally let go of the door to rub her arms. Despite the warmer air, she felt cold and so very alone.

"Everyone knew," she murmured, more to herself than to Jayson.

They all kept this from her. Jayson, Issac, Stas, Tom…

"Is he here?" she asked. Kiel told her he was alive. Everything else he said had proven to be true; would this as well? "Is Tom here?"

"Yes," Jayson replied quietly. "In the living room."

She nodded, her feet already moving.

Lizzie didn't bother checking her hair or her attire. She didn't care. Nothing mattered. These people had lied to her, kept secrets from her, and allowed her to grieve on her own. Were they ever really her friends?

She sensed the change in Stas months ago. Was that when she learned the truth? All this time, Lizzie had been nothing but supportive, a *good* friend, the best, and Stas had lied to her at every turn.

But none of that compared to the biggest deceit of them all.

Tom.

His funeral had broken her. She had cried alone in her room for days, because Stas had been too busy working. Lizzie thought her best friend just didn't care about Tom the same way she did, but no, that wasn't it at all. Stas didn't grieve because she knew Tom was still alive. And no one told her.

She followed the light in the hallway to an open space filled with people she recognized. At the moment, however, they all resembled strangers. Especially, the one in the middle watching her with a concerned expression.

Lies existed in those dark brown eyes.

She thought he loved her at least a little bit, but this proved all her emotions wrong.

Anyone who cared about a person would never put her through the pain of such a loss and say nothing.

But this man did.

The one she admired growing up, whom she thought she loved more than anyone else in existence.

Betrayed.

"Lizzie," he whispered as she approached him. "I'm—"

Her fist met his jaw with enough force to send him back a step, and a part of her was pleased with that hit, while the other part wanted to collapse under her grief. Because touching him made him real and alive.

All of it was true. She knew that, but to have proof changed the story entirely. "How could you?" she accused, her vision blurring with tears. "*How could you*?"

"It was the only way to keep you safe," Tom whispered.

"We needed John to believe he was dead," Stas said as she tried to approach, but one look from Lizzie froze her in midstep.

"You've known all along and didn't tell me." Her voice lacked the anger brewing within, something she chalked up to exhaustion. "I want to go home. To my condo. To be alone. Now."

"I would not advise that," Issac murmured. He sat beside a brunette with matching blue eyes.

His sister, Lizzie realized. A woman Issac had told her was dead over breakfast a few months ago. "All of it has always been a lie," she said, shaking her head.

"Amelia was only recently found alive," a voice said from her left. Balthazar cocked his head to the side, studying her. "When Issac told you she was dead, he believed it."

"He believed… But you… Did you just read my mind?" She shook her head. "Never mind. Of course you can hear my thoughts. You probably all can." She couldn't help the hysterical note of sarcasm, or the laugh that followed. "Take me back to New York."

Issac folded his arms. "As I said—"

"I don't care what you said," Lizzie snapped, her patience gone. "I've had enough for tonight. Let me go. Unless I'm a hostage?"

"Of course not," a blond man said from a recliner. "You're a guest for as long as you wish to be one."

"She can't go back," Stas whispered. "Not until she understands."

"You were the one who requested we stop taking away her choices, were you not?" the blond asked, arching a brow. "Her request is to return home, and I suggest we acquiesce." He stood, his height and strength reminding Lizzie a little bit of Jayson. "You are welcome back anytime, Elizabeth. We're but a call away." With that, he left the house.

"I'll get Jacque," Jayson murmured. "He can take you home."

"We need to talk about this," Stas said. "It's not safe in the condo, Liz. You don't understand."

"And whose fault is that?" Lizzie threw back at her. "I want you packed and out of *my* condo by the end of the week. It's not like you're there much anyway. Maybe your vampire, or perhaps John, will give you a free place to stay, but you and I are done."

"Lizzie, you're hurt, and I get that, but you need to give us a chance to explain." The authority in Tom's voice shoved her close to the edge of her sanity.

"You lost that chance when I buried you," she fired at him. "You're just another version that I never want to know. The Tom Fitzgerald I loved is dead, and frankly, I owe *you* nothing."

Stas gasped, "Lizzie."

She didn't even look at her. It hurt too much. "I want to go home," she said for the thousandth time. "I'm tired of being lied to and manipulated. It wasn't enough that I had to learn the truth from Kiel, so then you all tricked me *again* with that wake-up routine. And something tells me I didn't go to sleep by myself, either. I'm done. *Take me home.*"

"Okay. We can go," Jayson said.

Four words.

She understood them, yet didn't.

"I don't need a babysitter, Jayson," Lizzie told him. "You can stay here. I'll be fine on my own."

"It's not like—"

"Isn't it?" she countered before he could finish. "You said yourself that you were sent to New York City to protect me, right? And, what, when you didn't learn enough, you befriended me?" His expression confirmed her suspicions, which fractured her already broken heart even more. "You could have done all that without the added benefits," she added quietly.

How many times did he say they were just friends? She realized now what he'd been trying to do—push her away from any romantic notions. He never wanted to sleep with her, hence all those platonic kisses. It'd been an attempt to pacify her, but she had taken matters into her own hands during his party and kissed him, leaving him no choice but to respond.

No wonder he said they weren't having sex and refused to let her reciprocate.

He never wanted her. She didn't compare to his usual fare, something his friends had been happy to point out.

It'd all been a job to him. An obligation.

Why did that hurt most of all? Because everything else had weakened her to this point, or was it because she had started to care about him more than everyone else in her life?

I'm such a fool.

To ever think a man like him would want her…

At least she had confirmation about her feelings for Tom. His rejections had never hurt like this.

"I need to go," she whispered, her insides aching. "Now."

Because any longer in this room and she would break. She needed her room, her bed, and solitude before the tears came.

"Teleporting you back to New York so soon will make you a little queasy," a soft voice said. "But I will take you, if that's what you really want."

She met a pair of silver eyes filled with understanding and sadness. *Jacque.* The one who teleported her here, according to Jayson.

"You'll take me to my condo?"

"I will," he promised, holding out his hand. "If you'll allow me."

She didn't even think, she just pressed her palm to his. He could dump her in a fiery pit, and it would still be better than this place.

"Close your eyes," he whispered. "I'll tell you when to open them again."

The air shifted around her as she did as he suggested, and her stomach turned over at the unwanted inertia. It reminded her of an intense wind tunnel that stopped almost as quickly as it began.

"We're here," he murmured. "You can look now."

They stood in her living room again, and she nearly wept with relief. "Thank you."

He walked over to her sofa and bent to write something in the notebook lying open on the coffee table. "That's my direct line. Add the number to your phone, and call me when you're ready to come back. You're upset, and rightfully so, but they're still your family, Lizzie. And they love you."

Jacque disappeared before she could argue, leaving her more alone than ever before. Just as she wanted.

And yet, it only seemed to rip her apart even more.

I'm alone.

Well and truly alone.

Nothing would ever be the same now.

She didn't make it to her bed as originally planned, but instead she collapsed on the carpet and let all her emotions go.

It wasn't until much later—as Lizzie read Jacque's note—that she realized she couldn't call him even if she wanted to. That required a phone, one she didn't have because she'd left it at Cam's apartment with her purse.

CHAPTER FIFTEEN

A Free Spirit

> **Sleep deprivation logged at seven days and subject showing no signs of degradation. Benefactor requests simulation continues to test endurance.**
>
> **—Entry Log 105.07.4-7**

Jayson rubbed a hand over his face as Jacque disappeared with Lizzie.

"That went well," he muttered. Her pain had been a visceral thing, silencing anything he would have said.

You could have done all that without the added benefits. Her soft words had affected him in a way no others ever had. Because he *should* have protected her without touching her, but he had given in to the impulse instead.

Remorse mingled with frustration, because although he knew it was wrong, it had felt so right. How could he apologize for something he didn't fully regret?

"I expected her to be angry, but this…" Stas trailed off, her face paler than usual. "She can't stay there alone."

"She won't," Jayson replied. "I'll be there." It wasn't up for discussion. Lizzie didn't want a babysitter. Fine. He would be a guard instead.

Tom nodded, agreeing with Jayson's plan. He'd settled back onto the couch with Amelia at his side, but he didn't appear at all relaxed. His fingers traced his jaw, though Jayson doubted it still hurt from Lizzie's punch. The hit had been impressive, and startled most of the room, but also impactful on an emotional level, which showed in Tom's expression now.

"I can't leave it like this," Tom said. "When Jacque gets back, I'll ask him to teleport me to see if I can convince her to talk to me."

"I really think it should be me," Stas replied. "I know her best and—"

"You are not returning to New York City." Issac's tone brooked no argument. She opened her mouth to try, but he silenced her with an empathic, "No. This is not up for debate, Astasiya. Ezekiel knows you're a fledgling. Why he has not seen fit to act on that knowledge, I do not know, but this changes everything."

She was already shaking her head. "That's not your call."

"Indeed?" He arched a brow, daring her to disagree. "You seem to forget that your life is not the only one at risk in this situation. Should Ezekiel inform Osiris of your fledgling status, who will receive the harsher sentence?"

Her eyes widened, but the Ichorian wasn't finished.

"I have broken every Blood Law in an effort to support your decisions, Astasiya. And while it may be admirable, it ends now. I will not debate this with you. Call Jonathan and tell him you require a vacation, or quit, I do not care. As of this moment, you are not to leave Hydria until we determine Ezekiel's motives."

"And you?" she countered, clearly furious. "Will you be staying as well?"

"That remains to be seen," he replied coolly. "I have progeny to consider, as well as a company to run."

Stas folded her arms. "And I have nothing."

"You will have nothing if you are dead." A simple reply that didn't quite cool the fire brewing in Stas's eyes.

If Issac was trying to divert her attention away from the pain of hurting Lizzie, he was doing an excellent job of it. But Jayson suspected it ran deeper than that. Everything the man said was true, even if Stas didn't want to believe it.

"Why do you get to risk your life and I don't?" she demanded.

"Because I'm not nearly as valuable as you are," he replied without missing a beat. "Lucian has painstakingly allowed you to put yourself at risk with the CRF for a greater purpose under the promise that I keep you safe, and I can no longer guarantee that."

Her gaze narrowed. "And what happens when Ezekiel tells Osiris anyway?"

"That's for me to worry about."

"Fuck you." Tears brimmed in her eyes. "Fuck you for even thinking that! You believe you're the only one allowed to worry here? I sat through that Conclave, Issac. What Osiris did… You can't possibly think I would be able to sit by and allow that to happen to you, that I wouldn't fight for you."

"I know you would." He didn't flinch under the display of emotion. "Which is why you're staying here. I can't protect myself if I'm busy worrying about saving you." He palmed her cheek then her neck when she tried to move away from him.

"Don't, Aya. You're upset, and understandably so, but you cannot allow your sentiments to override the logical course, or we'll both regret it."

She looked ready to say more, when Jacque appeared, his expression somber. "I left her with my number in case she desires a lift back here," he said to the group before focusing on Jayson. "Ready?" The teleporter knew him well.

"Yep."

"I would stay out of sight for a few days," Balthazar suggested from his spot against the wall. He'd been observing the argument between Issac and Stas with a serious expression. All the Elders had agreed months ago that should her safety ever become a bigger issue than it already was, they would take measures to keep her in Hydria.

Unfair, but necessary, as Issac was right—Stas's gift for persuasion would be crucial during the next immortal war. And her life held more value than his, from a strategic point of view, anyway.

"I can't just sit here and do nothing," Stas said, shaking her head against Issac.

"It's for the best," Tom murmured. "As much as it sucks, they're all right. Your life is worth more than a few CRF secrets. We have what we need to keep Lizzie safe. There's no need for you to stay there anymore."

Stas freed herself from Issac's hold. He didn't try to touch her again but did watch her in that keen way he mastered through his brief centuries on Earth. "But we don't have Lizzie."

"Let me handle that," Jayson replied. "Give me a week."

Balthazar nodded. "From what I gathered of her emotions and her thoughts, Jay is our best hope right now."

Stas scoffed at that. "He barely knows her."

"I know enough," Jayson replied, irritated. This behavior had gone on long enough. He understood her distrust in the beginning, with everything being new and overwhelming, but now she just needed a swift kick in the ass. "You need to start trusting and respecting our experience, as it far outweighs yours."

Shock registered in her expression, replacing the frustration. "I… That's not…"

"It is," he insisted. "Your inability to have faith in our world has hindered your relationships with us from the beginning. I understand that you are not ready for immortality, but you need to accept your future. Perhaps you can use the next few weeks in Hydria to explore the world you'll be joining."

He didn't wait for her response. Rather, he focused on Jacque. "Let's go. Lizzie has already been alone too long."

~*~

Lizzie hesitated. If she knocked and no one answered, what would she do next? Call the cops from the phone she didn't have on her? Tell them that vampires exist and to please go check the Arcadia?

She almost laughed at the absurdity.

No one would believe her, and all the people she could confide in were liars.

"Just knock," she chided before the tears could start again. She already felt hungover from crying all night, not sleeping, and failing to eat or drink anything this morning. Or maybe the headache was a result of all the questions ricocheting through her head.

Who the heck knew, but she needed her purse and phone.

Her knuckles rapped against the door softly at first and harder as panic stirred. When Cam answered a minute later wearing her silky pajamas and a scowl, Lizzie threw her arms around her neck and hugged the life out of her.

"Do you have any idea what time it is?" Cam asked as she patted Lizzie on the back. "And why are you trying to suffocate me?"

"I was so worried," Lizzie admitted, her eyes dampening with relief. At least Kiel had told her the truth about Cam. She pulled away to look around the living area. "Is Kristin here too?"

"No, she took Zach home with her. Speaking of, Lars is still in my room, so… What do you need?" Typical Cam, eager to return to the man in her bed.

"Did he…?" Lizzie flinched as she spied the red mark on Cam's neck. "Never mind." He'd bitten her but hadn't killed her. *Yet.* "I need my purse."

"Oh yeah. It's still in the dining room. You can lock up on your way out."

She grabbed her friend's arm. The words she really wanted to say—*He's a vampire!*—refused to exit her mouth. So she settled on asking, "Are you sure about him? I mean, you just met."

Cam giggled and shook her head. "Oh, virgin Lizzie. You're so cute. I promise I'll be fine." She patted her on the head like one would a child. "Call ya later, chick."

Lizzie watched helplessly as her friend skipped off toward the bedroom. Even if she told her the truth, Cam would never believe her. She would probably laugh and tell Lars, and that wouldn't end well for any of them.

If he hadn't killed her yet, he probably wouldn't, right?

She could call Stas to ask, or that teleporter guy, or even Jayson, but would they tell her the truth?

Lizzie found her purse and pulled out her phone. What would she say? *Hi, just calling to find out if this Ichorian in the bedroom is going to kill my friend.* She snorted. That sounded ridiculous. And she didn't trust them anyway. Not after everything.

She had no one to turn to.

Her parents couldn't be trusted, especially after what Jayson and Kiel had said about the CRF. Her best friend had lied to her for months. The man she once thought she loved had faked his death and left her to live in misery without him. Then the man she started to well and truly fall for had turned out to be a babysitter sent to charm her into revealing information.

And her sorority sisters were shacking up with bloodsucking monsters.

She stared at her phone as if it could provide all the answers and noticed the nineteen missed calls. All from her mother. She'd sent a handful of text messages as well.

Lizzie had probably missed some sort of function. Or maybe they'd called to check up on her.

She snorted. *Yes, because they care.*

The last message came in twenty minutes ago. It wasn't like her mother to give up. Lizzie bet someone had been sent to her condo to check in on her, meaning she couldn't go home.

Not that she wanted to anyway.

Stas's stuff was still there. She could drop in at any moment to retrieve her belongings and move out, and Lizzie didn't want to face her or watch it happen.

If she called Jacque, he would teleport her to Hydria, which would be miserable but would at least provide some answers.

She shook her head. *Not ready for that either.*

"Damn it," she whispered, her eyes squinting as she strove for answers.

A piece of shiny plastic in her purse caught her eye. A credit card without a limit. One tied to her father's account, but with her name.

She checked the outer pocket for her passport as a plan formed. The devil popped up on one shoulder, while an angel sat on the other. She usually listened to the haloed creature, but today, the horned one spoke her language.

This isn't a good idea.

Are you kidding? This is a fantastic idea.

It's unsafe.

So is New York City, apparently. What could it hurt?

Everything!

Live a little.

I have to work tomorrow.

Seriously? That's your best excuse? Send an email and take the week off. You've earned this.

"Yes," she agreed. "I have." Living in a box and obeying the rules led to a lonely existence. Everyone else lied, cheated, and hurt her. Why couldn't she do something spontaneous and a tad dangerous?

There's a vampire in the other room, she thought with a laugh. She'd visited a club full of them last night, teleported to Greece to meet several more immortal beings, found out her best friend was apparently a part of that world for months without telling her, and also saw a man come back from the dead.

Yeah, a little trip on her father's dime was *nothing* compared to all of that.

A vacation was just what she needed. Somewhere to help her relax and think, away from all the distractions and troubles. When she returned, Stas would have moved out, and Lizzie could go on with life as normal.

Or not.

Either way, she deserved this excursion.

Decided, she sent an email to work stating she needed the week off. Her lesson plans were already done. A substitute would have no issue taking over.

That done, Lizzie left Cam's apartment and headed to the airport. Her navy shift dress was appropriate enough for a plane ride, and she could buy new clothes with her father's card when she arrived. He rarely monitored the account, and even if he did, he would just settle the bill as usual.

Sometimes it paid to have a rich father.

~*~

"We have a problem," Jayson said as soon as Mateo answered the phone. "Lizzie's at the airport and just bought an airline ticket, but I couldn't get close enough to find out where."

"I see," Mateo murmured. "Which desk?"

Jayson gave him the name of the airline.

"Any idea what card she used?"

"If I wasn't close enough to hear her, I obviously didn't see it," Jayson replied, his patience thinning thanks to the runaway redhead. She'd led him on a merry goose chase through Manhattan to a random apartment building before walking to Penn Station and boarding a train to Newark. He'd texted Luc to give him an update but hadn't anticipated her actually purchasing a plane ticket.

"Give me five minutes." Mateo ended the call as Jayson watched Lizzie go through airport security.

"Minx," he murmured. He sent a report to Luc with a shake of his head.

The woman needed a stern lesson on how to make smart decisions because this was not one of them.

He understood her fragile mental state, but to board a plane in response? Such an immature and bratty move. It weakened his regard for her intelligence as well.

He answered his phone as it started to vibrate. "Talk to me, M."

"Do you have your American passport handy?"

Jayson frowned. "No. It's in the condo."

"Okay. I suggest you ask Jacque to pop over and retrieve it for you because you're running out of time." A ding popped on Jayson's phone while Mateo was talking. "Congratulations. You've just been booked on the last available *Polaris Business* seat to Rome, and your flight leaves in sixty-seven minutes."

"Tell me the seat is next to hers," he growled.

"Of course. Safe travels, Jay." Mateo hung up again, and Jayson swore the man was laughing as he did.

"Fuck." The woman chose Italy for a last-minute flight? Did she not understand that the CRF was dangerous? That her existence was a mystery to them all?

He shook his head. Of course she didn't know, because she'd never given them the chance to explain. But to hop on a plane to Europe? Childish.

He punched in a message to Jacque, requesting his passport, and was still shaking his head when his floppy-haired friend arrived with the item in question.

"I'm very glad to not be the cause of that look," the teleporter said as he handed over the navy-blue booklet. "Try not to punish her too badly."

Jayson grinned. "Oh, when I get my hands on her, she'll never do anything this imprudent again." Fleeing the country, of all things. Damn foolish woman.

"Right, have fun with that." Jacque didn't sound so sure and even took a step back.

"I intend to," Jayson replied. And he meant it.

Because he was done playing nice.

Yes, he withheld information, but only to protect her.

No more.

If she wanted the truth, he'd wouldn't just give it to her; he'd show her.

~*~

Not for the first time, Lizzie wondered if she'd just made the stupidest decision of her life by boarding this plane. Then they came around with champagne, and she stopped worrying.

She watched the airfield workers out the window while she sipped her bubbly. The late-afternoon flight had worked much better than the option to Paris. Lizzie worried she would lose her nerve if she had to wait too long, so she'd selected Rome after reviewing all the departures on the board. Most European flights left later in the evening, but this one departed at half-past-five. She would watch a movie, try to eat something, and, hopefully, sleep.

The seat beside her crinkled as someone settled into it. Their business class chairs were close enough for chatting but also provided ample room for privacy. She'd still hoped the seat would remain vacant. Alas, her luck never prevailed.

"Welcome aboard, sir," the flight attendant purred. "Can I get you anything for takeoff? A drink, perhaps?"

"Mmm, yes," a familiar voice replied. Lizzie's lips parted as she realized just *who* had taken the seat beside her, but rather than acknowledge her, he remained focused on the flight attendant.

"I would love a whiskey neat, at least for takeoff," he said with a wink.

Flirtatious much?

"Of course, sir," the brunette replied before sauntering off while Jayson watched her with a smirk.

Lizzie wanted to hit him. Not just for checking out the attendant so brazenly, but for sitting beside her without a word. For following her. For acting like he didn't even see her staring at him right now.

He rested his elbow on the oversized armrest and eyed the woman's legs while she fixed his drink at the front of the cabin. It was as if Lizzie didn't exist, yet he'd clearly followed her onto this plane.

"What are you doing here?" she hissed, unable to hold back her irritation.

"That is an excellent question, Elizabeth." He buckled his seat belt before finally meeting her gaze with a decidedly unamused expression. "Rome?"

She swallowed, her ire disappearing. The energy rolling off him did not match his usual playful vibe. He seemed more powerful somehow. Because she knew the truth? Or was it something else?

"You know, it's a good thing this is a long flight," he continued. "It'll give us plenty of time to talk."

"Oh no, you're not—"

"International flight regulations state that no passengers can disembark once the boarding doors are closed, and I was the last one in line. Which means"—he glanced over his shoulder before refocusing on her—"you're officially stuck with me for the next eight hours and thirty minutes."

He relaxed into his chair just as the brunette approached with his drink. "Thank you, sweetheart," he murmured.

"Anything else?" she asked in a sultry voice.

Jayson ran his eyes over her and smiled. "Perhaps later."

Lizzie wanted to punch him again. As if the last twenty-four hours hadn't been hell already, he had to hit on the flight attendant right in front of her? Could he be any more heartless?

She'd only been in his bed two nights ago. Granted, that'd all been her own doing. She'd practically begged him to kiss her in the kitchen, though he was the one who invited her to his room—to pacify her, apparently.

"I'll be back to check on you once we're in the air," Flirty Skirt murmured.

"I look forward to it," he replied while Lizzie rolled her eyes.

Flirty Skirt added a sway to her hips as she left, eliciting a grin from Jayson.

"Maybe you should spend the eight-hour trip talking with her," Lizzie suggested.

"I doubt we would spend much time holding a conversation," he replied before sipping his whiskey. "And I'm not here for her. I'm here for you."

Lizzie masked the pain of his words by rolling her eyes and scoffing, "Right. Babysitter Jayson."

"Oh, Elizabeth, you have no idea how wrong you are on that." He captured her gaze. "*Babysitter* implies that I see you as a child, which is distinctly different from finding your behavior childish and immature."

"Excuse me?"

"You heard me just fine. I could beat your ass red for this stunt."

Her mouth fell open. "Did you just threaten to *spank* me?" She pitched her voice low but couldn't help the squeak at the end. Because he did not just say that!

"I haven't decided yet, but you'll be the first to know when I do."

She gaped at him, speechless. No one had ever threatened to spank her, not even in her youth. Jayson couldn't be serious. Men did not punish grown women in that manner. Did they?

Jayson's lips were suddenly at her ear, sending a jolt of electricity down her spine. "You would enjoy it if I did, which I'm not sure you deserve."

She shivered. His words held a promise she didn't understand, one that elicited forbidden feelings she had no business entertaining on a plane, let alone with him.

Vampires are real, she reminded herself in an attempt to stay grounded.

Eh, yeah, but that's old news now, her hormones responded. *And they're called Ichorians.*

So she was losing her mind. Awesome.

Jayson's palm went to her knee, bringing her back to the present.

Energy simmered beneath her skin as his hand traveled upward and slid under the fabric of her shift dress to her inner thigh.

She shouldn't have liked that nearly as much as she did.

He lied to her.

Everyone had.

But his touch seemed to unravel her frustration and replace it with a much hotter emotion. One that tightened her stomach in anticipation.

Her brain fired important questions at her unresponsive mouth—she couldn't seem to move her tongue or form words. The man had captivated her with his touch.

Wizardry.

"For the record, I may be far older than you can imagine, but that does not mean I have ever thought of you as a child." He licked the shell of her ear, pebbling goose bumps down her neck. "You are a gorgeous woman, Elizabeth. And babysitting is not an activity I consider in your presence. Far from it." He nipped her ear before returning to his personal space.

He left a rattled, confused mess in his wake. Lizzie was supposed to be angry with him, not… feverish and… whatever.

And he'd only befriended her to learn more, not because he liked her.

Except he called her gorgeous again.

And the way he'd just touched her was *not* very friend-like.

"Buckle your seat belt," he said as the plane pulled away from the gate. "Once we're in the air, we'll play a game."

It took her three swallows before she managed to say, "A game?"

"Yes. One where I make the rules and you obey them."

Yeah, she definitely didn't agree with that plan. "Good luck with that." The words lacked their designated punch. Damn hormones.

His brown eyes smoldered as he met and held her gaze. "I've been easy on you, Elizabeth. That ended the moment you decided to forgo common sense and flee the country on a whim."

She opened her mouth to contest that point, but he silenced her with a glance.

Okay, so maybe it had been stupid of her to get on a plane to Rome, but it wasn't like she didn't have several good reasons to react that way. Escaping had sounded like a solid plan at the time. She just hadn't anticipated anyone following her.

"By the end of this flight," he continued, "you will understand why I've managed to survive as long as I have and how I earned the title of 'Elder' among my kind. Afterward, you will agree to play by my rules because you want to, not because you have to."

That was never going to happen. "You clearly don't know me at all." There. That held a little bit more confidence.

Except he silenced that budding self-assurance with a predatory smile—a king grinning at his chosen conquest.

"Oh, that is where you're wrong." His gaze dropped to her mouth before sliding back up. "Your body speaks to me on a level you don't yet understand, but you will, and soon."

CHAPTER SIXTEEN

The Treaty of 1747

> **Benefactor is satisfied with subject's intelligence quotient and requests increased focus on subject's information recall functions.**
>
> **—Entry Log 106.09.4-7**

If Jayson called Lizzie by her full name one more time, she would scream.

He ordered her meal for her—*Elizabeth will have the filet*—then ignored her protests and made small talk while referring to her by her full name the entire time, and now he'd just requested a dessert drink for *Elizabeth* again.

Lizzie never thought she would actually miss her nicknames, but she certainly did now.

"What if I didn't want a dessert wine?" she asked, irritated.

"In that case, I'll have two."

"Do you always order for the women you stalk?" She'd started referring to him as a stalker since he disliked the term *babysitter*.

"Only the misbehaving ones," he replied as he relaxed into his seat and flipped through the array of movies on his private screen.

This was hardly what she had in mind when he mentioned a game. It seemed to be more a display of power than anything else and perhaps a subtle way of implying that he knew her tastes. Because the dinner he selected was the one she wanted, and she did enjoy dessert wine with chocolates.

But that wasn't the point.

He couldn't just waltz onto this plane and watch a movie. Not after everything she'd been through these last two days. The whole purpose of her escape was to forget, and as he'd made that impossible, he might as well give her some answers.

"Were you really born in Babylon?" she demanded.

"Yep." He continued playing with the movies instead of regarding her.

"To the son of a war god?"

He snorted. "Artemis fancies himself one, but he's just an Ichorian who can control and manipulate metal."

The background noise from the plane drowned out their conversation to others, spurring her onward on this quest for information. "Explain what you mean by that."

"Pick up your spoon," he said instead.

"I hardly see—"

He cut her a look. "You will, if you listen."

She blew out a breath. "Fine." She lifted the spoon. "Happy?"

He didn't respond, but the spoon bent in half, causing her to yelp and drop the item back onto her tray.

The passenger across from them gave them a curious expression, and Jayson said loudly, "Right. No horror movie."

"How did you do that?" she hissed. The metal returned to its real shape while she watched in fascination.

"Ichorians pass their supernatural talents on to their progeny, meaning Artemis gifted me with the ability to control metal. That spoon is a parlor trick, by the way. I can sense every nut and bolt on this plane, as well as all the watches, necklaces, belts, you name it. If I wanted, I could manipulate them all at once, or one at a time."

Her lips parted. "Really?"

He shrugged. "It's important to note that not all immortal gifts are created equal. I've met telekinetics who could only lift a stapler and others who could lift an entire house. Those of us with stronger skills live longer."

"So your father could do the same?"

"He can, yes." He finally met her gaze. "Artemis, the Ichorian who helped create me, is still alive."

"And your mom?"

"She died a very long time ago," he murmured. "Ezra, my mother, was mortal. Artemis killed her when I was ten human years old."

Lizzie's eyes widened. "Why?"

"Because she was aging." Jayson paused as if considering what else to say, then shrugged. "He could have turned her, of course, but he was bored with her. And rather than let her go, he killed her in front of me. He considered it a lesson in mortality and why immortals should never grow too close to humans. They die."

"That's…" She couldn't even finish. How horrible to do that to a young boy.

"I spent most of my youth trying to please him and prove my worth so I wouldn't suffer the same fate, but on my nineteenth birthday, he slit my throat." Lizzie flinched at the bluntness of his words, but he continued, unfazed. "He wasn't aging due to his Ichorian genetics and had hoped to assume my identity as the new ruler because he wanted to hide his immortality from the mortals. But I woke up the next morning. He tried again for good measure, but I recovered, and he proclaimed me his true Ichorian son."

The flight attendant returned at that moment with their dessert trays. She traded them for the dinner ones while Jayson murmured things to her in Italian. Her cheeks were flushed by the end, causing Lizzie to roll her eyes. The damn man had been flirting with the brunette all through dinner and again now.

It churned Lizzie's stomach and soured her taste for the chocolate laid out before her. She opted for the wine that came with it, needing the alcohol to numb her senses. If he walked off with the woman, she would lose it.

Not that he owed her anything. They weren't dating. She was just a temporary assignment to him. Nothing more.

Except when he touched her.

"What was I saying?" he asked as the brunette wandered off with an overstated sashay in her step.

"That you're a jerk?" Lizzie suggested. *Okay, maybe less alcohol.*

He grinned. "Jealous, Elizabeth?"

She glowered at him. "First of all, no. Second of all, stop calling me Elizabeth."

His lips curled all the more, revealing those two precious dimples. "I thought you disliked my nickname for you, or you used to, anyway."

"I… That's not the point. You're calling me Elizabeth like I'm in trouble."

"Ah, but you are in trouble." He selected a piece of chocolate from his tray and brought it to her lips. "Open."

"No, this—" He silenced her protest by sliding the decadent dessert between her lips.

"Yes, enjoy that while I continue my story." His gaze dropped to her mouth, where she reluctantly chewed. Spitting it out would be a waste of a perfectly good sweet and also very unladylike.

"Artemis believed me to be his own creation of an Ichorian, but he soon discovered that I didn't have a taste for mortal blood, nor did I require it. And I also boasted not one gift but two."

He selected another piece of chocolate and pressed it to her mouth. She really wanted to refuse, but saying no to such decadence seemed sinful. Besides, if he wanted to give her all of his dessert, she wouldn't complain. But she also wouldn't share her own.

"My secondary talent is from my mom's bloodline. I can more or less manipulate how others see me and leave them confused about my physical traits. I do it constantly without thinking, to the point where I have to actively want to un-shield my appearance, such as right now with you. You're the only one on this plane who *sees* me."

She blinked and swallowed. "What about Ms. Flirty Skirt?"

His brow furrowed. "Who?"

Lizzie gestured to the front of the cabin with her eyes. "The flight attendant you keep hitting on." She had given her name earlier, but Lizzie didn't remember it. Probably because the woman only focused on Jayson every time she stopped by.

Amusement crinkled his eyes. "I rather like you being jealous."

She rolled her eyes. "I'm not jealous."

"You are," he said, grinning. "And to answer your question, her recollection of my features is fuzzy, but she knows I'm attractive."

"That's not arrogant."

"It's not," he agreed. "Because it's true."

Another piece of chocolate appeared before she could respond to that. She grazed his finger with her teeth on purpose, earning her a heated look.

"Careful," he murmured. "Or I'll take that as an invitation."

To what? she wondered.

"Back to what I was saying," he continued as he studied her mouth. "I wasn't an Ichorian at all, something Artemis eventually deduced, and a meeting was called. It served as the first Conclave, actually, though they didn't refer to it as such at the time. The word used isn't one I can clearly translate given the dead languages, but it essentially implied they were gods."

He swirled his wine thoughtfully before continuing.

"Ichorians from all over gathered to discuss me, only to find that there were others in existence as well. That was the day I met Balthazar, Lucian, Alik, Eli, and about twenty additional immortals with similar traits." He smiled fondly, as if remembering it now, and shook his head.

"Some called us a gift from above, while others considered us a threat. Needless to say, the governing board, now known as the Conclave, voted to keep us alive to test our worth."

Lizzie sipped her water before setting it aside and focusing on him. "What does that mean? Test your worth?"

He studied her for a long moment before saying, "Nothing good. Let's just say they explored our limits in terms of death, powers, and otherwise. Not everyone made it."

Her eyebrows rose. "But you said they were your parents, right? Like, Artemis was your dad, so obviously Balthazar had an Ichorian parent as well?"

"Our fathers," Jayson murmured. "My kind are created when an Ichorian male procreates with a human female. And as to what you're implying, yes, they essentially tortured their children in the name of research. The one thing they never did was taste our blood because the Conclave had decreed it as disgraceful. Everything else, though, was considered fair game."

Jayson tilted his glass to finish his wine and set it down with a finality.

"That's awful," she whispered, her voice masked by the airplane's engines.

Their flirty attendant appeared to snatch up the dessert trays and frowned at finding them partially eaten. Jayson said something to her in Italian again, eliciting more blushing. Lizzie was still shaking her head when the lady flounced off.

She gasped when he stole a piece of food from her plate and popped it into his mouth.

"Hey!" She tried to smack his hand when he did it again, but he was too quick.

"I promised Rebekah we would be done soon."

"Rebekah?"

"Sorry, that's Ms. Flirty Skirt to you."

Lizzie grumbled a few choice words under her breath. Of course the woman had a sexy name to go with her long legs and curves.

This time when he tried to feed her more chocolate, she refused. Her figure certainly didn't need the fatty enhancements.

"To shorten a rather long story, the Ichorians eventually decided we could be useful as long as we were maintained. They treated us as second-class citizens—peasants—and exploited us for their own purposes. They also killed any progeny who could potentially overpower them and allowed only the useful children to be reborn into immortality."

"So Immortals can be killed?"

He nodded. "It's not easy, but it can be done by severing the head or burning the body to ash."

Lizzie flinched at the image that evoked. "Gross."

"There's also the matter of our blood being toxic to Ichorians, something that wasn't discovered until about a millennium ago. I'll come back to that after I explain where *Hydraian* came from." He stole the final bite from her plate and followed it with some water. "Do you want more wine?"

She shook her head. Two glasses were enough.

He signaled the attendant with one of his grins, and Lizzie wondered if little Ms. Flirty Skirt could actually see it. She must have because she brightened under the attention and almost bounced all the way over to them. Lizzie would have to ask him to explain the facial manipulation thing more in depth. After he finished this new round of flirting.

The trays disappeared, giving them space to move around again. Lizzie tucked her legs beneath her on the oversized seat and angled her body toward Jayson. He rested his ankle on his knee, giving her a nice view of his strong legs.

Dressed in khaki pants and a sweater, he resembled a fashion model. He even had the windswept-hair look and alluring eyes.

"After several centuries of testing our mettle and determining the best ways to manage the population, we were given a place to live on our own with limited resources. It was a way to hold sway over my kind, something most of us recognized, but we weren't going to turn down the opportunity at some semblance of freedom. And that's when we colonized Hydria."

She couldn't believe they were discussing this all so casually, yet it all felt so much more believable coming from Jayson than it ever did from Kiel. "So that's why you call yourself Hydraians?"

"Yes. Luc, whom you met briefly last night—he's the blond one—is a master of strategy and suggested we develop a term to promote unity among our kind." He smiled, his fondness for the memory and the man palpable. A moment of history that clearly meant something, perhaps one of the first to bring him happiness?

"Luc's commonly referred to as omniscient, but that's not quite right. His gift allows him to remember everything, no matter how trivial the details, and he's been alive for longer than I have and was born to an Ichorian with a similar ability. Between the two of them, they essentially know everything."

Lizzie caught the affection in his voice, so different from when he spoke about his own father. "It sounds like Luc's upbringing varied from yours?"

He chuckled. "It did, in more ways than one. My father created me for the sole purpose of assuming my identity after a certain period of time so he could hide his own immortality from the mortals. Aidan, Luc's father, actually loves him. He's also considered one of the oldest beings on Earth, and unlike most of his brethren, he craves peace and equality among the immortals. I believe it stems from his love for strategy."

"He sounds okay," Lizzie agreed. "Does his opinion cause issues?"

Jayson scratched his chin. "Well, yes, but as I said, he's old, and as such, he's respected. I mentioned that Hydraian blood can kill Ichorians, which was only discovered about a thousand years ago. The realization lent credence to those who already wished to exterminate our kind due to our dual powers, and incited centuries of violence."

He paused, his expression sobering.

Lizzie placed her hand over his on the armrest and squeezed gently, startling him from wherever he'd gone in his head. He cleared his throat and refocused, his eyes brimming with haunting memories.

"I lost a lot of friends, several of them among the oldest of my kind from that original meeting, but those of us who survived proved resilient. The Ichorians had gotten lazy over the years, their control over my kind was implied and expected, and they didn't realize that some of their children were extremely powerful, because our kind had learned early on to hide those talents.

"Alik, for example, can torture with his mind, something he never admitted. The Ichorians thought his telepathic skills—gifted through his father's bloodline—were his primary ability. For the longest time, he pretended that a minor language affinity was his other talent, but in truth, he can cripple an army of hundreds with a single thought."

"That's terrifying," Lizzie admitted softly.

Jayson nodded. "Yes, but also very useful. Pair his strengths with my affinity for metal, Luc's strategy, Balthazar's flair for manipulating emotion, a few Hydraians who can control fire, and several other combat-related abilities, and you have quite a formidable army. It helped that we developed weapons coated in our blood that kill on impact."

The attendant appeared again with bottles of water and a smile solely for Jayson, but this time he didn't return it. He merely dismissed the woman with a few words and refocused on Lizzie.

"In 1747, an armistice was established between Hydraians and Ichorians that created peace in specific regions. Hydria, for example, is a safe zone for my kind, while New York City is a haven for Ichorians."

She considered his words with a frown. "Isn't your being in Manhattan a violation?"

"No, it expressly states that we can venture over borders at our own risk. Meaning, if the wrong Ichorian found me in New York, he would be within his rights to kill me."

"Kiel is an Ichorian and a friend?" It came out as a question because Kiel spoke fondly of Jayson and they obviously hung out, but they were supposedly also rivals. Had Kiel meant that in reference to their warring factions or something else?

Jayson blew out a breath as he uncapped his water and took a swig. "Ezekiel isn't so much a friend as a respected adversary who is trained to kill fledglings, otherwise known as the progeny of Ichorians, who have not yet been reborn as a Hydraian."

He shifted while Lizzie waited for more. It was all so complicated, but he explained it in a way that helped her understand.

Stas knew about all of this?

How?

And where does the CRF fit in?

"There's a unique poison that essentially burns Ichorian blood when ingested, thereby killing fledglings. We call it the Nizari poison, after the band of assassins—of which Ezekiel is the primary leader—known to administer it."

Lizzie's lips parted. "So not a friend."

"Definitely not, though he seems to be playing by his own set of rules lately. I imagine it's a result of boredom that will end when he craves death again." He studied her. "Did he say anything else interesting?"

Can you read my thoughts? she asked, suspicious. Because she'd just been thinking about her former best friend seconds ago and his subject change seemed odd, but his expression remained politely curious.

Coincidence?

Possibly.

Lizzie considered her conversation with Kiel. Despite being shocked and emotional, she remembered almost every word.

"He said he arranged for me and Stas to live together our freshman year." Which was odd. "He also knew her full name, which I never mentioned to you or him, and 'Astasiya' isn't an easy guess."

"No, it's not, which means he knows more about her than we realized," Jayson replied, his expression thoughtful. "Is that all he said?"

"About Stas? Yeah," she replied. "He mostly talked about his youth and how Osiris took him in as a boy and raised him alongside his own son, Sethios. In Babylon."

He studied her for a long moment. "He said he grew up with Sethios? As in they were the same age as children?"

"Yes, that's what he implied, anyway." Lizzie had a knack for remembering facts and discussions; it was something that suited her well in college, because she never had to study.

"What else did he say about Osiris?"

She shrugged. "Not much, just that I would meet him someday and he's friends with Artemis. Why?"

He finished his water, his eyes narrowed in thought. When he finally looked at her again, she saw a sort of resolution in his gaze, as if he'd been battling something internally.

"Osiris is a being everyone fears, including Ichorians, because he can persuade others to do his bidding through vocal command." He let that settle, his expression hardening. "I'm guessing Ezekiel meant to imply that Osiris turned Sethios, or perhaps even raised him as a child similar to the way Aidan raised Issac."

"Uh… Aidan?" All these names were giving her a headache. He'd mentioned him already as Luc's father, but not in relation to Issac.

Jayson smiled, as if hearing that thought, and slid his hand to her nape, where he massaged some of the tension from her neck.

"The immortal who turned Issac into an Ichorian," he clarified. "He's also Luc and Amelia's birth father, but that's not important."

Jayson shifted into her personal space and palmed her cheek. "I promised myself the day we met that I would never lie to you, and I've kept my word, but I've also omitted quite a bit. Before today, I mean. But this is really something Stas should tell you, not me."

Dread pooled in her stomach, but she couldn't stop now. "You can't say that and not elaborate."

His thumb traced her bottom lip. "I've explained that Ichorians and humans produce fledglings—"

"What about a Hydraian and a human?" she asked before he could continue.

"Hydraians can't procreate," he replied. "But that's beside the point. What I want you to consider is *why* Stas would know about our world, and it's not because she works for the CRF."

Lizzie frowned. "Are you implying she's immortal?"

"Not yet, but close."

"A fledgling?" How could Stas keep something like that from Lizzie?

He nodded. "Yes, and her power is similar to Osiris's in that she can persuade through voice."

Lizzie's eyes widened. "What?!"

"Shh." His palm tightened warningly on her neck. "We don't want to cause a scene."

"You just told me my best friend can tell people what to do," she hissed. "I'm allowed a reaction to that."

"You are, but a quiet one," he replied.

She glared at him, but he merely smiled, amused.

"I understand. It's an interesting development."

Understatement of the year. Their entire conversation and the last twenty-four hours had been an *interesting development* in Lizzie's mind.

"Um, what's Stas's other ability?" Her voice had come down an octave, but her pulse still thrummed wildly at both Jayson's close proximity and their discussion. So much for this all being easy to believe.

"We don't know yet because she hasn't been reborn." Jayson's expression melted into one of compassion. "She has refused the next step for several reasons, one of which is you."

"Me?" Her eyebrows hit her hairline. "Why?"

"Because she can't work for the CRF as a Hydraian. She needed to remain human to become a Sentinel and gather intelligence. At first, she stayed on to save Issac's sister from captivity—which is another story we'll get into later—and subsequently, to help you. Tom found a file with your name on it while working there but had to retire before he could gather more information."

His palm slid to her neck, where his fingers massaged the tense area at the top of her spine. It felt divine but didn't belie the horror of his words.

"Do you have any idea what the file says?"

He shook his head. "No. We've spent two months trying and failing to gather more information, and we were planning to tell you everything, but Ezekiel beat us to it."

"I-I don't understand. What could they possibly have on me?"

"Whatever it is, you're valuable to them." Jayson settled back into his chair but kept his body angled toward her. "Do you remember that first night I stopped by? I believe a Sentinel stopped by right after, yes?"

Lizzie nodded. "Charlie."

"Does that happen a lot?"

She shrugged. "Sometimes. My mother likes to send them to check up on me."

"In this case, he stopped by to check on your surveillance equipment. I set off an interference with my watch to test their reaction time. It was impressive."

Lizzie blanched, and his palm covered her mouth before she could react vocally. She wrapped her fingers around his wrist to yank it down. "Don't do that."

"Don't scream."

"I wasn't going to."

He arched a brow. "Don't lie, either."

"You're one to talk."

"I've never lied to you, Elizabeth." The severity underlining his tone made her shiver. As did the intense way he studied her. "It was not my decision to keep all this from you, nor was it my place to tell you, even when I wanted to."

Lizzie swallowed.

It was Stas and Tom who kept all this from her. Jayson did, as well, but in a different way. They assigned him to guard and befriend her. That he wanted to tell her the truth said a lot, assuming he meant it. His eyes said he did, but her heart refused to believe anything yet.

"I need time," she admitted. "To think this all through."

"And although I appreciate that, running off to Rome on a whim is not the answer." He dared her with his expression to refute that, but she couldn't. He was right, not that she would admit it.

"Did you sleep at all last night?" he asked, his voice softer than before.

She shook her head slowly. "Not really."

"Then let's get some sleep now and start fresh in the morning. We can do a little sightseeing before deciding on our next destination."

"Really?" She perked up at that idea. "You're not going to send me to Hydria?" She half expected a welcoming party to be waiting at the airport for their arrival.

"Wherever we go next will be your choice." His lips curled as he added, "Just know that I'll be tagging along."

She toyed with a strand of her hair that had fallen over her shoulder. "You don't have to do that." It seemed unfair and dangerous from what he had said. "But I'm not ready to face them yet," she admitted, torn.

And to stay in Hydria? It would require leaving all she'd ever known.

Not that she had much to be thankful for in Manhattan. Her parents wouldn't miss her, and her friends would move on, just like they always did. She couldn't remember the last time she spoke to anyone from high school. Some of them kept in touch via text messages during freshman year, but everyone sort of moved on with their lives. That was when Lizzie met Stas, and their bond had felt so much more real than anything else in Lizzie's life.

Her chest ached with the loss of that friendship. It was irrevocably changed by the events of the last few months, and she wondered if they would ever be able to come back from this.

Jayson stood and stretched his arms over his head, revealing a sliver of skin between his red sweater and khakis.

Talk about a distraction.

Except she wasn't the only one who noticed.

Flirty Skirt gazed at him with a question in her eyes, but Jayson ignored her and turned to place his hands on Lizzie's armrests. His face was a scant inch from hers as he bent into her personal space.

"As irritated as I am with this last-minute adventure, I also understand your desire to run. Which is why I'm willing to overlook the foolishness of your actions, this time."

He tightly grasped her chin and forced her to meet his unwavering gaze. "But, Elizabeth, if you ever pull a stunt like this again, I will bend you over my knee and express my displeasure in a way that will leave you thinking about me for weeks. And I won't hesitate to do it in public, either. Do you understand me?"

Her mouth went dry. "You wouldn't—"

"I would," he promised.

She squirmed in her seat, uncomfortable by the feelings he'd awoken. A spanking should *not* intrigue her. It was wrong, yet the power in his stance as he leaned over her and the steadfast way he held her gaze unleashed something inside of her. A foreign desire that felt wanton and inappropriate, and oh-so right.

"What are you doing to me?" she whispered.

His mouth went to her ear. "I'm learning your limits, sweetheart. Now let's get some sleep."

CHAPTER SEVENTEEN

A Self-Guided Tour

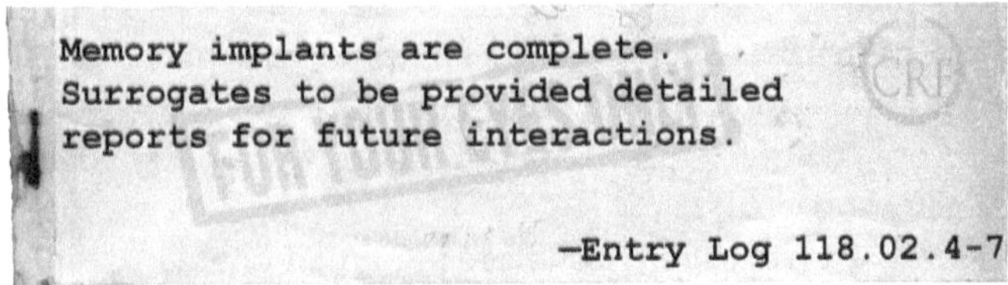

Memory implants are complete.
Surrogates to be provided detailed reports for future interactions.

—Entry Log 118.02.4-7

Lizzie woke to Jayson speaking Italian.

A peek through her thick lashes showed Flirty Skirt had returned. She had her hip popped against Jayson's armrest. His chair was upright while Lizzie lay curled in a ball on her flat-bed seat, and he seemed very alert.

The flight attendant blushed at whatever he said, and nodded. He fished his phone out of his pocket, murmured something sexy, and handed it over for her to type into. Which she did while smiling triumphantly.

Lizzie observed the exchange through narrowed eyes. Apparently, this was why he agreed to sightseeing and staying a little longer. He hadn't been able to sleep with the woman on the plane, so he was making other arrangements.

It shouldn't hurt.

But it did.

They weren't even dating, and he'd been clear about the purpose of their relationship, but why flirt with Lizzie? Unless she'd misread all his signals. Her experience in these matters was minimal at best.

He mentioned something about Balthazar as he returned the phone to his pocket, causing Lizzie to arch a brow. Tristan implied that Jayson enjoyed sharing women—was that what he meant?

Her stomach turned over.

They hadn't revisited their conversation from the other afternoon—the one where she learned about his penchant for bedding more than one woman at a time. And they'd yet to discuss his friend's comments from the party, either.

She clearly misread all his signals. One moment she swore he liked her, and the next, she was a mission again.

I need to get off this plane.

Lizzie sat up to check the flight monitor on her screen—one hour left. Good.

Jayson said something about her in Italian now, which caused the flight attendant to nod eagerly before scampering off.

"Rebekah is bringing you breakfast," he murmured.

Lizzie didn't acknowledge him as she shifted her bed upward into a chair. She tucked her legs beneath her and finger-brushed her hair, all while feeling his eyes on her.

Apparently, he expected a response.

Fine.

"I'm not hungry."

That's not petulant at all, Liz.

Screw you.

"That's too bad since you'll be eating anyway," he replied. "We'll be doing a lot of walking today, and I'll need you well fed for that."

She finally looked at him. Amusement radiated from every edge of his face. "And where will we be walking?"

"That depends on what sights you have in mind. I could provide a historical tour, if you're interested. Not the one provided by regaling tour guides, but one depicted from actual events." A boyish charm flirted with his features as he awaited her reply.

"You really want to show me around?"

"Of course I do. I wouldn't offer if I didn't."

Maybe his plans with Flirty Skirt were for after their day of sightseeing. Lizzie could attempt to exhaust him to the point of poor performance, though she didn't know if a man like Jayson ran out of energy.

Unwanted emotion poked her in the chest.

She had no right to be jealous. Sure, he kept touching her, but he also openly flirted with the flight attendant and exchanged numbers with the woman.

That was neither a faithful man nor one who would ever be interested in Lizzie.

"Why are you doing this?" she asked, confused. "Is it because you feel bad or something?"

He turned toward her. "Do I really need a reason for wanting to have fun with you?"

She stared at him. "You would have fun?"

He grinned. "Oh, undoubtedly. Probably more than I should, but as I've already broken all the rules with you anyway, what's a little exploration to add to the list?"

She frowned. "Rules? What rules?"

"Luc is a fan of edicts," he replied vaguely. "Now stop changing the subject and tell me where you want to go when we land."

His chocolate gaze pinned her in place, compelling her to comply.

Sightseeing could be fun… And he was right about the advantages of having a guide who walked the streets a thousand years ago. Two or three thousand, even.

How will I ever wrap my head around all this? she wondered.

Oh. The purpose of his request hit her smack dab between the eyes.

He was offering her a distraction. Because he pitied her, or something else?

Does it matter? No. She welcomed the reprieve with open arms.

"Uh, well, I've seen all the traditional points of interest, but it's been a while." She went with her parents about ten years ago? Her memories of that trip were foggy at best, reminding her more of a dream than a true experience. "Is there anywhere you recommend?"

He considered. "You've already seen Rome, right?"

"About a decade ago, but yeah."

"Did you visit Pompeii?"

She frowned. "That's not in Rome."

"I'm aware of that." He reached over to tug on a strand of her hair hanging near her breast. "Have you been?" he asked as the back of his hand skimmed her breast. If it was intentional, he didn't show it, but her body reacted anyway.

She forced herself to shake her head since her suddenly dry mouth no longer understood English. Because no, she'd never been. Her mother preferred shopping and fashion to archaeological sites.

"Then we'll head south for a day trip, have some Neapolitan-style pizza, and spend the night in Rome, if that's your preference." He let go of her hair and brushed his knuckles over her cheek. "You blush so prettily, Red."

Flirty Skirt chose that moment to return with the breakfast tray. No doubt well-timed on the flight attendant's part.

Jayson's hand fell to Lizzie's shoulder as he addressed the woman in English. "Thank you, Rebekah."

She replied in Italian as Lizzie busied herself with the table. She accepted the tray with a forced smile and muttered a "Thank you." Her mother taught her to be polite in all circumstances, this one notwithstanding.

Jayson's thumb traced the column of Lizzie's neck as he asked for two cups of coffee. Again in English. When he requested two sugars and a cream for Lizzie, her eyes widened. That was her preferred way to drink coffee, but they'd never shared a cup together.

"How did you know how I take my coffee?" she asked as the brunette wandered off.

"Observation," he murmured, his thumb circling her pulse point. "I've learned a lot about you these last two months—not in a stalker way but in a security-detail sort of way."

"Bodyguards need to know how their charges take their coffee?"

He smirked. "Perhaps not, but you stop by that coffee shop on Broadway every day before work."

Lizzie's eyebrows popped up. "You followed me?"

"Yes." No shame, just a straight response. "I wanted to see where and when the CRF intervened in your life."

"And did they?"

"Only once a month."

She frowned. "When?"

"Brunch," he replied. "Let's discuss it more after you eat. We'll be landing soon, which means you need to hurry up."

She wasn't so sure she wanted to eat at all now. "Brunch?" she repeated. "That doesn't make any sense."

"How about you work on that omelet while I explain." He worded it as a suggestion, but his tone indicated it to be a demand, not a request.

A compromise. Okay. She could agree to that even if the idea of breakfast didn't appeal to her.

Lizzie sliced off a piece of egg and, with a raised eyebrow, put it into her mouth.

Jayson grinned, appeased, and dropped his hand to the armrest between them. "All right, I'll tell you what we know, but I'm warning you right now that it's not much."

~*~

"A brothel," Lizzie said, her brow furrowed. "With a rock bed."

Jayson chuckled. "It kept the men from lounging around afterward."

She studied the small, preserved room of Pompeii and nodded. "I wouldn't want to lie there, either."

Their little venture to this archaeological site served as the perfect distraction from their conversation on the plane. Of course, every few minutes, Lizzie would mutter something about how unreal this all was, especially since Jayson possessed intimate knowledge of the former Roman city.

She ran her fingers over the walls before exiting into the sunshine. Her red hair glimmered alluringly, but it was her new outfit that captivated his attention.

Fitted jeans, black boots, and a flowy top.

Sexy. As. Fuck.

Lizzie picked up the outfit at the airport while he arranged transportation.

It'd taken all manner of restraint to travel here instead of finding a boutique hotel with a decent bed. Even now he wanted to pull her into one of the less populated sections, push her up against a stone wall, and devastate her mouth.

He clasped his hands behind his back instead.

"Does this place bring back memories?" she asked softly.

He shrugged. "It was primarily a trading port, so I never spent much time here. I preferred Rome." For a variety of reasons, but mainly for the women.

"No time in the brothel?" The teasing quality of her voice seemed forced, as did her smile.

"Do you really want the answer to that, Red?" He meant it as a taunt but also as a lesson. *Don't ask for details you don't really want to know.* He suspected that would be an issue between them given his age and her innocence. It was a challenge he wanted to overcome, but he didn't quite know where to begin. Or why he even felt the need to try.

"Probably not." Her gaze went to the ground. "Never mind." She picked up the pace, but he caught her hand and tugged her back to his side.

"Where are you running off to?" He linked their fingers and forced her to slow down.

"I wasn't, I mean, I just—"

"To answer your question," he said, interrupting her, "I don't pay for pleasure." He let that sink in before adding, "So, no, I did not waste any time in that brothel."

"Oh, I didn't mean…" She trailed off as color brightened her beautiful face.

"Yes, you did," he replied softly. And he couldn't really blame her. They had barely covered the surface of his experience, something that no doubt intimidated her, and rightly so. Still… "I can't apologize for my history, Liz." He squeezed her hand. "But I can try a new approach for our future."

She stumbled—something easy to do on the stone road, but he suspected his words were the true cause.

"Our future?" she repeated.

"Yes." He started to smile, when the hairs along his arm danced in warning.

Gunmetal.

Jayson's gift engaged on instinct alone, mentally grabbing the incoming bullet and dropping it to the ground long before it reached him.

A sniper. His location up in the hills gave him a perfect view of *Via dell' Abbondanza,* which meant Lizzie and Jayson needed to get off the main street. The former residences and shops surrounding them provided an ideal place to play hide-and-seek.

Jayson sensed two approaching handguns paired with blades.

Sentinels on the ground about a hundred yards out. He didn't bother searching for them. A battle among the tourists would result in unnecessary fatalities.

Only one option: run.

Jayson wrapped his arms around Lizzie and pulled her backward into a restricted area of Pompeii.

"What—"

"Sentinels," he explained as he yanked her between a pair of stone pillars and darted for another set. The way he forced her about would have caused a scene if anyone could see them. Fortunately, this area was roped off to the public and masked by ancient walls.

Thank fuck for preservation.

His back slammed into an old doorway as he subtly dismantled the Sentinels' guns with his mind. They were still close, but scattered, and wouldn't notice his meddling—something Jayson would use to his advantage as needed. He fucked with their knives for good measure as well and checked for anything else they could use as weapons from afar.

"Jayson," Lizzie breathed, her nails digging into his forearms.

"Sorry, Red," he murmured, easing his hold. He'd grabbed her harder than he meant to—a reaction to the approaching weapons. "We need to go."

"H-how do you know—"

"Guns," he replied quickly. "Now follow me." He grasped her hand and tugged her toward a side exit that was clearly not part of the original architecture.

His ability continued to scan for metal associated with gun power as he pulled a phone from his pocket. He'd texted Luc with an update when they arrived and also sent a message to Jacque to remain on standby.

Jayson had suspected the CRF would arrive and ruin their little field trip at some point, hence the necessary backup plan.

Jacque picked up on the first ring. "Yo."

"The CRF found us," he explained as Lizzie sputtered beside him. "We need a teleport. Now. Get B and have him explain to you where the *apodyterium* is located. He has fond memories of that place."

"On it."

The line went dead as Jayson leapt over a rope. He turned, grabbed Lizzie's hips, and hoisted her over it as well.

"I'm capable of doing that on my own," she snapped.

Jayson grinned despite the circumstance. "Probably, but this is more fun, Red." He winked and laced their fingers together. "Keep up."

She grumbled something incoherent, increasing his amusement as they moved at a brisk pace. At least her fiery personality hadn't died with the arrival of the CRF.

"We need to get rid of your phone," he said as they entered another home. They'd left her purse in the trunk of the car due to the Pompeii bag restrictions, but she brought her mobile, something he suspected the CRF was tracking. Or they had one inside her, like they did with Amelia.

Lizzie didn't argue. She handed him her mobile and watched as he smashed it into the corner of the room. "You're buying me a new one."

"Sure, sweetheart."

This time she took his hand in anticipation of being guided, eliciting a grin from him. She should have been terrified, but trust shone bright in her gaze. He supposed it helped that she didn't know about the sniper or have any idea how many Sentinels were on the ground.

"Remind me to kiss you later," he murmured. Completely inappropriate timing, but Jayson adored a strong-willed woman.

Her brow furrowed, but he didn't give her a chance to reply.

The *Stabian Baths* he desired appeared as he maneuvered them through another set of stone walls, and he increased their speed as they hit the open area.

Several tourists wandered about taking photos, providing what could have been decent cover if not for Lizzie's notable hair.

The CRF would identify her in an instant.

"In there," he said, gesturing to a solid doorway leading to the women's bathhouse.

"It looks like a dead end."

"Yep," he agreed as he guided her inside. "Keep moving."

She did, but slowed when they hit an open area filled with impressive mosaics. "Wow," she whispered as she tried to focus on walking and not admiring.

"I promise to bring you back here someday," he vowed. "But right now, I need your undivided attention. Move."

She nodded and continued the way he guided her until they hit a dead end. Jacque hadn't appeared yet, which wasn't a good sign.

"Uh, what now?" she asked, voice quiet.

"We wait or fight." He didn't have any weapons on him thanks to traveling by air, but he shouldn't need one. Jayson excelled in all manners of martial arts and a few other techniques not of this time period. Not to mention his affinity for metal.

"You're sure the CRF is here?" Lizzie whispered.

"Yes." He scanned the perimeter with his senses. The Sentinels appeared to be splitting up, which suggested either Lizzie's phone was the source of their tracking or something in these old walls was interfering with the signal.

"Okay." She sucked her lip into her mouth and chewed nervously. "I didn't see anyone I recognized."

"Not surprising. As much as I dislike them, the Sentinels are well trained."

She nodded. "Most of them are recruited from Special Forces, or the like. I always knew something was off with them. Nothing ever added up. Why all the traveling and secrecy?"

"They still do some good around the world," Jayson admitted. "But mostly to maintain their cover."

He sensed two guns enter the baths.

Four.

"They're coming," he warned. "Step over the rope and press your back to this wall."

She studied the mosaic on the floor and flashed him a skeptical look. "Isn't that illegal?"

Despite the situation, humor touched his chest. Just for a moment. Then he lifted her, set her where he wanted, and caged her against the wall with his body. "Don't move." Not that she could.

"But—"

He pressed a finger to her lips as a couple of tourists wandered in through the room's only entrance. They took in the sight with matching grins, snapped a few photos of the mosaic floor beside Lizzie's feet, and left.

I love this country. Displays of affection went unnoticed and undiscussed.

Jayson's amusement was short-lived as the gunmetal approached.

From the placement and nearness, he counted a pair of Sentinels carrying a duplicate set of firearms.

Easy.

CHAPTER EIGHTEEN

Trust and Conviction

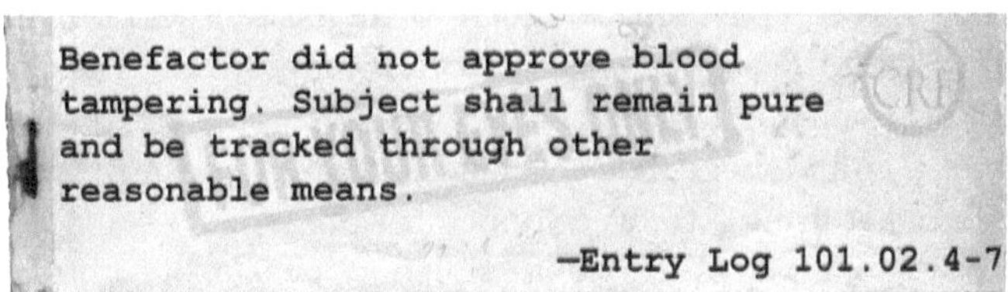

Benefactor did not approve blood tampering. Subject shall remain pure and be tracked through other reasonable means.

—Entry Log 101.02.4-7

"Try not to scream," he whispered as he stepped away to position himself on the other side of the entrance. Her rounded eyes touched his heart, but he needed to focus.

The Sentinels thought they were armed, giving Jayson the advantage.

Five.

Four.

Three.

Two.

As the first soldier stepped through the threshold, Jayson slammed his hand into the muscular man's throat, temporarily disabling him.

Unfortunately, that gave the Sentinel's partner enough warning to react. The blond tried to fire his useless weapon and threw it at Jayson when he realized it no longer worked. He followed it up with a punch that Jayson dodged and a kick to the ribs.

Evenly matched in size and strength, it became a dance of brute force.

Jayson went for the hit, but his opponent kept blocking and returning the favor.

Then the Sentinel made a fatal error by noticing Lizzie against the wall. Familiarity touched his features, and Jayson used the distraction to his advantage.

His fist collided with the blond's jaw, knocking him off balance and right into Jayson's knee. The Sentinel tumbled to the ground, where Jayson leapt on top of him and wrapped his hands around the man's throat. He sputtered and tried to grapple with him from the floor but failed.

"I'd say this isn't personal," Jayson said. "But that would be a lie." Because he recognized this jackass as the one lurking in Lizzie's building a few weeks ago. He'd been the one sent to check up on her after Jayson fucked with the surveillance equipment in her condo.

The blond's eyes dimmed as his oxygen supply depleted.

It would only be a few more—

"Jayson!" Lizzie squealed as the other Sentinel attempted to fire his weapon from the ground. The mechanism didn't trigger or move, causing him to pull out a knife instead as he climbed to his feet. He'd recovered faster than anticipated.

"Oh, that looks fun," Jayson said. He bent the blade with his mind while the blond beneath him lost consciousness.

"Code H, bathhouse," the Sentinel mouthed, but no sound came out as his windpipe had not yet recovered. So much for requesting reinforcements. And it seemed they didn't realize he was a Hydraian until now. Fascinating. What, did they think the sniper missed?

Jayson stood and took a defensive stance, when a familiar presence arrived, followed by a bullet firing into his opponent's skull.

Well, that was one way to handle the situation quickly, but a hell of a lot less fun.

"Next time, you need to be more specific," Balthazar chastised from behind him. "There were several baths I frequented in Pompeii, not just this one."

"There's only one *apodyterium*, B." Jayson turned as he brushed his hands against his jeans.

"In the historical records, sure," his friend replied. "But my memory is much vaster than a mere text."

"Can we go?" Jacque asked, holding out his hand. He and Balthazar both stood in the center of the roped-off area, while Lizzie remained plastered against the wall, eyes wide.

Right.

Not a good time to debate history with Balthazar.

He jumped over the rope and went to check on his startled companion. She flinched as he caressed her face. "Easy, Red. It's okay."

"You… you killed Charlie," she stammered.

That must have been the blond's name, and the way she said it sounded like she knew him well.

"He's just taking a nap, Liz. He'll wake up in a few minutes."

She met his gaze and blinked. "They tried to kill you," she whispered urgently.

"They usually do." He pulled her away from the wall and into his arms. "We'll have to finish our tour later."

"But this… I …"

"Shh," he murmured as he hugged her. "We'll talk more once we get somewhere safe. Close your eyes, Red." He gestured for Jacque to join the group hug with Balthazar and grimaced as the sensation of whirling hit his abdomen.

Jayson's living room materialized around them, followed by a startled yelp from the naked woman on the couch.

Amelia.

One of the most alluring females in existence with her dark hair, striking blue eyes, and porcelain features. She resembled an angel, though she didn't look so angelic right now with the blond, male head between her legs.

Not what Jayson wanted to walk in on considering he loved the woman like a sister. Good thing her real brother wasn't with the welcoming party, or hell would ensue.

Tom's reflexes didn't disappoint as he yanked a blanket from a nearby cushion and tossed it over Amelia while also jumping to his feet in nothing but a pair of tented boxer shorts. His unashamed expression morphed into shock at seeing who stood before him.

These two lovebirds really needed to finish building their own home.

Lizzie trembled, her face tucked safely into Jayson's chest and away from the romantic scene.

"Not bad," Balthazar said, eyes grinning with mischief. "I'd deduct points for execution, as you get a better angle from, say, the counter, but overall a flat seven. Jay?"

"Don't you fucking knock?" Tom demanded.

"Not in my own fucking house, I don't," Jayson returned. "And I'm not rating that scene, B."

Bright pink splotches colored Amelia's cheeks as Lizzie froze. She'd obviously recognized Tom's voice.

"Sorry, we weren't expecting you," Amelia murmured as she found Tom's hand and gave him a healthy tug. He landed beside her but remained fixated on Jayson, or rather, the redhead in Jayson's arms.

"Yeah, the CRF found us in Pompeii. Which reminds me: I need to scan Lizzie for tracking devices." Not that it mattered here. The Sentinels would never attempt to enter Hydria, but there were other types of technology that could be running through her system.

"Mine was at the base of my neck," Amelia said softly, her complexion paling. "Tom removed it."

"I'll check there," Jayson replied as he drew soothing circles on Lizzie's back. She hadn't said a word or tried to move during their exchange. He pressed his lips to her ear. "You still with me, Red?" His words were whisper soft and for her alone.

Her fingers curled into his thin sweater so hard that he felt her nails through the fabric. "I-I can't."

The broken reply prickled his protective instincts.

"Let's go talk," he murmured, low enough for only her to hear. To the others he said, "We'll be in my room."

"Whoa, hold on a minute." Tom was on his feet again. "I don't think that's a good idea at all."

Jayson lifted Lizzie into his arms and cocked a brow at the young immortal. "That wasn't a request."

He didn't wait for or acknowledge a reply before starting down the hall to the master bedroom and kicking the door closed behind him.

Jayson stood in the center of the room, holding Lizzie, and admired the view out the balcony windows.

He missed his home, Hydria, the water, and the sunshine. But never had it felt quite like this. It was as if a missing piece of him had returned, except it had nothing to do with the scenery or his room and everything to do with the woman cradled against him.

The weight of the moment slammed into his chest, warming him inside and out. Everything about it seemed right, as if he was destined to be here, right now, with *her*.

Jayson never believed in fate or soul mates. He'd lived far too long for any of it to be real, but this connection forming between them surpassed logic.

He wanted to blame the serum or claim it was some sort of unique pheromone in her blood meant to seduce him. But no one else felt it except him.

It's all Lizzie.

Her intelligence floored him almost as much as her heart did. Sincerity flowed from her in waves, caressing everyone she met, and he adored that about her. She was charming, witty, and so beautiful it hurt.

And he was so done for, but fuck if he cared anymore.

All that mattered was her.

He slowly lowered her feet to the floor and held her close while she steadied herself. Her nails bit into his biceps—a physical indication that she didn't want him to let her go, which was fine by him.

"Talk to me, Red," he murmured as he palmed her nape. He gently prodded the area by her spine for a potential tracker beneath the skin. No bumps or obvious marks. He checked her hairline, but everything felt natural there as well.

He slid his hand to her face and eased her head back. Big brown eyes locked on his as her lips trembled.

"I-I can't," she stammered. The same words from before.

He studied her pale expression. The fear from Pompeii had been replaced by a deeper emotion, one that darkened all her features and creased the edges of her mouth.

Pain.

Ah, he understood now.

"You're not ready to be here." He tucked a loose strand of her hair behind her ear. "Okay, Liz. We can leave, but I need to check you for tracking devices first." Because he didn't want the CRF following them.

She blinked. "W-where?"

"Where will we go, or where do I need to check?" he asked.

"The former," she whispered.

He traced her lip with his thumb. "Somewhere remote, just the two of us, while we sort all this out. But I need to know the CRF can't follow us there first."

Relief shone bright in her gaze as all her tension melted into warmth. She crumpled into him with a sigh. "Thank you."

His lips touched her forehead, then her temple, as he held her close and luxuriated in the rightness of it all.

Her arms wound around his neck as she hugged him with far more strength than he expected. He returned the embrace and rested his chin on her head. "How do you feel about Santorini or Turkey?"

"Aren't they close by?" she asked, voice small.

"They are, but both locations are beautiful." He paused, waiting to see if she would respond to that, but she stayed silent.

Hmm, we need something farther away.

Most European countries were out due to surveillance cameras, same with the United States and several countries in South America. The CRF had access to several systems worldwide, all with facial recognition software.

An island somewhere would be better.

The Caribbean was too close to New York City for his liking.

"How about the South Pacific?" he wondered out loud. "Tahiti, Fiji, or something similar?" All remote areas with little camera footage outside the airports. Since they would be using a teleporter instead of a plane, that wouldn't be an issue.

"Like Bora Bora?" she asked softly.

He grinned. "Sure, if you like that idea." They could go wherever she wanted. One of the perks of living forever was amassing unfathomable wealth. Most of his funds went into keeping Hydria healthy and thriving, but he maintained a private account as well.

She tilted her head back to see him, and the difference in her expression floored him. No more pain, only mild curiosity. He had accomplished that with a few words of understanding. Jayson rather liked the way that felt.

"That sounds warm," she said.

"There's a lot of water for cooling off."

"Bora Bora," she mused with a laugh. "Really? We can go there?"

"Well, we can't return to New York, and you're not ready to stay here, so why not go somewhere exotic. French Polynesia is private, beautiful, and far away from everyone. It sounds perfect to me." *And you'll pretty much be living in a swimsuit the entire time.* Nothing to complain about there.

She started to laugh, then paused, her eyes going wide. "I… Wow. I can't believe this is real life. I was in New York, Rome, Pompeii, now Greece, and now you're talking about the other side of the world." Her brow wrinkled as she laughed again with a touch of deprecation in her tone.

"The CRF sent people to kill me, and you're, like, three thousand years old, and Stas is a fledgling. Her boyfriend is a vampire, Tom is alive, and you totally kicked Charlie's ass. While I'm over here, just me, with a few added hormones. But why? I don't…"

He did not like where this rant was headed, nor did he like her paling cheeks or the look of despair shining from her beautiful brown eyes.

"This is all a mess, isn't it?" she continued, voice dropping to a whisper. "I'm a mess, I mean. And you're… Oh, you can't leave your home for me, Jayson. That's not fair to you, and I'm—"

He threaded his fingers through her hair and kissed her, hard. Her mouth opened, perhaps in protest, but he didn't care. That little rant set his blood on fire. Every word chipped at her confidence right before his eyes until she stared at him with an expression he never wanted to see on her face again.

Uncertainty.

Aimed at him.

And his feelings, his pride, and his place in her life.

Hell. No.

His tongue parted her lips and wasted no time in staking his claim. She moaned against him, spurring him on in his pursuit until every inch of her mouth belonged to him.

Mine.

No questions.

No arguments.

Fact.

"All bets are off now, Red." He licked a path down her neck. She knew the truth now, which meant no holding back. Luc's "no fucking" rule no longer applied, at least in Jayson's mind.

"I-I don't understand."

Oh, he doubted that. Her body understood every inch as it arched into him, begging for more.

But he could put it into words, if that's what she needed.

"Mmm, I intend to devour every inch of you, Lizzie." He brushed a kiss against her pulse and another over her jaw. "Inflict more pleasure than you can even imagine." His nose skimmed her cheek as he drew his mouth closer to hers. “And see how much of you I can make blush just by using my tongue.”

Her gasp tasted sweet against his lips.

“Yes, I think you understand just fine,” he whispered before taking her mouth the way he wanted—exploring, licking, and memorizing.

Lizzie melted against him, and he suspected the arm around her lower back was all that kept her upright. He would have grinned in amusement if the kiss hadn’t devastated him just as intensely as it did her.

All Jayson wanted was more.

And so he took it.

The restraints of last week no longer applied.

He could take this woman how he wanted, for as long as he needed, in any way he desired. Over, and over, and over again.

Except he craved this woman on a level he didn’t know existed. It went beyond lust and physical desires and hit him so much deeper. Her touch burned his soul, implanting her memory there for decades, maybe centuries, to come.

It overwhelmed and consumed him, but fuck if he could stop.

And as her arms tightened around his neck, holding him even closer, he knew she yearned for this connection as much as he did.

Her little mewls of satisfaction only deepened as he palmed her ass to pull her flush against his aching cock. Over two months without a woman’s touch, yet only she could satisfy him now. No one else would do.

She slid her palms down his arms to his hips and under his sweater to explore his heated skin. Eager little minx.

He adored how she came undone in his arms.

Beneath all the innocence was a passionate woman waiting to be unleashed.

He’d meant this to be a demonstration, not a claiming, but damn if he didn’t want to dominate her right here and now. The alluring woman held more control over him and his actions than he cared to admit.

But this was neither the time nor the place. Especially with their unwelcome audience.

He’d felt the metal move as someone opened the door, and recognized the newcomer by the gun in his hand.

Only one person would be naïve enough to enter Jayson’s bedroom armed. The man probably carried it out of habit, but the lack of a knock suggested a threat. As did the wave of angry energy rolling off him from the doorway.

Jayson slowly ended the kiss and brushed his lips over her cheek while maintaining his possessive hold.

“I wouldn’t,” he warned, his voice low with unveiled fury.

Lizzie’s hands stilled against his abdomen. “What?”

“He’s talking to me,” Tom replied, his tone equally livid. “I’m just here to check on her.”

“And as you can see, she’s fine.”

“Is she?” Tom countered, sounding every bit like the older brother. Jayson would have laughed if it didn’t piss him off.

Lizzie had tensed up again during the unwelcome conversation, infuriating him more. To the point where he wanted to put the young immortal's head through a wall for interrupting what was otherwise an enjoyable experience. He understood the protective reaction but also loathed the display of distrust.

"I suggest you remove yourself and your firearm from my room before something happens that upsets Lizzie more." A suggestion underlined with threat.

"Worried I might kill you?" he asked, cocky as ever. Jayson usually liked that trait in Tom, but not today.

"As entertaining as it would be to test the strength of your powers against mine, it would upset Lizzie greatly to watch *you* die," Jayson replied, confident. Tom was a strong Hydraian with impressive gifts, but age and experience would win this battle of wits.

Jayson finally met Tom's gaze over Lizzie's shoulder and let him see the severity of this transgression. "Amelia is like a sister to me, Tom. As such, I understand your concerns, and I'm willing to let this one instance slide. But try this again, and there will be consequences."

There was a reason Jayson had survived as long as he did, and it would be best for Tom to remember that. He let that conviction show in his eyes for a moment longer before returning his attention to the rigid woman in his arms.

"We'll be leaving soon," he whispered. "I promise."

She nodded slowly as faith dilated her pupils. That look undid him. He didn't know how he'd managed to convince her to trust him, but he would never take it for granted.

"I still need to scan you, and I think Luc will want to talk to you about a blood sample. Afterward, we'll go wherever you want, for as long as you need, okay?"

"Blood sample?" she repeated, sounding uncertain.

"He's out of options since the CRF serum doesn't tell us much."

"Oh…"

"But you can say no," he assured. "Everything that happens will be your choice. Always." And that applied to more than the research. He meant that in the bedroom as well.

She nodded again. "I've never been to Bora Bora."

He grinned. "You'll love it."

"Okay," she agreed, her lips curling into a small grin.

He nuzzled her nose. "Okay."

Their brief exchange, though meant to be private, must have appeased Tom as well, because he had left without a word.

Trust, it seemed, was the theme of the day.

CHAPTER NINETEEN

A Lesson in Confidence

> **Benefactor denied request to remove pleasure receptors, stating subject should feel satisfaction. Upgrade is forthcoming.**
>
> **–Entry Log 116.11.4-7**

Lizzie expected a hotel room with beach views, not this gorgeous, secluded cabin on the ocean. There were others like it, but each one was strategically placed to give a semblance of privacy. And it came equipped with a private dipping pool, as well as an open deck to the salt water below.

And one giant bed.

"This is incredible," she said as she opened the balcony doors.

Jayson's scanner hadn't picked up any devices—indicating they were free to enjoy their stay without interruption—and the two large suitcases Jacque had teleported with them suggested they would be here for a while.

Lizzie had mentioned her job, not that it mattered anymore, and Jayson said someone would handle it for her. Whatever that meant. Something told her she wouldn't be working for a while, if ever again.

Being coddled should have bothered her, but after the last few days, she welcomed it and didn't ask any questions. She was just grateful to be away from

Hydria and Tom. And Stas, too. The latter had showed up at the end of Lizzie's medical session with Luc and tried to express her regret, but it fell flat.

Lizzie wasn't ready.

She understood the reason Stas and Tom kept everything from her, at least on a logical level, but that didn't fix her broken heart. She needed time to think, and she couldn't do that with them barraging her with apologies.

This—the sea, the fresh air, and the new experience—was what she needed. And the fact that Jayson knew and understood that floored her.

She should be just as angry with him, but all the blame fell at Stas's and Tom's feet instead. Mostly because they were the ones who lied to her for months, even years.

Not Jayson. Everything he told her was a version of the truth with missing details. They were important omissions, but not nearly as devastating as the ones her best friends kept from her.

Tom was alive.

Stas controlled people and would someday be immortal.

Two very important facts that true friends would never withhold.

Jayson's only fault was knowing the truth and not saying anything, but it was never his place to tell her. She understood that after their discussion on the plane, and perhaps even before that.

Her initial hurt had been the result of her intense feelings for him and the overall situation. But it took time to learn someone's faults and secrets, and their friendship was still very new. She thought that might be why she could be so angry with Stas and Tom, but not with Jayson.

Or maybe it went deeper.

Her connection with him defied comprehension. Staying in a room alone with him should terrify her, yet all she felt was satisfaction and perhaps a little bit of anticipation. Especially with the way he was looking at her now.

"Jacque bought you some clothes," he said as he wheeled over the suitcase.

She frowned. "He did? But how did he know my size?"

"I gave him the information he needed."

She glanced at the bag then back at him, uncertain. Her sizes varied by store, something her mother loved to ridicule her about. Because apparently, Lizzie had control over the fashion industry. "Uh, are you sure you got it right?"

His eyes roamed over her slowly and thoroughly, leaving her a little breathless. "I'm confident in my measurements." He set the suitcase on a luggage rack and unzipped it. "But feel free to try them on, Red. I'll be changing into swimming trunks."

She swallowed as he sauntered off with his own bag in the direction of the oversized bathroom.

Swimsuit. Yeah. She could handle that.

Her whole sense of time was backward after hopping from Rome to Hydria to Bora Bora, but she thought it was morning. A glance at the clock confirmed her theory.

Talk about the longest day ever. She could get used to having a teleporter around.

Lizzie peeked at the contents laid out before her and grinned at the array of color. Sundresses, flip-flops, and several swimsuits.

Perfect.

Her jaw dropped as she found the lingerie. The French designer brand was one she knew well, but not one she ever purchased from.

"Oh, crap," she breathed. The gorgeously crafted handmade items were nothing like her usual flair, and very sexy.

Jacque picked these? Her cheeks warmed. *Oh dear.*

"I definitely think you should try those on," Jayson said as he entered the bedroom in a pair of black swim shorts. No shirt.

Her mouth watered at the sight of all that delicious muscle on display and, at the same time, dropped open at his comment.

"I… These…" She cleared her throat. "I'll just be putting on a swimsuit."

She grabbed one blindly and walked swiftly to the bathroom area. A huge round tub, a marble shower, and a double sink took up about a quarter of the space. The toilet was off to one side with an oversized walk-in closet across from it. Another long marble counter ran the length of the adjacent wall.

So much space for two people. No wonder Jayson only reserved one room.

Lizzie removed the outfit she purchased in Rome and folded it on the counter, and picked up the string bikini.

She held it up and nearly swallowed her tongue.

Not a full-piece bottom, but a thong with little strings at the sides.

That's what she deserved for rushing the selection process, but seriously, who wore thong swimsuits?

Lizzie pinched the bridge of her nose. She should have checked the swimsuit before undressing herself. Walking out there in a towel to dig through the suitcase would attract attention, as would putting all her clothes back on and starting over again.

Damn it.

Why would Jacque buy her such sexy outfits? Was it a European thing? Maybe all the women in Hydria wore thongs. Jayson probably wouldn't notice, right? Or he'd be comparing her to all the other women in his life.

No. She couldn't go there, or she'd lose all her confidence.

Right. Okay. She would wear it and cover up with a towel. Jayson would be none the wiser, especially if she jumped into the water after him.

The deep-red bikini top fit her perfectly, as did the bottom, though that didn't surprise her. Not a whole lot of fabric on a thong.

She found a towel, wrapped it around herself, and wandered barefoot into the bedroom, where Jayson stood waiting with the hotel phone in his hand. His other hand rubbed his chest idly, bringing Lizzie's focus to all that muscle again.

So hot.

Especially the way he drew his palm up to the back of his neck and squeezed, accenting his biceps.

Immortality seemed to gift men with insane sex appeal. Between Jayson, Issac, and Balthazar, the female gender didn't stand a chance. Neither did the males, for that matter.

As if hearing her thoughts, Jayson turned and winked at her while listening to whoever was on the phone.

"That sums it all up nicely, thank you." He hung up. "I arranged for an early dinner on the beach for after our swim. I figure we'll be hungry again by four or so."

"Uh, sure." She gestured toward the deck. "Okay. After you."

His gaze danced over her as he sauntered toward her instead of the open doors. She backed up into the wall and gulped as he entered her personal space without preamble.

"Why are you hiding?" he asked, voice deceptively soft. The heat from his chest radiated against hers, but he didn't touch her. Not physically, anyway.

"I-I'm not."

He traced the top of the towel, just over her breasts. "Liar."

Jayson tugged on the knot, and her hands flew up to catch the fabric before it fell. Butterflies took flight in her abdomen as he grinned at her instinctual reaction.

"I warned you, Red." A sharp yank sent the towel to the floor. "I'm done holding back."

Lizzie tried to cover herself, but he captured her wrists and pressed them against the wall on either side of her head. Warmth pooled between her legs at the show of dominance, causing her to squirm and Jayson to grin.

His gaze touched every inch of her bare skin, leaving her hot and bothered by the end of his exploration.

"This color looks amazing on you." Approval deepened his tone, sending a shiver down her spine despite the warm air. "I think we're ready to renegotiate limits."

She swallowed. "What did you have in mind?"

He slid her hands over her head, where he clasped one big palm around both her wrists. It left her feeling exposed and powerless, but she trusted her captor. And she was more than ready to further explore with him.

"This isn't about me, but about you, sweetheart." His free hand slid down her arm to her collarbone, and lower. Her nipples pebbled as he played his fingers over her cleavage. He tweaked one stiff peak without warning, eliciting a moan from Lizzie as she arched into him. It hurt, but the way he massaged it afterward felt so, so good.

"Mmm, I can work with that," he murmured as his touch shifted south. Her breathing escalated as he traced her belly button and ventured lower to the small patch of fabric covering her mound.

His eyes held hers as he slowly drew his thumb over the top of her bikini bottoms to her hip bone before continuing the path of her swimsuit along the crease of her thigh. Electricity hummed in her veins as anticipation thickened the air between them.

"Not a limit," she breathed, telling him with words and her body that she was ready for whatever he wanted.

But rather than take what she offered, he skimmed his knuckles along her thigh, around to her bare ass. He cupped one cheek and applied pressure, forcing her hips to meet his.

"Do you feel that, Lizzie?" he asked, his voice low and seductive. "Do you feel how much I want you?"

God, yes. She nodded.

"Words, Lizzie." He pinched her ass in reprimand, then soothed it the same way he did her nipple. "Do you feel how hard I am?"

She swallowed and started to nod again, when she realized his demand. "Y-yes," she managed to say, though it sounded more like a groan.

"Good." His hand slid to the strings decorating her thighs. "Never belittle yourself by hiding, Red."

He held her gaze as he continued. "I promised never to lie to you, and I make no exception now when I say, you're gorgeous, Elizabeth. I've thought that since the first moment I laid eyes on you, and my attraction has only grown." He punctuated the point by pressing his groin into her again and drawing another moan from her throat in the process.

"I went easy on you the other night, sweetheart," he whispered darkly. "But your limits have expanded, and I intend to explore them thoroughly."

"Yes, please," she breathed as she arched into him again. They could swim later. Or during. She didn't care as long as it meant more of that pleasure he introduced her to over the last week. It was unlike anything she had experienced, and she yearned for more.

He tugged on the bow at her hip until it came undone. Her heart rate kicked up a notch as he explored her freshly exposed curls with his thumb.

"I bet these are red too." His lips caressed her mouth with each word. "I can't wait to see how you blush down there while I'm tasting you."

Her knees trembled with the image his words evoked. What would it feel like with no barriers?

The other side of her bottoms came undone and fell to the floor between her legs. He licked her bottom lip before nibbling gently. "Hang on, Red," he whispered as he released her hands. "I'm going to devour you now."

That was the only warning he gave as he went to his knees before her and kissed her *there.*

"Oh God…" She tried to grab the wall and failed.

It was wicked, wet, and so very wild.

Her head fell back on a moan as his tongue explored her intimately. She thought the pleasure from the other night was intense, but it was nothing compared to this. His hands on her hips were all that kept her from falling.

His name fell from her mouth as a plea to never stop, but he controlled every move. She was a slave to his demands and the pace he set with his mouth.

"More," she begged, not knowing what she meant but knowing she needed something. Her thighs shook with the mounting pleasure, and she wondered how long she could remain standing.

He took the choice away from her by rising to his feet and kissing her soundly on the mouth. The taste of her own arousal knocked her legs right out from under her. Jayson lifted her into his arms without missing a beat and carried her to the bed.

The soft sheets soothed her heated skin, but only the man crawling over her could ease the ache between her thighs. She threaded her fingers through his thick hair and forced him to kiss her again. He grinned against her lips but placated her silent demand by sliding his tongue into her mouth and staking his claim on her soul.

Deep down, she knew no one would ever come close to making her feel as Jayson did. His skills set the bar too high, and she wouldn't have it any other way.

"Make love to me," she whispered. *Fuck me* were the words he probably wanted, but she couldn't seem to say them. They felt dirty and vulgar and so inappropriate for this moment.

He palmed her cheek and kissed her far too softly. "*Love* is not a word I use lightly, Lizzie." Another caress of his lips was followed by his tongue lightly dancing with hers as he untied the strings at her nape. He drew his nose across her cheek and pressed his mouth to her ear. "But it's a word I may just use for you."

Her skin burned as he trailed kisses along her throat to her breasts. His nimble fingers slid beneath her back to unfasten the top and tossed it aside. She bowed off the bed as he sucked her nipple deep into his mouth with a force she hadn't expected. Pain mingled with euphoria, confusing her nerve endings and heightening the pulse between her thighs. When his hand wandered down to explore her wetness, she moaned.

It was as if he had every button on her body memorized. He knew where and how hard to press to drive her insane with need.

Her hands were in his hair, tugging and pulling, as her body trembled uncontrollably beneath his.

And then he entered her. Not in the way she originally requested, but with two fingers twisting in a delicious pattern that brought tears to her eyes.

Heaviness weighed down her limbs as she fought for her elusive climax, but it evaded her.

Lizzie groaned in frustration as Jayson pulled away, and subsequently froze at the sight of him removing his swim shorts. He did so slowly, as if performing a striptease meant only for her, and tauntingly revealed the part of him she'd yet to see.

She licked her lips at the beautiful sight of him fully nude and longed to explore him for herself.

He caught her hand and brought it to his mouth for a warning nibble. "Touch me now and we'll be doing this an entirely different way," he murmured as he settled between her thighs.

"I don't care how it's done," she breathed. "I just want you."

His erection prodded her slick folds and found her entrance with ease. Her hips flexed in encouragement, but his palms held her down.

"Minx," he murmured, his tone holding a touch of admonishment. "You're forgetting who's in charge again." His thick head slid inside her while he spoke, causing her to still beneath him. "This is going to hurt, Red."

Her lips parted to reply, but a shocked gasp exited instead as he penetrated her innocence in one swift move.

His warning did not prepare her for the severe reality of the experience. She thought it would be slow and didn't expect to be split in half by his impressive length.

Tears pricked her eyes, and not the good kind. She clung to his shoulders, begging him not to move again.

"Breathe." He nuzzled her neck. "Concentrate on me, sweetheart. Feel my mouth"—he licked a path along her throat—"and my touch."

His hands drifted up her sides to cup her breasts. She whimpered as his thumbs thrummed her stiff peaks.

"That's it, Red. Feel me." He nibbled her jaw while his fingers worked magic around her nipples. She pressed into him and jolted at the reminder of the fullness below, but it didn't throb in the way she expected; it was more of a tingle.

Lizzie lifted her hips to test the friction and found the movement far more pleasurable than she anticipated. Another shift had her moaning in approval.

His hot length branded her insides, claiming her as his in a way no other man ever had or would. He would forever hold her virginity, a gift she would never give anyone else, and she was oddly at peace with that.

His mouth took possession of hers as his body began to move. Slowly at first, almost teasingly so, before steadily increasing in power and in ferocity. He grabbed her hip to control the pace as his opposite hand cupped her cheek.

Her arms were around his shoulders, holding on for dear life as he wrecked her inside and out. Every thrust pushed her closer to the edge of something intense, and each swipe of his tongue against hers felt like a promise of souls.

Mine, some part of her proclaimed.

An irrational response, but one she couldn't deny in this moment.

All that mattered was the man mastering her body.

Her nails scored his back, marking him as he continued to devastate her future. Because no one would ever compare to Jayson and the feelings he evoked inside.

"You're so perfect," he whispered against her lips. "So fucking perfect." His hand shifted from her hip to the top of her sex where he found her swollen nub. It sent shocks to every inch of her being and created a dark yearning she couldn't ignore.

"Put your legs around me," he urged. She locked her ankles together against his ass and screamed as he slid deeper and harder into her.

"Oh, Jayson…" Her eyes rolled into the back of her head. That new spot, coupled with his expert touch, obliterated her grasp on reality.

Sensation and breathing were her only thoughts.

And pleasure.

Such intense discomfort, yet rapturous.

She couldn't think.

Couldn't breathe.

Couldn't move.

Just reveled in the motions and the feel of his body commanding hers.

"Shatter for me, Lizzie," he demanded. "Let it all go, and come for me."

Her pulse hammered through her thoughts as her body yielded to his command. His thumb pressed down while he slammed into her harder than before, and her world went black, then light, as an explosion went off inside her.

Sounds she didn't even know she could make spilled from her mouth as she trembled from the most intense orgasm of her life. It rolled through her over and over and over again.

Sight failed her.

She was a puddle of bliss and nothing else.

Jayson groaned her name as he followed her over the edge after a few fierce thrusts. Warmth spilled inside her, joining her arousal and spiraling them both into a sea of ecstasy.

Lizzie panted from the onslaught of it all as her heart beat an unhealthy rhythm.

All her friends complained about their first times, but Lizzie could honestly say she had no regrets. Because that was phenomenal, and as soon as she could speak, she would ask for another round.

Jayson chuckled against her neck. "Don't worry, Red. We'll continue this exploration after we take a dip in the ocean."

She tried to respond but couldn't. It didn't surprise her at all that he sensed her wishes; he'd more than proven his ability to read her body language.

He went to his elbows on either side of her head. "How do you feel about swimming naked?"

CHAPTER TWENTY

Flirtatious Behavior

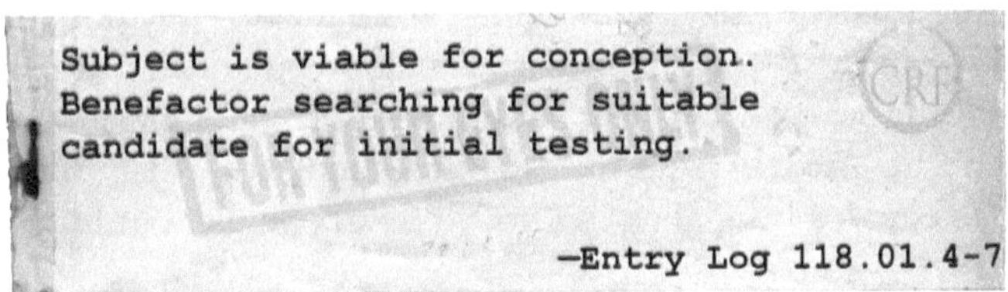

Subject is viable for conception. Benefactor searching for suitable candidate for initial testing.

—Entry Log 118.01.4-7

Lizzie resembled a mermaid on the beach with her damp red locks hanging alluringly over her blue sundress. She'd taken Jayson up on the skinny-dipping offer, something he thanked her thoroughly for. Twice. And she appeared well pleasured as a result.

"Why are you staring at me like that?" she asked.

He grinned. "Your naïveté floors me, Red." The woman had no idea how sexy it was to watch her twirl her tongue around that straw. He kept envisioning his cock in its place.

Jayson's goal to ease Lizzie into their sexual relationship rested on thin ice. He wanted to introduce her slowly to his darker cravings, but if she kept licking her straw like that, he'd have her on her knees in the next five minutes with his dick down her throat. And wouldn't that be lovely for the waitress to see?

Lizzie's cheeks hollowed as she sipped her drink while watching him, and damn if it wasn't the most innocently erotic thing he'd ever seen.

"If you keep doing that, we're not going to make it through the main course." Because he'd be devouring her instead.

Her eyes widened as the straw popped out of her mouth. "What do you mean?"

He curled his finger in a beckoning manner. "Come here, Red."

Lizzie glanced around the mostly unpopulated area of the beach. Jayson had requested a private dinner near the water rather than in one of the restaurants. It meant their waitress left them alone for longer periods, and allowed for a more romantic experience, but anyone could walk by.

She licked her lips. "I don't—"

"Now."

"Uh." She cleared her throat. "Yeah, okay."

She stood, walked around the table meant for four diners, and stopped beside him with an arched eyebrow. "Happy?"

"Not yet." He relaxed into his chair and patted his leg. "Have a seat."

"You realize I'm not a dog, right?" she muttered as she did as he requested.

He wrapped an arm around her waist to pull her firmly into his lap, right where he wanted her. His mouth found her ear. "Do you feel that, Lizzie?" He knew she did by the way she froze after settling her ass on his hard cock. "That's because all I can think about is replacing your straw with my cock."

Her lips parted at his vulgar words as two splotches of pink painted her cheeks. "Oh…"

"Yes, *oh*," he murmured as he settled his palm on her exposed thigh and slid upward. "You drive me crazy, Red—in the absolute best way possible—which is why all this 'going easy on you' is very *hard*. Do you understand?"

He traced the seam of her new panties with his index finger and held her steady when she tried to squirm. No one could see what he was doing, something he ensured by angling her body the way he did, but Lizzie wouldn't know that.

"We've only begun to scratch the surface of what I intend to do to you, Elizabeth." He pressed his thumb to her clit and massaged the little nub through the handmade silk while she fought to breathe. "My appetites exceed traditional standards—a result of age and experience."

He sucked her earlobe into his mouth as he applied more pressure below. Her arousal seeped through the thin barrier while she tried to shift to close her legs. His palm prevented her thighs from touching, and his arm around her torso tightened in warning.

"You're going to come for me," he whispered. "But you're going to do it quickly before our dinner arrives."

"Jayson, I don't know…" She trailed off on a whimper as he increased the intensity and pace of his touch. The dampening fabric confirmed her enjoyment even as her mind rebelled against it.

A crack in her mental barrier was all he needed.

"Focus on the pleasure, sweetheart. Do you feel how hard I am right now?

You're doing that to me, Red." He drew a hypnotic pattern with his tongue over her pulse before nibbling gently. Her breathing shallowed as her body tensed, all thought of their surroundings lost, just as he wanted. He hadn't meant to deliver this lesson over dinner, but he couldn't ignore the opportunity to play.

Jayson nuzzled her neck as she started to shake. "That's it, love. Give in to the sensations." He slid his palm up from her waist to her breast and pinched her erect nipple. "Let me feel you come, Lizzie. Now, sweetheart."

She shuddered and whispered his name as a benediction. He would never tire of that sound or the moan that followed as she crashed headfirst into oblivion and shook uncontrollably on his lap. His dick begged him to bend her over the table and fuck her until she screamed, but he reined in his yearnings and focused on the woman coming apart in his arms.

So much to teach her…

He would need years, maybe decades, to fulfill his craving for her.

I'm so fucked and don't even care.

His forehead rested against her shoulder as she came down from her high. He knew when reality returned, because she tensed and tried to scramble off his lap.

"Do that again, and I'll force another orgasm out of you, Red." He punctuated the point by roughly thumbing her sensitive bud. Her body jolted against his as another of those delicious whimpers left her mouth.

"What are you doing to me?" she asked breathlessly.

"Training," he replied against her neck. "And you're responding wonderfully to it." He removed his hand from between her legs and lifted his thumb to trace her lips. "Lick," he demanded.

She did with a tremble. "Oh God…"

"Mmm, I'll accept that nickname." He took hold of her chin and tilted her head back for a kiss. "You taste amazing, Lizzie. I think you'll be my dessert later."

Her cheeks darkened to that luscious shade he adored. "O-okay, but only if I get to taste you too."

The woman had no idea how fucking hot those words were, especially when spoken so innocently.

"I will absolutely be taking you up on that," he promised. "After we eat dinner." He helped her stand and fix her dress just as the waitress strolled over with a tray of plates.

"Excellent timing, Jana," he said with a boyish grin. "That smells amazing."

The petite female beamed at him as she started decorating the table with food. "I hope you enjoy, Mister Jayson."

"I'm certain we will," he murmured with a wink. "Thank you."

"Can I get you anything else?" The touch of innuendo in her tone should have intrigued him, but it didn't. Not in the slightest. In fact, it sort of irritated him considering his obvious date, but some women would see that as a challenge. Still, he couldn't be rude.

"Not at the moment," he replied with another grin he knew women adored. "Thank you, though."

"You'll let me know when you're ready for dessert?" Another insinuation, one that reminded him of his plans later.

"I definitely will." He smiled a little too eagerly as a vision of Lizzie sprawled out naked in their bed graced his thoughts. It would be a very pleasurable night indeed. "Thank you, Jana," he said in a polite attempt to dismiss her.

"You are most welcome, Mister Jayson." She flashed him a promising look before flouncing away with her tray, leaving Jayson to shake his head in amusement. The female was pretty enough, but nothing compared to the beauty across from him.

He unfolded his napkin and eyed the array of dishes on the table. French cuisine was one of his favorites, but his companion didn't seem nearly as excited by the fare. Odd—she'd been thrilled about the menu when they ordered.

"What's up, Red?" he asked, confused by her furious expression. "Why are you glowering at me?"

Lizzie's eyebrows rose. "Seriously?"

Well, that was a response a man never wanted to hear.

He sipped his water and waited for her to say more.

"You're a jerk," she finally said, throwing her napkin onto the table. "No, I'm sorry; that's not the right term. You're a *player*. Of course, I already knew that. I'm the idiot for thinking this, us, or whatever…" She shook her head. "You know what? Never mind. I'm not hungry." She pushed away from the table, but he caught her wrist before she could walk away.

"Sit. Down." Two words. Softly spoken. Underlined in demand.

"Or what?" she countered. "You'll force an orgasm out of me at the table again and later seek the waitress out for dessert?" Her eyes shone with unshed tears as she looked imploringly at him. "I can't watch what happens next, Jayson. Just…" She sucked in her bottom lip as it trembled. "Please let me go." The broken quality in her voice undid him.

"Lizzie—"

"Don't, please. I just…" She sniffled, her eyes closing. "I'm fine."

He stood and pulled her into his arms because she was very clearly *not* fine. She stiffened, which both infuriated and shattered him. How had their dinner gone from pleasurable and promising to *this*?

And what the hell was she talking about with dessert? Why the fuck would he want that from the waitress when he had Lizzie?

"You're going to have to help me out here," he admitted. "I just finished telling you what I wanted to do to you after dinner, but you're implying I want the waitress instead. How did you come to that conclusion?"

She scoffed and tried to push him away. "You can't be serious."

"I'm very serious," he growled, irritated by her words and antics. He threaded his fingers through her hair and tugged her head back so he could read her expression as he added, "I've been nothing but honest with you from the beginning. Yet you're acting like I've deceived you in some way and are saying unflattering remarks regarding my personality, and I want to understand why."

She swallowed as the first signs of uncertainty filled her features. Now they were getting somewhere. "You were flirting with the waitress just like you did with the flight attendant," she said. "In front of me. Like I'm not here."

"Flirting?" he repeated, frowning. "I was being polite."

"By hitting on them!" she snapped, her fire returning. "I saw the woman on the plane give you her number, and you just promised the waitress to follow up on her offer for dessert, which I know has nothing to do with food. I might be inexperienced and naïve, but I can recognize sexual innuendo, Jayson."

"I see." He debated which point to tackle first and settled on the waitress. "Do you know what I was thinking about when Jana asked about dessert?"

Lizzie paled. "I don't want to know."

"No?" He arched a brow. "That's too bad because it was quite the picture in my head and starred you—very naked—in our bed."

Her eyes widened. "What?"

"And as for Rebekah," he continued, ignoring her confusion. "She gave me her number to pass along to Balthazar, because their preferences in the bedroom are well-suited." He considered whether or not to add this next part but decided holding back would only harm them at this point.

"She propositioned *us* on the plane, Red. It seems threesomes with handsome couples are her thing. I politely turned her down and suggested she reach out to B the next time she's in Greece."

Pink splotches decorated Lizzie's cheeks as her mouth popped open in surprise. "A threesome?" she whispered, scandalized.

"Yes, it's not uncommon. But as I told Rebekah on the plane, I have no intention of sharing you with anyone. Ever." The words came out with more conviction than he anticipated, but it felt good to admit it out loud. "I won't even share you with Balthazar." Those words were for himself more than for her and sent a shock to his heart.

Jayson never denied Balthazar when he wanted to bed a woman.

But Lizzie?

Oh, he would be fucking denying that.

Jayson's blood boiled at the thought of B touching *his* redhead.

Well, that's new.

He always shared.

Not her.

"You're hurting me," Lizzie said, voice strained.

Jayson relaxed his arm around her back, as well as the hand in her hair. "Sorry, Red." He hadn't meant to squeeze her—or even realized he'd done it. "My mind wandered to something unpleasant."

She swallowed and nodded, her brow creasing. "So, um, you didn't plan to see the flight attendant in Rome?"

"Of course not. I expected the CRF to find us, though I hoped they wouldn't. At no point did I intend to see her again, nor do I have any interest in our waitress."

"But you agreed to dessert?"

"Yes, with you," he murmured, grinning. "If you heard desire in my response, it was not directed toward her, Red. Only you."

She pursed her lips, and he could tell she wanted to say something but kept second-guessing herself. When she shook her head and forced a smile, he knew this conversation was far from finished.

"Say what you need to, Lizzie. Don't dance around it or hide. I expect honesty between us and will accept nothing less. That's the only way we'll ever work."

She blinked. "You talk about us like we have a future."

"Don't we?" He searched her beautiful eyes for answers but only saw more questions. "You need to help me out here, Red. I thought you wanted something long-term. Am I wrong?" He had better be right because short-term wasn't going to work for him. Not with her.

"What's long-term to a man of three thousand years?" she asked. "I mean, from what I gathered from your friends, you enjoy bedding multiple women at a time and eating breakfast as a giant group after a night of sexcapades. Oh, and Tristan insinuated that you usually share. So, as the man with all the experience, you tell me—what should I expect?"

"I don't know," he admitted as he combed his fingers through her damp hair. "All my relationships have been ones of an open nature. Eternity is a long time to promise yourself to one person—something all my former long-term lovers understood. They usually took other partners to keep things interesting but came to me when they wanted something familiar, and vice versa."

She scrunched her nose and pinched her lips to the side. "Okay, so an open relationship where I sleep with whomever I want and you do too?"

His stomach twisted at the thought of another man touching Lizzie. "Absolutely not."

Her eyes rounded. "But that's what you just described."

"No. I mean, yes, I did, but that wasn't in reference to us." He dropped his arm from her waist to palm the back of his neck.

Why was this so difficult? Jayson understood women, adored them, bedded them all the time, and yet this one had him tongue-tied and irrational. She'd just thrown up the alternative to bed her for as long as he wanted with the option of remaining open, and he'd turned it down without hesitation.

He needed his head examined.

Jayson did not do jealousy. He was a free spirit, and her description fit him perfectly—except when it came to her.

"I don't want you to take other partners, Lizzie. With or without me, the notion of another man touching you is enough to drive me mad, something I can honestly say has never been an issue for me." He let go of her completely to take a step back, both of his hands going to his hair as he paced in front of her.

"I don't want to share you, either," she said quietly. "It hurts when you flirt with other women. A lot."

Her gaze fell to the sand as her shoulders hunched, indicating that those words were not an easy admission. But they were words he needed to hear.

Jayson developed his charming candor with females over the centuries with the primary purpose of attracting them to his bed. It came so naturally to him now that he didn't even think about it, he just acted. And it clearly hurt Lizzie.

He cupped her cheeks to tilt her head upward again and swallowed hard at the pain radiating from her beautiful eyes. "You were right," he murmured. "I am a jerk."

She started to shake her head, but he stopped her response with a brush of his lips against hers.

"I thought my firsts were well and truly in the past, but this—us—is definitely brand new to me." His fingers slipped into her hair as he pressed his forehead to hers.

"You make me want to try something different, Red. Something I've never considered before. But it's going to take patience and time because my habits are very old, and I'll need you to tell me when I'm hurting you, just like you did tonight. Can you do that, Lizzie? Can you be honest and tell me when I'm doing something that wounds you?"

The begging quality to his voice was one he didn't hear often, but Lizzie brought out a side of him he rarely allowed anyone to see. He considered it his weakest link, but also his greatest strength.

His heart.

He wouldn't say he loved her—they didn't know each other well enough for that—but he could see the potential *to* love her. She touched him in a way few ever had, and every part of him itched to stake his claim.

Mine.

A natural drive he rarely felt around a woman, but Lizzie caressed every possessive instinct he owned. The dominant in him understood patience, while the soul in him recognized his potential mate.

Lizzie licked her lips and parted them twice before replying, "I can call you a jerk when I need to."

He grinned. "Yeah?"

She nodded, her lips curling. "Maybe an asshole too."

He pulled back in mock surprise. "Did you just curse?"

"I curse. Sometimes. When it's warranted." Her brow came down. "My mother always said people used bad words when they couldn't think of anything more intelligent to say."

"Yeah, well, your mother's a fucking bitch, so I think I'll ignore that ineloquent deduction."

Lizzie laughed. "You say that like you know my mom."

"I may not have met the woman, but I watched her with you at brunch that day, and my summary is more than accurate. It took considerable effort not to throw her through the window."

Lizzie's eyes rounded. "You were at brunch?"

"Hormonal drinks, remember?" he prompted. "Speaking of which, we should probably eat our now-cold food. Unless you're still not hungry?" He cocked a brow, daring her to deny her need for sustenance. If she claimed not to be famished, his ego would be wounded.

Fortunately, she nodded in agreement. "Dinner." She gazed up at him through her lashes as she added, "Followed by dessert."

"As if that was ever a question," he murmured against her lips. "And tomorrow we'll have breakfast in bed."

Lizzie's lips curled into an impish smile. "I think I like the sound of that."

CHAPTER TWENTY-ONE

Let's Play a Game

> **Benefactor has requested his associate be allowed to taste the subject for tracking purposes. A supervised visit will need to be arranged.**
>
> **—Entry Log 107.11.4-7**

Two weeks of sex and sun looked good on Lizzie. Her cheeks held a healthy glow, her eyes shone with the secrets Jayson had taught her, and her lips seemed perpetually curled into a smile. The lingerie helped with the latter.

She clipped her silk stockings into the garters and adjusted her cleavage in the lacy top. Jayson had given her a tutorial last week on how to wear all the fancy French garments, and she'd enjoyed taunting him with that knowledge ever since.

Lizzie adored fashion. This newfound obsession with lace would not go away anytime soon. She loved how each set was strategically placed to appear revealing without actually showing anything truly intimate. And even more, she enjoyed Jayson's reactions.

Another once-over in the mirror produced an even bigger grin on her face.

Perfection.

A confidence boost was among the gifts Jayson had given her these last few weeks. After so many hours naked in his presence, it seemed silly to hide.

And the way he looked at her when she dressed up for him like this? Worth every ounce of hesitation.

She sauntered into the bedroom to wait for Jayson. He'd drawn her a bath in the oversized tub before venturing off to the market to procure some fresh fruit for the room, but she expected him to return any minute now.

Lizzie poured herself a glass of wine and admired the calmness of the waves. Jayson remarked last night that it reminded him a bit of home, something she took as a subtle sign that he wanted to return to Hydria soon.

Luc had visited twice, briefly each time, to ask a barrage of personal questions—similar to a physician—and to take more samples. She didn't really enjoy being his personal test subject, but she also wanted answers, so she allowed it.

Deep down, though, she knew if she *really* desired the truth, she needed to leave Bora Bora. The selfish side of her scoffed at the idea, while the part of her who adored Jayson dwelt on the unfairness of forcing him to stay here. Not that he seemed to mind, because he—

"Well, that's a sight to behold."

Goose bumps scattered down her spine at the familiar voice behind her. It came from a man she never expected to see again.

She swallowed her nerves as she turned to meet a pair of amused brown eyes. All his fatherly appeal seemed to be replaced by a man she barely recognized. The way his gaze danced over her in an appreciative manner stirred up bile in the pit of her stomach.

"Doctor Fitzgerald," she managed.

"Come now, Lizzie, I think you can call me John while dressed like that." He gestured to the armed blond beside him. "You remember Stark, yes?"

She tried to nod but couldn't. Not with the way both men had her cornered by the water. She could jump, but where would she go? To the beach? Her dancer's legs didn't translate well in the water, not to mention her lacy undergarments would weigh her down. The two men would either catch her or beat her to the sand.

And they probably weren't alone, either.

"Shall we go?" Stark asked, his voice bored. He hadn't bothered to glance at her or her seductive attire, something she felt minutely grateful for, especially with the manner in which John kept glancing at her breasts and legs.

Twenty-four years and he always treated her like a daughter. But it was all a lie, and she could see that in his lecherous gaze.

"Not yet." John closed the gap between them. He fingered a strand of her hair as he asked, "Would you care to change before we go?" Innocently worded and belittled by the smolder in his gaze.

Lizzie always wondered why John appeared no older than thirty-five, but now she knew it was a result of his Ichorian bloodline. "I would," she admitted, unable to lie. From what she understood, he excelled at forcing the truth out of people, and it was no different with her.

"Please do," he gestured to the suitcase. "You'll understand why it has to be in front of us, though. I already lost you once and can't afford for it to happen again. You're an expensive investment, after all."

She shivered at the bluntness of his words. "What do you mean?"

"We'll discuss it along the way," he replied. "You have two minutes to change. I suggest you use the time wisely."

Lizzie considered telling him to go to hell but opted for sense instead. She couldn't try to run in this outfit without garnering a lot of attention. Jean shorts, a tank top, and tennis shoes would be far more appropriate.

A snakelike sensation crawled over her skin as he supervised her removal of the garter belt and stockings. Stark still didn't acknowledge her but focused on the perimeter.

Scanning for Jayson.

If she could find a way to delay their departure, maybe he would return in time to kick John's ass.

Lizzie finished her show of dressing by pulling a tank top over her head and folded her arms to hide herself from John's view. She'd managed to keep the important bits covered, but his grin said it didn't matter.

This John—despite the similar features—resembled a stranger and left her feeling cold, used, and inadequate.

She shivered as his smile grew.

"I think we should play a game and find out just how far this infatuation goes," he mused. "Would you like that, Lizzie? To learn Jay's true feelings?"

"Do we have time for that, sir?" Stark asked, an edge to his tone that wasn't reflected in his bored expression.

"Of course. Why else did we come prepared?"

"Because we assumed he would be here, sir."

"And I suspect he will be any moment now." John touched his ear. "Any sign of the Elder?" He nodded at whatever the person on the other side of his communication unit was saying. "Excellent." He glanced at Stark. "I told you Patel's gadgets would work."

The Sentinel shrugged one shoulder as he drew a gun. "We won't know for sure until he enters."

"Fair enough." Dark chocolate eyes met hers. "Be a dear and come stand by me, please." So politely worded and perfectly John.

And yet, everything between them had changed.

This man was a monster—an Ichorian—who founded an organization meant to hunt other immortals. And he'd done something to her, though no one knew what. Then there were the things Jayson had told her about Tom and a Hydraian named Amelia.

Lizzie would never trust Jonathan Fitzgerald again. And she certainly didn't want him to touch her.

"No," she replied, surprising herself and him. Years of elegance training kept her hospitable even in the most uncomfortable situations, but no more. What did she have to lose? He'd already implied she was an 'expensive investment.' That meant he wouldn't kill her, right?

"Sir," Stark murmured.

"I heard it," John replied as he stepped toward Lizzie. She started to back up out of his reach, not that she would get far on the deck, unless she jumped—

She fell to her knees as something sharp smacked her upside the head. Right above her ear. It throbbed and distorted the room.

An arm around her torso yanked her up against a hard body as something razor sharp pressed into her neck.

"Careful, sir, or the benefactor will not be pleased," Stark remarked, voice cold and void of feeling. He could have been talking about the weather for all he seemed to care.

"You let me worry about that." John's response came from behind her, confirming he'd been the one to smack and grab her.

Had he hit her with the blunt edge of the blade pressed to her throat?

"Try not to move, Lizzie. This isn't your average knife." He sounded amused by that, and she could think of only one reason why.

It's not made of metal.

She tried to focus on the firearm in Stark's hand, but it wavered in and out of her vision. The tears collecting in her eyes didn't help matters.

John shifted to place his back to a wall while holding Lizzie in front of him. The arm around her waist reminded her of a contracting band as he squeezed the air from her lungs. A whimper escaped Lizzie's throat, which resulted in a chuckle from her captor.

"That's for forgetting your manners," he murmured against her ear.

She had no idea he could be this cruel. Hearing about it from Jayson and seeing it were two very different experiences. No wonder Tom had faked his death. From her understanding, John didn't know. He also thought Amelia was dead. If only she could escape in a similar manner.

"I found those baby bananas you love, Red," Jayson announced as he entered the suite.

Lizzie opened her mouth to respond, but John's constricting arm warned her not to while Stark positioned himself defensively beside them.

Silence followed, suggesting Jayson suspected the disturbance.

"By now you've sensed our weapons are not of the traditional variety," John said by way of greeting. "But trust me when I say they are just as deadly."

Bags rustled against the ground before Jayson stepped around the corner empty-handed. He didn't look at Lizzie but focused on the man behind her. "Hello, Jonathan."

"Jayson," he greeted back. "I wouldn't come any closer unless you want to see what a diamond-encrusted ceramic knife can do against skin."

Jayson lifted his hands in surrender, his expression expertly blank. "You have my undivided attention."

"Do I?" John mused. "Excellent. I was just suggesting a game to Lizzie. Would you care to play?"

"Depends on the parameters." Jayson folded his arms. "What did you have in mind?"

"It's simple, actually. You see, that gun"—he gestured to the one Stark had pointed at Jayson—"is filled with glass incendiary bullets. A new technology we devised specifically with you in mind. Your penchant for metal is a tricky one."

Lizzie trembled. Jayson told her the purpose for incendiary bullets. *They set the blood on fire, thereby permanently killing immortals.* Yet he merely yawned and waved his hand in a gesture to continue. "Go on."

"Well, the threat is clear, yes? But I'm willing to give you a choice. Consider it a way of respecting my Elders." The grin in his voice didn't seem to entertain Jayson at all. If anything, he looked about as bored as Stark.

Did he call Jacque for backup? Lizzie wondered. She tried to catch his gaze, but he remained fixated on the one behind her. John shifted his hold, raising his arm to cross her breasts instead of her waist, and she cringed at the intimate touch, but the knife at her throat kept her in place. At least her vision had cleared.

"Get to the point, Jonathan," Jayson demanded, his calm veneer cracking.

"I'll allow you to leave, unharmed, if you go now without Lizzie."

"Or?" Jayson prompted.

"Or Stark kills you."

"I'm not a fan of either option," Jayson drawled. "Surely you can be more creative than forcing me to choose myself over Lizzie."

"I admit, I assumed the choice to leave would be obvious."

"The last time an Elder trusted you, you shot him. I won't be making the same mistake."

John tsked. "Now, now, let's not live in the past. Not when we have a future to discuss." His fingers danced along Lizzie's arms, causing her stomach to churn. "All right, the third option is to let Stark collar you. It thwarts a fight and allows you to stay with Lizzie."

Her eyes widened. Jayson had mentioned the device that controlled Amelia. "No, Jayson—" The blade bit into her skin, silencing her instantly.

"Your betters are talking, Lizzie. It's rude to interrupt." He squeezed her again, hard enough to draw out another whimper. "You broke my product, Jayson. I have to say, I'm displeased."

"I'd argue I improved it," Jayson replied, his voice underlined with emotion. "I accept option three."

John stilled behind her. "The collar?"

"Yes." No hesitation, and he still refused to look at her. If he did, he would have seen her imploring him not to do this. Not for her. Not ever. There would be another way. There had to be.

"Truly?" John sounded surprised. "For her?"

"Yes."

"First Issac. Now, the renowned Jedrick of Babylon?" John laughed humorlessly. "The world must be coming to an end."

Jayson cocked a brow. "Are we done playing this game?"

John chuckled. "Sure. Be a good Elder and kneel for Stark."

"Don't!" Lizzie shouted, unable to hold it in anymore. She tried to say more, but the air whooshed from her lungs as John crushed her with his arm. Her ribs and chest ached at the show of strength as her heart shattered in two at the sight of Jayson going to his knees with his hands loosely at his sides.

Still he wouldn't look at her, but she caught the tension in his jaw. He was holding back. For what, she didn't know.

You'd better have a plan, she thought as black dots danced over her vision.

"Really, Lizzie," John chastised. "You're acting like a child."

And you're acting like a dick.

Stark pulled a collar from his pocket and stepped forward to wrap it around Jayson's neck. It sealed with a snick that seemed to ricochet through the room. He didn't move from his submissive pose even as the Sentinel backed away.

"Well, that worked out better than I expected." John sounded quite pleased as he finally loosened his hold enough for Lizzie to breathe. It struck her as odd that she hadn't passed out despite the darkness lurking in her gaze, but she didn't have time to think about it.

"I say we play one more round of truth," the monster behind her murmured. "Stark, send the text."

"Yes, sir."

Jayson finally looked up from the floor. "This isn't good enough for you?"

"Hardly," John scoffed. "There's a loose end that needs addressing."

"It's done," Stark informed. "I suspect we will know within minutes if your hunch is right."

As he said it, a buzzing sounded from Jayson's pocket.

"That would be your phone, I imagine," John surmised. "Let it ring."

Her lover shrugged. "As you wish."

"Oh, I'm enjoying this far more than I should."

"Enjoy it," Jayson replied. "It'll be short-lived."

"So confident for an immortal completely at my mercy. I did give you the option to leave."

Jayson's eyes smoldered as he narrowed them over her shoulder. "You did, and trust me when I say I won't be returning the favor."

"We'll see." John sounded more amused than frightened, something Lizzie suspected would be a mistake. Because Jayson's expression had transformed from polite boredom to lethally serious.

"We will," he agreed, voice colder than she'd ever heard it.

A frantic knock sounded at the door, sending relief to Lizzie's heart. That must be Jayson's backup, though why the Hydraian's would knock—

"Lizzie!" Stas's voice called through the door. "I know you're mad at me, but I need you to open up!"

Jayson flinched as John sighed. "And there's my answer."

"It would appear so, sir," Stark agreed. "Shall I let her in?"

"No, Lizzie will do that for us." The knife disappeared from her throat. "Be a dear and let Stas in, and don't even think to warn her, or Stark will put a bullet in Jayson's head. Actually…"

He removed his arm and turned her to face him, his expression excited.

"I'll allow you a choice, Lizzie. Warn Stas, Jayson dies. Don't warn Stas, Jayson lives, and, well, we'll see what happens."

"Oh, fuck no," Jayson growled.

Lizzie shook her head as tears collected behind her eyes. "That's an impossible choice." Jayson or Stas? She could never pick between them. As angry as she was at Stas, she didn't want to hurt her.

And Jayson… The idea of losing him twisted her up inside.

No.

She couldn't, *wouldn't*, let him die.

But Stas…

Another frantic knock had John grinning. "Tick tock, Lizzie. Make a decision. Now."

"I-I can't. You can't—"

"Shoot him," John instructed. "Now."

"No!" Lizzie jumped backward on instinct, placing herself between Stark and Jayson. "No. I'll… I'll decide. I'm deciding. I just…" She trailed off as a violent tremor shook her from head to toe.

Jayson's gesture of kneeling and accepting his fate left her without a choice.

She couldn't let him die. Not for her.

And John didn't know about Stas's immortality, at least according to their intelligence. That could be used to their advantage, as well as her ability to persuade.

Lizzie swallowed, her resolve solidifying.

This was the appropriate play and the only one that kept Jayson alive. Because the look on Stark's face said he wouldn't hesitate to pull the trigger, even if it meant shooting through her.

"I-I'll open the door," she decided as yet a third knock sounded, followed by Stas begging Lizzie to talk to her and Jayson's phone vibrating again.

"Excellent," John replied. "Escort Stas in here, please."

Lizzie nodded even as Jayson said her name in warning.

"You're not the only one who gets to make sacrifices," she whispered as she turned toward her fate. Her hands were shaking uncontrollably as she unlatched the door.

"Oh, thank God," Stas said as she threw her arms around Lizzie. "The CRF is coming. Jacque left for reinforcements, but I demanded he drop me off first to warn you and Jayson, who isn't picking up his phone."

Lizzie awkwardly hugged her back while her mouth refused to work.

Run, she wanted to say.

Stay, her heart begged.

Because Stark probably had his gun to Jayson's head, and the image sent a chill down her spine. She swore her soul cried at the thought. They had decided to be exclusive but never discussed their feelings.

This situation told her all she needed to know.

She loved him. More than she ever knew was possible.

Tom had been a crush.

Jayson? He was the real deal, and his life hung in the balance because of her indecision.

But her best friend… She loved Stas too.

An unfair choice.

She squeezed her friend as the emotions threatened to destroy her. "I'm sorry," she whispered. "I'm so sorry."

"Hey, that's my line," Stas murmured. "I'm the one who's sorry. I should have told you, especially about—"

"Don't," Lizzie said, cutting her off before she could say the name that would derail everything. *Tom.* "I… We…"

God, how could she walk her friend into the lion's den? How could she leave Jayson there to suffer?

He stayed for her.

He kneeled for her.

He took the collar for her.

It was about more than duty and protection for him. She knew with her soul that he felt the same abnormal connection, and saw it in the way he looked at her. Even if he wouldn't admit it out loud.

Love.

Or at least the beginning of it.

"You're shaking." Stas pulled back to grasp Lizzie by the shoulders. "I promise the CRF won't touch you."

Too late.

Stas's lips curled down as she studied Lizzie's expression and, worse, her neck. "How…?"

"I'm disappointed, Lizzie," John said as he joined them in the hall with a gun in his hand. "But not nearly as disappointed as I am with you, Stas."

Her best friend froze, her lips working on silent words as shock drained the color from her features.

"It's a shame," he continued. "You had so much potential, but I've suspected for some time that you were playing both sides. I assume your lover is as well, which is truly his loss. What me and my benefactor are creating is far greater than Issac can even imagine." He sighed dramatically. "Well, he can consider this a message. Goodbye, Stas."

The bullet cracked through the air before Lizzie could blink.

She yelped in response.

And screamed as the life drained from her best friend's eyes.

It happened so slowly.

Her body seemed to float in the air, suspended in time as death registered.

And suddenly she was falling to the ground, her green eyes wide with emotions left unsaid.

Lizzie collapsed as her knees gave out. "No!" she screamed, her heart breaking into a thousand pieces. "NO!"

She shook her head as the tears fell.

This couldn't be happening.

He didn't kill Stas.

Her immortal genetics…

Except he said they were incendiary bullets—specially manufactured to kill immortals of all types. Fledglings included.

"No," she sobbed, her body folding over the ground as the weight of emotion crushed her spirit. "No, no, no…"

"Lizzie," John said, his voice holding a sharp demand. "I need your focus."

She shook her head, unable to yield. He'd just killed her best friend. Without a single ounce of remorse. As a fucking message.

NO.

Quivers racked her spine as she fought to breathe through the pain.

Then the unthinkable happened.

Another gunshot.

This one at the end of the hall, leading into the living area.

She glanced up into Jayson's vacant eyes and blinked in disbelief.

No.

He wouldn't… That… He promised…

"You made your choice," John murmured as he holstered his gun above Jayson's corpse. "He paid the consequences of your indecision. But don't worry, Lizzie. You'll have a long, long time to live with the repercussions of this moment, as I suspect his life lives on inside you now."

She couldn't breathe, couldn't think.

Jayson…

Dead.

Because of her.

This had to be a bad dream.

Just yesterday he kissed her on the beach.

But his eyes…

So broken.

So… lifeless.

His lips were parted on words she didn't hear. Did he say her name? So shadowed in her own grief over losing her best friend, she didn't get a chance to say goodbye.

He would never know how she felt.

Jayson died thinking his sacrifice meant nothing, that she wasn't willing to make the same choice, that she didn't love him as he did her…

Oh, Jayson.

Something shattered inside her, rendering her immobile.

Her soul detaching from her body?

Her heart?

"I suggest we get moving," Stark said as he knelt beside her and pricked her arm with something.

She couldn't move.

Didn't care.

Escape meant nothing.

What was the point of living without the two most important people in her life?

Dead.

Because I couldn't decide.

Because I exist.

No longer.

Oblivion swallowed her, relieving her of this nightmare.

Blessed relief, lifting her to a dreamlike state where she searched for Jayson, for surely he would meet her here.

Except all she saw was darkness.

A future without friends or love.

A future in a cage.

Home, her subconscious supplied. *Where we belong.*

She blinked inwardly at that thought.

That's not…

A vision of white lab coats, cameras, and endless tests flashed behind her eyes.

Memories or nightmares?

Home.

We're going home.

Chapter Twenty-Two

Welcome Back

```
Subject's vitals are steady. Will
commence resuscitation at 0800 hours.
Need to create new log for Subject
4-7.1.

                 —Entry Log 124.11.4-7
```

Lizzie awoke in a sea of white.

Walls, blankets, furniture, and curtains, all pristine. Even her pants and tank top were colorless.

A sense of déjà vu overwhelmed her as she sat up in the fluffy bed.

Sunlight streamed through the floor-to-ceiling windows.

Where am I?

A bandage on her arm suggested someone had recently taken blood from her. She removed it and examined the healing mark, indicating the invasive procedure was in fact recent.

She shifted to stand and winced at the weakness in her limbs. *How long have I been asleep?*

That strange feeling of having been here before swept over her again as she moved toward the glass. Evergreens and a clear blue sky stretched out for miles. She'd seen this before, but the memory evaded her.

A gentle knock preceded the opening of the room's only door.

Familiarity hit her in an instant, but she couldn't recall the bald man's name. His ancient green eyes spoke to her on a level she didn't understand, and as his lips curled, a feeling of foreboding twisted her insides.

I don't like him.

She didn't know why, but the feeling of hatred toward him superseded reason.

"Don't worry, little one. Your memories will be returned to you eventually." He clasped his hands behind his back as he sauntered toward her. "How do you feel?"

"Confused," she admitted. "Where am I?"

"In my home," he replied. "For now, anyway. Jonathan would prefer you in the lab, but I think this will prove a less stressful environment for you. You can return to him once you've given me what I need."

She swallowed. "Which is what?"

He smiled. "Your progeny."

My what? How?

Lizzie blinked as images surfaced behind her eyes.

New York City. Campus. Stas. Tom.

Jayson.

It seemed lost behind a cloud, the information she needed on the cusp of her mind…

"Yes, Jonathan felt inclined to introduce chemicals to your system to keep you more compliant. As I do not want anything to jeopardize the life growing inside you, I've ceased the treatment. You are mine, after all."

"I—I don't understand."

"No, I imagine you wouldn't." He gave her a dismissive smile. "Reimagining your childhood was the only way to fulfill the final test, and I must say, it far surpassed my expectations. When they suggested giving you unloving parental figures, I questioned it, but the outcome worked just as they anticipated. You craved love and affection, thereby allowing others to easily manipulate your emotions. Fascinating, really. I can't wait to explore the depths of that programming myself."

She shook her head, not following. *Reimagining my childhood?*

"Now, your preference for dancing? That was my idea, as I've always enjoyed the ballet. And the beauty pageants were also my suggestion. Granting you second place after almost every competition instilled that drive to constantly do better while also ingraining a sense of elegance in you. I mean, the last woman I want is an insolent one."

He clasped his hands together. "Well, in any case, I'm pleased. I never expected an Elder to take the bait, but I'm thrilled that he did. It's the perfect final test before we begin."

Why the emotional profile?

And begin what?

A knock at the door caused him to turn with an arched brow at the female visitor. "Apologies, Sire, but Skye is having an episode."

"I see. Thank you, Jezebel. I will be right there."

"Of course, Sire."

Osiris, her brain finally supplied. That was this being's name.

How do I know that?

"We'll continue our discussion soon," he murmured. "For now, eat the food that is provided and behave, and I'll allow you to remain unrestrained in your room. I may even bring you some books. Assuming you still enjoy them?"

She frowned. Fortunately, he wasn't looking for a response. He merely smiled as if amused. "It's lovely to have you here again, especially now that your purpose has arisen. Enjoy your afternoon."

With those strange words, he left, the door latching firmly behind him.

Lizzie blinked several times, confused.

More images trickled through her thoughts, these more erotic in nature.

Jayson kissing her. She touched her lips with the memory as her heart sped up. Her breasts tingled as she recalled his mouth teasing her nipples before venturing lower…

She moaned at the thoughts assaulting her, the very real memories of him worshiping her body and her returning the favor in kind.

Two glorious weeks spent learning each other intimately and falling in love. Her heart ached for him and fractured on a cry as the final image broke her mind.

His lifeless eyes.

"No!" she screamed as she collapsed onto the pristine floor. "NO!"

Jonathan killed him.

And Stas.

"Oh God…"

She dry-heaved, but her empty stomach denied the follow-through, leaving her light-headed.

Lizzie curled into a ball as the pain lashed at her nerve endings. Tears unlike any she'd ever shed poured from her eyes, dehydrating her soul.

"Jayson," she whimpered, craving him more than she ever had.

God, she thought Tom's death ripped her apart. It was nothing compared to this loss.

She felt incomplete—like half of her died with Jayson. He had touched her in a way no one else ever had.

And I'm carrying his child?

Was that what Osiris implied?

That Jayson had impregnated her? And Osiris intended to keep the baby?

Her blood ran hot and cold.

Jayson said he couldn't procreate, but Osiris implied she carried Jayson's life inside her. Jonathan had said the same.

How was that even possible?

What am I?

* * *

Lizzie needed a plan, some sort of diversion that allowed her to access the outside. Then she could lose herself in the trees. They stretched on for miles, but surely a road existed somewhere.

A chill skittered down her spine as someone knocked and opened the door without preamble. She expected it to be Osiris again and thought it was at first, until she saw the man's mouth.

Oh God… It was sewn shut with razor wire.

His green eyes, so much like Osiris's, met hers as he set a tray of food on the table in the corner. Beside it was a wooden chair.

"Th-thank you," she mumbled.

He bowed his bald head and straightened to study her. Curiosity lit his expression, and she thought he might want to say something but couldn't.

Those barbs resting against his lips looked painful. What could he have done to deserve that treatment?

"That'll be all, Sethios," Osiris said as he entered with a brunette in a lab coat.

The silent man bowed again before excusing himself quietly from the room while Lizzie frowned.

Wasn't that the friend Ezekiel mentioned growing up with in Babylon? The one Osiris raised as a son? Why on earth would he sew his lips together?

"Lizzie, sit in that chair." Osiris gestured to the wooden seat, and her legs moved of their own accord. She couldn't have stopped them if she wanted to.

This is bizarre.

She sat.

"Eat your sandwich," he added.

She picked up what she thought might be egg salad and took a bite. Again, against her own free will.

What the heck?

The hairs along her arms danced as the bread met her mouth again.

Compulsion.

Jayson mentioned Osiris's ability on the plane, yet that wasn't how she knew. *I've met this being before.* The question was, when?

"This is Valerie." He gestured to the petite woman beside him. "I've borrowed her from Jonathan's research team and have requested her to oversee your progress."

The female's hazel eyes blinked once, the only confirmation that Osiris hadn't so much requested as demanded.

Lizzie commiserated with the woman. *This sandwich isn't even that good, yet here I am devouring it.*

"I'll leave you two to get acquainted," he said, leaving with the sound of another latch of the door.

Valerie set her bag on the floor and wandered the room with her arms crossed while Lizzie finished forcing the food down her throat. She didn't even like egg salad that much, but she couldn't *not* eat it.

Was that what Stas could do?

A pang rattled her chest. They never had a chance to discuss it, or anything, and the option to do so had been stolen from them by a bullet. To the head.

She sniffled into her glass of water.

If only Lizzie had agreed to return to Hydria, to talk to Stas… But no, she couldn't regret that decision, either. Not without regretting her time with Jayson, and she wouldn't give up those moments for anything in the world.

Valerie cleared her throat. "We should get started." She had a clipboard in her hand.

Lizzie swallowed and set down her drink. "Uh, with what?"

"I've already reviewed your records from intake, but I prefer to do my own exams." She gestured to the bed. "Over there, if you wouldn't mind." The hesitancy in her voice surprised Lizzie. She gathered from her reaction to Osiris that she might not want to be here, either, but the way her hazel eyes drifted from side to side confirmed it.

"Okay," she agreed, only because she suspected something unpleasant would happen to them both if she didn't.

The mattress creased beneath her weight as she settled against the headboard. Valerie's hands shook as she turned the page of the file to read the next page. Lizzie shifted subtly to see the top of the sheet.

Asset File: 4-7

Genotype: Nonhuman

Project Name: Rebirth

She frowned. "What is that?"

"A high-level summary of your progress," Valerie replied. "Have you ovulated this month?"

Lizzie blinked. "No, but—"

"Yes or no is sufficient." She wrote something down. "Do you know the date of your last cycle?"

"Yes." She didn't elaborate since she was told not to before.

Valerie met her gaze. "Date, please."

"No."

She arched a brown brow. "No?"

"No." If anyone was going to answer questions, it would be this woman. "Tell me what the file says."

"It's classified."

Lizzie couldn't help the laugh that bubbled out of her. "Look, I can tell you want to be here about as much as I do. How about we work together so we both survive?" Or better yet, perhaps they could help each other escape.

Unlikely, but worth a try. Maybe.

Valerie studied her for a long moment, then went back to reviewing her paperwork.

Lizzie blew a raspberry in frustration.

Okay, so that wouldn't work. She'd probably misjudged the doctor's reaction to Osiris. He did mention borrowing her from John's research team, which implied she worked for the CRF by choice.

So she was back to being on her own without a solid plan. The door locked from the outside, something she already confirmed, and her windows didn't open. They also appeared to be thicker than usual, not that she considered breaking them to be an option. Jumping from this height would result in injury and capture, thereby ruining that idea altogether.

Lizzie could—

"Asset 4-7 is the first successful attempt of birthing a child of Seraphim genetics from a mortal womb. All forty-six trials before this one failed or were exterminated due to unacceptable abnormalities at birth." Valerie looked up from the file. "Would you like me to continue?"

Lizzie processed the words but didn't comprehend them. "A Seraphim," she repeated. "As in the highest order of angels? The ones with the fiery wings?"

"Most people are not well versed in theology." Valerie flipped through a few pages and nodded. "Oh. I see Osiris designed your education curriculum. That explains it." She met Lizzie's gaze. "Yes. Seraphim are powerful immortal beings who are commonly worshiped in a variety of religions. And their wings are said to glow, though none of us can see them unless they take corporeal form."

Lizzie blinked. "Right." Why not? After everything else she learned, why couldn't angels exist too? Maybe they were friends with Ichorians and Hydraians. She suppressed a hysterical laugh and instead asked, "And you're saying I'm part Seraphim?"

"According to your records, you *are* a Seraphim." She read a few more lines and shuffled the papers around. "It seems our International Affairs Chief, George Watkins, agreed to use his wife as a host in exchange for a higher-ranking position with the CRF. Considering all forty-six prior hosts died during the process, I'd wager to say he doesn't care much for the woman."

She seemed to be musing idly to herself more than talking to Lizzie, but the information seemed accurate. George and Lillian were certainly not a love match.

"Lillian's pregnancy progressed at an accelerated rate that nearly took her life, but she survived your birth and was paid handsomely as a result." Valerie's eyebrows shot up as she said that last part, no doubt at whatever figure Lizzie's "parents" received for their sacrifice. That explained the family's wealth and her father's, or rather, George's, obsession with the CRF.

This is surreal.

And yet, it felt right.

All those brunches and parties and parading around in high society like a puppet; it always left her feeling empty inside. And Lillian's constant hatred toward her didn't help. But now Lizzie understood why.

Because I almost killed her.

Not that it was Lizzie's fault or that she ever had a choice in the matter.

She wiped her clammy palms against her white pants.

"Does it say who my real parents are?" Lizzie wondered out loud.

Valerie pulled a paper from the stack and read it with widening eyes. "There are no names listed, but it says you were created from a variety of biological samples, all based on Seraphim genetics." Her hazel irises flared as she met Lizzie's gaze. "And Osiris is the one who provided the live Seraphim subjects for testing."

"Why?" Lizzie asked. "Why did he create me?"

"To produce more Seraphim." Valerie looked at Lizzie's stomach. "You were genetically engineered to birth a new race of angelic beings, and if the child you are carrying turns out as Osiris anticipates, then the final phase will be for you to birth him a new son."

Chapter Twenty-Three

Move Your Ass

> The seer has informed the benefactor that it is time to collect the subject. Sentinel Unit notified that the destination for retrieval is French Polynesia.
>
> —Entry Log 124.11.4 7

Jayson. The cool, unwelcome voice penetrated the darkness.

Fuck off.

I wish I could. Now wake the fuck up.

Oh, when Jayson opened his eyes, he would kick the telepathic bastard's ass. He enjoyed his peace and quiet, as it rarely occurred. Alik knew that better than anyone.

Seriously, I'm going to toss you in the fucking ocean if you don't start moving.

You'll be the one going for a swim, jackass.

I doubt that.

Jayson stretched his arms and rolled his neck as he stirred from the deep slumber. His body ached in a way it shouldn't after sleeping so soundly. And he had one hell of a headache.

He winced at the sunlight spilling over him and groaned.

"Alik," he growled, furious at the disturbance. But his voice didn't sound right. Too scratchy, like he'd just woken from death.

He sat up with a start and regretted it as the room spun around him.

"Shit." He fell back into the mattress. It felt like a cement truck had run over his skull.

"Good work, Lara," Luc praised. "We'll take it from here."

"Of course," she replied.

Why is a Hydraian healer here?

"Because you were shot in the head," Balthazar replied, irritated. "As was Stas, but she's not ready to wake up."

"We pulled you out early because we need to know what the hell happened, and you're the only one strong enough to handle it," Luc explained. "Start talking."

He would if he could, but his addled brain refused to commit to anything specific.

"Someone shot you with a glass bullet," Balthazar prompted. "Stas, too."

Jayson shook his head. "Where's Red?"

"Excellent question," Luc replied. "We're hoping you know the answer to that."

He tried sitting again, this time slowly, and eyed his familiar surroundings. They were in his room in Hydria, which meant Jacque had teleported him here. Without Lizzie.

Jayson massaged his temples as he fought to remember what happened while striving not to panic. He went to pick up some fruit and other items from town and had been considering how to broach the topic of returning to Hydria as a couple. When he arrived…

"Stark and Jonathan," he said as fury clouded his vision. The image of a ceramic knife to Lizzie's throat, followed by the acceptance of the collar—he touched his neck to find it missing—then forcing her to choose between him and Stas. "They were incendiary bullets."

"No, they were hollow glass," Luc corrected.

Jayson shook his head. "Jonathan said they were glass incendiary bullets, but maybe the new technology malfunctioned?"

"I watched as Lara removed the pieces from your head," Luc replied. "They were definitely empty bullets, with no chemicals to stir up a fire upon entry."

"A ploy?" The note of disbelief in Jayson's voice conveyed his thoughts on that guess. Jonathan loved his games, but to miss an opportunity to kill an Elder? No. He wouldn't do that. "How soon did you arrive after Stas?"

"Within five minutes," Alik replied. "Your bodies were still warm when Jacque and I arrived."

Meaning Jonathan and Stark hadn't stuck around to confirm that their new technology worked—not that it would have been easy to tell. The incendiary bullets lit the blood on fire, killing an immortal instantly, but the corpse remained fine on the outside, minus the point of entry for the bullet. Impressive little things.

"Did you remove the device from my neck?" Jayson asked.

Alik frowned. "What device?"

"If you don't know, then they removed it before you arrived and took it with them." Because it was an expensive piece of hardware. He understood that, but the rest of it… Jayson scratched his jaw. "Something isn't adding up." Jonathan would have tested his tech before using it, but obviously, the bullet hadn't worked as intended. Why?

"You're thinking too hard," a cultured voice informed from the shadows. Ezekiel stepped out of his cloak, hands in the air in a gesture of surrender. "We all know my coming here is a huge risk to my person, so I suggest you hear me out before attempting to kill me."

Balthazar studied him. "How long have you been standing there?"

"Long enough." He smirked. "Upset that you can't access my mind, old friend? Shall we focus on that or the relevance of my appearance?"

"He's immune," Alik murmured. "That's new."

"Yes, I imagine you are quite displeased by that development," Ezekiel taunted. "Now, can we get to the point, or would you all prefer to continue wasting precious time?"

"Start talking," Jayson demanded.

"Brilliant." Ezekiel kicked back onto Jayson's chaise lounge, hands tucked behind his head, and crossed his boot-clad ankles.

"As to your discussion, they were indeed empty bullets, though Jonathan believed them to be of the incendiary variety. I would take credit for that parlor trick, but that would be deceitful and untrue. But that should not be the focal point for this discussion. As you all are apparently unable to determine Elizabeth Watkins's purpose—despite all the clues we have hand-delivered to you—I'm here to educate."

"We?" Luc repeated.

Ezekiel smiled. "Yes. But as I was saying, Elizabeth is the key. She was created by Jonathan as a token of appreciation for the CRF's benefactor." He glanced around. "Seriously? None of you know? Fuck, this is going to take longer than I expected."

"Keep talking," Jayson urged. "Preferably before I stick a knife in you."

Ezekiel tsked. "Tone down the threats and listen. You all must know Jonathan didn't create the CRF on his own, and you have to wonder why Osiris would allow an organization who enjoys slaughtering immortals to thrive in the heart of Ichorian territory."

"Because he's the benefactor," Luc translated, his omniscient ability gluing all the puzzle pieces together before everyone else. "I've suspected their partnership before but never knew what Osiris could gain from it. From what you're implying, Elizabeth is his prize."

"Partially, yes. At least that's the item I've come here to discuss."

"Meaning there's more," Luc interpreted.

Ezekiel merely shrugged. "Isn't there always?"

Cryptic bastard. Jayson needed Ezekiel to start talking faster.

The assassin grinned, as if sensing the impatience in the room and enjoying it. "I assume you ran a few tests on her blood?"

"Enough to infer her purpose," Luc replied. "The serum Stark so politely donated to our cause was a mix of hormones meant to encourage pregnancy."

"Politely donated," Ezekiel repeated, amused. "He'll enjoy that classification. As for Elizabeth, she is a being beyond labels, but mostly a Seraphim without any of the abilities. Her aging has slowed, indicating she'll be immortal very soon, and yes, she was created for the sole purpose of breeding."

Jayson's blood heated, cooled, then heated again as his emotions warred. *Breeding.* "With whom?"

And he had better not say "Osiris," or Jayson would lose it. His grip on his temper was already waning; it would not take much to send him over the edge.

"Ah, the debate of who would be first wasn't settled until very recently." Ezekiel smiled. "When Osiris learned of your interest in his prized possession, he decided to let it play out. Your talents are extraordinary, and he's curious to see how her genetics bind with yours. It also served as a way to test her compatibility with Hydraians, which I gather was successful."

Jayson's heart stopped.

As did his breathing.

He couldn't mean…

"I believe congratulations are in order, Jedrick. You're going to be a father." Ezekiel brushed a piece of lint off his leather jacket.

"How do you know all of this?" Luc asked as if those words hadn't shattered Jayson's entire being.

I'm going to be a dad?

And Lizzie… Oh, hell… Lizzie…

"Where is she?" he demanded, not caring at all that Ezekiel had been in the middle of responding to Luc.

"As I was saying," Ezekiel murmured, "I know all this because I've been involved in her project from the very beginning. Not by choice, but that's a conversation for another time. What matters here, however, is that I've tasted her blood. Which, as you all know, means I can track her."

"You're the reason they found her in Bora Bora and Italy," Luc mused. "Clever."

Ezekiel shrugged. "As I said, it's not a project of my choice."

"Which is why you're helping us?" Balthazar guessed, speaking up for the first time.

"My reasons are my own," he replied. "But I'm happy to give you her location."

"Do that," Jayson urged. "Now."

Ezekiel gave him a disapproving stare. "You really will need to learn more patience, Jedrick. I hear children can be quite troublesome little beings."

Jayson wanted to introduce Ezekiel's face to the wall but refrained. Not only was the woman he cared about in jeopardy, but so was his supposed child. Assuming Ezekiel spoke the truth.

It could all be a deceptive con meant to trap them, though his comments regarding the bullets added up. Jayson had seen the excitement in Jonathan's eyes when he pulled the trigger. He truly believed they were destined to kill.

And Lizzie's monthly hormone supplement did seem appropriate for a woman meant to conceive. If she was designed to breed with immortal beings, then her being pregnant now was a definite possibility. Especially after all the hours they spent in bed together.

He grimaced as pain touched his chest.

My Red.

She had to be so scared and alone.

And worse, she thought he was dead. That no one would be coming for her.

But he would. Even if it meant storming the CRF alone, he would cross the gates of hell for her.

Mine.

No one touched his heart.

Balthazar clapped a hand on his shoulder and nodded, as if to say, *I'm with you to the end.*

He returned the gesture and met Luc's patient gaze. "I want her back," Jayson said. "Osiris can kiss my ass."

"It may instigate a war," Luc cautioned. "Which I'm guessing is Osiris's goal."

"She's one of ours," Balthazar countered. "We don't leave ours behind."

"Is she?" Luc asked. "From what Ezekiel has implied, she's more Seraphim than Hydraian."

"She's carrying my child." Jayson let that statement settle before adding, "And even if she wasn't, she's still mine to protect."

"He'll go with or without us," Balthazar pointed out. "This bond they've formed supersedes logic."

"Alik?" Luc asked.

"Are you asking if I want to kill some Ichorians? Because I think we all know the answer to that already." He pushed off the wall. "Can I start with the one on the chaise?"

"And I believe that is my cue to depart," Ezekiel murmured. "I shall text you the address, Jedrick. But be advised that it's Osiris's home estate, and he's surrounded by some of the most powerful Ichorians in the world, including a clairvoyant."

He started to shift into his shadow form but reappeared to add, "Lucian, I am very sorry about what happened to Owen. He served a greater purpose in befriending Astasiya, and I am forever in his debt for his service. And I sincerely miss his company in my plight."

Ezekiel bowed his head in prayer and vanished from the room without another word.

Everyone gaped at the empty chaise lounge.

That was unexpected. Hell, the whole thing was unexpected.

But that's what Ezekiel excelled at—breaking the rules and looking out for himself first and foremost.

"A Nizari assassin protecting a fledgling? Now I've seen everything," Alik remarked.

"He could be lying." Luc's emerald gaze glowed in that eerie way that indicated the use of power. "However, I see no logical reason for him to add that information, or to give us any of the other details. Unless it's all a trap, in which case, he did an excellent job of convincing me it's not."

"Even if it is, I'm going," Jayson stated. "I'm not leaving her under Osiris's care."

"Tom and Stas will feel the same," Balthazar added. "And that means Issac will follow with Tristan and Mateo."

Jayson imagined other Ichorians would be willing to help as well, considering the alliance between Osiris and Jonathan defied the armistice. It meant the leader of their Conclave was actively allowing the CRF to hunt and kill immortals at will. Not many would approve of that agreement.

"Everything Ezekiel stated is logical and suits," Luc said, his green gaze dimming. "If it is the wish of the Elders to rescue Elizabeth, then you have my support. I fear it will incite a war, but I also believe that fate to be inevitable. And this is one battle I'm willing to fight."

Jayson's phone buzzed on cue. He pulled it from his pocket and read the address out loud to the others in the room. "Sounds secluded," he added as he set the phone aside.

"An excellent place to kill without drawing attention," Alik mused. "I'm game."

"We'll need a solid plan," Jayson admitted. He had a feeling they would have only one shot at securing Lizzie, and if they blew it, things would not end well.

"I'll call Aidan," Luc murmured as he started toward the door. "In the interim, please provide Issac your support. He's putting on a good show, but we all know he's not taking this well."

Issac might not be a Hydraian, but all of them considered him very much family. His pain would be felt through them all.

Balthazar nodded. "We're on it, Luc."

"Thank you," he murmured. "I would attend to him as well, but I sense my presence will only worsen his acceptance." With those solemn words, he left to strategize. Jayson was torn between following him, going to Issac, and leaving for the address on his phone.

But as always, it was Balthazar who grounded him. "Take a shower. Afterward, we'll talk. You can't help her on your own, but we can as a team. And given what Ezekiel said about her importance to Osiris, it's safe to assume she's unharmed. We'll get her back, Jay."

He nodded, believing his oldest friend. "You'd better be right."

"I always am," he replied, cocky as ever. "But seriously, grab a shower. This bloody look on you isn't appealing, and you smell like death."

Jayson tried to smile at the obvious attempt at a joke, but it fell flat. To feel complete, he needed his Red. Because without her, he had half a soul.

I'm coming for you, Lizzie, he vowed. *Just hang on.*

Chapter Twenty-Four

Resurrection in the Light of Disaster

> Subject was paired with a college roommate. Name: Astasiya Davenport. Age: 18. Origin: Havre, Montana. No known conflicts at this time.
>
> —Entry Log 118.08.4-7

Another nightmare.

Lost in the depths of the ocean.

Stas struggled against the binds, but her deteriorated limbs refused to move. She resembled a skeleton, lost in the waves of time, screaming for no one to hear.

Everything hurt, but her heart most of all.

So much loss…

It wasn't supposed to end like this.

"Aya…" Sandalwood and peppermint accompanied the nickname, but it didn't fit.

Help me…

Find me…

Free me…

Water suffocated her thoughts, granting her temporary peace in the world of silence.

Only to awaken again in hell.

Over and over and over.

A dark, unending dance of solitude and death.

When will they come for me?

"Astasiya." The voice grew stronger, pulling her somewhere new. Away from the familiarity of the ocean floor and into a world of sunshine.

Too bright, she thought, sheltering her eyes.

The vestiges of her nightmare disappeared into reality, revealing a room of mahogany and rich brown colors that didn't belong to her or the man holding her hand.

She swallowed, her throat dry from her deep sleep. A straw slipped between her lips, and she sipped on instinct, welcoming the freshly squeezed juice. It replaced the bitterness that always followed her visits to the deep sea.

Issac, she thought with a smile. He'd learned so much about her in their brief months together and knew exactly how to pull her from the nightmares in the sweetest ways. She waited for his kiss after the drink disappeared, but it didn't come.

Strange. He always kissed her after sleep.

She stretched her stiff shoulders and braved the light by opening her eyes. Issac sat in a chair beside her with his elbows braced on his knees, his expression carefully blank. A glance around showed they were alone and in one of Balthazar's guest rooms.

Stas struggled to remember how she ended up here.

She'd been staying with Eliza in Amelia's old home these last few weeks. The Hydraians had dubbed it the "Fledgling House" since both of them were unturned immortals. Stas disliked the idea at first but admired Eliza's strength and conviction. She was a remarkable woman, especially considering everything that had happened to her prior to arriving in Hydria.

"How do you feel?" Issac asked, his voice soft.

"Groggy," she admitted as she rolled to her side and tucked her arm beneath her head on the pillow. It throbbed a little, likely from the nightmare. "Why aren't you in bed with me?" He wore one of his trademark suits, minus the tie, and his midnight hair was freshly tousled from his fingers. She loved this look on him but preferred him naked.

"Aya," he whispered, his voice cracking as he dropped his head into his hands. He visibly trembled, stirring alarm in her chest.

"What's happened?" She sat up despite her body's complaints. "Is Lizzie okay?"

The last she heard, her best friend was in Bora Bora enjoying alone time with Jayson. Definitely not the type of man Stas ever would have recommended, but at this point, all she wanted was for Lizzie to be happy. She deserved it after all the pain, and he seemed to be helping her work through the process.

Issac shuddered again, and Stas couldn't take it anymore. She reached for him, but he flinched away from her touch, almost as if she burned him.

"You're starting to scare me," she admitted, hurt that he would reject her in such a way. "What's going on?"

He shook his head. "I'm trying." His broken voice shot an arrow through her chest, eliciting an ache deep inside that fizzled and burned.

"What's wrong?" she whispered.

He ran his fingers through his hair and pulled on the strands. "Fuck, I'm trying, Aya. You…" His cheekbones hollowed with the words as he struggled to say whatever he needed to say.

This was a side of him she'd never seen, and it terrified her.

"Trying to do what?" she asked, tears in her eyes. "What's going on?" She grabbed his wrist and squeezed when he grimaced. "Tell me what happened, Issac. Now." The command slipped out of its own accord, but she couldn't pull it back, not even as his damp eyes met hers.

"You died, Aya." Three words, uttered so softly she almost didn't hear them. Or maybe that was the wind tunnel suddenly taking residence in her head that distorted the sound.

"What?" She couldn't have heard him right.

"You went to Bora Bora by yourself—without backup—and were shot in the head."

She blinked as the memory began to surface. So lost in her nightmare, she hadn't realized the truth of the moment.

"John," she breathed. "Where's…?" Her voice faltered.

Oh, fuck.

No.

No way.

This can't…

"I…" She released his wrist to feel her forehead and found nothing but smooth skin.

Her heart stuttered as her breath caught in her throat.

I died. Her mind fractured beneath the assault of those two lethal words.

I…

This…

She didn't want to believe it, would have begged for a different outcome, but the agony radiating from Issac's blue eyes confirmed the truth.

"I'm a Hydraian."

Her fingers went numb.

"I'm…" She couldn't say it again. That made it real. Too real. Just like the tears trailing down Issac's cheeks. And hers.

"No," she whispered, shaking her head over and over as if that would take it all back and fix everything.

She wasn't ready.

They weren't ready.

Her vision blurred as anguish ripped through her abdomen, tearing a scream from her throat. "NO!"

It wasn't fair!

She didn't want this future. She wanted *him.* The man she could no longer have. The man who meant everything to her.

Her heart…

And the despair emanating from him…

They needed more time.

"I can't touch you," she whispered. "But I need…"

Oh God, how would she survive without touching him? Without kissing him? Without his love?

All those tender moments and nights.

The unspoken words.

Those looks that said he wanted to devour her in the best ways.

His tenderness in the mornings.

All of it hung in the balance and shattered behind her eyes.

Forever cementing itself the past.

Too soon…

"Issac." Her soul withered as it sought the connection she knew it needed but couldn't have. She couldn't go to him. But, oh God, she wanted to.

"I'm so sorry." The words sounded foreign to her own ears. Was that shriveled, broken rasp her voice?

Issac merely shook his head, because what could he say? Nothing could be done now. She sealed her fate when she went to save her friend without thinking things through.

And she lost *everything* in the process.

Her decision had shattered their bond.

Stas broke under a sob meant to destroy her being, her entire body convulsing uncontrollably.

This can't be happening.

Please…

I can't breathe.

Issac brushed his lips against her forehead in a devastatingly careful kiss, his fear of touching her evident, and yet saying so much. Sorrow, hurt, and *pain.*

Even now, he wished to comfort her, when they both knew he couldn't, and she longed to allow it.

It's all my fault.

I destroyed us.

"Oh God, Issac…" The words burned her throat and singed the air, forever separating them. Because he would never be hers again, not in the way she craved. Her heart would never recover. And her soul… It died when John pulled that trigger.

"Aya," Issac breathed, his internal suffering etched into that single word. He finally took her hand and squeezed, his head bowed as the tears fell silently from his eyes.

Stas couldn't help the whimper that escaped her. It felt as if her entire world had ended before it even began.

And now she had an eternity of suffering to live through. Alone.

She curled into a ball, her hand still clasped in his, and relived every memory of him behind her eyes. Every touch. Every kiss. Every word. She would dream of him every night, think of him every day, and miss him every moment. Even when he stood beside her, she'd miss him.

It would only ever be Issac for her.

Forever and always.

A silent vow.

"I love you," she whispered. She'd never said it out loud, and it wouldn't matter now, but he had to know… "It's only ever been you, Issac."

"I know, love," he replied, just as soft. "I know."

Chapter Twenty-Five

Wall of Fire

Subject's infatuation memories with Thomas Fitzgerald were implanted today. Team psychologist says it will counteract potential relationships with unsuitable mates.

—Entry Log 118.05.4-7

"Stas is awake but won't be able to help us in her current state," Balthazar said as he entered the makeshift war room. "Issac isn't in the proper frame of mind to assist, either."

Aidan nodded. "It's for the best. Strategically, I recommend keeping Stas hidden for as long as you can. The sooner Osiris hears of her existence, the sooner he will come for her."

"There's no denying that her ability to compel would be useful in this situation, but I am inclined to agree." Luc flattened a drawing on the table. "Which is why we've devised a plan that doesn't include them."

The omniscient father-son duo had drafted over a dozen attack plans before settling on this one, all while the rest of the room observed. They spoke too quickly for anyone to completely follow their logic, but Jayson understood the main idea.

"How are we going to counteract the wards?" he asked as he folded his arms. Luc and Aidan had been discussing them just before Balthazar entered.

"We'll handle them," Luc replied, indicating himself and Aidan. "Between the two of us, we should be able to draw some ancient runes that will counteract the wards long enough for us to volley an attack."

"Yes, I suspect the point of them isn't necessarily to keep an army out but to give Osiris enough warning to relocate," Aidan murmured, his eyes that same emerald shade as Luc's. "Hopefully, that relocation plan does not involve Elizabeth, or we'll be playing a game of chase."

"That's where I come in," Ash said as she tied her light-blonde hair up into a ponytail. "Ring of fire."

"Exactly," Luc agreed. "But we'll have to stay back, just in case. Especially with Jeremy manipulating the earth."

Jayson nodded. "And if we see Lizzie—"

"I'll grab her," Jacque announced from his spot in the corner. He had three empty pizza boxes beside him and a protein shake in his hand. Teleporting burned calories at an insane rate, and they needed him fully charged.

"Good. Any questions?" Aidan glanced around the room. Several of Hydria's most powerful immortals had volunteered to help even though they didn't know Lizzie. Their support and unyielding friendship were why they would win a war against the Ichorians. Luc ruled with love and affection, as opposed to Osiris, who chose fear.

"Do you think my father will make an appearance?" Tom had his arms folded over the back of the chair he'd flipped around to straddle earlier. He hadn't said much but listened intently while Aidan and Luc debated.

Tom's previous sniper experience and general military knowledge would be very useful. Not to mention his perfect aim. And he seemed to have an uncanny ability to turn off emotions, because the man had to be furious about his father's actions, yet he didn't show it.

"Likely not," Aidan replied. "He's done his part by handing over Elizabeth to Osiris, and he believes he's just killed Stas and Jayson. The smart move for him would be to protect his headquarters, as he's now owed retribution from Issac for killing Stas and from the Elders for killing their brother."

"Why not take him alive?" Tom asked, causing everyone to look at him in confusion. "Sorry, I mean Jayson. I've been trying to figure out why my father would kill him. He's a powerful Hydraian, just like Amelia. Not that I condone it, but why not take Jayson back to headquarters for testing?"

"Because I'm too powerful for him to contain." Not an overstatement, but a fact. "He could have tried with that device, but I would eventually have found a way around it, and that would have ended very badly for him."

"Or it's his ego," Aidan suggested with a shrug. "When it comes to my progeny and the Elders, Jonathan does not think clearly. He wants power and craves theirs, while also seeking to appease."

"If it's ego, he would have claimed Eli's death," Balthazar pointed out. "Instead he framed someone else."

"To hide Amelia," Luc added. "But we don't know if he plans to make some grand statement later, or if he already boasted about his kills to Osiris. I'm inclined to agree that all of this has been about improving his ego since he's always been very touchy about his weak ability."

Tom snorted. "Small Dick Syndrome, not that I inherited that problem from him."

Balthazar grinned. "We've all seen proof of that, Fitzgerald."

Jayson cleared his throat. "Are we ready? Because I can't stand around here doing nothing much longer. I need to see Lizzie, and soon." An understatement. This whole multi-hour planning session nearly killed him. All he could think about was holding his Red again and telling her how he felt. He never had the chance, and now he worried it would be too late.

Balthazar bumped his shoulder against Jayson. "We'll get her back, Jay. I promise you. No matter what it takes."

"How can you be so confident?" It hurt to ask, but he wanted to know.

"Because in three thousand years, I've never seen you regard a woman the way you do Lizzie. And I am determined to give that back to you." The solemn words were followed by one of his trademark grins. Balthazar never could be serious for long. "I also might want to see you play dad for a few years. Should be incredibly entertaining. I hope you have a girl."

Jayson smiled despite the circumstances as a picture of a beautiful little redhead crossed his thoughts. "She'll look just like Lizzie."

"She will," Balthazar agreed, clapping him on the shoulder. "Now don't lose that vision. Emotions can be a powerful motivator, Jay. Don't hide from yours."

~*~

Lizzie fisted the sheets of the bed while Valerie examined her as one would a lab rat. She drew blood, took on the role of gynecologist, and was now performing a spinal tap.

"Don't move," she cautioned as the needle slid into her back.

Ow, ow, ow…

Her vision blurred with unshed tears, but she'd agreed to cooperate in exchange for more information. After the familial lesson and declaration that Lizzie was here to give Osiris a "new son"—which still freaked her out—Valerie had detailed Lizzie's genetic profile.

All her records indicated she was a full-blooded Seraphim without powers. She apparently didn't heal as fast as others, but the records provided proof of her immortality.

Because she'd been killed multiple times—in various ways.

And she had survived it all.

Yet she possessed no memory of any of it.

Lizzie couldn't decide if that was a blessing or a curse. Maybe Osiris could erase her memory of learning his purpose for her.

And what did that mean for the child in her belly now? Would he take the baby from her? She couldn't bear losing that final connection to Jayson.

Her eyes stung with suppressed emotion. An inferno of grief whirled inside her, waiting to be unleashed, but she swallowed it.

Osiris wouldn't win. He couldn't.

I'm not having his child.

She'd die first.

Or at least try.

"Done," Valerie said as she stepped back. "You can get dressed again."

Lizzie swallowed her response. *Thank you* had been on the tip of her tongue, which seemed inappropriate considering their situation. Her surrogate mother would say otherwise, but Lizzie no longer gave a damn. Not after everything she'd learned these last few weeks.

She pulled on the white drawstring pants and a matching tank top, gathered her hair, and let it fall against her back. Valerie placed all her medical supplies on a desk against the wall. Beside it was an empty bookshelf and another one of those wooden chairs.

The oversized room also came equipped with a marble bathroom with a large walk-in shower, two sinks, and a toilet. As far as prison cells went, this one wasn't bad. Although, she could do with some artwork, books, a television, or anything entertaining to keep her mind busy. Instead, she was surrounded by white walls, glass windows, and a few pieces of furniture.

The bed provided the only comfortable seat. Lizzie sat near the headboard and tucked her knees into her chest while watching Valerie bag and label all her samples.

Lizzie shivered, feeling violated and exposed.

I need to get out of here.

But she didn't know how or where she would go. She didn't even know where *here* was, for crying out loud.

Would anyone come for her? Maybe. Maybe not. She hadn't been very nice to the Hydraians, or to Issac, or Tom. Why would anyone want to help her after the way she acted?

Not to mention it being her fault Stas and Jayson were dead.

She dropped her chin to her knees.

Even if she escaped, would it be worth it? She would forever be a prisoner to her emotions.

I have a piece of him inside me.

She caressed her belly and closed her eyes. Would it be a boy or a girl? Would the baby have Jayson's milk chocolate gaze? His dark, luscious hair? His dimples?

Lizzie grinned at the adorable image of a small boy running around and causing mischief. She would call him Jedrick, in honor of his father.

Her fingers drew a heart—a tribute to the life growing in memory of their love. Because she had no doubt that she loved Jayson, just as she would their child. Time meant nothing in the face of her feelings. Her soul ached without her other half. That had to be love. And if it wasn't, then it translated to a word that didn't exist.

I'll take care of you, she promised as she palmed her flat stomach.

Because she would escape, if for nothing else than to save the life inside her.

"Are you ready to learn more?" Valerie asked softly.

"Yes," Lizzie replied without opening her eyes. "Please."

Papers shuffled as the doctor found a good place to start, but an explosion outside rattled the windows, silencing her before she could speak.

"What was that?" Lizzie asked as she sat up.

Another crash shook the foundation of the mansion and forced both of them to run to the windows. Smoke and fire danced in the yard.

Valerie closed the file and tucked it into her bag before walking across the room to peer outside. "They are trying to get through the wards."

"Wards?" Lizzie repeated as she joined her by the window.

"Seraphim create them, just like runes. I don't know much about the magic, but there are several surrounding the CRF, and it seems Osiris's compound has them as well."

"What do they do?"

"They mostly prevent entry." Another blast slammed into what resembled a force field around the estate grounds. "And strip immortals of their gifts. These appear to all be protective runes, and they're working."

Fire danced in the air, playing over a jagged line. "Are you sure about that?" Because it certainly looked as if they'd cracked the surface of that bubble.

"We should probably take cover," Valerie replied as a loud shriek sounded.

Lizzie cupped her ears at what resembled a raven's cry and screamed, "What the heck is that?!"

The doctor shook her head, her face paling.

A flash of light blinded them, and Valerie knocked Lizzie to the ground just as the glass imploded inward.

"Shit!" Lizzie yelled as dozens of slivers sliced her exposed arms. The doctor took the brunt of it, having covered Lizzie with her body as they fell.

Ouch.

Valerie didn't move or speak, which was fine by Lizzie. That implosion had shattered her eardrums, leaving an incessant ringing behind.

Smoke billowed overhead, forcing her to cough. She tried to wiggle out from under Valerie, but the woman was dead weight.

"Move," Lizzie urged as she tried again.

It took some shoving, but she finally dislodged her with a heave and sat up to expel the bad air from her lungs. Only it continued to cloud her room.

"We have to get out of here," Lizzie said with a nudge to her companion. She still didn't move.

"Come on, Val…" Lizzie trailed off as she noticed the blood coloring the doctor's lab coat. She leaned around the woman and gasped at the jagged piece of glass sticking out of her back. "Oh God." She finally met the gaze of a very dead woman and scrambled back on a cry. "Shit!"

Valerie had saved her life by covering Lizzie during the fall. On purpose or by accident? She would never know. And as another vibration shook the floor beneath her hands, she realized there wasn't time to find out.

She ran to the door and tried to open it, but it didn't budge.

"Help!" Lizzie frantically pounded her fists against the door as she screamed. She still couldn't hear over all the damn ringing, so if anyone replied, she wouldn't know. But the door remained closed. The place above the knob seemed appropriate for a key. Would Valerie have one?

A glance at the dead woman left Lizzie gagging. Probably not, and she didn't have the stomach to check. But she could try her bag by the table.

Lizzie moved quickly, going through all the pockets and zippers, and paused when she found the file with "Asset 4-7" printed at the top. She didn't have time to read it now, but she might later. Carrying the papers would be an issue, especially if she needed her hands.

Hmm…

Lizzie lifted her shirt and tucked part of the file into the band of her pants while resting the majority of it against her belly. Not the most eloquent look, but functional. She secured it by retying her drawstrings as tightly as possible and laid her tank top over the file before searching the bag again.

No key.

That didn't surprise her, as it seemed Valerie was just as much of a prisoner as Lizzie.

She returned to pounding on the door, her fists bruising from her efforts, as smoke continued to billow through the windows. It would be a lot worse if the fire were in the room with her, but, damn, it still sucked to breathe. And it couldn't be good for her unborn child.

The lock clicked as someone pushed the door open. She jumped back and met the green gaze of the silent male servant.

Sethios.

He gestured for her to follow him, and for lack of a better option, she did. His legs quickly ate up the hallway, and she kept pace behind him. The floor reverberated against her feet as powers far greater than her understanding annihilated the residence.

A set of back stairs appeared at the end of the corridor, and he pointed downward. She waited for him to lead, but he shook his head.

"Where do I go at the bottom?" she asked.

He mimed opening a door and scissored his fingers in a way that indicated running.

"Outside?" she asked.

One nod.

When she didn't immediately move, he pushed her forward with an urgent expression. Then his lips ripped through the razors, causing her to cringe as blood poured from his mouth.

"Go now," he rasped. His eyes trained on the hallway they'd just run through, as if preparing for a battle.

"Sethios!" Osiris's voice ricocheted off the walls, sending a chill down her spine.

Her helper cracked his neck and grinned in anticipation. Or she thought it was a grin. She couldn't see through the gruesome mess of his mouth. "Run down the stairs, little one," he demanded hoarsely. "*Now.*"

Lizzie's legs started moving before her mind registered the action. She didn't pause to analyze the how or why; she just fled down the stairs as instructed and went through the door at the bottom. The papers shuffled against her belly but remained in place thanks to her waistband. Not that they would help her with this new predicament.

Fire blazed across the ground not twenty feet from her, forming an impenetrable wall. She darted right, only to find the same force field of heat and energy surrounding the entire back of the property.

Heat singed her skin as she went back the way she came, toward the front. Her pants stuck to her legs, her tank top to her back, and the file to her stomach.

She shook her head at the sight, her vision blurring with tears.

This was hopeless. Even if she found a way through the flames, she'd probably die of suffocation.

I can't give up.

She had no idea who had started the attack, but it offered her the only chance she may ever have to escape.

And maybe, hopefully, the assailants were on her side.

Because anyone who disliked Osiris was okay by her.

She took off at a dead run to the other side of the giant residence, hoping and praying to find a passageway. Her legs burned as she ran, but she pushed through the pain and ignored the scrapes to her bare feet.

The estate was long and vast, but she managed to arrive at the other side and ran right into a brick wall of male.

He appeared out of nowhere and halted her with an "Oomph" as her face met his chest. Hands grabbed her waist, and her vision swirled.

I'm going to be sick.

Wind whipped through her hair, and she stumbled as she fell to the sand.

A bright moon hung in a star-filled sky above as waves crashed against the shore behind her.

She spun in a circle and found herself alone.

No fire.

No mansion.

"Where am I?" she whispered into the darkness.

No one responded.

~*~

"Got her," Jacque announced as he returned to Jayson's side.

"How the fuck did she get outside?" Jayson demanded. He couldn't believe it when he saw that wave of auburn hair flying outside the manor.

Jacque gave him a look. "You want me to go back and ask her?"

"Someone obviously helped on the inside," Ash replied, her brow sweating from all the fire manipulation. "What now, boss?"

"Demolish it," he replied, furious.

"You heard the man," Ash said into the comms.

It'd taken far too long to get through all those damn wards, even with all of Aidan's and Luc's knowledge. They had to work quickly to find and draw runes over them, calling on millennia of ancient logic to solve the puzzles. A few booby-traps forced them to launch their attack prematurely, something that wasted a hell of a lot of energy, but once the protection spells fell, they were able to volley a sufficient attack.

And strangely, Osiris didn't return fire. So much for Ezekiel's comments regarding a clairvoyant and the substantial immortal gifts on site.

Grace stepped up beside him, her focus on the mansion. She stripped it with her mind, removing the roof first and sending it into the fire Ash created, followed by the walls.

Jeremy took a knee and palmed the ground, causing it to shake. His affinity for controlling stones of all kind came in handy during times like this, as did Jayson's ability to manipulate metal. He used it now to warp the support beams, not caring at all whom he crushed in the devastation.

Though, he suspected Osiris had long fled with his minions. Otherwise they would be outside fighting. "Why would he run?" he asked, his question directed at Luc over the comm. No one else would dare speculate.

"Our source mentioned a clairvoyant," he replied. "I imagine she provided him with the odds of winning, and they were not in his favor, so he chose to flee."

"Why not take Lizzie?"

"Perhaps he meant to, but someone intervened. We'll need her input to determine that."

Fair enough. Jayson destroyed the last of the metal structures while Ash, Jeremy, and Grace handled the rest. An entire army of Hydraians who volunteered to assist with this mission surrounded the estate, and he gazed upon them in pride.

The remains of the former palatial residence glowed as Ash weakened the flames until only a few embers remained. "That was a waste of a perfectly good home," she remarked as she wiped her brow.

"You did good," Jayson replied

"Of course I did." She grinned broadly and tossed her white-blonde hair over her shoulder. "Time to go?"

"Time to go," he agreed.

"On it," Jacque replied as he group-hugged four Hydraians, including Ash, and disappeared.

"He's going to eat all the food in Hydria after this," Jeremy said as he stood. He was one of the members of Jayson's guard, just like Grace, which explained why they were both flanking him on either side. The perceived threat might be gone, but one could never be so sure.

"You realize I can handle myself," he noted dryly.

"Says the jackass who was shot in Bora Bora after he refused to let his Guardians do their jobs," Grace sniped. "I'll be standing right here until Jacque safely escorts you back to Hydria, *sir.*"

Jayson shook his head, bemused. There would be no talking her down, not that he intended to try.

Jacque appeared across the way, picked up the Hydraians walking toward the main camp, and disappeared. Jayson frowned as intuition inched along his spine. Two of those immortals were B's Guardians, but the Elders were nowhere in sight.

Not proper protocol.

"Luc, what's your status?" Jayson asked as his stomach twisted with foreboding. *Something isn't right.*

Silence echoed over the line.

Grace took a defensive stance, her ebony gaze flickering around the field as Jeremy knelt to touch the earth again. *Guardians sensing a danger to their Elder.*

Jayson cleared his throat and tried again. "Luc?"

"I'm sorry, but Lucian is quite indisposed at the moment," a cool voice informed. One that froze everyone in place.

"Osiris."

"Jedrick, or is it Jayson now? It's so difficult to keep everyone's names straight. Did you hear that Ezekiel is going by Kiel now? Such an unbecoming name." He sighed dramatically. "Anyway, I daresay you owe me a new home. Quite rude to drop by unannounced, but to destroy my property too?" He tsked. "And all over a woman. It reminds me of Troy."

"That's a myth."

"Is it?" Osiris mused. "Alas, we should chat more. In person. Assuming you want your *king* returned unharmed."

Grace and Jeremy shook their heads in prompt denial, while Jayson rubbed a hand over his face. Luc would tell him to stand down, but they both knew how Jay felt about following the rules. Exhibit A: Lizzie Watkins.

"Where?" Jayson asked.

"Finish sending your Guardians home, and we'll go from there."

"No," Grace stated immediately.

"Mind your Elders, young one," Osiris murmured. "They could save your life."

"Fuck you," Grace replied.

"Manners, child," Osiris chastised. "Make him scream, Alik."

Agony filtered over the speakers, causing Jayson to go to his knees at the familiar sound. It reminded him of when Luc almost died during the last immortal war.

"Now that is obedience," Osiris murmured. "Such a good little Elder you are." Jayson pictured him stroking Alik's head like a dog as he used his commands.

Jacque appeared, grinning proudly. "Eighteen down and…" His silver eyes widened. "What—"

More groans filtered through the earpiece, shredding Jayson's heart. Because that last one was Balthazar. Osiris must have snuck up on Alik when no one was looking and used him to take down the other two.

Fuck.

Jayson knew this had been too easy.

"More," Osiris urged as the screaming increased.

"Stop," Jayson begged. "I'll meet your demands."

"No, I quite enjoy watching them squirm. Centuries later, and I'm still impressed that you all managed to keep Alik's fantastic talent from me for all those years. It's fascinating."

Jacque's eyebrows hit his hairline. "Where?" he mouthed, and Jayson just shook his head. Because he didn't know. These comms worked up to four miles away, and knowing Osiris, he had backup who helped him switch locations.

"Take Grace and Jeremy back to Hydria," he said.

Jacque shook his head, his loyalty kicking in.

"Aidan," Jayson mouthed. The master of strategy was still on the island and could advise them on how to proceed. For now, Jayson didn't have a choice but to comply with Osiris's demands. "And take care of Lizzie for me," he added, the unspoken *In case I don't make it out of this alive* hanging heavily in the air.

The teleporter nodded slowly. "Okay, Jay." He grabbed Grace and Jeremy before they could fight him and disappeared.

That left just Jayson and a very quiet Tom. He'd taken a position up in the hills somewhere, his sniper rifle at the ready even though he hadn't needed to use it. And he'd intelligently maintained radio silence the entire time.

Or maybe they'd discovered and killed him. It was hard to tell, but knowing Tom, he was healthy, alive, and scouting the ground for Osiris right now.

"I'm alone," Jayson announced.

"Excellent. Now disarm."

Jayson wondered if that meant Osiris could see him, or if he had men of his own stationed in similar positions to Tom. He made a show of removing his guns and knives, including the one in his boot for good measure.

"Done," he said flatly. "Now where are you?"

"I'm sending someone to retrieve you. I believe you're old friends."

Ezekiel appeared with a grin not a second later. "Jedrick, old friend, it's been a long time."

"You son of a bitch," Jayson growled. "I should have known."

Ezekiel sighed, "I don't think he's very excited to see me, Osiris. I thought he would at least grin considering we haven't seen each other in over a hundred years."

Jayson blinked at the subtle comment. They'd seen each other hours ago, but it seemed his master didn't know that.

Or was it another ruse?

"I can hear that," Osiris replied. "Bring him to me anyway."

"As you command, Sire." His words were formal and respectful, but the gold flecks in his eyes flashed. He stared at Jayson, his gaze conveying some hidden message as he dropped a silver box between them. It was subtle and masked from onlookers by the position of their legs. He revealed a matching one in his palm before saying, "Shall we go, Jedrick?"

A tracking device? *What are you up to, Ezekiel?*

"Sure," Jayson replied. It wasn't like he had a choice. "Can't wait."

CHAPTER TWENTY-SIX

Fractured Bonds

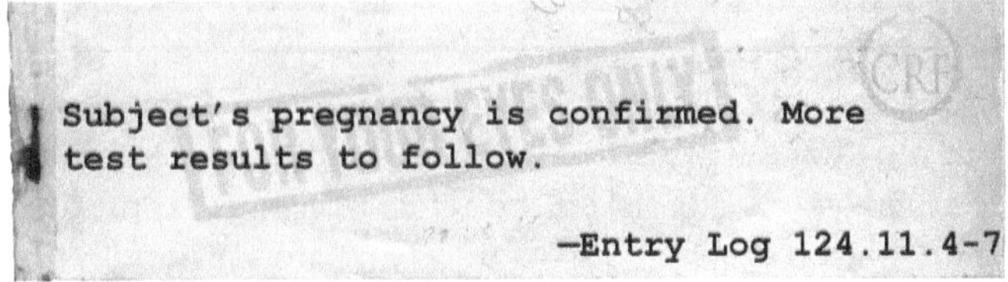

Subject's pregnancy is confirmed. More test results to follow.

—Entry Log 124.11.4-7

Lizzie paced the beach, sniffling.

She was too afraid to call out for help. It may have been Jacque who brought her here, but she didn't know for sure. There were no house lights or people, only the moon and the black sand beach. It seemed to embody her life—a constant state of loneliness.

"Lizzie!"

The familiar voice froze her in place. "Stas?" No. That was impossible. She saw her die.

So now I'm going crazy. Awesome. Why not? It seemed appropriate, all things considered.

And she was freezing thanks to her sweat-dampened clothes and the cool evening air.

"Oh God, Lizzie." The words were accompanied by a pair of arms being thrown around Lizzie's neck.

She blinked.

And now she was feeling things.

Lizzie did hit that man's chest pretty hard…

"I'm so sorry, Liz. I'm so, so sorry. Everything is such a mess, and I don't even know where to begin. But you're my best friend, Liz. And I hate that you're mad at me, but I need you so much right now. So much it hurts. Tell me what I need to do. Please. I can't go through this without you too."

Stas is rambling.

Which could really only mean one thing: Lizzie had lost her mind. She'd created a babbling figment of her best friend to keep her company in the darkness.

Not the healthiest coping mechanism, but she couldn't help returning her friend's hug and indulging in a false sense of closure. Lizzie clearly needed this temporary reprieve from reality to heal, and so she would use it effectively.

"I should have forgiven you," she murmured. "I'm not thrilled that you kept me in the dark, but Jayson explained that it was to protect me."

Too little, too late, of course. But at least Lizzie understood now. It still hurt, but not nearly as much as losing her best friend.

"We should have told you," Stas said, sorrow in her voice. "I wanted to so many times, but I also didn't want to take your choices away from you and force you into this world. I realize now that by not telling you, I still stole your right to choose, and I'm so sorry."

"I forgive you." Lizzie squeezed her tighter. "I just wish you hadn't died on me."

"Me too," Stas whispered. "Me too."

They hugged for several minutes while Lizzie waited for her phantom to disappear, but the moment stretched on. Was there more to say?

"Is Jayson here too?" she asked, hopeful. It seemed appropriate for her delusional state. Maybe she would have the chance to say goodbye to him too.

"He's not back yet, but Jacque's been teleporting everyone in, so I suspect he'll be here any minute."

Lizzie frowned. "Teleporting from where?"

"Osiris's house, apparently." She pulled back with a huff. "They went without me. Something about keeping me as their secret weapon since no one knows I'm a Hydraian."

"Wait…" Lizzie used the moonlight to examine her friend. "You're immortal now?"

"Well, yeah. Jonathan shot me."

She swallowed her hope. "No, he killed you."

"And I woke up," Stas replied, her voice sad.

"But they were incendiary bullets."

Stas shook her head. "Hollow glass, actually. Which means I'm a Hydraian now." She paused. "Hold on, did you think I really died?"

"Well, yeah!" Lizzie blurted out, unable to hold back her conflicting emotions. She'd spent the last however many hours or days grieving. "You're not dead?"

"Does that mean I'm not forgiven?" Stas asked, voice unsure.

Lizzie shrieked and threw her arms around her best friend to hug the life out of her again. She didn't even care if this killed her, because she needed the comfort and had to assure herself that Stas was really alive.

Joy unlike anything she'd ever felt filtered through her chest, especially as another realization hit her. "Jayson's alive too?" She held her breath, waiting and hoping.

"Yes," Stas breathed. "And you're suffocating me."

"I don't care," Lizzie admitted as she squeezed her tighter. "You're here. You're really here."

And Jayson too.

Her heart thudded wildly in her chest at the thought of seeing him again as tears pricked her eyes.

He's alive.

She would see him again, and, hopefully, soon.

Except… "Did you say Jayson is at Osiris's house?"

"Yeah, he led the rescue mission," Stas breathed as she thudded Lizzie on the back. "You're gonna kill me again."

She let her go. "And he's okay?" she pressed, needing to hear it again.

"As far as I know, the mission went as expected, and you're here." Stas grasped her shoulders as if needing to steady herself. "It's been a hell of a day." A touch of wariness highlighted those words, causing Lizzie's happiness to falter.

She was missing something.

Everyone's alive. They should be celebrating, but Stas didn't seem joyous at all. Thankful, maybe, but not in high spirits.

Dying would be traumatic, Lizzie imagined. As well as waking up fine the next…

Oh. Oh, no.

"You're a Hydraian," she realized on an exhale.

"That's what I keep saying. And what the hell is stuffed under your shirt?" she rubbed her abdomen. "It felt like hugging a tree."

"It's a file," Lizzie explained, but she also saw right through her friend's attempt to change the subject. She was upset. Really, really upset. And then it hit her—why becoming immortal would hurt her so badly. "Issac."

She covered her mouth as Stas's face crumpled. Lizzie knew better than to hug her again. It would only encourage the waterworks.

Stas was silent for too long before she whispered, "I'm not ready to talk about it yet."

"Oh, Stas," Lizzie murmured. "Oh God, it's my fault."

"No," Stas snapped. "Don't ever say that. Jonathan pulled the trigger, and I will kill him for it."

"Hold that thought," Issac said as he sauntered toward them. If he'd been watching in the shadows, he chose a heck of a time to make his presence known.

"We have a much larger problem to discuss." He glanced at Lizzie. "Welcome home, Elizabeth. I would allow this reunion to continue, but Astasiya is needed urgently. Amelia and Eliza have volunteered to keep Elizabeth company in the interim."

"What's going on?" Stas asked, her lips curving down as he came to stand beside her without reaching out to touch her. That missing gesture caused Lizzie's heart to break for her best friend.

They can't be together.

Because Stas died saving me.

"It seems Osiris has taken the Elders hostage," Issac murmured. "We tried to gather intelligence from the Guardians, but when we asked them what happened, they collectively slit their throats."

Lizzie gasped, her fingers going to her lips. "What? Is Jayson okay?"

"That remains to be seen," Issac replied, his tone far too formal for Lizzie's liking. "From what we have gathered, Osiris compelled the Guardians to leave the Elders unprotected. Then, in a grand show of power, he demanded they silence themselves when asked about the events of the kidnapping. It proves, unnecessarily, that distance does not dampen his power."

"Oh my God," Stas breathed while Lizzie tried not to faint at the gruesome image. "Will they survive?"

"Yes, with their memories intact." He paused to let that settle.

What a horrible thing to remember doing—and involuntarily, too.

She shivered. Osiris wanted her to have his child. What sort of monster would she have created for him?

Her stomach churned at the thought, followed by another more devastating one. It sliced through her chest, leaving her bleeding and pained.

"Jayson," Lizzie whispered, her voice cracking. To have him murdered, then resurrected, only to potentially die again by the hand of Osiris.

Oh God, her heart couldn't handle it.

"If Osiris intends to exterminate the Elders, he will do so in a grand fashion, which gives us time. My experience, however, suggests he's inviting us out to play, and Aidan agrees."

"You mean, you think he knows?" Stas asked, fear evident in her voice. "About your friendship with the Hydraians? About me?"

"I think he's always known," Issac murmured. "Ezekiel mentioned a seer. If that is true, it means Osiris has been playing us from the beginning. Although, Aidan believes a fortune-teller cannot predict all outcomes, and he has proposed a plan."

"Which is?" Stas prompted.

Issac studied her, his expression artfully blank. "He wants to send you to meet Osiris."

Stas paled. "What?"

"His plan hinges on Osiris being unaware of your talents, and he feels that the potential element of surprise is just what is needed to rectify the situation." Issac sounded so detached and very unlike the man Lizzie knew. Didn't he realize this behavior would only worsen the situation between them?

"What are your feelings on his plan?" Stas asked, her voice soft.

Issac remained silent for a long moment before replying, "My feelings on the plan are irrelevant. Aidan is a master of strategy, and I bow to his intelligence."

Pain filtered through Stas's expression at the far-too-logical response. Lizzie wanted to smack him for being so cold and heartless and would have opened her mouth to say so if her vocal cords still worked.

Stas nodded, taking on the same stoic air. "Well, so much for keeping me a secret. If I even am one, I mean."

"Indeed," Issac replied, his tone softening as he shifted.

The moon illuminated his features, causing Lizzie to stifle a gasp.

Sadness.

It emanated from his vivid eyes with such sincerity that it fractured logic. His formality may have hidden it in his voice, but that expression said it all.

The picture of a broken man.

"As always, you have my support, whatever you decide." He bowed his head in a way that spoke of reverence and torment—his throat convulsing with the words. "Always, Aya," he added in a whisper.

Agony destroyed Stas's features, breaking Lizzie's heart in two.

This was Issac's version of goodbye.

And her best friend had no choice but to accept it.

~*~

"Welcome, Jedrick," Osiris greeted, his hands open in a polite gesture belied by the scene before him. Luc, Balthazar, and Alik were all on their knees, heads bowed. A clear indication of where Jayson would soon be.

If he had access to his powers, he would choke the bastard with that gold chain around his neck. Alas, he seemed unable to use his gifts at the moment. No doubt a ward or a rune, or some other manner of voodoo created by Osiris himself.

Prick.

"Osiris," he growled as he stopped beside Luc. "Been a while."

"Has it?" Osiris blinked his ancient eyes. "I suppose it is a matter of perspective, but it feels very recent to me." He shrugged. "Well, now that I have you all. Kneel."

Jayson dropped to the ground at the single-word command but held Osiris's gaze. A direct challenge, one he knew the Ichorian would not appreciate, but Jayson didn't give a fuck anymore.

"What now?" he demanded.

"Are you in a hurry, Jedrick?" Osiris asked, arching a brow. "Perhaps you're hoping to return to a certain redheaded female you erroneously assume is yours?"

"There are no assumptions, Osiris. She is mine in every way." And he would do whatever he needed to do to protect her.

"Oh?" Osiris turned to Ezekiel. "This continues to fascinate me. I understood the attraction—she's a gorgeous specimen—but that sounded more like love. Have you been guiding him on the process?"

Ezekiel's nostrils flared, but his lips curled into one of his trademark grins. *Hiding the pain?* "I'm not sure I would be able to provide him much guidance given the circumstances, nor have I seen Jedrick in over a century."

Jayson wasn't sure what fascinated him more: Ezekiel's outright lie or the implication behind the words.

"Yes, I suppose you have been preoccupied with other tasks." The taunt in Osiris's tone was not lost on Jayson. Ezekiel mentioned not having a choice in his work as of late; were the two related?

"In any case," Osiris continued, his focus shifting back to Jayson. "What would you be willing to give me in exchange for Elizabeth?"

"Considering she's already safe in Hydria, I'd give you nothing."

"Safe is such a relative term. It can so easily change, you see." He started pacing, hands clasped behind his back. "Ezekiel could bring her to me right now if I asked. I ensured their bond after her successful birth, as I did not fully trust Jonathan to uphold his end of our arrangement. All it takes is a simple command. Would you care for a demonstration?"

Jayson bristled at the clear threat. "You son of a bitch, if you touch her—"

"I suggest you calm down before I decide to teach you some manners," Osiris chastised. "You could learn so much from Elizabeth. Perhaps I should allow you to keep her a little while longer, but I am still curious—what would you give me in return?" He strolled forward and ran his fingers through Luc's blond hair. "Perhaps your king? Would you sacrifice him for Elizabeth?"

Jayson's heart dropped to his stomach, impeding his ability to speak.

Luc for Lizzie?

He couldn't… wouldn't…

"Or perhaps your mind-reading best friend?" Osiris pet Balthazar with the words, almost as one would a cherished pet. "He's quite powerful. I could use him in so many ways or make an example of him at the next Conclave." He turned thoughtful. "Decisions. Hmm."

"Why?" Jayson managed. "Why do this?"

"Because you have decided to take something that belongs to me, Jedrick. Do you have any idea how long I've waited for her creation? How many times we tried to perfect it?" He paused, waiting. "No? Of course you don't, yet you dare claim her as your own? How incredibly ungrateful, after everything I've given you."

Jayson's lips moved, but no words escaped. How did one respond to a madman? The only thing Osiris ever gave any of them was death. Why would Jayson ever be grateful for that?

"Sire," Ezekiel murmured, gently interrupting the moment. "We are reaching the hour of the seer's prediction."

"Ah yes, the future." Osiris clasped his hands before him now and stepped back. "I so desire to know what it is our Skye cannot foresee."

Ezekiel's wince caught Jayson's attention.

Was it the name that hurt him, or the words?

"I would still love to know, though," Osiris added. "What would you give me in return for Elizabeth? If I vowed never to disturb her again, to wait for another of her kind's creation, what would you give me?"

"Your vow?" Jayson repeated, his voice hoarse with emotion. "Means shit to me."

"Perhaps, but that belies the point. I want to know what you would sacrifice for her. Give me a truthful answer. Now."

The compulsion wrapped around Jayson's heart and soul, forcing the response from his throat. He didn't want to say it, didn't want to think about what it meant.

Fuck…

It resembled a betrayal, a broken vow that was millennia old.

But deep within, he knew it to be true. As much as it hurt, he couldn't lie.

"Anything," he rasped, bowing his head in defeat. "I would give anything for her."

Because he loved her. More than anyone else in existence, including those he called his best friends and brothers.

A tear slipped from his eye as an ancient bond tying his blood to theirs splintered. For the first time in their existence, someone else had risen above their sacred connection.

"Fascinating," Osiris murmured. "Absolutely fascinating. I may just let you keep her after all, at least for now."

Jayson couldn't lift his head or say a word. What was there left to discuss? He'd failed his friends in the worst way, for a woman he cherished more than life itself.

It defied logic and all his principles, but Elizabeth Watkins was his to protect. And he would do everything in his power to fulfill that oath.

Even if it meant dying for her.

For she would forever be his heart.

I love you, Red.

Chapter Twenty-Seven

And So It Begins

> Subject's roommate has applied for an internship with the CRF. Benefactor informed of potential addition and has given approval for hire.
>
> —Entry Log 121.05.4-7

"This is a terrible idea," Tom stated.

"Maybe," Stas agreed. "But it's happening." She handed him a new earpiece meant for their team alone.

Several Hydraians, as well as Issac, Tristan, and Mateo, stood around them, dressed for action. Dark colors mingled with camouflage and a variety of weapons. Issac had worn dark jeans and combat boots, two items she didn't even know he owned. She'd donned long sleeves and pants, both forest green.

The plan was pretty simple. Send Stas in as a diversion, converge on Osiris and his minions while they were distracted, and free the Elders.

Aidan predicted their success to be around sixty percent. Better than all the other ideas, which were closer to forty.

Tom inserted his new comm unit. He'd muted the other one but kept it in his opposite ear to listen for any chatter between Jayson and Osiris.

"I have no idea where Ezekiel took him," Tom started, his words showering

Stas in ice.

"Ezekiel?" she repeated, her voice hoarse. "He's here?"

"Yeah." He frowned. "Sorry, Stas."

She swallowed and shook her head. "No problem." Except anyone who could hear the frog in her throat would see right through that.

Issac raised a brow, silently asking, *Can you handle it?* He knew her reaction to Ezekiel the first time hadn't been favorable. The man murdered her parents—brutally. She sensed the others weren't as sure of his guilt, but Stas remembered that night vividly. Those ebony eyes were forever ingrained in her nightmares.

"Astasiya," Issac murmured.

Everyone was staring at her.

She shook her head again. "Yeah, I'm good."

Her demon didn't look so sure. This was usually the part where he would hug her, but he maintained a polite distance.

Already pushing me away, she thought sadly. Not that she could blame him. One drop of her blood would kill him instantly, and they both valued his life more than their relationship.

Stas would rather see Issac every day and not be able to touch him than to never see him at all.

Hurt and loneliness wrapped around her heart, solidifying her resolve for the task ahead. She would focus on her inner frustration and devastation, and not on the fear Ezekiel evoked.

I can do this.

"I'm good," she repeated, stronger now.

Issac held her gaze for a moment longer before nodding. "Where did they go, Thomas?" he asked, his attention shifting to the plan.

"They disappeared into the underbrush." Tom gestured to the tree line. "I tried to track them but lost sight right about there." His finger lifted to a cluster in the distance.

"And that's where I come in," Brian, a Hydraian with decent tracking abilities, informed. Stas had seen the tall, lanky male wandering around Hydria but hadn't been formally introduced until tonight. His gift was the least defensive—being only able to track a scent, similar to a hound dog—however, their choices were limited.

"Hold on, mate. I sense something," Mateo said. "What happened there?" He nodded to the field beside what appeared to be a demolition site.

Tom followed his gesture. "That's where Ezekiel met Jayson."

Mateo grinned. "Brilliant. He left a tracker."

"You can sense that?" Tom asked, shock evident in his tone. Stas felt the same.

"I have a knack for technology," the blond replied with a wink. "Jacque?"

"Yep." He disappeared with the word and popped back not five seconds later with a silver rectangle in his hand. It'd happened so quickly that Stas didn't even see him appear and reappear.

Impressive.

Mateo plucked the device from his hand and started tinkering with it. Stas understood basic electronics, but she had nothing on this Ichorian. He flipped open a screen and grinned. "Now we have a location."

"They're still here," Issac said as he eyed the position. "That confirms my suspicions. He's waiting for us."

Tristan stepped forward to study the map. "Do you feel it's a trap, Issac?"

"I believe he wishes to issue a statement of sorts, though I fear what that may entail." Issac ran his fingers through his hair and sighed, "As for a trap, there is only one way to find out."

"On it." Jacque disappeared.

Issac looked to the spot the teleporter had just vacated, and shook his head. "Not what I meant. We have no way of knowing what wards Osiris has constructed to capture us or—"

"Scouted," Jacque announced as he materialized beside Issac. "Elders are alive, and only Ezekiel and Osiris appear to be on site. I popped around in a few places with no interference, and I have a good place to drop Stas now."

Everyone stared at him.

"That was a dangerous maneuver," Issac noted dryly.

"Then you would be really displeased to know that I almost teleported to Luc's side just to see if I could nab him, but I chose to come back here and report instead. Shall I go try now?" The sarcasm in his voice would have earned a grin from Stas any other day, but not now. She agreed with Issac on that being a cavalier move, though she'd done several of her own these last few months.

"You've grown quite insolent in your short years." Tristan grinned with the words, clearly meaning them as praise. "I'm impressed."

Issac cleared his throat. "We need to focus."

"Yes, and we need to relocate," Tom said as he started to pack up. "Time for the distraction."

Stas nodded and reached for Jacque. "I'll meet you all there."

Issac grabbed her wrist before she could touch the teleporter, his sapphire gaze blazing as he said everything through those two smoldering orbs. Her heart skipped a beat at the familiar intensity.

He didn't want her to go. She assumed as much—even as she agreed—but it was predicted as the most successful option.

And she could do this.

With his support.

"Issac," she whispered, aware of their audience. "This is what Aidan suggested."

"I am aware," he replied, moving closer. "That doesn't mean I'm thrilled by it."

She dared to lay her hand over his heart, her touch tentative. "You'll be right behind me."

Emotion flared in his pupils as he cupped her cheek.

Fear, she realized.

"I've trained for this," she reminded him. "It's sooner than we expected, but I can do this." She needed his faith, and she let him see that with her eyes. "Please, Issac. You have to let me go."

The words stabbed her in the heart, and his expression said he'd felt it too.

God, it hurt.

She hated this.

Hated fate.

Hated her cursed immortal blood.

Hated everything.

But most of all, she hated the broken way he nodded in acceptance. It felt like the beginning of the end. They both knew it was inevitable, but to have the choice ripped out of their hands seemed so unfair.

It will always be you, her soul promised. *Always.*

"Be safe, Aya," he whispered.

Issac took a step back, his eyes glistening with unsuppressed emotion.

"Thank you." She would forever cherish his unfettered confidence in her to see this mission through. He hated it, but he also had faith in her success. And that meant more to her than anything in the world.

"I'll be waiting for you," she said as she held out her hand for Jacque again. "Find me."

"Always," Issac replied.

Her environment changed as Jacque moved her deep into the forest about a hundred yards from the tracker signal. "Be back in a jiffy," he whispered.

Stas faltered as her emotions warred.

Focus, her brain demanded.

Cry, her heart begged.

There will be time to do that later.

She took a steadying breath and observed her surroundings from a crouched position. Their original plan had been to rely on Brian to point them in the right direction, but the tracking device worked much better.

The goal was to distract Osiris long enough to give the others a chance to take him and his minions down. It put a lot of the weight on her shoulders.

She shivered. *I can do this.*

It didn't help that she felt no different from before. Tom had mentioned the same when he awoke immortal. The others said it was "perfectly normal." Her gifts would trigger as she needed them.

Or so she hoped.

"We're in position," Issac murmured through the earpiece, his voice calming her in a way no one else could. "Give us a good show, love."

The endearment touched her soul, emboldening her.

He always knew what she needed.

She cleared her throat and grinned despite the dire circumstances. "That I can do."

All four Elders were kneeling at Osiris's feet in a clearing beyond the trees. Ezekiel stood beside him, hands clasped behind his back.

Where are all your minions? Jacque may not have found them, but Stas knew there had to be more.

Although, a man of Osiris's skill and power didn't really need an army.

Stas slipped between the trees, her boots silent over the forest floor. Stark had taught her a lot these last few months, especially about stealth and combat. He called her a natural in training, something she attributed to her inhuman birthright.

And then there were the sessions with Issac. So many evenings spent honing her gift and practicing the art of compulsion. She learned that her commands weren't attached to a definitive time frame but remained in effect for as long as she held the thread of control. As soon as she dropped the link, the persuasion ended. That would be the trick to remember with Osiris.

"...do I choose?" His ancient voice slithered through the air, dampening her skin.

The same feeling of familiarity swept over her as it did the first time she met him. So did the sense of dread.

Pure evil lurked beneath his formal facade. She'd witnessed his proclivity for torture from the front row in his amphitheater.

Sick fuck.

"You'll have to compel me again for that response," Jayson growled as Stas stepped out into the clearing.

"Or I could use Alik." Osiris smiled. "Inflict pain on..." He trailed off as he noticed Stas's approach. She was surprised it took him this long. It indicated he might be alone after all. Minus the assassin standing beside him.

"Oh, don't mind me," she said, her voice boasting a confidence she didn't feel. "I'm just wandering."

Jayson's head whipped around, his mouth falling open, while the remaining Elders remained bowed and unmoving.

Victims of control.

"Well, well," Ezekiel said, grinning. "Welcome to the party, Astasiya."

Osiris cocked a brow. "Astasiya?" He studied her. "You're familiar to me." He sounded almost curious, if a little bored. "When have we met?"

"You don't remember?" she asked, feigning disappointment. "I suppose you were busy preparing yourself for an evening of torture-filled fun." She stopped ten feet away and let her hands hang loosely at her sides.

Ancient green eyes looked her up and down, his expression indicating he found her lacking. "Your insolence is boring me. I'll deal with you when I'm finished. For now, stay—"

"Stop talking, Osiris." Three words, casually said but underlined in power. "It's rude to dismiss someone so quickly, especially when you know nothing about them."

His lips parted, but no words came out, causing his eyes to widen in apparent shock.

"See what I mean?" she asked as she wrapped all her mental faculties around that command and held it in place. If he couldn't speak, he couldn't persuade.

"Beautiful," Ezekiel murmured. "But, oh, don't mind me. I'm only here for the show." He displayed his hands in an *I surrender* pose and remained very still beside Osiris. "Please continue."

Stas considered muting him as well, but he appeared far more entertained than threatening. Osiris also appeared more amused than violent, his lips curling into an exuberant smile that nearly unsettled her resolve.

Apprehension prickled her nerves even as she forced herself to focus. She needed to free her friends. Then run far, far away.

Jacque had informed them all that Osiris had commanded the telepathic Elder to unleash his mental torture ability on the others. That seemed the appropriate starting place.

"Release your persuasive hold on Alik."

The tension in the air dimmed, but all three remained kneeling. Stas guessed all of them had been sent to their knees by vocal force.

She immediately dropped her command regarding Alik since it no longer held purpose, and tightened her mental grasp on the one forbidding Osiris to speak.

He appeared even more impressed now as he took her measure again. The bastard even applauded, which sent a tremor down her spine. She'd wanted to avoid his interest for as long as possible, but now she held his undivided attention.

He waved a hand as if encouraging her to do more.

And she had no choice but to comply if she wanted to save the Elders.

"Free Balthazar, Lucian, Alik, and Jayson from your persuasion."

Luc and Balthazar fell to the ground, their bodies trembling, while Alik sat back on his heels with a dead expression.

Jayson, however, stood. He'd obviously not experienced the same torture as his friends. "You shouldn't be here," he said in greeting. "Not that I'm complaining."

She ignored his remarks and unleashed her latest command, reaffirming her grip on Osiris's ability to speak.

The monster's grin widened in approval.

He spread his arms in a gesture that asked, *What are you going to do now?*

She'd expected more of a fight, but either the others had removed all the remedial threats or he really was here alone.

"Ezekiel, tell me where your backup is hiding." It took more effort than she expected to speak to her parents' murderer directly, but she managed with only a slight quiver in her voice.

The assassin smiled smugly. "You're looking at him, but I'm under strict instructions not to harm anyone." He glanced pointedly at his master.

Osiris shrugged, unconcerned. He still appeared to be far too amused for Stas's taste. She tested the speaking demand and found the binds strong and unbending.

"Are we ready to continue the show?" Ezekiel continued, his gold-flecked irises flickering to his left for approval.

Osiris nodded but kept his attention on Stas. He almost seemed delighted. Such a creepy emotion she never wanted to see on him again, especially in relation to *her.*

"Excellent. To the Ichorians on site, I have been instructed to inform you that your betrayal of your kind will not go unpunished, but for today, you are granted temporary amnesty." His gaze lifted over her shoulder. "And if you're thinking about shooting us, Thomas, I would advise against it. The seer predicted it would not end well. Besides, Astasiya seems to have Osiris well contained. Not bad for a pretty little angel."

The ancient one gave a subtle nod of acknowledgment, his eyes sparkling.

"How does that bastard know my name?" Tom growled through the earpiece.

"It would seem they expected this outcome," Issac replied. "Which would explain why Osiris merely tortured the Elders and didn't kill them. He wants us all alive, at least for now."

"And so, what, that means we should return the favor?" Tom asked incredulously.

"I am curious to understand the purpose of this meeting, so yes, I believe we should grant them the same reprieve. And as Ezekiel has insinuated, Osiris already knows we are here, which only intrigues me more. Besides, I'd say Astasiya has the situation under control." The pride in Issac's voice caressed her broken heart.

But that didn't mean she agreed that these two men should live.

They were murderers.

Evil, vile creatures who should be removed.

Kill them, a part of her encouraged. It would be so easy.

She could command the assassin to stab himself.

No.

She could force him to remove his own head.

A gruesome sight flashed behind her eyes, and her lips flinched upward.

A few words were all she needed.

Remove your head.

Monstrous.

It would satisfy my need for revenge.

And you would never forgive yourself.

But they would be dead.

Do it…

Her lips parted as she considered the demand. *End them.*

The compulsion wrapped a cloak of darkness around her, causing all her hairs to stand on end. It would be so easy—

"Aya," Issac murmured through the earpiece. "Focus."

Stas blinked, startled out of her dark thoughts.

She immediately tested the silencing command and found it hanging by a loose thread. Her mind emboldened it immediately as she closed the door on her wicked yearnings. They were always there, lurking, and ready to take her over the edge.

Her power was intoxicating and addicting. And could be used to wield so much pain.

She met Osiris's gaze and saw pride brewing in his lurid stare. It sickened her to the core.

He knew.

Because he openly embraced the wicked urgings stirred by this power. She'd seen him in action, knew what he was capable of, and witnessed how much he enjoyed it.

I'm not you.

He merely grinned. As far as she knew, he couldn't read minds, but that all-knowing look left her unsettled.

"Osiris is secure," she said over the comms.

"Yes," Ezekiel murmured. "And as a sign of good faith, Osiris has granted permission for the teleporter to retrieve the Hydraians' precious king."

Stas narrowed her gaze. "I sense a trap."

"No trap, Astasiya. Merely a token of temporary peace."

She studied the assassin and the content Ichorian beside him. None of this sat well with her, but they'd proven their knowledge of the situation at hand.

Because of the seer.

"I believe him," Issac said over the comms. "He has no reason to lie."

"I beg to differ, Wakefield. He has *every* reason to lie. Let me shoot him."

"Stand down, Thomas." The authority in Issac's tone rippled through her earpiece, soothing her in a way it shouldn't. "Jacque, grab Lucian."

Jacque didn't hesitate. He teleported to Luc and disappeared in a blink.

Ezekiel grinned. "There, that wasn't so hard, was it?"

"What was the point of all of this?" Jayson demanded, folding his arms. "A punishment for rescuing Lizzie?" He was still the only Elder standing. Whatever Osiris forced Alik to do to Balthazar had left him shaking uncontrollably on the ground, while the telepath sat motionless, staring off into the distance with dead eyes.

To be forced to torture your best friends… She trembled at the thought.

Ezekiel smirked. "Elizabeth is a key reason for our meeting tonight, yes. She's one of a kind, and Osiris would like her back."

"Over my dead body," Jayson growled.

"That can certainly be arranged," Ezekiel murmured as Osiris tapped him on the arm. They exchanged a long look that left the assassin grinning. "It appears my Sire has decided to grant her freedom. For now."

"For now?" Stas repeated. "What the hell does that mean?"

"I believe his objective has shifted, little angel." His gold-flecked gaze sparkled. "You are quite the enigma, darling one. And he's intrigued."

Ice dotted her spine as she interpreted his meaning. "I'm his new objective."

"So it would seem, for you should not exist." He checked his watch and sighed. "We have crossed several foreseeable outcomes now. Therefore, I do believe it is time for Issac to appear. Please. Osiris would like a word."

The ancient Ichorian nodded, his attention finally leaving her to gaze expectantly to his left. Her demon sauntered into view a second later, his expression blank, as Tristan and Mateo flanked him on either side.

"A test of loyalty," Issac mused as he walked directly to her side. "You've known all along."

The ancient lifted a shoulder.

"Partly," Ezekiel murmured. "The seer warned Osiris of this outcome, as well as several others, but her vision of the ultimate threat remained unclear."

"Stas," Jayson replied as Jacque reappeared to grab Balthazar. He vanished in a flash, but no one commented. "Your seer couldn't identify her."

"Precisely," Ezekiel replied, pleased. "And now that it's done, we can go?" He regarded his superior, who shook his head.

Those ancient eyes gazed eagerly at Stas.

"You want to be able to speak," she realized.

A nod.

"Absolutely not." She refused to give him even an inch. "I say we kill you instead."

He gave her a disappointed look and turned to Issac. A silent conversation transpired between them as everyone else observed.

"Is there a way for you to remove his persuasion but allow him to speak?" Issac asked, his concentration on Osiris.

"You want to hear what he has to say?" She couldn't help the skeptical tone in her voice. He couldn't be serious.

"I do," Issac confirmed. "Especially as it likely pertains to you."

"I agree," Jayson added.

"I say we shoot him instead," Tom replied through the comms. He seemed to be the only voice of reason.

"I wouldn't," Ezekiel warned, shocking Stas. "The seer already foresaw the possibility, Thomas, and you will fail."

Stas's brow furrowed. "You can hear him?"

"Of course not, but I know what was predicted. And Skye is never wrong." His lips twitched with that last sentence as if he was actively suppressing a reaction. "That said, you could all try, but you have no idea what you're truly up against."

"Immune," Alik rasped.

Ezekiel's lips quirked at the corners. "Yes, as Alik discovered the hard way, Osiris and I are both immune to Hydraian and Ichorian talents. And the incendiary bullets in your rifle won't penetrate our shields. But again, feel free to try."

"That's great, except I'm controlling Osiris right now," Stas said, proving his theory wrong.

"Indeed you are, young one. Well done." Ezekiel clasped his hands in front of him. "Shall we agree to a temporary armistice and hold a discussion, or should Thomas attempt to pull the trigger?"

"Stand down, Tom," Jayson said, his voice holding no room for argument. "I want to hear what Osiris has to say."

"Likewise," Issac agreed. "Astasiya, please?"

She met his vivid gaze, startled. Please? Really? Stas could never deny him when he asked nicely, and he knew it. But he couldn't be serious.

"He's a monster."

"Perhaps, but he has allowed Balthazar and Lucian safe passage to Hydria. He also granted us temporary amnesty, and I believe him."

Stas openly gaped at him.

"Trust your Elders, child," Ezekiel suggested. "They've been playing this game far longer than you."

She glowered at the assassin but refrained from replying. The man who murdered her parents saw fit to grant her advice. She had half a mind to demand he kill himself for sport.

The vision painted itself behind her eyes, eliciting a grin from a dark, dark place inside of her.

It would be so easy.

"Aya," Issac said, his hand brushing hers. "Please."

Twice.

She closed her eyes. The first time had been hard enough. The second, she couldn't ignore. "Okay," she whispered. "I'll do it."

They wanted Osiris's explanation, so she would give him back his voice. But they'd better at least consider killing him afterward.

Stas toyed with several phrases in her mind while the others waited. The command had to be concise with no flexibility to be interpreted as anything else, or this would go badly.

"Osiris, do not use compulsion on anyone within a one-mile radius of your current position."

He seemed much too pleased with her word choice and nodded, waiting.

She traced the mental strings to the order forbidding him from speaking and snapped the bonds.

"Thank you, child," he said. The fact that he felt the coercion lift implied far too much about his power. "You have much to learn, the first of which being that voice is never a requirement for persuasion. And as a second lesson, our shared gift is technically not called *compulsion.* My gifts have remained intact throughout our entire interaction, but I chose not to use them and will continue to do so now."

His amusement fled as he focused on Issac. Stas waited for Osiris to show his true colors and enact a horrid command, but he merely said, "The Conclave will be forever changed. I would request you all attend the next one, but I won't insult your intelligence."

Issac acknowledged the comment with a slight bow of his head, his version of respect. "I suspect we will see each other again soon, Sire."

Osiris returned the gesture. "You continue to impress me, Issac, even in your defiance. I may keep this entire interaction to myself, at least for now. Please give Aidan my regards. I will miss him."

"Of course," Issac replied in that cordial way of his, giving no outward reaction to the comment regarding Aidan.

"Best of luck to you. Until we meet again."

"Likewise, Sire."

Stas could not believe they were chatting like old friends. Just when she thought she understood this fucked-up world, the immortals in it went and held a pleasant conversation essentially underlined in threat.

Oh, by the way, I'm probably going to kill you soon.

Feel free to try at your leisure.

I will. No hard feelings, of course.

No, no, none at all.

Brilliant.

Seriously? This was why the world would end. They'd all sit back, enjoy a round of tea, and then beat the shit out of each other mentally.

Awesome.

Her inner sarcasm died as Osiris returned his ancient gaze to hers.

So old. So cruel.

"I daresay I am most pleased to make your acquaintance, Astasiya. Here I've spent the last few decades waiting to create a new protégé to replace my broken one, just to find that what I needed already existed. You." He turned to Ezekiel. "I'm quite impressed that Sethios managed to keep this revelation from me. His resilience truly is remarkable, yes?"

"Indeed, Sire," he agreed, his tone emotionless.

"Your gifts are quite rare, child," Osiris continued. "So rare, in fact, that they reveal your ancestry, daughter of Caro and Sethios." His lips curled into an avid smile while she fought to breathe. "Or would you prefer I call you 'granddaughter'?"

Her eyes widened impossibly more as her throat went dry.

What?

Daughter of Caro and Sethios?

She opened her mouth to refute his claim, then closed it as a sense of rightness overwhelmed her.

Stas's parents' names were Caroline and Seth, though her father frequently referred to her mother as Caro. And *Sethios* wasn't all that far off from *Seth.*

But "granddaughter"?

Was that why he seemed so familiar?

Green eyes… The same shade as her own. Her father's, too.

No.

She shook her head in denial.

No. That was just… No.

That was impossible.

His son would be a Hydraian, and Hydraians couldn't procreate with humans.

Unless another Lizzie existed, which Ezekiel implied as a possibility. Was her mother a product of the CRF?

"Osiris and I are both immune to Hydraian and Ichorian talents."

"Except I'm controlling Osiris right now."

"Indeed you are, young one. Well done."

The conversation replayed through her thoughts on repeat. A ruse? A lie meant to provide false hope? A hint? A way to fuck with their minds?

Osiris turned to Ezekiel. "*Granddaughter* is the appropriate title, yes?"

"Yes, Sire." Dark eyes met hers, and she swore a hint of pain flashed in his features.

"Excellent." Osiris pinned Stas with a final stare. "I look forward to our next conversation, my child. Might I suggest researching appropriate terms in the interim? Try, perhaps, *psychic persuasion*." He winked and grabbed Ezekiel's arm. "I will see you soon, Astasiya."

"Until next time," Ezekiel added with a nod.

They vanished into the shadows, leaving Stas gaping at the hole they created, both physically and mentally. She hadn't even had a moment to process the idea of attacking him after that information bomb.

"Grandfather?" she whispered, her psyche shattering.

"I have you, love." Issac wrapped her in his arms. "I'm not going anywhere."

She moved into his chest on autopilot, needing his scent and comfort. "He's…? I don't…"

"Go to Elizabeth," Issac said over her head. "I can take it from here."

"We'll need to discuss this," Jayson said.

"Indeed," her demon agreed. "Later."

"Yes," Jayson said. "Later."

Issac's lips brushed Stas's temple. "We'll figure this out, Aya."

The double meaning in those words destroyed the thin wall she'd built around her emotions. "Issac," she whispered, shaking as the world around her tumbled down.

She clung to him as her legs gave out, and he caught her, just as he promised, and lifted her into his arms.

Her energy fled with the last of her control.

Grandfather…

What did that mean for her?

Chapter Twenty-Eight

There's No One Like You

> Memories firmly erased and humanoid impressions implanted, as per the direction of the benefactor. Subject will be moved to the Watkins home briefly for simulation purposes.
>
> —Entry Log 110.03.4-7

Lizzie placed the file on the dining room table. "I have no idea where to start."

Amelia and Eliza sat across from her—two complete strangers who had taken it upon themselves to help Lizzie feel welcome in Jayson's home after Jacque had dropped her off.

The two women tried to distract her with a shower, fresh clothes, and a very large cup of hot chocolate. Lizzie's mind never trailed far from Jayson or his current predicament, but she tried to play along as best she could. Especially since Amelia and Eliza seemed just as worried as her.

"I suggest you start from the beginning," Amelia said as her elegant fingers flipped open the folder.

She mentioned her familiarity with the CRF during the initial part of their conversation, something Jayson had touched on briefly while in Bora Bora. He also informed Lizzie that Amelia and Tom were romantically involved. The news left Lizzie feeling like an outsider. Tom—the man who treated her like a sister—had run off and fallen in love, and she had no idea. She felt as if she didn't know him at all.

"It looks like a series of logs." Amelia scanned the words while she spoke. "Little snippets of details throughout your years in the lab." She flipped to the end. "And out, I think."

"It's a code," Eliza said, her ebony gaze sparkling as she reviewed several entries. "The first digit is always one, but the next number seems to increase at specific intervals. How old are you?"

"Twenty-four," Lizzie replied. "Soon to be twenty-five."

Eliza nodded as she flipped to the back of the file. "Then yes, your age in the file is the next two digits. For example, this one is one zero four, so you were four years old when they created this entry. And I bet the second set is the month since it never goes over twelve. The last is your project name, four dash seven."

"Huh," Lizzie mused. "So it's a chronological catalog of my life."

"It's a qualitative log," she explained. "Typical for researchers in labs. I'm guessing there's a quantitative report somewhere as well, but the one you have is more important anyway. The other would just be numbers and statistics."

Lizzie thumbed through a few of the pages, looking for her eighteenth year. She wanted to confirm a theory that had been planted in her head by Osiris—the one about her memory. With all the insanity of the last day, she hadn't been given a chance to consider it, but now she needed to know.

Her eyes scanned the file from her eighteenth year, month eight.

Eliza and Amelia read with her, both of them paling at the information detailed on the page.

"So it's true," Lizzie murmured. "None of my memories are my own. They erased everything and gave me a false sense of identity." That explained the fuzziness of her thoughts and the recollections that didn't stick. Like Rome. "Interesting."

What did that mean for her personality development? Her polite convictions were literally programmed into her, as was her innate innocence. She never desired men because they instructed her not to.

She flipped to the end of the file to search for any notes on Jayson.

Nothing.

So they didn't pair her with him—not purposely, anyway.

There were a few notes about her infatuation with Tom, though. Amelia's cheeks flushed as she read the lines, and Lizzie cleared her throat. "I… It's not like that anymore."

"It's okay." Amelia smiled, her cheeks flushing. "I quite understand the allure."

Eliza rolled her eyes. "You two really need to take your home back and just move in. I can crash with B."

"We're building a home," Amelia said. "It's almost done. Then Jayson can have his place back."

"Seriously, you know the offer stands," Eliza pressed. "I understand why everyone gave me space at first, and I appreciated it, but really, I can handle sharing a house with B. He doesn't, well, you know."

Amelia's eyes sparkled. "I do. He's always treated me like a sister and nothing more."

Lizzie swallowed. "He intimidates me."

"Oh, I bet," Eliza replied. "But I hear you're handling Jayson just fine, which tells me B would not be a problem."

"I don't… It's not…" She shook her head, flustered. "Jayson is the one I want." At their startled gazes she added, "He's the *only* one I want."

"Well, that is the best welcome-home present I could have ever asked for, Red," a deep voice murmured from right behind her. "Although a hug would be wonderful as well."

Lizzie almost fell out of her chair in her attempt to reach him. He caught her hips and hoisted her into the air as her arms flew around his neck.

Real.

He's real.

She hadn't wanted to believe—had refused to let hope capture her heart—until she touched him.

And he felt very much alive, and hot, and hard.

Wearing designer jeans and a long-sleeved forest-green shirt, he was just as she remembered him. Even the windswept brown hair was right.

She pressed her nose to his throat, inhaling his cedar scent.

Very, very real.

His palms went to her ass as she wrapped her legs around his waist. The shorts Eliza let her borrow rode up her thighs, but Lizzie didn't care.

"You're here," she breathed. "You're alive."

He chuckled. "As are you." He slid one hand up to tangle his fingers in her hair and gently pried her face from his neck. "I missed you, Red," he whispered after catching her gaze. "So much it hurt."

"I missed you too." She caressed his face with her eyes, memorizing every strong, masculine line. "I thought you died."

"I'm right here, Liz," he murmured. "And I'm not going anywhere. I promise."

She leaned forward to kiss him, but the clearing of a throat stopped her. Lizzie lifted her gaze to the man standing in the foyer.

"Sorry, I don't mean to interrupt." Tom dragged his fingers through his blond hair, looking a little sheepish. "I just wanted to say that I'm glad you're okay, Liz." The hesitancy in his tone stung. He'd never been uneasy like this around her. Granted, the last few times they saw each other hadn't been all that pleasant for either of them.

Jayson tugged a strand of her hair to catch her attention. "Do you need a minute?" he asked softly.

She swallowed. He was offering her a chance to talk to Tom, but only if she wanted it.

Did she?

Things would never be the same between them—likewise for Lizzie and Stas—but that didn't mean she wanted to hate him forever. They might not be best friends after this, but they could still be friends. Even close, over time.

And if what the doctor implied about Lizzie's Seraphim genetics was true, then her time on Earth would be infinite. Just like everyone else on this island.

Amelia walked around the table to enfold Tom in a hug, her lips at his ear. He nodded at whatever she said, but his eyes were so sad. Lizzie had never seen him like this. Was he hurting because of her? Because she didn't want to talk to him? Because she refused to forgive him?

He died.

She attended his funeral.

And he lied to her in the worst possible way.

Yet the pain of losing him had nothing on the agony she experienced after losing Jayson. And she understood, on a logical level, why Tom kept her in the dark. He meant to protect her, as he always did. That didn't excuse his behavior, but his heart was in the right place.

"I'd like to talk to him," Lizzie decided. "But don't go far."

Jayson captured her mouth in a kiss that knocked her world off-kilter. "I think you'll find it nearly impossible to get rid of me now, Red." He kissed her again before helping her stand. "Let me know when you're done. We have a few items to discuss."

The promise in his words, whether intentional or not, doused her in ice water.

In all the excitement of seeing him, she forgot about something very important.

The baby.

Was that what he wanted to discuss? No, of course not. He couldn't possibly know.

Oh God. How would he react?

Three thousand years of sex without consequences… No way would he be pleased by this news.

It threw her history in both their faces. She was a woman created in a lab. What man would want someone like that? Lizzie's classification didn't exist. A Seraphim created in a mortal womb.

"Lizzie." Jayson's hands cradled her face. "Don't give up on me yet, sweetheart. Talk to Tom, and afterward, we'll catch up, okay?"

She swallowed and nodded. "O-okay." He obviously had no idea, or he wouldn't be so calm.

One problem at a time.

Talking to Tom would be a cakewalk compared to the father of her child. She forced a smile, and Jayson traced the edges of her lips.

"Trust in me," he whispered.

Adoration emanated from his soft brown eyes, causing her heart to flutter with hope. This was the man who kneeled, accepted a collar, and died—all for her. He might not be thrilled by the idea of a child, but he would at least be open to discussing it. As for her being different, he already knew and never looked at her differently.

A lifetime of insecurity and being told she would never be good enough exploded in a single moment as she realized, *To Jay, I'm good enough.*

Because he loved her.

And she loved him.

"Of course I trust you," she replied with conviction. She'd trusted him from the moment he waltzed into her apartment uninvited—an innate, gut reaction to her soul recognizing his.

"Hold that thought, Red," he murmured with a smile. "Tom first."

She returned the smile. "Okay."

He brushed his lips against her forehead and stepped back to address their audience. "I'm going to provide Amelia and Eliza with an update on what happened. We'll be outside."

Tom nodded. "I understand."

"Is everyone all right?" Amelia asked as Jayson opened the front door.

"Physically, yes." His reply whispered through the room, causing Lizzie to frown.

"What does he mean?" she asked, her question directed at Tom.

"Osiris forced Alik to use his mental abilities on Luc and Balthazar, and he's not taking it well. And Stas found out that Osiris might be her grandfather."

Lizzie's eyes widened. "What?"

"Yeah…" Tom rubbed a hand over his face and scratched his jaw. "I'm not quite sure how that works considering Ichorian genetics."

"Do you believe him?"

Tom shrugged. "Honestly, after the things he knew tonight? It's entirely possible. Or he's fucking with us at her expense."

"God," Lizzie breathed. "Is she in Hydria? Because I should go to her. She must feel so alone."

"Wakefield's with her."

"He is?" After the way he acted toward her on the beach, that surprised her. "You're sure?"

"Oh yeah." Tom shook his head. "I might have my own issues with him, but he does right by her. I'll give him that."

She nodded slowly. From what she'd witnessed, he cared deeply for Stas, even if he'd been a bit distant earlier. "She's in good hands."

"Not sure I'd go that far, but okay." The air changed subtly between them as the focus shifted from their mutual friend to the elephant in the room.

"Fuck, Lizzie, I hate that you're mad at me. I know I deserve it, and if you never want to speak to me again, I will do my best to honor it. But you need to know that I never meant to hurt you. Ever."

He palmed the back of his neck. "It all went down so fast. Did Jayson tell you what happened?"

She cleared the emotion lining her throat and forced herself to say, "He mentioned you saved Amelia from a bad situation. And he said you both faked your deaths."

Tom nodded. "That's high level, but yeah. John put me on an assignment to watch Amelia out in the middle of the woods, and the things they were doing to her…" His fists clenched. "Let's just say, I couldn't let it continue. But the only way to protect her was to convince John we were dead, and I couldn't bring you into that, Liz. Not without endangering you too."

"So you left me alone in New York City with a hoard of Ichorians and the CRF." She couldn't help the sarcasm or the annoyance in her tone. Because really? That was probably the worst place to keep her.

"I only saw a glimpse of your file, and I overheard my dad once talking about the serum you needed, and Luc wondered if it was something meant to keep you alive. We couldn't risk removing you from the potential life source without knowing for certain, which was why we sent Jay." He dropped his hands to his sides in defeat. "I realize it left you alone, but there wasn't a moment that went by when I didn't worry about you. I've always adored you, Liz."

"When did we really meet?" she asked, curious.

Tom frowned. "What do you mean? You were, like, ten or something. We met at one of those damn brunches. You don't remember?"

She shook her head and picked up her file. "According to this, I lived in a lab until my eighteenth year."

He stepped forward to take the paper from her, skimming it. "This is bullshit."

"I don't think it is."

"No, I definitely met you as a kid. I remember thinking you were like the sister I always wanted."

She smiled sadly. "I think they implanted that memory." Just as they did all of hers regarding the childhood crush that never blossomed into anything more. "It makes sense. They wanted you to assume the big-brother role to protect me, and they wanted to give me a love interest that would keep me occupied." So she wouldn't be tempted by anyone else until they were ready for her to breed.

And then she met Jayson.

Tom read the paper again and set it down, his eyes blinking. "That… that…"

"Is really messed up?" she supplied with a humorless laugh. "Yeah, it is, but it's probably true."

He stared down at her, his tan face paling. "I had no idea, Liz."

"I know," she replied. "I don't blame you, and I understand why you did what you did. That doesn't mean I'm happy about it, but it's enough to start forgiving you."

Moisture glistened in his eyes. "God, when did you grow up?"

She laughed. "Really, Tom?"

"I mean it. You used to be this fragile, demure little girl. But this new you, she's not demure at all. I approve."

She rolled her eyes. "Six years, at least in my mind, I tried to get you to notice that I'm a woman, and *now* you work it out. Figures."

He chuckled and mussed up her hair. "You're still like a sister to me, Liz."

"A womanly sister, though."

"Sure," he agreed, his brown eyes grinning as he pulled her into a hug. They stayed like that for a long moment, his chin on her head and their arms around each other's backs. It felt right. Not in the same way Jayson felt right, but in a friendship kind of way.

"I've always recognized your beauty, Liz," he added softly. "But I respected you far too much to act on it. Stas, too."

"And Amelia?" she asked.

"Amelia," he repeated, his tone deepening. "I never stood a chance at denying her."

Lizzie smiled, happy for him. "You love her."

"I do," he agreed as he pulled away. "More than I should."

"Good," Lizzie said, meaning it. "I hope she drives you crazy."

"Excuse me?" He managed to sound both amused and floored at the same time.

"What?" She batted her eyes innocently. "We both know you deserve it, Tom Fitzgerald. Oh, and by the way, if you *ever* die on me again, do not expect me to attend your funeral. I've done that once already, and I refuse to do it again. So stay alive. Got it?"

He swallowed. "Yes, ma'am."

"Great. Now, if you wouldn't mind, I need to talk to Jayson."

Tom chuckled and shook his head. "You know, I worried about the two of you, but I think you'll handle him just fine. In fact, I'm looking forward to it."

"And what does that mean?" she demanded.

He shrugged as he started toward the foyer. "Oh, nothing. Just musing out loud." He turned the handle. "Jay, she's all yours. And, uh, good luck, buddy. Bye, Liz!" He popped out of the house before she could get in another word.

"Rude," she grumbled.

Jayson locked the front door. "Sounds like you two worked things out."

"I wouldn't say that," Lizzie replied. "Pretty sure I might want to kill him again now."

His lips curled in amusement. "Tom seems to have that effect on a lot of people, though his talents are unquestionably useful, so we keep him around."

She giggled, and it felt good. After so many hours or days, she needed it.

And then she sobered as she realized the importance of their pending discussion.

"So much has happened," she started.

"Yes," he agreed. "And before you start us down that path, there's something I need to say."

She swallowed. "Okay."

He wiped his palms against his jeans as he approached, his expression serious. She tried to read the emotions in his chocolate eyes, but they were vacillating between too many for her to catch.

Jayson stopped in front of her and took her hands. "I've debated all night on how I wanted to do this and what I needed to say, but no matter what words I form in my mind, nothing measures up to the magnitude of this moment."

He paused to clear his throat and wet his lips with his tongue.

He's nervous.

"In my over-three-thousand years, I never thought it would be possible to feel this way. The notion of a family didn't exist for me, and I was always okay with that because I grew up knowing that inevitability. But now, life has given me the most precious gift I didn't even know I wanted, in the form of you."

She bit her lip to keep it from trembling. The intensity pouring off him was almost too much. It escalated her heartbeat to what had to be unhealthy levels and, at the same time, stilted her breathing. Because she didn't want to miss a single word, and even a simple exhale was too loud.

He held her gaze as he dropped to one knee. "I can't begin to explain how it feels, Elizabeth, to suddenly have everything you never knew you wanted, given to you on the whim of fate."

He dropped her hands to grasp her hips.

"Knowing you has changed me on an irrevocable level. I thought my yearning for you was a passing infatuation, just as the others who came before you were, but the desire grew with each day until I couldn't deny it anymore. And so I broke the rules, and tasted you, but, God, Liz, it wasn't enough." His grip tightened as he pressed his forehead to her stomach. "I don't think it will ever be enough."

Tears glistened in her eyes as he lifted her shirt to place a reverent kiss on her abdomen. He stared up at her with a look of worship as he kissed her belly button.

"A family, Lizzie," he whispered. "I never thought I could ever have a son or a daughter, or even a wife. And I never knew how much I wanted all of that until you. I will spend every day for the rest of my life thanking you, loving you, and cherishing you. And I will do whatever you need me to do to prove that I'm worthy of this amazing gift, Elizabeth. To prove that I'm worthy enough to love you, and to raise our child."

She sniffled as he clasped her hands again and straightened his back while still down on one knee. "I want to marry you, Elizabeth. I realize it's an antiquated tradition, and that humans rarely take their vows seriously, but I want to promise myself to you in front of all our friends and family. What we have is so rare, Lizzie. And I need to do this right, not just for us, but for our future."

He cleared his throat as affection poured from his eyes. "A baby," he whispered, his voice awed. "I'm going to be a father." His gaze shifted upward as if in prayer. "It's the miracle I never knew I wanted, Lizzie."

"Jayson…" She could barely see him through all the water clouding her vision. And if he kept speaking, she'd be a sobbing mess. Of all the things for him to say to her, she never expected this. But it was so perfect, so heartfelt, and so extremely right.

He kissed her knuckles and bowed his head over her hands as tears streamed down her face. "I have the benefit of time and experience behind me, and I can say with utter certainty that no one has ever made me feel the way I do for you. It might seem fast, especially to you, but I know in my heart that this is it for me. There will never be anyone else, and I will wait, for as long as you need me to, for you to feel the same."

Moisture gathered in his gaze as he looked up at her again. "Eternity is a long time, but I want to spend forever with you, if you'll have me." He kissed her wrist, his eyes holding hers even through the tears. "Elizabeth Watkins, will you marry me?"

Chapter Twenty-Nine

Pizza Is Forever

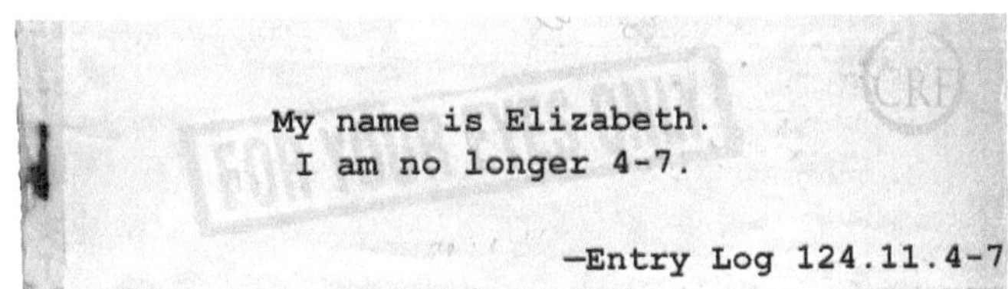

My name is Elizabeth.
I am no longer 4-7.

—Entry Log 124.11.4-7

Jayson's heart raced while he waited for Lizzie to say something. Anything. Even if the words *Fuck off* rolled out of her mouth, he wouldn't care, because the anticipation was killing him.

She licked her lips, opened her mouth, closed it, and opened it again, killing him more. Never had he needed an answer more than he wanted one now.

"Oh God, Jayson." She shook her head as more tears rolled down her pink cheeks. "No, that's not a no… hold on… I'm just… oh my God, I've gone and screwed it up already." She laughed and shook her head again. "Crap!"

Her face reddened even more, which he found both adorable and infuriating. The latter only because he wanted to kiss her, but he couldn't while she was still deciding how to respond.

She took a steadying breath, her hands gripping his harder than she probably realized. After several agonizing seconds, she finally met his gaze again and smiled.

"Yes," she said, her eyes matching the word. "Of course, yes. Always, yes. I… I don't even know where to start, but yes. I would love to marry you."

Adrenaline shot him to his feet as he wrapped her in his arms and kissed the life out of her. Her silky hair felt like heaven between his fingers as he coaxed her head to the angle he preferred. She melted against him, giving him what he needed as he returned the favor.

"I love you," she whispered. "I don't know how it happened, but it's true."

He smiled against her lips. "I love you too. And I also want you."

"Yeah?" She teased his mouth with her tongue. "Well, I *need* you."

"Minx." He lifted her into his arms to carry her to his room.

"Jay, this is a wedding-night tradition."

"In this house, it will be an every-night tradition. And maybe a morning one too."

She laughed as he dropped her on the bed. "Is that a promise?"

"Consider it part of the vows," he replied as he crawled over her. "Do you realize what you've agreed to, Red?" He pulled his shirt over his head while speaking.

"An eternity of staring at your abs?" Lizzie asked as she admired his torso. "No, an eternity of petting your abs." She ran her palms over his abdomen.

He caught her wrists and pinned them on either side of her head. "No, Red."

"Yes, Jayson. Definitely, yes."

He chuckled. "Mmm, no, you've agreed to an eternity in my bed."

"Our bed," she corrected.

Jayson smiled. He liked the sound of that. "Our bed," he agreed as he trailed his fingers down her forearms. "Don't move your hands."

"Yes, sir." The taunt in her voice stirred all his darkest desires.

"I'm going to enjoy teaching you the art of pleasure," he murmured as he traced her curves down to the edge of her shirt. "But we'll start slow." He rolled off of her and onto his feet.

"Slow?" Lizzie went to her elbows. "I'm not sure I like 'slow' if it means you leaving me all hot and bothered alone in bed."

"You moved your hands," he noted as he pulled open the top drawer of his dresser. "My future wife is not very good at obeying commands."

She snorted. "Your future wife will never obey commands."

His lips curled. "Good. I don't want an obedient wife. I desire an impish one." He found what he wanted and returned to stand beside the mattress with his hands behind his back. "Take off your clothes."

Lizzie's tongue peeked out to lick her bottom lip as she ogled him openly. It took her about three seconds longer than he anticipated for her to comply. Her tank top went first, followed by the shorts and the lingerie underneath. Normally, he would require a slower reveal, but this worked for tonight.

He took his time studying her in the low lighting of his room. "You look amazing in *our* bed, Red. I think I'll keep you here for a while."

She relaxed into the pillows with a come-hither expression. The innocent woman he fell for existed beneath the surface, but a vixen prowled on the outside. His dick more than approved.

He let her see the item in his hand as he placed a knee on the bed.

"A blindfold?" she asked, her voice breathy.

"Starting slow," he repeated as brushed the silk over her cheek. Her flaring pupils told him she approved. "Close your eyes." She did, and he secured the fabric around her head. "Good?"

She nodded. "Yes."

He stood again to remove his jeans and did so as silently as possible. Her nipples pebbled under his gaze, and her thighs clenched—all signs he scanned for in an aroused woman. *Someone approves of the blindfold.*

"Do you feel my eyes on you, Red?" he asked, voice pitched low.

She nodded as her pink tongue darted out to dampen her plump lips. "I want you to touch me."

"Show me where," he said as he slipped out of his boxer shorts.

Lizzie touched her chest far too lightly for his taste. "Here," she whispered.

"Just like that?"

She shook her head. "No, harder."

"Show me," he murmured as he palmed his cock and gave it a lazy stroke.

She swallowed visibly but grabbed her breast and squeezed. Her moan teased the air in the sweetest way.

"Only there, Red?" His voice had taken on a husky quality caused by the show on his bed.

"N-no." She whimpered as her fingers traveled down over her flat stomach to the thatch of red curls between her thighs. "This is wicked."

"It is," he agreed. "Now tell me how wet you are."

"Oh God." Her back arched off the bed. "This shouldn't be turning me on so much." Her hand slid lower, stirring a violent tremor from her. "So wet…"

She stilled as he knelt beside her on the mattress. "Let me see your hand, Red."

Her thighs squeezed together in protest. "I'm so close, Jayson."

"I know, sweetheart. Now give me your hand."

Lizzie trembled but relaxed her thighs for him. Her sweet arousal scented the air as she lifted her palm for his inspection, causing his abdomen to clench in yearning.

My future wife.

He drew his nose across her soft skin, inhaling deeply. "Mmm, I think that might be my new favorite smell, Red."

She squirmed beside him as he held her wrist. "You're killing me."

"The feeling is definitely mutual." He wrapped her fingers around his shaft and groaned at the sensation of her wet heat caressing his sensitive flesh.

She stroked him from head to base and back again, nearly undoing him. And that tongue of hers, licking her lips in anticipation, only worsened matters. He learned during their time in Bora Bora that she enjoyed sex of the oral variety, but he wanted to come deep inside her tonight, not in her mouth.

Jayson needed to claim her.

He gently removed her hand and grinned at her responding growl. "Someone's impatient." He kissed her wrist before stretching her arm over her head and introducing her fingers to the iron bars decorating his headboard. "Hold on to this, Lizzie." He caught her other hand and positioned it similarly. "Spread your legs."

She complied with a sweet moan, and he admired her damp, red curls. Her legs shook as she waited for his next move, but he purposely prolonged it, heightening the tension. He shifted subtly without touching her.

"I could admire you all night," he admitted softly. "So beautiful." He leaned over to blow against her sex, and she bowed off the bed in response. "Mmm, so needy too."

Sweat glistened over her skin. "Please, Jayson." Her raspy tone prompted his balls to tighten in anticipation.

Mine.

He knelt between her legs and drew a finger through her slick folds. "An eternity of loving you will never be long enough," he whispered reverently. "You're perfect in every way."

"Take me," she begged. "I need you inside me."

His palms slid beneath her ass to lift her pelvis from the bed as he thrust into her waiting heat. She cried out from the intense position, and he gave her a moment to adjust, even as his body implored him to take her the way he needed. *Hard and fast.*

"More," she demanded. "More, Jayson."

He smiled. "As you wish, future wife." He pulled almost all the way out and drove back in to the hilt on a groan that she echoed through the room. *So, so good.* He repeated the action faster and faster until her screams of pleasure rent the air.

God, he loved that sound.

And he would hear it for the rest of her very long life.

Fuck.

He wanted to own every inch of her, and he did with each hard stroke. Her legs quivered as her orgasm mounted, but he knew she needed more. He remained inside her as he lowered her to the mattress and found an angle that would send her over the edge.

His mouth met hers as he slipped a hand between them and found her clit with unerring precision. It took two circles to send her over the edge into oblivion, and, fuck, it felt amazing. Her walls clamped around him so tightly, so deliciously, he couldn't help but follow her into ecstasy.

"Lizzie," he groaned as his essence combined with hers in the most intimate way. But he couldn't stop. He craved more. And he wanted to see her eyes this time.

Jayson removed her blindfold and smiled at her sated expression. Mmm, they were nowhere near finished. "Arms around me this time, sweetheart."

"Oh, yes, sir."

~*~

Lizzie was never leaving this bed. Ever. The silky sheets smelled of Jayson and sex. So much sex.

She smiled as she stretched languidly, feeling more than satisfied.

"All right, I need you to help me solve an age-old debate," Jayson said as he returned with a pizza box in his hands. He set the greasy deliciousness beside her on the bed.

She flipped open the top to grab a slice of pepperoni as she asked, "What's the debate?"

He took his own piece and relaxed into the pillows beside her. "B says pizza isn't a romantic food. I say he's wrong."

"He's totally wrong," Lizzie mumbled around the cheese in her mouth. "It's sexy."

"Right?" He took a bite, chewed, and swallowed. "I think pizza should be a requirement post-sex."

Lizzie nodded eagerly. "I approve of this rule."

He grinned. "Then it's settled. Pizza multiple times a day, post-sex. And they say marriage is hard."

She giggled. "Sex multiple times a day as well?"

"Obviously," he replied. "I'm making that a rule too."

She enjoyed another dose of cheesy goodness while considering. "You're going to take that back when I get fat." Lizzie frowned. "Oh God, I'm going to get fat."

He stole her pizza and flattened her beneath him. It happened so fast she didn't know where the food went. Hopefully, in the box.

Okay, maybe pizza in bed isn't very sexy after all.

He kissed her soundly on the mouth before nibbling her chin and neck. His lips created a path that led from her throat to her belly button, where he paused.

"Do you have any idea what the image of you carrying our child does to me, Red?" He looked up at her so she could see the heat in his gaze. "The problem won't be me not wanting you, Red; it'll be me wanting you too damn much."

She shivered. "I think I'll enjoy that."

"I'll make sure you do," he promised with another kiss to her stomach. "If the tests could already show that you were pregnant, I'd say this birth might be accelerated. Did the CRF files mention how far long they thought it might be?"

She shook her head. "We didn't get that far before you walked in."

"That's okay. We have several physicians in Hydria, including B." His expression darkened. "No, not including B. I don't like that idea at all."

Lizzie giggled. "I'm sure he would be professional."

"Oh, he definitely would be, but no. That's not happening. We'll talk to

Lara. She's a Hydraian with healing abilities as well." He nodded, deciding. "Yes, I prefer that plan."

"Jealousy," Lizzie mused. "That's very interesting, Mister Masters."

"You're mine," he replied simply. "I'm not sharing."

"You've mentioned that." She smiled down at him, happier than she'd been in a very long time. "I'm okay with not sharing."

"Good." He relaxed his lower body against hers and rested his chin on her stomach. "You still owe me cookies."

She laughed. "I do. I'll bake them tomorrow."

"I think it's only fair that you bake them naked considering I've had to wait so long for them. While I supervise, of course."

"Will you also be naked?"

He shrugged. "If the chef requires it."

"She does."

"Then consider me naked." He grinned. "I better tell Tom and Amelia to find a new home." His grin slipped. "Actually, that may be more difficult now that several Ichorians are moving onto the island."

Lizzie ran her fingers through his hair while she asked, "What do you mean?"

"Well, rescuing you from Osiris didn't quite go as planned, and several of our Ichorian allies were outed in the process, including Issac."

She paused. "What?"

"Right, you weren't there. Let me fill you in."

He told her what happened after Jacque teleported her to Hydria, how Osiris managed to sequester all the Elders, and about his showdown with Stas.

"So now he knows which Ichorians are not on his side," she said when he finished. "And you think this will start a war?"

"Yes. Their defection tips the scales even more in our favor. Aidan's bloodline is very powerful, and all of them have officially chosen our side. It's possible more will request asylum as well, or go into hiding."

Lizzie considered everything he said while combing her fingers through his hair. He hadn't moved from her belly, his chin resting right over their future child.

What kind of world are we bringing you into, little one?

"I'll protect you both with my life, Red," he vowed, following her thoughts. She imagined the concern had flashed across her face.

"What about Jonathan?" she asked with a shiver. "He's still out there."

"Not for long." Something dark flashed through his eyes as he said it. "His time on Earth is short-lived. He's created too many enemies."

"But you said he's partnering with Osiris?"

He grinned. "My guess is that partnership is one-sided, in Osiris's favor. And I'm not worried. Jonathan will die. I promise you that."

She studied the conviction in his expression and decided, "I'm okay with that." It surprised her. Violence and death were two subjects she avoided. But the idea of Jonathan dying? Yeah, she could get behind that. "What if he's immune to your gifts like Osiris is?"

"Then we'll kill him the old-fashioned way. With a bullet." He kissed her belly. "I will do whatever I need to do to guarantee the safety of you and our child, Liz. I promise you."

"I believe you," she whispered. "Now come up here and kiss me."

He grinned. "Forgetting who is in charge again?"

"I might require another lesson on that."

He crawled upward to cage her between his hard body and the bed. "I'm happy to teach you, Red—every day, every night, for the rest of our very long lives."

She wrapped her fingers around his nape to pull him down for a kiss. "I love you," she breathed against his lips.

"I love you too," he murmured. "Forever and always."

* * *

Lizzie wandered up the hill in the direction of Luc's home. Jayson had given her directions earlier after saying Issac and Stas were staying with Luc for now.

His home wasn't near the other houses and seemed almost secluded up here, but the view was breathtaking. Dark blue waters rolling from almost every angle, white homes with blue tops, and cobblestone streets. So gorgeous.

Lizzie admired it all, including the adorable architecture of his home, before knocking softly. Jacque answered without his usual grin.

"Oh, hi." He palmed the back of his neck. "Uh, Luc's not feeling up for visitors right now."

"Is he still recovering from what Alik did to him?" Jay had explained everything that happened, including what it meant for Alik to use his gifts on someone.

Jacque nodded. "Yeah. They all are. I can tell him you stopped by."

"Oh, I actually came to see Stas. Is she here?"

He shook his head. "No, she went down to the beach with Issac. Want a lift?" His eyes brightened with that last part.

He likes to be useful.

"Actually, yes, that would be lovely." She could totally walk by herself, but she didn't mind the teleport, and his responding smile at being needed confirmed her choice.

He held out his elbow, and she accepted. The scene dissolved into the beach a second later. "That's a really cool talent," she admitted.

"It's awesome," he agreed. "Exhausting, but awesome." He nodded toward the beach where Issac and Stas strolled hand in hand, deep in conversation.

"I, uh, I think they're officially ending things," Jacque whispered. "We should leave them alone."

"What do you mean?"

"I mean, I think they're finally having *the talk.*" He glanced at them with a grimace. "You know, breaking up."

"But…" Lizzie paused as Issac stopped to face Stas, his expression tightened with despair. "Couldn't he just, I don't know, not bite her?" It seemed simple enough to her. Most couples didn't bleed around each other, right?

Jacque gaped at her. "Whom is he going to feed from?"

"Donors?" Lizzie suggested.

"Feeding is a sexual process for Ichorians, and also, our blood is alluring. If he loses control for one second during intimacy, he'll die."

Lizzie frowned. "From what I've seen, Issac is very determined and in control."

Jacque considered, nodding. "True, but a relationship of that nature between an Ichorian and a Hydraian is unheard of."

"Just as I imagine having a bunch of Ichorians moving onto this island is unheard of as well," she pointed out.

"Touché," he replied. "Regardless, it's considered impossible, and the others wouldn't approve."

"It's not really up to them, though, is it?" Lizzie said, slightly irritated on her friend's behalf. "If they want to try, they should."

Jacque shrugged. "I guess we'll see."

Lizzie had hope. If anyone could figure this out, it would be Stas. Her best friend was the strongest woman she knew. "I should probably talk to her later," she said as Issac cupped Stas's cheeks and pressed his forehead to hers. "They look pretty caught up in their conversation." And it felt a little weird watching them.

"Back to Jay?"

"Yes, please. I owe him some cookies."

"Cookies?" Jacque repeated. "Sign me up."

Lizzie grinned. "I'll have to make a few batches, because Jayson doesn't share."

"As he shouldn't," Jacque agreed.

Stas tilted her face up for a kiss that Issac tenderly returned just as Jacque teleported himself and Lizzie from view.

Lizzie's lips curled into a smile.

Their story is nowhere near finished.

EPILOGUE

One Week Later...

Jayson stood outside Luc's door, hesitating. This had to be done. He had to walk in there and explain how he could pick a woman over his brothers, but the words escaped him.

An apology would be a lie. When Osiris demanded the truth, he gave it.

Anything. And he meant it. He would give anything to protect Lizzie, including the lives of his best friends.

Fuck, it hurt.

He never wanted to choose between them, but Osiris had forced him to express his feelings out loud. And now the three men inside this house knew.

Jayson rubbed a hand over his face as he searched for his confidence. He hadn't seen Alik, Balthazar, or Luc since the incident. No one had, aside from a handful of Guardians who assisted with their Elders' recovery. Jayson had given them all space, waiting for the inevitable summons.

It arrived this morning via Jacque.

Stop being a caitiff and knock on the fucking door, he told himself. *They know you're here.*

Hell, Balthazar could hear every thought. That he hadn't demanded him to enter yet, however, left Jayson feeling even more inadequate.

It wasn't like B to leave him hanging outside. Alone.

Unless this was to be his punishment.

Shit, if that's how they wanted to play, then so be it. He wouldn't apologize for giving his heart to Lizzie. She was worth whatever pain his friends intended to inflict on him.

Yeah, fuck knocking.

He turned the handle and let himself inside without announcing himself.

Balthazar stood just inside the house, leaning against the wall, wearing one of his trademark grins, and appearing completely at ease. A sense of tranquility settled across Jayson's shoulder at the sight of his best friend—healthy, alive, and smirking.

"Well, that was amusing." Balthazar cracked open the beer in his hand and held it out for Jayson to grab. "Welcome back, Jay. Sorry it took an edict to force you to come visit."

He gripped the bottle and cocked a brow. "Seriously? You ordered me up here to share a beer?"

"He wants to talk about your bachelor party," Luc said as he joined them in the foyer. The dark shadows beneath his eyes were the only indication of his suffering a week ago. "As we understand, congratulations are in order?"

"Yeah, the fuck is that about?" Alik demanded from the living area. "We have to hear these things from Jacque now?"

"I was letting you rest," Jayson said, only partly meaning it.

"Bullshit," Balthazar replied in an uncharacteristically irritated tone. "You were hiding. Choosing Lizzie over us is one thing. Not being able to confront us on it is an entirely different conversation."

"Trust," Luc added. "You didn't trust us to forgive you, not that we feel there is anything to forgive."

That wasn't entirely true. "I needed time to find the right words."

"And have you?" Luc asked, his gaze brimming with curiosity.

"Honestly?" Jay palmed the back of his neck with his free hand and blew out a breath. "No. I have no idea what to say. I can't apologize, even though I feel like I should. And I don't know how to explain any of it. Osiris forced me to choose—"

"He asked what you would *give* to save her," Luc interjected. "And you gave him the honorable answer, because if you would give less than anything to save her, then you wouldn't deserve her."

Alik walked into the foyer, hands in his pockets, brown eyes clouded with memories and pain. "Did you not accept me when I chose Jenika over all of you?"

Hearing the name sent a shock through Jayson's system. Alik hadn't uttered those six letters in several centuries, and the agony of it etched a pattern over his features that all of them felt to their souls.

"Alik," Jayson breathed. "You don't need to do this."

"Yes, I do." Darkness shrouded his features even as determination lit his gaze. "You all know I would sacrifice anything to bring her back, but that doesn't belittle our bond. We're brothers and always will be, but love, *true* love, surpasses all the rules. Including those implied by our history."

"He's right," Balthazar murmured. "What you have with Lizzie should be cherished. We would never expect you to put us first, and you can guarantee that we will always be there to help you fight for it."

"Your happiness is our happiness, Jay." Luc clapped him on the back and pulled him into a hug. "I could sense how much that answer cost you, but I couldn't have been prouder."

"We all were." Balthazar joined the group embrace. "You'll always be our brother, Jay. No matter what."

"Loving her doesn't weaken you; it strengthens you. Hold on to that gift, Jay. Because you never know what life will throw at you next." The grave, but wise, words came from Alik.

He didn't join the group hug, not that any of them expected him to. Jenika's death had irrevocably changed him. None of them had understood, having never been in love themselves, but Jayson could appreciate that reaction now. Lizzie was his heart. Without her, he would cease to be.

Alik met his gaze over Luc's shoulder.

Now you know, he whispered telepathically. *Protect her, Jayson. Protect her with everything, and never stop cherishing your love.*

Jayson nodded once in reply, a solemn vow to do right by her. *Always.*

"You're going to be an excellent father," Luc whispered. "And an even better husband."

"After the bachelor party," Balthazar added with a pat on Jayson's shoulder as he pulled away from them.

Leave it to B to lighten the otherwise somber mood.

"After the party," Luc agreed as he released Jay.

Alik snorted and turned away as he said, "Yeah. Good luck convincing Lizzie to let him go."

Jayson welcomed the lighthearted change in topic but grimaced as he considered Alik's comment. "You're not planning anything too extravagant, are you?"

Balthazar grinned. "Would I call a meeting to discuss anything less than phenomenal?" He waggled his brows. "Step into the living room, Jay. We need to review the blueprints and my proposed timeline."

ABOUT THE AUTHOR

USA Today Bestselling Author Lexi C. Foss loves to play in dark worlds, especially the ones that bite. She lives in Atlanta, Georgia with her husband and their furry children. When not writing, she's busy crossing items off her travel bucket list, or chasing eclipses around the globe. She's quirky, consumes way too much coffee, and loves to swim.

ALSO BY LEXI C. FOSS

Immortal Curse Series
Blood Laws
Forbidden Bonds
Blood Heart
Elder Bonds
Blood Bonds
Angel Bonds

Blood Alliance Series
Chastely Bitten
Royally Bitten
Regally Bitten

Dark Provenance Series
Heiress of Bael
Daughter of Death
Son of Chaos

Elemental Fae Academy
Book One
Book Two
Book Three

Mershano Empire Series
The Prince's Game
The Charmer's Gambit
The Rebel's Redemption

www.ingramcontent.com/pod-product-compliance
Lightning Source LLC
Chambersburg PA
CBHW020534310726
48979CB00014B/2328/J

* 9 7 8 1 6 8 5 3 0 1 1 6 3 *